F
Ogilvie

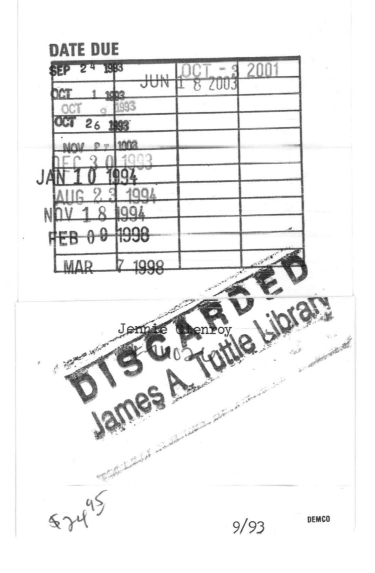

$24.95

9/93

DEMCO

Jennie Glenroy

BOOKS BY ELISABETH OGILVIE

* Reprinted by Down East Books

High Tide at Noon*
Storm Tide*
The Ebbing Tide*
An Answer in the Tide*
My World Is an Island*
The Dreaming Swimmer
Where the Lost Aprils Are
Image of a Lover
Strawberries in the Sea
Weep and Know Why
A Theme for Reason
The Face of Innocence
Bellwood
Waters on a Starry Night
The Seasons Hereafter

There May Be Heaven
Call Home the Heart
The Witch Door
Rowan Head
The Dawning of the Day
No Evil Angel
A Dancer in Yellow
The Devil in Tartan
The Silent Ones
The Road to Nowhere
The Summer of the Osprey
When the Music Stopped
Jennie About to Be
The World of Jennie G.

CHILDREN'S BOOKS

The Pigeon Pair
Masquerade at Sea House
Ceiling of Amber
Turn Around Twice
Becky's Island
How Wide the Heart

Blueberry Summer
Whistle for a Wind
The Fabulous Year
The Young Islanders
Come Aboard and Bring
    Your Dory!

Jennie Glenroy

ELISABETH OGILVIE

DOWN EAST BOOKS
Camden, Maine

Printed and bound at Arcata Graphics Fairfield / Martinsburg

2   4   6   8   9   7   5   3   1

DOWN EAST BOOKS
P.O. Box 679, Camden, Maine 04843

BOOK ORDERS: 1-800-766-1670

Ogilvie, Elisabeth, 1917–
    Jennie Glenroy / Elisabeth Ogilvie.
        p.   cm.
    Sequel to: The World of Jennie G.
    ISBN 0-89272-326-2 : $24.95
    I. Title.
PS3529.G39J43   1993
813' . 52--dc20   93-12684
                                          CIP

Synopsis of *Jennie About to Be* (Book I)
And *The World of Jennie G.* (Book II)

IN 1809, MARRIAGE WAS the best a spirited and healthy and intelligent girl could hope for, especially if she was an orphan without a fortune. Jennie Hawthorne, in London with an aunt who swore she'd make a good marriage for her, hated being exhibited as prime wife material, and she was desperately homesick for the family home in the north country. Then she met a dazzlingly handsome young officer in the Household Cavalry, Nigel Gilchrist, and fell in love. When they married, he resigned his commission to go to Scotland to manage the family estates for his older half-brother, whose heir he was. Jennie was enchanted with Linnmore. She made friends at once with the crofters and planned to start a school for the children, buying supplies from the thirty gold guineas left her by her father.

A grimly sardonic man, Alick Gilchrist, told her that the crofters were to be evicted, their homes destroyed, and the land turned over to sheep; and that Nigel had come to do the dirty work because his half-brother was a coward. Jennie could not believe this, because Nigel had told her this would never happen at Linnmore. But Alick had told her the truth; she saw it happen.

She rode out on the moor to give Alick some of her money to use for the refugees. Nigel followed her and came to blows with Alick. At the end of the struggle, Nigel lay lifeless in the heather. Alick disappeared into the hills to escape being hanged. Jennie, in shock, wanting only to get home to England, went with him. They became friends on the long and sometimes dangerous walk through the hills to a port where he hoped to get passage to America.

There was an immigrant ship ready to sail: the brig *Paul Revere*, owned by the son of earlier immigrants. He offered land and work, but there could be no bachelors over sixteen except for widowers with

5

families. Feeling responsible for Alick's exile, Jennie proposed posing as his wife to assure his passage, and after he was settled she would come back to England.

And so they sailed westward.

Arriving at Maddox on the coast of Maine, in June after a month at sea, the Highlanders were welcomed ashore by General Colin Mackenzie. On a whim of his wife, Lydia, because she liked their looks when they stepped onto the wharf, Alick and Jennie were offered a cottage on the grounds of Strathbuie House; Jennie was hired as governess to the General's children, and Alick went to work in the General's shipyard, studying at night with the village schoolmaster. Jennie's plan to return home at the end of the summer, when Alick should be settled and she would have earned her passage, was blown up when she found she was pregnant by Nigel. Though she was strong and healthy, she was afraid of childbirth (rightly, in those times), of dying so far from home. Alick was a strong and sensible friend, helping her to fight her terrors as she had helped him.

They both made friends in the village. There was a black time when Alick incurred the rage of a couple of young toughs. One stayed out of trouble after being called up before the General, but the other, Zeb Pulsifer, was savage. He ambushed Alick at night, and his frantic mother once assaulted Jennie on the street.

Alick welcomed Jennie's daughter into the world. Earlier she had expected to go home with the baby in the spring, but when spring came she did not want to leave Alick, and told him so. He had been silently in love with her since they first met, but was resigned to losing her.

While they were looking at a farm they might buy, they were locked in a barn where the hay had been set afire. They were saved by the young son of the tragic family who had once lived there: David, a deaf-mute boy who had been living in the woods since his mother killed herself. Everyone thought he had run away. (By chance Alick had been the man to lift her body from the water. Unseen, David had watched from the woods.) The arsonist was the vengeful young man from the village. Alick was able to catch him, but restrained himself from holding Zeb's head under water.

The farm was theirs, and a year after leaving Scotland, with both sorrow and fear, they began to make a new world for themselves.

Jennie Glenroy

"A land of love and a land of light."
—from *Kilmeny*, by James Hogg

Prelude

THE SHIPBUILDER'S WIFE stood apart by choice from the crowd at the launching, remembering another May, another country, another name.

Eighteen years ago, almost to the day, she had walked away from a man lying dead by a Highland burn and followed another man, whom she hardly knew, into the hills, and was never to be seen again in the place called Linnmore.

In retrospect, the breath-stopping wonder of the journey from there to here, from then to now, was its inevitability; each step, struggle, danger, anguish, and precarious joy, had led them along a predestined road to this hour.

Today she could not resist defying the Fates just a little. Surely it was owed her, she had resisted for so long.

We came with nothing, not even our own names. But behold us now!

9

One

J ENNIE GLENROY HAD not stood beside Alick at a launching ever since
she had christened *Artemis*, the first-born, that lovely little cutter
built by Alick and two old shipwrights who thought they had retired to
farm until Alick pried them out. Young David Evans had run errands and
tended the steambox, and the owner had worked on her when he could
be there. He was a transient schoolmaster, and a bachelor. Since then
there had always been wives, daughters, sisters, and fiancées to break the
wine bottles under the remote stares of the figureheads. She had never
resented this; the moment belonged to them and their men. Besides,
nothing could compare with the birth of *Artemis*, which meant also the
birth of the Glenroy Yard.

Even so, whenever one of his ships was about to come to life Jennie
always moved unobtrusively away from the crowd; in solitude, she was
with Alick for the climactic moment. On this fine windy May day of
alternating brights and darks, the river went from slate to sapphire and
then to icy viridian under a fresh glitter of crests on the high tide
crowding upriver from the sea. Jennie had gone up to the road to look
down across the scaffoldings and buildings of the yard, from the sail loft
to the smithy, where David Evans sat on the shed roof with his knees
drawn up and his sketchbook open upon them; from the bare yellow ribs
of the new ship on the stocks to the big sloop herself in the glory of new
paint and varnish and dazzling brightwork.

And thence to Alick, as a compass needle drawn inexorably north.
He had commenced the afternoon dressed for the occasion, but had
pulled off his coat to give the men a hand, revealing the blinding tartan

11

waistcoat Priscilla had made for his birthday. He swore such a tartan had never been seen in this world, but he was wearing it unabashed.

Young William stood at his elbow on the temporary platform, worshipfully holding his father's coat, which Alick would never remember now. Behind the clear, strong features and the calm dark-gray eyes, and the voice which had never lost the Highland softness, Alick was as anxiously joyous, as much caught in superstitious dread, as he had ever been at the birth of his children. When it was all over and everyone had gone, and his beauty had sailed out into the world beyond his touch forever, he would be wrung out.

"It's seeing them go and not knowing what will become of them," he told her, "when they've been under my hand and my eyes for so long." *Artemis* was long gone, they didn't know whether she still lived or not; but so far all his other ships had survived, which had given him a reputation for building luck into his boats. He never wanted to hear this spoken aloud.

If there were such a thing as luck, it came with the bit of rowan wood always built somewhere into a vessel, and the men who knew about it respected this practice from the Highlands, where their familiar mountain ash was considered a tree of grace and magic. If the Old Man believed in it, and it worked, who were they to scoff? They had too many hard and fast beliefs of their own. He could be right; likely he was. Alick himself said to Jennie, "It is superstition. But if I left out that bit of rowan, and something happened to the ship on her first voyage, I would be forever blaming myself. It is only a scrap of wood. Yet I feel safe with rowans in our dooryard." He smiled. "At least I am not praying to them."

He had no objection to prayers and blessings at a launching if they were requested, as long as the owner didn't object to the piper. He had never launched a vessel yet that hadn't been piped down the ways by Rory Mackenzie in full Highland dress. The minister, who was also a Scot, was always in enthusiastic agreement.

"Let us pray," he said now, and tipped back his bare red head as if to look God in the face. His prayers were always mercifully short; he'd grown up in a fishing village on the east coast of Scotland, and knew that the tide would not wait for him to tell God what the Deity already understood. As one man to another he asked that this bonny ship be guided safely into the safe haven where she wished to be. His smile when he finished was mightily reassuring, as if he had just received a firm promise from on high.

"God bless this ship and all who sail in her!" Mrs. Whittier's voice soared like a bird. "I christen thee *Ariel!*" With an astonishingly powerful sweep of the arm for such a slight woman she broke the beribboned bottle of Spanish wine over the bow. Simultaneously the blocks and wedges were knocked clear, and *Ariel* slid down the ways and into the water to a fanfare of applause, whistles, cheers, whoops, and the bagpipes playing through the noise as if through the havoc of battle.

The gulls circled high, their cries ringing like the pipes. Up on the road the horses tethered in the shade of the trees nervously shifted their feet, stretched their necks, and tossed their heads, making uneasy sounds in their throats. Their large eyes turned toward the noise in astonishment and alarm. Jennie moved along the rail, soothing them and touching them, while she still watched the scene below. From the pasture the family animals called jealously for her attention.

The Whittier men on *Ariel's* deck raised their hats to a fresh explosion of applause. Captain Martin Luther Whittier, after whom the town of South Maddox had renamed itself, was the town's daredevil privateering hero of Mr. Madison's War. His slim figure and narrow, Indian-dark face looked no older than his sons', even with the sun turning the gray in his hair to a glitter of frost over black.

He took the wheel, and the young men moved smartly to raise the sails. There'd be no bringing her alongside the wharf, she was as eager as her captain to take to open water. *This is what I was born for.* The big mainsail rose flapping and snapping in a creamy splendor of new canvas, to a salvo of cheers out on the river from the ship *Marmion* sweeping into view past the long rampart of Misery Wall. She was coming home after seven months away. Her captain was Stephen Wells's younger brother, and Stephen was out on the wharf swinging his hat in wild circles over his head.

Marmion flew on before the southwesterly wind that filled her sails to the curve of gulls' breasts. And now, clear of the bobbing planks, wedges, chocks, and the small boats salvaging the cultch, *Ariel* came about; tall and graceful, her bright new ensign whipping from the masthead, her canvas shivering and filling, she sprang forward like a great bird into freedom.

As usual Jennie had no handkerchief and had to catch a tear with a knuckle, hoping that her nose wouldn't run. Alick and his superintendent were shaking hands. A caulker jumped onto the platform; others swarmed up and surrounded Alick. He and young William were lost to

Jennie in the exhilarated crowd. "Mr. Glenroy," the men called Alick to his face, and "the Old Man" behind his back—a compliment, the traditional unofficial title given by a ship's crew to her captain.

Rory had been given another dram, and he and the pipes were well and truly warmed up by now. He was walking up and down beneath the ribs of the ship on the stocks, with his wild music flung crazily about him on the wind, and all the young children marching behind him. Bell Ann was there. The twins were out in the dory among the other small boats collecting the débris from the launching; Carolus was rowing and Sandy stood up, gazing after *Ariel* as she ran before the wind. Priscilla's yellow head showed up in a hilarious knot of boys and girls out on the wharf. There was one more to count, not as her child but a member of the household; David Evans was just dropping off the lower edge of the smithy roof.

Suddenly a change came over them all, as palpable as a whip-around in the wind. *Ariel* was about to sail past Basto's Point and disappear, and everyone was turning away, calling to the children, hurrying the slow-pokes. No one would endanger the sloop by watching her out of sight, even for this short sail upriver to her home anchorage. The custom was honored by its great age.

Oh, but she is lovely, lovely! Jennie thought. Who was not in love with the beauty today?—She turned away like the rest, keeping the precious image imprinted on her inner vision. She patted the crowding noses at the pasture fence: Shonnie, Perry, Blanchard, Diana. The pony, Brisky, kept thrusting greedily at her hand. When she looked around again, *Ariel* had disappeared and the people were drifting toward the spruce grove.

She left the horses and walked back down the field. She would be forty in October, but she rarely thought of that, and whenever she did she didn't believe it. She was a thin, straight woman wearing a Jaconet cambric dress striped in green and gold. From a little distance she looked like a thin, straight girl who had just recently put her hair up in a knot, leaving a few loose brown curls to fall where they chose. Her eyes were the color of her hair, but lighted like amber with the sun shining through it, and set in the fine creases that time and living bring to an expressive face. She was already tanned—she disliked hats and bonnets as much as she ever had—but the threat that her skin would turn to shoe-leather had been wiped out by soft rainwater, her own country knowledge, and Hat Shenstone's herbal mixtures.

She entered the coolness of the grove, where drink for all ages and shallow baskets of shortbread had been set out on plank tables. At the birth of *Artemis* she had decided to make the shortbread a tradition for launchings, as Alick had begun with the piper.

A quick look around, catching eyes, smiling, nodding, and she saw neither Alick nor Stephen Wells. She was hoping for some talk with Stephen, who had been at sea all winter. He would be gone again as soon as his ship was overhauled; *Bel Fiore* would make no money tied up in Maddox Pool.

After making sure no workman's wife was passed over, she could dip her cup of claret lemonade and sit down to visit with her two oldest friends in America: Anna Kate Mackenzie, who had crossed the Atlantic with her, and Lucy Clements, the second American woman she had known. Anna Kate had an ageless rawboned durability. Lucy had grown as snugly plump as a setting hen, but her leaf-green eyes were unchanged. Their men were off in an all-male group, but neither Alick nor Stephen was part of it.

An hour later everyone was still there, though the rum and the claret lemonade were gone; the last toasts had been drunk in the Canary wine contributed by the General. The children's punch bowl was empty, but a bucket of spring water was on the table. For anyone who had stock to tend there was still plenty of afternoon left in which to bask in the euphoria of the occasion.

"What do you suppose Mrs. Mackenzie is telling Elsie Lockhart?" Lucy Clements said. "Whatever it is, Elsie is fair mesmerized."

"I hope she isn't terrifying the poor lass with the horrors of child-birth," said Anna Kate.

"More likely she is telling her how to avoid becoming pregnant again too soon," said Jennie, "and Elsie has never heard anything like it in her life."

Eighteen years ago, when Jennie first met her, General Mackenzie's wife had been heavily pregnant, but managed to look both exotic and opulent. That child was now a Bowdoin College student and part of the uproarious game of blindman's buff going on in the field. His mother was even more opulent and more exotic as to gowns, shawls, and hats. The minister's wife was a big, fair young woman who never took her large eyes off Lydia's face. Her lips were parted in either awe or stupor. Her child was due this summer.

The General, as usual, was surrounded. There were a few of his veterans left, and to succeeding generations he was an authentic hero, one whom George Washington had called by his first name. His hair was white now, but still thick and wavy; his coloring was high. He leaned much harder on his stick these days, but he would always refuse a chair as long as he could.

The three women's conversation lapsed into companionable silence as they watched their children. The younger ones were playing King of the Castle up and down the granite whaleback between the Yard and the sandy beach. Bell Ann, seven, was screaming as loudly as anyone, a hoyden in sprigged dimity. In the field, Allan Robert Mackenzie, the General's son, stood blindfolded in the center of the moving circle.

"Bobbety, Bobbety, Bob!" Priscilla chanted, and he made a dash at her voice, missed her, and the chant was taken up from somewhere else. Priscilla, seventeen, was tall for a girl, with hair yellow as maize streaming down her back. She was trying to suppress her laughter; it was too unmistakable, perilously close to a guffaw. The twins would be fifteen this summer. Sandy, Alexander (or Alasdair) for his father and grandfather, had the tawny Hawthorne coloring and slender build, but Carolus, named for Jennie's father, was looking more and more like his great-uncle, the Old Laird in the portrait at Linnmore. He would never know the name Gilchrist, never know of the painting, or of Linnmore itself, and it gave Jennie a dizzy sensation to contemplate the queerness of it, as if the fetch of her son walked the halls of the red granite mansion between Meall na Gobhar Mor and the dark glass of Linn Mor.

"This way, Bobbety," a girl called out softly, and Robin lunged again and seized air. A boy's syrupy falsetto, "Oh, Robin, be my Valentine—," and then he nearly doubled over laughing.

"They make me feel old," Septimus Frye said. "Good afternoon, ladies." He flipped up his cinnamon coattails and sat down beside Jennie, stretching out his long legs in snug pantaloons and top boots. "Da—dashed old." He was twenty-four and looked all of twenty-one, with short-cropped hair like a black lamb's fleece and a dimple in each cheek.

"Hear the boy," said Lucy. "Old is when you have a sixteen-year-old sewing for her bridal chest, and you have two more to go through the same thing. You grow old just thinking about it."

"Old is when you are wishing to be thirty again," said Anna Kate, "and the children still small enough to croon them to sleep, and there is always dancing somewhere, and you at it."

"My dear Septimus," Jennie said. "I am old enough to be your mother, if I'd had you at sixteen or so. And you feel *old*?"

"Too old for *that*," he said ruefully, looking at the noisy circle in the sun. Robin plunged, yelling like a corsair, missed a girl, and got giggling William instead. "Those girls would consider me a lecherous old rake," Septimus said broodingly.

"Besides, they might muss you up," said Lucy. "That's a most handsome outfit."

"Thank you, ma'am," he sighed, and his chin sank into his fashionably high stock. He was as much of a dandy as Maddox tailoring and boots and his pay would make him. He was a notary public and justice of the peace, and occupied his uncle's office when the Senator was in Washington. With both charm and competence, Septimus attended to the complaints of the constituency.

He was also agent for an insurance company in Hartford, and this accounted for his presence at the launching; he had insured the new ship.

"And the boys would likely resent me ferociously," he continued. "I would make them feel so childish."

"Yes, you would," Jennie agreed demurely. Robin had recognized William's giggles and sleek round head. William was only twelve and had been kindly invited to join the circle by some of the older girls, who made a pet of him. He was blindfolded and pushed out into the middle, still giggling. May he always be as happy as he is right now, Jennie thought, knowing it couldn't be so. But there was no harm in hoping. She knew how his brown eyes were squeezed shut now, even with the blindfold, the better for him to pick out a certain voice.

" 'Oh, where have you been, Billy Boy, Billy Boy?' " the girls chanted. " 'Where have you been, charming Billy?' " William circled slowly in place; his ears were keen as a fox's.

Septimus rose abruptly, excused himself, and strode away toward the horses.

"He has an eye for Pris," Lucy said. "Madame Mackenzie had better not catch him at it. She'll have his head on a platter like John the Baptist."

"Och, you can plan these things until the Little People come trooping up the glen in broad daylight," said Anna Kate, "and still they never work out as you want them."

"If Pris ever sees Robin Mackenzie as anything but a brother, I shall be the most surprised of all," Jennie said.

" 'Did she set for you a chair, Billy Boy, Billy Boy?' " Caroline Goward had a strong voice for such a flat-chested wisp of a girl. Her straw bonnet hung bouncing down her back, and her white-blond curls were shaking loose into wild ringlets. She was so happy that she teetered on the edge of rowdiness. If her mother could see her now, she would likely have a seizure, Jennie thought unfeelingly.

"If that young one goes home with a sunburn," Lucy remarked, "her mother will send her to bed without her supper. How did Julia dare let Caroline out of her sight, and *here*?"

"When you say *here*, do you mean with the Godless Glenroys?" Jennie laughed. "Pris asked her because she was sorry for her, and then she asked the Lockharts to stop for Caro. It is hard to refuse the minister, especially when you want your daughter to marry one. I can't say that Caroline and young Fred Coombes are enchanted by the idea, but their mothers certainly are."

Lucy slapped her hands down on her knees and laughed aloud. "William's pounced!"

William had seized Thankful Basto. When he was four he had grandly promised a nine-year-old Thankful that he would marry her when he grew up, and sometimes Jennie thought he considered the promise still valid.

His brothers cheered him, girls clapped, and it didn't seem as if he could smile any wider; it was a case of a smile wearing the boy. Thankful mischievously kissed the top of his head, and he didn't even blush but looked completely blissful.

Thankful planted herself in the center, her hands on her hips. One day she would be stout like her mother; now she was as delicious as her mother must have been at that age, tinted like a ripe peach, and with astounding black lashes and eyes like a little Spaniard. She didn't waste any time catching and guessing Simmy Mayfield, perhaps by the way his thick fair hair lay like the thatch on a roof. His father had been in the crew of the brig *Paul Revere* when he was born (the year when she brought a cargo of Highlanders to America), and when Chet heard the news from a fisherman, a day away from port, he had been wild with triumph at the birth of a son. Simmy wasn't much younger than his father was then, and his grin was the same.

Now he was blindfolded and propelled into place, still grinning. "We'll see that you catch her, Sim!" someone yelled. In the grove the piper began to play for the General, and the horses tossed their heads and whinnied, not at the pipes but at another horse that came galloping down the road.

Two

W HO'S *THAT?*" SHOUTED a voice from the ring around Simmy, the slow circling stopped as everyone turned to stare, and intimations of disaster spread like the first fevers of a killing epidemic. But deeper in the grove the pipe music danced on, hands clapped out the time, and small children jigged and leaped like infant witches prancing to the devil's tune. Everyone was accustomed to the pipes by now, either loving or loathing them, and those who couldn't endure them simply moved a good bit away and tried to drown them out with vigorous con-versation. Some of these saw the horse up there in the sun, and fell silent.

The rider was Guy Rigby, one of the General's clerks, and he was out of the saddle almost before he'd pulled the animal up. He hitched the horse at the end of the line and came running down the field. The ring was broken, and the boys streamed after him to the grove, but the girls held back, bunching together as if in dread. Simmy, deserted, pulled off the blindfold, and followed the others at a lope.

"A fire in Maddox, God help us," someone whispered. "The whole waterfront could be going up."

"Or *Marmion*'s brought bad news."

Guy was breathing hard through his mouth, and his knobby face was red and wet. He was given a clear path to the General. The pipes stopped in mid-phrase, and the General looked all at once old, pleasure draining away from his face like blood. Guy Rigby arrived panting, looking wretched enough to throw himself on the ground and beg forgiveness for what he was about to say. Robin came past him and stood beside his father's chair.

"What is it, Guy?" the General asked quietly. "Do you need to wet your throat before you can talk?"

"No, sir." The boy licked his lips. "*Marmion*—"

"Yes, we saw her. Does this concern Captain Stephen Wells? Robin, go find him," he said irritably. "I've seen neither hide nor hair of him for an hour."

Guy shook his head. "Captain Orrin Wells is not sick or injured. He sent you a message, sir. He thought it was not right to wait any longer, because of needing to tell the families." His face streamed with new sweat and he pulled out a handkerchief and wiped it. "The *Maid of All Work*, sir—they spoke her drifting dismasted about two hundred miles southwest of Savannah, foundering and burning. No sign of life, all her boats gone. Very rough seas. Been a westerly gale, before *Marmion* left New Orleans."

"Somebody bring this boy a drink!" the General shouted. He pushed himself up from his chair by bracing his hands on the arms, and Robin handed him his stick. A young boy brought Guy a mug of water, which he gulped audibly. "Guy, rest the horse before you start back to town," the General said, "and don't hurry him. You've no cause to hurry now."

"Yes, sir. It's Young Joshua. Corny Sayers said to take him because he's fastest."

"Quite right," said the General. The *Maid of All Work* was one of his lime carriers. "We must assume—," he lifted his voice to carry, "that Captain Mayfield ordered his men into the boats before the *Maid* was blown so far out, and they are all safe ashore somewhere."

With surprising speed for one so large, Lydia had reached his side, and the minister moved to the other. The General limped off between them toward the road; each knew better than to offer an arm.

"*Simmy*," Robin said, aghast, and sprinted past his parents. Simmy was already bolting for the horses. Jennie shut her eyes and took a deep breath, bracing against what she'd forgotten until now, that Chet Mayfield was the captain of the *Maid*. A hand encircled her wrist and squeezed. She turned her head and looked into Anna Kate's pale, deepset eyes. Neither spoke. Then Anna Kate sighed and let go. "I will just be gathering up my family now," she said. Jennie longed for Alick and resented everyone and everything that crowded between them at this moment; she could not even see him, which seemed an added injustice.

Stephen and Alick came in time to see the General off, and everyone else left quickly after that. The joy had gone out of the day, and even the smaller children were subdued. Only Stephen remained, and that would not be for long.

"You and Alick have been mysterious all afternoon," Jennie said, "and I haven't had the chance even to pass the time of day with you."

"Believe me, Jennie, I would stay if Orrin hadn't come home this afternoon. We've seen each other just once in the past nine months, in Havana, and it was no pleasure because we each had men dying with yellow fever."

"Then this will be a grand evening for you and your parents," said Alick.

"Except that I will be riding around first to see Dorinda Mayfield," Stephen said grimly. "Lord, I can't figure Chet gone! It's not possible he isn't kicking up his heels somewhere. He's no fool for all his foolery. He's a good captain, and he's got them all safe."

"And looking for a dance," Alick suggested. Stephen smiled.

"When he was just a tyke he told Elder Mayfield he wasn't going to heaven if they didn't allow dogs. Later it was dogs and dances."

"At least we can be happy that Orrin had a safe voyage home, and I hope he has become very rich," Jennie said.

"He's a good Yankee trader, that boy." Stephen and Alick shook hands. "If I don't see you again before I sail, I will come to supper when I'm home again, Jennie. I'll confirm it in every letter."

"One can ask no more. We wish you a safe voyage, Stephen, and safe return."

Watching man and horse go away from them toward the road, Jennie's lips shaped the words *Safe voyage and safe return*, and she knocked gently on the pasture rail. Stephen had been her first American; first mate on the *Paul Revere*, he had received the Highland immigrants as they came aboard. Jennie had been quaking until she reached the top of the ladder and met his young blue eyes. She and Alick had both spoken to him in English, and he had exclaimed, "Thank God for English speakers!" Jennie stopped shaking. She'd been living from one hour to the next, then; she could not have imagined her American family-to-be, and this hard-bitten young man as a friend of it.

"Did you know," Alick was saying, "that Charles Wolcott was on the *Maid of All Work?*"

"Wee Charlie?" she asked incredulously.

"Wee Charlie could look down on the top of my head when I was last seeing him," he said. "He was taken on as cook just before she sailed, because the other one broke his leg. Charlie was wild to go, Stephen told me. He'd been promised a berth on the Daughters Line in the fall, but he wanted to be at sea while he waited. He hated farming."

Charlie was a Whittier boy, Priscilla's age. When they were small (and he was shorter than Priscilla in those days), he would go a mile out of his way to walk home with her, always barefoot except in winter, always silently trailed by two younger Wolcotts. He was consistently mute in Jennie's presence, but with an amazingly wide smile. She saw it now, and pressed her thumb and forefinger against the inner corners of her eyes as if to press back tears. "And Chet is gone too," she said. "I'm glad we don't know the others. This is bad enough."

"Come, *mo graidh*, it is cruel to them to give them up so soon. They could be finding their way home, even now. No one knows how long she was abandoned and drifting."

"Oh, I shan't give them up," she said fiercely. "But what a way to end the day! I can see why the ancients slew the bearers of bad news. Not that I'd want to slay Guy Rigby, but if he hadn't come we'd all still be happy for a little while longer.—You will have to put a gag in Vincent Taggart's mouth." Taggart was the most excessively superstitious of Alick's men. "At this moment he is probably telling everyone that *Ariel* is now cursed."

"I shall make him remember it is better to be silent than to sing a bad song," said Alick. "But she was a beautiful sight, was she not? Nothing can change that! And I am thinking that we could find something else to contemplate besides what all those horses have left for us."

"The poor creatures had nothing better to do," said Jennie. "All the fun was down at the shore." She patted Young Joshua's neck. The horse twisted his head around to stare up the road, his ears moving eloquently. A small gray horse was trotting toward them. The driver of the gig had a large round face like a smiling red moon wearing a top hat.

"Good afternoon!" he cried, saluting them with his whip.

"Good afternoon, Mr. Babb!" Jennie called back with spurious enthusiasm. Alick rubbed his hands tiredly over his face.

"He loves to be looking at his ship," he said. "I cannot be faulting him for that."

Mr. Babb pulled up, and Alick stepped to the small gray's head. "How is Dapple Gray today?" Mr. Babb laughed delightedly. "Capital name for him, but they call him Dandy. That's a mighty handsome weskit, Glenroy. Would it be your family tartan, now?"

"The Glenroys would be lucky if they had five whole shirts among them," Alick said dryly, "let alone a tartan."

Through the men's voices Jennie saw, as if through a small round window into the past, the cart trundling away along the Fort William street, Andrew Glenroy walking beside the horse and Elspeth Glenroy waving goodbye to them with both relief and sadness. They had sold their passage and their name to Alick and Jennie because at the last minute Elspeth was afraid to sail. Jennie thought about them often, wishing she could know if their baby survived, if they all still lived, if they had finally come to America, and where.

Creaking, and cautious, Mr. Babb was descending from the gig, puffing, but shaking his head at an offered hand. His torso continued the moon-shape on a larger scale. "If we could just go and have a look at my beauty. Not that I want to take up too much of your Saturday. But I am at my brother's home in Warren and it was a splendid afternoon to drive over to see her. So if it's agreeable to *you*—" He had the innocent complacency of a child who never expects a *no*.

"Certainly," said Alick, the epitome of Highland courtesy. They went down to the Yard, Mr. Babb expressing his pleasure in loud words and excited arm-wavings.

Jennie found the twins in the field, lying on their backs in the grass, hands behind their heads. They didn't hear her approach. "Would you rather drown all at once," Carolus was asking, "under one monstrous wave, or be tossed over and over till you died of exhaustion? Would you keep on fighting or just give up, to make it quick?"

"If there were sharks," Sandy said, "then you'd have no choice, and it would be quick, your blood flows so fast."

"But you'd be thinking while you bled. You'd know what was happening to you. I wonder if it's true about seeing your whole life pass before you."

"Well, we'll never know unless they come back from the dead and tell us," said Sandy, not flippant. "Or when it happens to us."

"And then we can't tell anyone," said Carolus.

Jennie stood by their heads, and they rolled their eyes up to look at her. "Why don't you ponder all this while you are cleaning up after the horses?" she asked. "The chore will keep you in touch with reality."

"It *is* reality," said Carolus. "The *Maid*'s crew is lost."

"We don't know that yet," Jennie said. "Now to work. You may take the tables apart too."

She saw them off and went across to the aromatic chill of the grove. In her bones she too believed that the crew was lost, but to deny death while there was the faintest breath of doubt was one way to stave it off for a little while.

William sat at one of the trestle tables, his father's coat in a bundle on the planks before him, his arms folded on it and his chin resting on them as he watched Priscilla and Thankful putting punch cups and mugs into large baskets. They had obviously been crying, but Pris carried her head very high, either to defy sorrow or to keep her nose from dripping. Bell Ann huddled in a captain's chair, her knees drawn up under her chin and her dress pulled down tight over them, thumb in her mouth, staring with glazed eyes at Guy Rigby. He slumped in another captain's chair, his long legs shoved out before him, his elbows on the arms and his chin braced on his folded hands. He seemed to be watching the girls, but he looked desolate.

"William! Bell Ann!" Jennie clapped her hands. "Who is going to let those poor dogs out of the barn?"

Bell Ann released her parboiled thumb and became instantly alert. She slid out of the chair. "I can do it. I don't need William."

"Yes, you do, if I say so," said Jennie. "All hands on deck, William! Take Papa's coat into the house and don't just toss it onto a chair for Garnet to lie on, and then you and Bell Ann can take the dogs for a good walk."

William sighed. He bundled the coat into his arms and said in a deep voice, "Step lively, Tail Pig."

"Mama, he called me Tail Pig!"

"William, you know what your father and I think about that. So mind your failings." She shooed them with her hands. Bell Ann turned back twice, but thought better of it each time and tramped off after her brother, an indomitable little figure whose dimity dress and white stockings had suffered greatly this afternoon. There was no point in telling her to change before the walk; nothing much worse could happen to her clothes.

Guy Rigby was struggling to his feet. "Mrs. Glenroy, ma'am, excuse me—"

"Guy, I think you need something more than cold water, but I'm afraid the wine is all gone."

"I promised my parents I would not drink wine or spirits until I am of age." His blush looked hot as a burn.

"Then you must have a good strong cup of tea."

"This is the first time a vessel has been lost since I became the General's clerk." He rubbed his forehead hard with the back of a big knuckly hand. "I had no idea, no suspicion, of what it would be like to carry such news. I never thought I'd *have* to."

"I know a little about it," Jennie said. "Just be grateful you were not obliged to tell the families. Your part is over. Priscilla!" she called across the tables. "Take Guy up to the house and brew a pot of tea. Drink it slowly," she said to Guy, "and it will help. Young Joshua is serene, he has Mr. Babb's horse for company." The girls were galvanized into cheerful authority, and escorted Guy away.

Three

SHE LEFT THE grove and walked around the landward end of the granite whaleback into another field, which had once been an alder swamp. Alick had rooted out the alders and cleared a path to the sandy cove, and turned part of the reclaimed land into a garden, enriched by years of leaf mould. It never turned powder-dry even in time of drought. The rest was green field where Jennie now picked her way among snowy scatterings of wild strawberry blossoms. Violets were sudden blue flashes in the mixture of dead and new grass. The minute yellow flowers of cinquefoil, the purple Gill-over-the-ground, and even smaller plants Carolus hadn't yet identified, could turn a square yard of field into a swatch as finely detailed as a calico print.

In the woods, green fountains of fern sprayed up from a floor of old spruce spills, and the trout lilies were opening. A small woodpecker worked high on a dead spruce, and all around her there was the busyness of chickadees and the tiny living jewels that were warblers.

She went deeper into the woods, until the wind became only a vague stir in the tallest trees. The little cemetery was in a clearing bounded by a stone wall Alick and David had built. They had found the Evans baby's grave here when they were exploring the woods during their first spring on the property. They were looking for the ruins of an old stone fort when they came upon the little clearing and the small grave outlined by white stones, almost lost in the dense groundcover that grew wherever the sun could reach through.

They had set to work then with their bare hands to tidy the little plot, while Pris lay on a shawl kicking and talking to the chickadees.

26

When Evans disappeared and his wife drowned herself, the children had been taken to Maddox. David, deaf and mute, was literate with a pen, but would not mention the baby. Gwynneth a bright, articulate little girl, told Jennie that David had built a box, and the two of them had bathed and dressed the baby in the best they could find, while their father lay insensibly drunk in his workshop and their mother was slowly losing her mind. David carried the box into the woods, Gwynneth took the spade, and small Geraint plodded stolidly behind them bearing a hatchet whose blade they'd wrapped in an old stocking so he couldn't gash himself. David dug the grave, and they buried the baby, whom their father had named Olwen, though they and their mother had called her Daisy.

"I wanted to say some words that day," Gwynneth said. "Something nice. But David ran away so fast. Geraint and I went to the beach and picked up white stones and put them all around it. Then I said 'The Lord is my shepherd'—all of it," she said proudly. "Mama never once asked us where Daisy was. It was as if there'd never been a Daisy." Her silver-gray eyes filled with tears. "I was going to put daisies there when they came in summer."

"We will put daisies there together," Jennie promised. She kept the promise, but even if their changes to the house had exorcised the drowned woman's ghost, Jennie was still haunted by the little grave and the picture of three children burying the baby. She and Alick had a small granite marker made, with the dates Gwynneth could guess at; David's eyes turned to dull glass when anyone approached him about it. Should the name be Olwen or Daisy? Jennie asked the child, and she said, "*Daisy*. Papa said Olwen, but he never looked at her. I hate Papa," she said calmly. "I hope he never comes back."

"If he did, the General and Mr. Dalrymple would never make you go and live with him," Jennie said.

"I hope he's dead. I think he probably is, and I can stay here, forever." *Here* was the home where the Overseers of the Poor boarded children left with no families.

She was living near Boston now, married to the first mate on a ship of the General's transatlantic fleet, the Daughters Line, and young Geraint was on another vessel of the fleet.

A week after the Glenroys moved into the house, David had appeared at the door, having walked from the orphans' home in Maddox. He let them know he would sleep in the shed with the cow and the horse, or in his brush camp in the old fort, but he was there to stay. He would do his own washing, and work for his board. The General, as his legal guardian, consented, and they made a room for him in the attic which was warmed in winter by the chimney coming up from the kitchen below.

He would turn his hand to anything he saw to do, or was asked to do, in the house or out of it. He spent his free time alone outdoors with the sketch books they gave him, or up in his room, even when they asked him to sit with them. When their prospects improved, Alick gave him an allowance, which he spent on drawing and painting materials.

He was now twenty-eight, and had been a professional artist ever since the General bought his oil painting of a launching.

Sitting on the wall, Jennie had let her mind travel far back, and was now working slowly, selectively, to the present, as if to escape contemplation of the second stone. Though she came here almost every day because of it, there was always this first flinching away from the actual sight of it.

They had named the fifth baby April for her birth month, and she was eighteen months old when the measles took her and almost killed three-year-old William. When she was gone, the house seemed full of her scraps of laughter or crying, and her own words for things like a flock of little birds chattering and flitting everywhere.

Alick had been walking the floor with her when she died; he thought he had lulled her to sleep with her favorite song. "Hee horo, my bonny wee girl, Hee horo, my fair one," he sang. "And will you come along with me, To be my own, my rare one?"

Jennie had been making tea when all at once the strength left her hands, and the presentiment nearly stopped the breath in her chest. She could have howled like a dog and run away until she fell from exhaustion in the dark, pushing her mouth against the earth to silence it and pressing her hands over her ears so that no one could tell her. It was as if she were doing all that, she was seeing herself doing it, even as she walked toward Alick and said with what voice could come from her, "Let me see."

Her face told him something, and he swung the child away from her, saying roughly, "She's asleep. Don't be waking her."

"Let me see, Alick." In a moment she *would* howl; it was rising in her throat. Finally he let her turn the blanket away from the small, perfect, sleeping, dead face.

Even then he denied it and would not give up, whispering Gaelic endearments to the child and brushing her face with light kisses. This was how it began for them, the hideous birth of grief. Though Alick felt himself to be Priscilla's father in all ways but one, April was the first daughter of his body. Lucy warned Jennie not to shut him out as she had shut out Harm when their first-born had not survived his second summer, but her warning was not necessary; Jennie and Alick had shared too much in their lives about which no one else would ever know to be separate in this.

During the days, neither could weep where the three grieving older children would see, and William was still weak and needed much care. But at night they could give way in each other's arms, under Alick's plaid; she'd brought it out to cover them like a magic mantle that took them back to the Scottish hillsides where they had first slept in each other's arms, not as lovers or bereft parents, but as fugitives fighting the cold and their separate terrors.

Three years later Bell Ann was born to them, their ragamuffin, gypsy, tomboy tyke with not even a wraith of resemblance to the lost one. Fate made the choice for us, Jennie thought. All we wanted was April back, if the baby was a girl. But we made Bell Ann instead, and perhaps her uniqueness was a special form of healing.

If April had lived, would Bell Ann have been born? As Jennie hadn't been able to imagine life without April, she couldn't now imagine it without Bell Ann, any more than life without Alick—the life she had actually been prepared to live with Nigel if he had not met Alick below the Pict's house that day.

She had never been glad of Nigel's death, but it had happened. The woman she had become could hardly believe that she had passively contemplated living with him, having children by him as her duty, after all the cold-blooded conspiracy of lies.

It would have endured possibly a few days, she thought, but never through another dinner with his family. No, I would not have stayed with him. If they wouldn't let me go in a carriage I'd have run away to Inverness like a tinker woman, and I'd have found passage back to England, home to Northumberland.

But then—still no Alick, except for those few meetings on the moors before the evictions and the burnings. No twins, no Sweet William, no April for a little while, no Bell Ann. You would have had Priscilla and never missed the rest, she told herself, but here it came again, the terrifying swoop into infinite space. How could all these who had been her life for nearly half of it not have *been*, simply because she walked on a road to the east instead of to the west? She fell back on a self-torturing trick she'd pulled on herself as a child: what if I have dreamed it all, and they never did exist?

Her forehead was wet and she heard her own hard breathing as she stared around the clearing. But there were the two small granite markers, and the woodpecker was still cheerfully hammering away as if to jar his brain loose, and crows were badgering an owl somewhere. She was wearing the wedding ring with which Alick had replaced Nigel's as soon as he could buy it.

She blew hard and shook herself. "Och, Cheenie, Cheenie, ye'll be off wi' the fairies yet," she murmured. It wasn't often she was tempted, or had the time and the privacy, to let herself go like this. In the eighteen years since Nigel had died she had learned to keep him where he belonged, even when he was present in a turn of Priscilla's head, in the light along a cheekbone, a gesture of her hands, in the way she sat a horse when she rode astride and galloped Diana across a field to take a wall like a hunter. Sometimes Nigel laughed at Jennie from his daughter's eyes, and that would be like a thumb pressed hard into the hollow of her throat, but only for an instant.

Within an hour of his death she had known that her survival depended upon her putting him into her past as soon as possible. There had been no time to weep for him and her lost innocence.

She turned the ring on her finger. As if this had conjured Alick to her, she sensed rather than heard his footfall behind her.

Four

S HE LEANED HER head against his chest. "I can feel the colors of that
tartan burning into my brain."

"Mr. Babb liked it fine," said Alick. "He was speaking of it again."

"One could almost be compelled to speak of it, to relieve the strain
of trying to ignore it."

He swung a leg over the wall and sat down, putting his arm around her
waist. The woodpecker had stopped. The brawling crows had flown
across the river. Silence and shade flowed together into the clearing until
over their heads a white-throated sparrow whistled his long pure notes,
and was answered.

"Babb has decided she will not be *President Jackson*, but *Governor
Lincoln*," Alick said. "He promises Aaron can begin work on the figurehead, and even brought drawings of the man. Now his only struggle is to
decide whether it should be *Governor Lincoln* or *Enoch Lincoln*. Och, it is
a mind-knotting question."

"Alick, I have not given thought to the *Maid of All Work* since I sat
here, and I am ashamed, with those families suffering."

"But there is nothing you can do about their suffering. We all know
the risks when a vessel goes to sea, whether she is carrying lime or salt fish
and barrel staves, or just going out to fish within a few days of here. When
I let our children sail on the river, I feel as if I am putting their death into
their own hands."

"But you don't let them know it."

"This is the coast and I am a shipwright. I cannot be forever clucking
on the bank like the old hen in Bell Ann's song. All I can do is put a

31

respect into them for tides and wind, and hope they will have more common sense than brilliance. I swear to myself that more vessels survive than sink, or else no one would ever have gone to sea at all. And then where would you and I be?" He nuzzled her neck, and she turned her mouth to his. "Isn't it the shameless pair we are," he said, "in broad daylight, and with such news black upon us?"

"But we've been apart all day," she said, "except at dinner, and then you were in disguise as *paterfamilias*." She held his face and kissed him again.

"We have all night," he said. He reached under her shawl to hold a breast.

"But as Papa and Mama we fall asleep the instant our heads touch the pillows."

"Not always, *mo graidh, mo leannan*." How astonished the rest of the world would be to know how seductive Mr. Glenroy could be with his eyes and his voice and his hands. She sighed pleasurably and settled against him. Gaelic was a language for lovers.

"What were you and Stephen talking about all afternoon? Is Stephen engaged to the daughter of a rich merchant in Oslo or the Canaries? I *know* she's not good enough for him."

"No, no," he said, laughing. "Not yet! But I'll have no word of our talk go beyond you and me and Stephen until our business is under way. Now it is an idea that I am to build a grand big ship for the China trade, and he and I will be partners in the venture."

"When will you begin?"

"Not tomorrow," he said with a smile. "Stephen will not be back until the autumn, and I will be working on the plans. Then the agreement is to be drawn up, and the timber cut and hauled out. *If* he is of the same mind when he comes back."

"He will be, he will be." She couldn't sit still any longer. "Oh, fiddlesticks! I must think about supper and all I want to think of is that lovely ship, and you and Stephen partners. Alick, when we met him at the head of the ladder at Fort William, if we could have ever *dreamed*— but it's better not to, I suppose. It makes the surprises all the more wonderful, and we can't brood about the tragedies when we don't know what they'll be." She looked involuntarily at April's stone, and his arm tightened around her in a spasm.

They had found how to live with it, but press ever so gently against it and it would bleed. Yet they would not, from choice, let it go. Mary Lamb had said it for all parents:

> Thou straggler into loving arms,
> Young climber up of knees,
> When I forget thy thousand ways,
> Then life and all shall cease.

They left the woods with their arms linked, hands palm to palm and fingers locked. "Are you ever worried about steam?" she asked. A Dutch vessel had recently crossed the Atlantic under steam, and there was talk in Maddox that a steam packet would be visiting this summer.

"We'll be dead and gone before ships are done with canvas and the four winds," said Alick.

"That's meant to be a comforting thought, I suppose," said Jennie, "but it makes me hear footsteps walking over my grave."

"Och, the Glenroys themselves may be building steamships one day, but if it takes a brave man to go to sea under canvas, it will take a hero to go to sea under steam. You can escape from a ship with burning lime, but not from an explosion."

Outside the woods, the sun's heat drew a sensuous and aromatic warmth from the earth. They stopped at the garden for a satisfied look at the symmetrical green rows and the new beanpoles. They had all worked hard at it; Bell Ann had dropped the seed potatoes in one row which she now called her own. At the head of the long slope, the spring sunlight had turned the late daffodils to a sheet of yellow light. It transformed the brass *Artemis* on the barn weathervane to a little ship of fire, and they watched her switch back and forth, blazing in the wind with the barn swallows swooping about her like attendant spirits. David had given her to Alick for his birthday the year after the launching. Not knowing what had become of the original still tormented Alick; he had never seen her after the hour of her launching, when her owner took her at once downriver on a northwest wind and an ebbing tide. She had flown past Misery Wall in her virgin beauty, and that was Alick's last sight of her, after she had shared his heart and soul with his family for half a year.

Some days later she was spoken by a home-bound Maddox schooner off Georgia's Sea Islands, but no local men had ever seen her again in all their travels.

In the past, when Jennie had caught Alick watching the weathervane, she used to say, "I am sure she is alive and sailing somewhere," but he wouldn't answer, so she had given up. Today he looked for a long time, his eyes half-shut against the light, and then he said, "I am listening to the silence. Our children must have all run away from home and taken the dogs."

"How considerate of them," said Jennie. "But Garnet refused to leave us to grow old without kit or kin." The gray tabby came through the orchard at the run, her striped tail erect with an eloquent crook at the end, and she was talking all the way in penetrating accents.

The small gray huddle of a house where the Evanses had lived, which Jennie had seen from the water when they entered the river on that distant Sunday, was larger now, clapboarded, and painted white. The herbaceous border was beginning to flower all along the front of the main house, except where tall lilacs grew on either side of the granite front doorstep. The roof had been raised to allow for dormers, the chimneys had been rebuilt, and an ell had been added at the western end of the house for the parents' bedroom. The kitchen ell on the eastern side had been lengthened to add a woodshed-workshop. David's room had become his skylighted studio.

When Alick and Jenny took the house, they did not move down the river to it at once. He went on working at the General's shipyard, learning more about the trade, and making the house livable with his scant spare time and money. Jennie continued teaching the General's children, to pay the rent on the brick cottage. Sukey's and Frankie's disappointment at not attending the town school was alleviated by the joy of keeping Priscilla at hand, as they had already chosen her for Allan Robert.

Harm Clements and Hector Mackenzie worked on the house with Alick, and the wives drove down with them on fine Saturdays, served meals, and did anything else they were allowed to do. The madness and speechless pain which seemed to have soaked into the walls were exorcised with new plaster and light colors. Partitions were removed to make large rooms out of tiny ones, and bigger windows brought in all the available light.

There was a shed for their first horse and their first cow, with a lean-to on the side for their first hens. The barn-raising came two years later. The Methodists fed well at their raisings, but they didn't hold with rum and dancing; the Glenroy barn had gone up with plenty of food and rum both, and a dance afterward on the clean new floor.

Kindling snapped in the kitchen stove when Alick and Jennie came in. Priscilla was in the pantry, which opened into both winter and summer kitchens; she was washing and drying the glassware and mugs, singing something melancholy to herself. She had tied back her hair and changed her muslin dress for a serviceable poplin one, and wore a large apron over that. She came out to gaze at her parents with wet blue eyes, then rushed at Alick and kissed him.

"What have I done to deserve this?" he asked.

"You're *alive*, Papa! I've been trying to imagine what it must be like to lose my father, but I can't bear to. I keep thinking about Simmy, and poor Charlie. It is too *awful*."

"No one knows yet that Simmy's father and Charlie are dead," Jennie said.

"But Simmy thinks his father's dead, and the Wolcotts think Charlie's gone, so it is all the same to them. If Papa was missing or you, I would believe the worst. I would be *positive* about it."

Like mother, like daughter, Jennie thought, putting on her own apron. "You are not going to lose me to the sea," Alick said to Priscilla, "so that is one less worry for you." He took his coat from the chair where William had tidily folded it and went through the house to the bedroom.

"It's natural to prepare ourselves for the worst," said Jennie. "But it's also natural and healing to hope for the best." She added more wood to the fire and brought out from the pantry the iron pot of haddock chowder she had made this morning, with all but the milk, and set it over the fire to heat. Garnet talked loudly; Jennie scooped out some solid chunks of haddock while it was still cool and put them in the cat's dish.

"Some people are always hoping and praying for the best," Pris said, "but they seem to get the worst, mostly."

"I think that to hope is a good *human* thing to do," said Jennie. "Because you never can tell. Men have come back before. When Paulina Revere's father was kidnapped by the press gang, we were sure he was as good as dead. When he was released after the War and came home, his wife had never given up hope. She was being courted like Penelope, but Roddy didn't murder all her suitors, as Ulysses did," she added meditatively.

"Do you suppose they still had the same dog?" Priscilla asked. "And he knew Roddy when no one else did? That part always makes me cry."

"I don't like to disappoint you, but when Roddy reached Liverpool— and he'd had a long walk, mind you, being discharged at Portsmouth— there was *Iolaire*, of all the ships in the world! Like his dreams, he said.

He could hardly believe it, and as he stood there staring, somebody aboard her recognized him, after seven years and a beard."

"In a novel no one would have known him," said Priscilla. "Mrs. Roddy would've married someone else, and Roddy would go away nobly with his broken heart, without ever letting her know that she was living in sin and her new children were illegitimate." She dabbled dreamily in cooling dishwater. "But he'd not have gone without a glimpse of his little girl. He'd have invented a reason to speak to her and hear her voice. He asked where he could find a meal and she pointed out the way and called him *sir* in her sweet little voice. She had eyes blue as larkspur, and—" She caught her breath and said mournfully, "How beautiful it was, and how sad."

"And it didn't happen. Have you considered writing novels as a profession? Because you've made a good beginning."

"If I thought I could support myself writing novels, I'd give it a good try. I would like to be a self-sufficient woman. — David has gone again. Guy Rigby told him that an old chapman is doing exact likenesses over in Wiscasset, so he loaded his saddlebags and left. His sketches of the launching are on the chest of drawers under the clock. Guy and Thankful were *so* impressed."

"David has been impressing me since he was twelve," Jennie said. Of course David had gone to look for his father again, drawn by the obsessive devotion that still existed seventeen years after his father left him.

"Where is everyone, Pris?" she asked.

"William and Bell Ann and the dogs have walked home with Thankful. The twins haven't cleaned up after the horses yet. They changed out of their good clothes, and Carolus said he was going botanizing, the dung would wait until he got back, it wasn't going anywhere. I told him that if the dogs rolled in it, he and Sandy would have to wash them."

"And Sandy?"

"Oh, I don't know," she said vaguely. "He's such a flea sometimes. Guy Rigby kept calling me *Miss* Glenroy. But he appreciated the tea and thanked me five times, and sent his thanks to you. He was really distraught."

"Poor Guy. When the General hired him he could think only of the glory and drama of great commerce. How did Caroline enjoy herself, before the bad news?"

"She was so happy, Mama! I have never seen her really romp around having fun. Between washing and combing and buttoning the pygmies, hearing their letters and drilling them on their sums, and being constantly told what's right and proper for a minister's wife, school is the only place where she can call her soul her own, and even then Fred Coombes is there. He's not bad—it's as if they had a silent agreement to ignore each other." She reached into a crock and came out with chunks of crumbly yellow johnny-cake. "How did this ever survive a day with these rapacious children?" She dropped the bread into a pocket. "But then Mrs. Goward puts her through an inquisition when school is out. 'Did you sit with Frederick at dinner time? Did you sing a duet with him today?' Caro simply freezes, and never says he *hates* sitting with *her*, and he can't sing even if he wanted to."

A chorus of bawling commenced across the road, and Pris said fondly, "Louisa is even louder than her mother." She ladled warm water into a pail. "Caro does not know *how* to milk, and she winces at the thought of washing Ianthe's udder, let alone squeezing milk out of it. She thinks I am a heroine." She continued the list on her way out. "She needn't wash dishes, or clean windows, or weed the garden, or even pick berries, because she must keep her hands nice. As if even *poor* minister's wives never have to do menial labor. And of course that disagreeable brat Bethiah resents this like a fury."

"I can't say that I blame her," said Jennie. "Pris—," but Pris cannily escaped, still talking about Caro. Keeping an unwelcome subject afloat while a child tried to drown it was a talent a parent must learn early or be forever swamped in succeeding floods. She moved swiftly. "*Priscilla,*" she called strongly, "where is Sandy?"

The bawling reached a crescendo, and Pris snatched a sun-dried cloth off a lilac bush and ran with the slopping pail to the gate. When she disappeared around the far side of the barn, the tumult stopped, which meant the cornbread was being distributed. "I think you were lying to me by omission, my girl," Jennie said, "and I intend to know why, very soon."

Five

_____

T ALKING TO YOURSELF?" Alick asked behind her. "Or are there Little
People here and I cannot see them?"

"I asked Pris where Sandy is, and she eluded me like a fish," said
Jennie.

He was not quite smiling, but near enough to amusement to make her
say with some warmth, "Whenever she doesn't gladly tell me what one
of the twins is doing, my thumbs prickle." She wiggled her thumbs
between her face and Alick's. "The last time these told me anything
strongly was when the twins played truant and walked to Maddox to see
the Spanish ship."

"Ah, yes," said Alick. "For the educational experience, Carolus
explained. Och, it was most educational, they discovered when they
spent Saturday and Sunday in their room except for their chores. . . .
Listen." A whistling Carolus was coming up the road, his black-japanned
vasculum slung over his shoulder. "One of Rory's tunes," Alick said.
" 'The Black Watch Leaving for Flanders.' All that's lacking is the swing
o' the kilt."

"He'd wear it well, wouldn't he?" Jennie said. Carolus's shirt was
dusty and his boots were plastered with mud. His black hair flapped over
his forehead. When he saw his parents at the gate he stopped whistling
and broke into a run.

"Wait till you see what I found lurking at the edge of the cranberry
bog!" He opened the vasculum and revealed to them a yellow moccasin
flower. "_Cypripedium calceolus_," he said. "I cannot believe there have
always been yellow ones here and I never knew till now. And _this_," he

38

lifted a long-stemmed flower, winged and delicate, in shades of pink. "*Arethusa bulbosa*," he said reverently. "I have seen yellow moccasin flowers, but never arethusa, anywhere. There are nine more. Can you credit that, Mama? Papa?" His eyes were shining like Bell Ann's. "I picked two. One is for Mr. Lockhart's collection. I went straight to them, as if something told me to go there, right now. *Today*."

"They are very fine," said Alick. "Do you have any idea where that other rare plant, your brother, is?"

"Oh." Familiar expression of polite interest.

"Aye, *oh*," said his father.

"I am not sure," Carolus said thoughtfully. "No, I don't really know. I should take care of these plants." He moved, but was immobilized by Alick's hand on his shoulder.

"He is not where he was when I last saw him," Carolus said earnestly.

"And where was that?"

Carolus pointed down the road. "There by the turn, by the old apple tree. You can't see the spot from here."

"And what was he doing? Preparing to leave home? Or to take wing, perhaps?"

"He was feeling sick." A familiar panic took Jennie by the throat. *Typhoid. Black diphtheria. Scarlet fever.*

"How sick?" she asked sharply. "In what way?"

"Not *sick* sick," said Carolus unhappily. His eyes slid from her face to his father's, and he licked his lips. Color burst into his cheeks. "He was drunk."

Relief and then consternation silenced Jennie for the moment. Alick took his hand off Carolus's shoulder and folded his arms, studying the boy's face as if memorizing it. Priscilla's voice came fragmented from the barn; she was practicing declamation while she milked.

"Drunk with what?" Alick asked softly. "Do you know?"

"Yes, Papa." Carolus gave up with grace the uneven struggle. "It was the General's wine. There was a bottle underneath one of the tables, and when we were taking the planks off the sawhorses we found it. The bottle was about half full. We both tasted it," he volunteered, "but I didn't like it much."

"How much did your brother drink?" Alick asked.

"Most of it," said Carolus unhappily.

"And why were you not stopping your brother?" Alick's voice took on strong Highland intonations.

"I was trying," said Carolus in unconscious imitation. "But when was Sandy ever listening to me? He was hot and the wine was cold. He is the oldest, he told me, so he knows the most. He said it was no different from cider, and he drank it fast."

Jennie worried about many diseases that could threaten her children, but she had never considered drunkenness; it was a plague that came to other families. Now she had a drunken son somewhere, five weeks short of his fifteenth birthday. His voice had not even begun to change! She found she was hugging herself hard enough to make her arms ache.

"And you are not knowing where he is at now." Alick hadn't raised his voice.

"No, Papa. We put the chairs away, but already he was dizzy. We started for the house, and he was laughing and singing, and spinning, and trying to dance. He fell down by the apple tree, and I couldn't get him up again—he kept slithering out of my hands like a sack of water, and laughing. So I left him there and came here to change my clothes. I'll begin cleaning up after the horses right now," he said eagerly. "The plants can wait."

"So can you," said Jennie. "Was Priscilla here?" He turned to her with frank relief.

"Yes, and Thankful, but Guy Rigby was gone, I told Pris in the pantry so Thankful and the young ones didn't hear. She said he would likely fall asleep where he was, and if you and Papa found him, he must dree his own weird. And he *was* sleeping when I went past him to go botanizing. I tried to wake him but I couldn't. What a snore!" He started to grin, but thought better of it. "He wasn't there when I came back."

"You can be at your work now," said Alick.

"Yes, *sir*!"

"Run upstairs first and look," said Jennie. "He may have come in and gone to bed."

He gave his boots a token scrape on the sisal mat outside the door, and they heard him running through the house.

Jennie loosened her aching arms and put her hand on Alick's sleeve. "*Drunk*," she murmured.

"It would take very little for a child not accustomed to it." Alick didn't sound unduly distressed. He put his hand over hers and said. "What cold fingers."

"But half a bottle for a child, and *our* child?" The leaves suddenly stirred over their heads, and she said, "Our rowans are not bringing us much good luck today. Perhaps they think we've had our share."

Carolus came running back, saying, "He isn't up there!" He ran to the barn as Pris had gone earlier, a bird released from a cage.

"Come along, my Jeannie," said Alick. "I am beginning to have the Sight about one of my children." They walked past the eastern end of the house, out by the old barn cellar toward the wash house. They heard Sandy moaning and retching before they found him sprawled behind the building. Evidence of everything he had eaten that day decorated the tangle of young growth around him, and a powerful scent of sour wine superseded everything else. He groaned and apparently tried to burrow under the plants, and a faint, plaintive cry was heard as his face encountered a thistle.

"*Mach'a seo*, Alasdair, *mach'a seo!*" Alick said vigorously. He picked up Sandy by the back of his shirt and the seat of his breeches and walked him around to the front of the wash house and propped him against the wall. Sandy was alarmingly white, and the thistle scratch was bright red across his nose. He kept his eyes squeezed shut and protested in small inarticulate sounds. Alick dipped a bucket into a butt of rainwater.

Priscilla had predicted correctly: if Sandy's parents found him, he must dree his own weird. The first bucketful of water took him in the face, and he caught his breath in a whooping gasp. Alick dipped the bucket again. Jennie was undecided between overseeing the remedy or sparing Sandy the humiliation; perhaps it should be an all-male occasion. She went back to the house, hearing behind her another splash and a yelp.

She was glad William and Bell Ann were lingering at the Bastos' with the new lambs and Carolus was still heaping up horse dung, assiduously keeping account of his share. Pris was now reciting Milton with tremendous brio. " 'Hence, vain deluding joys, The brood of Folly without father bred!' " Jennie remembered doing the same piece up in the lofty attic of Pippin Grange, where the acoustical properties were superb.

When she returned to the wash house with towels, dry clothing, and his barn boots, Sandy was stripped to his drawers. His hair was flattened down his neck and cheeks in long dripping locks; water was running off his eyelashes, his nose, his chin, down over his rib cage and concave belly, and the soaked linen drawers clung to the flesh that showed through them. He stood in a puddle of water. He gave his mother a quick look, then shut his eyes again and shivered in his martyrdom.

Alick seemed neither angry nor gratified. He opened the wash house door. "Go dry yourself and dress." Sandy groped his way into the building. His father took the clothes to him, and came out saying, "I am expecting to see you at work in twenty minutes." He picked up Sandy's shoes. "They'll be needing a bath in neat's-foot oil," he said cheerfully. "It's fine he wasn't wearing his Sunday pair."

Jennie beckoned him away from the building. "I don't know what I feel about all this," she said in a low voice, "supposing that he's now discovered it, he—"

"Don't be so anxious, *mo leannan*. He is not tottering toward a drunkard's grave. I had my first drink of whisky when I was fourteen, and after I stopped the gasping and the choking, I was that elated! *Merry* is the word."

"I'd love to have seen you merry at fourteen. And did you look like Carolus? Who was the corrupter of the young, or did you steal it?"

"Lachy was only trying to warm me after I fell out of a boat into the loch in November. I learned to swim that day too," he said. "Before that, I was always in fear of the kelpy, the black wolf, drowned witches, and whatever else we thought was living there. I'd never dip a toe in, only the oars. But I was swimming *that* day! *Dia*, I could feel them snorting all around me and clutching at me with their icy claws. And mind you, I was all of ten feet from the shore." He grinned. "But man, I was a hero when I crawled out, I had beaten them all. Then Lachy poured me a dram. What a day that was!"

They spread out the soaked clothing on the bay bushes at the edge of the woods. "The whisky ran like water in the glens then, but it was made to smuggle away through the hills and put a few pounds in poor Highland purses. What was saved in the cottages was medicine for the chills or to open congested lungs, or to make a bad pain bearable. No, that one sup didn't send me so mad for it so I'd be stealing from Lachy or Parlan. Besides, I would have been beaten for it."

"How will you punish Sandy if he does it again?"

"If. *If*. How can I know? Today he did not set out to get drunk, he gulped down a cold drink like the child that he is. But now he knows it was more than cider or raspberry shrub. Och, from the looks of it back there he has brought up everything but his own gut, and he will be remembering for a long time. Also the cold dousing," he added with a quirk to his mouth.

"I hope so," she said. "But somehow I can't help wishing they were all still under twelve."

"I will tell you honestly, Jeannie, that I have more worry about Sandy going to sea than becoming a sot."

"He can't go without our permission for six years, Alick. Let us not forget that." She put her hand on his cheek. "I will stop worrying about the drink if you will stop worrying about the sea."

"Done." He turned his head to kiss her palm. In the next instant Bounce, the terrier, was hurling himself at their legs, all lolloping tongue, wet paws and whiskers, and passionate little yelps. Darroch, the black Newfoundland, was booming out his return from between the barn and the springhouse. William and Bell Ann were behind him, shouting and waving as if just come back from a voyage around the world. They had not changed their clothes, but they had left their good shoes at home, which was a blessing of sorts.

Six

T HEY WERE POTENTLY scented with calf and lamb, and Bell Ann could have a lamb next spring if her parents allowed; she had no doubt of that, and was listing names over the din of hens wanting their supper.

There were two bull calves at the Bastos' farm, destined to take over the work when Bob and Barry were retired. "Why can't Ianthe and Louisa have bullocks, Papa?" William asked. "I could train them and hire them out, and haul lumber for the yard, and everything."

"Euphemia, Geraldine, Marguerite!" Bell Ann chanted.

"You will have to take the matter up with Ianthe," Alick told William. "Louisa is too young."

"I can't talk to her," William said crossly. "She doesn't understand English. Cows *don't*." He knew the Bastos' bull was involved, but suspected that Ianthe willfully chose to deliver heifers, and her daughter would do the same.

"Lucinda, Sarie Jane, Caroline," Bell Ann recited. She was marching now, stamping her bare feet.

"If the animal is ignorant of English, it is not your older sister's fault," Alick said. "She is giving the beasts a grand education in literature. You will have to speak to Ianthe in poetry. Try Sir Walter Scott."

William's dark brows came down and he pressed his lips tightly together. Alick laughed and took him gently by the nape of his neck; William ducked his head to hide his smile and bumped his forehead against his father's side.

"Abigail, Olivia, Beatrice," continued Bell Ann. "Don't you think they are all beautiful, Mama?"

44

"Music to my ears." Jennie stopped the procession by the woodshed door. "Your feathered friends are waiting yonder for their supper." Bell Ann plumped herself down on the bench and became as limp as her rag doll. "I'm too tired." Black lashes sank over her eyes and lay ravishingly on carnation cheeks.

"A girl as bright as you can do chores in her sleep," said Jennie. "Up with you now." William commanded his imaginary team to stand, and Bell Ann dragged behind him into the woodshed for cracked corn.

While they were inside, Sandy tramped across the road to the barn. Alick looked after him and then quizzically at Jennie. Both understood the unbearable rawness of pride, when one is too old to cry and too young to take a stand. When he met Priscilla coming from the spring house, she spoke to him but was obviously not answered. She shrugged and came on, carrying the milk bucket and cloths to be washed and a jug of cold milk from the morning.

"Can't you make them go faster?" Bell Ann whined.

Pris turned to her parents. "Make who go faster?"

"His oxen," said Jennie.

"He'll be wanting to take them upstairs tonight, they're just away from their mothers," Alick said, and they laughed. Sandy was just leaving the barn with his shovel, and even from here Jennie could see how red his face was.

Damn and blast! she thought, he thinks we're laughing at *him*. But to call after him and say it wasn't so would only draw attention to his humiliation.

While Pris was busy in the pantry, Jennie fed the dogs. The chowder was boiling and she moved it to the back of the stove. When the bubbles ceased, she poured in the milk, breathing with pleasure the aromatic steam. Alick was outside on the bench smoking his pipe, his elbows on his knees, gazing down toward the river. But not seeing it, Jennie thought; he was already building his and Stephen's ship.

She poured hot water into the big tureen to heat the ironstone before it received the chowder, then began to set the table. Priscilla was unnaturally quiet as her mother walked back and forth behind her; because of Charlie Wolcott, Jennie thought.

She lined up the soup bowls and laid split common crackers in the bottom of each. She brought butter from the cold cellarway under the front stairs and set out a fresh loaf on the scarred board with the bread knife beside it.

Pris, coming out with the wet cloths in her hand, said abruptly, "Mama, I didn't want to tell you about Sandy."

"I know that now," Jennie said. She gave Pris's arm a reassuring pat, and Pris went out singing to hang up the cloths. Jennie wondered if she had really wanted to spare her, or if it was clan loyalty to her brother in spite of their frequent arguments.

Never mind, she thought, it's over until the next time. And I promise myself that I shall remain tranquil, no matter what. At least on the surface, she qualified, and if it's not a matter of life and death.

Alick stopped William and Bell Ann outside and made them wash their faces and hands, and finally their feet, in the basin kept beside the corner rain barrel. Jennie handed out washcloths, towels, and a bar of Hat Shenstone's soap. When they came in, damp and lavender-scented around the edges, Jennie sent them upstairs to change their clothes; Bell Ann was to put on her nightgown, and they were to bring down what they had taken off and leave it in the big basket in the woodshed.

Carolus too washed by the rain barrel and left his boots in the woodshed.

"Where is Sandy?" Alick asked him mildly.

"Oh, he did his share and marched off to the shore. I don't think he's very hungry, but I am starved. Sandy was not inclined to conversation," he remarked. There was a slight tremor in his voice which suggested that he found the whole episode very funny, even if he didn't dare show it. He and Pris were noticeably avoiding each other's eyes. Each child knew a way to hit a favorite target; Sandy was shorter than his sister and his twin, so his specialty was to behave like Cock-of-the-walk, with frequent references to himself as the oldest son (he was born ten minutes before Carolus) and to Priscilla as a female (the word mere silent but understood).

William was too involved with his bullocks to miss Sandy, but Bell Ann asked at once where he was.

"He has an upset stomach," Jennie told her. "When it is settled, he can eat."

"Did you give him ginger tea?"

"Nannyplum tea is just what he needs," said Carolus, but Alick's sideways glance warned him.

"Bell Ann, eat, and you can talk afterward," her mother said. William ate solemnly, brown eyes watching his team waiting outside the door, just beyond the two dogs lying across the threshold. All safe, Jennie thought, even the animals in the barn. Sandy was safe somewhere down on the shore, comforted by solitude, a benison in short supply around here. But she wished she could stop seeing Charlie Wolcott as a small boy and Chet Mayfield as a big one.

Priscilla's spark of mischief had been quenched by sadness. Carolus was either thinking of the lost men or was wandering somewhere far from home finding the plant that had never before been seen in the New World and would henceforth carry the name *Glenroysia* after its family classification. Bell Ann prattled on about her new lamb.

"P'raps it will be a boy lamb, so I am already thinking up boy's names, and p'raps it will be a black lamb, and then his middle name will be Ebony, but I can give him two other names besides, and—"

"Why don't you write them all down on your slate tonight?" Jennie suggested. "Don't tell us any more now. Surprise us."

Bell Ann nodded and went on eating, but between swallows her lips were seen to move. Jennie wished, not for the first time, that she had never told the children about Ebony, the black wether of her childhood. He'd provided a flow of bedtime stories over the years, but after a while most of them were spun out of Jennie's imagination.

If they allowed Bell Ann to have a lamb, even a black wether, he could never live up to her vision of Ebony. Besides, there was nothing more domineering than a cosset lamb after it left off bottle-feeding and grew up. Besides that, a lamb raised by its mother would never touch the dangerous things that pet lambs ate. They sometimes died of their foolhardiness because they did not know how to be proper sheep. Bell Ann could never stand losing one, and if there was any kindness at all in fate she would be wanting something else by next lambing season. To be safe, Jennie would have a word with Nick Basto.

"Papa," William asked, "Will we ever build a lime carrier?"

"If someone is asking for one, we will be building her." He ladled more chowder into William's lifted bowl.

"Well, I hope nobody asks us to build one," William said flatly, "because having the lime catch fire is an awful way for a ship to die."

"All ways are awful," Alick said.

"A slaver is the worst thing to build," Carolus said suddenly. "Papa, you would know, wouldn't you, if a ship was meant for a slaver? I mean, with the special quarters below where they keep them, and all that."

"I would know, and I would not be building her. It is also against the law."

"Do you think Mr. Babb makes some of his money from slaves?"
Priscilla asked. "He has interests in Boston, and everybody knows how
many immoral men there are growing rich in the slave trade. I read about
it in the *Argus*."

"If a slave trader can name a ship for Mr. Enoch Lincoln," her father
said, "who hates slavery with a passion bigger than he is, that man is
hypocrite enough to make Satan blush, and I would not have him step
foot on my land. Does that answer your question?"

"Yes, Papa," Carolus and Pris said meekly together.

Sandy hadn't returned by the time they finished the meal, and Alick
sent William to find him and tell him to come home. William set off with
his bullocks and both dogs. Alick went to the ell bedroom where he could
sketch and figure by the strong light from the west. The twins usually
washed and wiped the supper dishes; tonight Priscilla took Sandy's part,
while making a public note of the fact that he owed her a chore. He could
do her share of the churning next time; they all hated to churn. Bell Ann
wiped the cutlery, one piece at a time. Her eyes were angelically lifted as
if she heard heavenly voices, but she was trying to make sense of a
conversation kept cryptic so she wouldn't guess it was about Sandy.

William was a long time gone, because you cannot hurry oxen. The
dishes were put away, the hot water kettle refilled by Pris, fresh water
brought by Carolus, and now he was cutting kindling out in the woodshed, keeping his own score against Sandy.

Jennie walked Bell Ann across the road to the Necessary. The barn
was dusky but not a frightening place, with the chattering swallows
coming and going under the roof. Bell Ann had to say goodnight to each
face that looked out at her over the mangers. Jennie used to do the same;
it was one of the unlooked-for gifts of parenthood along with its woes,
this re-creation of one's own childhood. However, she broke off the
adieux after the third kiss on Brisky's nose, and Bell Ann cried despair-
ingly, "What if he drops dead during the night? Or I do?"

"He won't," said Jennie, "and neither will you. But I promise to watch
you both the way Garnet watches a mousehole."

"Oh, the poor mouse!" All the children had rescued so many things
from Garnet to be released in the woods behind the wash house that they
called the area the Old Soldiers' Home.

Bell Ann's prayers were short. Jennie's theory of divine indifference
was kept to herself and Alick, and with the children she stressed being

more thankful than greedy. God could not possibly grant everyone's requests, there were so many people in the world.

"Sarie Oakes says God can do *anything*, the tiniest and the biggest," Bell Ann said.

"Well, perhaps," said Jennie, "but I think he'd appreciate a 'thank you' instead of 'please give me' from little girls like you, who have so much."

"But what if it's something I just couldn't stand being without? And I'd die if I didn't get it?"

"The world is full of people who *didn't* die from not getting their own way," said Jennie. "There are more of us than the other kind. Don't you think there are hundreds of things your papa and I would like to have?"

"But you're grown-up. You can just go and buy them."

"Oh no, my poppet. We are not rich! And some things cannot be bought, even if we had all the money there is. And just because I needn't ask permission before I do something, that doesn't mean I can do and have everything I desire."

Bell Ann bounced upright. "What do you *really* want that you can't have? What do you want to do the most in the world?"

"At the moment I want you to go to sleep," she said. "And you are keeping your children awake. They're all lying here thinking, 'Will that girl never stop talking?' Poor Bear has circles under his eyes."

Bell Ann gave her an enchanting gap-toothed grin and a tight hug around her neck. "I will go to sleep trying to think up things you want, and ask you tomorrow. I wish I could be your fairy godmother, Mama."

"And I yours," said Jennie. "But since neither of us lives in the chimney corner among the ashes, perhaps we don't need one."

Seven

A LICK SAT BY the western window of their bedroom, holding a slate on his knee and writing figures on it, whispering to himself, erasing, beginning again. He glanced absently at her, his lips moving, then returned to his slate. This was the preliminary incantation, the casting of the runes, that would result in his and Stephen's ship sliding down the ways.

She let herself quietly out the front door between the purple lilacs. The wind was still blowing, but the rustling of the orchard leaves was not loud enough to dull the evening song of the resident robin or blot out the calls of the veeries in the woods.

It was nearly low water in the river. The channel was a band of ultramarine and gilt ripples flowing between broad stretches of exposed flats and mussel beds on either side. Weedy ledges, invisible at high tide, were now appearing like a scattered herd of prehistoric bison. A few gulls picked about on the opposite shore where the wet mud reflected the western sky like glass. Fields, forest, and buildings were washed with gold, the windows full of fire.

It was a perfect hour for wandering among the fascinations of low tide, which William and Sandy must now be doing. Why am I not down there myself? she questioned. Why is it all left to the children? Because I would have to change my shoes first, and this dress, and by then the sun will be behind the trees, and then the twilight comes on too fast.

Garnet came from the orchard. A barn swallow shot down at her and straight up again as if bound for the zenith. Garnet ran chirruping to Jennie, who let her into the house.

She walked out to the road and discovered a conference under the rowans between Priscilla, Carolus, and William. No Sandy. He was still sulking, then, very hungry but waiting until he thought everyone had gone to bed. The children spun toward her with the effect of coming to attention. William said rapidly, "The dory's gone. He must have taken her out a long time ago, because the tide's way out beyond her mooring." He nervously fingered the side seams of his breeches. "I didn't miss her at first because I walked all the way to Misery Wall to see if he was digging around in the shell heap. When I came back, I saw she was gone."

He was gratified by his moment of importance, and awe-struck by his news. Sandy had taken the dory out after supper without permission. What *next*?

"William thinks Sandy's gone to sea," Pris said. "Like Bobby Shafto, but without the silver buckles."

"He's tide-nipped on a ledge somewhere." Carolus sounded bored. "The dory's high and dry, and he has to wait until she floats again, but he has about two hours to go before the tide turns. He is thinking of chowder and drooling like Darroch when he watches us eat gingerbread. I'll wager we could see him from the end of Misery Wall."

"Shall I go look?" William asked avidly. "I didn't go way out."

"No, love," Jennie said. If he went and didn't see Sandy, the event would be somehow threatening.

"Mama, I am wheeling up *all* the manure," Carolus said. "So Sandy owes me for it. Will you take note of it?"

"Don't either of you ever do the other a favor which does not have to be repaid?"

"Once you start that, it's as bad as irresponsible lending or borrowing," Carolus explained as if she were William's age. He picked up the handles of the wheelbarrow and trundled it away.

"You know, Mama," Pris said, "if you can put someone in your debt for three or four chores, it's as good as money in a dish on the shelf. It's a pity you couldn't have given William and me each a twin to sharpen our wits on."

"I thought one pair of twins in the family was enough," Jennie replied.

"I don't know if I'd want a shadow anyway," Priscilla said. "And what if *she* saw me as *her* shadow? What horror! —Take a walk with me, Mama?"

"I am going to stay with Papa," William announced.

"Wash the clam flats off Bounce first, and dry him before he can run upstairs," Jennie said. "I'd like to walk, Pris."

"I'll get us some shawls, then. It's cool now, with the sun down."

Waiting by the rowan trees, she heard Carolus whistling behind the barn and Brisky's response, the heavy shifting of the horses' feet on the barn floor. Behind her, William and Bounce were noisily enjoying the bath by the rain barrel.

Remember, she warned herself, you are going to remain tranquil, *no matter what*. She would not have been nervous for herself out there—she wasn't afraid of the water, and the dory was as safe and dependable as Darroch—but one's child was a far different matter, especially after dark when she wanted them all under one roof. Was the breeze freshening? Louder in the darkening trees? A going tide and an opposing wind could give you a fine run for the money if you had rage enough to work off, but before you knew it you had a prodigious long row back.

She knew that uncontrolled apprehension could be the first deadly vibration to set free the avalanche of panic. Her sister Ianthe had written to her from Switzerland about an Alpine village's death under a snow-slide, and Jennie had found the metaphor for her vulnerability.

The wet terrier threw himself at her, and William leaped after him with a towel and flung it over him, threatening to cut his tail off behind his ears. Bounce got his head free and seized a mouthful of William's hair. Jennie laughed dutifully, William went giggling to the house with his squirming bundle, and she was alone.

If I see Sandy first tonight, she thought, I shan't wait for his father to do the switching. She had gotten over expecting her own death as the logical end of every pregnancy; it was ridiculous, given the way she bloomed while carrying, and her easy deliveries. To worry about children was natural in a world where too many of them never made old bones, but common sense and her own experience as a child told her that not every fever, rash, or upset stomach was a portent of disaster. The three older children had sailed through measles without either eye trouble or lung congestion.

But when April died, and William nearly followed her, she and Alick crossed into a world of nightmare. Now it had happened to them as it had happened to almost all the other parents they knew; now a flush, a cough, or vomiting could mean another child was beginning the descent to death.

She and Alick had their first real quarrel when he told her she could turn the children into shrinking little creatures with fear forever at them. It was in their bed one night, when Carolus had just fallen asleep in the small chamber behind their room after a bout of summer complaint.

"What do *you* know about it?" she had whispered wrathfully. "*I* am their mother; *I* carried them in my body."

He seized her so fast and so brutally that she was shocked speechless. She could not move even slightly in his grip, and he spoke to her with a chilling composure.

"*I* am their father. Do you think *I* am not afraid in my gut and my heart? Do you think *I* am not knowing there is always something at our backs, and we not daring to turn and face it for fear of recognizing it? But what are we doing to *them*? And to *us*? *Dia*, it takes more bravery to be a parent than I was ever dreaming of. But you were always brave."

"You know that is not so," she said stonily. "I was always a coward."

"Not about ghosts of murdered excisemen." She knew he was smiling then, referring to a night in the Highlands when he had been afraid and she hadn't been. But she wanted only not to be reasoned with about her rightful terrors.

"I cannot help it. I cannot simply fold my hands and say whatever happens is God's will."

"I could not do that, because I am not such a believer. But they have a right to expect strength from us. If we can be driving away their nightmares, we can be driving away our own."

"I cannot," she insisted bitterly. "Not after—" She still couldn't say April's name, and she knew there were nights when he didn't sleep, he still walked the floor with April in his arms, singing "Hee Horo, my bonnie wee girl," to her, trying to find the missed moment when she had stopped breathing. *She went alone*, he had repeated that night. *She was so little, and she went alone without even a kiss from us.*

No, Jennie told him, she was not alone, she was safe in her father's arms. She went to sleep, as she had always done, to your singing. Jennie had painfully scraped together the strength for him, and she could do it for the children in the ordinary trials and alarms of existence. But she seemed to have no control over the sensation of dissolving bones, crushed lungs, and a heartbeat gone wild, until the day came when she saw reflected in a child's eyes not fear of the hurt, but of *her* fear.

Alick had been right, and she told him so. "But Alick, I have the same horror of losing *you*. I don't know how I could live without you."

"Every time one of them was born I went down to hell and back, thinking your heart might stop or you would bleed to death." He rocked her in his arms, whispering, "*Tha gradh agam ort-sa.*"

I love thee. He had said it to her for the first time the night they first made love. To her there was never such a language for tenderness: she always responded to it like a child who had been comforted by it in the cradle and never forgot.

The light had changed to the clear, shadowless medium after sunset, and Alick, Priscilla, and William came out to her from the house.

"So Sandy has gone downriver," Alick said. "Well, he will be coming home under the stars then."

"I wish I was with him," said William. Alick turned the boy toward the house.

"Set up the chessmen, and we will have a game before you go to bed." He took Jennie's shawl from Priscilla and laid it over her shoulders, running a finger up under the loose hair on her neck.

"He will be all right," she said.

"Och, I am sure of it."

"You're lying, of course," she murmured, and they both smiled. Priscilla looked at them indulgently.

"Watch out for witches and warlocks," Alick said, and returned to the house, calling the dogs. Jennie and Pris walked up toward the town road, meeting Carolus coming from the barn. "Good night, ladies," he sang out. "Beware the phantom Hessian soldier who is forever seeking his old regiment!"

"There were no Hessian soldiers around here, you idiot," said Pris.

"Then if you meet him, ask him who he really is," Carolus went on, whistling "Yankee Doodle."

The wind was a soft roar in the trees now, working around to the west. Pris tucked her arm inside her mother's. "I love going through the woods when they're so dark, and the wind in the treetops hides the beat of mysterious hoofbeats. I really think I should give serious thought to being a novelist. I shall have to think up a pen name, like Bell Ann thinking up names for her lamb. But, seriously—" She stopped Jennie. "Mama, what will become of me when school is out? I cannot be going to the parsonage forever, just to keep busy. I want to *do* something, work at something *real*, not stay home embroidering pillowcases for my marriage chest and waiting to be courted." Keeping her voice low intensified the emotion in it. "You don't know how I envy Fred Coombes, going to college in Waterville this year. He is so dull and timid that it will all be wasted on him. I don't mean *I* want to be a minister," she said with a shaky laugh, "but—well, I try not to envy Carolus's chances. I don't want him *not* to go to Bowdoin College, even if I cannot, because he is brilliant and he should go." Her voice wobbled childishly. "If only I'd been born a boy, then the whole world would be mine, as it belongs to the twins, and to little Sweet William."

They began walking again. "But Mama, when I catch myself speaking as if Maddox and Tenby are the world, then I know how bound, haltered, *chained* a female is. No matter how much freedom you and Papa give us here, the world outside is forbidden me. So what waits for me when I am twenty-one?"

Jennie's father had heard it often. The Hawthorne girls had never lacked for words; their father, she often thought, had been either a genius or a saint. She put her arm around Pris's waist. "Women have so few choices in this world. It is not fair."

"*You* broke free," Pris accused. "Your aunt wanted to arrange a good marriage for you, and she thought it would come off on your visit to Scotland, but you met Papa out on the moors and you chose him even though he was poor and uneducated. I think it's as wonderful and romantic as anything Sir Walter Scott ever wrote. But the most important thing is that you *dared* to strike out into the world. You didn't know whether you'd survive the ocean crossing, or what you'd find when you got here. You must have been frightened many times, but you still *dared*. And look at you! You're more than just a mere wife to Papa; you are his equal partner. All because you *dared*."

My darling, it wasn't a bit romantic, Jennie thought. It wasn't heroic either; I didn't make choices out of any wild, glorious, spirit of freedom. The vision of the tall gray house called Tigh nam Fuaran and the daffodils beside Linn Mor crowded in upon her; she even smelled the tang of peat fires. And then—the burning thatch was rank in her nostrils, even now after eighteen years.

"What are you thinking?" Pris asked. "Do you ever imagine what your life would have been with the other one? Tell me what he was like," she teased. "Was he handsome?" Pris believed that "a Highland gentleman" had been Aunt Higham's choice for Jennie, and it had been let go at that.

"Oh, love, handsome enough, but by now he is only a ghost to me. I hardly knew him, you see."

"He must have suffered dreadfully," Pris said. "I know it would kill us to lose you. Perhaps by now he has died of love."

"I gather you don't intend to do that," said her mother.

"It's not that I don't want to be in love! I *do*. I want to have a lover who will be my husband. I want to have babies. But not before I've accomplished something else. It all cooks down like maple sap to what I can actually do: *face facts*. The first one is that a woman in our society has no right to strike out into the world unless she is a widow who can set herself up in her own business, whether you're a milliner like Mrs. Loomis or a doctor like Mrs. Neville. *Dr.* Neville, I should say."

"Not everyone thinks it's quite decent for Dr. Neville to follow her husband's and father's profession," Jennie said.

"But that doesn't matter to *her*! She's as free as any woman can be today! If you can't be a widow with your own business, the other thing to be is a very rich eccentric spinster whom everybody kowtows to. Even if they still think you are a brazen, immodest hussy, it's no skin off your nose," she said inelegantly.

"I agree," said Jennie. "I always felt the same. Well, let us concentrate on what you wish to do and what you *can* do. You have never wanted to be a teacher, and that would be a profession. Would you reconsider? You could go next year to the seminary in Wiscasset."

"No, Mama, I do not want to be a teacher," she said firmly. "I have never seen myself successfully instructing the young. I have often thought I would be a good lawyer, like Portia, but a woman would never be allowed to do that."

They had reached the town road and turned toward the west, not far enough to set the Shaws' dog barking. The first stars floated in the deepening blue above the swaying black treetops. "No phantom Hessian," Jennie said. "No mysterious hoofbeats. Perhaps we'd do better at midnight. Listen to the frogs." Since late April the tree frogs had been piping in every patch of swamp, but now their sweet trills were being replaced by the deep, guttural throbbings of their ground-dwelling cousins.

"I am a realist, Mama," Pris said crisply. "I know what I can do well, even if it's not something tremendous and adventurous. I am practically an expert shirtmaker and dressmaker already."

"And you are superbly free of false modesty."

Pris giggled. "I am honest. Oh, Mama, what it would be to have my own shop with a beautiful sign painted by David; 'Miss Glenroy, purveyor of fine shirts, handsome waistcoats, rich cravats,' and if Aunt Ianthe will send me the fashion books from London and Paris, I could produce London and Paris modes as well as anyone. If we lived in Maddox, I could have a little shop, and board at home. I would be independent but still be with you."

"If wishes were horses, we would have a very crowded pasture," said Jennie. She turned them back toward their own road. "Pris, don't be in such a scurry and a scuttle to grow up. It's good to dream and plan, but you need not decide tonight whether you'll wade in or jump in with a great splash. You will be a grown woman for a long time. Touch wood." She tapped on the nearest tree trunk. "Now your business is to be our dear daughter and the children's big sister, and to have some good times along the way. You could go back to the parsonage this fall and study something mind-stretching, like Greek, and more mathematics. Then, next year, we shall see. There may be an apprenticeship possible, who knows?"

Priscilla was still young enough to see a promise in *we-shall-see*. "Wedding gowns a specialty," she murmured. "Elegant mourning. It will have to be a *big* sign." The apprenticeship might be in Tenby, or even in Portland. Her sigh was that of a child satisfied that now she could think of something else.

"Sandy should be starting home soon from wherever he's been stranded," she said with amusement.

If *stranded* was the word. It sounded so safe, somehow, as long as you saw him high and dry. Jennie tried to think instead of a future for Priscilla. The Misses Applegate had long since passed on, but they would have taken on the Glenroy daughter without hesitation. Perhaps she could make arrangements with the successors, on the chance that one of their girls might leave next year. Pris would have to be placed to board with a trustworthy family, but both Anna Kate and Lucy lived too far out of town. Of course the Mackenzies would raise a fuss, wanting her at Strathbuie House, and outrageously spoiling her.

I wish they were all under twelve, Jennie thought again. Pris wouldn't be all in a ferment about life, and Sandy wouldn't be downriver somewhere alone in the dark.

Darroch recognized their footsteps and came to escort them to the house. Sandy wasn't there, of course. In the winter kitchen the chessboard was on the table between two candles, and William was doggedly trying to play his father, his chin resting heavily in his hands, his eyelids sagging. At the other end of the table, with two more candles, Carolus was making sketches of his specimens. Alick was not as calm as he looked, sitting back smoking his pipe while William sleepily pondered a move. She could tell by the way his head came up when she came in; the meeting of their eyes said all that was necessary.

Eight

J ENNIE WOKE UP on the camp bed in the candlelit winter kitchen, horrified to realize she had actually dozed. Alick lay on the outside, turned toward her with his arm over her. He was asleep. The Simon Willard clock that had marked off their first hours in America struck first, then the long-case clock across the hall followed. Counting, she hated them both. When April had died, she had damned the relentless procession of hours bearing her farther and farther away from her baby's life. Like the seas carrying away the crew of the *Maid of All Work*. *Seas carrying Sandy.*

Eleven o'clock. What would the morning show?

Darroch snored under the table, Bounce was curled in a chair. William had been sent to bed, and Pris had gone up to lie on Sandy's bed and keep him company until he went to sleep, so he wouldn't be worrying about the usual occupant. Carolus had been to the shore several times with a lantern; now the lantern burned on the bench outside and Carolus was asleep in a rocker, his feet on another chair and the cat in his lap.

How could they all have fallen asleep when they didn't know where Sandy was, when he could have lost an oar in that chaos of cross currents at the mouth of the river or been knocked overboard when he tried to put up the little sprits'l? Dories were supposed to be safe, riding like ducks on the roughest seas, and Alick and Thad had put this one together. Thad was a master hand at dory building, and Alick had been learning then about small boats; even now he said he could approach the construction of a schooner with more confidence than the creation of a perfectly balanced dory. He believed they had accomplished it with this one. And he had also included that bit of rowan wood in the form of a pair of thole pins. So Sandy should be perfectly secure, she thought with the clear-sighted irony that comes with the acceptance of disaster.

The older ones had been using the dory freely for several years now, and she was a living, trustworthy being to them all, like one of the horses. But not now. Not ever, Jennie thought. I believe not in holy spirits dwelling in rowan trees or that a boat receives a soul when she is joined with her natural element. I believe in the awful randomness of events. All over the world at this moment people are dying horribly, with prayers of supplication on their lips to whatever gods they worship. If they escape, it is again due to randomness, not to something swooping them to safety as the children rescue bees struggling in the rainwater butt.

I know, she thought, that Sandy could already be lost to us. The wind was taking him, the white crests were rushing him through the dark. *Time, like an ever rolling stream, bears all its sons away; they fly forgotten, as a dream dies at the opening day.*

She sat up, shivering, and Alick was instantly awake, saying, "*Dia,* how could I have been sleeping?"

"I must go out, or burst," she whispered. He rolled himself noiselessly off the couch. Bounce jumped down when he saw Jennie wrapping herself in a shawl, and slipped out with her, but he was not the coura-geous tyke to dash around barking in the dark, and stayed close by her legs except when he stopped to lift one of his own. Alick came behind her with the lantern. The wind had dropped while they slept; the silence was dense, as if the entire world had ceased to breathe. The only sounds came from their footsteps and Bounce's pattering paws as they walked in the aura of lantern light toward the barn.

A heavy stamp of hooves inside brought a sweet relief; something else lived, after all. "Sleep. It is not morning yet," Alick said in Gaelic to the animals; for them, too, it was the language of gentling.

The barn was warm, but Jennie seemed to have always been cold. When they left it, Bounce growled and crowded against her leg, trem-bling with suspense. He could be hearing or scenting almost anything, for all the wild things were out at night. She picked him up and put her hand around his muzzle; his heart was beating hard, and so was her own. Alick was holding her with one arm, but his attention was strained away from her. A deer nearby, or a moose? A bobcat coming through?

Bounce convulsed into a frenzy, sprang from her arms, and was gone—and then they knew, even before they heard the lagging footsteps. The dog yelped with joy and jumped at the shadowy figure. When Sandy knelt down, something long and pale flapped at his side. "All right, all right," he muttered, shading his eyes from the lantern as it approached.

"Carolus?" he whispered.

"Try again," said his father. Sandy stood up, nearly falling over the leaping dog. He smelled sweaty and dirty and like dried salt fish; he smelled *alive* in Jennie's arms. He hugged her with a ferocious young strength, but hers almost equaled it. The long, pale objects flapped stiffly against her back, with Bounce jumping for them.

When Sandy turned to his father, he still didn't drop the fish, and Bounce didn't give up reaching. Jennie put her hand to her mouth to hold back laughter. She'd had him swept out to sea either alive or as a drowned body, and he came walking home carrying two slack-salted dry codfish from which, by his breath, he'd been tearing strips to eat as he walked.

He and Alick embraced briefly, then Alick stood the boy off from him, and Sandy held the dried fish against his chest like a shield, breathing quickly, while Bounce went round and round him in frustration.

"Now," said Alick without raising his voice, "you will please be explaining yourself, from the beginning."

"I wasn't really wrong to take the dory without permission," Sandy said rapidly. "Because it wasn't after supper yet."

"I am in no mood for splitting hairs," said his father. "But because you choose not to eat supper does not abolish suppertime. Go on."

"I'm some thirsty," Sandy said plaintively. "I've been eating strip fish for miles." He waited, but neither parent spoke. He is here, Jennie rejoiced. Now let him squirm a bit.

Sandy sighed. "I did it because I never felt so rotten in my life, in every way, and Carolus kept—" He discarded that. "I just didn't want to speak to anybody or be spoken to. So I took the dory and went." A statement of fact, neither defiant nor contrite. "It was a good stiff row into the wind, and it made me feel better, head and guts both. I was going to sail back when I was ready, with the wind behind me, so I kept going and going because it made me feel so good to head into those seas, and I pretended I was sailing alone around the world. But outside the river with the tide and wind fighting each other, it wasn't so easy to raise my sail, and—," his voice trembled slightly, "somehow I lost an oar when she rolled way down in a deep one. And the wind changing didn't help any. And there was no point in dropping killick out there, even if there'd been enough rode-line. It couldn't have held her."

He gave them time to contemplate the drama of it, but they offered him no help. Even Bounce gave up and lay flat on his belly, patiently waiting for the fish to descend to him.

"Some Keelers picked me up," Sandy said. "Coming back from a day of fishing outside. It was Mr. George Gunn's *own boat*. I had to make a stupendous jump for it, you know," he said. "I had to move exactly right when the dory and *Blue Jay* came together between seas. If I'd *missed* it—," he paused to let them imagine this. "But I didn't, and I remembered to take the painter with me. *Some* people wouldn't have. A tremendous black man grabbed me up, laughing like thunder and calling me the biggest fish he'd ever caught. I was all out of puff by then, and I lay on the fish all the way in, but my own bed never felt so good. I could talk better if I had a drink."

"Swallow a few times," said Alick unfeelingly.

"They took me back to the Keel, and they began dressing the fish by torchlight down on the beach, but Miriam was there, and she took me to their house, and Mrs. George Gunn gave me a meal. Lobster chowder. Why don't you ask Miriam how her mother makes it, Mama? It was *some* good! They offered me a bed for the night, but I knew you'd be worrying," he said righteously. "I asked if they would rent me a horse and I would ride him back tomorrow when I came for the dory, but one was too old, and the other'd been working in the woods all day. So I set out on shank's mare.—Oh, they sent you these." He held out the codfish, and Bounce arose in hope. "I like to wore my boots through by the feel of them. Might as well be barefoot. And I've been chewing these all the way, and I've got no more spit. I'm drier than a cork leg."

He waited, but release was not yet and he knew it. He sighed. "Harry Shaw was out prowling around with a pistol, and he held me up with it. When he found out who I was, he asked me what in Tophet I was out on the road for at this hour. As if I had no right to be. As if I was up to no good! It's a wonder he didn't shoot me first. He could be *dangerous*, Papa," he said indignantly. "Stopping honest folks on the road like a highwayman! I wonder that you keep him on at the Yard."

Alick said, "We are still waiting."

Sandy gave in at last, in a rush. "I apologize for all the trouble I have caused you. I didn't do it on purpose, but I won't do it again."

Oh yes, you will, Jennie thought. You might not take the dory and nearly drown yourself, but you will do *something*, many somethings, without meaning to.

"Will you accept my apology?" The tremor in Sandy's voice nearly did her in. She slid her hand into Alick's.

"Yes," they said, almost together. "But there is more," Alick said. "You think that by saying you are sorry it wipes out what you have done to all of us tonight. It is not that easily washed away. You are too old to whip, and I think this time the wine has punished you, and so have the seas and the tide and wind. The question is—will you remember? Or do you need an hour with the grindstone to fix it in your mind?"

"Oh yes, Papa, I will remember!" Sandy said devoutly.

"Good. But after you bring the dory back tomorrow, you will not be taking her out again until I give the word. Come in now and get your drink."

"Yes, Papa." Sandy took a few steps and then stopped. "When may I start calling you Father and Mother?"

"Tonight if you wish," said Alick. "At least for me."

"I agree," Jennie said with a faint pang.

They left the fish in the woodshed so Garnet wouldn't be chewing on them during the night. When they went into the house, Sandy headed for the water bucket and drank so long that his father called in to him, "You'll be having to take oars to bed with you."

This woke Carolus. He was stiff and cross and stared resentfully at his brother. "You should have had to walk fifteen miles and been chased by a bear."

"If it's any satisfaction to you, old Go-to-loo'ard, I think I heard a bear. I didn't know whether to run or look for a good tree, so I just tiptoed away. And then Harry Shaw nearly shot me for an outlaw," he added nonchalantly.

"*Honestly?*"

"Carolus, get your brother's nightshirt," Jennie said. She shut Sandy into the pantry with a candle for light while he shed his fishy clothes and washed up. Carolus stayed with him, curiosity conquering jealousy. Sandy had broken a family law and been rewarded with an adventure, but Carolus was not about to cut off his nose to spite his face. He didn't believe in the bear, but he had never been to the Keel. It was an axiom that the Keel never bothered the rest of Whittier, and Whittier never bothered the Keel.

Once the boys were in bed and Jennie had looked in on the others, she and Alick undressed by the cool light of the stars. She loosened her hair but was too tired to braid it; she would deal with the tangle in the morning. The beds had been changed that day, and the sheets smelled of fresh air and lavender. "Oh, what bliss to lie down," she said, "and know they are all in their beds."

"It is not true that children keep you young," Alick said. "They age you very fast. That young amadan has taken five years off our lives tonight. If he keeps this up, we will be ancient and decrepit before he is of age, and then he will try to finish us off by being lost at sea, appearing six months later, and saying, 'I apologize. I am sorry. I will not do it again.' And I am thinking—," he turned over with a groan and put his arm across Jennie, "that if we are still living I will not be accepting the apology."

"But you will give him a drink of water, won't you, if he's been living on salt fish?"

"Och, I'd do the same for any poor body who appeared at the door, my son or not."

"Carolus is being eaten with envy," she said drowsily, "because Sandy has been at the Keel. He will be thinking there is no justice."

"He can go with Sandy to bring the dory home." He was almost asleep, but she lay there thinking about the Keel, that enclave which had been temporary or permanent sanctuary to many a lost or frightened one ever since an Indian family had taken in the first George Gunn over a century ago, when he swam ashore from a fishing vessel that would have carried him back to Scotland. He had taken his chance with unknown dangers, wild beasts, and possibly murderous savages, rather than cross the Atlantic again, with its threats of lethal weather and the possibility of being blown up by French ships or outrun by British naval vessels seizing able-bodied men for the Royal Navy.

The prohibitions about visiting the Keel were unwritten but well observed. Genuine criminals were not encouraged to stay, so there was no need to see the place as a kind of malignancy. Keelers were never out on the road after sundown without good reason, and some were never seen, though a few would work for various people and a small group came to church. Taxes were paid on time, the Keel portion of the town road was worked upon, the Keel's children educated at the Keel's expense, never sent to the district school. The present minister was usually welcome, not as a minister—they never called him for their weddings and funerals—but because he was a North Sea Scot, and even knew the minute village from which the first George Gunn had sailed so long ago, and from whose name the word "keel" was the remote derivation. The doctor was welcome if there was a problem they couldn't cure; there were not many of those. Like the minister, she was carefully uncurious and never censorious. Nothing to be censorious about, Carlotta Neville said. The houses and cabins were clean, they had rules about sanitation and refuse, and Mr. George Gunn's word was law; fortunately he was a benevolent despot.

The first George Gunn had married the daughter of the Indian sagamore, and they had been given the land as a wedding present. At that date, there were no other white men around except upstream at the fort and trading post in Maddox. By the time the long series of French and Indian (really French and English) wars was over, the Oquissocs, never a large group and not particularly aggressive, had been decimated by old age, illness, and the loss of their young men to larger tribes. The Gunns had the area to themselves. They could have claimed the whole territory, but they did not. Surrounded by squatters in the grand rush to the Maine coast after the Treaty of Paris, they required only to be left alone, and they were, except when a Shaw instigated a raid on the Keel at the start of the War of Independence; he claimed they were Tories and Royalists, a nest of traitors to be burned out. The raiders were ungently ordered off the land, though left bruiseless, and received scant sympathy from their other neighbors. Besides, one of the Keel young men had sailed to Boston with a cargo of salt fish in time to join the Boston Tea Party.

The present George Gunn was sometimes referred to as George the Fourth, though no one would ever dream of calling him that to his face when he made his infrequent appearances on the town road. His daughter Miriam "helped out" through the town, and her brother Moses peddled fresh fish.

"Do you think," she murmured to Alick, "that George Gunn was made to swim ashore that night over a hundred years ago so that his descendants could be in the certain spot tonight to save our son?"

He didn't answer. He was already asleep, and she was glad he hadn't heard such selfish foolishness. How many lives had been salvaged one way or another when the Keel became a haven for the lost or dispossessed? How many went on, born again, and how many stayed because the world outside was not for them? Here the pathetic and mutilated dead, found drifting or washed up wrapped in banners of kelp, were given the dignity of burial.

"God," she murmured as she glided toward sleep, "if you ever really bless people, please bless the Keelers."

Nine

S UNDAY MORNING EVERYONE slept well past sun-up, and the life outside the house, both domestic and wild, was in full voice by then. A portion of the uproar was slightly muffled by the barn and henhouse walls, but the local family of crows teetered among the apple blossoms, shrieking sociably at one another. The peremptory robin shouted from the ridgepole just over Jennie's head, *Giddyup, giddyup, giddyup!* Herring and mackerel gulls sped low over the house uttering warnings, greetings, and maniacal laughter.

Jennie sat up, squeezing her eyes shut, hugging her knees and resting her forehead on them. *Sandy is safe.* Alick's fingers walked up her spine under her nightdress and he asked drowsily, "Are you praying or cursing?"

"What about Charlie's mother? I'd clean forgotten the *Maid of All Work*," she said, ashamed. In a passion of superstitious guilt and gratitude she twisted around until she could kiss Alick, then she slid out of bed before he could take hold of her.

The children arose, protesting or eagerly, depending on their natures, and went to their chores.

When everyone was washed and combed, the dogs in place on the threshold, the door opened to the morning, they sat down to eat. William gave thanks for the Sunday bacon and eggs to come, then those who had slept through Sandy's return last night wanted to hear the details. Sandy's narration was restrained by his parents' presence. Carolus, having heard the whole story when it was fresh and suitably garnished, maintained a scholarly detachment while he ate. William was frustrated by Sandy's vagueness and shrugs.

"What are you going to do to him, Papa?" he asked.

"Does he have to turn the grindstone?" Bell Ann asked. "Can I watch?"

"Time for you to watch when you yourself are turning it, my bonny wee girl," Alick said.

"I am *never* going to turn the grindstone," she said.

"Don't be too sure," Pris warned her. "I've done it more than once in my life. Females are absolutely equal in this house when it comes to hearing Papa's opinions while he takes forever to put an edge on an axe."

"But I won't *ever* do anything bad," said Bell Ann. "I will be the only perfect child in this family. What did *you* do, Pris?" she asked greedily. "Was it simply disgraceful?"

"I am not going to give you any ideas," said Pris. "I wouldn't want to spoil your pursuit of perfection."

"My *what?*"

Everyone laughed, and Bell Ann was furious. "I know what you did! You *swore*. Or kicked. Or broke something on purpose! Did you *spit?*"

"Bell Ann," said Jennie. "Be quiet."

"Then will you please excuse me?" Bell Ann asked haughtily.

"Gladly," said Jennie. "Bounce and Darroch can share your egg and bacon." Bell Ann sank back with a sigh.

When breakfast was over, Jennie prepared for roasting two anonymous hens from the Basto farm. No Glenroy birds were ever eaten, all having been given Christian names at birth. Priscilla scrubbed potatoes to be baked, and trimmed the ends of the early asparagus. Alick washed the breakfast dishes, assisted by William and Bell Ann, while the rest dressed for church. Alick never went to church, Bell Ann was too young to sit through a service, and William was inclined to have nightmares Sunday night if the sermon had been especially dramatic. Mr. Lockhart's preaching drew a good house each Sunday, but it was not for children. To Pris and the twins it was as thrilling as they imagined the theater to be.

In the lower grades they learned Bible verses by rote, usually the grimmer ones; at home they argued happily about what colors were actually in Joseph's coat and whether Esau's mess of pottage was beef stew or pea soup. The boys fancied David, not only for killing Goliath, but for the way he had crept like an Indian into Saul's camp to cut off the hem of the king's garment as he slept. Bell Ann wondered why Papa didn't build them an Ark like Noah's, just in case. Pris as a small girl wished she had known Jesus, but how could a man who wasn't a wizard actually turn water into wine? Did Papa believe it?

"Och, it could be that the presence of Himself could make water taste like the finest wine," he said, "the kind of man He was."

Mr. Lockhart was a brawny young man who had been ordained a Presbyterian minister in Scotland but began to suffer serious doctrinal doubts, lost his church, and emigrated with a view to teaching. By roundabout travels through the states he fetched up at last in Maine, where the climate was much like Scotland's, and in Maddox specifically, where the town was still mourning the death of the teacher Liam O'Dowda. Ian Lockhart was filling in when the Baptist minister asked him to preach for him when he had a quinsy sore throat. He was then invited to the Baptist church in Whittier when Mr. Street dropped with a stroke, and held the church together so well in spite of the strong pull of Methodism that when Mr. Street died he was invited to remain, provided he became a Baptist. He accepted, provided *he* could teach at the parsonage. (He called it the manse.) He became *deus ex machina* for the few parents who wanted more education for their children after they'd gone through their local schools but didn't want to send them away from home to board, even as near as Maddox Academy.

The twins set off early in their Sunday suits. Sandy's was bottle green, and Carolus wore Spanish blue; the buttons were gilt, and their white cambric shirts had frilled collars. They were not yet obliged to wear high cravats, only small neat bows, and Pris had made two from what was left from Alick's waistcoat. They wore tasseled caps, but wouldn't keep them on for long. Jennie warned them that at almost fifteen they were expected not to walk in wet places in their best boots.

She and Priscilla drove in the chaise behind Diana, keeping the boys' Bibles with them. Church was an occasion for dressing up; there weren't many in Whittier. Priscilla wore her blue cambric and had trimmed her summer straw with blue ribbons and silk cornflowers. Jennie wore the green-and-gold striped dress, and her bonnet had a wreath of small green leaves and little yellow flowers. Each had a light summer shawl. Each had a reticule and gloves—nuisances like the boys' caps. A lap robe protected their skirts from the dust of the road.

Priscilla was not yet allowed to drive out alone, but she had good hands and managed Diana well; on this fresh bright morning, the mare saw every other horse as a challenge to a race. They exchanged greetings with the Bastos as they passed the imperturbable Charley Horse. In turn, they were passed by the Shaws' big black colt, who, even more than

Diana, seemed to think he was born for the race track. He was driven by the massive Mrs. Shaw, whose son had stopped Sandy last night. She gave Jennie and Pris an unsmiling nod as her light trap sped by them. She was always in mourning for near or distant kin, and had never been seen at church in anything but an ensemble of black crepe, feathers, ribbons, and gloves. A little girl sat beside her like a life-sized doll in a pink coat and bonnet. She was Bell Ann's age, and the variety of her school dresses and matching pantalets flabbergasted Bell Ann at least once a week.

They drove by green meadows and ploughed fields, past orchards, tidy houses, healthy cattle, people leaving for church, or non-churchgoers out to sniff the morning in seventh-day idleness.

Contrasts shocked by extremes; a blackened chimney was a monument to a long-ago fire when a whole family had died without anyone's knowing it until the next day. The men couldn't sort out the bodies, except to say which were adults and which were children.

They passed on their left the schoolhouse in a well-trodden yard, with a buzzard hawk perched on its miniature belfry. The flagpole in the dooryard was varnished like a spar on a vessel.

Next came the South Whittier post office, in an ell added to the Phippses' house. Behind the farm buildings, sheep and goats moved across a steep pasture like clouds across an emerald sky; the voices of the new lambs and kids carried on the erratic breeze.

They were now passing and greeting more and more walkers; some of the men worked at the boatyard while the wives and children worked the farms.

"Where would a man be without the woman at home?" Jennie asked.

"I will never be simply The Woman at Home," Priscilla said grandly.

Crit's Brook was heard long before it was seen, tumbling in small rapids out of the woods and running noisily through a culvert under the road. Then it flowed more quietly across the fields of Three Corner Farm to the great loop of Crit's Cove, a brimming lagoon at high tide and a lake of mudflats at low tide. This morning the tide was slowly coming back, sending an intricate network of little blue streams across the flats.

Where the brook splashed into a pool on the landward side of the road, the churchgoing Keelers were washing their feet in the icy brown water and putting on their clean stockings and good shoes. Sandy balanced on a rock at the brink, talking all the time, and Carolus was poking around in the miniature arboretum where the brook left the woods.

So much for telling them to keep their feet dry, Jennie thought.

There were seven Keelers who came regularly to church, starting out early to walk the ten-odd miles. One was a dignified gray-headed black man who kept a grandfatherly eye on the younger children in the group. Depending on the observer's fancy or prejudice and the children's coloring, the youngsters showed Indian, black, gypsy, Irish, German, English, or Portuguese blood.

"Morning, Mrs. Glenroy!" Miriam Gunn cried happily. "Morning, Pris!" Miriam worked at several houses in the lower town and was as ingenuously friendly as a pup.

"Morning, Miriam!" they called back. Sandy nearly fell off his rock and leaped onto dry land while his mother was watching. Up on the hill the church bell began to ring.

At Three Corners the road was crowded with traffic from North and Center Whittier. This was very exciting for Diana, who wanted to plunge at once into the flow. The Keelers and the twins took a shortcut through the woods, and by the time Jennie and Pris reached the church, the boys were there to assist their mother and sister to alight, and take Diana to the open carriage shed. The bell tossed its brazen voice out over the cove, echoing from the woods behind the church, sending crows flying, setting dogs to barking for a good distance around. The minister gave the children turns at the bell, boys and girls alternating; through the open doors this morning two young sisters could be seen pulling on the rope with all their might.

Jennie liked to sit at the back of the church, because on very warm days the doors were left open. Priscilla went to sit with Thankful, and the twins were with friends from North Whittier. The hard-of-hearing had a front pew to themselves, one of the minister's innovations.

The scripture, prayer, and sermon today were all on the subject of Hope. It was too soon, the minister said, to consider Charles Wolcott and his shipmates dead. They might still find their way home from some lonely lee in which they had found shelter.

He had called on the Wolcotts last evening. "They worship with our friends the Methodists," he said. "But in the larger human scheme we are all one family." The Scottish accent grew more pronounced. "Young Charles is one of us. I do not say *was*. Parents, he is your son; boys and girls, he is your brother."

A smothered sobbing somewhere. Blowing of noses. The woman in the pew beside Jennie was dropping tears on her Sunday gloves. Jennie felt tears in her own eyes. I *will* not imagine myself Charlie's mother, she said savagely to herself, or I will disintegrate on the spot and disgrace my children.

"If only we could all hold out our arms and cry with all the force of our longing, 'Charlie, come home!' But no matter how passionately we yearn to do that, *we* cannot bring him home. It is only our Lord and Saviour who can do that."

No, he can't, Jennie thought, and you know that, even if you qualify it by saying *He can* rather than *He will*. Why should God have whimsically decided to save Sandy last night, when He has let whole families burn in their beds and ships go down with no lives spared? She intended to ask Mr. Lockhart sometime if his was a God who could *do* absolutely anything but wouldn't, or one who was loving but helpless. That hen who hatched out ducklings and clucked frantically on the bank when they took to the water—if she'd had any sense, which most hens lacked, she'd have turned her back on the lot as a lost cause. God must have done this some time early in the Old Testament, when people began killing each other in the most revolting manner possible and saying He told them to do it. He must have said, "What are they doing to my lovely earth?" and turned away in despair.

There was a flurry of light footsteps out through the vestibule; Pris and Thankful had disappeared.

" 'Faith is the substance of things hoped for,' " Lockhart quoted Paul. " 'The evidence of things unseen.' Our faith is often sorely tried; it is natural and very human to question His will. We have all done this, and God forgives us like the loving Father that He is. But Hope is one facet of Faith. No matter what, we can always hope. We *must* hope. We *must* cherish this priceless freedom to hope. Never kill it or allow it to die of neglect." His voice dropped to a new tenderness, but every word sounded like a note of music in the silence.

"Hope, like the gleaming taper's light,
        Adorns and cheers our way;
    And still, as darker grows the night,
        Emits a brighter ray."

After the benediction, the twins and their friends were the first to escape; Jennie sat on for a few minutes, watching the outward flow. There were some downcast eyes and furtive, embarrassed little sniffles, not just among the women. Jennie half-closed her eyes, watching the light change color and tremble on her eyelashes.

"Well, Jennie, are you waiting for a direct revelation?" Carlotta Neville's deep voice said behind her.

Ten

I ARRIVED JUST IN time for the benediction," she said. "So I waited in the vestibule. Mr. Lockhart must have really surpassed himself. More people came out snuffling, and—oh, yes—when I drove up there was a covey of girls outside, having a good cry."

"He spoke about Charles Wolcott so simply, without an excess of sentimentality. Of course the girls dissolved, and I wanted to."

"He is a superb speaker. He makes a poem even out of the benediction." She walked around the end of the pew to one of the tall windows and stood looking out, an attenuated dark figure against a flood of light.

Jennie said uneasily, "Are you losing a patient? Or have you just lost one? Or are you yourself ill?"

Carlotta turned around. "Can you tell that I am really on fire with rage?" she asked rapidly. The fire was on her high cheekbones, and her gray-blue eyes had the brilliance of fever. She slapped her gloves hard across her palm. "And I must talk about it to someone, or I shan't be responsible for the consequences. But I cannot discuss it in church—you see, I am still a model of propriety in some ways."

"Then let us go down to the carriage shed." Jennie arose and moved out of the pew. She felt an uneasiness in her stomach; she knew Carlotta had taken many more slings and arrows in the past nine years than her friends could number, enduring them in a stubborn silence as something to be expected by a woman in a man's profession. But Jennie believed most of the calumnies had ceased now, except for some superficial carping about the way she dressed, using an elegant simplicity to make the most of her six-foot height. "As if she's *proud* of it!" one woman had said, incredulously.

"Good morning, Dr. Neville!" the minister called over intervening heads, and she smiled and bowed.

"I love the man more every time he calls me that," she murmured to Jennie. She moved in apparent serenity down the steps. She had told Jennie and Priscilla once that Mary, Queen of Scots, was six feet tall, and when someone taunted a young Carlotta about her height she had tried hard to walk like a queen. She had succeeded, but there was no suggestion of regal condescension in the way she let people detain her, as if she had all the time in the world and nothing on her mind.

Waiting while Carlotta accepted an invitation to heft an infant and see how he'd grown since she'd birthed him, Jennie was amused by the oblique glances cast from the die-hard critics, avidly absorbing details of the claret-colored fine delaine dress, cut as simply as a riding habit, and the wide silk scarf in a shimmering mosaic pattern draped casually over her shoulders. Her bonnet was plain except for the wine ribbon around it; she rejected plumes, saying they made her feel either like a horse drawing a hearse or a Roman centurion, depending upon her mood.

The Keelers had gone, and all the other non-socializers, but a few older boys loitered at the edge of the woods, chipping off spruce gum with their knives and casting resentful and yearning looks toward the tight confederation of girls with their heads together and their arms around each other.

Sandy was talking to Captain Whittier, who listened with his head canted courteously. Carolus waited outside Mr. Lockhart's court, shifting from one foot to another; Jennie could all but see the rare arethusa blooming in glory behind his eyes. The minister's wife stood with two young women nearly as pregnant as she was. They were laughing gently, their hands laid on the swell of their bellies as if to calm the occupants, their eyes sliding complacently toward their husbands.

Carlotta took Jennie's arm. "Let us move before I'm called to another consultation." Her black and white piebald was at the far end of the rank, next to the road.

"Last night," she said, "I attended the birth of a great ten-pound, eleven-ounce beauty of a child. I won't tell you the family's name, only that they live in North Whittier. The woman had been eating for three or four, I think. I have troubles with women who don't eat enough, or who follow some outlandish diet old Granny Grunt swears to, so the baby is born undernourished and the mother has lost more teeth. No chance of that *here*, but she was a dreadfully long time at it, and I was afraid her heart would give out. She has no female relations around, and a neighbor had terrified her with stories of babies having to be killed in the womb to get them out.

"So there were the two of us at midnight, by candlelight, and the husband—" She made herself take a few even breaths. "Well—I bless the hired girl! She is not very bright, but she is loyal. She had come for me, and she did stay within call, even if she was down in the kitchen and frightened out of her wits. But the *husband!*" She had to stop again, half-laughed at herself, shook her head, and ran her hand over the piebald's shoulder.

"He disappeared when her pains began. Well, I've had this happen before. It transpired that he spent the whole time in the barn, drinking himself senseless. If she had been dying, we couldn't have gotten him up the stairs to her. This morning I went around to see how she was, if she was bleeding again or had any other complications. She's exhausted, of course, and I told her she must stay in bed and sleep all she likes, doing nothing more strenuous than feeding the baby. The girl left to come to church with her family, and when I went downstairs, I met the Sleeping Beauty face to face. He told me he could not bear to see her suffer, and he was so grateful to me he very nearly groveled. And a groveling man just crawling out after a night of drunkenness is not a pretty sight."

"No," Jennie agreed as if she too had experienced such a scene.

"I went into the pantry to wash my hands." Carlotta kept stroking the horse's shoulder, as if the motion and the contact gentled her. "Jennie, I have been patted. I have been flirted with. I have been patronized, lectured, and even preached to. I have been told that I was indecent. I have been accused of 'unnatural practices.' All through it I have been deliberately obtuse, and they knew it, and that was the end of it. But this is the first time that I was not only enraged, I was sickened, and I broke my own rule."

"Did he curse you because you were short with him?"

"That would have been simple." Carlotta flashed a glance at her. "He came into the pantry as I was washing my hands and he seized me around the middle from behind, and pressed his belly and the rest of him hard against me, burrowed his bristly face into my neck, and made an absolutely foul proposition."

She showed ironic amusement at Jennie's expression. "I could not move at first. The man has the brawn and the strength of a gorilla without, I'm sure, the charm. But with his vile breath roaring in my ear, and his fingers trying to dig into my breasts, and what was prodding me from behind, my paralysis was short. There was a slab of meat on the dresser by the sink, and a butcher knife by it." She turned to squarely face Jennie. "I have never felt anything like this before in my life, Jennie. I've been furious many times, but not murderous. I seized the knife and said, 'Which hand shall I slash first, left or right?' He swore and let go, and I turned around and put the point of it to his shirt, over his heart, with enough force to prick through the fabric. Oh my God, his *face!*" She laughed aloud, then stifled it as someone spoke farther along the line of horses.

"I'm still astonished at myself," she said just above a whisper. "I think I should have gone on the stage. 'A woman may kill in defense of her honor,' I said, 'and your filthy handprints are on my apron to prove I was assaulted by you. After I kill you, I shall go directly to the constable while the dirt is still fresh.' As I was saying it I had a sudden vision of poor Nate's face when confronted by Lady Macbeth, and I wanted to laugh. At the same time I really ached to drive the knife into that gut. *He* was so frightened I think he lost control of his bladder. He backed out, holding onto everything on the way, and just before he bolted he shouted that I was a rack of bones full of pisspot airs, and he'd sooner cohabit with a skeleton. 'Cohabit' is my word, not his, you understand." She waited while a chaise went out past them. She and Jennie bowed to the occupants with impeccable gentility.

"I drove home and changed my clothes and came on to church, hoping you'd be here." She shrugged. "That is all, and thank you for listening. One must have at least one person to trust. I used to have my father, and then Simon." She said it without self-pity.

"You honor me," Jennie said. She tried to sound as dispassionate as Carlotta. "Will you go back there?"

"Oh yes, but she is gaining, and she has good milk, so the baby should thrive. The hired girl is clean and capable. The existence of her father and brothers keeps *her* safe in that house. I imagine they'd happily hang him by his thumbs and horsewhip him if he touched her. But I am a lone woman and fair game."

"But not now," said Jennie. "I wish I'd been a fly on the wall to see it, but as a fly I wouldn't have appreciated it. Do you think he'll be abject, once he's sober?"

Carlotta laughed. "Hell hath no fury like a man who's been made a fool of by a woman. Or worse, who's made a fool of himself."

"Come home to dinner with us, Carlotta," Jennie said. "I promise that a few hours in the Glenroy house will knock everything else out of your head. It happens to me, often."

"Oh, I wish I could! But I must be at home. Babies are no respecters of the Sabbath, and I've another one due."

"The invitation is always open."

"Thank you. I regard your home as an oasis." She unhitched her horse, and Jennie looked around for her children, seeing only Sandy, who had now captured Captain Blackburn's attention. The captain was an Englishman from Hampshire, once an officer in the Royal Navy. He was large without being stout; Sandy looked like a tawny little bantam rooster beside him, but didn't seem abashed.

" 'Seek to be good, but not to be great,' " Carlotta recited. " 'A woman's noblest station is to retreat.' Advice to a lady, which I am not, apparently."

"Neither was Molly Pitcher. Or Boadicea. Or myself."

"Good morning, ladies!" Captain Blackburn came toward them, lifting his hat. Sandy bobbed at his elbow. "Or should I say Good Noon?" The captain took out his watch and regarded it with humorous affection, as if it were a small pet he kept in his pocket. "It's just high noon, and a glorious one, eh?"

"It certainly is," said Jennie. "Sandy, will you collect Pris and Carolus? Where is your Bible?"

"Somewhere," he said with a smile meant to be disarming.

"Then find it," Jennie said gently. "Give it to Pris, and remember it will still be Sunday on the way home."

"Good day, Dr. Neville, Captain Blackburn." Sandy left with proud deliberation.

"Your children are so poised, Jennie," Carlotta said.

"You could call it that, I suppose. All I know is that if Sandy appropriates your ear, it is very hard to get it back. Thank you for your patience with him, Captain Blackburn."

"Oh, I enjoy the lad, he's so full of ginger. High-spirited but single-minded, with his eye firmly on his own star." The Englishman's square chin was deeply cleft, and his thick fair hair was brushed back from a wide forehead. His coloring was youthfully fresh, his blue eyes as ingenuous and eagerly observant as a child's. "It's a pleasure to teach your children,

Mrs. Glenroy," he told her. "They each pull a strong oar, and they'll all come through with flying colors, whatever they do."

"And she has two small wonders at home," Carlotta said.

"I meet them on the road from time to time. *Splendid* children!" He stroked the piebald's nose. "And what a grand chap this fellow is!"

"Because I have no children, he kindly praises my horse," Carlotta said. "Never mind, I love my Michael. When I went to the Gowards' to look for a horse, Mr. Goward kept passing him by, thinking I would believe him ugly. He was running around the pasture with another colt, and there was something in the way he moved—and then he came straight to me when I whistled, even though we'd never met before. How could I leave him behind after that? If everyone thought him ugly, what chance would he have in life?" Michael nuzzled her bonnet. "So I said I wanted him for his individuality, and it turned out he has a character to match. We plain ones must compensate for our lacks."

Moving swiftly, she was up onto the seat before the man could put out a hand. The horse backed away from the rail and turned toward the road, seemingly all on his own. She smiled down at Jennie and the captain. "You see how I am about my horse. If I had children, I should be so disgustingly proud no one could endure me, not even those very children. Good day, Jennie, Captain Blackburn. Home, Michael."

Blackburn looked after her. "What can her lacks be?" he exclaimed. "If she thinks she is plain, she is wrong. *Handsome* woman! And there's no doubt of her intelligence. Game, too. Courage of a fighting ship. My admiration grows every year. But she's not a woman to know, if you catch my meaning."

What Jennie caught was a touching wistfulness, as if a bashful and adoring youth lived on in him though there was gray over his ears.

"But she told *you* the story of Michael, and I'd never heard it before," she said mendaciously.

"Really?" He laughed delightedly. "I say!"

Eleven

PRISCILLA DIDN'T ASK to drive home. She was pensive and melancholy, sighing often. Jennie heard her as one hears a clock ticking. She was thinking about Carlotta; Captain Blackburn had helped to wipe away some of the nastiness, but the outrage was still there. Fair game, Carlotta said. Legitimate prey. It was unconscionable that some drunken clod could see a woman like Carlotta as nothing more than available female flesh, and assault her as he might have seized the hired girl if he weren't afraid of her relatives.

Carlotta had come from Connecticut nine years ago. Her father and husband had died from Spanish influenza within a week of each other after weeks of overwork in a stricken countryside; she had carried on their practice until she could sell it, and then she had fled the state. She came to Maddox from Boston on the weekly packet, took a room at the St. David Inn, and called on the local doctor. Once Dr. Waite had made up his mind about her qualifications, he suggested she settle in Whittier. There were so many more people about now that, even with his young assistant, it was difficult to attend patients down the river in what used to be South Maddox before the town renamed itself for Captain Whittier.

Dr. Waite's blessings and the welcomes of an enlightened few weren't enough for the many. But in time Carlotta was generally accepted because she would go anywhere at any hour and, without turning pale, take charge of the bloodiest of accidents. This was considered one of her indecencies, but not by the persons involved. She began to be admired, detested only by the chronically censorious.

"They must have a target," she said indulgently. "And if I am *it*, well,

that is life for a professional woman. Shakespeare broke trail for us with
Portia, but even then he had to disguise her as a man." She could smile
at the letter, signed "Five Concerned Women," that had urged her to
leave Whittier while there was time for her salvation. It came after she'd
been called out in the night by a panic-stricken woman whose husband's
mumps had developed characteristic complications.

But today she had been severely jolted, perhaps because for the first
time she had felt helpless. Until she'd seen the knife.

"Mama," Priscilla said suddenly. "You look so *savage*."

"Do I? My thoughts were savage. Uselessly, I'm afraid. We're so
helpless against so much, like feathers on the wind."

"If we shouldn't give up hope about Charlie, we still have to face the
probabilities, don't we?" Pris said. "I'm either too old to be so trusting or
I haven't enough faith, but I'm sure in my heart that we'll never see
Charlie again. And if he is truly gone, how do we know he wanted to go
to Heaven so young? He will never see the Indies or China! He will never
grow up to have his own ship! I would bitterly resent being snatched
away before I was ready, though I'd be afraid to let God know. It would
be a thousand times worse than Papa disapproving."

"I should think so," said Jennie.

"Except that God probably doesn't express himself in Gaelic," Pris
said, and they both laughed.

"There's something else," Priscilla said abruptly. "I know you won't
tell it. Just Thankful and I know it now, besides Caro."

"I promise."

"Caro is *very* sad. She had to hurry out of church today before she was
overcome. It was bad enough for all of us who are—who *were*—his
friends. But I don't think I'd have blubbed," she said reflectively, "if Caro
hadn't. She was especially grieved, and it was over such a little thing."

Jennie waited, waved to small children picking dandelions by a gate,
and finally decided she was meant to ask about the little thing, and did so.

"It was huge to Caro. A matter of conscience, and you know how hard
that can be. It came over her all at once, when Mr. Lockhart was talking
about calling Charlie home, that she would never have a chance to
apologize to him for something she did once."

Priscilla had a gift for making the most of her stories, even when she
was sincerely moved. She wiped her eyes and blew her nose. "I know how
I'd feel. But I don't think it was all for guilt because she insulted Charlie
when she was twelve years old and now can't take it back. *I* think this is

the first time Caro realized how final death is. She has never lost anyone right in the family the way we have."

"Did she ever tell you how and why she insulted Charlie?"

"No, because that monstrous little Bethiah came around the corner and said," Priscilla whined it out, " 'Mama and Papa want to know what ails you. Why are you crying? It was just a Wolcott.' "

" 'Just a Wolcott!' " Jennie's exclamation made Diana toss her head. "Why didn't she say, 'Just a human being,' and let it go at that?"

"Almost what I said to her! I don't believe Bethiah would weep for *anyone*, she's such a self-centered little beast. And she's so jealous of Caro she can hardly look at her without squinching her face up as if she were eating a lemon."

"She must be a very unhappy child," Jennie warned her. "There has to be a reason for it."

"But she makes it hard for anyone to think that, when she puts herself out to be so disagreeable," Pris said.

"Well, perhaps if Caro talks to you and Thankful about the guilt it will wear off. I know what it's like. Most of us do." But she was thinking of Bethiah, the plain second daughter, seeing her pretty sister being raised as a sort of princess, intended for a prince—in this case, the clergyman into which Fred Coombes was meant to evolve.

Diana turned without prompting onto their own road and attempted to gallop the rest of the way.

There followed another of those periods of ritualized confusion, with Jennie finishing the dinner preparations while being an audience for William's account of his morning, and giving Bell Ann a report on what Lily Shaw was wearing. Bell Ann longed to play with Lily apart from school, but the Shaws did not allow it.

The twins arrived, noisy with hunger and from the strain of preserving a Sabbath decorum on the road. Finally they could all sit down at the table; the dogs and cat took their usual strategic places. Carolus offered the grace, and Alick began to carve. For a few minutes everyone ate in silence, except for parental reminders about manners. Pris had laid aside her sadness like her Sunday bonnet and was enjoying her dinner.

"Carolus, did you confound Mr. Lockhart with your plant?" Jennie asked him.

"No," Carolus said glumly. "There's a batch of arethusa in the woods behind the parsonage."

Sandy cleared his throat. "I've arranged with Captain Blackburn to study navigation next term. Captain Whittier told me I couldn't have a chance with him for a long time yet, but he said it would be better when the time came if I knew navigation."

"And have you discussed the cost of all this?" Alick asked.

"Oh, yes. I know it will be extra over what you pay already, but I intend to make up the difference."

"How?" asked Carolus skeptically.

"Well, I have my pocket money, and I usually get some on my birthday—" His voice broke, for the first time. The other children were too surprised to laugh, and Sandy stepped neatly across the crack. "And my militia money."

Carolus lay down knife and fork and stared at him. William said, "But you've been saving for that forever! What about your musket?" He sounded about to cry.

"I shall hire out," Sandy said. "I can do more besides what I do here, and be paid for it. And I can dig clams and pick mussels and sell them, and catch mackerel. I can get work in the woods. I can—" Another more disastrous crack. William and Bell Ann snickered. Sandy slumped back in his chair and stared at his plate. His father reached over and lightly touched his shoulder.

"All right, William," said Jennie, "your turn will come. And Bell Ann, take care."

"I didn't make a personal remark," she protested.

"It is just as bad to laugh at something a person can't help."

"Fred Coombes says Captain Blackburn's family pay him to stay in America," said Pris, "because he disgraced them in England, and the Prince Regent made him go. So how do we know he was ever in the Royal Navy at all, even as an ordinary sailor? Just because he knows higher mathematics is no proof of anything else. Maybe he will be studying navigation like mad all summer long to be ready for you."

Sandy, head still down, was breathing hard enough to whiten his nostrils.

"If Fred Coombes is to be a minister," Jennie said, "he'd better leave off malicious gossip."

"Well, he did say it after Captain Blackburn told him he was wasting his time trying to learn calculus," Pris said. "Fred was furious, but he doesn't think he should show ordinary feelings like common folk. He takes on this sickly sanctimonious smile as if he's forgiving the world."

"In case anyone is interested," Alick said, "the General saw Captain Blackburn's credentials before he sold him the property on Crit Hill. He is not in disgrace, and he resigned from the Royal Navy after the Treaty of Ghent."

"Isn't it strange to think he was once our enemy!" said Priscilla. "He makes geometry so clear, it is almost beautiful! Navigation should be lovely too, all about the stars."

Sandy said scornfully, "There's more to it than stargazing."

"What does the word mean, that Sandy wants to do?" asked Bell Ann.

"How to steer a boat," William said.

"But he can do that already. He can row and everything."

"That is certainly true," said Pris. "When his ship is becalmed in the Indian Ocean, Sandy can row her home."

"If the oars are long enough, and I can locate the Big Dipper," said Sandy, "we should fetch up right here in the dooryard."

Everybody laughed.

"Anyway," Sandy continued, jaunty now. "I expect to buy my own books and everything else I need, including my militia gear."

"Who is going to sew up the holes your money keeps burning in your pockets?" asked Pris. "Will you ask somebody to tie you down when you go near a shop? Like Ulysses and the Sirens?"

"When a person has a true purpose in life," Sandy stated loftily, "those trivialities become insignificant."

"Hoity toity!" said Pris, and Carolus grinned.

"Pris, will you bring the tart?" Jennie asked. She and Alick communicated without words down the length of the table. On principle they never discouraged enterprise; Sandy would find out just how gifted a juggler he was with chore-time, hired-out time, and the free variety.

The money was another challenge. Sandy could not see merchandise without buying something, even if it was no more than a colored handkerchief, a pencil, or a ribbon for Bell Ann from a pack peddler. The Whittier store at Parson's Cove was a cavern of dazzling treasures; trips to Maddox were luckily few, because he suffered from such horrid crises of indecision among so many shops. His desperate last-minute choices were always regretted on the way home, and he was no silent sufferer. He'd done magnificently to have saved anything at all toward his militia equipment. Perhaps the vision of himself parading with a musket on the first Muster Day after his sixteenth birthday had been his True Purpose until now.

By the time they were eating rhubarb tart with thick yellow cream, the subject had been changed. If, after an honest, persistent, self-denying try Sandy hadn't made what he needed for the books and extra tuition by the end of summer, his parents were already silently agreed to pay; after all, they were setting aside money for Carolus to go to Bowdoin College.

The meal was followed by an argument that looked bad for the Sunday china, with four children crowded into the pantry. Pris and William were each determined to be the third to go to the Keel and sail home the dory. The twins were equally resolute about going alone, hoping to linger at the Gunns' a while. Sandy felt he had a legitimate excuse for that because they had taken him in.

The Keel was Far Cathay to William, and then there'd be the sail home upriver. He was close to tears as he argued for his right. Priscilla, who was just as greedily curious but wouldn't admit it, was haughtily articulate.

"I suppose I mustn't even *think* of it because I am a mere female, even though I am useful enough to row people for *hours* when they are trolling for the mackerel they plan to *sell*."

Bell Ann curled up on the camp bed against the wall in the winter kitchen, listening blissfully to the skirmish until she fell asleep as if to a lullaby. When Alick had had enough of the wrangle, he silenced it by appearing in the pantry doorway, and told them that they would *all* go. "And quickly, while I still have my hearing. And my patience," he added.

Priscilla radiated triumph, William could hardly believe his luck, and the twins were taken aback but not for long. The company of an older sister and a younger brother couldn't spoil everything. Meanwhile, Bell Ann slept.

Jennie brought a stoneware pot of marmalade and another of strawberry jam from the cellar and put them in a basket for Pris to carry to Mrs. George Gunn. "And thank the right person for the strip fish. Say we are much obliged, we will be having it tonight."

"Yes. Yes." Sandy was in a rush to be gone, so was William, carrying the spare oar. Carolus slung his vasculum over his shoulder, in case there was a rare plant at the Keel found nowhere else on earth. "There's just enough wind to send us flying home without heeling over."

"I like *that*," Pris was saying as they went under the rowans. " 'Give me a rapt ship running on her side so low, that she drinks water and her keel plows air.' "

Sandy stopped them all. "Let us agree here and now that you are not going to be declaiming all the way there and back. At least William doesn't know all that poetry."

"No foolish chances, now!" Alick called after them. He whistled Bounce back and tucked him under his arm. "Ah, Jeannie, those children," he said softly.

"There's not much wind, and it's broad daylight," she said.

"It's not that. It's the wondering from time to time where they really come from." He set the wriggling dog down. "Whose souls do the wee creatures snatch from the air and keep for their own?"

"Why, Alick," she said happily. "What a poetic thought! And a profound one too."

"We Gaels are the great ones for poetry and profundity. You should be knowing that by now."

"And I am loving it," she said, kissing his cheek. Darroch watched benevolently, slowly waving his tail. Just so had his grandfather been a witness to the clasped hands and the promises over Priscilla's cradle.

"Tell me this, *mo graidh*," Jennie said. "If a ship must have a soul, could the soul of a lost one move into her?"

He didn't smile at her whimsy, but looked past her up at *Artemis*. Then he said, thoughtfully, "I don't know, but I feel it is there. Something. . . . I will be at the yard for a wee while now." He kissed her and left her, thinking of his ship, she knew, and an uninterrupted hour in his office.

She turned toward the house and the mail she hadn't had time to open, and met Bell Ann, who held Evelina Ermintrude against her cambric chest and looked resentfully at her mother from under drawn dark brows. Her lower lip was out.

"They all went, didn't they? Even William. Everybody else can go to the Keel, and see the goats and Miriam's house, but I can't do *anything*, because I'm *nothing*."

"You're my baby, and you're Papa's *nighean dhu*."

"But what are we going to play? No cards because it's Sunday. We can't sew for Evelina Ermintrude, and she needs everything new, she is so hard on her clothes."

"We can go down to the shore and build a sand castle, and perhaps find an arrowhead."

"I don't want to do that." Having a good grievance, Bell Ann cherished it. "Everyone else is doing something wonderful!"

"Let's go sit in the swing and decide what we'll do." Bell Ann stamped along behind her, as much as one could stamp in bare feet on thick grass. They took opposite seats in the swing under the apple trees. Bell Ann curled herself up tightly and scowled at her mother. She always awoke in a bad mood from a daytime sleep and went through this tiresome ritual of objecting to everything.

"We can walk to the trout pool," said Jennie. "We could take some rods along."

"I don't want to. I never catch anything anyway. Mama, are we bad to fish on Sundays? Some of the children at school keep saying we should think about God all day on Sunday, but I don't know what he looks like! He doesn't even have a skin face, so how does anyone know he's really there?"

You are your father's true daughter, Jennie thought, no matter where you snatched your soul from. "I don't know," she said. "It's something people have been arguing about for hundreds of years. We have this great planet Earth to live on, and there are others out there, like Jupiter and Venus and Mars. You know those. There are stars by the millions, we have night and day as the earth turns, and there are the seas with the fish in them, and the whales—"

"And mermaids!"

"Perhaps mermaids," Jennie agreed. "Well, something or somebody had to begin all this, Bell Ann. Something or somebody had to plan it all out and know how to make it work. And that is what we call God."

Bell Ann nodded impatiently. "Like a king with a kingdom. Like in the Bible. 'He is the King of Glory.' But nothing says what He *looks* like." She uncurled herself. "Supposing God is not a man king at all, but an eagle, and He watches us from way up there." She pointed straight overhead. "Or what if He is a great wise horse, much bigger than Shonnie and Perry, and He has green pastures and a barn like a castle up there in a land of clouds?"

"It's a beautiful thought!" Jennie was captivated by a heavenly horse galloping across celestial meadows.

"A holy horse," said Bell Ann happily. "He can think and do *anything*. And when it says He created us in His own image, it could really mean horses and not us. We just like to *think* it means us, because we can have churches and everything. But the horses know the truth. He's *theirs*, and they are *His*."

She set the swing in gentle motion. "I can think about Jesus, because I've seen pictures of him. And I think of him not just on Sundays. He was

a good man, like Papa and David, and I *hate* the people who hurt him."
She narrowed her eyes menacingly and doubled up a fist. "I just wish I'd
been there. . . . Today Papa and William and me read about the loaves
and fishes. I don't think Papa or the General could do anything like that,
and I wonder how Jesus did it. But he *did*, because it's written down."

"It's also written down that Jesus is called the Son of God, and he calls
God his Father. So God couldn't very well be a horse, even a most noble
one."

"Why?" Bell Ann wasn't impertinent, but immovable. "Whoever
made every creature would be a kind of father, wouldn't he! So he could
be anything he wanted to be. *Couldn't He, Mama?*" She stared into
Jennie's eyes. "I know it because I dreamed about Him. His coat was gold
and His mane and tail were silver. I was lost, and I thought nobody else
was alive but me, and then *He* came, and He told me to get on His back,
and His beautiful silver mane was so long I could pull myself up by it, and
He galloped like the wind but He didn't even touch the ground, and He
brought me home."

She fell back in her seat and gazed triumphantly at her mother. "Now
I think I'll go ride Brisky. I promised him."

"Change first." Jennie untied Bell Ann's apron and unfastened the
back of her dress and pulled it off over her head. "Bell Ann, don't tell the
other children what you think about God. It will only upset their
parents."

"I shan't tell them *anything*. They say such stupid things. Lily Shaw
told me God made her fall out of a tree and nearly break her arm because
she should have been thinking of Him and not playing on Sunday. I told
her it was an accident, but she said *I* was wrong, not her. Poor Lily." She
said it with kindly condescension. "I still like her."

She trotted away in her shirt and drawers, carrying her dress and
apron over her arm.

Between us Alick and I created this marvel, Jennie thought. I wonder
if God felt this way about Adam and Eve? Marveling at His work but
apprehensive. If Bell Ann has created a new Deity at seven, even the old
one can't know what she'll come up with at seventeen. Surely nothing as
tame as a dressmaking shop.

Twelve

W AITING FOR Bell Ann, Jennie leaned on the pasture gate at the far side of the barn watching the three horses who grazed in the shade across the field, their tails gracefully whisking away insects. Ianthe and Louisa were lying down in the sun closer by, chewing their cuds. Brisky fed along the upper fence; the sun brushed golden highlights onto his *café au lait* coat, and his mane and tail were almost white. He had been given to the twins on their seventh birthday, when Priscilla's pony, Dolly, also became officially theirs; at nine, Pris was long-legged enough to ride Diamond with the stirrup leathers shortened.

Dolly, a neat little sorrel, had been sweet-tempered and placid; Brisky established his independence from the start. Anyone who attempted to train him to jump even the smallest obstacles spent more time picking himself up off the ground than riding on the pony's back. He refused to be hurried, but was often seen tearing around the pasture in an ecstasy of high spirits.

The twins had named him. Having grown up with Bertie (for St. Cuthbert) and Nelson (for Admiral Horatio), Jennie suggested several distinguished American names, but they coined Brisky from "brisk" and "frisky," and were as proud as if they'd invented the wheel.

Dolly and Diamond (their first horse) and the cow Peggy had each been buried with honors amid flowers and tears in the lower eastern corner of the pasture. Realistically, the children designated a place for Brisky; unrealistically, they did not expect him ever to die.

Bell Ann's breathy inexpert whistling preceded her from the barn. She always whistled whenever she wore William's outgrown breeches and shirt. But she couldn't do the boys' two-fingered variation, so she yelled through her hands at the pony, who came at a moderate canter for his lump of sugar. He was quite gracious today about accepting his bridle, allowing Bell Ann to be ostentatiously efficient from the top rail while he rolled his eyes at Jennie.

"There!" Bell Ann swung a leg over the pony and slid onto his bare back. Jennie opened the gate, and Bell Ann clicked her tongue. (Brisky did not respond to heel-proddings.) The pony walked out, and Darroch arose from where he had been lying in the shade.

"We'll start at the top today," Bell Ann said. "Brisky likes a change." He walked sedately up the road, Darroch pacing beside him, and then turned left toward the woods behind the wash house. Bell Ann and Jennie blew kisses to each other, and Jennie returned to the house. A small brown projectile narrowly missed crashing into her legs; Bounce was on his way to catch up. He disappeared up the road, yipping.

Jennie took a volume of Wordsworth and the parcel of mail down to the orchard. She laid the mail aside to sort when Alick came, and opened the book, but she forgot to read. It was poetry itself to be quietly seeing, hearing, and breathing May; to be drifting on the tide rising toward summer. When Alick arrived she smiled drowsily at him. "Bell Ann is doing the Square," she said. "Sit down and let me tell you before she comes back. She says that God is a Great Horse, and all the horses know it. The other animals do too, I should imagine. It's an immense concept, isn't it? That one day all the abused creatures will rise up and hold their own Day of Judgement?"

"It's as reasonable as any. We should set her at Lockhart. He would find her a hard little nut to crack."

"Especially since she's seen the God in her dreams, so she can describe him perfectly. And Brisky gave me a certain *look* today."

"He is a great one for certain looks. Now that we are alone, do you think I could be reading my newspapers like a gentleman? Since I cannot bed my wife without bringing everyone home at once like a clap of thunder?"

"Och, the poor *bodach*," Jennie crooned. "The poor *cailleach* too, now that I think of it. Light your pipe, and I shall sort."

Garnet arrived during the sorting, rushed up a tree, scattering the birds, and lay on a limb over Alick's head, looking down on him like a miniature and friendly tiger. Somewhere Bounce was barking at a squirrel, the only form of four-legged wildlife he considered safe enough to challenge. Jennie handed three newspapers to Alick.There were no letters from any of her sisters, but David had two. She sniffed them and studied the handwriting, postmarks, and seals without shame. "Neither hand looks feminine. I hope they're commissions to do tremendous things."

Finally, there was a letter from Scotland. She said more soberly, "We have word from Nancy MacNichol. Shall I read it to myself?"

"Read it out now and have it over with." He reached for it, and with his pocket knife pried up the seals. "I love the woman, but not her news."

Jennie and Nancy had exchanged several letters a year ever since the first one Jennie wrote to tell her they were safe in America. Nancy's Highlander had come home whole from the Peninsular Wars; they had prospered, and the redhaired boy Angus was doing well in Canada. This wasn't the sort of news Alick hated. But the forced emptying of the Highlands, a trickle when Alick and Jennie left, had become a flood of exiles. Thousands of acres had been turned into sheep walks, deer forest, or grouse moor by landlords whose forefathers had died in battle among their clansmen, or had been hanged as traitors by the English because of their loyalty to their own. The stone walls of roofless cottages were all that remained.

As the emigrants left (few so fortunate as to be under the auspices of men like General Mackenzie), the English returned, but not as another butchering army. Poets and artists who had never ventured north of the Borders discovered a savage and romantic beauty in the Highlands; only a very few knew how recently the picturesque cottages had been destroyed. Sightseers came to Fort William to walk up Ben Nevis in the mist and rain, hoping it would clear long enough to show them wave on wave of mountains with names like music. The MacNichols enlarged their inn and now called it the Hotel Ben Nevis. It was almost always full from early spring into the late autumn.

"I wish I could read it in her accent," Jennie said. "I can 'ear 'er, but I can't sye it. She says 'MacNichol gets into monstrous takings of guilt, to be doing so well when so many get drove out with nothing and go to nothing. If he has too much to drink, he carries on about it to the guests. The kitchen is always open to the worst cases. You were two of the lucky ones.' "

"Aye," Alick said heavily. "We were two of the lucky ones, because of you and your courage—and your gold, to make a practical point."

She leaned forward and put her hands on his knees. "Alick, when you walked out of that room to go and find a ship, I was bereft, even though I expected I'd be going home soon. I could only think that I'd never see you again, never know what had become of you. And when you came back—and drank all the milk from the jug, remember?—what joy! I would have a second chance to say what should be said between us, *if* I could think what it was. There, is that thoroughly confusing?"

"It is one of your charms, that I am never knowing what you are about to say, and Bell Ann takes after you."

"What do you suppose ponies are in the heavenly scheme? Cherubim and seraphim? I can clearly see Dolly with little wings, but not Brisky. He would object violently to flying."

"But not Mata," he said smiling. The name of his beloved garron made her eyes smart. "The Elliots were kind to him, I am sure of it," he said quickly.

"I am sure too," she said. "But I think of Morag and Aili, and the little boys I pulled from the brook. The red-headed man who had been a soldier. Morag's mother, with that wonderful smile. What became of them all? It's as if I see them through blowing mists, and we stretch out our arms to one another, but the mists come thick between us and then there is nothing." She wiped her eyes on a corner of Evelina Ermintrude's apron.

"And him too?" It was just audible. "Do you see him?"

She shook her head. "Hardly ever. Do you?"

"It is not a thing a man forgets. But it belongs to another life. I am no believer in a day of judgment when he and I will meet face to face."

"Especially if the Great Horse is directing the event," she said.

A throat was cleared. Someone said tentatively, "Good afternoon?"

Septimus Frye stood by the lilacs, holding his hat against his breast like someone watching a coffin go by. Apparently he thought he had caught them in an intimate moment. Alick whispered something, and Jennie squeezed his fingers.

"Good afternoon, Septimus!" she called. "You are just in time for a cup of tea."

"I would appreciate that, Mrs. Glenroy," he said with more assurance. His horse was hitched to one of the rowan trees, contentedly cropping fresh clover.

Jennie looked out once while the water was coming to a boil over the spirit lamp, and saw the men standing and talking in the orchard's dapple of trembling light and shadow; at least Septimus was talking, expressing himself with wide gestures. Garnet sat up on her tree limb staring at his hat as it rose, swung in an arc, swooped, and rose again.

When Jennie went out, Septimus recklessly scaled the handsome hat across the grass and ran to take the tray. By now he must have known that Priscilla wasn't about, but he had come glowingly to terms with it; he would make the most of this.

He was easy and mannerly at tea, praising the brew and the cakes. He congratulated Alick on the launching; he'd stopped at Parson's Cove today and gone aboard *Ariel* again. "She feels different when she's afloat. *Alive*." This was the right thing to say to Alick. "She's sailing tomorrow morning for New Orleans. She will do you proud, Mr. Glenroy."

He referred modestly to his uncle's speech in Congress about Nullification; it was reported in full in most Maine papers, including the *Tenby Journal*. Alick said he had not reached it yet, but he was looking forward to it.

Then all at once Septimus was quenched. The dimples nearly disappeared. He ran his hand over his lamb's-fleece hair, and his dark eyes shifted dismally between Alick and Jennie. His tongue touched his lips delicately as if they hurt.

"I am sorry the children aren't here, Septimus," she said. "Bell Ann is within reach of a good shout, but the others are out sailing."

"Actually I am glad they are not here, Mrs. Glenroy." He was turning a rich scarlet. The ebullient young insurance salesman, justice of the peace, embryo congressman, had been replaced by a youth floundering between a tortured self-consciousness and a reckless hope.

"I would like permission to call on Priscilla. Formally. I mean with honorable intentions." He seized his cup and drank till it was upended, like Bell Ann with her mug. Alick looked over at Jennie, soundlessly exhaling the long, slow breath of exasperation, Jennie's reaction was a dismayed pity. She nodded slightly, for Alick to speak first. Septimus touched his mouth with his napkin and his eyes were as shinily expectant as Bounce's.

"Priscilla is seventeen, Septimus," Alick said. "She is not old enough to be courted."

"But she *looks* it!" he blurted out. "And girls of *sixteen* marry all the time! Just last week I stood up with my cousin, and he is thirty-three and the bride just sixteen, and very happy they are!"

Alick hid his annoyance well. "It is of no concern to us, how or when other parents give their consent. We are in no hurry to see Priscilla courted."

"But is *Priscilla?*" he appealed ardently to Jennie. "Of course she's thinking about it! All girls do! What else is there for them? She's mature for her age, and she won't want to be a schoolgirl forever. Mrs. Glenroy, *you* are a woman, *you* have been courted, and—"

Jennie reached for Alick's cup. "Would you like more tea, my dear?" She winked with the eye away from Septimus and saw his mouth relax.

"I was twenty-one, Septimus," she said. "And there is a great gap between a girl of seventeen and a man of twenty-four. A man of the world like yourself," she added shamelessly, and gratification glinted through his emotion. "Priscilla may be tall, but she is not mature for her years. And only last night she told me she wants to do many things before she settles down. I understand because I had the same wishes."

Septimus gazed glassily at her. In a very few minutes the wind had been taken out of his sails and he had fired off only one round before he was sunk; he could not understand it. He stood up. "I had better go. I am sorry if I have overstepped," he said. He went to fetch his hat from where he had thrown it.

"You had a right to ask," Alick said. "How else would you know?" He sounded very kind. They walked to his horse with Septimus and shook hands. "You are always welcome," Alick told him, "as a friend of the family."

"Thank you for your generosity," he said stiffly. He swung himself into the saddle and raised his hat to them with a smile meant to be sadly ironic, Jennie thought, but sad irony is hard to manage with dimples. Then he galloped away, raising quite a dust.

"Poor boy," said Jennie. "I wanted to tell him he would feel better tomorrow, but that would have made him feel worse."

Alick was pale around the mouth. "The lie is lodged in my throat like a fishbone, I would choke to death on it. Telling him he is always welcome! What kind of man am I, not giving him the truth, that I will not have this — this *politician* making himself free of my daughter's company!"

"How free would it be, with four other children clustering around him like honeybees?"

"Even with them there, and you and I never far off, he will ingratiate himself. How else has he managed to be selling so much insurance in the little while since he began?"

She took his hand. "My darling, last night we had Sandy gone forever. Today we have the first young man to ask to be Pris's beau. It is

like the first crack in Sandy's voice, inevitable but not the end of the
world." She faltered a bit on that. "It's the beginning of the end of their
childhood, and I hate that too. I *loathe* it!" She brought his hand up to her
mouth and pressed her lips against the knuckles. "But Pris is no fool. He
cannot sell himself to her the way he sells a policy on a house or vessel."

"How do you know? He is no fool either, you know. Granted, he
thinks highly of himself, all cock-a-hoop to succeed, as they say, and that
is neither sin nor crime. But Priscilla is ambitious too, and he could be
mesmerizing her into seeing herself as a senator's wife, or the Governor's,
or even, God save us, the President's Lady."

"It could be dazzling," Jennie agreed, but she was disturbed more by
Alick's reaction than the prospects he was describing.

"And if none of this happens," he went on, "and he becomes no more
than a small-town office holder, all the bloom and the passion turned to
a frost-killed garden, what is happening then to Priscilla?"

With her own proclivity for anticipation, pleasant or otherwise, she
could see Priscilla married to an embittered, frustrated man who had
loved her for her élan but didn't propose to allow it in his wife, who would
not set her up in a little shop or even a dame school, but keep her heavy
with young as a woman's primary purpose for existence.

"I'm home!" Bell Ann shouted from the barn, and the spell was
broken.

"Listen to us!" Jennie said. "What a pair of ravens croaking disaster!
Pris thinks any man in his mid-twenties is middle-aged, unless he's
another Lord Byron or a hero in a novel. But if Septimus *does* turn out to
be a spellbinder, we'll have three years for the spell to wear off."

"If she takes it into her head she wants to marry before she is twenty-
one, she'll be thinking we cannot refuse her her heart's desire."

"Then she will find out that we *can* refuse. Blue eyes shimmering with
tears may be beautiful as dew-wet violets, but Papa and Mama can resist
them. They've had years of practice."

He laughed at her and at himself; a sort of renewal came often to them
at unexpected moments. It was not only recollections of their dangerous
walk through the Highlands that could do it; this was an event of the
Here and Now.

Thirteen

O N EVERY OTHER Monday morning Miriam Gunn came to help with the washing, until school was out for the summer. Since the last of April she had come in bare feet, with her homespun skirt pinned halfway up her muscular brown calves to keep it dry on the long walk from the Keel along a narrow track through juniper and bay and then the Glenroy woods.

At once she built and kindled the fire under the hanging iron wash-pot, which the twins had filled the night before. Coming from chores, the children always asked her to breakfast, but she always refused, saying she'd had a ding-clicker of a feed before she'd left the Keel. She whistled "The Devil's Dream" as fast as the best fiddler could play it, all the while she was stirring in the soft soap and pushing linens under water with the forked hardwood washing stick.

Now the men would be coming to work at the yard. The older ones teased her in an avuncular way; one of them always shouted, "Whistling girls and crowing hens always come to some bad end!" She would shout back, "I'm just making a joyful noise unto the Lord!"

By the time Alick had gone to the Yard and Jennie was filling the white cedar dinner buckets on the summer-kitchen table, with the windows open, the younger workers were coming in. Harry Shaw, who had held up Sandy on Saturday night, always came first, alone and walking fast, with a slouch hat pulled low over his face, ignoring Miriam and avoiding Bounce's friendly advances. Two others behind him kept together, tossing ribald quips at Miriam like rotten apples, knowing Alick was already at the Yard and taking a chance on Jennie's not hearing them. But she often did.

The indecencies seemed to bounce harmlessly off the girl, who kept on whistling. But after Carlotta's story yesterday, it seemed to Jennie that their words were substitutions for physical assault on permitted prey, a female *and* a Keeler. Miriam kept her back to them, still whistling, until they gave up and walked on, laughing loudly and hitting each other in the ribs.

Jennie imagined confronting them on the road, swinging a full dinner bucket in each hand, breaking first one nose and then the other, perhaps knocking out a few teeth as well. Luxuriously she imagined their horrified astonishment and the blood running down over their lips, the taste of it washing away that of their obscenities. Of course it couldn't be done, not by Mrs. Glenroy, but wasn't it delightful to contemplate? She was still wistful with unfulfilled desire when she tucked napkins over the food. William and Bell Ann shared one bucket at noon, and the larger one fed Priscilla and the twins.

Setting out with their schoolbags and dinners, the children could not linger with Miriam. She was a favorite for being herself, as well as being exotic for belonging to the Keel, but tardiness was considered a cardinal sin at school, ranking with locking someone in the privy or throwing stones in the schoolyard. At the parsonage, Mr. Lockhart stood on the steps studying his watch while the dilatory ones came panting up with their excuses, knowing the lost moments would be basted onto the end of the day.

When Jennie joined her at the wash house this morning, Miriam was overflowing with admiration for the children. "Of course *I* knew them already, and I've told Marm about them, but her meeting them in their real flesh and blood is some different! She was so taken with Sandy when we brought him in that night. He was so *polite*, even if he was soaking wet and worn out, and then when Carolus and Pris and little Will came with him yesterday—*Well*! She knows what's finest kind!"

"They were taken with her too. They came home boiling with excitement yesterday, all talking at once. Their father had to tell them not to make nuisances of themselves. We don't want *your* father to be sorry he ever picked Sandy out of the ocean that night."

"It was Elias did that," Miriam said, being literal. Now where did *he* come from? Jennie wondered, but knew better than to ask.

Alick had delivered a strong message over the hot cornmeal mush and strip fish at supper. "You are not to be running in and out of the place, though with all the miles between us it would not be easy. There are folk who keep to themselves, and it is their right. I will not have you destroying their privacy. Is that understood?"

"Understood, Papa," Pris said, and Carolus nodded.

"Yes, *Father*," Sandy added.

"Yes, Papa," said William. "The bad men must have all been hiding yesterday; I didn't see anybody that looked really evil. Rupert Foss says there are murderers there of all colors, who would just as soon cut your throat in your bed as look at you."

"Rupert Foss says a great deal more than his prayers," said Pris, "*if* he says those."

"Mr. George Gunn is a law-abiding man," Alick said. "I am doubting very much that Rupert Foss's father says what Rupert reports. Mind that you are not reporting that either."

"I wouldn't," William protested. "Miriam and Moses are already our friends."

"And Orono," Bell Ann put in, jealous for Moses' fish-carrying donkey.

"And now we know Mr. and Mrs. George Gunn," William said, "so they are friends too. Anyway, if there are some murderers at the Keel, I don't think it is their *business*, like a shoemaker or carpenter. Probably they didn't mean to do it, whatever it was."

"In school tomorrow, young Wim," Carolus said in an off-hand older-brother way, "either you hold your tongue about the Keel, or you will never go anywhere with us again."

"You don't make the laws here," William said saucily. "Papa and Mama do."

"We know you are dying to brag," Sandy said indulgently. "Just resist the temptation to make a tall story out of it, full of cannibals and buccaneers and Chinese pirates and suchlike."

"It is safer not to speak of it at all," said Alick. "It's another offense against privacy to gossip about people."

"Is it true, Father," Sandy appealed earnestly, "that there always has to be a George Gunn?"

"I am not knowing if it *has* to be. It is the way it has always been."

"But it will be Moses some day," Carolus said thoughtfully. "Mr. Moses Gunn. It lacks the authority of 'Mr. George Gunn.' But then so does Moses."

"Who is only eighteen," Pris said tartly. "But his middle name is George, Miriam told me, and so one day he will be George the Fifth. Just think, an American dynasty." She looked very pleased with herself.

Carolus sighed and shook his head. Sandy said, "I don't think they'd enjoy being called that. After all, George the First—I mean, George Gunn—was running away from that foolishness. We're all Americans, and we hate royalty."

"*I* don't," said Bell Ann. "I *love* stories about queens and princesses and castles. I may," she said, preening, "grow up and marry a prince, because I look just like one in my fairytale book, the Sleeping Beauty."

"They're such real little gentlemen," Miriam was saying, "and we know about that; there have been some real gentlemen at the Keel since it began." She stopped as if a hand had clamped across her mouth. Lord, what a set of stories this sturdy black-eyed young girl knew, Jennie thought enviously. Who had come, and why? Who had gone, and where? A separate nation's separate secret history.

She squashed her temptation to ask questions and inspected Sandy's fishy clothing, left soaking since Sunday morning. "Miriam, I heard what Asa and Elmo said to you this morning. I can't reprove them, but Mr. Glenroy can, and he will, if I tell him about it. They have no more right to insult you than to throw rocks at you."

"Bless your heart, Mrs. Glenroy, those gorms don't mean no more to me than those swallows. Not as much, because the swallows are pretty things. You take that Asa. If he caught me in the dark he'd be scairt to lay a finger on me. He's all gas and gaiters, and Elmo's the same. If I'd taken a step toward him this morning and asked what he had in his breeches—I beg your pardon, Mrs. Glenroy—he'd have run. But . . . you notice Harry Shaw wasn't saying a word?"

There was a gloss of sweat on her face and throat and strong bare arms. She had scooped her curly black hair off her neck and tied it up with a piece of twine, and it bobbed at the back of her head with every movement.

"It's Harry's kind I'm leery of. They ain't exactly evil, they're just menfolk, but not the best kind. They have to try me, like some old rooster skipping around the yard jumping on and off hens till he gits one that'll scooch for him to tread." She laughed. "Somebody's always hoping I'll scooch for him."

Together they began to wring out a sheet and transferred it to a tub of sun-warmed rinse water, then fished out another with the washing sticks. Jennie's hands were strong, but Miriam's were stronger, and she seemed to use no effort; she had been rowing, digging clams and potatoes, and hauling up lobster hoopnets with her brother from the time they could hardly see over the side of a dory.

"Are you ever afraid?" Jennie asked.

"Scairt he'd ambush me, you mean?" She cocked her head like a gem-eyed raccoon. "He did once. Come out in the road and stood in my way. It was real dark, and he looked mighty mysterious. But I moved him quick. Pa wouldn't let me away from home without a few tricks, seeing as the Shaws are always trying to prove we got no rights to our land, and the old man, *he* won't give up till he's dead, and Harry, *he* won't give up till he's tumbled me in the bushes." She grinned. "But the way I was brought up, I won't be bedded, even by a man I fancied, without a minister and a ring. We got too many woods colts running around as it is. But, Lord above, who'd wed me?" she asked without rancor. "Anyone *I'd* look at twice ain't reckoning to pick a Keeler, even one that ain't a come-by-chance. They'd be scairt of having a baby with no wits, or with a tail, or coal black, or born with a little tommyhawk in his hand."

"I think a man would be lucky to get you, Miriam," Jennie said.

"Ayuh, he could hitch me to the plow when the horse is ailing," she laughed, but Jennie caught the taint of sadness. The girl was far from stupid; at eighteen, she knew too well what life was withholding from her. It would have been a kinder destiny for her to be thick-witted than to need to brace herself so young against wanting the world outside.

She giggled, like any girl her age. "It's comical about the Shaws. Missis buys fish from Moses, so the old man has to put up with a Keeler walking up his road once a week. Mostly he's out working on the farm, but if he comes back to the house for something, all he can do is blow hard through his nose and stare at Moses like looks could kill and Moses will drop dead any minute. Missis don't turn a hair."

A new and provocative picture of Mrs. Shaw emerged, but it was not altogether a surprise, given the way she drove that big colt.

When they had the linens spread on the grass and the next batch of laundry steaming in the hot suds, they went down to the house. The breakfast fire had gone out, but Jennie made coffee over the spirit lamp, knowing that Miriam considered this an ineffable elegance. No other house where she worked had anything like that.

"You're a lady," she said, "and you're out there wringing out sheets with me, just like you never had servants back there across the ocean, like the King and all."

Jennie spread thin bread with butter, another delicacy to Miriam, and added gooseberry jam.

"I didn't grow up with servants, Miriam. Just someone to keep house and look after us and our father. We four had to do our share of the work."

There was an uproar from the dogs, quickly stopped. Jennie and Miriam went out to look. The dogs were with David at the barn while he unsaddled Blanchard. All his motions were slow, as if he were very tired. He had taken off his coat, and his white shirt clung wetly to his back. He was about Alick's height, broader of shoulder and with harsher features. His black hair was coarse and rough, with the luster of a crow's wing.

"*Is* that him?" Miriam whispered behind her. He had never once happened to be home when she was there. "That's *him* who painted you and the Mister, and drew all those pictures?"

"That's David. Let's go in so we won't be caught staring at him."

Miriam was at a loss. "Should I go back to the washing?"

"Of course, not! Come in and have your coffee."

"But what will he *think?*"

"Nothing," said Jennie, "and he may not even come in."

But he did come, escorted by the pleased dogs. He dropped his coat and saddlebags on the bench outside and stood in the doorway, looking in at them. He had very light gray eyes, strange with the dark skin and the black hair; the paleness was not watery, it was assertive in itself, of the hue and opacity of silver.

Jennie pointed to the two letters on the mantel, and he crossed the room to get them. "We are having coffee." She gestured toward the table. "Would you like a cup?"

"No, thank you," his lips and expression answered.

"This is Miriam Gunn, from the Keel. She knows an ancient magic spell for removing paint stains from your white shirts," she wrote on the slate.

A quick smile illumined him; Miriam was too stunned to acknowledge it and his little bow. When he went up the stairs, she sat as if listening for supernatural voices. Finally she sighed and drooped. "My, he's handsome," she said in a low voice. "Ain't it a dreadful shame? Don't you pity him?"

Jennie shook her head. "He's lost only his hearing. He doesn't need to hear or talk to be independent. He has a great gift, and all the work he can do."

"But he can't be happy," Miriam fretted. "He looks most dreadful *un*happy. Is he in love?" She could be as romantic as Pris, for all her earthiness. "Maybe she won't have him because he's afflicted, and their children would be so."

"That couldn't be. David wasn't born deaf," Jennie said. "He learned to read and write before he fell sick. He remembers how he woke up to a silent world, and how terrifying it was." He had no idea what his illness had been; his father had never taken him to a doctor.

"Then his pa went away and left 'em paupers on the town?"

"They were never paupers," said Jennie. "Their father was buying this house before we bought it. The General invested funds for them to the amount their father had paid, and when the youngest reached twenty-one the money was divided three ways."

Miriam said raptly, "It's just like a story in a book." She kept looking toward the door for David to reappear. Jennie had never seen her so impressed.

"My mother was left a pauper, over in Amity," the girl said unexpectedly. "Fourteen she was, and the house burned up one night and took her folks along with it. She was out, gone by herself to prayer meeting. They'd had nothing, didn't even own their house—her father was one of them 'Come-day, Go-day, God-send Sunday' fellers. So the town bound her out to the lowest bidder."

Jennie tried not to look greedy, but Mrs. George Gunn, who had so impressed her children, was too good a subject to miss, and if Miriam wanted to talk about her, she was happy to prime the pump. She poured more coffee and pushed the cream jug closer.

"We never have coffee at home," Miriam said, and drank deep. Lifting her head she said, "Marm ran away the first night."

"Now that's a girl after my own heart," said Jennie. "How did she manage it?"

"She was sent to bed in the open chamber and she climbed out onto the shed roof and dropped off'n it, and she was *gone!*" Miriam was luxuriating in all this. Her eyes sparkled. "She wasn't scared of bears or wolves, she was that desprit. She just couldn't stand the disgrace of it, and losing her folks like that. She come over Crit's Hill in fog thick as dungeon. They used to have some real dreadful stories about old Crit haunting his house. But she didn't care for none of it. Not Marm!" Her voice sang with pride in the valor of that fourteen-year-old.

"She thought she was going to Maddox to friends of her folks, and if they wouldn't help her, she would drown herself in the river. Had it all planned out. That's Marm! Well, in the fog and the dark, and being light-headed too, she took the wrong turning. She kept trudging on and on, thinking she'd come to Maddox pretty soon, but she never did. Just her own footsteps for comp'ny in the fog, except when she scared a deer. And when she was weary enough to drop, she got off the road and curled up to sleep. She never had no fear of wild things—they'd let her come all this way in peace, didn't they? She said her prayers and went to sleep expecting she'd never wake up again."

"And what woke her?"

"My Auntie Tamar was putting her to bed in Grandsir's house. His dog found her, Old Bet, when she was scouting around at daylight. She come and got Grandsir, and he carried Marm home and she never woke up, she was that tuckered out. Well, to this day she thinks the sun rose and set in Grandsir. He never asked no questions, and after Auntie Tamar married Manny Joe, she kept house for Grandsir and the boys, and nobody laid a finger on her. After two years she and Pa stood up one day before Mr. Atkins and was married."

"Thank you for telling me, Miriam. It's a lovely story," Jennie said. "I wonder what they thought over in Amity."

"They advertised for a while, Pa said, and then they gave up."

"Tell me about Mr. Atkins. Was he a minister?"

Miriam grinned. "Claimed he was. Nobody knew where he come from. He's dead now. He'd been in bad trouble, but he was a pretty talker when he wasn't rum-sick. He said the right words over Marm and Pa, so that makes it true, don't it?"

"Yes," said Jennie. "The right words always make it true." She and Alick had said the right words to one another across Priscilla's cradle, with the baby and the General's dog for witnesses, and she couldn't have felt more married.

Fourteen

M IRIAM ATE DINNER with them. She was always perfectly at ease with Alick, but whenever David passed anything to her she jumped as if he'd offered her either diamonds or serpents. It was a wonder she could even eat. She was fascinated by the blend of sign language and lip-reading which kept David effortlessly in the conversation, and she did not relax until he and Alick left for the Yard.

David had brought some cherries from Whittier's store; they had just arrived on a schooner returning from the South. When Miriam was ready to leave, with her earnings tied up in a handkerchief in one pocket, Jennie filled her other pocket with cherries to eat as she walked to her next place, and Miriam recoiled as if they were stolen gems.

"You sure he won't care? He brought 'em for *you*."

"He brought them for all of us. He'd like you to have some, I know." Miriam blushed with pleasure and walked dreamily away toward the road.

Jennie was now presented with at least three free hours before the children came home. Her basket of darning was challenged by the new Scott novel David had wickedly left beside it on the chest under the Simon Willard clock. She did not like darning, but it reproached her like a basket of hungry orphan kittens. She delivered herself from temptation by putting the book in the top drawer of the chest without even opening it. Then, forgetting the darning, she went outdoors.

It was just past noon, warm and still. She was so used to the variety of sounds from the Yard that she barely heard them. Only a few birds sang at this hour, and even the gulls were quiet. She walked to April's grave, but not alone; Bounce went ahead, Darroch plodded behind her, and while she was there the cat came out of the woods and jumped onto the stone wall beside her. There were more lilies of the valley out now, scenting the little glade with delicate, sad fragrance.

On the way back she found some large dandelion greens in the lower field, and she went home for a knife and basket. She dug the greens and sat on the ground to clean them. Bounce and Garnet went mousing, optimistically, and Darroch lay in strawberry blossoms like a Sybarite.

Back at the house, she considered saddling Diana and riding for an hour. But it was beginning to cloud up, and the darning was still there. Feeling unjoyfully virtuous, she took the basket outside to the bench, where lilacs and a humming bird were of some compensation. When she was pregnant for the first time she had resentfully seen her future as a blizzard of white flannel, but it had turned out to be an unending storm of stockings. At Pippin Grange Sylvia had coerced her with gentle but unyielding threats into learning how to knit and to darn, so in spite of her distaste she did both things well. Her polished maple darning egg had been a whimsical housewarming gift from Sylvia, along with an assortment of the best Milwards needles.

Carolus was the first one home from school, interrupting the letter she was writing in her mind to Nancy MacNichol. His shirt bore signs of his botanizing on the way home, its pockets damply stuffed with greenery.

"Mr. Lockhart's given me a mammoth assignment," he said. "It's to map our whole property and mark exactly what grows in every section, from the tiniest plant to the tallest tree. And I am to catalog *everything*, with map references. It will take all summer, and it will be the most ambitious thing I've ever done." He was trying without success not to smile.

"Splendid, darling!" Jennie said. "I'm so proud that he thinks you can do it. It's a really scholarly project."

Scholarly pleased him. "Yes, it *is* scholarly, and it will be very important, especially if I find something new. On this whole place I should make at least one discovery, shouldn't I?" His gloss dulled a bit.

"It seems so, but even if you don't, the map will still be of incomparable value."

Incomparable pleased him too. "I'm starting at the Basto line this afternoon, as soon as I change my clothes."

"You may as well keep that shirt. What about a few armfuls of wood before you leave, if you expect baked halibut tonight?" They had brought home a small one from the Keel.

"At once, Mama. *Mother*," he added self-consciously. "It sounds strange. Which do you like best?"

"Use whichever *you* like," she told him.

"*Mama* then, but I'll practice the other." Later he came out with a mug of milk and a thick slice of bread soaked with molasses, on a plate to catch the drip. He sat down beside Jennie, who prudently moved her workbasket to her other side.

"Sandy is looking for work," he said. "He is stopping wherever he thinks anyone has two pennies to rub together."

Pris arrived wearing the expression that meant she had much to say and wanted privacy for it.

"William is playing in Hewitt's brook, and Bell Ann is walking *very* slowly with Lily Shaw. They keep stopping to talk." She went on into the house.

"I stopped by them," Carolus said, "and Bell Ann flapped and squawked at me like a blue jay after a cat. I must have interrupted a profound secret."

"Little girls," murmured Jennie. "I know. I was one."

"Big girls too," said Carolus. "I'll tell you one thing, Mama. If Sandy thinks I'm going to do his share of the work here, he will be paying me for it, in money, so I may be sure of it. I have as much need for money as he has, and I've told him so. There are times when he peacocks about as if he is already a captain." His mouth tilted up at one corner. "I reckon I love him, but he puts a mighty burden on my patience."

"That is mutual," Jennie told him. "And I think you both do wonderfully well. I would have hated to have a sister just my age."

"And a few minutes older," Carolus reminded her. "Now he claims he will be the first to shave, because his voice is changing first."

"My darling," said Jennie, "go and botanize. The clouds are sinking lower and lower."

He tossed down the rest of his milk and gave Bounce his fingers and plate to lick. "Fare thee well," he said, his hand on an imaginary hilt, and strode toward the gate, where he met a glum Sandy. Carolus slapped him on the shoulder. "Avast there, Cap'n sir!"

Sandy looked affronted. Carolus broke up into giggles like William and marched away singing "The Minstrel Boy." Sandy advanced slowly; he'd walked quite a few extra miles today. He gave his mother a desolate look. "Go and get a strupach," she told him, "and then come and tell me."

When he came out with an immense slab of bread and jam, he looked less wan. He told her where he had gone, the flat refusals and the *We'll sees*.

"The trouble is, everyone has all the children or hired men they need, or some of both. If we lived in Maddox, I could find all sorts of work," he said gloomily.

"I know that working for your parents wouldn't be as interesting as working for someone else," Jennie said, "but there must be several things that you and Carolus could do here for pay this summer."

"I want something I can do *alone*. Money doesn't mean as much to Carolus as it does to me."

"There are materials and books to do with botany he'd like to buy."

"If he wants extra money he should be out looking for it, as I am doing. Mother, I am *different*. I believe a man can never have too much money, no matter what he does with it. Carolus is a dreamer, but I am a man of action."

It didn't seem the time to remind him of his spendthrift habits. "Will the man of action please fetch a fresh pail of water?"

"I haven't given up, you know. There's work somewhere for me."

He went in for the water pail, and when he came out he said, "I shall have to have a sextant and compasses and begin studying Nathaniel Bowditch's book on navigation. Captain Blackburn says if I make the acquaintance of Bowditch during the summer, the lessons will come easier in the fall." He went off to the springhouse. When he brought the water back he said, "I forgot to tell you, Bell Ann and Lily Shaw are sitting on a log on the side of the road, and Bell Ann told me not to come a step closer to them. Lily was all eyes, as if I were a dragon." He laughed. "I am going to the Kilburns now. They might need an extra man, if Samuel goes to sea this summer."

He left, singing at the top of his lungs, "A-roving, a-roving, since roving's been my roo-eye-in, I'll go no more a-ro-oving with you, fair maid." His voiced cracked on the highest note, but he finished the line.

"I thought those infernal boys would never leave!" Pris erupted from the house like a genie from a bottle. "I would like to talk about something extremely important *without* a young audience."

She had changed from her gingham school dress and left off her shoes and stockings. Sitting cross-legged on the grass, she wriggled her bare toes with unconscious pleasure. "This is exciting to *me* because it is just about the most tremendous thing in Caro's life. She has made her own decision about something other than choosing ribbons. Mama, she's never even had the choice of goods for a new dress! Everything is decided for her with Fred Coombes's mother and aunts in mind. What will *they* think? Is a stripe too *daring*? Is a floral too *gaudy*? If it is too dark, it will fade her coloring; if it is too delicate, it will look too extravagant for a minister's intended." She laughed scornfully. "Mama, Fred Coombes can hardly bear to *look* at Caro. You needn't caution me; I shan't be disre-spectful about Mrs. Goward or Mrs. Coombes, except to say that between them they have two dreadfully unhappy children."

She grasped her ankles and rocked back and forth. "I fully intend to be madly in love with the man I marry, the way you were with Papa. But Caro cannot even let herself *dream* of love. She is an innocent victim who is to go to prison for life as soon as Fred is ordained a minister. If he ever reaches that pinnacle, which I strongly doubt. He is a victim too, unless he suddenly goes mad and asserts himself. But he needn't go mad," she said reasonably. "Caro has made her decision, and *she* has not gone mad."

"This is a very long story," Jennie said. "I am tingling with suspense, and listening for William and Bell Ann to come arguing."

"I will be quick. I *knew* Caro was different when we met on the hill this morning, but the rest were there, so she couldn't tell me why. We were kept working very hard, preparing for our examinations, until noon. We took our dinners outdoors, and Mr. Lockhart came out and sat with us. He said we should talk about Charlie, because he must be in all our minds, and this could be a sort of memorial service, more personal than yesterday at church. It took a little while, but Noah Whittier led off by telling us how he and Charlie were always going to run away to sea when they were small." She smiled with a tender indulgence for two little boys. "They stowed away on a Whittier vessel, but Noah's father had seen them sneak aboard. It was really funny, and made us laugh, even while we were sad. After that, almost all of us had something to tell about Charlie, and to be sad together was a relief, even for the boys. Do you know what I mean?"

"Indeed I do," Jennie said. As the twins were becoming young men by fits and starts, Pris was already a young woman for at least seventy-five percent of the time.

"But when it was Caro's turn, she blushed like fire and bit her lips, and said in a stiff little voice that she had a good deal to think about, but she couldn't speak it. I knew she was too ashamed to tell how she had hurt Charlie's feelings, but if she told us, or at least Mr. Lockhart, it might stop her feeling so guilty. It wasn't *her* fault that she had been raised to think the Wolcotts were not good enough for a Goward to speak to. But then she asked me after school to walk home with her, and she told me, and she was *resolute*."

"Quickly," Jennie commanded, trying to imagine Caro resolute.

Pris kept rocking back and forth, her eyes distant as if she were watching two girls walking slowly along a quiet road. "Once, when we were about twelve years old, Charlie brought a big sack of apples to school. They were so pretty and red, and he had polished every one. The Wolcotts didn't have much, but they did have that special tree, and he was so proud to bring each of us an apple from it, and to Mrs. Swan too. I remember those apples and how good they were, and Charlie's great grin as we took them. I didn't remember that Caro put her hands behind her and backed off shaking her head as if he'd offered her a—a horse bun. But she has never forgotten how he looked so hurt. Now she can never apologize, and she has become very angry—I never dreamed Caro could be so very angry!—at being raised to do such a cruel thing and be tormented by it now because she cannot undo it."

"Poor child," Jennie murmured.

"But it's not 'poor child' at all!" Priscilla said. "She has had a revelation, like lightning, and now she is thinking about her own life, how her future has been laid out for her all these years like her Sunday dress. At least Charlie had plans, and he had made a beginning, even if he cannot carry them out. But she hasn't even dared *think* except the way she's been told to do. Mama, it is so exciting! The words 'second chance, second chance' kept dancing through her head all night. No second chance to apologize to Charlie, and *he* had no second chance either, but she is *alive*, and she is going to think something for herself before she loses all her chances the way Charlie did. Do you remember how transformed she was at the launching? Well, today she is transformed in a different way. She is going to begin by telling them that she does not want to be Fred Coombes's wife."

Jennie applauded softly. "That's what *I* did," said Pris, "and she was all of a glow, as if freedom were the finest wine and she'd been secretly sipping at it all day." She giggled. "She certainly looked it, with her eyes so bright, so intoxicated at the idea of simply thinking her own thoughts, just enjoying *Now* without marriage to Fred Coombes like a spectre at the feast. The only thing was, she didn't know how to begin, she wanted me to tell her because she knows I can say anything to you and Papa. She was afraid she would end up crying, 'Forgive me, Mama. I'm sorry, Mama. Yes, Mama, I'll never do it again!'—and all in front of Bethiah, too."

"Her father," Jennie began, and Pris snatched at that.

"I told her perhaps she could begin with him, ask for a time to be alone with him. Or to write it all out, everything, and give it to them when she goes to bed. She could say she would never care for Fred and he certainly does not care for *her*, but she would never make a choice that would disgrace them. Oh, if only I could write it for her!" Pris said hungrily. "We were talking about it at the gate when the younger ones came from school, and Bethiah gave us this disagreeable little grin and went by without speaking. Caro watched her go up the lane, and then she said in a low voice, 'Another thing—they have made Bethiah hate me. And I loved her so much when she was my baby sister.' It made me feel so bad for her. . . . And I'll tell you, Mama, she was so upset by Bethiah right then, I wouldn't be surprised if she walked straight into the house and blurted out *everything*."

"Oh, Lord, I hope not," Jennie said. "Mrs. Goward is a very determined woman. She will not easily give up a parsonage for her daughter." She reached down and lightly slapped Pris's shoulder. "Let us take the washing in. Those clouds are full of rain."

Bell Ann straggled in, unusually tidy. "I am going to wear shoes to school," she informed them. "It isn't nice to show your bare feet to everybody." She pointed sternly at Pris's feet. "What if somebody should come?"

"Fiddlesticks!" said Pris. "If this is what walking home with Lily Shaw does to you—" Pris lifted a foot and wiggled the toes defiantly. "We thought you were our friend, Bell Ann Glenroy!" she squeaked. "Now all us little piggies hates you!"

Bell Ann put both hands over her mouth, and her eyes squeezed shut in silent laughter.

"How did it happen that Lily let you walk with her today?" Jennie asked later. She was preparing the halibut for the oven, and Pris was hanging shirts and underwear on the folding clothes horse.

"I ran after her and then I stood in her way like this—," Bell Ann put her hands on her hips and set her feet apart, "and I asked her straight out why she couldn't play with me. *And*," Bell Ann said victoriously, "she told me! It's because of William."

"*Our* Sweet William?" said Pris. "Our Billy Boy? What in the world did *he* ever do? Are those people out of their *minds?*"

"He didn't do anything, but he is a boy, and boys do nasty things."

"Shaw boy," Pris grumbled. Jennie stopped her with a look. Bell Ann tipped up her mug like a thirsty harvest hand.

"What sort of nasty things?"

"I *told* her William wouldn't show her his thingamajig," she said. "*I've* never even seen it. But her mama says boys are always doing things like that, and if you are not careful, they will do worse." She tried to lick off her milk mustache. "Lily says she doesn't know what worse things, but we are very wild children." A touch of the braggart.

"Was there anything more?"

"*Oh* yes!" said Bell Ann happily. "Her big brother met Sandy on the road late one night, and he said if Whittier had a curfew Sandy would be arrested. I told her he was coming from the Keel and *she* said," Bell Ann went into Evelina Ermintrude's most petulant voice, " 'Oh, my goodness, they have bedbugs down there!' "

"Did you talk about anything that wasn't disagreeable?" Jennie asked.

"Dolls and our playhouses, and dresses," said Bell Ann. "She must have about a hundred times more than I have. And she wears white stockings *every* day. If I go to church, will you make me pantalets with three ruffles on them? No, four."

"No, *none,*" said Jennie. "And you are not going to church until you are much older. Of course, if you want to live like Evelina Ermintrude and her sisters, you could be ruffled from head to toe. But you are not a doll, you are a very active little girl. Now, if you wish to wear shoes and white stockings until the end of school, you may. You may also wash your own stockings."

"I'll decide tomorrow," said Bell Ann. William was calling to her to do chores. "But I think *Lily* thinks I have more fun than she does."

Fifteen

WHILE THEY WERE gathering eggs, Bell Ann told William that Lily considered him a desperate character, and he came back to the house in a lather of inarticulate indignation.

"Don't be thinking ill of the wee girl," Alick told him. "It's the queer ideas her people are putting in her head. Walk on the other side of the road and pretend she is not there at all, because if she stubs her toe and soils her apron she would be putting the blame on you. Go and wash now." Privately he said, "Next they will be accusing the boy of interfering with her. What sort of people are they, to be poisoning a child's mind with such things?"

"What sort of people?" Jennie was sprinkling and wrapping the clothes to be ironed tomorrow. "Oddbodies, to be sure. It must be a grim household, and in the midst of it Lily like a living Evelina Ermintrude. Perhaps Mrs. Shaw never had a doll. Perhaps a childlike heart beats under all that black crepe."

By the time they finished supper, the southeast wind was tossing rain by the bucketful against the front windows, and masses of low black cloud rushing across the river darkened the house early. Pris and the twins studied by the bright light of the Argand lamp in the winter kitchen, while Alick and David played chess at the other end of the table. Jennie and the younger two had a lesser lamp in the summer kitchen. She was knitting new heels and toes into the worst cases among the socks while she gave William words from the speller open before her at the table. He sat with his hands folded, staring at a point between her and the lamp, slowly and correctly spelling each word as if he were choosing the letters from an invisible notice board. Bell Ann, singing under her breath, was drawing capital letters on her slate from the models elegantly executed by the teacher in ink on a strip of stiff paper. After many weeks, she was now down to X, Y, and Z.

At half past seven it was time for Bell Ann to go to bed. Jennie read *Puss in Boots*, with Bell Ann frequently exhorting Garnet to pay attention. William was sent to bed at half-past eight, and Jennie read from *The Swiss Family Robinson*. He was a good reader himself, but he clung to this special privilege of early childhood, and Jennie cherished it, in the certain knowledge that one night he would tell her, shyly or gruffly, that he would read to himself. He would kiss her and his father goodnight, and be henceforth trusted to carry his own candle upstairs.

The rain was beating on the roof close to his head and blowing against his window, and the wind was whining somewhere. "It's like being in my berth at sea," he said drowsily. "In one of Papa's ships. I wouldn't go in anybody else's."

"Even if Sandy were skipper?"

"*Sandy?*" He giggled. He could not imagine Sandy a man.

She blew out the light and said, "Where are you?" There was a little snort of laughter. "Here. Lean down." She did, and he hugged her around the neck.

The chess game was drawing to its end, and at nine o'clock the twins and Priscilla would put away their books. Jennie would make a pot of tea, and the family would take turns reading from *Ivanhoe*, the new Scott novel. David had begun it on his own; while the others read aloud, he would make sketches for a projected large painting of the family around the table in lamplight.

Sandy yawned and slammed his book shut, and simultaneously a heavy hammering began at the back door. It catapulted everyone out of serenity, and the dogs set up enough bass and soprano volume to nearly drown out the pounding.

"Hold the dogs," Alick said on his way to the door with David. The simple unlatching of the door let in a great howling buffet of wind that sent the lamp flames wildly fluttering. Alick pulled a man in by the arm, and David drove the door shut behind him. The traveler's sodden hat brim sagged low over his face, and his long coat was heavy with wet.

"Get this off," Alick said, taking hold of the collar. "It must be weighing you down like an anchor." The man pushed him away, took off his hat and slapped it violently against his leg; water flew and flames shuddered again. The man was Eli Goward, Caroline's father. He was breathing in noisy heaves, and his usually unremarkable face was beaten red with rain and wind and deeply scored with either rage or pain.

"Sit down, man, and catch your breath!" Alick urged.

"No!" Goward said hoarsely while they watched with alarmed suspense. "Is Caroline here?" Squinting against the light, his eyes went to all the faces, and stopped at Priscilla's. "*Is* she?"

"No, Mr. Goward," she said respectfully.

"She been here, then?"

"No, Mr. Goward," she answered again.

"You lying to me?" It was the rough shout of a driven and frightened man.

"I would not lie to you, Mr. Goward."

Goward began to shake. "Come, man," Alick said, "let me give you a dram to take the chill out of your bones."

He pulled himself up and managed a tremulous poise. "Thank you, Glenroy, but Temperance is my watchword. We don't know when she slipped out. Nobody saw her go. She had words with her mother. Never did such a thing before." He looked accusingly at Pris. "Like to give her mother a stroke. She sent the girl to her room, and we forbade the younger ones to go near her. Around eight she went up to see if the girl was ready to apologize, and she was gone. *You* walked home from school with her; the young ones saw you at the gate. If she didn't come here, where is she? What'd she tell ye?"

Priscilla looked very young and uncertain. "We talked about school, and—," she faltered, looking across at her mother.

"Then she's out to give us a scare. What fancies you been putting into her head, Missy, eh? Oh, I'll give her mother some blame and take a share for myself; I gave in to the woman's foolish ideas, knowing the female brain is too feeble for such education. What we got for our money is a creature ruined for any use, all in a fever from heathen poets and music written by immoral men, and—" His eyes fell on the schoolbooks on the table. "What do they intend *you* for? A rich ship owner, or the MacKenzie pup?"

"That is enough, Goward," Alick said quietly. "Now David and I will be joining in the search along the roads."

"I won't have you! This is a nest of vipers here. It's not for nothing you're called the Godless Glenroys! When she thinks she has punished us enough, she'll come home. And then she will not be seeing *you* again,

Missy, or that cussed parsonage. We will be going over to the Methodists." His voice broke, and he turned blindly, pulling his wet hat down on
his head.

David was taking the lantern from its hook in the wall. "If you want
nothing from me," Alick said courteously, "perhaps you will be letting
David light you to your horse. He has never done you any harm."

Goward kept his face turned away, but he didn't move while David
lighted the lantern from a candle and put on his coat. Alick held the door
open just enough for the men to slide out one at a time. When he shut
it behind them, Pris burst into tears. Jennie put her arm around her,
murmuring, "There, there. . . ."

"I am *angry!*" Pris sobbed. "The female brain is *not* feeble!" She
looked around at them all with appalled eyes. "What if she *was* on her
way here, and something happened?"

"What could happen to her on the road?" Carolus asked. "There's
nothing wild out there that wouldn't run from her before she even saw
it." The dogs were intensely examining the floor where Eli Goward had
stood.

"She could be safe and dry at home by now," Alick said. "And the
poor man half-crazed with fear. It is sad, very sad." He looked it.

"We'll have our tea now." Jennie sounded too loud even to her own
ears. "I think we need it." Priscilla was staring out into the dark beyond
the reflections in the windows. David came in with his black hair
whipped up into a wet crest, and Alick handed him a towel.

Beginning the new book was a charm to lessen, if it didn't destroy, the
anxiety they all felt in varying degrees. Eli Goward's anguish had shaken
even the boys. Still, while they took turns reading aloud around the
table, the troubled present was displaced by a past so ancient that its
tragedies had been distilled into myth and romance. Ten o'clock struck
too soon.

The rain had ceased and the wind had dropped enough to let them
hear the dripping from the eaves. They all went out, sniffing at the night
as the dogs did; for the humans it was scented with soaked lilacs, wet grass
and earth, rockweed cast up on the shore. Great black clots of cloud
moved across the sky on the dying wind. With the passing of the storm,
the emotional atmosphere had also cleared; voices were cheerful. The
men and boys went around the house, and Priscilla and Jennie walked to
the barn.

"I'm not really worried about Caro tonight," Pris said. "It came over me when we were reading. I am sure I know where she is: out in the horse barn, safe and snug in the hay, probably sleeping. She likes to hide out there whenever she can slip away, because it is the only place where she can have real peace, and the horses are company. But she will pay for it tomorrow. You heard what Mr. Goward said."

"The poor man was desperately frightened, Pris," her mother said.

"But Mama, Caro needs a friend," she said obstinately, "and I will always try to be that."

Light from the windows showed the beaten petals of apple blossoms strewn on the grass. "Poor pretty things," Pris said. "Why does there always have to be a storm to wreck them?"

Sixteen

J ENNIE WENT TO sleep quickly, lulled by Alick's breathing. But she was awakened by a chaotic dream of calling voices. She was out of bed before she was completely awake, and listening at the foot of the stairs, but no sound came from above. She walked to the back door and listened, all was quiet at the barn. She might have heard a night heron, a fox barking, even the scream of a bobcat. Now I will be awake for the rest of the night, going over and over this Goward business, she thought crossly.

The broad, smooth floorboards were comfortably warm under her bare feet. Darroch stirred in the kitchen but didn't get up; Pris had taken Bounce upstairs. The parlor was not dark, with its pale walls, and the windows were gray with the fog outside. Between two front windows was the space reserved for a pianoforte, if she ever achieved one. Standing there in her nightgown, she played scales and chords on phantom keys, and a few flourishy arpeggios. All the children watched from their frames on the walls, from David's earliest drawing of Pris with a kitten in her arms, to Bell Ann in drawers and a short shirt, squatting in a tide pool picking up periwinkles. April was there, her head thrown back in laughter, small starfish hands clapped together in patty-cake. Jennie didn't need to see them, she knew them by heart.

She and Alick, in oils, watched the children from across the room, side by side over the mantelpiece. The portraits were so good that Jennie had thought, If Alick dies before I do, I shall destroy that painting, because I could not bear to look into those eyes and not have them change at sight of me. — Since she often entertained captains' and owners' wives in the parlor, it was a useful gallery for David's talent, and frequently secured commissions for him.

She was pleasantly chilled when she got into bed; the warming-up was the most exquisite of creature comforts, and the sweetest drug. She hoped Caro was sleeping snugly in the hay of the horse barn.

She was half-roused by Alick's sliding stealthily out of bed, and she kept her eyes squeezed shut so as to hold onto sleep. Almost at once it covered her again, and she dreamed something crowded and noisy, from which she woke all at once. The tall clock was striking four. Alick had not come back, and the windows were still gray with fog.

She bounced out of bed. A dim light met her in the hall, coming from the summer kitchen where the lighted lantern stood on the table with a napkin-wrapped bundle and a stoneware bottle beside it. Alick was pulling on his boots. Darroch opened an eye at her approach, then shut it again.

"How long have you been up?" she asked Alick.

"About ten minutes." He stood up to stamp his feet down into his boots. He had a look she knew well: withdrawn, absorbed, concentrated on a single objective with no room for anything else.

"Where are you going?"

"To find her. I think she is on the shore between Crit's Cove and here. I have been seeing her all night."

A nastily familiar coldness went rippling down her back and along her arms and legs. She had learned to expect surprises, good and bad, every day of her life, but expecting was not the same as accepting without a tremor.

"She may have been coming here to Priscilla," he said. "And she has fallen, and is huddled up somewhere cold and in pain. I am not sure, mind you, but I must be looking."

He put the package into one coat pocket and the bottle into another. "She will be hungry, the poor wee thing."

"I am going with you," Jennie said. "I do not intend to sit here until broad daylight wondering if *you* have broken a leg. I shall be ready in five minutes." She pointed a finger at him like a sword. "Don't you go without me."

"I would not dare, the woman is such a tyrant."

When she returned to the kitchen dressed for a wet and rough walk, David was there, also ready to go. He was buttering bread, and handed her a slice, then began eating the other one. Alick took nothing. For someone who denied having the Sight, any such happening could be disturbing; he was probably hoping that this one wasn't genuine, just his own dreaming.

Half-past four struck as they left. They didn't need the lantern; the light would have simply glared back at them from a wall of fog so thick that they couldn't see the old apple tree at the turn until they were only a few yards from it. Beyond that, everything had disappeared; there was only the familiar road under their feet. They were hazy even to each other.

At the Yard the three separated and searched every building down to the smallest shed. In the fog, with no visible surroundings for comparison, the *Enoch Lincoln* towered above them like a man-of-war. Moisture fell steadily, like rain.

They left the Yard for the shore below the eastern woods. The fog brushed softly around them, beading their eyelashes and their clothes, wetting their hair. Strands of rockweed were slippery, and they picked their way carefully along the detritus marking the last high tide. Daylight and the tide were slowly returning. Outside the river the seas were still high, and the unremitting thunder of the rote was a roaring in one's head, separate from the stillness here.

David went ahead. He had spent more time on this shore than anyone else, beginning as a small child, and he knew each slant of ledge, each isolated boulder, every variation of color, texture, and conformation. It was he who had shown them the glacial scrapes running from north to south.

Alick walked in isolation, not only physical. Each time David paused and then went on without beckoning to them, he closed his hand more tightly around hers.

"Caroline wanted to object to being handed over to Fred Coombes," she said. "She was growing desperate, and Charlie's being lost was the last straw. She saw how short and uncertain life is."

"Aye," Alick said absently. David had stopped on a ridge, then went on out of sight. They followed him down to the small gravel beach of the Bastos' cove, where sandpipers flew up with tiny peepings. The tide licked at the stones. Loose rockweed floated on it. The sandpipers returned to feeding before the human beings had left the beach.

The birds of the woods were waking now; they found Caroline to the flutes of white-throated sparrows. At first she seemed only another parcel of débris left by the tide, entangled in kelp, lying across a split in a wrinkled gray rock. The three stood a little way off in a common refusal to discover what one does not want to discover; that it was not simply a bundle of kelp and old branches; that they did see a hand; that by moving closer they would see a white face.

It was not completely white; it had been battered almost unrecognizable as last night's surf and high tide tossed her body back and forth. Her hair looked like soaked and bleached Irish moss.

The men moved quickly to clear away the branches and loose weed, but when they tried to lift her, they could not. Alick swore at the entwining kelp and tried to find the end of it under the body. David went forward onto his knees and pushed his hands down into the narrow crevasse. After a moment he gave up and walked away and stood with his back to them.

Alick worked in silence and patience to free the leg. When he lifted it and laid it across the rock, the foot dangled from a broken ankle. The shoe was left behind, and the soiled white stocking looked dead itself. David carried her up to the high ground, and Jennie could not leave the broken foot dangling, but supported it as if it could give pain. It was cold enough to chill more than her hand.

Alick went ahead, and just inside the woods he cleared old leaves and twigs away from a little grassy spot. David placed Caro on it as gently as if she were sleeping. Jennie gave him a scarf from her cloak pocket and he folded it and put it under Caroline's head, while the pale eyes looked up past him like a doll's. Her dress had been tattered into long strips, which fell away from her. Her stockings had been wrinkled down, the garters gone.

David gave Jennie an appealing look, and she set her teeth and worked the stockings up over abraded legs to where they should be, trying to keep her finger tips from touching the rigid cold flesh, incredulous all the while because this was Caroline. Or what was left, and how could it be?

She laid the ripped lengths of calico together the best she could. Then she took off her cloak, and the two men tucked it around the body from over the fine fair hair to under the toes. Alick gave his jacket to Jennie. She didn't want to take it, because he was shivering, but he shook his head impatiently at her and held it for her to put on.

"Will you go and tell them?" he asked David. "Someone should stay with her, and I will be doing that."

David indicated that he would go up to the Bastos' farm, which was nearest, and borrow a horse. He questioned Jennie with a lifted eyebrow.

"I will stay with Alick," she said quickly.

"Oh, no," Alick said. "You will be going along with David, to the children." He took her by the arms and lightly shook her. "I am fine, *mo ghaoil*. Grief is at me for the child, but no fear. To watch with her is the least I can do."

They embraced, kissed, and she followed David, who was already walking away. As a child he had watched his mother drown herself, and then he had watched Alick lift her body from the water. The child had been numb with it, and Alick had been sick with it.

"Alick, be careful on the ledges when you come home," she called back, unable to resist.

He waved her on. But just the same she felt safer for saying it.

As she and David walked side by side up through the woods, she was preternaturally aware of physical details. Every sight and sensation was so intense, it was like a weather-breeder of the brain—the fog drip, the loose, warm earth softly giving underfoot, the spangle of pale lavender toadstools among blackened trunks, the blinding white of bunchberry blossoms on brilliant green, a flash of black and scarlet feathers—yet she was still at the shore seeing a dead child. One foot slipped on wet moss, and instantly David had her arm in a hard grip.

"A fine thing for me to break an ankle after telling Alick to be careful," she said, but his eyes were as blank as silvered glass.

While Nick and David were saddling a horse, she told Nora Basto and a dumbstruck Thankful what had happened. She wouldn't sit down. "The children will think we've been stolen by gypsies," she said.

Mrs. Basto walked with her to the path. "And Alick knew where to go!" she said. "Well, I've heard of these folks. But right next door—and him such a quiet man!"

"Please keep that part to yourself," Jennie said. "I told you because we're old friends and neighbors. But if it spread around town—you know they think we are odd enough down here." Nora muted her laugh in deference to the occasion and gave Jennie a motherly hug. "You're white as skim milk. Take care walking home, and eat a good breakfast even if you have to force it down. Something like this sucks your strength away without you even knowing it, until you drop."

When she left the woods Brisky saw her and came galloping, snorting with suspicion until he recognized her, and thrust his head over the fence. She put her hand on his shaggy neck. "Art thou the clever lad, then?" she murmured. She felt as if she could stand like this forever, or for at least an hour, just leaning on the fence in the warm fog.

Priscilla came running from the springhouse. Bounce passed her and threw himself at Jennie; she had to pick him up to quiet him. "Ulysses's dog never acted like this," she told him. Darroch delivered the New-foundland equivalent of a twenty-one gun salute, and Jennie was sur-rounded by all her children.

"Papa is all right," she said quickly. "David is all right, and nothing has happened at the Bastos'."

Bell Ann wrapped her arms around her and pressed her cheek against Jennie's midriff. "I missed you and missed you and missed you—"

"We all missed you," said William belligerently. "Why are you wearing Papa's coat, and where is he?"

"If I may go in and take off my wet boots, and have a good cup of tea—," Jennie began. Immediately Bell Ann was yanked away by a stern William. All the way to the house she heard how everyone had waked up, or had been unkindly waked up; what everyone had thought and where they had searched; and how much time had been consumed convincing Bell Ann that people were stolen by the fairies only in fairy stories. When they realized that David was gone too, but not his horse, the older ones thought a ship might have run into Misery Wall in the fog, and a seaman had struggled up to the house for help. So they had all streamed down there, to nothing.

"Anyway, there was no blood anywhere in the house, so we didn't think you had been murdered by bandits in your bed," said William.

"And there's no porridge," said Bell Ann.

"Darling, no one had the time. Now go and get ready for school, and then we will have a good breakfast. Hurry, because I am hungry. You too, William."

William glared at the twins. "They wore their barn boots into the house," he said.

"They'll take them off and wipe up any soil. How are your feet?"

"Clean. I wiped off all the hen turd in the wet grass."

"So did I!" Bell Ann yelled from the stairs. William left reluctantly, suspecting secrets behind his back. He would know about Caroline later, but right now she wanted no young audience. She beckoned to Pris, and they went outside to where the twins were shedding their boots. "I hope Sweet William won't turn into Sour William one of these days," she said. "I'd like to have one little boy left for a while."

"Oh, Mama, we were all at sixes and sevens around here when we couldn't find you," said Pris. "That's what's at William!"

"Everything was all tapsalteerie, as Mr. Lockhart would call it," said Carolus.

"Brought us up all standing," Sandy was tersely nautical.

"There is no subtle way to tell this," she said. "Your father was out of bed before four this morning, saying he was sure that Caroline was somewhere on the shore between Crit's Cove and here."

They couldn't really have stopped breathing, but that was the effect. "David and I went with him." She took out the napkin-wrapped bread and the water bottle. "He thought she might have sprained her ankle and curled herself somewhere to wait, he took this for her. — Caroline is dead, my dears," she said. "Drowned. We found her just past Bastos' cove. She had somehow jammed her leg down into a crack in the rock and she hadn't been able to free herself before the tide came up." As she said the words she wanted to vomit.

Sandy's mouth opened as if in protest, then he tramped away from them around the house and out of sight. Carolus looked a little dazed, as if he couldn't believe what he was thinking, and followed Sandy. Pris remained alone with Jennie, frowning; she might have been trying to decipher a statement spoken in a foreign language. Suddenly she said with an odd little laugh, "Oh, my goodness, I forgot to strain the milk!"

Remembering herself in her youth, Jennie knew she must not follow yet. She was relieved to have the news out, and she felt tired enough to drop where she stood. Garnet came to her, sleek and dark with wet, and leaned heavily against her legs as if in solace. "Let us go in, Cat of Cats," Jennie said.

Carolus said behind her, "Where is Papa?" He had not gone far.

"He and David got her free, and now he is waiting with her for David to bring Mr. Goward back."

"Poor Papa. Poor David," Carolus said. "Poor you."

"Poor Mr. Goward. We all set our teeth to do what had to be done. My cloak is covering her, and that is why I'm wearing your father's coat. Now let us do something about breakfast."

"I built the fire," said Carolus with modest pride.

She changed her boots for knitted wool slippers that warmed her feet. Water was boiling, and she made a pot of tea and sipped from her cup while she cooked a skilletful of scrambled eggs. Carolus poured milk and toasted bread, Bell Ann set the table, and William was sent down cellar to choose jam for the toast. This gave him a happy ten minutes trying to decide, with Bell Ann shouting suggestions down to him. Sandy came in with an unsolicited armful of wood and left with an empty water bucket. When he returned, Jennie asked him what Pris was doing.

"She's perched on the Squaw Rock, not saying a word, and I pretended I didn't see her." It was one of these unexpected touches of delicacy with which her sons could surprise Jennie.

Bell Ann asked William severely why he did not bring up raspberry, as she hated blackberry, and he replied, "Because I wanted blackberry." The arrogant simplicity of it flummoxed her into silence.

When the children were well into their meal, and Jennie was somewhat revived, she kicked off her slippers and walked on bare feet up to the springhouse.

The Squaw Rock was a huge boulder on the far side of the building. Anyone who sat there couldn't be seen by the ordinary passerby. Priscilla had named it herself, in a continuous narrative the older children used to tell about a mythical Indian family who had lived here long before the white men came. The mother of nine sons, with no daughters to help her, had become very tired of having to chew enough moosehide for all those moccasins year after year, and never being allowed to canoe on the shining river or to go roaming in the dark forests. One day when the men came home, there was no camp fire with a stew bubbling over it, there was many a moosehide left unchewed, and the squaw was sitting on this rock with her arms folded. She was deaf to orders and entreaties until the three older sons promised to find wives so she would have someone to chew away at home while she roamed the dark forest and canoed the shining river.

Pris sat higher than Jennie's head, with her arms around her knees. She flicked a glance toward her mother, then away. She had not been crying.

Jennie took a perch halfway up the side. "Whatever happened to Mrs. Ho-ho?"

"Who cares?"

"I care!" said Jennie. "It's a pity William and Bell Ann are growing up without the Ho-hos."

"They are all," said Pris hollowly, "in the Happy Hunting Ground. No moose has to die, and women's teeth last for eternity. Oh, Mama!" she cried. "She must have been on her way here! I can't *bear* to think of how she must have died, so frightened and alone, begging for someone to come, and the rain and the surf beating her, and how she must have kept calling until the water filled her mouth." Sobbing, she bowed her head onto her knees.

Jennie reached up and felt for Pris's bare feet and clasped her hands around them.

"I wish I had never let her talk to me," Pris railed through her sobs. "And then her father would not be blaming me, and *I* would not be blaming me, and she would still be alive, and— Oh, I shall *never* get over this, as long as I live!"

Jennie squeezed a foot hard. "Listen to yourself, Pris. It is all I, I, I, how *I* am suffering! Soon you will want to blame someone because you are so uncomfortable, and it will be poor Caroline. Cry for *her*, not for yourself. You might even spare some pity for her family, and what they are suffering now. But do it *without* sackcloth and ashes for yourself."

Pris angrily snatched her feet free and lifted her chin. "I wonder if *you* have ever felt—" She stood up and jumped off the far side of the rock. When she came around to Jennie she had capitulated without a word, and they walked back to the house with their arms around each other, like sisters.

"Would you like to stay home today?" Jennie asked.

"No. We have examinations in Latin and mathematics. I'd like to think about something else besides what has happened."

"And besides, if you stayed home I'd give you ironing to do."

"Not that, not that!" Pris said with feeble humor.

After breakfast Jennie told William and Bell Ann, with no details, that Caroline had been drowned. They listened in awed silence, not really taking it all in; the questions would come later.

When they had all gone with their schoolbags and dinner buckets, she thought of going down to the Yard to tell the men what was keeping Alick, but the children would be telling anyone they met coming in. She considered lying flat for fifteen minutes before washing the dishes, but she couldn't have stopped thinking. Alick came in with the dogs, and without speaking she took him into her arms. He looked haggard and pale.

"Are you all right?" she asked him.

"Yes. You? And Priscilla?"

"I am functioning in my sleep, as you see. Pris chose to go to school."

"*Gle' mhath.*"

"They had all the chores done, but it takes Papa to tend the porridge. We had scrambled eggs. I'll fix some for you when you are ready."

"Thank you. I will just be shaving first." He took the teakettle into the pantry and she followed him. "David rowed Goward down; he has no boat at all," he said. "They had to go around to Three Corner Farm to borrow one, but Goward was letting no one else come with them. He wanted no talk. Well, he would get only silence from David."

He mixed a mugful of hot water and Hat Shenstone's liquid shaving soap, and began to lather his face. "*Dia*, when I was hearing the oars in the fog coming nearer and nearer, it was like the old tales that used to send the cold bony fingers of skeletons clutching at our bellies. And it seemed as if the birds stopped singing. And then to see him sitting in the stern, glaring past David's head as if I were the Earl of Hell himself. Och, but I was sorry enough to weep for the man." He took up his razor. "I was thinking, what if it was one of ours lying there? —They had brought a litter from Three Corner Farm, but it was not easy to arrange her, she was so stiff. He was not saying even one word, and his lips were gray as ash. I thought he would drop dead beside his daughter."

Jennie shut her eyes. *One of ours*. Not dying in our arms but in a far-off place where she had cried for us without our knowing; and then to bring home a grotesquely angled, stiffened object that was once flesh of our flesh, blood of our blood.

Alick's voice had ceased. She opened her eyes and he was staring at her in the mirror, the razor motionless. She swallowed. "Alick, I've been worried for you, because of that other time. I wish anyone but you and David could have been the ones."

"Och, so did I, when we first found her. Before, I was so sure she'd be living, you see. And to find her like that—I cursed my visions! I've never had the Sight, and I never wanted it." He resumed shaving. "With David you can never be telling anything until you see a little tic beside his mouth. Well, it was there then and when he came back with Goward. —The *coldness* of her. I remembered that from the other time. You cannot believe it was ever living, it is so cold."

"I warmed you then, didn't I?"

"That you did, and if I were to have my heart's desire at this moment it would be to have you in my arms and ourselves in our bed. But since I have a business to go to, you could be cooking the eggs now."

Seventeen

S HE WASHED THE dishes and set the flatirons on to heat. Waiting, she put the carcasses of Sunday's chickens in a pot to slowly simmer with a good many onions, reflecting that if Caroline's death was a shock too deep for tears, she was weeping anyway from slicing onions; one was bound to shed tears somehow. Meanwhile she had a mountain of ironing in a hot kitchen, with all the windows and the door open to the soggy smother of fog. The day was lightening to a white glare and then abruptly darkening, open-and-shut. Against it her thoughts played like actors on a stage. She was not the only woman thinking of Caroline this morning, but the knowledge would yield no comfort to Caroline's mother. To know that your child ran away from you could only compound the agony. That is, Jennie qualified, if you blame *yourself*. Perhaps the Gowards were crying, "O Lord, why did this thankless child do such a terrible thing to us?"

Jennie's mother had died of childbed fever at Sophie's birth, when Jennie was six. She and Sophie were so mothered by the two older sisters, and their father was such a strong presence, that the lack of their mother hadn't been a brutal physical and emotional deprivation. But, growing older, they envied Sylvia and Ianthe the jeweled details of complete memory. They were greedy for something, *anything*, to give life to the slender woman in the painting in Papa's study. It was harder for Sophie than for Jennie; Jennie could remember being rocked and sung to by their mother, but Sophie remembered instead the face and the arms of the local woman who had been her wet nurse after her own child died.

When Jennie became a mother, her treasury had been magically enriched by recollections she hadn't known she possessed. She heard her mother calling her in her dreams, and wondered if her own voice was like her mother's. When she rocked a child and sang about the fox going out one winter's night, or if Bell Ann came home from school singing "Lavenders blue, dilly dilly," a shaft of pure recognition could run her through, not with pain but with near-joy.

But what had it been like for Ianthe and Sylvia? They, like Papa, had grieved in private for her sake, but they had been children themselves. Could one be worse than the other, she pondered—to be a parent and watch your child die or to be a child watching your mother die? And what if Papa's heart had stopped years earlier, when they were still very young?

She knew she shouldn't have gone this far, to imagine leaving her children. But *please*, she was entreating, not both of us before they are grown! It was not a prayer; honor forbade treating God as any port in a storm, crying, "God, if you are really there, will you grant me these few small favors? *Please.*"

When David walked in, surprising even the dogs, she was so glad to see him and be saved from her thoughts that she hugged him and was embraced tightly for a moment in return. He looked gaunt and very tired.

"I will make you a proper breakfast," she said. He shook his head and pointed at himself, meaning that he would do it. "Tea, then," she said. "I would like a cup myself." She set all the irons on the back of the stove and pushed the teakettle forward.

They took their food out to the bench; the sun was burning through the fog now. Jennie had no wish to discuss Caroline and knew that David was of the same mind. She brought out the message slate.

"Did you find anything useful in Wiscasset?" she wrote.

He mimed humorous ignorance. "What do you mean?"

"If you ever find your father, what will you do?"

He shrugged, and spread his hands in a very Gallic gesture. Then he took the slate pencil. He had a small neat script, between writing and printing. "What makes you think I am looking for him?"

"Intuition."

He wiped the slate clean. Then he wrote slowly, as if he were shaping the words in his mind first, "I have wanted to strike him down ever since that day. I swore on my mother's grave that I would do it when I was big enough. Now I am not sure. We don't need him now. Perhaps he needs us, but he doesn't have us. I would like him to know that."

"Could you forgive the way he let you run behind the wagon and he never looked back?"

"I hated him for it, yes, but we survived. We were better cared for without him. But I can never forgive him for what he did to our mother." The pencil hesitated. "One other thing. I would like him to know that I am a better artist than he is."

She laughed with pleasure and relief. "I don't know," she teased him. "Those miniatures of the General's children are very beautiful."

"No more than those of the Glenroy children!"

"Vanity, vanity, all is vanity," Jennie wrote.

Still smiling, he patted himself on the head. "He gave me talent, not because he wanted to, but because he couldn't help it. He also made us illegitimate. We didn't need *that* gift."

Gwynneth had told her about the last day, their mother screaming at them, "You are bastards, *bastards*! You must die to be saved!"

"My mother," David wrote, "taught me how to read and write and how to notice everything, so when I became deaf I wasn't helpless. I owe her the most. But for his gift I owe him something besides a blow and a curse."

"Well, I hope you will find out soon whether he's alive or dead, so you can put it all behind you. But what makes you think he is in Maine? He could be anywhere, even back in Wales."

He shook his head. "I don't think he would go back there. When I could still hear, I once heard him talking to himself, or to somebody not present, when he was drunk. —But if things haven't gone right for him, and he is alone, he may come somewhere near to get a word or a glimpse of us. The farther my name travels, the better the chance of it. The old man at Wiscasset does flat likenesses without shading. They are not dear, and he sells a good many. He told me I put him in mind of someone, but he is old as Time, and he couldn't remember. I have my mother's eyes, so it couldn't have been that, unless—" The pencil hesitated, and then resumed. "He might have seen us all together before we ever came here."

"Will you go to Belfast and Hallowell both?"

"Belfast first, and a letter to Hallowell. If they want me, they should be willing to wait." He had an objective consciousness of his own worth.

He took hot water up to his room, and she returned to the ironing, refreshed not only by the strupach but by the change from her painful introspection to something positive and creative. When David was ready to go, she walked out with him and stood by while he saddled Blanchard, and when he was mounted she said, "Safe voyage and safe return, David."

He leaned down from the saddle and kissed her cheek. The dogs escorted him up to the main road, and while she went back to her work, her fancy went with the man and the horse. They would be quitting the town as fast as hoofs could take them. The little bundle of death he had carried in his arms would be left more than miles behind him. *Worlds.*

Arranging a finished shirt on the rack, she thought, I wasn't praying for favors a little while ago, and I expect none, I have had so many. I was *hoping.* Hope is a fact of faith, Mr. Lockhart says. We must never let hope die, but we cannot hope without faith. Well, I shall simply have to have faith that Alick and I will live to be very, very old.

When Alick went back to the Yard after dinner, the fog had burned away except for a few gauze draperies transparently veiling a series of pale pastel watercolors. Then the wind sprang up from the northwest, and all at once the day shone like a souvenir plate of green and blue porcelain, with a gilded edge scalloped by the flight of goldfinches. It had been about nine hours since Eli Goward first saw his daughter dead. At first, time makes nearly imperceptible progress away from the moment of your child's death, and then suddenly it flies so fast, too fast, and behind you the beckoning little figure grows smaller and smaller, and you cannot go back for it.

Jennie was on her knees weeding the herb garden when Pris and Carolus came home. Pris waved to her and went into the house, but Carolus dropped onto his heels beside her. "Mr. Lockhart didn't know anything about it until we told him this morning," he said with a melancholy satisfaction. "Nobody knew. It was quite a shock," he added moderately. "Mrs. Lockhart was feather-white. All the girls gasped—you know how girls are—and Fred Coombes looked pretty queer."

"You gasped," Jennie reminded him, "and looked pretty queer yourself, as I remember."

"I reckon so," he said sheepishly. "Anyway, Mr. Lockhart saddled up and went straight to the Gowards'. Captain Blackburn gave out the mathematics examinations, and Mrs. Lockhart took the music girls into the parlor, so we sat around the dining room table trying to do geometry and algebra with them plunking away in there. But I daresay the Glenroys managed pretty well, even Pris, bad as she felt. We always do."

"Try not to be so superior about it," Jennie advised him. "Pride goeth before a fall, and so forth."

"Mr. Lockhart didn't stay very long at the Gowards'." He picked a leaf of mint and chewed it. "He said we should go to the funeral on Thursday, to show how much we all thought of Caro. *I* shan't go," he said placidly. "I don't believe in funerals. I don't even want one for me. I shall just vanish."

"To be one with the Universe, I take it." Jennie went on tidying the rosemary. "None of you three need go. Where is Sandy?"

"He is digging up a garden spot for Mrs. Taggart. She is setting out tomato plants, and Mr. Taggart says they are poison, so he won't have anything to do with it. Sandy didn't make a bargain before he commenced, so he may be paid with a doughnut instead of money."

"You hope," said Jennie.

"No, I don't!" he protested, trying not to grin. He gave her an affectionate pat on the head, and went in to change his clothes. Soon after, he departed with his fishing rod and his vasculum.

William came next. Bell Ann was dilly-dallying with Lily, he said. He was in a hurry to take his rod and follow Carolus, rashly promising enough trout for an evening's meal. After he had gone, Priscilla came out and sat cross-legged in the grass near Jennie, without speaking. Bounce brought her his toy, a pair of old stockings tied into a hard knot with flapping ends, and kept pushing it into her hands until finally she took the ends and he pulled on the knot with all his might, bracing his legs and growling in a frenzy. Darroch lay watching with mild interest.

It was impossible to be half-hearted about anything with Bounce, so in spite of herself Pris was laughing when Bell Ann came running, swinging her schoolbag in wide circles. "Mama! Pris!" she cried. "Bethiah and Grace and Nellie and Samuel and Henry—," she flopped gasping on the ground, "didn't come to school today, and William and I told Mrs. Lennox it must be because Caroline drownded. My, she was *surprised!*"

Pris's brief sparkle went out. Her hands went slack. She turned her head and kept it strained away. Bounce tried to move her hands, but gave up and rushed at Bell Ann.

"And guess what," Bell Ann continued, bracing herself against Bounce. "When we came out of school, they were all there but Bethiah. They can't come to school till after the funeral, but they ran away, they said, because it was terrible at home. Mr. Goward whipped Samuel just because he started to whistle. And they miss Caro *awful*. She's in her room and they won't let them see her." Bell Ann was beautiful in the bloom and brilliance of her indignation.

"Bethiah doesn't want Caroline to wear her new best dress because *she* wants it. It's blue, with silk embroidery, and Caroline's hardly ever worn it but she loved it. Mama, Caroline doesn't *know*, does she?" She didn't wait for an answer. "Why does she have to look nice for everybody else if *she* doesn't know it? It is like a big party, everybody is bringing things to eat, and Bethiah says *she* will fix Caro's hair and put flowers in it, and will lend Caro her best brooch."

There was no benefit in stopping children in full spate, telling them not to think of certain things, sloughing off their questions. Besides, Bell Ann had attended pet burials in her life, comforted by the family discussion of the Dear Departed's welcome in Heaven from the animals that had gone before.

"She is going to take it back before they put down the coffin lid," Bell Ann said. "What is a coffin?"

Oh Lord, Jennie thought. Pris was motionless. "A coffin is a sort of bed for Caro to lie in."

"But can she get out of it? Why don't they wrap her up in her quilt? That is what *I'd* like. And let her wear her best blue dress," she added judicially.

"I'm sure the grown-up people will take good care of Caroline," Jennie said. "Now go into the house and change from your school clothes, and—"

"Grace and Nellie and Samuel and Henry," she continued with ruthless clarity, "*hate* Bethiah. Henry and Samuel said they could shoot her with a bow and arrow, and say it was Indians done it, but nobody will believe it. Do you know why she *specially* doesn't want Caro to have her new best dress? Because Caro is going to burn forever, and that dress will be all ruined."

Pris said in a choked voice, "If anyone should burn for eternity, it's Bethiah." She looked ill. Not able to reach her, Jennie reached out for Bell Ann and drew her close. William came out and stood silently by.

"Did she say why Caroline is going to burn?"

"Because she drownded herself, and that is a sin, so God doesn't love her, God *hates* her!" She was furious. "I said, that's *your* God, not mine! I wouldn't have a God like that! I would not speak to Him, no matter what He did to me!"

William said stolidly, "I asked them why they thought Bethiah was telling the truth. They said even Bethiah would not dare make up a story like that. I said, 'Oh yes, she would, just to make you cry.' " He gave his mother a long dark look. "She woke them up early this morning and told them Caro was dead and when they put her in the ground she would just keep sinking down to H-e-l-l and begin to burn."

Bell Ann leaned hard against Jennie. "It's not true, is it?" she whispered fearfully. "*Forever?*"

"No, it is not true," Jennie said, and Pris echoed her, emphatically. "It is *not*. What else did Bethiah say, William?"

"She said Caro was impertinent and disobedient, and when her mama scolded her she went out and drowned herself."

"It was a terrible, terrible accident," said Jennie.

Bell Ann sat up with more confidence. "I told them that, because you told me, and you never tell lies. And I said God wouldn't hurt Caro, He'd have saved her if He could, but He must've been somewhere else, but He will come and get her. They have to put her in the ground first, like planting flowers, and she won't go down to *that* place. She will go up to heaven, in her best blue dress."

Rising up through the clouds to an azure heaven, riding the Great Horse with her hands secure in his silver mane. Jennie longed to share the image with Pris.

"But Mama," insisted Bell Ann, "how can they sleep tonight? Nellie says she will be afraid to go to bed, having to think about it. They won't believe us instead of Bethiah, because she talks to them all the time about it. She comes in and whispers."

"*I* told them they should ask their mother and father," William said.

"That's what I told Caro," Pris said, "and look what happened!" She sprang up and ran into the house. The younger two looked after her with alarmed respect, as if they were afraid she would never be her familiar self again; they had never before seen her like this.

"Well, children," Jennie said, removing Bell Ann's thumb from her mouth, "this is one of the times when we cannot help, no matter how much we want to. We can only hope that things will cure themselves. Poor Mr. and Mrs. Goward have a terrible burden of grief, but if they knew what was going on with the children I'm sure they would stop it."

"We could write them an anonymous letter," William suggested. "Or we could send Bethiah one, with a skull and crossbones, and everything."

"No, we shan't do anything like that. Perhaps one of them will have the courage to tell, or they'll be crying out with nightmares and *then* tell." She unhooked the back of Bell Ann's dress. "Now, go and have your strupach. You've done all you can."

When they'd gone in, attended by the optimistic Bounce, she sat back against the clapboards and shut her eyes. The existence of Bethiah was almost enough to convince one of Hell and its legions of foul fiends;

one had to forcibly remember that Bethiah was a child and a most miserable one. But the torture was not to be excused by the torturer's personal misery.

Pris came out and sat down beside her.

"Would you like to know how Caro will go to heaven?" Jennie asked in a low voice. "It might comfort you a bit. But it is Bell Ann's secret, and she keeps it very well. So you keep it too."

"I love it!" Pris said at the end. "I love *Him*! And Caro loved the horses so! It almost makes me happy, and that's a strange thing to say when I feel absolutely murderous and I'm hoping that little fiend is haunted every night of her life. I hope if Bethiah gets the blue dress it burns her skin like fire and leaves her covered with blisters. Oh, Mama!" She suddenly wept on Jennie's shoulder. "I've done so well all day, but now I can't seem to bear it. It hasn't been twenty-four hours yet, and at this time yesterday Caro was bursting with hope and resolution. She even *joked*." Pris had to stop and blow her nose. "She said, 'Today I am going to make Fred Coombes a happy boy!' And now it's as if Bethiah is killing her all over again, by slow torture. I could strangle her with these two hands. Are these vile thoughts?"

"I have been having some vile thoughts of my own," said Jennie.

"You know why I love you, Mama?" Pris exclaimed. "Because I can blaze away with the most awful, shocking, unladylike things and you don't turn a hair. You know exactly how I feel."

"When your aunts and I were girls, we honed our talents on each other. Out of your grandfather's hearing, of course. I don't mean we brawled all the time, but none of us was a bit reticent about grievances. That way things were quickly over with. I think Papa knew more about it than we gave him credit for."

Pris said wistfully, "I'd like to fly away right now to Pippin Grange, and back in time, too, so I could know Grandfather Hawthorne. Mama, will you go to the funeral with me? I don't *want* to go, but I am still Caro's friend. So, please?"

"Yes," Jennie said. She didn't want to go either, but Pris was not asking for enthusiasm.

"I think I'll ride Diana now," Pris said, standing up. "Since I cannot fly away to Pippin Grange. Do you suppose Diana knows about the Great Horse?" A quick smile, and she was gone.

Eighteen

B LACK CLOTHING HAD no place in Jennie's and Priscilla's wardrobes, another sign of Glenroy intransigence, but Jennie had a dark blue lawn, and Priscilla could wear a plain lavender dress she hadn't yet trimmed. Mrs. Phipps at the post office shop kept a supply of black ribbons and gloves.

Priscilla was bound to go; both parents opposed it, but not openly. In bed Wednesday night Alick said, "It will do her no good. She is already so miserable, and trying to hide it."

"It is a matter of pride with her," Jennie answered. "Or honor, if you like. I am proud of her, but I shan't be disappointed if she loses heart by tomorrow noon. I hope she does—I hate black gloves as much as anything."

"If I go before you," Alick kissed her hand, palm and back, "promise me, no black gloves. No funeral at all—"

She put her free hand over his mouth. "Let us promise each other the same thing here and now, and let that be the end of it."

Any students of the parsonage classes who intended going to the funeral were dismissed at noon. The minister told them he would not be officiating. "I'm sure he would have said something beautiful and exactly right for the children," Priscilla said. She had come home alone and had no appetite for a meal. Alick found a practical reason to object to her going to the funeral.

"You will not be doing the poor *chailin* a kindness, and with them all crushed together in these rooms in the heat, who knows what will be at them by tomorrow? I have three men out now. You will be putting yourself in the way of the fever and the flux and the summer colds running wild, and the lass never knowing you are there."

"We shall try to sit near a window," Jennie soothed him, "and surely they will keep the doors open."

"Then eat something, Priscilla," he ordered her, "or you will be fainting."

"I have never fainted in my life!" she objected. "Caro does—*did*—sometimes." She appeared to swallow the word. "It is tight lacing that does it, and Mama doesn't allow that."

That morning the twins had rolled out the chaise and wiped it free of the inevitable barn dust. William and Bell Ann were assigned the wheels, though they complained reasonably that their work would be all undone by the time the chaise reached the Goward house.

Priscilla had nothing to say on the ride, and Jennie didn't try to make conversation. She half expected—and fervently hoped—that Priscilla's resolve would break down at the Gowards' gate. But it did not, and Jennie drove on, resigned.

Just where the lane curved sharply into the maple shade before the house, there was a long view down over the fields to the river; beyond a fenced meadow where mares grazed and their foals scampered, the family cemetery stood on a little hill overlooking the water. Seen from up on the lane, the dark rectangle of the open grave was like the entrance to the allegorical Underworld. Jennie hoped Pris hadn't seen it.

The dooryard was crowded with rigs, and as Jennie halted Diana, looking for a space, a fattish man detached himself from the nearest group of men and trotted toward her, taking off his hat. It was Vincent Taggart, he of the omens and portents. "I'll take her, Mrs. Glenroy." His bass voice was at odds with the face of an aging cherub. His smile when he handed them down was a nice blend of approbation and piety.

"Sad, sad," he rumbled. "The Wolcott boy, and now this one. There'll be a third before all the hay's in."

"Knock on wood, Mr. Taggart," Jennie said.

"That won't break the spell," he answered sorrowfully.

She knew all the South Whittier men, most of the Center people, and a few from North Whittier. Eli Goward's brother, a prosperous saddler, conveyed his disapproval of her and Priscilla by the way he lifted his hat to them, and she wondered just what had been said to him about the Godless Glenroys.

Priscilla didn't look left or right. They were at the steps when Jennie realized they hadn't put on the black gloves. Priscilla still carried both pairs, and a little nosegay gathered from the flowers at home. The house was so crowded it hummed like a beehive; the low buzz poured through open doors and windows on waves of sweetness from the double-flowered white narcissus that was too strongly scented for indoors. If they have banked the coffin with it, Jenny thought, the nearest mourners will be falling like autumn leaves.

She put her hand under Pris's elbow, and the girl's arm felt as hard as iron. She was so pale, and her gaze so fixed, that Jennie involuntarily stopped, but before she could hold Pris back the girl was going on like a sleepwalker, she had so steeled herself for seeing Caroline in her coffin.

They crossed the broad new piazza the Gowards had added last summer; it had been a nine days' wonder at the time. Fred Coombes leaned against a post, looking as if he would rather be shot than stay here. He gave Jennie a vacant nod.

Then all at once Bethiah Goward appeared in the doorway and stared at them with her mouth open. She was in a black frock without a touch of white, either hastily cut down or quickly run up by an aunt. It turned the fair family complexion to tallow and washed the pale blue from her eyes. Her blond hair was plastered to her round head without a curl.

"*Ma!*" she shouted. "*They're* here!" She rushed away from the door, and Jennie and Pris stepped into the hall. Nora Basto looked out from the parlor and whispered, "Two chairs in here, Jennie."

Pris turned toward her, still the somnambulist. Mrs. Goward, pallid as her daughter, rustled through the hall from the kitchen, carrying a rough bundle held away from her black crepe as if it were filthy, and Bethiah hovered excitedly behind her.

"If you came for this," Mrs. Goward said, "take it, and go. You are not welcome here." She threw Jennie's cloak at her. "And *you*, Missy!" she shrilled at Pris. "Not one step more toward that room!"

Pris held out her flowers. "Mrs. Goward—"

"Not a word from *you*, Missy! Have you no decency, no *respect?*"

The woman is half-mad with grief, Jennie reminded herself, reaching protectively for Pris.

"You knew what my poor innocent was up to, you led her into the ways of evil—"

"I did not!" Pris cried, brutally stung awake. There was a stir through the crowded rooms like the wind rising in the trees. Priscilla rallied. "All I said was that she should talk to you!"

"Oh, she did, right enough!" The voice was strident with anguished wrath. "And I suppose that is how you talk to *your* mother! She would never have thought of it *herself*. But everyone knows how the Glenroys raise their children, they aren't called the Godless Glenroys for nothing!" Her hands flailed the air as if summoning curses. "Or you can call it *raising*! Oh yes, we know all about the *Glenroys*."

For the space of a breath Jennie was transfixed. How could anyone here—in all America—know about *Nigel*? Then she was back in the suffocating scent of narcissus and crowded overheated bodies, trying to move an immovable Pris, and Eli Goward was saying weakly, "Now, Mother. Now, Mother," and looking fit to collapse.

"I cared for Caro," Pris stammered. "I was her friend."

"Of course you were, my dear," a man said. "And you miss her, but we know that she is safe with Jesus now, don't we? Beyond all sorrow and pain."

It was the soothing yet authoritative voice of the Methodist minister from Maddox. "Please, Mrs. Goward, calm yourself. Caroline would not like you to attack her friend. And remember the little ones."

The little ones were pinned on the stairs by Bethiah at the foot; left to her care, they would have good reason to never stop missing Caroline.

"Thank you, Mr. Coates," Jennie said. "We are leaving."

"You haven't heard the last of this!" Mrs. Goward shrieked after them. "You'll pay for what you have done to this family!"

Pris balked and tried to turn back. "I have something to say."

"No, you have not," her mother said. Mrs. Goward collapsed in loud sobbing on the minister's chest. Her husband looked very ill. With her left arm shielded by the cloak, Jennie deliberately squeezed Pris's forearm until the girl gasped. "Mama!"

"*Be quiet.*"

She forced Pris around and out the door, meeting Fred Coombes, who said weakly, "Uh—Pris—," and stood aside.

"Down the steps, Priscilla," Jennie said. "Don't look back." Or you'll turn either to salt or stone, she wanted irrepressibly to add. Nick Basto was waiting for them at the foot, a big and beaming guardian angel.

"I'll see you off, Jennie." He stepped between them, put a big hand firmly around the elbow of each, and walked with them toward the chaise. The other men obeyed a silent signal from the door and began moving reluctantly into the house.

"You'll be late, Nick," Jennie said.

"The guest of honor ain't hurrying away," he said. "I may stay outside anyway. Strange, but I always get to sneezing something fierce when I'm shut up with a crowd in a hot room. Unless there's dancing going on. Now *that* clears the passages something stupendous. Some folks act mighty strange at times like this," he went on. "You're well out of it."

"Alick would agree. He didn't want us to come."

"Wise man, Alick."

Priscilla tossed bouquet and gloves into the chaise, angrily untied black ribbons, ripped her bonnet off, and laid her forehead against the mare's nose.

Nick watched her with a bemused kindness. He used to bounce her on one knee and Thankful on the other, roaring "Ride a horse to Boston, Ride a horse to Lynn," holding them in place by the backs of their dresses.

"What were you thinking, to come to this funeral?" he asked. "We couldn't have dragged Thankful along for love nor money."

"It was for Caroline," Pris's voice was muffled.

"Well, if she's not beyond knowing, she'll take the intent for the deed. I can't have my little Sunshine wearing such a long phiz."

She gave him a watery smile. "That's better," he said. "Now up you go."

Jennie handed the cloak to Pris, who pushed it down behind the seat. "You drive, Pris," she said. "It will do you good." Nick gave her a lift up and unhitched Diana.

"Thank you, Nick," Jennie said to him. "I was as glad to see you today as I was when you came through the woods all those years ago when the barn was burning."

"Lord above, we were some young then, weren't we?"

"Ah, but we don't grow older, Nick. We mature, like fine wine."

"Now that's handsome of you, Jennie. I'll be studying on it all through the next hour." When they left the dooryard, Jennie looked back and saw him walking slowly toward the house, the only person left outside.

She untied her bonnet and rubbed the place where the bow had chafed her skin. Because it's *black*, she thought unreasonably. She leaned back, trying to relax her tight muscles and give herself up to the beauty of the day. It is over, forget it.

"As soon as they've put her in the ground and shoveled in the dirt," Pris said in a harsh, unfamiliar voice, "they will all go back to the house and have a feast. Couldn't you *smell* the beef through all the flowers and the sweat? It was *sickening!* And while they are stuffing themselves, nobody will give Caro a thought."

"Her father and mother will be thinking of her, Pris, and they will go on thinking of her."

"They are to blame," Pris answered coldly. "Because of them she is put away like a wax doll in a box." They drove in silence until they were almost home, when Pris made a small, soft plea. "Must we tell Papa what happened?"

"Yes, we must, the instant we get there, before the others come home from school," Jennie said.

"Then there is something else I suppose I must tell you," Pris sounded braced for the last ditch. "If I can be glad of anything, I am glad of *this*. Yesterday I finished my French examination before the others, and I asked Mrs. Lockhart if I might go out, and she gave me permission. It must have been meant, Mama!" A bit of her own bright self sparkled like mica in a rock. "Otherwise why did it happen like that? I was going to the brook, and I met Bethiah and the four younger ones coming up the hill, taking a horse to the smithy. Bethiah was riding it—wouldn't you know it?—and was talking in a low, steady, monotonous voice. The young ones were all sniffling—no, Nellie was crying *hard*—and Henry was stamping along so heavily it must have hurt his feet. I stepped out in front of them, and they had to stop. The children looked shocking: wrung-out, red-eyed, and dirty-faced. Poor Caro, if she could have seen them! Such pitiful little objects. I knew I couldn't let them go by like that. You wouldn't have, either, Mama," she said.

"Just tell me what you did, and if it's actionable," said Jennie. Priscilla surprised them both with a feeble chuckle.

"I don't know how they could make an action out of what I said. I called each of the young ones by name and said, 'Have you told your mama and papa yet what Bethiah has been telling you about Caro?' She had the brazenness to grin at me, sitting up there on her high horse, but Henry spoke up bravely and said, '*She* says Ma and Pa feel so awful about Caro going to *that place*, if we ask them it will be like the Devil driving pitchforks into them.' There was a loud wail from Nellie, then Grace joined her, and Samuel was rubbing his knuckles into his eyes so hard it made me wince. I said, 'Well, boys and girls, if Caro's going anywhere, it is straight to heaven, because there was never a better girl, and you know that she loved you very much. She even loved Bethiah, if you can believe that.' The way they stared at me. . . . I didn't look up at Bethiah, and she didn't move. 'As you are afraid to ask Ma and Pa,' I said, 'and if you can't believe William and Bell Ann and me, then I will find someone else to convince you.' Poor Henry gave up being brave and blubbered with relief. There they all stood howling, except the monster, and I was thinking, Whom can I tell? Mr. Lockhart isn't welcome there, but perhaps he could pass it along to Mr. Coates. So I did."

"You did *what?*" Jennie stopped Diana.

"I told Mr. Lockhart. I believe he drove to Maddox after classes yesterday. Mr. Coates must have spoken to the children at once, when he arrived today. They looked better to me. I think he was giving me a message, later." She sighed. "Mama, I couldn't pass them by, I just couldn't. That is why I know it was meant for me to go out when I did. Otherwise, why would I have found them like that?"

"You handled it very well, very tactfully. I'm proud of you."

"And now I would like never to talk about it again," Pris said wearily, "but I know we must tell Papa."

"Yes, it is better to talk it out instead of burying it."

Priscilla said, "Shall we have a good cry right here in the road? Or shall we wait and half-drown poor Papa with our tears?"

"Do you have two handkerchiefs? I refuse to wipe my nose on these odious black gloves."

"I always have two." She passed Jennie one. "I am so handy; I must take it from my father. Oh, let's hurry! I can hardly wait to be home, and I'll dissolve the instant I see him. I shall make the most of it before I'm too old for it."

Priscilla did make the most of it. Alick held her with one arm and dried her face with his handkerchief, but it was some time before she could stop the flow, all the while hiccuping apologies and wailing, "I don't know why I am *doing* this!"

Jennie suspected that it was not all grief and rage for Caro's sake, but a little for herself, because she had come to the end of her childhood and the sorrows that could be healed by her father's arms and a song. Still, this outburst helped; she had needed to give in to it, and she was very calm when the other children came home. They were all respectful, and not even Bell Ann commented on her pink eyelids. Pris went to bed when Bell Ann did and took over the reading. When Jennie went up later, Pris was deeply asleep in her own room, with the cat sprawled across her stomach. Garnet purred at Jennie's presence without opening her eyes.

"Hold me," Jennie commanded Alick when they were in bed. "Until my ribs hurt. I hope nothing ever again makes me feel the way I did this afternoon when my child was attacked. I felt as savage as a bear seeing her cub in danger. But at the same time I could sympathize with that poor woman, half out of her mind and having to blame another child for *her* child's death."

He settled her against him, smoothing her hair back from her face with long, slow strokes, but though she made herself lie still she could not let go. At her age no one had the right to be stupidly lulled by illusions of security. Into the festival that launched a handsome ship comes the black blow, another ship lost with all her crew. Because of that, a child dies. When was life ever safe? She shivered with the peril of it. Tonight all her children were under one roof, and she and Alick lay in one another's arms, but it might be for only tonight. How simple it had all been out on those Highland hillsides, when she and Alick had only their own lives for which to fear.

Nineteen

E ARLY ON A DRY, bright, windy morning, Jennie put on a dress of blue and green English gingham and her summer straw bonnet newly trimmed with cornflowers and tied with green ribbons, and prepared to drive Diana to Maddox. There had been a long fog mull, during which the wash didn't dry and the black flies enjoyed a renascence, and a new generation of mosquitoes took wing. Fortunately the hay had been made before the fog came in. This year the twins mowed for the first time with their father and David, but were incensed to find they were still expected to go out every day with their mother, sisters, and William to rake and turn the new-mown grass as soon as the dew had dried on it.

School had closed, with proper last-day observances in both the district school and the parsonage classes. Now and then several little girls came to play for an afternoon with Bell Ann, and she was often convoyed to their homes, usually by William. But Lily Shaw and her playhouse and the glory of her wardrobe remained as if on a distant star.

The wild strawberries had come and gone, and in the old barn cellar the asparagus had long since turned to feathery fern and the rhubarb to tall columns of creamy blossom. The raspberries and blueberries went on ripening in the warm fog. The garden flourished with a tropical verdure, but some of the beans rusted. Bad tempers also flourished, along with mold, mildew, and biting insects. Sleep was too heavy to be satisfactory, and the sheets always felt damp at first touch. But with the return of dry weather everyone was exhilarated, and the fog mull was forgotten like the pains of childbirth.

The list of errands for Maddox had grown. Even though the Whittier store had a great variety of goods with two family vessels in trade, there were some things to be had only in Maddox.

The men were coming in to work, and Alick was already down at the Yard. Sandy had gone to the Kilburns', where the man of the house was on crutches with a broken foot. Carolus had done all the mucking-out, made their beds, fetched in water, and had gone off to work on his botanical project. Warned by Alick to settle their differences quietly or be put to work without pay at something neither would like, the twins had made a private treaty, and their parents expected to hear no more arguments unless one twin reneged.

Pris was churning, with Bell Ann teasing for a turn at it; having never yet churned, she thought it must be the most exciting and desirable experience ever, infinitely preferable to dusting, wiping dishes, snapping beans, and tidying her room. William left with Jennie in the chaise, on his way to fly his kite at Three Corner Farm.

William was always silent when he was happy. He sat with his dinner bucket in his lap, his bare feet braced against the dashboard, and from the corner of her eye Jennie could see the wriggling of his toes like ten blissful little brown creatures. There was something singularly huggable about William, though of course now that he was twelve one did not give in to the impulse too often without a legitimate excuse.

The kite whispered behind them like something alive. David had made kites for all the children, even Pris, last Christmas; great, glowing winged creatures like prehistoric beauties with brilliant eyes, painted in splashes and coils and flares of vibrating color. Until the early spring flying, they had hung from a beam in the attic chamber; whenever anyone walked beneath them, they moved slightly and made a secret susurrus among themselves, like creatures stirring in their sleep. Everyone, even Alick and Jennie and David, had participated in their April launching. Now in late July there was another perfect spell of flying weather, and the Fosses of Three Corner Farm, who had admired William's kite in the spring, had asked him to come and fly it with theirs.

It had eyes of black and gold, and William called it Iolaire, one of the handful of Gaelic words the children commonly used. It meant "eagle." This morning Diana had reacted so dramatically at the sight of Iolaire's gorgeous wings that the kite had to be handed up to William while Pris held the mare's head and distracted her with pet talk. Even then she was suspicious, and her ears were eloquent.

As they approached the first gate of Three Corner Farm, Jennie said, "Have a happy day, sweetheart, and say good morning to Mrs. Foss."

"Yes, Mama." He quickly kissed her while nobody could see. She pulled up at the gate, where Diana was distracted by the cows on the other side so she didn't see the kite being handed down to him. He didn't bother to open the gate but went over the bars, looking as if he had grown glorious plumage. The kite struggled to go free in the wind; running past amazed cows, letting out the line, William seemed about to launch himself into the air.

"Well, at least he'll have something to eat while he flies," Jennie said to Diana's expressive ears. She pictured William winging out over the river in a convoy of gulls while munching bread and cheese and scattering fragments of eggshell.

"Bonny lassie, will ye go?" she invited Diana, who would indeed go, at an invigorating and stylish pace.

The fifty-first birthday of the Declaration of Independence, and the twins' fifteenth birthday on July fifth, had all been appropriately celebrated. The Declaration had received public homage, speeches, bonfires, exhibition drills by the local militia companies, and fireworks. The twins received congratulations and gifts from family and friends. Their parents gave Sandy *The New American Practical Navigator*, by Nathaniel Bowditch, and gave Carolus *A Selection of the Correspondence of Linnaeus and Other Botanists*. New penknives came from William and the pets. Priscilla made them waistcoats of gaudily striped Marseilles cloth with silver buttons. Bell Ann sewed handkerchief cases of the leftover material; each one held a linen handkerchief hemmed and initialed by her. David gave Sandy a set of compasses and Carolus new watercolors and a packet of special paper for recording his specimens.

The "sweet season of sonne," was not only the season of blossom, berries, and birthdays. The black flies and mosquitoes were kept somewhat under control by the swallows and the bats streaming out from under the eaves at dusk, but it was also the time of the catarrh, which kept some poor souls red-eyed and sneezing until the first frost; at its worst, they wheezed and gasped for breath while gulping down mullein tea by the mugful. None of the Glenroys suffered this way, but there were the fire-filled bites, the mysterious summer bumps and rashes, cooled down by poultices of mashed plantain leaves, touch-me-not, and burdock; packets of wet tea leaves in gauze soothed the thickened lids of eyes too swollen to open.

There were specifics for the seasonal stomach and bowel complaints variously called the distemper, summer complaint, epizootic, and other more graphic names the children were not allowed to use, at least in their parents' hearing. Carlotta said the decoctions worked as well as anything she could give, cautioned against the overuse of a certain few, and emphasized the rules of hygiene.

So far it had not been a bad summer for cholera infantum. Jennie, who could never count her own blessings without feeling guilty about someone else's loss, was happy to be passing houses which had not yet been visited by the baby-killer.

She felt wonderfully young and free today. None of her children was into mischief, the *Enoch Lincoln* was proceeding flawlessly toward her autumn launching, David was painting a family in Augusta, and a letter from Stephen, written in Naples, had been delivered the week before by one of the Dalrymple twins, both captains. In the last news from England, everyone was well there. Ianthe, on the continent, had sent Priscilla a new packet of fashion drawings and some French ribbons and lace, and Bell Ann a Paris frock of eyelet-embroidered pink voile, with a silk slip and ruffled pantalets. Bell Ann was now agitating to go to church, so she could stun Lily Shaw. "She will just *die*!" she said happily.

"Bell Ann Glenroy, what a terrible reason for wanting to go to church!" Pris scolded her. "To show off your clothes and make other people envious!"

"*You* dress up," said Bell Ann. "And you prink for an hour first."

"That child is growing saucier by the day," said Pris over the twins' unkind laughter.

At the top of the hill above Maddox bridge, Jennie stopped by a pasture wall beyond which three donkeys grazed, until they saw the mare and came for a closer look. This occupied Diana while Jennie contemplated Maddox proper climbing from the river to Main Street. With this wind, the view was unhazed by the smoke from the lime kilns. The opposite waterfront was crowded with wharves, sheds, and vessels, and behind it Water Street traffic was heavy and varied. A concert of shipyard hammers resounded in the clear dry air from both sides of the river, their pitch and volume depending on what work they were doing. The General had been more eager to see the town prosper after the depression of the war years than to remain its principal magnate, so he had sold much of the shore, while retaining his own enterprises there.

The Pool was roughened to a peacock-blue chop by the northwest wind and crowded with the wood-carrying schooners that came to feed the kilns. Bows to wind, they waited for the tide to rise so they could unload and depart downriver. Those with British ensigns had come from New Brunswick. There were other foreign ensigns on some of the ships at the wharves, emblematic of trans-Atlantic commerce.

Between Water Street and the crown of the land there had once been only a scattering of houses among green fields. Now Quarry Lane was a road running from Main Street down to the bridge, and another new road descended between Quarry Lane and Ship Street to Water Street.

There was a thunderous echo from the bridge as a horse galloped across it. The rider was Septimus Frye. He had not been back since he had left with his humiliation that Sunday afternoon, and Jennie didn't think he was likely ever to be back. If he could be welcomed wherever else he went, delight whomever else he met, that would doubtless mean far more to his self-esteem than the pursuit of one young girl under severely limited conditions.

Walking his horse up the hill, he saw Jennie and lifted his hat high to her, like a popular hero greeting a cheering multitude; he was exquisitely dandified even in a plain brown suit appropriate for a morning business errand. His linen dazzled, his boots shone.

"Good morning, Septimus," she said.

"*Good* morning, Mrs. Glenroy!" The dimples were delightful. "What a superb day, eh? Makes me see what the poet was getting at. 'Full many a glorious morning have I seen/ Flatter the mountain-tops with sovereign eye,/ Kissing with golden face the meadow's green,/ Gilding pale streams with heavenly alchemy.' "

He sat back in his saddle looking tremendously pleased with himself. "Why, Septimus, how lovely," she said. "Shakespeare, isn't it?"

"One of the sonnets, actually. I've forgotten which, but it's a favorite of mine. Always comes to mind on a day like this."

Either he had unsuspected depths of erudition, or he had memorized the verse in order to impress. She was sure her reaction hadn't disappointed him.

"Is Mr. Glenroy at the yard this morning?" he asked.

"He was when I left, so he still must be there, unless he has been stolen away by the Little People and won't reappear for seven years."

"Mr. O'Dowda was always threatening us with them. The truth is, Mrs. Glenroy, it wasn't fear of God, the General, or our fathers that kept us on the straight and narrow, it was the fear of the Little People. We thought he'd brought his private army over from Ireland."

They laughed, he lifted his hat once more, and gave Bolivar his head. They went off with a thrilling drumroll of hooves which made Diana try to dance in the shafts.

"Goodbye," Jennie said to the donkeys. She drove down the hill, restraining Diana, and crossed the bridge thinking of Liam O'Dowda, whose devotion to his pupils was so complete that he died while saving a child who had tumbled into the flooded and fast-moving creek below the school. He had held her with one arm and hooked the other around a low-leaning willow sapling, until the older boys could push off a skiff and reach them; as they took the child from him, his heart stopped.

The school was much larger now, and had two teachers, the general's daughter Frances (Frank) and Nabbie Frost. The school chorus had been kept alive as a memorial to Liam, but it seemed as if no one else could draw such music from young throats.

They met considerable wheeled and foot traffic on Water Street. Between Diana's curiosity and her sociability, she was prone to sudden halts unless her driver was in complete control. Turning up Ship Street, they met a load of new barrels going from the cooperage to the wharves; Diana was astounded enough to stop short.

"This isn't the first time you've seen a load of barrels," Jennie said, and took her smartly past the wrought-iron gates of the formal entrance to Strathbuie House and on to Back Lane. It was not until they had turned into this green and breezy passage that she thought of Septimus again, and his question about Alick. It might concern insurance only, but she had a strong intimation that Priscilla was going to hear that quotation this morning.

He was likely to catch her barefoot, swigging down a beaker of buttermilk like a harvest hand. Pris would not be disconcerted; there was little of the spun-glass damozel about her. And however Septimus reacted, with either delight or shock, Bell Ann would be the audience, with the sticking quality of a burr in a spaniel's ear.

Then, if Alick should come up to the house for something and discover the young squire-and-dairymaid scene being played out in the dooryard, Highland hospitality would have a hard time of it. Jennie smiled.

Diana stopped at Strathbuie's rear gate, and Corny Sayers came limping to open it, scented agreeably with hay and horse. He had lost some fingers and become permanently lamed in a quarry accident, and

the General hired him when Benoni Frost retired. He had not many
teeth left, and he grinned at Jennie like a jack-o'-lantern when he
handed her down as if she were eggshell china. He had often publicly
stated that the Glenroys had saved him from the gallows, because they
interfered when he and Zeb Pulsifer ambushed two Highlanders within
the General's gates.

He talked about it now while he was unhitching Diana. "Who knows
but what I'd a been with him when he torched that barn with you and the
Mister and the little one in it?" He always mentioned it whenever he met
her or Alick. "Not that I'd of let him do it, mind you! *Never*! But he could
of laid me low, you remember the size of the fist on him, and I'd of been
hanged along with him just for being there."

"Corny, we all know that your father threatened you with battle,
murder, and sudden death if you so much as passed the time of day with
Zeb. So he's *the* responsible one."

"But you and your man stopped us that night, and it was on account
of you we was hauled up before the General. So it's on account of you that
I've got a good woman and some good young ones of my own, and Pa's
proud of me, which I never thought could happen. . . . Come along, my
girl." He led an eager Diana to the paddock gate. Young Joshua whinnied
at sight of her, and she cantered toward her friend. Prince and Nixie, two
old ponies now, watched through their thick forelocks.

Jennie took her basket and walked up Ship Street. The hillside above
Back Lane was still wooded, but the opposite side of Ship Street was
closely built up now. The Frost farmhouse and buildings were still
halfway up the road to the Ark and the flagpole, but the roomy pasture
from which the cow Columbine had escaped daily to promenade Main
Street was gone; it was all fenced yards.

At the head of Ship Street, the flag snapped in the wind with the
sound of pistol shots. The Ark had been turned into a boarding house for
respectable bachelors. Across the street, the St. David Inn had added a
ballroom where dances and concerts took place, and "Good Noon
Dinner Daily" was advertised outside.

The trees along Main Street were tall enough to shade the hitching
rails and wooden sidewalks, but the traffic was heavier than ever, and in
dry weather it raised a perpetual duststorm. The selectmen had sworn in
a special constable just to keep order and make it possible for those not
fleet of foot to safely cross the flagpole intersection. There were many
more shops now, and hardly any need to send to Boston for anything,

unless it was something exotic like a harp or a piano. Columbine would have had windows to gaze at from dawn to curfew; Jennie missed her serene, drooling, self-sufficiency and the debonair indifference with which she dropped her streaming manure on the sidewalk and went on with a flirt of her tail. Life had been so uncluttered then; nowadays who would tolerate an errant cow on this very commercial thoroughfare?

Most of the older shops were still there. Ten years ago Mr. Barron had daringly put up a new sign shaped like a boot. Whynot, the barber and hairdresser, looked like an elderly Regency beau in a novel by Bulwer Lytton; Mrs. Loomis, the milliner, appeared exactly the same, even in dress, as she had seventeen years ago. The stationer's premises were greatly enlarged, a whole section given over to the latest novels and books of poetry. You must not look in *that* window, Jennie admonished herself, until you have done everything else. *You must not.*

She left three pairs of shoes with Mr. Barron to be mended. He was a little wispier, a little grayer, but his eyes swimming brightly behind the magnifying glasses were incorrigibly young. At Jennie's first meeting with him, he and she had joked about the brownies who mended shoes; she thought he looked like a species of brownie himself. He had an apprentice elf now, a hunchbacked boy who looked up from his bench with a shy smile and nod, and went back to his tap-tap-tap.

After a gracious exchange of courtesies, it was agreed she would return for Alick's new boots when the rest of her errands were done.

She stopped in next door to buy embroidery floss and lace frilling from the successor to the Misses Applegate. Could *she* consider another apprentice? The thought was done away with at birth; the niece was as different from her aunts as chalk from cheese. Besides, Pris was already too accomplished to begin as an ignorant apprentice, except in tailoring. Would the Porters take her, for a fee? Would they be shocked at the suggestion, or simply not want to bother with her? They had a silent young man there now who did excellent work and played clarinet duets with Mr. Porter in the evenings. Oh, well, no harm in asking! They couldn't bite; they could only politely refuse.

She crossed the street, visited Mrs. Loomis, and bought a plain chip bonnet for Bell Ann, some sweet peas to trim it, and peach-colored ribbons. Mr. Whynot called her Dear Lady, as he always did, and inquired after the family. At the ironmonger's and apothecary's windows she looked at everything with a solemn attention that reminded her of Columbine without the drool.

Outside the Masonic building, erected where a house had burned down, the notice board told her that the Temperance and Debating Societies would be meeting there next week, and tomorrow night a renowned professor of Greek history would lecture on the gallant struggle of the Greeks against the vicious Turks. Donations would be solicited.

Everyone admired the Greeks, so the donations would be substantial. Jennie walked on past the Dalrymple and Wells houses; the older people were gone, but sons raised families behind the fanlighted doors, and children played on the shady lawns behind the palings. The square spacious houses had been lavishly enlarged at the rear, so the classic façades faced the street unmarred. Spinster sisters, lone cousins, invalid aunts, elderly uncles, and bachelor brothers like Stephen Wells all had accommodation under the spreading roofs.

Seen in broken glimpses through the traffic, Maddox Academy, across the way, was insulated by a long lawn from the dust and din; the Greek Revival building stood gleamingly aloof in fresh white paint against a backdrop of oaks. When there was a short gap in the traffic and a thinning of the dust cloud, Jennie saw for an instant the granite milestone where she had once been set upon by Zeb Pulsifer's mother and two fiercely squeaking henchwomen. The memory would never die, but it was simply something that had happened once; your life was made up of many things that had happened once, and you could not carry all the dreadful or merely unpleasant ones with you forever.

Beyond the Wells house, Church Lane led off to the left, to the Baptist Church, and on to the countryside beyond, and Main Street began its steep descent to the creek. At the foot, Sawmill Way also turned off to her left, where she had often passed the sawmill on her way to the Clements Farm. The Porters lived and worked in a tall, narrow house on the opposite corner, only a few buildings away from the bridge over the creek. She waited while a load of new-sawn boards came out past her; the big horses headed across Main Street toward Fish Street and efficiently held up the downhill traffic, while the flow from the east was halted on the far side of the creek by an ox-drawn load of logs that took up most of the bridge. There was much good-natured noise but not much movement.

In this hiatus, Posy Pulsifer suddenly appeared, walking swiftly from beyond the Porter house toward Sawmill Way. Jennie had seen her from time to time ever since she was a tall gawky child looking very much like her father, but they had never come face to face.

It was about to happen now. Jennie had an impulse to dart across Main Street past the load of boards, and escape ahead of it into Fish Street.

But she did not, and the girl came on, her wide tanned face unsuspecting. She had a thick, curly brown mane like Zeb's, but longer, and the same high color in her face. She carried easily a washing basket balanced against one hip; she had a reputation for doing fine laundry.

You have no reason not to be meeting this girl's eyes. It was Alick's voice, and it kept Jennie moving. *She was as much her father's victim as we were, and we are always wishing her well.*

She walked rapidly across Sawmill Way and met Posy on the Porters' corner. "Good morning, Posy," she said, hoping she hadn't chirped in what she and her sisters used to call the vicar's-wife-voice.

When Posy stopped, it was as if some great force of nature, a waterfall or an avalanche, had halted in transit. Her mouth worked, her cheeks sucked in. She spat in Jennie's face and then moved impassively on.

When the saliva hit her cheek, Jennie's first reaction was surprise. Automatically she took a handkerchief from her reticule and wiped off the trickling wetness, afterward crumpling the handkerchief into a ball and wishing she could fling it away from her, but it was one that Bell Ann had embroidered. Then came the incongruous guilt and shame, as if she had been caught in a nasty trick; the furtive look around to see who had seen. But of course two women on a corner weren't worth noticing, and the ox team had crossed the bridge now, everything was moving again with an increase of noise and dust.

She whirled around, and shouted, "*Posy!*" Long experience of making herself heard by oblivious children carried her voice over the rumble of wheels.

The head never turned, the long stride never lessened. The house of her stepfather stood a short distance in from the main street, and Jennie walked swiftly behind her. On their right, the sawmill was silent after its morning's work; the ox team was turning in ponderously behind Jennie. She wanted to catch Posy before she reached the dooryard where most of her mother's five children by Ki Bissett were playing something extremely noisy, assisted by at least three barking dogs, bleating goats, and their unseen mother's shrill cries telling them they were enough to make a minister swear, they'd give any ship a bad name, and their father would warm their jackets if they committed any more crimes, which she enumerated in detail. As far as Jennie could tell, neither threats nor promises made any difference whatever in the pandemonium.

This was the last place where she wanted to confront Posy. The piercing two-fingered whistle learned in her hoydenish youth stopped the girl as if a dart had struck her between her shoulders, but she did not look around. She began to walk again.

"You had better stop, Posy," Jennie said coldly. "If you don't, I shall bring a complaint against you."

Posy spun around, her face crimson, "It's only your word against mine!"

"But if the matter becomes public, how many people will want to know *why* you did it? There are new people in town who know nothing about the past, and others have put it out of their minds. Do you want to rouse it all up again? Do you want it whispered behind your back and your mother's when you walk on Main Street? What about those children?" She pointed toward the dooryard. "Do you want *them* to know?"

The girl stood her ground in marmoreal silence. Jennie had to look up slightly, but that was no disadvantage; she was invigorated by a sudden charge of energy, as if there were nothing she couldn't do, but her sense of power was tempered by pity. As a child the girl must have heard a cruel plenty from other children about her father. With her own baby safe, Jennie had known a bitter sorrow for the other baby, whose father had been hanged. That he hadn't wanted her, that he'd tried to run away when she was born, would have been only shallow wounds beside the enormous one of the hanging.

"Posy, you have no call to hate me," she said.

"If it wasn't for you, my father would be alive now. You lied about him, so you just as same as killed him with your bare hands."

"Posy, nobody lied," she said gently. "And we did not want your father to die. We asked the court for mercy, because we were alive to ask for it, no thanks to him. But still we were grateful to be alive, and we did not want to be the cause of *his* death."

She couldn't seize the girl and shake her out of her monolithic passivity, but something should do it. "My baby was with us that day, Posy. Did you know that? She was four months old. He wanted to burn my baby alive."

Posy blinked. There was the impression of a slow shudder, as if of a giant waking up. "I tried to keep feeding her, to calm her, and I was praying for us to die quickly so she wouldn't suffer. You know how a burn on your hand feels. I could not bear to think of that little body feeling the terrible pain as it burned to death."

Something—too vague to be called expression—was passing over Posy's face like flying clouds. Her eye lashes flickered as if the glare of that long-ago fire were hurting her eyes.

"How do you know *he* did it?" She flung it like a stone. "You took the word of that dummy! How do you know it warn't *him*? He was queer enough in the head, didn't know enough to speak like a Christian."

"David broke the door open with an ax and saved us. Zeb ran away. Why did he run if he hadn't done it? My husband caught him and wanted to kill him on the spot, but he stopped himself." She saw Alick with his knee in Zeb's back, holding his head by the thick curly hair and pounding his face into the water and gravel.

"We've always wished you and your mother well, both Mr. Glenroy and myself," she said. "We shall always wish the best for you."

They remained facing each other long enough to hear Malvina Bisset threaten someone with never reaching his twelfth birthday, then Posy turned, shifting the laundry basket to her other hip, and walked away.

Jennie watched her go, wondering if she would look back. She felt weak, nor from the confrontation but from the memory of the night they had lain awake, listening to the clock striking, knowing they had done all they could. "They will be better off now," Alick said heavily when the time of execution had passed. "She has family to be taking care of her, and she can marry again. If he was in prison, he would be a millstone around her neck."

But he had been cold in Jennie's arms, colder than she was. "It is not that he is on my conscience," he said. "*Dia*, the man would have murdered us without a prickle of conscience. Still, I am not rejoicing because he is dead. I have dreamed too often of the gallows myself."

They might as well have spoken Nigel's name, it was large enough between them.

But that had been long ago, and now all at once the color and gloss and cleanliness of the day burst upon her again. She had done it! She said what had needed to be said for all those years. Whether or not Posy believed her, she didn't care. She had said it. She felt remarkably cheerful, and she was as hungry and thirsty as the child Jennie coming home from a day on the hills.

She decided this was no day to approach the Porters about teaching tailoring to Pris. Reincarnated as a fourteen-year-old tomboy, she recklessly ducked, dodged, and scampered her way across to Fish Street and was on her way to Strathbuie House, shamelessly pulling off her bonnet.

Twenty

A T THE BACK DOOR of Strathbuie House, Darroch's brother Ozzie (Ozymandias) arose from the cool bricks to meet her. She scratched behind his ears and went into the house, swinging her bonnet. From along the passage she heard Eliza Bisbee in the kitchen, delivering a salty pronunciamento. Mrs. Frost and Benoni had sold their farm on Ship Street and were farming to the west of Maddox; their dairy was a blessing to the town dwellers who didn't keep a family cow and hens, and these were in the majority now. Eliza had succeeded Mrs. Frost as cook, an event which often astonished her, especially when, after the ritual panic, she turned out an elegant dinner for the frequent "from away" guests.

She'd been a plain, gaunt young woman when Jennie first knew her, in charge of the little Mackenzie girls. Now she was not only cook, but she had been left the family farm, her brothers all going to sea. She preferred to have a tenant on it and live in town at Strathbuie House. Time enough to putter around with a farm when she was old, she said.

"When it comes time for you to be courted, you will be!" she was saying with her customary emphasis, like punching down rising yeast dough. "Even *I* was courted once." She laughed, apparently at her audience's expression. "And it was my choice not to have him, I wasn't chancing my luck on a seafaring man." There was a murmur, and she answered vigorously, "Blessed be, child, you'll have a bust when it's ready, just be thankful you ain't likely to have too much of it."

Jennie knocked lightly on the door jamb, causing a lively silence in the kitchen. When she put her head around the door, she met Eliza's aggressively resentful stare for an intruder; at the sight of Jennie it turned into a broad smile.

With time, Eliza had achieved a sort of equine handsomeness, like a rangy Roman-nosed mare. "Come in, come in! We're just resting our face and hands." She and Sibba, the plain, dark little maid, had cups of tea and a plate of buttered muffins before them. "Jump up, Sibba, and get a cup for Mrs. Glenroy," she said. "She's in dire need of it, from the looks of her."

"I do feel as if I'd been wandering in the desert for years and years, like the Children of Israel. Good morning, Sibba."

"Morning, Mis Glenroy." She was always solemn, seventeen but looking an undersized fifteen in her pink print, starched white fichu, cap, and apron. The Mackenzies had taken her into Strathbuie House when the rest of her family died in one of those too-common winter fires.

"Hand me the cup, Sibba," Eliza said heartily. "If you've et your piece, take the molasses jug and run down to the shop and get it filled. No, don't run," she added. "We don't want you stubbing your toe and cracking the jug or your knee. Take your time, young one."

Sibba glanced anxiously toward a breakfast tray. "Never mind that," Eliza said. "If she rings before you come back, I'll take it up. Git along with you, now."

Sibba slipped out as silently as a breeze. "Never thought I'd ever be mothering," Eliza said, pouring Jennie's tea. "Take a muffin; they're still warm. There's strawberry preserves, too. They entertained last night. *Gambled* is more like it. You know how the Missus loves it. Whist, bezique, euchre, backgammon—anything she can wager on. If 'twas us common folks doing it, we'd be shiftless, not worth the powder to blow us up Ship Street." Her tone and the saucy tilt of her head indicated she did not consider herself common folks. "And that Robin," she went on fondly. "Half-past ten is his curfew, but only he and the Lord knows when he crept up the back stairs last night. Still, he's a good young one. His room never smells like a rumshop in the morning. He and his father were on deck at the stroke of six today, eating their porridge right at this table," she slapped it with her hand, "and the two of them bright as guinea gold. — How are all the Glenroys? Doing stavin', I hope?"

Jennie knocked on wood. "At this moment, as far as I know, they are."

"I don't suppose for one minute that Pris worries about catching a boy's eye."

"Not that I know of. She *does* think she's too tall. Of course I can't read her mind, but at the moment she seems mostly caught up with declaring independence for women."

"That Pris," Eliza said affectionately, "she always did know her own mind. As sure of herself as she could be without being impertinent. Knowing she could have her pick from more boys than she could shake a stick at, when she gets around to it. It's the poor souls who think themselves homely as a hedge fence that begin fussing young about being courted, thinking they'll have to settle for what they can get." She laughed, but not cynically. "I'm glad I'm out of *that* tangle. I'm not saying I didn't go through all that romantic foolishness, but I am thankful every day of my life that I warn't desperate enough to make a snatch at John Fernald, with him lost before he was thirty. Being an old maid can be quite pleasant at times, specially if you have a good situation and own property. Of course, you can't think like that when you're seventeen."

Jennie agreed.

Eliza went on in a conspiratorial voice, "There's them that think nothing would become this house like Priscilla being the mistress of it someday, and it's not just Robin."

"Ah well, they both have a long way to go," Jennie said tactfully. "In the meantime they should be enjoying their youth."

"If you could see the way the girls of this town flock around that shop with their foolish errands! It would be disgraceful if it wasn't comical. Robin pretends it's Guy they're after, and that poor young one is red as fire most of the time."

The bell jangled, and Eliza rolled her eyes. "Are you going up?"

"I will give her time to return to full consciousness without an audience, while I look at the new draperies in the drawing room."

"They're some handsome! Real English chintz!"

Jennie had first walked across the square, skylighted hall in a wool and linen gown over a tartan petticoat, wearing coarse stockings and deerskin brogues. She had been escorted up the airy curves of the staircase by a maid for whom the adjective *pert* was created. Hannah was now married to a captain who was building an imposing house on the new street between Ship and Quarry Lane; in fact, the street was named for him. Hannah was a stout matriarch now, and Tony Mackenzie, who'd been forever pulling her apron bow loose, was now his father's business manager in Boston. Young Robin could never be as mischievous and satirical as young Tony had been; Jennie wondered if Priscilla would see Robin as more than a brother if he were more like thin, dark, twinkling Tony.

She opened one set of the double doors into the drawing room, and they swung noiselessly shut behind her and latched with the faintest of clicks. Such was luxury, and the sheen of daily-dusted mahogany, and carpets that looked as if they'd been picked clean by hand. The English chintz pattern was an Oriental proliferation of flowers, vines, birds, and butterflies. The long room had changed many times since she had first seen it, but always the tints and contrasts were luscious; Lydia had a felicitous greed for color.

Jennie turned back the lid of the square rosewood piano and sat down to play it. It had always been kept tuned, even in the past when Lydia hated it and would not allow it to be played in her presence. Jennie played softly now, knowing the sound could not go through the doors, up the stairs, and into the bedroom. At the first touch she felt a thrill of pure bliss. She attempted nothing complicated, but began with the songs they had taught the children. The effect was like the silkiness of tepid rainwater when you buttoned yourself into the washhouse for a long bath in the oval cedar tub. No child could reach you, no four-footer could hook a paw around the door and follow it in. She laughed at her similes as she played "*Mo Nighean Dhu,*" Alick's song to a black-haired daughter.

Her hands had changed from the slender pair that showed young Charlotte Higham how to play scales in Brunswick Square and had accompanied Archie singing his beloved Jacobite ballads at Linnmore. Her hands had always been strong and capable, because of her unpampered youth, but in the past eighteen years they had become the hands of a woman who kept house, dug in the garden, split kindling when it was necessary, fetched water from the well, swung a scythe, made hay, washed all the family clothes and bedding, and was proud of her strength in wringing out sheets; she had hired Miriam only in the last few years, as a small luxury. She had done all the ironing until she could train Priscilla to help. She had scrubbed and painted floors and woodwork, caught and cleaned fish, and dug clams. Hat Shenstone's mixtures and mild soaps had helped to hold back the signs of wear, but the hands were larger now—she took a bigger glove—tanned and muscular, but not noticeably knuckly, for which she was grateful. And she could still play the piano, and she longed for one of her own.

When will I have it? she wondered as she played. When our ship comes in—literally? What will she be, a brig like *Paul Revere*, but larger? Or something along the lines of the *Enoch Lincoln*, or the General's grand new barkentine, *Whimsey*? She was nothing now to Jennie but a collection of sketches and figures, but surely Alick and Stephen saw their ship throbbing with life from her keel to her skys'ls.

Jennie now played an impromptu and fanciful arrangement of all the sea songs she knew. Brig or barkentine or schooner, it didn't matter; their ship was a tall ship, and she had been to China. The eyes of her figurehead—and what would that be?—had seen what most living eyes here could find only in books and dreams. She was sailing upriver now, dressed in new sails bent on for this occasion; they were filled with wind, and there was a boiling of diamonds under her bowsprit and flashing along her sides, and her wake spread out in a train of coruscating ruffles.

For the first time since *Artemis*, Jennie would be christening a vessel. What would she be called? Not Eugenia, Jennie had never been called that, and Alick had always called her Jeannie. 'Jeannie Glenroy' had a fine rhythm to it. Stephen might want to include his mother's name. Mrs. Wells, gone now, had once wistfully confided over teacups that she wished she could come back in another life as a man and go to sea like all her sons. It would be nice if she could know that at least her name was going to sea.

Jennie accomplished a triumphant arpeggio, and as she lifted her hands to commence another, Lydia Mackenzie said, "You look very pleased about something."

She stood in the doorway, majestic in a loose-flowing morning gown that rivaled the new chintz. "I've been listening for some little while. What was it? I have no ear for recognizing tunes, but it was charming."

"You flatter me. It was all improvisation, and it improved only after my fingers loosened."

Lydia settled herself on a loveseat covered with rose linen for the summer and drew a tapestry frame toward her. "The devil hates idle hands, I'm told, and besides, Christian's birthday is in two weeks. — When will you have a piano, Jennie?"

"When my ship comes in." The phrase was common enough not to suggest facts.

"It would be no great undertaking to bring a piano from Boston," Lydia said seriously. "Tony writes that a Mr. Chickering is turning out a fine instrument."

"We have children to educate before that luxury comes into the house. And we are clever at making our own music. Alick's very good at mouth-music. You would not believe it if you haven't heard him. It's a way of singing the dance tunes; the Highlanders do it when they have no pipes or fiddles at hand. Teaching the children and me a reel and singing the tune at the same time, he's another incarnation entirely."

"I can believe it," Lydia said with amusement. "So that is what you all get up to on winter nights."

"Just one of the things. Lydia, when I first knew you, you abhorred music. It made you actually ill, I understood. It gave you a sick head-ache."

Lydia smiled at her work. "That headache was one of my most efficacious escapes. If you can ever imagine me timorous, unsure of myself, with a trembling stomach and a desire to burst into tears ten times a day—no, you cannot. But when I married Colin I was so horridly aware of his first love, and so afraid." She looked across at Jennie with an unguardedness Jennie had never seen in her before.

"I wanted to be this wonderful man's only love. I should not have resented Desirée, *I* was in possession. *I* was in his bed, if I may say this without shocking you."

"You may," Jennie said dryly.

"But that bed was in the house in Roxbury where she had borne their children. It wasn't the actual bed, but there was I, an overgrown, overblown lump of a girl," she laughed at Jennie's expression, "in *her* house with *her* children, who not only looked French, but spoke it like their native tongue, and I had only my pathetic finishing-school French, so I was forever suspecting the mites of discussing me in their own language. And Tony and Christian were musical prodigies, to add the killing blow. So I became physically ill at the mere sound of the piano. It was not all acting—until I found out how well it worked. No more musicales, please; cards and conversation instead. I think it was to my credit," she said candidly, "that I didn't turn against the children or demand that the piano be removed. I couldn't have done that anyway; it was theirs. Nor did I stop their lessons or their practice, as long as I was not obliged to listen. But we could have all made life miserable for one another, except that we all adored Colin. At last he and I had two babies in the nursery when Desirée's two were long out of it, and then I gave him another son. These days Christian and I are two mothers with sons in college, and the boys are friends; we have that and the General in common. Tony and I have always sparred, but I think we love each other. There, confession time is over once and for all. You see that I trust you with my heart's deepest secrets," she said ironically. "Because I have always known you to be deep as a well."

"I thank you for the honor," Jennie said soberly.

"And now to business! A theatrical company, such as it is, is going to do 'Macbeth' at the Masonic building Saturday night. Why don't you send Pris and the twins up in the afternoon, and they can stay the night here. William too, if you think he'd enjoy it. We're making up a little theater party, ridiculous as that sounds in Maddox, with Frank and

Nabbie and their young men, and we will have supper here afterward."

"My crew will be in raptures. Who are the girls' current young men?"

"Septimus Frye is Frank's, Nabbie's is the new Greek master at the academy. Tomorrow night he is taking her to the lecture. They must have painfully intellectual conversation. William will be the youngest, do you think he will be bored?"

"William is never bored by anything that allows him to be up late, and 'Macbeth' is such fun, with the witches and Banquo's ghost. But are you sure you want to bother with him?"

"Certainly I do. When William smiles at me, I quite melt. He's a little boy now, but when he is a big boy, watch out. He has his father's quietly dangerous charm."

I can hardly wait to tell Alick that, Jennie thought.

"Wouldn't you and Alick like to come? We can put you up with no trouble."

"I would love it," Jennie said truthfully, "but there is Bell Ann, and even if we left her at the Bastos', we would never leave the place alone for a night. David is away."

Lydia asked her to stay for the noon meal. "Colin would be pleased, and it will be just the three of us. Robin and Guy Rigby sail in their noon hour if there's any wind at all, munching hard crackers and cheese and tippling cold buttermilk." She shuddered. "Grisly, isn't it? Still, it could be worse; it might be gin they were nipping at. Robin says they are escaping from girls—can you believe it? Do stay, Jennie, we've hardly begun."

But Jennie had had enough of town. She always enjoyed the ambience of Strathbuie House. But she was anxious to be home among her own lares and penates. It was only the piano that she briefly mourned; if she ever had one, it would be the Jove of her household gods.

She and Lydia kissed goodbye at the door to the kitchen passage. Lydia herself never walked it;. When she first moved into the house, she may have once or twice entered the territory beyond the door to see the kitchen and the laundry, but never again. She had a sublime faith that these regions were kept immaculate without her personal inspection. There was an olympian egotism about her confidence. Her men might eat breakfast in the kitchen, the children had lived half their young lives at the back of the house, and family friends came and went that way as they pleased. This did not irk Lydia; she simply bade them farewell at the door in the hall.

Twenty-One

E LIZA WAS ALONE, washing salad vegetables. She dried her hands and walked out to the door with Jennie, who was just remembering that she hadn't gone back to Mr. Barron's; Posy had knocked everything galley west, as Stephen would put it.

"Oh, fiddle," she said crossly. "I've forgotten my husband's new boots. Well, no help for it. I shall walk up while Corny's prying Diana away from her friends in the paddock."

"Let me go," Sibba said behind them. They hadn't heard her approach. "There's time," she appealed to Eliza, who nodded. With the air of a competent athlete preparing for a race, Sibba unpinned her cap and tossed it at the settle outside the door, her apron followed the cap. Withy-thin, she lifted her pink print skirts and ran. When she disappeared around the curve of the walled garden, Jennie said, "I'm keeping you from your work, Eliza. I'll sit here on the settle and wait for Sibba. I can visit with Ozzie." The Newfoundland rested his chin heavily on her knee.

"Like the young one said, there's time." She sat down beside Jennie. "Lord, it's some good to set outside this time of year and listen to the birds." She gave Jennie a colorful report of Maddox news until Sibba came in view among distant trees, running like a nymph pursued by a lecherous young god, or an angry one whose boots she had stolen; one dangled from each hand. She was pink-cheeked when she reached them, with a sparkle in her eyes. "Now who's been winking at her?" Eliza asked dryly.

Corny had coaxed Diana away from young Joshua, and they were on the way down to Water Street in the refreshing hush of noon. The road was almost empty, and all work had stopped around the waterfront for the early dinner hour. Out where the wind-whipped Pool became the river, Robin's sailboat was heeling over so far it seemed as if her sail must dip into the water, and the two boys were perched on the high side, leaning back with their feet braced.

To the beat of Diana's homeward-bound gait, Jennie swung back briefly to Posy. Whether any of Jennie's words had sunk in or if Posy had set her mind against hearing, Jennie would never know, but at least she had told the truth. She might discuss it with Alick, and then again, she might not. Uneasily she shed the business like a too-warm shawl.

Septimus was a pleasant change of subject, especially since he'd settled on Frank. A practical choice too; the General's third daughter was an energetic, intelligent, forthright girl who would love to push her man into politics, and her father could only be an asset.

Jennie had gone through North Whittier and was in Center Whittier, rounding the miniature bay of Parson's Cove. The Whittier wharf and store were behind her, looking deserted at noon, except for the cattle and horses in the pastures that reached to the river's edge. On her right the Captain's big square hip-roofed house stood on a rise behind a row of copper beeches. Next came the track that led away across the meadow to a Whittier farm, and now she passed Roger Williams Whittier's lane of chestnuts and lindens.

Carlotta was driving away from the distant white house, down through the long lacy dapple of leaf-shadows. She saluted Jennie with the whip she never used on her Michael. She was wearing the color 'Damask Rose,' which Priscilla had identified at church last Sunday as the very latest in Paris and London, according to news from her Aunt Ianthe. Carlotta could never have afforded her wardrobe on a country practice where a good part of her fees came in food or services. She had been left money by her mother, and it had been invested by a financially acute cousin.

She indicated with her whip that she was going north, so Jennie waved and went her own way. The man who had tried to assault Carlotta had been giving her a wide berth ever since. "He is sickeningly respectful," she told Jennie. "The mother has taken the bit in her teeth and chosen the baby's name herself. Carl Otto, after me." She laughed. "He sounds like a German princeling. Of course I am honored, and have given him a silver porringer, engraved."

"Take care," Jennie advised. "After this, you will be having name-sakes and be handing out mugs and porringers all over town."

"But don't you see, I am beginning to belong here in a way I never dreamed possible! One day I shall be known as the doctor who brought a whole generation of townspeople into the world. Or most of it," she added. "I shall be a leading citizen even if I did come 'from away,' which always seems to indicate a spot up there among the Pleiades."

At the Goward farm the horses and cattle stood in pools of shadow under the trees, and the family would be sitting down to dinner in a hot farmhouse kitchen. But only the small children would eat with satisfac-tion, the parents would eat only to keep up their strength. They must still be seeing in their fine parlor what Jennie hadn't seen, but could so relentlessly imagine; and always they would have in their nostrils the overpowering scent of the double white narcissus.

Bees must have come in the open windows that day. It was as if Jennie had actually been in the parlor and seen them crawling in and out of the white ruffles, like the bee on Nigel's forehead the last time she saw him.

As she approached Three Corner Farm she saw the kites first, dipping and soaring against towering clouds in a sky by Constable, then the children running into the wind down the long slope to the water, their voices small and high like gulls' cries sounding from blue space. "William's having a lovely day," she said. Diana flicked her ears and moved faster, as if to say, Give up any thought of stopping me now.

"I wouldn't dream of it," said Jennie, "but it's not suppertime, if that's what you think." She didn't see William at once, but there were several children down by the river, unrecognizable at this distance against the blinding glitter of the water under the wind. William's Iolaire was not flying; perhaps it had tangled with another kite and they'd brought them both down to free them.

She was well past the farm when she saw William plodding along ahead of her; he had his dinner bucket but no kite. Hearing hoofs, he stepped off the road without looking around. His shirt was half out of his breeches, his calves were crisscrossed by red lines of bramble scratches, and he was limping.

Diana stopped before Jennie could pull her up, and gave him a vigorous bunt between the shoulder blades that almost knocked him down, and he dropped his dinner pail. He whipped around, lifting a doubled fist, and said in a choked voice, "Cuss you, Diana, I got no sugar on me!" He glared at his mother, then scrubbed his fists hard against his eyes. His face was smeared with a mixture of dirt, tears, and blood from more scratches.

She wanted to cry out to him in pain and wrath, "What is it? Who has done this to you? Where is your kite?" She wanted to take him into her arms and rock him. But she said matter-of-factly, "Come aboard, William, and ride home with me."

"I'd rather walk." He folded his arms and turned his head away.

"As you wish. Give me your dinner pail." He wanted time to get over whatever it was, but she was not going to drive on and leave her Sweet William out here trying not to cry. "Behave yourself, Diana," she said. "Never mind if William hasn't smuggled any sugar to you today. You are almost too spoiled to be useful. I suppose you claim the Great Horse as a close relative, but I'm sure *he* does not countenance this self-centered behavior."

It caught William as she'd hoped. His round dark head turned toward her. "What Great Horse?"

She didn't want to give him anything to use against Bell Ann when he felt impish. "A little girl I used to know thought that God for horses and ponies was a Great Horse, with a golden stable in the sky."

"It could be true," William growled, looking away again. A sigh shook him, the quivering exhalation of a child who is clogged and bleary with long crying.

"Where is your kite?" she asked him.

He shrugged, staring at his bare toes.

"The string slipped from your hands, and Iolaire escaped, is that it?"

As if hearing the beloved name mentioned was unbearable, he shouted at her. "They cut her off! She's gone, way out there!" He pointed at the woods but meaning the river beyond.

"Oh, William!" She restrained herself from getting down and going to him. "Not the Fosses, surely?"

He shook his head. "They came over Crit's Hill. You know that little house on the far side of the crick, almost to the back road? Well, they just moved there from somewhere away. There's a boy bigger than the twins, and one my age. They think they know *everything*," Now that he was under way, nothing could stop him. "He, the big one—Joseph—*he* said my kite was too pretty and I was too vain, so he—," he might have been describing the murder of Bounce or Garnet, "*he cut the string.* I ran and I ran, but I couldn't catch her. I could just—just—" There was a poignant little squeak.

"You could just watch her go." She took on his despair as he watched the magnificent wings rising against the clouds, going higher and higher over the river, growing smaller and smaller above the St. David peninsula until they disappeared out over the sea.

"Didn't anyone say *anything?*" Had they all been jealous then, the little beasts?

"Patience cried." He wiped his face with the backs of his hands, snuffled mightily, and finally blew his nose on his shirt tail. "Joseph laughed like a crazy man and yelled, 'See her go!' Nobody else said anything. Maybe they were scairt he'd cut theirs off. I could *kill* him, and maybe I will! He said, 'It don't do to think too proud of anything, because God'll take it away from you.' I told him God didn't take my kite, *he* did, because he's the Devil's git, and then he said, 'For that I'll cut your heart out! You're nothing but a Nancy-boy, and God hates *them!*' Mama, he *did* take his knife off his belt, and I ran and I ran, and I went through the bushes and I climbed over the fence onto the road, and—well, if a Nancy-boy is a coward, I guess I am," he said bitterly.

"No, you were sensible. None of us would like it if someone cut out your heart."

"I wish," William said, "that the Great Horse would come down and kick his head in."

"So do I," said Jennie. "Come up now, William, and you may drive."

"*Really?*"

"Really." There'd be no risk. Diana would take herself home and stop in the barnyard even if no one held the reins.

Everyone had scattered after dinner. There was no one around to see William at the helm, so to speak, but no one to see his smeared face either, and that he was returning without Iolaire. Only the dogs.

Together Jennie and William unharnessed the mare, and William ran to get her a sugar lump before she was let into the pasture. "I was pretty sharp with her back there on the road," he explained. Accompanied by the rejoicing dogs—Darroch even managed a prance or two—they carried Jennie's purchases into the house. Then William went out and took a long look at the sky across the river, as if he could still see some speck that was Iolaire, as if by some miracle she was returning to him. It was too soon to say to him, David will make you another one. But later she would tell him that he was invited to join the theater party.

Twenty-Two

S HE TOOK WILLIAM'S dirty shirt and sent him to wash, including his scratched legs. "Never mind if it stings," she said. "Soap and water are best for them. After you are all shipshape and Bristol fashion, you can go down and see if Papa has a few minutes for you. You will feel better after you have told him what happened."

"I will never feel better," he assured her desolately, but he obeyed. He had eaten his dinner before the tragedy, but he was almost always hungry, no matter what, so he took a thickly buttered slab of gingerbread with him when he left for the Yard with Bounce, who was strenuously living up to his name. There was no doubt that Alick would have those few minutes he always had for any of them.

The girls' workbaskets were gone, which meant they had gone across to the Bastos', where Bell Ann would spend more time with the young animals than practicing buttonhole stitch. Carolus, with his work done, was somewhere on the forty-odd acres, mapping and sketching. The clocks ticked with that preternatural loudness possible only in an empty house.

The rooms were still pleasantly scented with the noon meal Pris had prepared. Jennie helped herself to food from the chilly cellarway. Cold boiled mackerel and a mealy potato were good with a little salt, and she dripped vinegar over boiled young beet greens. Garnet materialized on the chair beside her and stared at the mackerel; no doubt she'd had a whole mackerel for herself earlier, but every tidbit was welcome. Darroch lay over the threshold, shifting heavily each time Garnet received something; Jennie gave him a larger piece now and then. If she weren't so angry about Iolaire, she could have been quite happy at this moment, she thought resentfully.

Alick stepped over Darroch and came in. She held up her face to him and they kissed, slowly and appreciatively.

"It has been strangely empty here today," he said. "With ten children but not you it would have been the same." He picked up Garnet and took the cat's chair; she settled along his thigh. "None of them is within a hundred yards of us at this instant," he said. "I put William to work sweeping my office." He took her hand and kissed the palm.

"Why, Mr. Glenroy, what will your men be up to while you dally like an uxorious husband? I love it, but they may be holding wild revels among the shavings."

He separated her fingers and kissed each one, his eyes on hers. "Alick," she protested in a whisper, "this isn't fair."

"One of the first English sayings I learned from my wife was 'All is fair in love and war.'"

"Speaking of war, was Septimus here today?"

He kissed the inside of her wrist. "Aye, the politician was here. He has a new insurance scheme, and I told him I would be thinking about it. What is war having to do with it?"

"I met him this morning at the bridge, and he asked me if you were home. I thought that if he lingered with Priscilla, and you should come up to the house. . . ." She left it there.

"Och, the two *chailins* were already out on the river fishing for mackerel. He could hardly keep his eyes from the sight of the dory. It was a kindness to listen to the lad until his fever broke." He kissed the inside of her elbow; Garnet tried to roll over, in expectation that the caresses would reach her, and fell off Alick's leg. Looking down on Alick's head, and the first gray threading through the dark, Jennie thought, How lovely for a woman nearly forty to be moved like a twenty-two-year-old by a man of nearly fifty who is such a lover.

"He may have been in a fever," she said, "but he is now officially Frank Mackenzie's young man."

"A brilliant choice." He began his way back to her wrist.

"You are a tease, Alick," Jennie said huskily. "For two pins I could lead you straight into our bedroom and button the door, and then Mr. Babb would drive in, all the children will come home at once, and someone at the Yard will break his arm, and Vincent Taggart will have foretold it."

"*Dia*, you are right. And I was about to give you the two pins." Ceremoniously he gave her hand back to her and stood up. "Wasn't it the grand life, when even the oldest was in bed and asleep by sundown? William has told me about the kite, in my arms. The boy is heartbroken. No other kite, however beautiful, will be Iolaire. I have given him a sweet piece of pine to begin a new boat. A Baltimore clipper, we are thinking."

"Alick, that is perfect! And I have a surprise for him, for all of them." She told him about the theater party. "William will have good things in his head when he goes to sleep tonight, not just Iolaire flying away from him out over the ocean. . . . I hope she flew a long way before she went down."

"Perhaps she is still flying, and men are looking up from the decks of ships and crying, 'What is *that*? For the love of God, what is that bird? No, don't shoot, it may be an albatross! No, it is a bird of paradise!' "

They both laughed. She said, "You must tell William that; it might make him smile. Alick, I am concerned about those new boys when school begins again. They can make William's life terrible."

"You are always saying we have three years, or five years, before it is time to worry about one thing or the other. Now we have five weeks, and tomorrow night William is going to see a play."

"And Bell Ann will be hurt and angry," she said sadly.

"I was forgetting!" He laughed like a boy, "I lost my memory at sight of you! When Peter Oakes came back from his dinner today, he brought a message from his wife asking Bell Ann to come Saturday afternoon to play with Sarie and stay the night. His boy would be bringing her back early Sunday, if one of ours could be delivering her there on the Saturday. Can you believe that?"

"No, I cannot," she said. "Something will go wrong. It is altogether too much of a miracle to expect."

"Why should we not be expecting and receiving a miracle now and then? And this is just a wee one, a night for us, with the children all safe and happy elsewhere."

"And you and I will be alone with your quietly dangerous charm."

"My *what*?" Alick kerflummoxed was a joy to see.

"That is what Lydia calls it," she said gravely. "She says William takes it from you."

"I shall never be able to face that woman again!"

"Oh yes, you will," said Jennie. "You have always known that she has had an eye for you ever since she saw you walk ashore that day. Just think, your first moment on the American continent—I cannot say *soil* because it was a wharf—you were set off from the crowd by the keen and discerning eye of a lady. Are you blushing?" she teased him. She laid her palms on his lean cheeks, pretending they were hot to the touch, and he seized her hands and kissed first one and then the other.

"Och, I am afraid to be thinking of Saturday," he said in a low voice, "for all my daft talk of miracles, it will be wearing me out."

William came in, announcing, "Finished sweeping, Papa!" He was carrying his block of pine. "She will be a Baltimore clipper," he told Jennie. He went on into the winter kitchen, where he stopped and looked up at the shelf where his little model of *Ariel* sat in her cradle beside the Simon Willard clock. Then they heard the soft thudding of bare feet running up the stairs.

Peter Oakes was chief of the sail loft, a widower with a nearly grown son. A good and honorable man, he had married again last year, a young widow with one small girl. Sarie and Bell Ann played together whenever it was possible, and often had an overnight visit at one home or the other. Jennie had known Eudora Oakes as a young Phipps daughter, and then a woman whose husband was lost at sea before Sarie was born. Like many a wife for whom the sea was the widow-maker, when she married again it was to a man anchored to the land. Eudora was lusciously, healthily pregnant this summer, like the minister's wife; they bloomed like peonies and had a gently joking wager as to who would deliver first.

It was agreed that the older children would leave Bell Ann at the Oakes farm, well beyond Three Corners, on their way to Maddox Saturday afternoon. William was speechless at being included with the older ones. He couldn't help smiling whenever he thought of it; pleasure and sorrow passed in turn constantly across his round face like sunshine and clouds. The older three were sympathetic and angry about Iolaire, without mentioning the beloved name. They conspired to keep reminding him of the grand events awaiting him; that night when he called out in his sleep in a frantic, breaking voice, someone up there had quieted him before Alick or Jennie could go to him. They settled back into bed again, gently warmed by the kindness of their children to one another in times of stress.

Twenty-Three

F OR BELL ANN, a good portion of the pleasure in making a visit or receiving one was the preparation. When she wasn't talking about
staying with Sarie, she was up in her room packing for the adventure.
Time enough at the last minute for Jennie to remove all but the essentials
from the satchel. Evelina Ermintrude with her large wardrobe must go, of
course, and Bear, who was softer to sleep with. He had come from
Switzerland, by way of Ianthe. But she needn't take two dresses with
matching hair ribbons, two petticoats, two spencers, her best black
slippers and white stockings, *and* the Paris frock.

Sandy fluctuated between despair and elation as he sought for someone to do his chores at the Kilburns' through Sunday morning.

"What is really a dagger in his heart," Carolus said, "is that he will
have to pay with real money, not promises."

"Is that what you are receiving for taking over Sandy's chores?"
Jennie asked. "Promises?"

"Never fear, Mama," said Carolus. I have my ways of collecting."

"Pine slivers under the fingernails," Pris said. "Sandy's pride won't let
him scream. Come along, Shipmate," she said to William. They were
going fishing for mackerel on the far side of Misery Wall. William was
pleased; he could not be out of sight in the dory unless he was accompanied by someone older. He looked quite cheerful this morning, with so
many good things in prospect, though he would quietly grieve for Iolaire
for a long time.

Carolus accompanied Ianthe and Louisa to the upland pasture, taking a strupach, and his new water colors to make a painting of an unusual plant he'd discovered yesterday. Upstairs, Bell Ann talked to herself and her family as she emptied her chest of drawers. Jennie went out to the barn cellar to pick raspberries. The dew was heavy, and her shoes and hems were soon soaked, but the wet wasn't cold, and her bare feet squashed enjoyably in soggy shoes. The sun was shining, the roofs and woods steamed in the heat, and a strong whiff of barn added character to Nature's other scents. There was a rejoicing of birds all around, at least it sounded like rejoicing, though Carolus swore that what the ignorant called songs were territorial challenges. She didn't believe that could explain the musical flight of goldfinches or the way the catbirds went on trying out new themes and cadenzas.

The dogs lay in the shade of the house. Bounce pretended indifference to the hens let out to forage; wearing a dead hen around his neck for a whole day in his youth had convinced him that the game wasn't worth the candle. As for Darroch, young chicks could climb over his paws with impunity. Garnet had left for the woods where nobody could see what she was doing and the swallows couldn't swoop down on her.

Each sound from the shipyard fell separately into the hush, emphasizing its depth. From here, the confusion and dust of Main Street in Maddox were as difficult to imagine as the sensation of Posy Pulsifer's spittle on one's cheek. She hadn't told Alick, and she had waked up today knowing she would leave the affair between her and Posy and let time bury it.

There was a soprano view-halloo from Bounce, and Darroch rose up, looked, and lay down again. Moses Gunn and his donkey were stopping by the springhouse, while Brisky gave them a loud welcome.

"Good morning, Moses!" she called, making her way through the thicket. Bounce whimpered in frustration and lay flattened where he was, afraid of the donkey's hoofs.

Moses took off his hat. He had a thick fall of black hair down his nape past the neck of his collarless shirt, and he was tawny rather than brown, his eyes the opaque flat black she had seen in the faces of gypsies at home in Northumberland.

His sister Miriam's face was as lively and changeable as moving water; his gave away nothing. Chewing on a stem of grass, he watched her approach with less expression than Orono, the donkey, whose moist brown gaze anticipated treats.

"Morning," Mrs. Glenroy," he said. His voice was always a surprise with that wooden face and those eyes. It was boyish and pleasant. "I've got some real good cunners."

"Then I'll have a dozen," said Jennie. "The children keep catching trout and mackerel, but I cannot resist cunners. We may be eating fish three times a day."

"They smarten up the brain, I hear tell," he said. He reached inside one of Orono's finely woven panniers. "Two cents apiece they'll be."

"I'll get some money and a pan." She ran toward the house, lifting her drenched hems. She was counting out money from the coins kept in a cup in the pantry cupboard when Bell Ann said plaintively behind her, "I will need a *big* satchel for all my things."

"We'll worry about that tomorrow morning," Jennie said. "Will you take a strupach to Orono?"

Bell Ann forgot the ecstatic anxiety of planning a visit. "I want something for Moses too." Jennie gave her a piece of dry johnnycake for the donkey and a square of raisin gingerbread for Moses, and Bell Ann skipped out. When Jennie got there, Moses was eating, and drinking water from the bottle he carried, and Orono was crunching away on his cornbread while Bell Ann stroked his big rough head. When the donkey had finished he went to the watering trough, drank, and remained to exchange stares with Brisky. Moses hunkered down and began cleaning and skinning the fish with swift, efficient slashes of his knife. Bell Ann knelt beside him, watching him with the same unblinking attention the pony and donkey gave each other. The firm, pinkish glistening meat went into one pan, and the entrails, head, and tails went into another for the hens.

"You are much faster than any of my family," Bell Ann told Moses, who said, "That so?" He washed his hands in rainwater, wiped them off in thick grass, and dried them along the sides of his britches.

Someone came galloping through the woods. The dogs arose barking as Garland Shaw rode out into the open, a small man on a big chestnut roan. He pulled the horse up short at sight of them, and his face was so red and distorted under his broad hat brim that Jennie thought some terrible accident had happened at the farm, sending him in search of help where he had never come before.

"What is it?" she called to him. "What's wrong? Bell Ann, run down and find Papa!"

"Save your steps, girl, I don't want nothin' of your Pa!" It was like a whiplash snapping out and laying open a cheek. The facial contortion Jennie had mistaken for terror turned out to be rage, turned on Moses. "What did you take in my house, you thievin' little bas—— scoundrel?"

"I never took nothing, Mr. Shaw," Moses said calmly. "I wasn't raised that way."

"*Raised?* Is that what you call it, with your father a black and white and likely red mongrel, if he *is* your father? And your mother the good Lord knows *what* from who knows where, and likely *He* couldn't even put a name to her!"

"*Mr. Shaw!*" Jennie said, and it startled him into stopping with his mouth still open. Moses, just for an instant, was more deadly than stolid; there was no slow color rise under the tawny skin, no visible flinch, and she only sensed it, but she knew it was there.

"Mr. Shaw," she said more quietly, "Moses is here on business. You are not. Unless this is a social call, you are trespassing."

"I have a right to pursue a thief!" Shaw shouted. Like his horse, his voice was large for a small man. "I come up from the field sweating like a hog and go into the springhouse for a cold drink, and there's a pan of them things," he pointed at the cunners as if at excrement, "setting there, and my wife gone with the young one since before seven this morning!"

Today's funeral must have been a long distance away for her to start that early, Jennie thought.

"We're none of us deaf, Mr. Shaw," she said.

"Mr. Shaw," Bell Ann said brightly, "may I come to play with Lily sometimes?"

He gave her a half-demented look and snarled at the nervous horse to stop his infernal dancing.

"No, you may not, Bell Ann," Jennie said. "You had better go back to your packing."

"But you said—"

Jennie shook her head. "Goodbye, Moses," Bell Ann said languishingly. She kissed Orono's nose, then she climbed up on the bars and kissed Brisky. At last she went very slowly toward the house, where Bounce met her with frantic joy. Shaw seemed to explode into a convulsion that shook his light frame and startled the horse.

"You were in my house!" he shouted at Moses. "And my wife warn't home! What did you *do* in there? What'd you lay your thievin' hands on?"

Moses remained mute and immobile.

"Dumb insolence," Shaw growled. "I will be at the Keel with a constable and a warrant before sundown, I promise ye."

"Won't do you no good," said Moses in a soft slow voice. "Because I never took nothing. Never went inside. I cleaned eight cunners for her and threw the orts to the hens, same as I always do."

"Who told you to leave the fish?" Shaw cried triumphantly. "Did that on your own, did ye? Give a good chance to nose around, did it? By God, if I had my pistol along, you'd be turning out those baskets on the ground so I could see what you lifted in my house."

"Mrs. Shaw left me a note and a pan," Moses said mildly. "She said to leave some of what was best, and she will pay me next time."

"You can read, can ye?" Shaw laughed loudly to show his contempt. "You expect me to believe *that?*"

"Yes, sir," said Moses. "The note is still there under the conch shell on the top step. She trusts me, and I trust her."

Jennie paid him and he put the money away into a deep deerskin purse with a draw string, which he returned to his shirt pocket. He touched his hat to her and clucked to Orono, who came away from the pasture bars with no apparent regrets, though Brisky whinnied after him.

"And as for that jackass of yours," Shaw said, showing his teeth in that predatory grin, "you want to make sure you keep him tethered close to hand, because if I ever catch him away from the Keel, he's a dead jackass. Is that clear?"

Jennie did not have to see Moses' response to know it was there, by the cold at the back of her neck and a tightening of her scalp. Then Moses was walking out past Shaw's horse with Orono behind him.

"Goodbye, Moses," she called after them. "I will see you next week." Moses lifted one hand without looking around, and went on. "Mr. Shaw," she said coldly, "if anything should happen to Orono, we'll all know whom to blame."

She knew that *whom* held a wasp sting. *Airs and graces, Miss Lady; should have stayed up there under the General's nose.*

"Those Keelers," Shaw said. "Those Gunns. All alike. Got nothing much but a hide like tarred canvas. Outlaws, every one of 'em. You hear all these stories about the first George Gunn, old Geordie? Well, he was a scallywag and worse, no matter which one you believe. Come and squatted here and nobody ever had the belly to turn him and his git out."

"According to the General," she said gently, determined to hold her temper, "Old Geordie had a deed that Mrs. Mackenzie's grandfather respected when he took over his grant."

He jabbed a finger at her. "*Ha!* Who from, eh? That's the puzzle, Missus." A small man must feel like a giant when he sat a big horse and pelted a woman with hard words. "Before *her* grandfather, 'twould have to be from an Indian, wouldn't it?" The finger stabbed the air before her face like a sword being run through a haystack to kill a fugitive. "In that case, 'twouldn't be worth the paper it's written on. Or the birch bark." He snickered. "If old Prothero respected it, it was because Geordie had so much Indian kin hereabouts a man could never be sure the bloody brutes wouldn't come on him in the middle of the night. Oh, Old Geordie'd made his pact with the Devil all right. He'd drunk with the Devil and married his daughter. But times are different now."

He took off his hat and wiped his forehead with his arm. He had fine features and thick fair hair barely touched with gray; with a different temperament he could have been almost handsome. "I can challenge *Mister* George Gunn, you know. I can fetch *Mister* George Gunn to court. If there's a deed, they have to bring it out. And if it's signed by some savage calling himself a chief, the court'll make short work of it."

She had a cruel desire to spoil his glee. "But what would that do for you?"

"*Do*, Missus? The whole Keel should belong to me! Shaws have been trying to get it back since the Froggies left Castine."

"Get it back?" she repeated. "Do you mean you had it *once*?"

He reddened. "We should have had it first hop out of the box. Would have given us a good junk of the shore and now it wouldn't be Robbers Roost down there, and worse. Old fool Prothero tells Grampa, 'You can have it if you can get it off the Gunns fair and square.'" He spat with a contemptuous juiciness. "Fair and square. Those words never meant anything to Old Geordie's git. And Grampa never dared tell him to bring out his deed, on account of the Indians."

"I don't think," she said provocatively, "that people can be evicted from where they've been living for generations. If they could, that land would likely still belong to the Prothero heirs."

That did it, to her satisfaction. "They ain't ordinary squatters! That lascivious crew down there, criminals, sinners, couples laying with each other out of wedlock and mixing up the races . . . them unholy Maddox sea captains dropping off their concubines before they sail upriver like heroes—" Bubbles appeared at the corners of his mouth. "Place ought to be burned down like a plague house, scoured clean back to God's good ground."

"I've heard it said that a raid on the Keel might turn up more than a missing cow," Jennie said. "Perhaps a black sheep or two supposed to be miles away or safely dead all these years. It could be embarrassing."

From the way he looked at her, she might have, in all innocence, touched a fact that was sore as a boil. He wrenched the horse's head around and galloped out. Jennie got a mucking shovel from the barn, scooped up a pile of still steaming manure left by Shaw's horse, and deposited it around the roots of a small maple that had seeded itself behind the house. She contemplated the neat heap for a moment and decided it was more useful than Garland Shaw.

Twenty-Four

A T NOON WHEN the family collected for dinner, Sandy had finally found a responsible boy—a younger brother of Charlie Wolcott—to do the Kilburn chores through Sunday morning. He declined to state what he was paying, but made much of his canniness in giving him half his pay in advance

"Supposing they like him better than you," Carolus suggested, "and they keep him on?" Sandy smiled in a superior fashion at the impossibility.

"They could be sorry for him," Pris said, "and think he needs the work much more than you do. After all, his father and poor Charlie are gone, and you are almost rich by comparison. Not *almost*," she corrected herself. "You *are* rich."

Sandy ignored the reproach. "If they keep him, so be it," he said grandly. "I am nothing if not a risk-taker. That is how a man succeeds in this world: by never being afraid to take risks."

"Aye, aye, your Captainship, sir!" Carolus pulled at an imaginary forelock. There was the ghost of a giggle from William. Bell Ann, having been left out too long, burst into her really sensational news.

"Mr. Shaw was here today, and he is going to kill Orono!"

The effect was all she could have desired. Intoxicated by success, she shouted over the din, "You should have heard what Mama said to him!"

Alick rapped for silence. "You had better hear it all now, and then we will be done with it." He nodded at Jennie.

She tried to make a short account of it, but with such an eager and articulate crew briefness was hardly possible. They were outraged that

175

Moses was called a thief, and the donkey threatened even though there was no chance of his straying. They wanted Harry discharged at once; no Shaw was fit to set foot on Glenroy property. They managed to be vehement while enjoying crisp fried cunners.

"Don't be telling your father how to conduct his business," Alick said. "Unless you are all applying for partnership. The lad is not a charmer, but then I am not paying for charm, only honest work, and that I receive."

"I wish I could have heard you, Mama," Pris said enviously, "and seen him fit to explode up on that big horse!"

"I made a few hits close to the bull's eye," Jennie admitted. "I was always good at archery. But I'm not very proud of myself for having words with him. The Shaws have handed down their rage about the Keel from father to son like a family curse. It keeps them sour and miserable, I'm sure, and no arguments, even legal ones, are going to drive it away."

"But could they really gather enough people together to raid the Keel, the way he threatened?" Carolus appealed to his father.

"The last time that was attempted was about fifty years ago," Alick said, "and the raiders made grand fools of themselves."

Exhilaration succeeded indignation; they were as jubilant as if the Keelers were their own, which was so in a certain sense ever since Sandy had been landed there. But the cautions followed. "I know you are all dying to tell this at Strathbuie House tomorrow," Jennie said. "But it must not be repeated *anywhere*, at any time. You know how stories grow; this one could be the size of a herd of elephants in a week, and completely beyond recognition. So, keep the rules in mind, no matter how tempted you are to tell how magnificent your mother was."

"People should know," Carolus threatened mischievously, but she knew they would obey.

"Bell Ann, do you understand?" Alick asked her.

"Yes, Papa." Bell Ann dipped demurely into her raspberry cranachan, a Scottish confection of toasted oatmeal, heavy cream, sugar, and fresh berries.

"Remember it when you are visiting Sarie," he said. "We are not carrying unpleasant stories from this house, no matter how exciting they are."

"Yes, Papa." She put down her spoon, slid out of her chair, and went around the table to his lap.

"Someone is homesick already," he said. "Someone will be better staying home tomorrow."

"Not me!" Bell Ann struggled free of his arm, and the rest laughed.

"Don't you want your cranachan?" William asked, reaching for it.

"Don't you dare touch that, William Farrar Glenroy!" She stamped back to her chair. The whole Shaw incident was now part of the past. Jennie could not imagine Harry carrying on the family tradition with his father's energetic venom. The obsession would die with him.

There had been a few objections to including William in a (nearly) grownup party.

"What if he snores when he falls asleep during the play?" Carolus asked. "It will be embarrassing."

"I will not fall asleep." William spoke through clenched teeth.

"I'm glad Sweet William is coming with us." Pris ran her hand fondly over his head. "He's such a dear wee boy."

William's ambivalent expression said he appreciated the support but jibbed at the description.

"I don't look forward," Sandy said, "to having a little brother tagging me from one end of Maine Street to the other. A person likes to gaze into shop windows and cogitate without a talking Bounce at his elbow."

"Columbine must have been cogitating all those times," Jennie said to Alick, who grinned.

"*Alasdair*," he said.

At the Gaelic version of his name Sandy came to startled attention. "*Sir?*"

"I am sure you will not be doing anything unfit for your younger brother to see."

"Of course not, Father!" Sandy sounded shocked.

"Perish the thought," said Jennie. "Just be thankful your parents will not be with you."

"Anyway," William said, "*I* am not interested in Main Street. I would not be *dragged* into that hooraw's nest. I only care about what happens on the wharves."

After kisses all around, and as few parental injunctions as possible, they left in the wagon early on Saturday afternoon, with Perry (Oliver Hazard) between the shafts. Four were dressed in their second-best outfits, suitable for an afternoon in town. Bell Ann wore a rose-budded dress with a fresh pinafore over it, and her new straw bonnet. She and William, Evelina Ermintrude, and Bear sat on the chest that carried the clothes for the party. Evelina's many outfits, Bell Ann's one change, and

her overnight necessities went in a much smaller satchel than she had
wanted. The twins and Pris sat on the wagon seat, and Carolus had first
turn with the reins.

"Good heavens!" said Jennie. "What handsome children! Who are
their fortunate parents? Do you know, Alick?"

"We are orphans," said Pris. "We intend to ask the General to adopt
us."

"But we will return your horse first," Carolus said. "And you will still
have Bell Ann, and William if you cannot bear to part with him."

"Remember," Alick told them. "It is a warm day, and Perry is not to
be hurried. You are not rushing munitions to besieged troops or rescuing
refugees from the plague. Be off with you, then. Enjoy yourselves.
Beannachd leibh!"

"*Beannachd leibh!*" they answered. Perry moved, and Bell Ann stood
up, crying, "I forgot to kiss Brisky and Diana and Garnet, and Bounce,
and Darroch, and—" Perry was moving faster. "And Louisa and Ianthe!"
Bell Ann shrieked.

"I will give them all kisses from you!" Jennie called. William forcibly
sat his sister down as Perry's pace picked up. Standing with the dogs,
Brisky whinnying resentfully over the wall, Alick and Jennie took hands
as if watching their children approach a foreign frontier. It was the first
time they had all gone at once, the first time William and Bell Ann had
ever spent a night away from home.

"I am wondering if Sandy has taken all his money with him," Alick
said.

"Surely not to spend," Jennie protested. "Not everything he has been
saving toward his sextant and his militia gear. He simply loves having it
where he can touch it."

Before the wagon had quite disappeared, Pris began to declaim: " 'Is
this a dagger that I see before me, handle toward my hand? Come, let me
clutch thee—' " She was drowned out by noisy objections.

Laughing, Alick and Jennie walked back toward the house. The
sound reassured the dogs that their world had not completely disappeared in the twinkling of an eye. Under the rowans Jennie put her arms
around Alick's neck.

"We are alone! Can you believe it? For the first time since Pris was
born!"

Bounce cavorted around them, and Garnet returned home from a
morning on her own, leaning against their legs. Out of sight, Brisky was

complaining, pleading, or merely showing temper, and Diana joined him. Alick lifted his head. "Was it *alone* you said?"

"Darling, they do not argue, they do not ask difficult questions, they do not need an endless supply of fresh laundry, they do not go through shoes and stockings like a mower through a wheatfield, but I'm glad they cannot talk. We would never get a word in edgewise."

Alick ran his hand down over her hip. "First the pieces to shut them up, and then we will be taking the dogs in and locking the doors and pretending we are all away from home."

"When did we last make love in the daytime? Not since Priscilla was an infant in the cradle. Alick, remember those noons when we didn't eat dinner?" Even through dress, petticoat, and drawers, his hand could raise pleasurable prickles along her skin. "When have we taken the time to look upon one another?"

"*Dia*, we'd best be going into the house before someone drives in. I am in no condition to be meeting anyone."

Inside the summer kitchen door they were in each other's arms again, kissing as if they had been wandering in separate deserts for half their lives, until an uproar from the dogs slowly penetrated their wilderness. Alick swore under his breath and went to the back window.

"*Babb!* I should have known. He has not been here for three weeks. He has his brother, and his nephew following on horseback. They will eat up the afternoon." He went into the pantry where he stripped off his shirt and doused his head in cold water, and splashed more over his chest. "Let us hope this will take care of the rest of me," he said. "There is no time to jump into the river."

Jennie handed him a towel. "We have tonight. *All* night. We can go to bed before dark and make love in the sunset."

"Please do not be speaking like that," he said through the towel.

"Darling!" she whispered. "I feel as if I were your mistress. When I am giving them coffee they will never guess what a wanton woman I am."

She stood in the doorway while he greeted the Babbs, called "Good afternoon!" to them, and then went into the bedroom to take a quick sponge bath and change into a fresh dress. She brushed and pinned up her hair at the back of her head, but she could never quell the curly tips that sprayed loose from the knot.

A touch of French scent (from Ianthe) behind her ears and at the base of her throat behind a modest frill was for Alick; never mind the others. She ground beans for coffee and set a tray with the Lowestoft coffee service, linen napkins from Sophie, and silver spoons from William and Sylvia. She took Brisky and the horses each a cut-up potato for their strupach, and brought back cream from the springhouse.

She was too keyed up to sit down and quietly occupy herself. So she went for a walk instead; there would be plenty of time. The dogs had gone with the men, so she went alone through the field to the woods. Now the way led through tall yellow St. Johnswort and past billows of blossom-ing wild rose bushes entangled with the vibrant blue and violet spires of meadow vetch. April had lived long enough to stagger through the field flowers, picking them by the fistful and thrusting them into her parents' hands, beaming with the rapture of giving.

Jennie sat for a few minutes on the stone wall by the babies' graves, meditative but not sad. It had been a long time before she could conquer her obsession with what must be happening to her baby in the ground, all turned to a handful of bones, nothing left of the small satiny body, and the strong little voice that could already carry a tune, "Bobby Shafto," which was William's favorite at the time.

When Jennie was small, whenever a pet died Sylvia and Ianthe told her that their mother had welcomed it into Heaven, and then it became *her* dog, cat, lamb, or bird. Jennie's belief had comforted her. After April, she had told her children that there were two sets of grandparents to care for April, and they had been solaced as she had been. But this was comfort for children, not for the parents who would never hold April again in this life.

Priscilla, no older than Bell Ann was now, told the five-year-old twins that April and Daisy were best friends. No one knew what David and the other Evans children thought about their lost baby, but doubtless their little sister lived on in a hundred ways as April did.

Garnet, who had arrived making conversation, accompanied her through the woods to the trail that led gradually upward to the old fort beyond Misery Wall. It was really the remains of a fortified dwelling, now only a partial enclosure of fieldstone which must have been much higher once when it surrounded the actual house of an extraordinarily brave Englishman some two hundred years ago, long before the Gunns. Gabriel Mannering had farmed the land, he had fished in the river and had sailed far beyond its mouth for the great codfish. He traded with the local Indians, who were for the most part as peaceful as Geordie Gunn later found them. But when there was trouble—inspired usually from the outside, he had written in later years—he kept his stock and his family inside the walls and prayed not to be overcome before help could arrive from the Fort Point garrison at Job's Harbor.

The walls had almost completely fallen down, half lost in blackberry vines and bracken. It was a marvelous playground for imaginative children. According to Mannering's account, he had rocked up a spring in one corner, but the twins had never been able to find it with all their digging, though they turned up an almost whole pottery jug, a coin issued in the time of Queen Anne, and a corroded sword blade. These occupied a shelf in the parlor with the Indian treasures.

Occasionally the twins camped here overnight, alone or with friends, refusing William because he was inclined to see the ghosts of Indians or pirates creeping up on them. But they had been so busy this summer that the fort had been neglected, and fresh wild growth flourished inside the walls. Jennie climbed by the boys' toeholds to the top of the side overlooking the river. Garnet made it in one leap.

The river lay in sunlight, peacock blue, under the prevailing southwesterly wind. The tide was high and there was a steady traffic in departures and returns. The arrivals ran exultantly before the wind; those leaving beat their way downriver.

William would be spending his Maddox afternoon at the wharves, every moment an adventure. Sandy would be up on Main Street, probably Carolus too. Priscilla had friends in Maddox to see, unless Robin wanted her to sail; if so, there would be no argument.

She would attend the play tonight dressed in the silky lilac muslin that Jennie had worn to her first dinner at Linnmore House. For years Jennie had found reasons for not unlocking the trousseau trunk. Long ago she had opened the one which held her dearest personal possessions, and they had allowed her to share her childhood and youth with her children. Then, one day early this summer, she had at last confronted the trousseau trunk. She had been alone in the house; the children were all at the shore, good for an hour or more of playing in the water like seals.

It had not been terrible at all. Sylvia had repacked everything with potpourri sachets between the layers, and when she lifted the lid, all her summers at Pippin Grange came out at her, because they always made potpourri as the rose petals fell. Besides, she had hardly worn the things, her stay at Linnmore had been so short; the associations were not as hurtful as she expected, she had traveled so far since then. The scars were barely visible or had disappeared. Lifting out the bronze riding habit, she wondered what had become of the plump and talkative young artist who had painted her wearing it, and what they had done with the portrait when it arrived at Linnmore House. But it was rather like wondering about the end of a story in a book.

None of the wedding gifts had been sent to the rectory with her personal effects. Perhaps they had brightened Tigh nam Fuaran for the next factor's wife, unless Christabel had taken a fancy to some of them; she was greedy enough. Jennie did not even try to imagine her successor. The tall gray stone house appeared briefly to her like a ship showing through thinning fog and then vanishing again.

Priscilla had been incredulous and then overjoyed to be given the freedom of the trunk. She didn't know that she was handling a trousseau; the simply cut white and silver wedding dress could have been a girl's first ball gown. She loved the slender graceful lines of the Empire period and shrugged off Thankful's vivacious prattle about adding huge full sleeves, gores, and braid and ruching.

"Foofaraw! Fussbudgetry! When I am an arrived *modiste*, I shall make this style high fashion. It is too beautiful to be lost."

Bell Ann was wrapping herself in one shawl after another. Why couldn't the lilac and purple silk shawl be made into a dress for her? she cried, stroking it. "It would not be suitable," Pris said. "Besides, I shall wear it with the lilac muslin at the very first opportunity. I suppose it would be too ostentatious for church—"

"Yes, it would," said Jennie. "But the time will come." Tonight it would make its American debut at Strathbuie House. "I shall pretend I am going to the theater in New York or London," Pris said grandly.

Bell Ann finally settled on a cambric morning dress patterned with rosebuds, and Priscilla made her and Evelina each a frock from it, with new pink ribbon sashes. They were wearing them today.

Jennie found neither poignancy nor irony in the circumstance that put Nigel's daughter in a dress her mother had worn as Nigel's wife, and that Nigel's arm had been around Jennie when she wore it to Linnmore House and his hands had draped the silk shawl over her shoulders. It was another of those things that had happened once, and then time had swept her swiftly away, as the wind in the sails swept the ships along the river.

"Look, Papa, I've made over one of Mama's dresses for myself," Pris had said, revolving before Alick. His smile was tinged with a sadness only Jennie sensed. He had never seen her in the dress, it meant nothing to him except that the girl wearing it was becoming, too fast, a beautiful young woman.

All at once Jennie realized she had been sitting on the wall for a long time, seeing nothing before her on the sunlit river, and the shadow of the woods was slowly flowing down the rocks toward water. A flurry of chickadees told where Garnet was. "I'm going," Jennie called to her. When she left the woods, the men were just walking up to the house; they stopped for a long discussion under the old apple tree at the turn, and by the time they came into the house the coffee was brewing and Jennie had set out a plate of sugar-and-spice wafers. It was as if she had been sitting there all afternoon with her embroidery or her mending or, as might be expected of an educated woman, her book.

Mr. Babb's brother was as courtly and genial as he was, and his son was one of those young mariners who looked too downy and virginal to be captains. But young Babb was already a veteran, and he would be skipper of the *Enoch Lincoln*. He gave Jennie the earnest homage due an attractive but respectable older woman.

"I thought they would never go," she said to Alick, smiling and waving as they rode out.

"It was your fault, *mo chridh*. They could not bear to leave you. In five more minutes, the young man would have commenced his life story, if he could have seized the time from his uncle and his father. Now the fear is at me that someone we are not even dreaming of will make us a *long* evening call."

"If we cannot foil that, we are mighty poor specimens. My love, we will be naked in the sheets before sundown, I promise."

Twenty-Five

W HEN THE CHORES were done and the dogs and cat fed, Alick and Jennie were hungry for nothing but each other. The sun was still up but it was dusk when they fell voluptuously asleep. They awoke in the dark, hungry.

They groped for their nightclothes in air that brushed their skin like silk. They smothered their voices like surreptitious lovers in a houseful of people, and laughed at themselves for it. The clocks began to strike eleven as they went barefoot to the kitchen and the welcome of Darroch's tail and Bounce's toenails as he scurried around them. Garnet was crying outside the door, and Jennie let her in and the dogs out while Alick lit a candle.

The night was warm, thick with stars, with fireflies around the lawn. Jennie was very conscious of the emptiness of the house, of no children upstairs. Bell Ann should be sleeping deeply now, tucked in with Sarie; they'd have talked and giggled until they dropped out of consciousness without even knowing it was happening.

The others would be at Strathbuie House enjoying their after-theater supper; the older three acting extremely grown up, or trying to, and William flummoxed to be in such company, which included two lady schoolteachers (even though he had known them all his life) and a professor of Greek. However, he would not be awed out of his appetite.

She and Alick stood smiling at each other. There was high color on his cheekbones, and his dark hair fell youthfully over his forehead. "Now I know what you must have been like at twenty," she said.

"I was never this happy at twenty. Never as happy as I have always been with you. It is not only to do with making love, to be in you, to be one flesh with you. It is everything that you have brought to me, all that I never expected to have in this life, and I had no great hopes of the next one."

She put her arms around him. "You have given all this to me, too. I thought I was happy when I was young at Pippin Grange, and I was, but it was as a child. One day when I was twenty-one I believed I'd had all the happiness allotted to me in my life, that the chance of more had ended with my childhood, and for the rest of my days I would simply endure."

That had been the day when she saw Nigel ordering the burning of the cottages on the moor, and Alick knew it. His mouth moved gently over her temple and cheek.

"My life as an adult woman began when I walked away from Linnmore," she said. "I could never have left you by the next spring, Alick. I had grown closer to you, by the time you heard me screaming and saw me exposed and helpless beyond shame as Pris was born, than I have ever been to another person in my life, even my sisters."

Nothing more needed to be said. They took their tray to the bench outside the door, with the fireflies; it was not black-dark but starlit. They had hot tea, warm hard-cooked eggs he had boiled in the teakettle, a fresh cucumber sliced as they wanted it, bread and butter, and Nora Basto's damson-plum jam.

"A feast," she said.

"We've had many a feast."

"No trout has ever tasted so good as those you caught just before Fort William."

"Where you taught me to write my own name of Gilchrist that I have never written since."

The dogs were enchanted by the unexpected picnic, but Garnet was satisfied with their company alone. Jennie leaned back against the clapboards, sipping her tea and looking at the stars.

"I don't have to know all their names," she said. "It is enough to simply marvel at a million points of light."

"I know where the pastures of Heaven are," Alick said. "Where the Great Horse is folding his wings and grazing in Paradise. Above, it is all rich meadow, and the sun shines even in the showers that water the grass."

"Tell me more, O prince of knowledge!"

"The Great Square of Pegasus, do you remember? Last winter when the older ones went skating at the Bastos' and came home one night in a ferment about the stars, and we went out with them to look. Sandy could show us clearly for the first time the Great Square of Pegasus. Bell Ann missed it, being asleep, but in the morning William told her about it and showed her a picture of the winged horse in your father's Mythology."

"So it all spun together in her head," said Jennie. "Heaven, the stars, a winged horse, and a place marked off for him up there—what else could he be but a god? It's so perfect, it makes a feather run down my back. — Oh, dear, I forgot to tell Bell Ann firmly not to take her new gospel to Sarie! It could really upset the Oakses. As long as she keeps him to herself, he will exist, and I should hate to lose him, myself."

"I am becoming fond of the beast," Alick admitted. "He is so benevolent. When I was Bell Ann's age I went in terror of the water horse carrying me into the loch to drown"

It was midnight, and summer mornings came too soon. She wanted to touch him again, and sleep with no fabric between them, which was not possible when they could be roused by a child.

Now they fell onto the bed in a fervent tangle of arms and legs. This time their lovemaking was unsubtle and merry, as if they were two very young rustics tumbling about in a field.

"But without bruises from awkward roots," Jennie said afterward as they lay entwined. "And no mosquitoes on defenseless flesh, and the possibility of poison ivy."

"But is there the possibility of a wean?" he asked wryly.

"I don't think so," she said. "I am *almost* sure. But if I find myself celebrating my fortieth birthday with a newcomer making itself at home here," she patted her belly, "I shall always remember the night it was conceived as one of the most magnificent of my life. Not that all my nights with you are not magnificent in one way or another."

He laughed. "My Cheannie," he said, as he used to before he lost so much of his accent. "Och aye, it's chust Cheannie," she murmured against his chest. Through the clouds of approaching sleep she heard Darroch's deep-throated deliberate barking; they had left him outside. Under the bed Bounce picked up the alarm, and Jennie sprang up straight, feeling for her nightgown. Bounce was now racing for the kitchen yelping and growling, Garnet came skidding over the threshold into the bedroom.

"*Dé tha sin?*" Alick asked groggily.

"I don't *know* what it is! My God, Alick, will you get *up*? Something is out there. It could be a bear! Darroch could be killed!" She was pulling on her nightgown with shaking hands. Suddenly the Newfoundland had ceased to bark, and that was ominous. Bounce was now attacking the inside of the door.

"There has not been a bear in South Whittier for years," Alick protested.

"That doesn't mean there cannot be one!" She threw his dressing gown at him and ran out to the kitchen. Bounce sprang to meet her and then rushed back to the door and kept jumping at the latch. On the other side of the door, unbelievably, Bell Ann was saying, crossly, "Stop it, Sarie. You *know* he won't hurt you!"

Jennie unbuttoned the door and the children stumbled in. Darroch squeezed in with them, and Bounce spun in mad circles. "Mama!" Bell Ann cried, and burst into tears. Jennie knelt and tried to hold both at once. They were barefoot and in their nightgowns; beside Bell Ann, Sarie felt as fragile as a bird.

Alick came, carrying a lighted candle, and Bell Ann wailed, "Oh, Papa, robbers, robbers! And they killed Enoch!" Sarie seemed to be trying to burrow into Jennie's breast. She was sobbing and shaking. Bounce danced around and was told to lie down.

They carried both children to the camp bed, wrapped them in blankets, and dried and warmed their feet. Cradled in Alick's arms and within reach of her mother, Bell Ann quieted first. Sarie went on crying, less violently, in Jennie's embrace, now and then drawing a quick trembling breath.

"Now tell me, *mo nighean dhu*," Alick said to Bell Ann. "How can I be helping if I am not knowing what has happened?"

"There was a terrible crash that woke us up, and Sarie's mama was screaming," Bell Ann began, short of breath at the start, but gathering strength. "And the dogs outside were barking so *loud*, I don't know how those men *dared*, but they must have crept up the stairs, because Sarie's mama was screaming harder—" She reached out convulsively and seized Jennie's arm.

"And Papa was shouting," Sarie lifted her face and hiccuped, "and we think one of the men was hitting him, but the other one was galloping away, we heard a horse—" A long crescendo of shivers. "We think he killed Enoch when that crash happened, but we were afraid to go see."

"So I said we should run away and get you, Papa," Bell Ann said, "because you are so brave. We went down the back stairs, Sarie was afraid even to move, but I made her come." A little pride blazed forth. "The dogs didn't even see us. They were too busy barking."

Dear God, with all the houses between there and here, Jennie thought, all this way in their bare feet and nightdresses, and no knowing what they left behind.

"You were very brave, and we are proud of you," she said.

"But my Mama and Papa and poor Enoch—" Sarie was overcome again, shaking violently.

"I had better be going," Alick said, and went to dress.

"Now everything will be all right," Bell Ann assured Sarie. "And we are nice and safe here, aren't we, Mama?"

"Yes, you are." Gently she loosened Sarie's arms. "Darroch won't leave you. Bounce, up with you." She patted the camp bed, and Bounce jumped onto it and began kissing any ear he could reach. "Bell Ann's papa will go to see what is wrong, and I shall make you something good to drink."

She tucked the blankets snugly around their feet and followed Alick, wanting to run, but for the children's sake she walked. She sat on the bed beside him while he pulled on his boots, wanting to cling to him like Bell Ann, and wail and beg, but she held onto reason in the face of the unthinkable.

"*Robbers*," he said. "I cannot believe it, but there could be queer folk straggling down the road." He stroked her back as he had often done in other times of terror and grief. "I will be as cautious as a cat. Garnet is no fool, and neither am I."

"Then stop at the Bastos', please. Nick will go with you, or one of the boys."

He kissed her, and she knew he would not be waking up Nick Basto or anyone else. He would have no pistol, either; he had never owned but the one, left to him by his grandfather, a beauty made by one of the master gunsmiths of Doune.

In the kitchen he lit a lantern. "My papa will take care of those men," Bell Ann said proudly to Sarie. "Take Mr. Basto with you, Papa!" she said when he leaned down to kiss her uplifted face. He smiled, and kissed Sarie too.

"He is not going alone, dear," Jennie said. It wasn't a lie; Shonnie would be going with him. She went and waited until he led the horse from the barn and hung the lantern from the hook at the corner nearest the road. She listened to Shonnie going away, walking at first and then moving faster, so that by the time he reached the town road his gallop was weirdly multiplied by its echoes. She returned to the children, who were sitting up watching for her. Sarie's brown eyes were inflamed by weeping and rubbing. With her round face and fluffy fair hair, she would have looked like a doll if it were not for her very human misery.

"I love my brother Enoch," she wept. "I never had any brother till him. I *know* that is why Mama was crying. She says he is as good as any son of her own could be. And he is handsome too. I'm glad *you* were there, Bell Ann," Sarie said thickly, and Bell Ann put a protective arm about her. "Because I saved you," she said.

"Now we'll have some warm milk and be all cozy together," said Jennie.

Both children were still shivering even in the blankets. She brought two of Bell Ann's flannel nightdresses from the winter clothes and helped them change. Making reassuring little mother-sounds, she thought, Is Alick there yet? Has he changed his mind and taken someone?

She sweetened the milk with maple syrup, "Do you want bread and butter?" Sarie mutely shook her head, but drank deeply. Bell Ann *would* have bread and butter; she was like William.

Jennie had brought out Alick's plaid with the nightgowns, and when the children finished their drinks she had them use a chamber pot and crawl back among the blankets, and then she covered them with the plaid. "This is something like a magic blanket, Sarie," she said. "If you are sick or cold or afraid, it always helps. Doesn't it, Bell Ann?"

"Only Jesus can do that," Sarie protested feebly. "Magic is evil."

"Not *this* magic," Bell Ann said. "We always have it on our beds if we are sick, and it makes us better."

"But you have to pray too," Sarie insisted.

"Would you like to say your prayers now, Sarie?" Jennie asked.

"No. I already said them once." Sarie lay down between Bell Ann and the wall. Bell Ann began, rather smugly, "I said my prayers to—"

Jennie put a finger to her lips, and Bell Ann said, "And I needn't do it again, either."

We shall have to do something about the Great Horse before too long, Jennie thought. Someday she will tell and we will be the scandal of Whittier.

Bell Ann talked foggily about the plaid, but not for long. They were asleep by the time Jennie returned from emptying and rinsing the pot.

She took Garnet's rocker and put her feet in another chair, tipped her head back, and tried to make herself go limp. But the Simon Willard clock, striking every quarter of the hour, had no mercy; that it had timed more good hours than bad ones was no defense.

It had struck through the long night of April's dying and they had been too superstitious to stop it. Besides, April had loved the clock from her earliest days and would stand transfixed to hear it strike; in case she was still hearing it, they could not take it from her.

The night before Bell Ann was born, Jennie had lain on the camp bed under the plaid (for luck), timing her pains by the clock. She had been afraid of conceiving for a long time after April died; they both feared bringing forth another small life to lose. *This* small life had been strong and busy in the womb for months, but so had April been.

The vivid little scene on the base of the clock had looked alive in the tremulous candlelight. The trees swayed in a phantom breeze, the blue water rippled, it had been hypnotic. She moved into it; she heard the leaves whispering, smelled the perfume of wild strawberries in the grass, strong as incense. Bemused, she felt her body floating, and when the clock struck half-past three it had been like a reassurance that the pains would not come too fast. She needn't wake Alick to go in the dark for the doctor.

She had gone to Carlotta first when this tall young woman had newly come to Whittier. (Uglier than sin, someone called her. She'd do real good stuck in a cornfield to scare off the crows.) Dr. Waite was miles away in Maddox. If Jennie had gone to him he would have listened like a kind uncle to her self-conscious complaints about her nervousness and insomnia and lack of appetite and told her it was natural after her ordeal. Then he would have prescribed a tonic, told her to drink wine with her meals, to let the work go sometimes and read the latest Scott novel. She could not have told him what the real trouble was.

She could not have discussed it even with Lucy and Ann Kate, who had both lost children. But here was a woman who could be objective, not grieving with her in loving friendship. The Whittier family had spoken up for Carlotta; she had cured a young Whittier wife of ceaseless, incomprehensible weeping, apparently by inducing her to talk through many long visits as she would talk to no one else.

Jennie was desperate that late spring afternoon when she drove to the Neville house, telling no one first; Alick thought she intended to look at a shipment of new fabrics brought home by a Whittier ship. She would know in five minutes whether or not she could talk to this woman, but she was ready to turn and run before she lifted the knocker.

Within three minutes of her entrance into a room filled with books and flowering plants, she was saying, "Our little girl died last October, from measles. Since then we are afraid of my conceiving. But my husband and I have needed each other so much, we have always been everything to each other." Her voice was shaking. "And it has been so long."

"Yes," the doctor said, and with that one word she ended the trembling. She asked a few questions about Jennie's general health, and then began to explain her theory, which had been her father's and her husband's.

"Though healthy females must put up with twelve periods of bleeding a year, a very complicated and unkind joke on the part of the Creator, they also have corresponding periods of infertility, as any female animal has. Both my father and my husband kept records of certain patients' menses and their dates of conception. These were intelligent women who wished to control their childbearing and could persuade their husbands to agree. A true pattern emerged." She spoke with a quiet, radiant passion, and henceforth Jennie would never again see her as a plain woman. "I am so *happy* that you are allowing me to tell you about this! To put it simply, you and your husband may enjoy each other in safety within certain limits, *if* you are regular in your cycle. If you are not, it may not always be successful."

"I am as well regulated as the moon." Jennie's euphoria was like Diana attempting to gallop and being held back to a decorous trot. She wanted to believe what she was hearing, but could not, quite. "And I have no women's complaints."

"Then your chances should be good, if your husband is willing. Sad to say, the subject is unmentionable in too many households."

"There is nothing my husband and I cannot discuss," Jennie said with pride.

"You are fortunate," the doctor said. "The problem of making their husbands understand is insurmountable for some women. I am seen as a bold and lewd woman—calling myself a doctor has already made me *that*—who is interfering indecently with the masculine privilege of taking their pleasure whenever they wish it."

"My father raised four daughters to think for themselves as much as possible, given the world's general opposition. I could not live with a man who looked down on me. Are you keeping records?" Jennie asked shyly. "Because if you are, I should like to help in your research."

"Oh, would you?" Carlotta asked eagerly. "That's very generous of you!"

They had decided Jennie's pattern that afternoon, and according to calculations she was in a safe period; in bed that night she explained it to Alick, and they made love for the first time since before April fell sick. It was a calculated risk; her instincts told her to trust Carlotta's theory, but she was apprehensive until her menses began on the twenty-eighth day, and she knew that she had begun to live again.

She still wanted Alick to have a daughter, and Bell Ann was another calculated risk; she might have been a boy.

"There is no way to foretell that," Carlotta said. "Not yet! You might as well guess by a fortune teller's cards or by a wedding ring swinging over your abdomen, or what you've been eating, or whether you're carrying high or low."

Jennie didn't tell her that she kept dreaming it was a girl; she knew that could be because she wanted a girl. I would love a little boy just as much, she assured herself, and listed boys' names as well. But the dreams were like promises.

"You have your girl, Jennie." Carlotta's voice had said over Bell Ann's first angry squall.

"Alick's girl," she answered, wanting to weep with pride and happiness.

The clock striking two roused her from her waking dream. So this is the most magnificent night of my life, she thought cynically. If ever I spat in the face of Providence, without even knocking on wood first, it was when I said that. *Where is he?*

She went out and listened for hoofbeats in a silence that had become terrible. The soft call of an owl was no delight but like a message from a grave. She could not leave the children to go to the Bastos for help. Bloody visions passed before her, and she was nauseated with the poisonous certainty that she had conceived on the night her husband would be murdered.

When she heard the leisurely sound of a walking horse, she thought Shonnie had come home on his own. But when the horse came into the lantern light, Alick was riding him, and as usual she was ashamed of her own weakness. He looked tired but intact. "It is all right," he told her at once. But he said nothing more until they were in their room; by candlelight he looked very profound, and maddeningly intent on taking off his boots.

"First, who is hurt?" she urged him.

"No one, but there *was* an invader, a poor creature with nothing much of his own, not even a decent suit of clothes to cover him. Och aye! And a savage one, from the howls of rage, but they had him well in hand." He was silently laughing. "About this long," he said, measuring. "About eight pounds, I would be guessing. Bald, poor wee lad, but eyes like the bluebells of Linnmore, and och, what a voice!"

"Then Enoch—"

"He was the robber galloping away to fetch Dr. Neville. *She* was there, the whole house lit up, burning candles and oil as if they had three ships at sea. Mrs. Oakes fell downstairs, you see, and it started the little one coming, and it frightened her and Peter—he told me it had been so long since he had been a new father, he was fairly losing his wits. The boy had to have sense for the both of them."

"What I have gone through!" Jennie said. "What I have *imagined*! I am no older than those two in the kitchen."

"Come to bed," he said drowsily, falling back among the pillows. She slid into his arms between the chilly sheets, and the warm comfort of each other's body was narcotic.

"He was fair astonished to see me, and horror-struck to know that the children were gone, and so far in their bare feet and nightgowns. I said we would keep Sarie here for all tomorrow, and Enoch will come for her late in the day. Peter said to tell Sarie she had a little brother now, as well as a big one."

"You know what this will mean?"

"What?" He was yawning.

"After Bell Ann finishes asking us why it took so much noise to bring a baby home, and how far they had to go to get it, she will be asking us about *her* little brother or sister, or possibly one of each at once, like the Kilburn twins."

Twenty-Six

I N A FEW HOURS everything was noisily awake except for the two children, who slept curled together like kittens under the plaid. They didn't wake until all the chores, including Bell Ann's, were done, and the porridge was bubbling gently while Alick stirred it, and Jennie was setting the table. Bell Ann sat up yawning, flushed with sleep; Sarie still nestled under the plaid, as if by accepting the magic she had become loath to leave it. She warily gazed at Jennie over the edge while Jennie told them the news.

"Your mother tripped and fell down the stairs, and that was the crash you heard. It frightened her and your papa too, in case she had broken any bones. Enoch very sensibly decided to get Dr. Neville to come, and you heard *him* galloping away, not a robber. *Well*—" She drew the word out to whimsical length, which Bell Ann recognized as the prelude to a sensational disclosure and settled herself comfortably, like a hen on her nest, gray eyes wide with pleasurable anticipation.

"*Well*," Jennie said again, "your mama hasn't broken any bones. She is feeling very well, and now you have a little brother, as well as a big one."

Sarie burst from the covers like a jack-in-the-box and cried, "Oh, I wish I'd stayed home so I could be there when Dr. Neville brought him!"

"You were too afraid to stay," Bell Ann said with annoyance. Her cheeks were a deeper red. "You were *positive* it was robbers and murderers."

"That was *then*," Sarie crooned. "But now I know. A baby brother! I can hardly wait to see him!"

"We could go paddling and ride Brisky," Bell Ann said coldly. "I s'pose those things don't matter now."

"Oh yes, they do, Bell Ann. You know how I always love to play here. But this is different."

"You may as well make up your mind to play," Jennie advised her, "because they are all going to get their sleep today, after being up most of the night. Enoch is coming for you this afternoon."

"All right," said Sarie agreeably. "I expect he prob'ly needs *his* sleep too. What are we going to do first, Bell Ann?"

"Get washed and dressed," Bell Ann was crisp. "I'll choose a dress for you. Then we have breakfast. Then we can go play."

There was a certain amount of ritual giggling as they ran barefoot outdoors to scamper in chilly dew across to the Necessary, but the usual contented babble upstairs as they dressed, and the laughter and squeals as they brushed one another's hair, were missing. Jennie recognized the symptoms. Something was souring Bell Ann; she wanted to complain, but manners forbade it. Instead of being joyful with Sarie about the baby, she was actually displeased; could it be that she was disappointed because they hadn't made a death-defying escape from thieves and murderers? How could she thrill and impress her brothers and sister *now!* A glory had certainly departed.

During breakfast, while Alick was occupying Sarie—in her euphoria she had become extremely conversational and confidential about her favorite dog, her pet hen, her beloved stepbrother, and what she would like to name the baby—Jennie called Bell Ann into the parlor and shut the door behind them.

"Now tell me just what is wrong, honeybunch," she said. "You are very unhappy. Tell me quickly, and you will feel better."

"No, I won't." Not insolence, simply a prediction. She hunched one shoulder, then the other, pushed out her lower lip, bit it back, pleated her pinafore with her fingers, and then gave Jennie a blazingly hurt and angry gaze. "Dr. Neville is s'pose to be *our* special friend. Why didn't she ask *you* if you wanted that baby?" For an instant Jennie was a lady with a parasol walking a tightwire, with a sudden breeze springing up and no net below. Looking back into her daughter's accusing eyes she had not a coherent thought except about the length and thickness of those black lashes, and then the threatening gust subsided, her balance was intact, and she was answering with deceptive ease.

"As a matter of fact, I told Dr. Neville some time ago that we did not need a boy *or* a girl." And what about last night? she thought, surreptitiously knocking on a chair arm behind her.

"But you didn't ask the rest of us," Bell Ann said. "*Me*." She didn't dare add, "You should have," but it was implicit. "And I am the only one in this family who doesn't have someone littler. Pris has got four, and even William has me. But I am Tail Pig."

"Oh, darling," said Jennie, pulling the stiff little figure into her arms. "There are some matters that are for the parents to decide, not the children, and your papa and I have decided what is best in this case. Things don't always come about for *us* the way we'd like, but we go on without pouting or sulking. You have so much more than some little girls have, not having a baby brother or sister is not going to ruin your life."

"Yes, it is," Bell Ann insisted. But suddenly she relaxed in her mother's arms, hugged her hard, pulled loose, and ran back to the kitchen, saying, "First we can walk to the fort, while the boys are away!"

The children and dogs gone, the idea of church and a big Sunday dinner dismissed, Jennie was washing the dishes when Alick came into the pantry and turned her around, kissing her with a vehemence that she returned in kind.

"Goodness!" she said breathlessly. "All this fire after last night!"

"My fire is eternal. It was merely banked for a wee while." He took a towel and dried her hands. "Let us have some fresh coffee in solitude. We deserve the spoiling after a midnight rescue, and then doing all our children's work for them while they will be sleeping deep in the lap of luxury."

They went out to the bench. It would be a hot day, but now it was all dewy fragrance and coolness. "Sunday morning," he said. "Two bonny words, no matter what the weather. And this is perfect; there is even a patch of mackerel sky to promise us the rain we need. Mind you, I was expecting we would be alone like two honeymooners now, the way the night began."

"It was heavenly, Alick, even with the midnight adventure. Can you guess what was displeasing our youngest this morning?"

"Och, she will be praying to the Great Horse to bring her a baby, if she cannot be trusting us and Dr. Neville." He was smiling. "And who knows but what he might be hearing her?"

"He had better not. And I had better be right. Oh, I think I *am*," she said hastily. "You haven't been down to the Yard for your Sunday morning inspection. How do you know the ship is still there? Perhaps the fairies have stolen her away and left you a square-rigged mussel shell in her place."

"So we will sail away to Kilmeny's land. —Och, the beauty! You can see it in her bones. But I'm thinking she will look strange carving her way across the seas with a man in a coat and cravat under the bowsprit. A waistcoat too, and a chain across it. Mr. Babb was most particular about that."

"Supposing Mr. Lincoln hates the sea," said Jennie, "and the very thought of his image riding the waves gives him *mal de mer*. Dipping, rising, up and down, roll and pitch, for thousands of miles. The launching of her could be his undoing. I shall have the brandy at hand."

"Perhaps he is like me, a man who loves ships but not to sail in one unless there is absolutely no other way."

"What of your and Stephen's ship? How real is she by now, or is she still a phantom of delight, like Wordsworth's maiden?"

"She is glimmering just here." He touched the back of his head. "And more than a ghost. When Stephen comes home and the black flies and mosquitoes have gone, he and I and a crew will go into the woods and choose her timber. He has all the oak and hackmatack down east that we will want."

"You will have to go and come by water," she said. "I hope you have remembered that."

"Have I not! But a short sea voyage along the coast is a small thing compared to embarking upon the whole venture. My fiftieth year is nearly upon me, and Stephen is forty-odd. There is no fool like an old fool, unless it is a pair of old fools."

"*Old?*" She fluttered an imaginary fan. "La, sir! Who was in my bed last night? Young Lochinvar?"

"*Dia*, these Highlanders have no shame."

"All the better for a woman who has no shame."

"When can we be sending them all off again?" He sighed. "Though I love them to the last drop of my heart's blood."

The children were coming through the orchard, hand in hand, Bounce ahead and Darroch plodding behind. Bell Ann's head was bent, and Sarie looked solemn. "Very sad, all at once," Jennie murmured. "Now what?"

The children arrived like mourners at a kitten's funeral. "Mama," Bell Ann almost whispered, "I forgot Evelina Ermintrude and Bear last night, and I never remembered them till now."

"You had other things on your mind, sweetheart," Jennie said. "They will be safe until they can be fetched. I am sure the other children will love going to the playhouse without Evelina along being supercilious."

"She is that way," Bell Ann agreed, not knowing what the word meant.

"So is my Gwendolyn," said Sarie in proud ignorance. "But I think she will let Evelina Ermintrude sleep in her bed, Bell Ann, and Bear can sleep with me until they can go home."

"Oh well, all right," Bell Ann agreed, dubiously. They hurried upstairs to collect the other dolls. Sarie was given a child for the day, and they went off to the playhouse with loaded arms. It was halfway between the barn and the Basto line, just off the path between the farms; a rather elegant playhouse, its rooms marked off by lines of blue mussel shells, its own broom to keep the floors swept clear of spills and broken twigs (after storms); cupboards and furniture knocked together by the boys from scrap lumber. It had first been Priscilla's and the twins' playhouse. They had been ceaseless collectors of whatever they could cadge in the house or salvage on the shore, and so now Bell Ann's house was luxuriously furnished with the advantage of never having to be dusted. (Dusting was Bell Ann's most detested task of all her chores.)

The children played there all morning until Jennie rang the bell for dinner, a picnic meal in the orchard, which always enchanted Sarie and gave Bell Ann a chance to be especially gracious. Brisky refused to be ridden in the afternoon, staying stubbornly in the shade at the far side of the pasture, so the girls went down to the beach to play in the tide pools, wearing old drawers and dresses of Bell Ann's and wide-brimmed straw hats. The tide was so far out there was no danger of anyone's tumbling down and drowning.

Jennie ached for a nap, but she would not sleep with the children unsupervised. She urged Alick to seize the moment. "Not if you cannot," he said. She took her own broad-brimmed hat and a book, and he walked with her to where the wagon track turned off toward the Yard. "*She* will be keeping me awake," he said. "The Phantom of Delight. You were no phantom last night, but you were all delight." And he put his fingers delicately on her throat where the blood was rising.

"On the day we first met under Highland skies," she said, "how could we have ever imagined that all these years later you would be making me blush under an American sky?"

Twenty-Seven

B ELL ANN DECIDED she had been a heroine after all, because believing there were robbers was almost the same as *knowing* it; she could hardly wait to tell the others.

They heard the rest of the family before they could see them, singing at the top of their voices about the oak and the ash and the bonny ellum tree, all a-growing green in their own countree. The wagon rattled into the barnyard, with Priscilla driving and William beside her, as the last notes reached an operatic conclusion. Robin Mackenzie cantered alongside on his horse Sinbad, so named because as a colt he had been saved from a wrecked vessel.

Enoch Oakes rode in the back of the wagon with the twins; he'd been singing too, but gave up with a grin of embarrassment when he saw Alick and Jennie. Sarie thought he was handsome. In this case beauty was surely in the eye of the beholder, but that he was a kind and responsible boy was known to everyone. He was sixteen.

Robin was not part of the chorus, but wore what Pris called his mumpish look. Bell Ann danced around, trying to tell her story at a shout while the other four were also talking. They had met Enoch on the way, and they had heard about the new baby. The play had been tremendous, *everything* had been. They were going swimming right now; the tide was perfect, they had time before chores. Jennie and Alick prudently stayed apart from the havoc, and miraculously it was all sorted out, Shonnie in the pasture, and the four gone in to change for swimming.

Enoch carried Bear and Ermintrude in an Indian basket on his back.

"And don't think your twins haven't been plaguing me like sin," he said to Alick. "Well, little Sis, you ready to set sail?"

She beamed, as proud of him as Bell Ann was of her brothers. Jennie gave them each a good wedge of shortbread to be going on with, and Bell Ann and the dogs walked up to the town road with them.

A momentary silence descended upon the world, and Robin was left standing with Sinbad under the rowans. "I feel as if I'd been suddenly struck deaf," Jennie said. "Were they this noisy at your house, Robin?"

He shook his head, with a brave attempt at a smile.

"I hope they didn't come all the way through Whittier singing like a wagonload of roisterers rolling home from a tavern. After all, it *is* Sunday."

"No, they didn't start until we passed the post office." His mouth was so stiff, he hardly moved his lips. It was impossible to ignore such boiling resentment or pure anguish, whichever it was. And perhaps he didn't want it to be ignored; he was only eighteen.

"Well, Robin," Alick said, "things are not right with you. Would you walk down to the Yard with me to take a look at the ship?"

"No, thank you, Mr. Glenroy." Robin spoke with a poignant dignity. "What is not right with me is neither here nor there." He blushed so vividly that his freckles almost disappeared. "I don't mean to say it is not your business, sir, but—"

"It is not my business." Alick smiled and patted his shoulder.

"Come and swim with us, Robin!" Carolus shouted on his way by.

"Thank you," Robin called after him, "but I will be riding home as soon as Sinbad is rested." He kept watching the door as if waiting for Priscilla to come out again, but visibly losing hope.

"Let me water Sinbad for you," Alick said. "He is such a clever handsome beast, it is a pleasure to handle him."

Robin politely gave him the reins, and Alick led the horse up toward the trough, speaking to him in Gaelic as he had talked to his garron Mata long ago. Robin didn't accept the offered opportunity to confide in Jennie or to be tactfully comforted.

"Are you sure you wouldn't like to swim?" she asked. "We could fit you out with something. Or would you have a cold drink?"

"No, thank you, Mrs. Glenroy." He gave her a formal little bow, and turned and walked after Alick and the horse. His shoulders were very square and he carried his red-blond head gallantly high. Bell Ann, coming back from the corner, gave him a hearty salute, which he gravely acknowledged with a few soft words. She followed him to his horse telling him about her midnight adventures; at last she had a listener. Briefly. When he rode away, she sped toward the house and indoors to prepare for swimming. Alick returned and sat on the bench with Jennie.

"He made his farewells like a man going out to hang himself," he said. "He was hoping, he said, to have a few words with Priscilla, but evidently it was not to be."

"All for the love of a lady," said Jennie. "If you can call Pris a lady. Though she may be one, some day."

"I was noticing that she never once looked him in the face. Well, if unrequited puppy love is the worst grief the lad suffers, he will be fortunate."

"But it is no help to be told you'll get over it," she said. "Were *you* in love at eighteen? There must have been someone. You did not grow up a monk, I know *that*."

He laughed, picked up her hand and laid it on his thigh and stroked it as if it were Garnet's back. "Who was *he*, the one when you were eighteen?"

"Let us save that for the night when you tell me why you laughed when I asked about *you*."

"You know," he said, "I feel as if we have made a brief journey into the land of our youth, and we have returned as swiftly as Iolaire was flying away from William."

"Are you satisfied to return?"

"Och, aye. If only we can run away there again."

At sunset the family was still at the table, leaning on elbows amid the empty plates. Bell Ann had moved to Alick's lap. The play had been temporarily done with, though the subject would be bobbing to the surface at unexpected moments for days to come, especially with William, who stored much. He had spent most of his free time on the wharves with some congenial town boys, and had seen a Spanish ship come in and the Customs inspector go aboard. Late Saturday afternoon the *Lady Lydia* arrived from Boston, and he had seen the actors coming ashore, talking in high style, with gestures; and he had earned five cents carrying a lady passenger's bag to the hotel. She was very elegant and talked fancy. The actors caught up with them, and they all bowed to the lady as they passed; she told William they were thieves and mountebanks.

The twins had traveled the length of Main Street, missing nothing. At the sawmill they watched the great wheel in motion and Ki Bissett and his crew sawing out broad white pine planks from some of the ancient giants.

"It did not seem right, somehow," Carolus said. "After they had lived so long. Think how much history they knew without even knowing they knew it."

Carolus had then gone along the riverside behind the mill, and Sandy went to Morse's second-hand shop on the eastern side of the bridge to see if by some magic a sextant had appeared. One had. Mrs. Morse had bought the entire contents of the attic of a house on the east bank; the heirs were from away and not seafaring.

"It's perfect!" Sandy gloated. "She said she'd save it for me, so I made sure she put it out of sight while I watched. Now if I can just—" He went from gloating to a worried silence, always a deep plunge for him.

There was no mention of Posy. One of the Bissett youngsters had tagged along with Carolus, asking bright questions and leading him to a flowering swamp plant he'd never seen before. He'd given the child a penny and brought home a sample wrapped in his handkerchief.

Pris had gone sailing with Robin. "We raced Mr. Heriot in *Vixen*, and I had the tiller all the way down to Parson's Cove and back. *Allouette* simply *flew!*"

Alick did well not to visibly flinch. Too often he had seen *Allouette* heeled over until her big mainsail just skimmed the water. "Mr. Heriot blew kisses to me when we passed him," Pris said, laughing. "And Robin called him an old roué and a popinjay."

"I believe the aged reprobate is not yet thirty," said Alick.

"And besides, his wife was with him, waving and smiling," said Pris. "She's as good a sailor as I am. Well, not quite, because I won."

"My dear, you have too much modesty," Jennie said.

"Well, I suppose I must give some credit to the captain and to *Allouette* herself," she admitted. "But not much."

They had all loved the play because it *was* a play, the first professional one they had ever seen. The older three had read it in school and had told the story to William on the way to town that afternoon. He liked best the witches, Banquo's ghost, and the swordplay. Everyone had a favorite most-thrilling part to describe, and to act out as far as the others allowed it. "We almost had to sit on Pris," Sandy said, "or we'd have had Lady Macbeth all the way home."

"How about you two with the dagger scene?" she retorted. "Trying to outdo each other, with your eyes out on sticks, and your voices down in your boots! Papa, the men wore kilts—what do you think of that? And some of them had perfect legs for it, too."

Carolus observed that historically Macbeth hadn't been a bad king at all, any more than Richard the Third had been. "But I *will* say that old W.S. gave us some mighty rampageous good drama."

"If W.S. hears that, he must be humbly grateful," said Jennie, "to be recognized at last."

"Eliza and Sibba had been given tickets, and Captain Blackburn and Dr. Neville were there. He looked so hearty and handsome and deep sea-ish," Pris said, "and *she* looked like an empress!" She went into a lyrical description of Carlotta's dress and hair.

The captain and Carlotta had been invited to join them at supper, for lobster salad and scalloped oysters. "Three kinds of cakes," William said, "and ice cream. And lemonade."

"Everybody had wine but Robin and us," said Carolus. "I thought the way Sandy got drunk after the launching would make a good story, but Sandy said he would kill me."

"And then, after all that food, we danced!" Pris said. "We taught them "The Braes of Moidart." Can you picture it? None of us can do the mouth-music and dance at the same time like Papa, but Professor Stebbins caught the rhythm perfectly and fiddled music to fit it, right out of his own head. He wouldn't dance because he said he looked like an animated scarecrow when he tried it, and he didn't want to disgrace his partner. So Carolus was Miss Nabbie's partner, and she could have been Highland-born, Papa, the way she skipped through it. The General clapped the whole time, stamping his good foot. Even Mrs. Mackenzie liked it. The way Captain Blackburn kicked up his heels, I'm sure I shall never regard him again as I have in the past, and Dr. Neville was quite marvelous to watch."

"Who was your partner, Sandy?" Jennie asked.

He grinned. "Miss Frank. Because Septimus Frye—"

Priscilla went silkily on as if there'd been no interruptions. "Mrs. Mackenzie asked William if he danced at home, and he said yes. Sibba was watching from the hall, so Mrs. Mackenzie called her in, and they made the dearest little couple." She smiled at William. "She's not much bigger than he is, you know. And with a tiny waist he could get his arm around."

William, surprisingly, looked pleased, even a bit smug.

"Light-footed, is she?" his father asked.

"Lighter than any girl in *this* house," William said. "But I reckon Septimus Frye thinks Pris is thistledown."

"Oh, William" Pris said. "What *nonsense*."

"It's true," Sandy burned bright with mischief. "He *had* to dance with Miss Frank sometimes, but when he could get away with it, especially when she played the polka, he made a beeline for Pris like Garnet going for a mackerel. And he caught her before Robin could, each time."

Pris sat very straight and spoke with scorching hauteur. "Thank you, Alexander Glenroy. You are not only very *un*flattering, but you are giving an entirely false impression of what occurred."

"Hoity-toity!" said Sandy. Carolus chuckled, and William tucked in his mouth trying not to laugh. "Didn't he beat out Robin?" Sandy appealed to them. "And whenever he had a chance to put his arm around her, you could *see* how he enjoyed it. Fairly made his teeth water."

"Comparing me to a mackerel again, I see." Pris tried for ennui, but was not successful.

"And you enjoyed it too, Pris. You know you did!"

"Papa!" she appealed. "Mama! Are you going to allow this—this hectoring and harassing?"

"Enough, Sandy," Alick said.

"What did I do?" He was aggrieved. "I wasn't telling tales! What harm if he liked dancing with my sister and she liked it too? It would have been unmannerly if she showed she *didn't* like it. I don't think Miss Frank was upset. Robin turned mighty black, though."

"He had no reason for that!" Pris snapped. "Between his glowering at me from corners and Septimus prancing around me with his dimples and all his flourishes, I was dreadfully embarrassed. Thank goodness Miss Frank didn't take it too seriously, but I was almost wishing I hadn't come."

"Ho, ho!" said Carolus. There were some snickers, which were quickly stifled when Alick looked around the table.

William cleared his throat and said in an elderly tone, "Bell Ann had quite an exciting experience, didn't she?"

"Yes, I did!" Bell Ann sat up on Alick's knee.

"I hope you all appreciate how brave Bell Ann was," Jennie said, "to walk home that distance in the dark—"

"And *Sarie* was so scared," Bell Ann reminded her. "I had to keep telling her we were safe." Reluctant to give up the floor, she said, "Sarie says dancing is bad because it leads to fornication. Do you know what that word means?" she addressed William like a schoolteacher.

"No," said William. "Do you?" She shook her head.

"Sarie doesn't even know. It is something bad, though. Stealing, perhaps, or saying dirty words."

The twins were abnormally sober. Pris coughed shatteringly into her napkin and blinked wet eyes at her mother. "It was either that or explode."

Bell Ann leaned her dark head against Alick's shoulder. "If God made music and dancing, how can they be bad?"

"Some of us are not believing that," Alick told her.

"William," said Jennie, "did you see the lady again? The one who said the actors were thieves and mountebanks?"

"Oh yes," he said, off-handedly. "She was Lady Macbeth."

Twenty-Eight

MACKEREL SKY, TWENTY-FOUR hours dry. It was usually right. This time it took longer, but the scent and feel of the coming rain was strong enough Monday morning to discourage thoughts of washing, and Jennie secretly rejoiced. Sandy went to the Kilburns', Carolus did his and Sandy's work and set out on his own. He had had a dream last night, he said, about the old fort. He'd been wandering about in it in an odd sort of twilight in which everything was as clear as if at noon, and outside the wall, where Gabriel Mannering's garden used to be, there stood one tall, single, superb bloom. He had never seen anything like it before.

"It's queer," he said. "The dream was in color, I remember how green everything was and the river was so blue. But I can't remember what color the flower was, except," he was beholding it in bedazzled memory, "that it was what you'd expect to find growing in Paradise."

Pris was washing the milk pails. She said, "You are lucky to have such a dream. You will probably always remember it." She had been very quiet this morning.

"Yes, I always shall," he said simply. "Until I find it."

"You sounded envious," Jennie said after he left. "Why? You must have lovely dreams sometimes."

"Yes, but I don't expect them to come true. I'm too old for that." They were interrupted by the return of William and Bell Ann with the eggs. They were going to pick huckleberries before it rained, and continue to be each other's audience for tales of their recent adventures.

"Mind you keep picking while you're talking each other's ears off, if you want huckleberry fool for supper tonight!" Jennie called after them.

They were already into their stories when they passed the springhouse. Bounce saw some of the men coming in and went to meet them. Jennie passed the time of day with them when they went by the rowan trees, and seeing Harry Shaw coming behind them (for once) with his characteristic loose-footed gait, head down, she waited to speak to him rather than seem to snub him. So much had happened since his father's intrusion on Friday that she had forgotten it until this moment.

Harry would have slouched past, pretending she wasn't there, but she said, "Good morning, Harry," and he touched his hat without glancing toward her, mumbling, "Mornin'."

"How is your mother keeping?" Jennie asked. "Well, I hope."

He stopped and took off his hat, so unusual for him that she was startled. "She's good. Always is." He seemed immobilized, staring at her with surprised greenish-hazel eyes. With his thick, slightly curling, fair hair, his fine features, and those astonished eyes, he appeared hardly older than the twins, though he was in his twenties. *Vulnerable* was the word that came to mind. She suspected that his father bullied him, and she spoke as if to a painfully shy child.

"Harry, couldn't you bring Lily along with you some morning, so she could spend the day with Bell Ann? I would send a note by you to your mother." She rarely thought of him as Lily's father, by a hired girl, when he was seventeen or so. The girl had run away.

His fingers busily worked at his hat brim, but at least he was looking her in the eye. "Marm don't allow the young one off the place without her, 'cept for school." She wondered if *he* ever thought of himself as Lily's father.

"I'm sorry about that," Jennie said. His eyes swerved away from her, looking over her shoulder. Pris had come out.

"Good day, Harry!" she called.

He mumbled again, and went on.

"Well, we know already that Mrs. Shaw doesn't let Lily out of her sight," Jennie commented.

"Bell Ann is going to write Lily a letter," Pris said, "and I have promised to see that it is mailed."

"I hope Lily will be allowed to read it."

The air was stifling with late summer heat, but very clear. On the river two small fishing sloops were becalmed on water like colorless glass, and the crews were getting their sweeps out. The sky seemed to drop lower and lower, and a veery in the woods was unnaturally loud in the hush, as Pris was unnaturally quiet. Jennie would not ask anything, but she was relieved when a peapod flew out of Pris's hands, scattering peas all around, and she exclaimed in a brief fiery burst.

She apologized afterward. "But I feel so itchy and nervy and depressed this morning. I *hated* being a hypocrite about Septimus Frye! I sounded such a fool at the table. I kept expecting somebody to say 'the lady doth protest too much,' but the twins don't remember that in Hamlet, or else one would have used it!" Her eyes glistened with appeal, not defiance. "Because I *did* like it, Mama. Septimus is an older man, and he dresses so beautifully and wears such heavenly cologne, and his dimples are so—so beyond description. I don't suppose *adorable* is the word for a man. I've never really looked hard at him before, but when you are dancing with a man, and he is holding you, it is different. Suddenly it is all very different."

"Yes, it is," said Jennie.

"I wouldn't have offended Miss Frank for the world, and I don't think she *was* offended. But Robin behaved as if I were either a seductress or a ninny *asking* to be seduced. No one else looked at me like that."

"Robin was very unhappy yesterday afternoon," Jennie said.

"He was sulking! Of course," she added offhandedly, "I may have made it a little worse, I was so cross with him. I smiled at Septimus as if we had a secret, that sort of thing. Flirting, I suppose. I've never had much opportunity for that, and it was fun."

"I remember how much fun," Jennie said. "With Squire Robard's son, and now he's married to your Aunt Sophie. Imagine, he is your uncle!"

Pris ignored that. "When I woke up Sunday morning I felt I'd gone a little too far, and I was prepared to be Miss Pris Propriety, but Robin must have waked up sulking. He came downstairs all humped up like a hog going to war, and he kept it up all morning, except before his father and mother. And *except* when he was making such a fuss about Margery Dalrymple outside church. Well!" She flung back her head. "I took the wind out of *his* sails! I behaved as if Margery was a perfect dear, adored her dress and her parasol, and I congratulated Robin on his good taste until he wanted to slap me, but it was his fault in the first place for being so— so *proprietorial* about me the night before, like a possessive prig of a husband."

"That's a well-turned phrase if I ever heard one," Jennie said. Pris laughed, uncertainly.

"It *was* good, wasn't it? Of course he revenged himself by *not* taking me sailing after dinner, and he knew I wanted to go again. Simply walked off without a word to me and took William instead."

"That was nice for William."

"But Robin had no right to glower when they came in and found me playing croquet with Seven and Miss Frank, and the twins. We were not alone, for goodness sake! We were not even partners."

"*Seven?*"

"That's what his closest friends call him. He hates the name Septimus, and since he's a seventh son he prefers to be called Seven. It's different, don't you think? I said I could not imagine having six brothers—*three* felt like a dozen. At supper last night, Mama, I felt positively inundated by brothers. Even William is growing pert. Who ordained that women should be the born victims of male conspiracies?"

Jennie began to laugh, and Pris scowled. "It is not funny, Mama! It is a terrible *fact*."

"Yes, it *is* a fact, except that men sometimes think they are the victims of female conspiracies, so they are always expecting an ambush."

"Papa is not like that!"

"No, he is *sui generis*."

"Himself!" Pris said triumphantly. "Like no one else. One of a kind."

"And so was your grandfather Hawthorne."

"I feel as if I know him, you have told us so much about him. But I wish I knew more about my Glenroy grandfather. Papa says only that he was a soldier, and he is buried somewhere in America. I'm sure he must have been very brave, but I wish he hadn't died so far from home, never knowing his little boy. It always makes me so sad to think of it. At the same time I feel so fortunate to know *my* father."

She was still troubled. "It's a relief to tell you about Seven, and all that, but Robin and I have never been at daggers drawn this long before. Usually we have one grand battle, and that is the end of it. I *hated* having him go home like that, but why should *I* be the one to end it? I didn't begin it."

"Probably he feels just as injured as you do. So it will go on until one of you says 'To the devil with pride!' and stops it. It depends upon how much you want peace."

"I suppose." Pris looked disconsolately out at the silver glass of the river. The sloops had rowed themselves out of sight. "But even if I wanted to, Maddox is a long distance, and before I see him again he's likely to be really wound up like a ball of yarn and tucked away in Margery Dalrymple's workbasket."

"You shouldn't mind, if you don't want him for a beau, just a comfortable brother or a cousin."

"I *would* mind," Pris said, "very much. Because Margery will be thinking that he *was* my beau and she has taken him away from me, and she will gloat."

Remembering herself at seventeen, Jennie didn't attempt to discuss the logic of this. "Will you go down to the shore and cut some greens? The orach is thick, I noticed yesterday."

Priscilla got a knife and a basket and went away whistling a doleful tune. Jennie was free to think of something else. William, for instance, dancing with Sibba and being so nonchalant about it afterward. Neither twin would have shown such *sangfroid* at twelve. Perhaps Sweet William was not going to be a shy man after all. She felt a pang for his little-boyhood, but decided that it was a trifle early for nostalgia.

As for Pris's pleasure in Septimus, she had once experienced the same sensations; she hadn't had to wait until Nigel to know them, those first flares of surprised and joyful recognition, as if with the first taste of ice cream and the realization, *This is what I was born for*, promptly wanting more.

Yes, she knew, and along with knowing she was discovering a mother's reaction to the phenomenon. Had they waltzed? No one had mentioned that. But there'd been quite enough with the reels and polkas. She was glad Maddox was a good distance away. She was almost positive that Septimus was cautious enough not to risk losing Glenroy business by coming to court where he'd been forbidden.

Of course he could always find an excuse; after Saturday night and Pris's eager response, with the little frills she'd added to enrage Robin, how long before he came riding down with another perfectly legitimate reason? Pris couldn't be out fishing every time, and even if he couldn't see her alone, nobody could stop the messages. A touch, a glance, one word—

Courage, Jennie! she admonished herself. Just think how much fortitude will be called for when the twins are old enough, so you're likely to have three in love at once, and William apprenticing for it, and their father trying very hard to keep his composure.

The rain began before dinner, and not in delicate showers. The berry-pickers came back temporarily talked out, and huckleberry fool was assured for supper. Carolus returned, and Sandy walked in with his hair plastered to his head and his clothes to his body, water running off his earlobes, his nose, his chin. He looked as he had when Alick dowsed him the night of the launching. He wasn't needed to mend harness, tradi-tional chore for a rainy day; Mr. Kilburn preferred to do it, so Sandy was excused until the evening chores.

William whittled on his Baltimore clipper. Sandy went upstairs to read Bowditch, but fell asleep to the music of rain on the roof. In the same room Carolus worked on his herbarium. Pris and Jennie took turns reading aloud while the other let out hems and sewed on buttons and Bell Ann basted a bib for the Oakes baby. Pris wanted to read poetry. Wordsworth was not romantic enough for her, Grandfather Hawthorne's Cavalier poets did not suit either, but Shakespeare did.

" 'For valor, is not love a Hercules, still climbing trees in the Hesperides?'" she read with feeling while Bell Ann breathed hard over her needlework, and William whittled and heard nothing around him. Darroch snored, Bounce chased squirrels in his sleep, and Garnet watched him sleepily from the other end of the camp bed.

"Subtle as a sphinx; as sweet and musical
As bright Apollo's lute, strung with his hair;
And when Love speaks, the voice of all the gods
Makes heaven drowsy with the harmony."

Pris gazed into space, her lips parted. Seeing Love as nymphs and shepherds dreaming in each other's arms on the slopes of Olympus? Or a dancing Septimus with those adorable dimples? Jennie hoped Priscilla's appetite for ice cream would not grow extravagantly fast.

The rain was intense while it lasted, and then all at once the wind veered around to the northwest. Untidy bundles and frayed rags of cloud were blown out to sea, leaving a polished blue sky seemingly held aloft by spruce tops hung with diamonds. A rainbow bridged the river from the Basto barn to a hilltop church. Everyone but Sandy ran out onto the wet grass, into air aromatic with drenched woods and flowers. High on the barn *Artemis* flashed in the wind; an osprey family fished, an eagle rode high as the rainbow.

Sandy came downstairs disgruntled because he had slept so long and so hard, and now had to go up the road and do chores. Jennie took pity on him and told him to take Perry. By the time he could lay hands on a horse who did not want to leave home this late in the day, he was completely awake, and rode away in a happier mood.

David walked in just before supper. No one could express so much in complete silence as David did. His smile made manifest his pleasure at being home, the very movements of his hands were eloquent as he brought out his gifts. Whenever he completed a commission, he also sent presents to Gwynneth's family and banked an equal sum for Geraint. This time he had brought Alick a meerschaum pipe, and for Jennie a scarf of peach-colored silk gauze fine enough to draw through a ring with room to spare. Bell Ann had a little locket, Pris an Indian-woven workbasket of sweetgrass. Books for the twins: *A Captain's Adventures* and *Travels of a Botanist*. William received a collection of miniature blocks and anchors for his models.

David had also stopped for the mail, but that could wait to be enjoyed after supper.

The children did not hang on David just for the fairings he brought them. He had always been in their lives, like their parents. Priscilla had been an infant when the boy appeared at the door signing that he had come to work for them. Earlier he had saved their lives, and this house had been his home, grim as the existence had been; what else could they do but make room for him?

Watching his talent ripen had been a privilege for Jennie and Alick. For the children, learning from babyhood to communicate with David had been another sort of gift and privilege. He was eighteen when April died, and if he shed tears for the child who used to stand on the toes of his boots, hugging his legs to be walked about the house, her parents never knew, but he had been a rock for the twins and Pris. He sacrificed hours of his free time from the Yard to row or walk them on long excursions up and down the river, where they cooked their food over a campfire like Indians.

After supper tonight they all went out with him for a walk. They had much to tell him, and it meant giving one another time to make each story full and vivid. They would be polite because otherwise they would make no sense for David; he would simply laugh at them and walk away.

"David should have children of his own before he is much older," Jennie said. "If the right woman would chance him, she'd be very fortunate. But if the wrong sort took advantage, I'd be as ferocious as any mother could be."

"He is not looking upon you as a mother," Alick said dryly. "He has been in love with you since he was twelve years old."

"Children take fancies. William is twelve, and he worships Thankful."

"It is different with David. You came into his life at a terrible time for him."

"He came into our life," she corrected him, "at a terrible time for *us*. He saved us, so we belong to him. I think he loves you and me as one entity, the *Us*."

Alick smiled, and she put her forefinger on his nose and pressed. "If that expression is intended to be enigmatic, it's not working." She opened the package of mail. "A lovely thick letter from Sylvia; she always writes a book. And what is this, for Alexander Glenroy, Esquire; Ship Builder, South Whittier?" She held it up. "From Edward Jennings, Attorney at Law, Wiscasset, State of Maine. Such beautiful calligraphy. And, judging by the thickness of the paper and the amount of sealing wax, this is extremely important."

He reached out and plucked it from her hand. "A mysterious benefactor," she rambled on, "has left one of our intelligent and handsome children a fortune. Mind you save the wax for William."

He slit the letter open, then she took his knife to open Sylvia's, saying, "What does Mr. Edward Jennings really want? Does someone need you for a witness?"

Twenty-Nine

H E DIDN'T ANSWER; he had become a different man, with lines gone deep in his face and a grayness around his mouth, which had thinned almost to invisibility. He was staring down at the letter in his hands, and his grip on the paper was so tight he seemed about to rip it into shreds. She felt the familiar shutting-off in her throat, the necessity to force a breath and to swallow.

"What is it, Alick? *What is it?*"

His head came up. His eyes were opened wide, but it was as if he did not see her.

He spoke just above a whisper, and his speech was a river of sibilant Gaelic; she had enough of the language to know he was cursing as he had once cursed a man in her hearing. Except for the time he had nearly killed Zeb Pulsifer, she had never seen him so angry since, and *anger* was a feeble word to use for this. He thrust the letter at her. It took her a dazed few moments to see what prowled among the convoluted legal phrases. Then it sprang out at her with bloody claws, the threat of Edward Jennings' client's action in a court of law against Alexander Glenroy on the grounds of slander, if said Alexander Glenroy was not able to restrain his minor child Priscilla Glenroy from disseminating malicious lies with intent to destroy the good name of Caroline Emma Goward, deceased. Substantial punitive damages would be demanded.

Her head rang as if she'd been suddenly boxed hard on both ears by invisible demons. She sat down and read the letter through again. "They must have taken leave of their senses!"

"They will be returning to their senses very soon," he said, "before I sleep tonight."

She reached out and seized his hands. "Alick, you can't go now, you are beside yourself!"

He wrenched his hands free, "Of course I am, woman! And so should you be!"

"I am! So much that I—but listen, if you go to them now, like this, they will bring an action for trespass or criminal threatening, even assault and battery if you so much as brush your hand against Goward's arm. Tomorrow morning we can drive to Maddox and see young Mr. Dalrymple."

"Do you think we can endure until then? You may, but not myself. I am telling you, Jeannie, I am as afire with this as I ever was at Linnmore."

She went around the table and tried to embrace him. "With the way you look," she said, "and the way I feel, I am positive we should not go near them tonight. If we take the time to approach them through our attorney talking with theirs, it could all burn off like morning fog."

She was not half so reasonable as she sounded. Her hands shook partly from the desire to seize Bethiah Goward by the shoulders and shake her half-senseless, and then to slap her face scarlet. She knew the girl was to blame for whatever this was, because Pris had interfered between her and the younger children. But if they claimed grounds now for legal action, whatever Alick said tonight in the Gowards' own house would give them ammunition of which they had never dreamed.

"We know what has happened, and they do not," she said. "Bethiah has been concocting stories and then reporting them to her parents as malicious gossip. They aren't cold-blooded in this; they are grief-stricken to hear their dead child abused."

"Grief-stricken! They have taken the devil's own time to be getting there! 'Substantial punitive damages.' Does that sound grief-stricken? Will a raid on our savings and perhaps the ruin of our business mend their grief? Dia, the poor chailin, they are using her in her grave to make money for them, for new carpets or dresses, or a champion stallion for the horse farm. How much grief can one put a price on, and how high a price will dry a parent's tears?"

The Gael was in full dramatic spate, and she could have enjoyed it under other circumstances.

"The deaf man will aye hear the clink o' money. So will the heartbroken man, it seems. No, I will be having no lawyer writing to *his* lawyer for me. But first I will be hearing it from Priscilla's own mouth that she has not said one word which could be made into a slander, and then they will be hearing that we expect an apology either in private, on the spot, or it is I who will be bringing an action."

"She will be devastated to have to hear all this."

"It concerns her," he said implacably. "She has a right not to be cosseted as if she is no older than the other children."

"And after you speak with her, you are going to see Eli Goward, tonight?"

He nodded. "Then I am going with you," she said defiantly.

"I was not thinking otherwise." He gave her a quick, hard squeeze and went out to find Pris.

Priscilla's first reaction was the same as her parents'. She was not wounded to the heart, she was outraged. "What awful people they are! They were so mingy and mean when she was alive, making her a slavey at home and then driving her to those classes she hated, just in hopes of turning her into a minister's wife. And then—," she half-choked on tears, "they wouldn't even bury her in her favorite dress because greedy, sneaky little Bethiah wanted it, and her coral beads. "I *know* that because Thankful's mother said Caro wasn't in her best blue, Bethiah's been seen in it since, *and* the beads."

"Bethiah has been doing more than wearing Caro's best blue and her coral beads," Jennie said.

"You are sure you have said nothing that could be made into trouble?" Alick asked.

"I think of her often, when I least expect it. At school we all missed her—it was so strange—one day she was there, and then she wasn't anywhere. Even Fred Coombes was changed by it. Sometimes Thankful and I remember that day when she was so happy at the launching, and we speak of it often when we are sewing. But Papa, if you will fetch out the Bible, I will swear on it that neither I nor any of Caro's friends have ever blackened her name. What bad thing could we say? The really bad thing is the way Bethiah tortured those children. I shall look very hard at Bethiah as I swear on their Bible, and she will know that eye hath not seen and ear hath not heard what I would do to her if I could. And still may do," she added, "if I ever catch her alone."

Even Alick smiled at that. "No need to swear before them. If they refuse to take my word, they can be hearing it in court. Don't be telling the others."

"I am going with you. It is my affair, Papa, and I mean to speak for myself, and I shan't blubber." She took Jennie's arm. "My dear Mama, you must change to your green and gold and wear your cashmere shawl and the bonnet I trimmed for you, and gloves, and you will be truly impressive."

"I think your father will be impressive for all of us," said Jennie. "But I was not intending to go in my housedress and apron, nor he in his shirtsleeves."

"I will wear my sky-blue." She departed for her room with conscious dignity. Her parents looked ruefully at each other. Alick shrugged. "It is her choice."

"I have a business call to make," Alick told the others when they found him harnessing Shonnie. "Your mother and Pris are going with me, and no one else. And no more questions."

"But will this mean a new ship, Papa?" William asked. "Who in town—"

Alick gently pinched the boy's nape. "Don't be guessing, William, *mo graidh*."

The sun was still high enough so that leftover raindrops coruscated on every bough and shrub. The northwest breeze was fresh and cool. Could Priscilla possibly be as calm as she looked? Her arm didn't tremble against her mother's, but waves of unrest swept over Jennie, slightly nauseating her and then causing cramps; it was like the onset of summer complaint. How awful to be seized away from home, and especially at the Gowards'. How utterly disgusting! The prospect was restorative; she would exert mind over matter and will the nastiness out of existence, at least until they were on their way home, no matter how many times Alick had to stop and let her escape into the bushes.

The sensations disappeared altogether when Alick got down to open the Gowards' gate, and she took the reins to walk Shonnie through while Alick latched the gate behind them. No one moved about the house under the elms in which a robin was singing. A dog barked from out of sight, probably tied near the barns. It looked as though no one was home; Jennie didn't know whether she was relieved or disappointed.

But the front door stood open, and Bethiah appeared in it as they drove into the dooryard. She seemed to be anticipating callers, but not these. Her expression changed to alarm, and she backed away from the door and slammed it shut.

Imperturbably Alick alighted, fastened Shonnie to the rail, then came around to assist Pris. "Thank you, Papa," she said in a clear, carrying voice. He kept his hands tightly on Jennie's waist even after she was on the ground, and they looked into each other's faces. This voiceless communication occurred before every action or decision they undertook together, ever since the first one by the Pict's House at Linnmore.

Then he released her, drew her arm through his, and Pris took his other arm, and they walked toward the piazza. Eli Goward came out and stood with his hands on his hips, impassively watching them approach. He was in shirtsleeves, work breeches, and riding boots; an attenuated version of the man who had come to their house that rainy night. He'd been haggard enough then, but now he looked as if he hadn't eaten a decent meal for weeks, his cheeks were so hollowed and his eyes sunken.

Suddenly children burst out behind him as if a dam had broken, and he turned and waved an arm at them. "*Bethiah!*" he bawled with unexpected volume. "Take these young ones down to the shore! They can paddle if they've a mind to, and keep your hands off Henry's ears; you'll make him either deaf or foolish!"

"Our business concerns Bethiah, Eli," Alick said courteously.

"How could that be?" Goward's voice was uneven with nerves.

Alick took the lawyer's letter from an inside breast pocket. "You must have seen this, or a draft of it when you consulted Mr. Jennings." He held it out.

Goward made no move to take it. His face changed as if he had gone into hiding behind it. "I have nothing to say to you."

"Very well," said Alick. "I will now be seeing my lawyer, and you will be called to answer my complaint that the existence of this letter," he shook it gently, "constitutes a libel on our daughter." He started to turn away.

"Whoa there!" Goward shouted. "Coming up here with that—what in Tophet did you think you could do about it?"

"Threaten you," said Alick blandly. "I have just done so, and I am prepared to back it up in a courtroom. Good evening, sir."

Goward's color was an unhealthy dark red. "Look here, it needn't come to that." He was talking rapidly. "Bad business, neighbors going to court. An apology published in the *Tenby Journal*—that would end it."

Jennie's indignation rose like her supper in her throat, but Alick spoke first. "Would that indeed be ending it?" he asked with a smile. "An apology from *me*, publicly libeling my daughter? I will tell you how it can be ended. You will be giving me the name of the persons who have brought you the cruel gossip about your girl, and the names of those from whom they received it. This is what my attorney will be requiring from you. If you wish to answer him instead of me—"

"How could I?" Goward was nearly stammering. "It is everywhere like a disease. All I know is, *she*—your girl—was the one who started it."

"Started what, Mr. Goward?" Priscilla asked respectfully. "And if it is everywhere, why have we not heard of it? Seeing that I never speak of Caroline except with sadness and affection, I have a right to face my accusers."

It was all Jennie needed. "We would like to speak to Bethiah."

Mrs. Goward burst out of the house, squawking like a broody hen. "Your Priscilla—*she's* to blame for my poor little girl being in her grave! She admired her for her free and easy ways, and your *Priscilla*," she said the word like spitting out phlegm, "encouraged her, and filled her with all kinds of sinful thoughts she shouldn't have been thinking. Making her defy her parents, and that is why she is dead, and when she is in her grave she is blackened and made into a sinner by your precious Priscilla, telling everyone she drowned herself!"

Goward said tiredly, "Julia, go back inside." He took her by the arm and tried to steer her toward the door, but she fought him off, striking at him with her fists.

"My little Bethiah came home from the store just sick with what was being said about Caroline! Your girl has spread a trail of filth from one end of town to the other."

Alick's iron poise was terrible in its own way. "If we are not allowed to be speaking with Bethiah here," he said, "it will be in a court of law."

"Now will you hold your tongue, woman?" Goward shouted at his wife. "If that girl hasn't gone to the shore yet—if she's listening on the other side of the door—send her out here."

She broke into ugly weeping and blundered into the house. Goward, swearing under his breath, flung it open and dragged Bethiah out by her shoulder. The children crowded out behind her, big-eyed.

Bethiah had her arms folded tightly across her apron front, as if holding herself all together, and she kept licking her lips. Her gaze moved rapidly from Alick's face to Jennie's, and then to Priscilla's cold composure. Her father shoved her at them.

"All right!" he said. "Have it out! It is all sending me out of my *mind*!"

Bethiah was fighting, and Jennie felt both admiration and pity. She was a child, still, no matter how ill-intentioned, and she was brave after her own fashion; finally she hardened her face into stolidity, and even put up a hand to daintily touch a curl.

"Now, *mo chailin*," Alick said. "Priscilla has something to say to you."

"Henry, Samuel, Nellie, Grace," Priscilla said steadily. "Do you remember the things your sister said to you when poor Caro died?" They stared witlessly at her. "And Bell Ann and William told you God would not punish Caro like that, and William said you should ask your parents. And then I met you on the way to the smithy and you were all crying. All but Bethiah. She was riding the horse and kept telling you that Caro would be burning forever in hell because she was a sinner. And do you remember what *I* said?"

For a horrifying moment, they seemed paralyzed. So did Bethiah, tallow white and swallowing, unable to turn her face away from Priscilla's.

"Henry?" Pris said gently. "What did I say? I know you are afraid, but your father will protect you."

But it was one of the little girls who spoke. "You said if anybody should burn up, it was Bethiah for saying such things. And you said someone would tell us Caro wasn't burning. And Mr. Coates did."

Now the dam was breached, they all wanted to talk. Both the girl and her father had listened as if stunned, even Mrs. Goward was silent behind the door.

Then the back of Goward's hand across Bethiah's face knocked her head sidewise so hard Jennie thought she heard her neck crack. Tears spurted from Bethiah's eyes and she was for the moment simply a shocked and injured child. Jennie took an involuntary step forward, but Alick's hand closed on her arm.

Bethiah turned so fast she nearly fell down, and rushed into the house, howling.

"I hope you're satisfied!" Mrs. Goward shrieked out at them.

"We are not satisfied to see all the trouble in this house," Alick said. "Only to have our daughter's name cleared."

"And what about *our* daughter's name?"

"It was not blackened except in this house, to those children. It was the torment of those little ones that was the worst crime."

"Are you letting them walk away when it was all Priscilla's fault to begin with?" Julia Goward demanded of her husband, as if nothing that had been said had gotten through to her.

He strode across the piazza and shut the door in her face. Then he came back. "There's fault and fault. I never did find out what was said that sent the girl out of the house that day, a gentle girl like her wouldn't say Boo to a goose." His eyes filled, and his voice thickened. "I know one thing, that second one of ours has got a lot to answer for, the besom."

"Whose was the idea about the damages?" Alick asked.

"Not mine! The lawyer, he's a cousin of my brother's wife, said it was usual and it would scare you into seeing that the talk stopped." His laughter was a hoarse, breaking sound, as if otherwise he'd have been weeping. "He was so da—— so cussed helpful, and all the time it was right in our own doughdish."

"I misjudged you about the money," said Alick. "I apologize."

"Apologies all due from this side." He put out his hand, at once desperate and tentative, as if he expected it to be struck away, but Alick took it. "That Bethiah. I don't know. I don't know." He walked down the steps with them.

"Sometimes it is not easy being the second child," Jennie said. "Sometimes they cannot help being jealous."

"We have a saying in the Gaelic," Alick said. "There are three things which come without seeking: love, fear, and jealousy. And it is not easy raising children even under the best of circumstances. No two are alike."

"And four more to come after her," Goward said despondently. "She's nothing like Caro with 'em."

"I am sorry for your trouble, Eli," Alick said. "I know what it is to bury a child."

Goward nodded. His bloodshot eyes looked blind. He made a weak gesture toward Shonnie. "Fine animal, John Paul Jones. I knew his dam, Columbia. Too bad he's a gelding; he'd have made a great sire with that bloodline. Shows in his eyes and the way he carries himself. Clever, is he?"

"Och, he is not quite a horse angel," Alick said. "Clever enough, but he has a strong will of his own. Haven't you now, *mo gille donn?*"

Goward smiled painfully and put a hand on Shonnie's shoulder. The brief conversation had salvaged a shred of his pride. When they drove away he was still standing there, as if he dreaded going into the house.

"*Mach'a seo!*" Alick said under his breath. The horse knew it for "Let's go," and broke into his best trot toward the gates.

Pris said finally, "Thank you, Mama and Papa, for letting me go. I'd have never slept a wink tonight with it all boiling up like a sickness. I really enjoyed telling that little fiend off! But I was terrified that she had the pygmies too afraid to speak up. You are always saying Bethiah is unhappy, Mama, so she can only strike out, but that was a monstrous way to do it. I think," she said with satisfaction, "she deserved that slap, even though it made me flinch."

"The man has been driven beyond endurance, between his sorrow and that woman," Alick said. "But I hope there are no more slaps. That is no way—she will only pass them on."

"Now that it is over, I can't help being sorry for the child," Jennie said.

Pris was silent for a bit, then she said reluctantly, "I can see why, a little, I don't think Mr. and Mrs. Goward are people who can show affection as you do to all of us. When you are angry with one of us, it is a terrible thing to know we deserve it, and none of us goes off thinking with clenched teeth, 'I am going to get even with them.'"

Suddenly Alick began to whistle in time to Shonnie's hoofs. He broke it off and said, "I would like to dance. I would like to be going to one now. If no one else is having a reason for a dance soon, we will be giving one before we are forgetting how."

"I would love a dance, Papa," Pris said. "I want to think of something merry. I can remember the one when the barn was built."

In the amethyst glow between the last of sunset and the onset of twilight, David sat on the Squaw Rock, smoking his pipe. He got down and came to take Shonnie's head; Alick told him briefly what had occurred, and he gave Pris a smile and a compassionate touch on the shoulder.

"Thank you, David," she said. "I think that I was quite impressive."

With Shonnie attended to and the chaise put away, the three walked together toward the lamplit and not very quiet house. The dogs were in the summer kitchen with the children, except for Bell Ann who was in bed. The rest were entertaining Thankful Basto and Simmy Mayfield with a card game Pris and the twins had invented; it called for any number of players, several packs of cards, and a good deal of noise.

At the sudden entrance of parents, everyone fell into a Sabbath quiet, decorously studying cards.

"They must be holding a prayer meeting," Jennie said.

"Och, but their prayer-books are ill-bound," said Alick. The twins snickered, Simmy's cards flew out of his hand and he disappeared under the table to find them. Thankful held hers before her like a fan, and rolled her dark eyes at Alick. A jaw-cracking yawn caught William unawares.

"Play on, children," Jennie said grandly as she and Alick went through the winter kitchen. Priscilla caught up with them in the parlor.

"Thank you again." She gave each a quick hug. "I felt really grown-up. Papa, you were superb, as always, and so were you, Mama, even if you did forget your gloves."

"Priscilla, if you turn into a female who is obsessed with gloves—"

Pris laughed. "Never! But you both looked so handsome when we came in just now, I was proud. Simmy was so impressed he didn't know where to look."

"Under the table is aye a safe place," Alick said.

"I think he is still down there, unless Thankful has hauled him up. They're *courting*. Can you believe it? May I make chocolate?"

"You may," said Jennie. They went into their own room and shut the door. "Ah, sanctuary," said Jennie. "Well, my dear, we have enough in the house for a dance."

"The humor is off me now," he said. "I could not make mouth-music to save my life. Why did we not raise all our children to be fiddlers, so one could always be playing while the rest of us danced?"

"And we could hire them out, for a pretty penny."

She was putting her bonnet away in the closet when there was a subdued knock at the door. "May I speak to you?" Sandy asked diffidently; his mouth was very close to the panels, so no one else would hear.

"Aye, lad," Alick said. He had taken off his coat and was loosening his cravat. He gave Jennie a humorous look and rubbed fingers and thumb together as Sandy came in; of course the boy was about to ask for an advance on his pocket money so he could buy outright the sextant in Maddox.

"Don't light a candle," Sandy said tensely. "Please don't light a candle. This will be easier in the dark. Well, almost dark."

It was as if the room had dropped into the cellar. Jennie was aware of havoc in the brain but, whatever Alick thought, his voice was dispassionate.

"Sit by me, Sandy. You too, Jeannie."

They sat on a row on the side of the bed, Sandy in the middle, facing the western window and the black forest across the field, which seemed to be moving stealthily closer with the approach of night. Sandy was so taut it was as if fine tremors shook the very air about him, and Jennie wanted to put her arm around him to ease her apprehension as well as his, but she folded her hands tightly in her lap and waited.

"I lost all my money," Sandy said.

The five words made no sense; she was still waiting for the confession that must be made in the dusk.

"How?" Alick asked.

"It was a lottery," Sandy said desolately. "Last Saturday. Well, it was more than one. I know how you disapprove of them, but people do win, and why not me? You see, there were three, and if I'd won just *one*, I'd have had enough for the sextant, and I could buy my militia gear now too, and have it all taken care of, you see." His parents' attentive silence weighed heavily on him, and he hurried. "I'd have had enough to buy Carolus's gear too, just think of it! Then he wouldn't have to save toward it, he could spend his money on books and all the foofaraw that botanists like. I *really* wanted to do this for Carolus, and I know he would do the same for me, if he was as brave and adventurous as I am."

"Brave and adventurous," Alick repeated thoughtfully.

"It *does* take bravery and a talent for adventure," Sandy's voice cracked, "to gamble in a lottery."

"In three of them," Alick commented. "I don't know if I would be calling it that—well, yes, perhaps, with a few more adjectives. You were feeling very lucky, is that it?"

"Yes!" By now his voice was hard to control, but he charged valiantly on. "All the signs were right! I stubbed my toe going upstairs that morning, and my left hand was itching all the time I was walking on Main Street. And I'd had this dream of finding gold. Everything looked so *right*! How could I lose? So—," he let out a long tremulous breath and slumped between them. "I used all my money, fourteen dollars. There was forty-eight cents too, but I kept that. The rest is gone. Forever. I'm sorry," he said in a muffled voice. "I know how you feel about lotteries."

"We are sorry too," his father said. "For you. You are the one who has worked so hard and so long at anything he could find to do. Now you have it to do all over again."

There would be no advance, and Sandy knew it. "I didn't *intend* to lose it all!" he said loudly.

"You are never intending," Alick said. "What would happen if you ever set out with intent? Would we be weeping or rejoicing afterward? You would make gamblers of us all."

"Are you going to punish me?"

"You have punished yourself. Unless your mother has something in mind?"

"No," said Jennie. Poor Sandy, forever falling into traps of his own making. She'd have liked to hug those defeated shoulders, but Life would not embrace him for his mistakes. "Do the others know?"

"No, they'd never let it die." He stood up. "Well, at least I have confessed it to you. Now I shall just have to face what comes. Carolus will cart it to me till I feel like committing twinicide."

"Look at the bright part," Alick suggested. "You are not completely a pauper; you still have forty-eight cents. Men have built fortunes from less."

"What men?" Sandy asked skeptically.

"Go out and have some hot chocolate," Jennie said. "It will cheer you up."

"If they left me any." He arose, walked slowly from the room. They listened, and heard his step quicken as he crossed the hall, and then his voice joined the others. They moved close together on the side of the bed.

"You told me he would not become a drunkard," Jennie said. "Now can you convince me he won't become a gambler?"

"No, but he may become a man who built his fortune from forty-eight cents, and we will be looking back fondly on this moment and saying, 'Och, but the lad always had enterprise!'"

"I know what happened after your first drink," Jennie lifted his arm and put it around her, and his hand closed comfortably over a breast. "What did you first gamble on?"

"I don't remember. You know how children are with their surmises and guesses. Gambling was one of the Seven Deadly Sins in the cottages, and we were on our way to That Place we couldn't be mentioning, ruled by That One we couldn't name. But we gambled just the same, without a penny amongst us."

"We did too, and we did have pennies to lose, and we received no more pity from Papa than Sandy received from us."

"And then one day you and I met, and gambled on each other." He kissed her. "I staked my life on you. I hope the gods of luck will be as kind to Sandy."

Thirty

T HANKFUL AND SIMMY left with their lantern, escorted on their way by
Pris, the twins, and the dogs. William was sent to bed, and when
Jennie went up to kiss him goodnight, he said that he'd told David about
the kite. "He will make me another, but not like Iolaire. If I can't have
her, I don't want something almost like. — Do you think Thankful will
marry Simmy?" He sighed and turned over without waiting for an answer.

Jennie, Alick, and David sat down to finish the chocolate. David had
received a letter from Gwynneth, saying that Geraint had broken his leg
on the *Susanna*'s last voyage from Liverpool and was staying with her in
Charlestown until it mended. It was a good time for the three to be
together for a visit if David would come. David could; he was not needed
at home, and he was between commissions. He would be gone before
they arose in the morning, riding to Maddox with Levi Winter, from
Job's Harbor, who took a load of garden stuff to town every Wednesday,
and passed the Glenroys' road sometime between four and five in the
morning. The family could mail their list of errands to Gwynneth for him
to do.

Jennie and Alick read Sylvia's letter in bed; it was a perfect antidote
for the scene at the Gowards'. Even though William was now a bishop,
Sylvia's letters always seemed to have been written in a country rectory;
it was as if she carried that element with her wherever she went, an
ambience of old gardens growing green and sprawling into a jungle of
blossoms and bees at the foot of high hills that changed their carpets with
the seasons. One instant they were mirrored perfectly in the broad
stretches of sky-colored water far below, and the next instant the images

were swiftly wiped away by the wind, which Jennie swore she could sniff and hear in the written pages. In summer there was the scent of heather and broom, and the cries of the lambs following their mothers; in winter it carried the pure, unscented, nose-pinching cold before snow, and made its own, often tumultuous music.

The children could read the letter tomorrow. Their English cousins were as exotic to them as they were to the English, and they had spasmodic bursts of correspondence which always petered out because on both sides their moment-to-moment lives took all their attention. Yet the contact remained, tenuous as it was, and they loved their aunts' letters. In moments of severe discontent or frustration they thought their cousins must be living lives of infinitely greater satisfaction than their own.

The next day was perfect for washing, with no escape. Jennie arose early to get it over with as soon as possible. By the time the first kettle of water was heating and Jennie and Pris could begin, Carolus had finished the mucking-out and gone to the fort, taking William with him. The image of the dream flower and its location was still so clear, he thought the dream could have signified the location of the missing well. William just might find water; none of the rest were dowsers, but they had never tried William.

"In a family like ours," Carolus said severely, "which is quite talented, by and large, *somebody* should have the gift."

William was amiably ready to try anything. Bell Ann resented not being invited; dolefully she helped with the washing. Spreading wet towels and pillowcases on the grass was not fun, but she cheered up when it was time for the mid-morning strupach. By noon everything was either dry or out of the rinse water and into the sun. It was a superb day, and David would be having a fine sail on the Boston packet. Jennie envied him that without wanting to visit Boston, but Pris said wistfully that she would like to go. It was at least possible one day, not a dream like London, Paris, or Carolus's wondrous flower.

The afternoon was the free property of all, with no dilemmas or crises at the Yard or in the family. A good afternoon, like a ripe red apple, packed tight enough to burst with healthful juices that brought more delight to the palate than Spanish wine. It washed away any lingering aftertaste of the session at the Gowards'. Bell Ann sewed a frill on the Oakes baby's bib, anxious to reach the embroidery; Pris would print out his name when they knew it.

"I s'pose I won't like it," Bell Ann said, "but it's not *my* baby brother." Pris was making a nainsook cap for him.

In the late afternoon William and Carolus came from the fort and found Jennie reading in the orchard. She listened straight-faced to Carolus's complaints, and William tried without success to look humble while his brother blamed him for not being a dowser.

"He kept *giggling*. No wonder it wouldn't work! And then he ate most of our food!" William was sweetly unrepentant. He had his own methods of neutralizing the twins' seniority.

The dogs went hungrily ahead of them to the house. "Well, Carolus," she said, walking with her hand on his shoulder, "the flower could mean something else. Perhaps it signifies the way your career is going to bloom."

"If there is anything left for me to discover by the time I begin it," he grumbled. "*They* are out there, all over the world, laying claim to everything that grows even if it's too small to see without a glass."

"There will always be something new to discover," William said earnestly. "Won't there be, Mama? Same as there'll always be ships to build."

"Yes, so we needn't weep like Alexander because there are no new worlds to conquer," Jennie said. She gave Carolus's shoulder a squeeze, and he acknowledged it with a quick sidelong smile and flash of dark gray eyes very like Alick's.

It was chore time, and as the four straggled toward their work Carolus began telling Pris about William's failure as a dowser, but by now he could see the humorous side of it. Thus the only cloud on a perfect afternoon—hardly a cloud at all—disappeared.

Jennie was feeding the cat and dogs when the bell sounded for the close of work at the Yard. She imagined Harry first off the mark as usual, solitary, always hurrying. To *what*? He was a skilled joiner, but so odd and inarticulate that no up-and-coming girl would chance her luck with him, and he must have known that.

She was kneeling before the stove, scraping out noon's cold ashes, when Miriam Gunn spoke outside the back door as Jennie had never heard her speak before. "Just *what* did you think you was about, Sandy Glenroy?"

"Saving *you*, that's what I was about!" Sandy snapped back. "From that—that *poltroon*!"

"What's a poltroon, some fancy kind of rooster? I can save myself, and I don't need any child nigh unto getting himself killed for me!"

"*Child!*" It was an ignominious squeak. Jennie arose from her knees and went out. They were both extremely flushed and extremely agitated. Miriam was roughly brushing twigs, spruce needles, and dirt off the back of Sandy's shirt while he tried to squirm away from her.

"Look at you!" she scolded. "If you ain't some sight! It's lucky it's not blood I'm wiping off—" She saw Jennie and stopped, but not meekly. Sandy, looking murderous, tried to push past his mother into the house, but she caught him by the arm. "What has happened?"

Miriam was now rubbing her right wrist. The encircling marks were a dark, angry red on her brown skin. "Did Sandy do that?"

"Oh no, no, Mrs. Glenroy!" Miriam protested. "He never did anything but get himself knocked about, and there wasn't any need."

"*Harry Shaw!*" Sandy pitched the name at them. "He had hold of her! I turned in off the road just in time, or he'd have—I don't know what, but I know what it looked like, and she wasn't liking it one bit!"

"I've never seen one of them stinkards I couldn't take care of!"

"Then tell me what happened. You met Harry and he laid hands on you, is that it?"

"Yes'm, because I wouldn't stop and talk. I was coming down to take the shore path home. I've been helping out at the minister's. He called me—" She caught her lower lip under her teeth. "That don't signify. He grabbed my wrist and gave it a twist. *Well!*" Her eyes took on the glaze and shift that Jennie had once seen in her brother's eyes. "I'd have made him some sorry if Sandy hadn't jumped him so sudden, it was like he dropped from a tree onto him. Harry threw Sandy off him so hard I was scared Sandy'd smash his head on a rock like an old punkin."

"He had to let you go, didn't he?" Sandy's voice skidded out of control again.

"He would've anyway, when I kicked him hard enough." Half her rage was from being cheated out of that, Jennie thought.

"You couldn't have got a good kick in, the way he muckled on to you! He was going to drag you off into the woods like a Sabine woman—"

"A *what?*"

"Sandy," Jennie said, "will you please finish cleaning out the ashes?" He went in, grumbling to himself.

"Mrs. Glenroy, I just didn't want him to be hurt." Miriam dropped her voice. "That Harry is some strong for his size."

"Well, so far the only injury is to Sandy's pride," Jennie said, "and I'd rather have that than the bloody kind."

"My pride's a mite bruised too," Miriam said ruefully. "I reckon I needn't have been that hard on Sandy, but I don't know how to make believe I'm one of those damsels in distress in books."

"I never did very well at that myself," Jennie said. "Well, no harm done, but Harry should be warned."

"Please don't, Mrs. Glenroy. He might take it out on Sandy." The girl was politely insistent. "Leave him to us. If he makes me any more trouble, Pa will talk to him." And Harry's father will likely invite Mr. George Gunn to a duel with axes, Jennie thought. It would be like some feisty little tyke the size of Bounce challenging Darroch.

Sandy came out with the ashes and strode past them without a look.

Miriam had been working at the parsonage all day. She was elated about her earnings and looked forward to more work when the baby was born. "River Farm and the Parsonage—that's where I am happiest," she said. "She is a real sweet woman, and *he* makes me laugh when he talks Scotch, and all that poetry." Mr. Lockhart was addicted to Robert Burns.

"You must have something to eat, Miriam, with all the walking."

"I had tea and Scotch bannock before I left. Then Mrs. Shaw drove along when I was just past Three Corners. She and Lily had been to a funeral way up in North Whittier, a Mrs. Erskine. I've heard of her. Pa knows just about everybody there is and ever was in Whittier and half of Maddox. Well, it's natural; Gunns was here before any of 'em."

Jennie was only half-hearing the vivid young voice. She wondered if she was missing something by not knowing Mrs. Shaw, but any neighborly overtures she'd made through the years had met with arctic rejection. Shaw could be one of those men who did not want callers, and his wife avoided provoking his temper. But he could not completely dominate her; big Major was hers, and she drove him when and where she pleased. Most funerals could be turned into legitimate social occasions, if you humored your man by staying away from quilting parties, tea-drinking afternoons, ladies' reading clubs, and other such female foolishness.

"Lily's a pretty little thing." Miriam's voice, which had seemed to fade away while Jennie mused about Mrs. Shaw, was literally returning. The girl came from the house with a mug of water and sat down again, as comfortable with Jennie as if they were the same age. "She looks a dite like Harry, but I can see her mother in her." She took the water in meditative sips. "*She* came down to the Keel not twelve hours after the baby was born. Ran away when everybody was out of the house. I remember. She was white as milk, with these blue places under her eyes," she traced half-moons on her own face with a sturdy brown forefinger, "blue as violets, and she was nearly fainting, she'd walked so far, and she'd had a hard time birthing such a big baby. Of course I didn't know that then. . . . My aunties, they'd been getting crabapples up near the track when she came stumbling down, didn't even know where she was going. They brought her to us, and Marm put her to bed and dosed her up with motherwort tea. That's the best thing after childbirth," she explained kindly.

Jennie said, "I see." I'm sitting here being instructed about the neighbors by a child, she thought, but I'm not a bit ashamed, I'm enthralled.

"You know what she told Marm? Why she ran away from her baby and all? She said Mr. Shaw was going to drive her over to Waldoboro way and leave her by the side of the road, and if she ever stepped foot in Whittier again, she'd be warned off as a pauper or arrested as a vagrant."

"Could he have that done?" Jennie was incredulous. "*Legally?* To a girl who had just given birth to his son's child?"

"Pa said Shaw would be in trouble, not her, because she was so young and been put in their care when they bid for her, but *she* wouldn't believe it. Well, you can see why Marm coddled her the way she did, after what *she'd* been through. . . . Mrs. Glenroy, Saffy'd been *interfered with*. That Harry came into her room in the attic, and before she knew what he was about he had her pinned down and helpless, and afterward he said his folks would never believe if she told it, because she was a nothing. When they found out she was in the family way, they never spared her none. But it wouldn't look good for them to put her out. And everybody'd think it was Harry's even if she never told. Besides, Mrs. Shaw wanted the baby."

Jennie could only shake her head.

"Do you know what Mr. Shaw said she could do after he left her? Be like a squirrel, he said. Use her tail to cover her back. Mrs. Glenroy, she was only fifteen!"

"Is she still there at the Keel? No—I'm sorry I asked that. It is not my business. But I'd like to think she is safe somewhere and has some happiness. Do you know *that* much?"

Miriam shook her head and looked down at the mug in her hands, moving it so that water circled gently. "When she was strong enough, she sailed to Boston on Cap'n Alley's lobster smack. She said she had kin up there. He said he'd do what he could to help her locate 'em. And you know we *never* found out? Old Cap'n was took bad, died, and was buried over on Vinalhaven almost before we knew it, and his nephew, who's Cap'n Alley now, he gave up fishing to take over the smack, and he never knew a thing about Saffy."

"Saffy?"

"For Sapphire. Isn't it pretty? We've had four little Sapphires at the Keel since then. . . . When I was riding along with Mrs. Shaw today, I pondered what *I* knew and *she* didn't." She spoke with a serene and adult satisfaction. "What would they say if they knew where Saffy ran to, Mr. Shaw feeling like he does about the Keel? What if they ever suspected it, and they think she—," she whispered it, "is still there?"

Garland Shaw's look that day, when Jennie mentioned turning up black sheep and skeletons at the Keel, answered this. Perhaps it was coincidence; how could a man of his combustible nature have endured living for the past seven years with even the faintest suspicion that the girl was close by?

"We first heard of Lily," she said, "when Bell Ann was only a few months old. We heard that they'd taken in an orphan baby to raise after someone's widowed niece had died in childbirth. The pauper girl was said to have run away when the rest were all gone overnight to the funeral in Belfast. I don't know just how it got about that *she* was the mother of the baby and Harry was the father, and she wanted to be free of the child and had run away with a peddler, hiding in his wagon. The story must have satisfied the Overseers of the Poor, and of course they could never trace the peddler, who probably didn't exist. No wonder they never found her; she had gone to earth right under their noses."

Miriam emptied her mug. "Poor Saffy. I hope she's happy somewhere."

Bell Ann and William were coming with their eggs, pleased to see Miriam and disappointed that she was leaving, but they were allowed to go as far as the fort with her.

Sandy must have told Carolus about his adventure and put a high polish on it, to judge by their conspiratorial air when they came in. Priscilla had been kept in ignorance, but by tomorrow Sandy would be unable to resist telling her what a fine fellow he had been. But Alick had to know at once, and Jennie made the time after supper by inviting Alick for a walk.

Down at the shore in the roseate sunset light, they sat on the driftwood log among thick patches of mint in blossom, and late-working bees. Sandpipers ran along the shore, always in conversation, like chickadees. The twins were rowing the dory across to the opposite shore. Two home-going fishing boats idled by on coral-tinted water, their sails colored to match.

"I will be having a word with Harry," Alick said. "I'll not have the girl molested on our property. If it happens again, I will be letting him go."

"Miriam begs us to leave it to the Gunns, for fear Harry will take it out on Sandy. She says her father can take care of it."

"Very well," he said reluctantly.

"The Keelers know a good bit about the Shaws," she said, crushing a mint leaf and sniffing it. "For instance, Lily's mother ran away to the Keel because Garland Shaw had her terrified. It was not twelve hours after the baby was born, and she was a child of fifteen, told that she would be turned out to make her living as a prostitute."

"All this going on in the neighborhood, and us not knowing!" said Alick. "Dia, I am glad the child had the Keel to run to; we were certainly no help to her in our ignorance."

"It's chilling, isn't it?" She wriggled her hand into his. "Feel how cold I am. We go along thinking only of ourselves and our children, and all the time there is a horror waiting in ambush, if not for us, then for someone close by. Would you mind putting your arm around me?"

"Not in the least."

The twins had touched the opposite shore and talked with some boys over there, and now the dory was heading home. They were using two pairs of oars, and the dory skimmed the pastel water like a living creature, some kind of water insect with four narrow flashing wings.

"I'd better be speaking with them both," Alick said thoughtfully.

"What are you going to say?"

"Stay and listen," he invited.

"No, this should be a father-son conversation. I was simply wondering if you would advise them not to leap to a girl's defense because they might get the worst of it."

"I am proud of Sandy. I will tell him so, and I think Carolus would be no coward, either. But they should do as Miriam asks, leave him to her and her family. What I am asking is for them to ignore Harry. It is too easy to provoke him, and he has enough of that at work." Then he looked at her with a mischievous, one-sided grin.

"Did Sandy really say 'poltroon'?"

Thirty-One

O N SATURDAY AFTERNOON, while the whole countryside and the birds and the river seemed to drowse in a windless heat, Jennie read Miss Austen in the orchard. The scents of midsummer ripening toward autumn surrounded her. The dogs lay asleep in the grass. Pris had gone with Thankful to help piece a bridal quilt for a betrothed friend in Center Whittier. Carolus was somewhere on the property. William was playing at Three Corners Farm; the alien boys had worn out their welcome there some time ago. The family had moved to Amity and the boys would not be attending the South Whittier school this fall.

Bell Ann was out in the playhouse. Alick was cherishing a few hours of pure solitude in his office at the Yard with his ship plans.

And now Sandy's whistling preceded him into the somnolent shade of the orchard—a brisk, martial tune. Darroch lifted his head and let it fall again, but Bounce ran to meet him, and Garnet sat up on her tree limb and stared toward the sound, her tail switching. Sandy halted on the lawn, gave his mother a sweeping wave of his straw hat, marched down to her, came to a military stop, and saluted.

"I've been discharged," he said jauntily.

"Are you really that happy about it, or are you putting a good face on it?"

"No, I'm happy." He looked it. "Merry as a grig, whatever that is. Some cousins just drove in from Vassalboro and probably saved my life. Mr. Kilburn was not eager to have me paint the house, especially the high bits, and to be honest, I wasn't either. But I was prepared to be valiant. You know, 'Cowards die many times before their death, the valiant only taste of death but once.' " His grin broadened. "I was afraid my taste would come when the ladder and I fell over backward with a crash."

"I don't think your father and I would have been overjoyed, either," Jennie said.

"Glenroys never quiver with fear, at least not in public. But one of the cousins has a great head for heights and also may be part monkey. You should have seen him threatening to do a dance on the ridgepole! They will be here for a week or more, and Mr. Kilburn's foot is much better, so I am not needed any more. I was paid for the whole week, and *this*—," with a conjuror's flourish he held two silver dollars between their faces, one in each hand, "is my bonus."

Her response pleased him; his amber eyes sparkled like a brook in sunlight. He laughed and dropped onto the grass and stretched out, fending off Bounce. "Och, it was a long walk home!"

"Weighed down with all that money."

"But I was not objecting to that, mind you," he said with his father's intonation. He grinned up at her, looking about ten years old. "Och, man, it's a great thing, money."

"Will you be starting out Monday morning to find more work?" she asked. "You've gotten used to all this wealth. You are a plutocrat to the others."

"No," he said, rolling over on his stomach to seize Bounce, who quickly danced out of reach. "I'm rich again, or almost. I can buy my sextant, and I must spend time with Bowditch; he has been on my conscience. And—," he lay on his back again and said, rather shyly for him, "I've been missing them, and this place, and our own animals, you know?"

"We have missed *you*, Sandy," she said.

With this new shyness he said, "Well, I would not like it if you stopped missing me. I would not like it at all, if suddenly you looked at me when I came home as though you are thinking, 'Oh, it is *Sandy*! I forgot him the instant he was out of sight this morning!' "

"My darling, your father and I are not likely ever to stop missing you, even when you are halfway around the world."

"Oh *that*." He dismissed it with transparent relief. "It will be different then—I will be a man—but I have a long way to go until then."

"Yes, you have," she agreed. He sat up and began wrestling vigorously with Bounce. "Sometimes Bell Ann and William look at me like that," he said through the scrimmage.

"They are young," she said. "They can be totally immersed for hours in what they are doing. So can you. But the ties and the love are always there." Bounce seized a mouthful of thick brown hair, and Sandy yelped. "You are getting as shaggy as Brisky," Jennie said. "Your father had better be shearing you tonight." It gave her a chance to lean forward and run her hand over his head.

Hugging the struggling terrier against his chest, he looked up at her with happy anticipation. "Monday morning I am going out with old Carolus, and perhaps we will find the incomparable, supreme, unique plant that will make Mr. Lockhart speechless for once."

When they returned from church the next day, Alick had had a visitor, a young Winter from Job's Harbor, the fifth Job in a direct line. When he turned twenty-one he had refused to join the clan's mass visit to Maddox every Sunday for a long day of churchgoing. He was building a boat, and though he kept the Sabbath in his own way by not literally working, he had ridden up from the Harbor to ask Alick's advice on a problem. He was willing to pay for both the time and the advice if Alick would come to the Harbor and look at his work.

"I told him no fee was necessary," Alick said. "I am too pleased to be getting a look at the competition. He is a bashful lad, but he has a smile to light up the sky. This will be a fine afternoon for a drive, Jeannie, not too warm for us or Shonnie. Shall we be going to Job's Harbor, just you and I?"

"Yes!" Jennie didn't stop to consider. Pris and the twins laughed, but William and Bell Ann were hurt not to be invited, for they had taken a fancy to Job Winter. "There is no room for the two of you," Jennie said, "and we surely would not take one and leave the other."

"Why not?" Bell Ann passionately thought up reasons why she should be the favored one. William suffered in silence, but Bell Ann had to be told to be quiet and eat her dinner or she would have no dessert.

The day had a patina of August gold, under which everything took on a special grace. When the Keel territory began, with a growth of superb spar pines and oak, Alick said dryly, "No wonder Shaw's mouth is watering. There is a small fortune in lumber here, besides all the rest of the land down to the river."

"If George Gunn the First married the sachem's daughter," Jennie said, "then all his descendants have authentic American blood to some degree, and everyone else is a Johnny-come-lately. I wish I'd said that when Garland Shaw came charging in on his high horse."

"Och, he is one who is believing in the divine right of white men."

Job's Harbor was several farms and woodlots beyond the Keel. It was deserted this afternoon except for the young boatbuilder and the live-stock. The houses and barns, all belonging to Winters, were randomly scattered around the harbor; gardens were fenced off from the common pasture. Split and salted codfish were drying on the flakes where the land sloped down to the wharves and workshops. Fishing boats rocked lightly at their moorings in the puffs of south-west wind that came over Winter Head. On the eastern point stood the remains of the old garrison, on which Gabriel Mannering had depended for help against hostile Indians. One of the town's earliest houses kept it company; though much built over, this was still lived in.

"Haunted," the young Job Winter said. "But my uncle don't care. He says they're all kinfolk and won't never do harm to a Winter. But my aunt gets a dite upset with them creaking up and down the stairs half the night and shifting her cultch around in the ell chamber."

He was building his boat in his father's barn, and Jennie left him and Alick in consultation under the skeleton, with hens walking around their feet, and went out on Winter Head and down to the open shore with two friendly dogs whose ancestry was so mixed they could have been the start of an entirely new breed.

It was more than a pleasure to be out on an open sea beach again, to be half-deafened by the roar of breaking seas and the loud rattle of the popple rocks as the undertow dragged them. The wind, hearty with salt and rockweed, whipped at her dress and tore at her hair. She'd left her bonnet behind. With no one to see but the dogs, she took off her shoes and stockings, held up her skirts, and let the water rush foaming around her ankles, pulling the sand out from under her toes as it withdrew for another assault. Gulls cried in the wind and circled above her on tilted wings, watching. The dogs ran back and forth barking and splashing, keeping out of reach of the surf, bringing her sticks and rolling in the glistening windrows of fresh weed. After a time she found a little patch of hot, dry sand at the brow of the beach and dried her feet in it, but she hated to put on stockings and shoes again.

There were shells here that they rarely saw up in the river, some never, but she had nothing she could carry them in, so she took what her hands could hold. Her cheeks and her nose were hot with fresh wind-burn. When she left that tumultuous shore the air at once turned smotheringly close. She realized that she had barely thought of the children until she began to pick up shells, and leaving the beach was so painful she almost wished she hadn't come. It had been home again, and she had not known until now how much she missed it. As she and the wet and sandy dogs followed the footpath among granite outcroppings, the noise of the shore was diminished; she smelled grass now, and barn scents melding with the clean hot reek of drying nets beyond the fish flakes, and she felt a visceral pain of exile which she had not known before except on the night she and Alick left Scotland.

Alick and Job were standing outside the barn smoking their pipes. Longing dropped from her like a wet cloak sliding heavily off her shoulders and leaving her free. Exile now would mean life without Alick, 'O my America, my new-found-land,' John Donne had written in adoration of the woman he loved, and Jennie knew exactly what he meant as she walked toward Alick.

Job was a stocky, sunburnt young man, bashful as Alick said, and he'd been right about the smile. They were treated to cold creamy milk and raisin cake in a spotless kitchen.

"I like it when everybody's gone," Job said. "The place belongs to me and the critters. I can stand out there and scratch the pig's back for an hour if I feel like it." He tossed a hunk of cake to each dog. "Do this, too. Marm don't approve. I take after Old Job, I reckon. Day he got married he wrote in his journal, 'Goodbye, peace and quiet.' "

"I wonder what she wrote in hers," said Jennie.

"Judas, I never thought of *that!*" Job tipped back his chair, laughing, and slapped his thighs. "I hope it was a good one! Well, they was both pushing ninety when they died, and neither had tunked the other one on the head with a stick of stovewood in all that time, so I guess they made do."

He gave them two handsome cod from the flakes and invited them to the launching in the spring. "You may be married by then," Jennie teased him.

He threw up his hands and backed off, shaking his head. "No *ma'am!* I'd have to build me a house first. Can't take her into Marm's kitchen, nor keep her aboard my boat."

"Unless you name it the *Pumpkin Shell*," said Jennie, which made him laugh until his eyes ran water. Alick invited him to the *Enoch Lincoln* launching, and he said reverently, "I'll surely come."

"What a *good* afternoon," Jennie said when they drove away. "Could you help him?"

"Och, aye, it was a simple enough wee thing." He explained, and it was anything but simple to Jennie, but she pretended that she understood perfectly. "The lad is talented," Alick said. "But he chooses to be a fisherman, not a shipwright. Fishing is his calling, he says."

Shonnie was in a tearing hurry for his supper and had to be held in and gently admonished in Gaelic. Finally he settled down to a pace that suited Alick and himself. The interlude on the sea beach was far behind Jennie now, not only in physical distance. It would be dear to her in recollection, like the memories of Pippin Grange; cherished, but not grieved for.

Alick said suddenly, "He is building this boat by himself, for himself, and she will always be his."

"The ships you build are like children who go out in to the world to seek their fortunes," Jennie said. "But what about yours and Stephen's?"

"Och, she will be the One," he said with quiet satisfaction. "The queen of them all. And I will be making at least one voyage in her."

"You *will?*"

He gave her the quizzical look that could baffle the children and sometimes her. "And won't she be expecting it of me, to show that I trust my own?"

"How long will this voyage be?"

"You sound exactly like Bell Ann," he said. "Belligerent and suspicious."

"I know. I heard myself." She put her cheek against his shoulder. "I don't want to lose you off Cape Horn, or to a typhoon in the Pacific."

"A voyage could be as far as New York, or only Boston, and not without you. But it's a long time until we lay the keel."

"I shall try to possess my soul in patience. But imagine you and me and Stephen on the same ship, and you the builder and half-owner, and then remember how we all met." He nodded without speaking. She took his arm and pressed it against her side for a moment and then released it.

When they came to their own road, Bell Ann and Brisky were just turning into it, an apparition that astonished Shonnie as well as his passengers. He tossed his head and whinnied, and Brisky stopped short to reply. He and Bell Ann were unaccompanied. She was wearing William's old breeches and shirt, and she was wiping her nose on a sleeve. She stared blearily at her parents and then opened her mouth in a loud cry of either despair or rage. Jennie was down from the chaise almost before the horse stopped; Alick took Shonnie off the town road and walked back to them.

Bell Ann's eyes overflowed like never-failing springs, tears ran unceasing down over her burning-red cheeks and dripped off her chin. "Darling, tell me!" Jennie implored, which brought out new freshets.

"Now then, *mo chridh*," Alick said, and handed her his handkerchief. She buried her face in it, blotted the drip, blew her nose, and told them between hiccups and long snuffles that she had gone to the Shaws to see Lily, and Mr. Shaw had called her a shameless little slut dressed like that and sent her away. "And Mrs. Shaw wouldn't even let Lily come out!" she howled.

Jennie wanted to sweep the child out of the saddle into her arms, and knew Alick felt the same, but there was such a thing as due process.

"You know you are not to wear those clothes on the public road," she said. "You know you are not to be out on the public road alone. Where is Priscilla?"

There was an especially long bubbling snuffle. "I s'pose she's pouring tea for Mr. Frye."

Alick's hand quivered slightly on the pommel. "And the boys?" he asked.

"They went somewhere, and I *know* they are having a good time, the way boys can do. *They* don't care how Mr. Shaw talked to me." The injustice of it threatened to drown her eyes again. Brisky muttered in his throat and stamped a foot, just missing Jennie's.

"Come along, Bell Ann," Alick said. He and Jennie returned to the chaise, and Brisky trotted along on Jennie's side. Bell Ann looked up at her mother and said plaintively, "Pris *said* I could go, and Mr. Frye saddled Brisky."

"And did Pris say you could be out on the road?" Jennie asked. "Or just that you could ride Brisky?"

Silence, head down, then a sulky and muffled answer. "She said I could ride Brisky."

"And when you ride Brisky alone," Alick said, "it is all around the fields and the edge of the woods, is it not?"

"Yes, Papa." She looked up at them with those appealing eyes, fringed with wet black lashes. "But I wanted so much to see Lily's playhouse, I just—I just *did* it, and I never even *saw* her! And Mr. Shaw was *horrid!*"

She stopped at the sight of Septimus Frye and Bolivar cantering toward them. "Good afternoon!" Septimus called exuberantly, doffing his hat with a sweep appropriate for a cavalier's plumes. "I was hoping to see you!"

"Oh? And why was that?" Alick asked dryly. Septimus chose to be amused, and laughed, holding in the restive Bolivar with one hand, negligently dangling the hat at his side. He was sprucely turned out today in fawn and Spanish blue, and with this, his smile, his excellent teeth, and his dimples, he would have been an enjoyable sight under different circumstances.

Then he saw Bell Ann, and exclaimed in concern, "What happened to *you*? Were you thrown?"

"No," she said in a small piteous voice.

"Bell Ann went on an unauthorized excursion," said Alick. "It seems that her sister was not noticing."

"I must apologize for that. Perhaps I was a distraction," Septimus said with a manly air of contrition.

"It was not your responsibility," said Alick. "Good day, Septimus." Shonnie began to move. Septimus bowed to Jennie with a rueful little grimace of regret and humorous dismay, and rode on.

She left Alick and Bell Ann at the barn unsaddling and unharnessing, and walked to the house carrying the dried cod Job had given them and her bonnetful of shells. The boys weren't in sight, and it was almost chore-time. Priscilla was in the pantry, dismantling the best tea tray, singing, " 'Drink to me only with thine eyes, and I will pledge with mine. Or leave a kiss within the cup—' "

She beheld her mother with happy surprise. "Mama, would you like a cup of tea? There's some left, and it's nice and hot under the cozy."

"Thank you, but no," said Jennie. "Do you know where Bell Ann has been?"

"Riding Brisky," said Priscilla. "Did you meet Seven going out?" Her expression was all bright innocence.

"Yes, we did," said Jennie. "And we also met Bell Ann coming in."

That brought Pris out of the pantry, a plate in one hand and a cup in the other. "What do you *mean*? Where was she?"

"Up on the road. She'd been to the Shaws."

"That little minx!" Pris was shocked and admiring.

"I'm afraid she's not very proud of herself. It turned out badly. Where are the boys?"

"I haven't the faintest idea. Likely not far." Priscilla was perfectly carefree. She saw no reason for blaming herself for Bell Ann's transgression; the child had always been trusted to stay within earshot of the house. She felt no guilt about having been alone with Septimus; the question had never come up between her and her parents. She ran on trustingly about the visit. He had brought her a book, *The Language of Flowers*. Inside, he had written in flourishes, "To my young friend, with deepest regards, Septimus Frye."

"Wait until the boys see it. I'll never get it back. They'll be making up all kinds of messages, except that we don't have half the flowers listed, as far as I can see."

"It has charming drawings and verses," Jennie leafed through it, wondering what the book would represent to Alick.

"And he gave each of the boys a half-dollar! They think he's rich as Croesus. Ostentatious, isn't he?" She giggled. This was reassuring to Jennie, and she was sorry Alick wasn't there to hear it. He came with Bell Ann a few moments later, looking much as usual; when Alick chose, not even his wife could guess at his thoughts. Bell Ann was not happy, but she was not tragic either. She smelled strongly of her afternoon with Brisky.

"Never mind washing now," Jennie said. "Wait until after you've done your chores."

"I shan't start before William," she warned her mother.

"Oh, I think you will, dear," Jennie said pleasantly. "And after that you may go upstairs and bathe, and put on your nightgown before supper."

She could not stay up after supper, then. Her mouth trembled, but she was too proud to give in. The three boys arrived together, scuffling and hilarious outside the door. William looked positively beatific at being upended by Carolus, a rare sign of equality. They went at once to their chores. Priscilla went to milk. Alick, thoughtful and uncommunicative, strolled down to the Yard.

At supper the children presented a panoply of luminous youth and transcendent innocence. Could combed hair and washed faces make such a difference? No, it was the amity among the boys; as if in the space of an afternoon the three elements had coalesced into one, with an inner glow of its own. Tomorrow it would shatter apart, but it was very nice tonight.

The twins had been teaching William to sail, and he couldn't seem to stop smiling. Bell Ann was scented with Pris's favorite carnation soap and her cheeks were nearly the red of cherries, her black hair brushed sleek, the frill of her nightdress setting her off like a valentine. Pris, of course, was floating on a separate plane, having spent the afternoon conversing with a captivating older man over her mother's best teacups, with the assurance that she had been equally captivating.

Jennie knew all about it; she also remembered a certain tilt to Papa's eyebrow and a certain dry intonation in his response to girlish transports. He must have missed having someone to talk it over with in bed.

The flower book made the rounds of the table. Sandy composed an anonymous message for Harry Shaw, but Pris told him it would do no good unless he included a translation with the bouquet. "Besides, we don't have all the right flowers." Carolus was both tantalized and depressed by all the names he had not heard before, and threw himself back in his chair with disgust. "I shall *never* know all the plants, *never!*"

"Och, it's early days to be giving up your profession," Alick told him. He had read the inscription with no obvious displeasure. Since Pris was not jealously keeping the book in her own hands, obviously it was not precious to her. She might have enjoyed the attention, found it flattering, but the book was no more than a whimsy.

"I can hardly wait to show it to Thankful and to the others," she said. "We'll have some fun!" So it wasn't going to be kept under her pillow like a marked volume of Keats, though that might come later.

The twins wanted to sleep at the fort tonight. Earlier, the mosquitoes had been too many and too ravenous, but now they were much less, and summer was going too fast, so why couldn't they begin now? They wouldn't take anything for breakfast, just a jug of water and some food to see them through the night, and they would be home in time for chores.

"But tonight is your turn with the dishes," Jennie reminded them, "so it would be dark before you got there."

"If we can strike a bargain with Pris, may we go?" Sandy was expert at dividing his most winsome appeals evenly between his parents. Meanwhile Carolus gazed eloquently at Pris with dark gray eyes like his father's and Bell Ann's, and said intensely, "*Anything.*"

"Oh, go ahead. I'll think of something," Pris said. With the pantry to herself she could let her thoughts flow undisturbed. "But you may regret your impetuous promise."

Carolus grinned. "Thank you, Pris. I trust I'm not mortgaged for life."

"And we will take William with us," Sandy announced it like a proclamation, and William looked up from his plate with not very convincing astonishment; he had known beforehand.

"We are s'pose to clear the table," Bell Ann told him. "You and me. So *you* can't go."

"I will clear it, honeybunch, because you'll be in bed." Pris said. "William can do something for me sometime."

"Why can't *I* ever go?"

"For the same reason William couldn't go till now," said Carolus. "Too young. Every time anything moved in the woods or a night heron squawked, you'd be punching us awake thinking it was ghosts, or wolves, or an ogre, or Heaven knows what."

"William must have promised," said Pris, "that he won't wake them even if he sees a boa constrictor slithering toward them. He will just quietly get out of the way and let it squeeze them to death."

"That's right!" said William. Alick laughed.

"You'd best be setting out now, then. No lantern, no fires, and home by sun-up. Is that understood?"

"*Understood!*"

They left with a stone jug of water in a rope sling for easier carrying, and a loaf of bread sliced and buttered and done up in a cloth with the corners tied together. Each boy carried a blanket roll on his back. The dogs went with them to the edge of the woods and were sent back.

Bell Ann's tears did not win her a chance to stay up a little while. When Jennie went upstairs to tuck her in, she found her still crying, but quietly. "Mr. Shaw *hates* me, and why? I am just a little child."

"Mr. Shaw is a very unhappy man and that makes him hate almost everybody, not just you. But you know, Bell Ann, if you hadn't disobeyed our rules, he couldn't have said those things to you. You would not have been there."

"But I like Lily so much! And she likes me!"

"I know, sweetheart. I know." Jennie rocked her in her arms. "But remember you have Sarie Oakes for a friend and be thankful. Tomorrow is another day, and we can put all the bad things of today behind us."

"*You* didn't have any bad things today," Bell Ann pointed out. "Nobody did but me."

"But you did it to yourself, love, and when Papa and I met you on the road, that was not a very nice thing for *us*."

"I'm sorry." She yawned, and Jennie tipped her into bed and pulled up the sheet. "I wish I decided to be a boy. Peter Paul Glenroy—isn't that pretty? That would be my name. But I s'pose it's too late now. If we have a baby boy, we could call him that."

"Goodnight," Jennie said.

The house quieted early with the boys gone. Priscilla affectionately kissed her parents goodnight and went upstairs humming "Drink to me Only with Thine Eyes," which led Jennie to believe Septimus had quoted it over the teacups, if he hadn't actually sung it. She wouldn't have been surprised if he had one of those sweet lyrical tenor voices, like that of the curate who had been Aunt Higham's choice for Jennie. She decided not to tell Alick this.

When their books were laid aside, the candles blown out, and the only sounds the long unbroken trill of a cricket competing with Garnet's rumble at the foot of the bed, Alick said suddenly, "This was not an accident. He came to see *her*, and she has been blooming ever since."

"Pris is always blooming." She made herself sound sleepier than she was. "She's of an age to bloom." She forced a yawn and snuggled against his side. "You told him yourself he would be welcome to visit with the family."

"But he singled her out; he brought a gift, and he gave each boy a half-dollar, and they left him alone with her."

"The boys would be off on their own anyway, and Bell Ann left when she was bored," Jennie said. "Can you imagine anyone saying to one of our boys, 'Here is some money; have you no plans of your own for the afternoon?' They'd *never* go! They'd stay, out of curiosity."

He admitted that. "But it is *at* me, this politician making himself so free here. Will we be finding him with her every time we come home? Tonight her head is full of him. If she is sleeping now, she is dreaming of him. I cannot in all fairness cancel my policies to be rid of him, but why cannot the amadan remember and do what we asked him? Or am I the amadan for expecting it of him?"

"My darling." She slipped a hand under his neck and kneaded the taut cords. "You are no amadan, you are a father."

"The two are not mutually exclusive," he said drily.

"Being a mother doesn't necessarily mean possessing the wisdom of the ages, either. I can only guess that Pris isn't in love with him *yet*; she's flattered. But if we tell her she must not see him alone—"

"It could be putting the idea in her head." He sounded tired and sad. "Jeannie, getting herself born she was not half the trouble and the anxiety of *now*." He turned his head toward her. "He is the one I must be speaking to again, hoping he is a man who has some notions of honor and responsibility, and not to be amusing himself with putting a spell on a young girl. Talk about the water horse! That one is a kelpie right enough."

"I agree. And now let us talk about something very strange."

"What is that?" He kissed her temple.

"Why are the twins being extremely *nice* to William? I thought first they had simply stopped regarding him as a nuisance. But taking him to the fort for the night—it was all talked over beforehand. I have intuition if not omniscience. William knew he was going; it was like the aura around a candle flame."

"What does your intuition say?"

"It asks, 'What does he know about them? What have they been up to, and when?' If you want to know what could keep me awake tonight, that is it. What are they *talking* about? Not the stars, I'd swear to it."

Thirty-Two

I T WAS VERY warm and still at four in the morning when Jennie and Alick arose. After he built the breakfast fire and set the water to boil for the porridge, she made tea and they drank it out on the bench. They barely spoke, relishing the silence. The swallows had gone, and *Artemis* looked bereft without her attendant sprites; other birds were heard, but not with the extravagance of the spring's dawn chorus. The dogs and the cat wandered about, sniffing at the tracks of the night's travelers. The sun rose huge and scarlet in a sky like gray velvet above the serrated black wall of woods to the east, and as if the blaze were transmuted into a trumpet call, the boys appeared suddenly in the lower field.

Their clothes had obviously been slept in, their eyes were heavy, and William was inclined to fall over his own feet when he yawned. No, he had not seen wolves, Indians, or an early settler's ghost.

"He is growing up," said Carolus, patting William's head.

"I hate having my head patted." William was amiable but firm.

"I beg your pardon," Carolus said gravely.

Priscilla came out tying her apron. "I suppose you have been running through the woods all night playing pirates. You certainly look it."

"And I hope the mosquitoes bit you like anything," Bell Ann said uncharitably. She was ignored, which at times was necessary with Bell Ann, and everyone went to work.

"What can the twins have been up to?" Jennie wondered aloud, bringing out the porridge bowls. "It had to happen during the week. I don't know where the twins were every moment, but I thought I knew where William was."

247

Alick was adding the dry oatmeal to the boiling water in a thin stream from one hand, stirring constantly with the wooden spurtle he had made for the purpose. "There is more in William than meets the eye," he said.

"And I don't know if I like what it seems to be."

"Come now, *mo graidh,* you could not be expecting any one of our children to be a simple wee soul, as easily read as Bounce and Darroch."

"I suppose not." Jennie laid out the spoons. "Perhaps William isn't blackmailing them, but I can't think what else it would be."

"The wee lad is entitled to his choice of weapons," Alick said.

"I would just like to know *what* and *why,*" she answered.

There were never any long dawdling conversations over the weekday porridge. Alick was always at the Yard before his earliest-arriving employee, and the children had other work to do before they could be free.

The air was enervating, clothes felt clammy and constricting even without stays. The skin was constantly damp with perspiration. Jennie loathed it, but Priscilla was euphoric enough to make her mother tired. In the midst of changing the boys' beds she pulled *The Language of Flowers* from her apron pocket and read aloud a verse from Keats. "Isn't that absolutely perfect?" she demanded. "I really adore this book."

"But what does it *mean?*" Bell Ann asked. "What is a Sensitive Plant? Does Carolus know? I'll ask him!" She darted out of the room.

"Careful on the stairs!" Jennie called after her from habit, but Bell Ann drowned her out, yelling, "Carolus!"

"If she keeps that up," Jennie said, "by the time she's grown no one will ever be able to say 'her voice was ever soft, gentle, and low, an excellent thing in woman.' Your grandfather threatened us all with that."

"You threatened me too, and listen to me now." She began to read 'Gather ye rosebuds while ye may,' in tenderly expressive tones, with eloquent gestures of her free hand. At the end Jennie applauded, and Pris dipped in a low curtsey. "Perhaps I shall become an elocutionist," she said.

"Seriously, Pris," Jennie asked, "is that how you feel? That time *is* flying too fast? That if you do not hurry you will miss all the rosebuds and be an old lady before you know it?"

"No, Mama!" she protested. "Well, at least not always. Sometimes I want to hurry, but sometimes I want time to stop right where it is for a while. When I was younger I wanted to go back before April—" She still could not say *died.* "I used to think that if we could go back, *knowing,* we would be warned and we could save her."

"Your father and I know that longing too well. 'O! call back yesterday. Bid Time return,' that is a line to break one's heart."

"But I discovered that you shouldn't wish your Now away, either backward or forward. You should not waste what each hour brings you, because tomorrow you might not be here." Pris punched a pillow with passionate vitality. "I don't dwell on morbid subjects, Mama. I am so glad we had April, even if we could not keep her. But the hole was so deep until Bell Ann came." She tilted her head toward the door, smiling, "And here Bell Ann comes."

"Carolus says *I* am a Sensitive Plant!" she was shouting on her way. "And Sandy and William *laughed*." She stamped into the room. "William is becoming horrid. You shouldn't let him be with those twins, Mama. He is too young."

"Thank you, dear. I will think about your advice," Jennie said. Pris was leafing through the book, smiling a private smile, delicate, wistful, yet unconsciously wise. If we were two girls of the same age, Jennie thought, folding pillow cases into a parcel for Bell Ann to carry, I could say, Do you like Septimus? Do you fancy him? Did you write in your diary last night, over and over, 'Septimus Frye, Priscilla Frye, Mrs. Septimus Frye'?

" 'Currant,' " Pris read aloud. "That means 'Thy frown will kill me.' " She hooted. "Does it mean you send one lonely little currant or a whole bush?"

So much for romance. Suddenly the whole day improved for Jennie.

"*And*," Bell Ann went on, "they are all going to see this man find water at the Post Office Farm."

Pris dropped her book into an apron pocket. "That must be the famous one whose mother is a witch!" She seized a bundle of linen and ran downstairs.

"A witch!" Bell Ann said wildly. Then, in black despair, "I s'pose no one will invite *me*!"

"Let's find out, shall we?" Jennie suggested.

The boys were out by the washhouse. They had kindled the fire under the washpot, and Sandy was explaining that the dowser didn't like to have the sun at its nooning; the rays then were like lightning striking a chimney, they interfered with the natural psychic unity between the dowser, the forked hazel twig, and the unseen water below. This glib explanation was received cynically by Pris and Carolus, and with admiration by William and Bell Ann, who hadn't the slightest idea what he was talking about.

"If this man does not wear a special costume and charge admission," Jennie said, "he is lacking in business acumen. Does he do sleight-of-hand too, and pluck coins out of little children's ears?"

"*Mother.*" Sandy was offended.

"I want to see the witch!" Bell Ann kept repeating loudly.

"There is no such thing as a witch except in the fairy tales," Jennie told her. "She is probably a nice old lady like Mrs. Shenstone."

"Anyway, she is too old to be out and about. She won't be there," Sandy said.

"But can't she come on her broomstick?" Bell Ann asked anxiously. "I would like to see that."

"Who wouldn't?" asked William, and was gratified when his elders laughed.

Jennie decided that they might all go, including Bell Ann. "And if I hear one groan about that, everyone stays home," she promised. Nobody groaned. "Now to work, then."

They dispersed joyfully, and they were still joyful when they left after dinner, washed, combed, shod, and decently dressed. Priscilla wore blue gingham with a fresh white fichu and tied on her broad-brimmed hat with a blue ribbon. Bell Ann was restrained from putting on her Paris frock, persuaded that her pink gingham dress and pink ribbons turned her into a fetching picture. Dressing up on a weekday burnished the familiar with a peculiar magic; *anything* could happen once they set foot beyond their own boundaries—the possibilities had no end.

Jennie and the dogs walked to the Yard with Alick. "Lachlan Campbell, he calls himself," Alick said mildly. "Not long from Cape Breton, they are telling me, and all wondering why he left."

"But wouldn't you like to meet him and have a wee blether with another Gaelic speaker?" she teased him.

"Not that one! But mind you, those who would be paying him deserve to lose their money. As if there are not men and women in Whittier who could be finding water without half the noise and asking nothing."

"Ah, but it's paying in hard coin that makes some think the service is more valuable than what is freely given."

"The sort who'll aye be reaching deep in their pockets to give their last penny for a bonny apple from a peddler while the cow eats their own." He shrugged, smiling. "Och, the Phippses and Campbell will be giving half the children in town a grand afternoon, so nothing is wasted."

She whistled Bounce back from the Yard, where he was enthusiastically visiting, and walked home, wondering if the afternoon was really hers. She washed the dishes, singing songs of her childhood; in the scullery at Pippin Grange Ianthe had taught her and Sophie part-singing as Pris taught William and Bell Ann.

Then she took her writing materials down to the orchard table and began a letter to Ianthe. Her sister's letters from Zurich, Rome, Paris, Vienna—wherever Casimir was performing—were like chapters in a long novel in which Ianthe was the observant heroine. Paradoxically, Ianthe considered Jennie the heroine of a novel she was composing by living it. She found the details of Jennie's American life endlessly entrancing.

"Imagine ships being built in your front garden, so to speak! Papa would be *enthralled!*" She said Alick must be one of the most irresistible men on earth, besides her Cass; Ianthe had a gift for hyperbole, but Jennie enjoyed it. (Ianthe had also told the children she was flattered when they named a pretty calf for her.)

Jennie had gotten to the dowsing, and Bell Ann's hope of seeing the witch arriving in glory on her broomstick, when the dogs warned her of a visitor. Garnet disappeared higher up in her tree, and Jennie wished she could do the same.

The dogs weren't barking now. They knew the caller, but it was not Mr. Babb. Carlotta's chaise was under the rowans, and Carlotta was just coming away from Michael. "I apologize for the intrusion," she said. "But your oasis is too tempting."

"I'm overjoyed!" Jennie said. "I don't see you often enough. Come down to the shade, such as it is."

"It sounds like heaven." Carlotta was elegant as usual in spite of the heat. Her dress was a flowered Jaconet muslin with a turn-down collar open at the throat; the locket she always wore lay in that revealed hollow. The brim of the Leghorn hat she'd tossed into the chaise was turned up at the back with a flat yellow bow and a spray of daisies.

"Look at you!" said Jennie. "Even Solomon in all his glory, and so forth."

"The assurance of being always *soignée* is my armor against Fate, even though the poet James Shirley claims there is none."

"There is such a thing as moral support, and besides, you have turned mundane existence upside down for Mrs. Loomis and Mrs. Trescott."

"Come now, I am not the only vain woman to be hatted and gowned by them."

"But think what you have done for their creative instinct," said

Jennie. "You are the only woman of such style and daring in the county, Pris claims—having been no farther from home than Tenby."

"Pris flatters me. Is it she who sees that her mother is always charmingly turned out?"

"You mean especially now?" asked Jennie. "Barefoot like a tinker woman, except that some of those would put me to shame with their ear bobbles and splendiferous shawls. Come along, let us get a pitcher of lemonade and go down to the orchard."

"You invited me once to consider this place an oasis," Carlotta said, "and that is exactly what it is."

She unbuttoned the cuffs of her bishop sleeves and turned them back. She waved to Garnet, peering down at her from among the leaves. "This really is an oasis," she said. 'Annihilating all that's made to a green thought in a green shade. . . .' I have just been to see Lily Shaw."

Jennie's apprehension showed before she could hide it, and Carlotta shook her head. "It's not dangerous, merely a little upset that Mrs. Shaw has already cured with ginger tea. She'd left a note with Polly yesterday afternoon when I was away from home, asking me to come to see Lily, but when I arrived this afternoon I found the child cutting paper dolls on the doorstep." She folded her long clever hands in her lap and smiled with humorous resignation.

"She wanted to give me advice; since I saw Lily through lung fever last winter, Mrs. Shaw has never ceased to be grateful in her monolithic way, and it seems she is disturbed for me."

"Is it the Five Concerned Women again? Have they been—"

Carlotta shook her head. "No, no, I am sure there is nothing more than the ordinary chronic babble over the teacups. No, she has reached these conclusions on her own and was impelled to share them with me, and I listened with a solemn and, I hope, grateful expression." She poured more lemonade for herself. "This is between you and me, Jennie. And Alick, if you want."

"I'll wait and see. I am breathless with suspense."

"She says I must marry to protect my reputation, and Nicholas Blackburn is *the one*. She does not advise me to give up my medicine; I am too useful. Whittier needs me. But I need a husband to drive me to all my calls, especially the night ones, and who would be with me when I attend male patients. A chaperone." Her smile broadened. "I quote Mrs. Shaw. 'A woman can be very free inside marriage, if she is determined enough.' "

"Which she has proved, to a point," Jennie agreed. "Sometimes I would like to know that woman better. I often hear things that surprise me. She is very kind to Moses and Miriam Gunn, for instance, while her husband can't speak of the Gunns without having a seizure. But then she keeps that child a prisoner—it's a wonder she lets her attend school."

"She admires Captain Blackburn in her way, even if he *is* an Englishman, and feels he would be the perfect husband for a woman in my position. If Nicholas heard all she has in store for him, he would be in the next state by now."

"I don't think so," said Jennie, amused. So she was calling him *Nicholas*. "I've seen the way he looks at you, and apparently I'm not the only one who notices. Another facet of Mrs. Shaw."

"Jennie, do *you* think I should be married to make an honest woman of me?"

"Oh good heavens, *no!*" Jennie was shocked. "Are you *serious?* That was just my romantic streak showing through. You have become respected as a doctor without the protection of a husband, so there is the answer. . . . Are you sure there has been no new gossip?"

"If there is, it's been created out of boredom. This is the low period when they are tired of summer and all the work in boiling hot kitchens, and wish the children were back in school, and cannot abide their husbands. In comparison my life must seem an idyll of pleasure. I have my home to myself, someone to prepare my meals and do my washing, and wherever I go I am expected and wanted and welcomed."

"And always handsomely dressed."

"That helps to aggravate the grievance like a sleeve rubbing against a burn," Carlotta agreed. "And I am responsible only to myself. They must see it that way, not realizing that I am responsible to anyone who makes a claim on my help, at any hour, day and night. But I can see why some of the women I attend think I have it all. I don't know if Mrs. Shaw envies me—she seems to have Garland well in hand—but she really believes I should have a husband. At least she sees nothing wrong with a charming one. She actually almost smiles when she speaks of Nicholas."

"Now I'm positive I should know that woman better." Jennie laughed. "How long has it been 'Nicholas' between you and him?"

No coloring, no shift of the long fingers. "Ever since he brought a very bloody little Collier lad to me, and held him while I sewed up his slashed leg. He'd found him by the side of the road, the boy had been cutting sweetgrass with a sickle. A strong man who is not afraid of blood is very helpful; I've had fathers and husbands faint at the sight and be no good at all. But, dear Jennie, I am not about to propose to him because he doesn't blanch at the sight of gushing blood and knows how to apply a tourniquet. Well, now I've talked to you about it, and shall put it out of mind except to smile at it now and then, and cherish my *friendship* with Nicholas. I shall drive home and see what is waiting for me. I needed this half hour in your oasis, Jennie. You're part of it, you know. You listen so well."

"I've had a great deal of practice, with five very articulate children." They were walking toward Michael.

"Ah, Jennie, if I've envied you anything, it's the children!" Carlotta exclaimed. "All those bright young faces."

"Priscilla admires you tremendously," Jennie said. "The boys have grown up thinking it is perfectly natural for a woman as well as a man to be a doctor. But Bell Ann was very displeased with you when she thought you gave a perfectly good baby to the Oakeses instead of us, until I convinced her that Alick and I had refused the gift. So then she was angry with us instead of you."

"I am relieved. I should hate to be in Bell Ann's bad books."

"Remember this when you think of raising children: a parent's life is a perpetual performance. I'm waiting for Bell Ann's next question: who brings the babies when Dr. Neville doesn't? When God sends them directly, how does He do it? Bell Ann's picture of God is far different from the usual images, so she will be wondering how He arrives unseen and unheard. She can be relentless."

"I hope I live to see what sort of woman she becomes. Pris, of course, will be a fighter for the rights of women, and I suppose Bell Ann will be carrying the banner beside her."

"Right now she is going to marry either Moses Gunn or David Evans, and she's a bit taken with Sarie Oakes's stepbrother," Jennie said.

"Where are they all this afternoon? I'm glad we had this time to talk, but I miss them."

"They have all gone to the Post Office Farm to watch some exotic stranger find water. He enjoys a large audience. I don't know if he has a little page to pass among them collecting money, but I wouldn't be surprised."

"I've been hearing about him. Good heavens, Gib Dixon found a wonderful never-failing source for me without putting the glam on me, as the gypsies say." She unhitched Michael and stepped up lithely into the chaise.

Thirty-Three

SHE HEARD THE boys and Bell Ann coming with a concert of dog howls, Indian war whoops, and someone's teeth-jarring imitation of a bobcat's scream. None of this deceived the dogs, and the horses looked interested but not alarmed.

They had been a long time on the way home. They had attempted to find water in someone's pasture until a bull appeared, when they all ran for the fence, dragging Bell Ann and hurling her over the top rail. They had played follow-the-leader along the top of a stone wall and jumping back and forth across a brook, not always successfully. They had warred with pine cones and green apples; they had competed to see who could climb the highest in a stand of mast pines, but were intimidated by angry ravens. Sweat had made dirty tracks on their dusty faces and they were sticky with pitch.

Bell Ann was still at the manic stage. The dowsing had been both mysterious and dull for her, with everyone hushing her, and she'd seen no witch on a broomstick. But the way home had been glorious. She had lost one hair ribbon, her dress was soiled, she was scratched, her shoes were wet, her stockings falling down, and she had green apples in her pockets. She was almost too hoarse to speak, but she kept on talking anyway.

The four squabbled giddily around the rainwater hogshead at the end of the woodshed, tossing dippers full of tepid water at each other, spilling the basin over Bounce, and once on William's head. William was not offended; he turned a scoop of water over Bell Ann, who screamed for the joy of screaming.

When the havoc had died down to isolated little bursts, Bell Ann shrieked at Jennie, "Look at me, Mama!" Her black hair was plastered to her head, her nainsook shirt and drawers to her body.

"I see a little herring," Jennie said. She began drying Bell Ann's hair. "I don't suppose your sister wished to travel home with the savage hordes."

Sandy scrubbed at one palm with a lump of pumice to remove pitch. "She was sitting under a tree with Thankful and Hester and Candace when we left. Heads together, tongues clickety-clack. Wasn't about dowsing, I'll take my oath." He aimed a sly grin at Carolus, who ignored it; he was combing his damp black hair with his fingers, scowling when he encountered pitch that would have to be cut out.

"Septimus Frye has a fancy new gig!" William said. "She's some handsome, Mama! Dark blue, and shining like a glass bottle. He must've stopped and wiped the dust off her before he got there. I'll have me one like that some day, and a horse like Bolivar, when I'm a big shipbuilder."

"I'm sure you will, my darling," Jennie said. "Now, all of you, hurry, it's getting on for chore time."

"Pris is *late*," Bell Ann said disapprovingly. "Why do we have to start now?"

"Because I said so." She gave Bell Ann a light spank and sent her toward the door. "Comb your hair before it dries into a bird's nest. Let Carolus part it for you."

Even out of sight, the children thronged the place; they left invisible but distinct wakes of passage washing away everything that was not immediate.

She was measuring flour for scones when Bell Ann came in and said severely, "Ianthe is very upset."

"Pris is probably on her way home from Thankful's house this minute," Jennie said.

"I wish *I* could milk."

"Perhaps next year, when Louisa is in milk and your hands are bigger, you and she can start out together."

Bell Ann went from disbelief to incandescence, and rushed out, shouting, "William, next year I can milk!" She collided with her father, who caught and held her by the shoulders. "Papa, next year I can milk Louisa!" she told him.

"Now isn't that the grand adventure to be looking for? And for Louisa too. And did The Campbell find water this afternoon?"

"I don't know," she said blankly. He let her go, and she hurried on, calling William.

"I haven't heard a word of water," said Jennie. "Only that they went all round Robin Hood's barn on the way home."

"And how was your afternoon?" His eyes held her as his hands had held Bell Ann. "Och, I am no gentleman to come near you after a day like this one. We were sweating like beasts and the water running into our eyes and off our noses. The lads were jumping overboard, but I will be having a bath."

He took towels, and soap, and clean clothing from the skin out, and went up to the wash house. Jennie put eggs on to boil and made a salad of young spinach and onions, cubes of cold boiled beet, and thin translucent slices of cucumber, to be eaten with a dressing of vinegar, sugar, and celery seed. The first scones would go on the griddle when the family began to collect for supper. She fed the dogs and the cat and went outside for a respite from the stove's heat. Ianthe was indeed upset, loudly so, and Louisa was joining in. There was not a child in sight; they'd all be at the pasture bars self-righteously criticizing Pris for forsaking the poor dumb animal who depended on her. It was not often they had such an opportunity, and she would face five censorious faces whenever she appeared.

Alick came strolling down, looking as spotless and at leisure as a gentleman who has bathed after a day of pleasure in preparation for an evening of the same. At the same time there was a light quick percussion of hoofs from the woods, and Bolivar appeared, extremely smart and mettlesome, drawing the glossy new rig as if it weighed nothing at all. Septimus sat back at ease in his green coat, his hat on his cocked knee, and he was smiling. Priscilla's hat hung down her back, and she was driving.

The children burst into sight and chased the gig. Their shouts brought the dogs from the house.

Jennie saw nothing but the girl driving the horse. She was as incandescent with bliss as Bell Ann had been about milking. For a breath, Jennie was swept back to Hyde Park with the bright little equipages flying past the barouche, and the girls and women driving. If Nigel had not died, Pris might be one of those; yes, and at seventeen too. The daughter of a man so proud and indulgent, she'd have been driving his two-horse phaeton in public at fifteen.

Pris brought Bolivar to a stop in front of her parents and sat beaming down at them.

"Well, how did I do?" she asked pertly.

"A handsome sight, was it not?" asked Septimus. He sprang down, but Alick was already holding out his hand to Pris. With a nervous little laugh and a quick glance at her mother, she accepted her father's help.

"Thank you, Papa," she said with great sweetness as he set her down. Septimus came around past Bolivar's head, bowed to Jennie, and spoke with glowing self-assurance to Alick. "I hope, sir, that you approve of my giving your daughter a ride home."

"I am not sure of the circumstances," Alick said pleasantly. "We were thinking Priscilla was with her friends for all this while."

"I was really grateful for the lift, Mama and Papa," Pris assured them. "The dust in the road is so thick."

"I know. Your brothers and sister came home wearing half of it," said Jennie. Bell Ann leaned possessively against her mother, gazing at Septimus. William was stroking Bolivar's head, and the twins were examining the gig from all angles, frowning like prospective buyers. The dogs seemed to have multiplied into three dogs each, and the over-wrought Ianthe was now bellowing.

"Hear my darling Ianthe!" Pris said sentimentally.

"You had best be going to her," Alick said in a soft voice. Pris's chin jerked up, and her mouth compressed to a straight line. The blue flash of eyes toward her mother was both surprise and shock for Jennie, recognizing a woman's resentment, not a child's. There was no martyred *Yes, Papa*. High-headed, she put out her hand to Septimus and said, "Thank you, Seven. It was lovely. I shall never forget it."

"It was entirely my pleasure." He released her hand with a tender reluctance, and she gave him a sad little smile and walked into the house as if she were wearing a train. He looked wistfully after her, his light beaver hat held against his handsome Loretto silk waistcoat.

"And the rest of you," Alick said, still quietly. "Have you nothing better to do than stand around like beggars at a fair?"

William ducked back under Bolivar's head and reappeared behind the gig on his way to the woodshed. The twins moved speedily toward the barn. Bell Ann leaned harder against Jennie.

"You too, Bell Ann," Jennie said.

There were times when no one argued, even the youngest. "Farewell, Miss Bell Ann!" Septimus called after her, and she gave him a flirtatious smile over her shoulder.

"One day she will be as beautiful a young woman as her sister," Septimus said to Jennie. Pris came out with her apron over her arm and her boots in hand, smiling gallantly at Septimus, and went her way. He looked after her with a small poetic sigh, then turned to her parents with a confident flash of dimples and excellent teeth. "Well, I suppose I must be heading home, though parting from River Farm is always such sweet sorrow!"

Alick said courteously, "I do not recall giving you permission to be alone with our daughter."

"But surely on the public road—" He turned appealingly to Jennie.

"You cannot be as naïve as you sound, Septimus," she said. "And you allowed her to drive, which is quite enough to tear a girl's reputation to shreds."

He was the picture of hurt astonishment. "But—"

Alick was pleasant but implacable. "I blame myself for not telling her what I told you. I was not wanting to give it so much importance, you see. I was thinking that a word in the ear of an honorable man was enough."

The violent color ran up into his black fleece. "If you are accusing me of dishonor, sir, I resent that! Upon my word I do, sir!"

"I am not yet calling you dishonorable," Alick said. "But if her brothers were an hour or more on the road with their games and their foolery, and you were not arriving here until an hour or more after that, what are her mother and I to think?"

"If you are thinking that I have ever treated Priscilla with other than the highest respect, I—I—" The stammer humiliated and enraged him as much as the reproof. He fairly leaped up into the seat and loosened the reins. "Good day, Mrs. Glenroy! Always a pleasure!" Alick was elaborately ignored. He turned Bolivar's head, and they left at a good clip.

When he had driven into the woods Alick said, "Was I unfair? Too hard on him?"

"You sound neither doubtful nor repentant," said Jennie. "No, what you said was necessary. He is old enough to know better, but he has been trusting to his charm for too long."

"Priscilla is not happy with me. I am sorry for that."

"For goodness' sake, don't let her know it!" She put her arm through his, and they walked toward the house. "She's tough, Alick. She can endure having her feelings bruised now and then, especially if we are as honest with her as we can be."

Alick asked the boys if Lachlan Campbell had been successful. Yes; at the spot where the pull had nearly wrenched the hazel out of his hands, they had dug and found water at six feet.

"And was he having his own piper go before him playing 'The Campbells are Coming'?" Alick asked. The twins laughed, and William said longingly, "Wouldn't it have been splendid?"

Priscilla came in with the milk pails to wash, and a jug of cold milk from the morning, which she set on the table. When she saw her parents her face went as blank as a slate wiped with a wet sponge.

"Well, Mama, Papa, have you anything to say to me?" It was just short of arrogance.

"What would it be?" Alick asked. He went on lighting his pipe.

"Only *you* know." She looked icily around at her juniors, and Carolus said, "*Must* we leave? When can we eat?"

"I suppose," Sandy said dourly, "we can be looking forward to more of this than less, now that she's feeling her oats."

"Go," said Alick. "All of you. Everyone is entitled to some privacy in this house. And now it is your sister's turn."

"But what did she *do?*" Bell Ann asked. Carolus took her hand and led her out. "In just half an hour," Jennie called after them, "I'll ring the bell for you. That's a promise."

"You must have something to say to me," Priscilla said. "Obviously you had something to say to Seven, for him to go off like that without saying good-bye to me. He offered me a ride and I accepted. Is that a *crime?*"

"I am not angry with you, *mo graidh*," Alick answered, "and neither is your mother. But with Septimus—yes. Perhaps you will be telling us the reason it took you so long to come home."

"We didn't come directly home. Is that a crime or a sin?"

"Be careful, Priscilla," Jennie warned her.

Pris laughed shakily. "Or shall I be turning the grindstone for an hour?"

"Not yet," said Alick. He succeeded in getting his pipe going. Between puffs he said, "Where were you? Making a call on one of your friends?"

"Didn't he tell you? Or didn't you give him the chance?"

"He was not offering to tell. He was too offended when I mentioned it."

"No wonder. There was no harm in it! He took me over Crit's Hill to show me the house his brother has bought, down below Captain Blackburn's." She appealed for a friendly interest. "You know the big square house with the beeches and the chestnuts?"

"The Aldridge house," Alick said agreeably. "And was his brother there?"

"No, but it is all ready for him and his wife to move into, when they are married next month." Encouraged by their amiable attention, she went into details of the painting and varnishing. "And from the cupola on the roof you can see all the way down Sweetgrass Creek to Bugle Bay."

"So you were not in the public eye all this time," said Alick quietly. "You were prowling around an empty house with this man."

"Is *that* wrong?" she flung at him. He shook his head and walked across to the windows and stood looking out. Jennie knew the negative was for Pris growing up too fast and all at once seeing him as an enemy. She wanted to go to him; she wanted also for Pris to be small enough to be held in her lap while she explained.

"Not wrong of you, Pris," she said. "But wrong of Septimus. He is much older than you; he knows more of the world. He should have know he was exposing you to gossip."

"But he did nothing bad. *That man*, as Papa calls him, was a perfect gentleman. He did not even touch me, except to offer me his hand in stepping down from the gig, and then up into it when we left." She was beyond tears in the dry white heat of incredulous indignation. "Mama, you are the one who quoted to me, 'They say—what do they say? Let them say.' "

"There is a difference, and we will sit down and discuss it like philosophers when we are all calm. For now, the point is that you are seventeen, you are still under our care, and perhaps we've been remiss in not laying down certain rules before now. If we had done it earlier, there wouldn't be this trouble now. But it needn't be trouble—it needn't amount to anything. It is over."

"No, it isn't. Papa is too angry."

"Not with you, *mo ghaoil*." Alick came back to them. "With Septimus Frye. He was told some time ago that he was welcome here but not to be seeing you alone. However, he has managed it twice in two days. The first time we could be naming it an accident; the others went away and left him with you. He might have excused himself and left, but he did not. Today it was no accident, and he is no longer welcome here."

Priscilla ripped off her apron and threw it at a chair, and ran upstairs. When her door slammed shut, Alick looked tired—and worse, defeated.

She put her arms around him and kissed his cheek. "We have four other children, and the evening to get through, and then you and I can talk about this all night." She was as shaky in her stomach for him as for herself, and for Pris too. This was a new and terrible event for all three of them.

"You behave," he said, "as if you have been through all this before."

"I have," she said, "but as the seventeen-year-old girl."

"I wish I had known you then."

"I looked like Sandy, with curls, before his voice began to change."

Pris didn't quite dare to refuse to come down to supper, and Jennie was glad to see that her regal isolation hadn't harmed her appetite.

The others kept their curiosity to themselves and gave a minute-by-minute account of the afternoon from four viewpoints; even William was unusually voluble. The boys left early for the fort, and Pris went to bed soon after Bell Ann. Before she went upstairs she made a little speech she must have been composing while she washed the dishes, alone from choice.

"You will not have to worry about Mr. Frye ever again. After what you must have said to him, he will never want to lay eyes on me. I will be as deadly poison to him. It will probably be that way with everyone, so I might as well resign myself."

She left before either parent could answer.

"Exit the Tragic Muse," Jennie murmured when they heard the door close.

"How can you be so calm?"

"Because I was once seventeen, remember. And before that I had two older sisters to observe when *they* were seventeen. Pity my poor father."

But nothing would reassure him, and being so sorry for both Alick and Pris gave her no time for self-pity, if she'd been inclined to it. She wanted only to stretch out in cool sheets beside Alick and hope it would all be swept away by the tide of night.

"Do you think she is weeping herself to sleep up there?" he asked as soon as they were shut in their room.

"She was not when I looked in on Bell Ann a few minutes ago."

"She would be too proud to let you hear."

"Alick, my darling." She reached for his hand. "She will have to suffer it out. After all, it is not the end of the world. We have not torn her away from her one and only love. I am not hard-hearted, I would like to take her in my arms like Bell Ann, but for us to apologize would be false. We haven't blamed *her* for anything."

"She has been so innocent in all this. I am sorry to see the end of such innocence."

"Come into my arms, and let us be sorry for each other." He rolled toward her and she embraced him as she had done on their first night, to warm him. "She is growing up, and you cannot walk the floor with the little head bobbing on your shoulder while you sing to her."

"We were everything to her. We answered all her needs then. Are our children only loaned to us, Jeannie? To be taken back, or to go away?"

"Thousands, millions of parents must have wondered the same thing. But Alick, no matter how delectable Septimus is, she cannot marry him until she is of age. *We* are still sailing this ship—never forget that. Right now we are aching for her, and she is aching both for herself and for us, because it is terrible to be so upset with your parents. But we will all survive it."

"What makes you so brave?"

"I am not brave, my love. I am merely a desperate optimist." He was amused, and she felt the tension leaving him. But her release came more slowly. Lying entwined with Alick in the dark, she remembered the creak of saddle leather, the scent of horse, a polished boot and a long doeskin thigh, and Phoebus Apollo smiling up there. How could a dimpled young popinjay become Phoebus Apollo to the other god's daughter? Preposterous! But then, Nigel had been no god, not even a noble human being.

"Are you asleep?" she asked the head on her shoulder. "Because I want to tell you about this afternoon."

"Tell," he said. "How could I be sleeping when I am wishing to be alone with you somewhere? *Anywhere.*"

Thirty-Four

T HE WEATHER CHANGED overnight; the heat would be dry, the shade as cool as a drink fresh from the spring. But Jennie awoke in a bad temper. She wished she could have jammed all the ironing away deep in a closet, but then she would have to hang it all out again to shake away the wrinkles. She hated Septimus Frye; she was annoyed with Pris; she wished she could walk away to the western most limits of the property and stay there all day, without children. By the time she was up, washed, and dressed, the ironing was safe, she was ashamed of hating Septimus and had moderated that to a permissible irritation. The annoyance with Priscilla had gone with the sleep washed out of her eyes.

Pris went about her work in a marble silence; she may have talked to the cows, but no one knew for sure. The other children knew that Septimus had left in a temper and that Pris was in a Hawthorne flink. The twins suspected why, but they were too involved in their own affairs to give it much attention. To them, Alick was as he always was in the morning, but Jennie knew the truth; Alick had never received such a cold "Good morning, Papa," from Pris.

"I thought she would be all over it in the morning," he said when Jennie walked to the Yard with him. "Surely she knows how much we love her. Yesterday she should have known our action was *for* her, not against."

Jennie slid her hand down his arm to cover his hand and grip it. "She knows. That is part of it. She is reaching the age when she will love another man besides her father, and she won't be able to help herself. She knows that, too."

"I am no amadan, woman!" he said irritably. "I know the nature of life! But I will not have her throw herself away on that—that *politician*!"

"We have two girls' husbands to think about, and three boys' wives. The brutal truth is that if only one or two suit us we shall be very fortunate."

"Is this more of your desperate optimism?"

"No, that consists of reminding ourselves that none of this is going to happen tomorrow or even next year. What I just said is called 'facing facts.' "

"My Jeannie," he said with a sigh, sliding his arm around her waist. "I am in no mood to be building ships this day, I am wishing to run away with my wife to Kilmeny's Land."

They released each other as the first workmen appeared below the turn by the apple tree. "Some day you will build a ship you will call Kilmeny, and nobody will know why," she said, "but I will be the woman to christen her."

"*Dia*, I would name the new ship that if she were to be all mine!" he said. "And can you not see the figurehead, beautiful as the day? We would have to be finding a real artist for that! David could do it."

Thad Eubanks called "Good morning!" and they answered cheerfully. "Don't be anxious about Pris," she murmured. "What I am going to do is take a long walk—*alone*." She pressed two fingers against her own lips and then on his, and left him.

When she left off ironing at eight o'clock, the boys were preparing to go clamming. Late each summer the Clementses and the Hector Mackenzies brought their children to River Farm for an all-day picnic; it had become a tradition that it never rained on that day, and that they would always have clams, no matter how much other food there was. The boys would dig every morning between now and Saturday, keeping the clams cold and alive in net bags hung off the end of the Yard wharf. Bell Ann wanted to have a go at it with her little spade, and Jennie was glad to see her out of the house before she dressed for her private walk.

"You can take over the ironing now," she called up to Pris. "I am going to walk to the post office." Conscience demanded a reason.

Pris descended the stairs like a queen going either to her execution or a forced marriage to an ugly suitor. "So I am to do all the rest of it as a punishment," she said.

"It's not a punishment. Go as far as you like and then stop. It is nowhere engraved in stone that all the ironing must be done on Tuesday."

She brushed her hair again and did it up more carefully, and put on a paisley print in brown and copper shades that would be impervious to the road dust. It also had a deep pocket for her purse. When she went out to the kitchen to have Pris do up the tiny buttons at the back, Pris tried to remain impassive, but couldn't resist a fashion note.

"Sleeves are much bigger now."

"These suit me," said Jennie. "Any larger, and we shall all take to the air squawking like distraught hens."

Pris was not amused. "*There,*" she said, fastening the last button, and went back to her ironing.

"I am buying more candles and some sealing wax," Jennie said. "Is there anything you would like? Not that there's an exciting selection."

"No, thank you, Mama." Pris fussed unnecessarily with a shirt sleeve. "Am I to be trusted alone in the house after my monstrous indiscretion?" Her voice trembled at her own sarcasm.

"It was neither monstrous nor an indiscretion. We are not angry with you, Priscilla, but you are angry with us. You feel humiliated because of what was said to Septimus—"

"Discussing me behind my back! Talking about me as if I were Bell Ann's age! Isn't that enough to humiliate *anyone?*"

"But you are blaming the wrong person." Jennie wished she could take the flushed and furious face between her hands. "If Septimus had done as we requested, you would not be so unhappy now."

"Ignorance is bliss, I suppose," Pris said bitingly. "What I want to know is why I was ever a subject for you and Septimus to discuss in the first place!"

Alick was still dead set against telling her about the courtship offer; coming from an enchanter like Septimus it would dazzle the girl half out of her senses, he said, and Jennie was not yet ready to go against his wishes.

"Put your iron back on the stove and sit here," she said, patting the camp bed. Pris obeyed stolidly.

"Septimus came the afternoon you went to the Keel to bring back the dory. He thought you were older than you are," this was poetic license, "and wanted permission to call on you. Your father and I agreed that he would always be welcome here, but not to see you alone. You were too young to have gentlemen callers. A boy of your own age, like Robin, is one thing, but Septimus is seven years older than you."

"Papa is seven years older than *you.*"

"I was twenty-one when we met. I was of age."

"Well, now I can see why you and Papa were upset yesterday," Pris said reluctantly, "if he promised and then broke his promise." It was grudging, but one could always depend on Priscilla to try to be fair.

"He didn't promise in so many words, but we made our wishes known, and he didn't argue. I don't believe he said anything but 'Good afternoon' and rode off. It's commonly believed that silence gives consent, so that is how we took *his* silence." His angry, thwarted, embarrassed silence.

"He is so *nice*, Mama. So much fun, and a perfect gentleman as well! I wish I could explain to him about yesterday." Her voice trailed off, she sighed and looked into space.

Pris, he knows, Jennie thought, but he is brazen. He thinks his dimples will win him anything.

"When *may* I have gentlemen callers?" Pris asked.

"Not this year," said Jennie. "And after you are eighteen your parents will still have the right to approve or not. — I thought Septimus was Frank Mackenzie's young man."

"Seven told me he is *not*. He says they played together, and they are more like brother and sister, just like Robin and me. — Are you going to wear your gloves?" She grinned, and Jennie wanted Alick to see that sunny face.

"Will you run down and tell Papa where I've gone?"

"Gladly!" Pris kissed her and turned toward the Yard. Afterward she would return contentedly to work in solitude; without guilt, she could weave the most exquisite romances with herself and Septimus as the doomed, enchanted, or blessed lovers. Certain family laws were immutable, and there was no use in rebellion, but her pride had been assuaged. She could *think* as she pleased; no one could censor that.

With Alick forgiven, and Pris off her mind for the time being, Jennie found her walk exceptionally enjoyable. She had gotten herself and Alick aboard the *Paul Revere* knowing full well that the brig and all aboard could disappear in a mid-Atlantic storm. Having survived all that and six childbirths besides, here I am, she thought, walking along this road on a perfect August morning, in a country that is no longer foreign to me; my husband is a respected man, and I know where all my children are at this moment. Who could ask for more?

At the post office she said greeted to the old men who came early to talk and smoke on the bench outside. The flag snapped like a sail in the

northwest gusts coming down over the trees. She told Phipps, the
postmaster, that it looked especially handsome, and congratulated him
on his new spring. He was a tubby little man who spent more time out of
the post office than in it, yarning with the bench-sitters while his wife
did the clerical work inside.

Jennie was passing the time of day with Mrs. Kilburn when a strange
chaise rattled into the yard.

Thirty-Five

A VOICE CALLED, "Good mornin', all!" A long-legged driver, unknown to them, jumped down, hitched the horse to the rail, and strode toward the building, taking a rolled paper from one large pocket of his loose linen jacket and a small hammer from the other. He flattened the paper and began to nail it to the notice board beside the door.

"Who in tunket are you?" Mr. Phipps demanded. The old men on the bench were twisting their heads around to read the paper, some of them creaking to their feet. Mr. Phipps spoke in his official big voice. "Just what are you nailing on my board, Mister?"

"I'm simply exercisin' my rights, suh," the stranger drawled. "Advertisin' for my stolen property." He was a tall, gaunt man with a leathery red-brown face, big-nosed and lantern-jawed. He wore light-colored trousers strapped over Wellington boots. His shirt was open at the neck under the linen jacket; his clothes hung on him as if he were no more than big bones. He pushed his broad-brimmed hat back on his untidy graying head to give him better visibility for his business, and drove in another nail.

"What stolen property?" Phipps huffed suspiciously. Two of the men from the bench were reading past the stranger's shoulder as he drove in his last nail. He stood back with a mocking bow. "Be my guests, gentlemen. I reckon you don't often get up to much excitement in these parts."

The Foss grandfather said in slow amazement, "Well, I be da—" He stopped himself. "Never thought I'd see something like this in *these* parts." He read aloud, slowly, his spectacles pushed far down his nose. " 'Reward: Fifty dollars offered for information of whereabouts of Jerome,

269

a black man aged forty years, sound of wind and limb, expert carpenter. Property of Edward Fitzwater, Esquire.' There's an address here, in Charleston, South Carolina."

He stood back and looked the stranger up and down. "You a slave catcher?"

"I am the owner, suh. I am Edward Fitzwater."

"So that's what one looks like," the old man said as if viewing an elephant for the first time. "Almost human, ain't he?"

Mrs. Kilburn made a small sound of shock and distress. Phipps had been reading the poster for himself; now he turned on Fitzwater like an embattled bantam rooster.

"I will not have that trash here, Mister. You tear it down or I will!"

Fitzwater was two heads taller, and unalarmed. "Either I post this now, or I go away and come back with an officer of the law."

"If you're talking about the constable for South Whittier," Old Cathcart offered, "he ain't available. He's gone fishing for cod to dry for winter."

This was ignored. "I have the right," Fitzwater said with a smoothly overriding arrogance. "I can display this poster at a United States Post Office anywhere in the nation."

"Not *here*," Sam Phipps said. He had to stand on tiptoe, but he ripped it off, leaving only the ragged bits around the nails. He crumpled the rest and tossed it at Fitzwater. "Now you can just *git!*"

Fitzwater put his hands in his pockets and laughed at the men and women who gazed back with varying degrees of distaste. "What kind of folk are you up here in this backwoods state? Up the road, the Whittiers just about ran me off their property—U.S. Post Office and all—and your famous Captain Whittier, your tin sailor you named the town for, *he* knows where my property is, but he gives me that black-eyed look like an Indian figgerin' to scalp you in the next breath, and says, 'You're talkin' through your hat, Mr. Fitzwater. You better start lookin' elsewhere for your *property!*' " He laughed again. "Says it like it's such a dirty word he's got to spit it out fast. Well, they couldn't stop me from nailing up signs on trees, and I aim to keep on doin' it—after I put another one up here."

"Be careful where you drive your nails," one of the old men said. "Us backwoods folk are mighty tender with our trees."

"You reckon you have a private fiefdom here, under your famous general?" He was just on the verge of shouting. "Does the old toy soldier own you all, even this far down the river? I paid my fare on one of his vessels, and my money was good enough, but no *suh*! 'You cannot put up your notice on this wharf. It is private property and not a public landing.' "

"General tell you that himself, did he?" old Foss inquired.

"No, suh, a sassy young rooster who needs his tail feathers pulled out by a good old South Carolina hound dog."

Robin, thought Jennie, wishing Pris could have seen him speaking out like a man to this creature.

"Won't do you no good to insult the General or his boy," one ancient said. "Him and his veterans, and I'm one, built up this place after we won the war."

Fitzwater laughed. "You must have been a great soldier, old Daddy. Well, somebody's stolen a valuable piece of my property, and I mean to have it back before I leave this den of thieves." He swung back to Phipps, who faced him with his doubled fists on his hips. "Is this or is it not a United States Post Office?"

"It is a United States Post Office in the State of Maine, mister, and the State of Maine abhors slavery! I'd no more allow a slave catcher's sign here than I would a blasphemy, because slavery *is* a blasphemy. It stinks in our backwoods nostrils, and it must stink in the nostrils of the Almighty."

"I'm not a slave catcher!" The Southerner was stung at last. "The man's my property, bought and paid for!"

"What makes you think he is here?" Jennie surprised herself, and he looked around as if the building itself had given tongue. He smiled, removed his hat, and spoke in a honeyed drawl. "Why, ma'am, the ship *Ariel* was in port, and a Castine vessel was there at the same time. I hired out my boy to the Castine captain to make some changes in his cabin. I've had him trained as a finish carpenter, and that makes him a heap more valuable than a field hand." When he smiled he showed large, long, tobacco-stained teeth. "He was seen being talked to like a white man by a couple of Whittier men on the dock one day. Both vessels left at high tide that night, and I didn't know till late the next day that Jerome never came back to his quarters." His open-handed gesture was probably meant to be appealing. "What is a man to *think*?"

"But why couldn't he have gone on the Castine ship?" Mrs. Kilburn asked.

"Oh, ma'am!" He laughed jovially. "As I'm not partial to life on the ocean wave, and also suspicious of those Whittier men maybe trying to lure him away into this foreign territory where he'll likely freeze to death come winter, I came to the nearest port. Of course, if I don't turn up the black rascal here, I'll be obliged to find my way to Castine, but I won't go by water if there's such a thing as a road."

He turned back to Sam Phipps, "I'll wager my soul on it, that boy's here *somewhere*, and somebody'll want the reward." He pointed a finger at Sam's round belly. "Either you allow my poster up, or I will be back with a warrant from the court."

"You'll have to drive to Wiscasset for that," said Phipps, "and if your man's here now, he'll be halfway to Nova Scotia when you get back, and hid so deep in the woods it'd take a passel of Indians to dig him out—if we had any Indians. You'd have to go up-country for 'em, and then they wouldn't know this territory, so—"

Fitzwater, foxed by the country oafs, tried to recover the *sangfroid* with which he had driven into the yard. He made sweeping bows all around, cried, "*Good* mornin', ladies!" and climbed into the chaise and drove off.

The third old man, who had not spoken before, said diffidently, "Just the same, a man's property is his property, if he paid good money for it under the law."

The other two simply looked at him, but Phipps swung around. "Gemini, Abel, this is a human being, not a cow or a horse! You got no right to buy or sell human beings! If a white man indentures himself, he can work himself free, but how'd you like a gang of bandits to come down on you like the old press gang, and put chains on you and take you away from your wife and young ones, and throw you into a stinking hold on one of them hell ships, and think you no more than a beast because your skin is black? If there's a God in Heaven, why does He allow it?" He shook his fist at the sky. "You hear me up there? Strike me dead if You ever said You created the blacks to be the white man's beasts of burden! It was likely writ down by some Old Testament reprobate who used You for an excuse for any deviltry he felt like getting up to, including plenty I'd never mention afore ladies, and saying You told him to!"

He tramped into the building, leaving behind him a reverberating astonishment at such fire from a supposedly simple little man. The old fellow who had spoken up for property rights studied his boots. Mr. Cathcart said, "The poor critter's not around here. The Whittiers are too law-abiding, even if they hate slavery like the devil hates holy water."

"Well, wherever he is," Jennie said, "let us hope it's a safe haven in Canada."

"Amen to that," old Foss said. Mrs. Kilburn wiped her eyes.

"I don't know as I'll sleep very well," she said to Jennie, "thinking how this kind of awful stuff has come into our town, like the plague."

"He'll be gone tomorrow," Jennie said, "and the man *has* to be safe somewhere, by now."

"But nothing will be the same afterward," Mrs. Kilburn said. Jennie walked quickly away from the post office, wanting to be alone, to get home as fast as her legs would take her.

She came suddenly upon the hired rig, stopped on the right-hand side of the road, and she crossed to the other side. Fitzwater, whistling, was nailing a notice on a fence post. He gave her a cheery wave of the hammer. "We meet again, ma'am! I am a fortunate man!" He cocked his head at the poster. "Don't that tell it all? Fifty dollars reward. *Fifty dollars.* Now that is going to look mighty beautiful to *somebody.*"

Jennie didn't answer, but walked faster, hoping he wouldn't catch up with her. That particular poster wouldn't stay there for long; it was on the Post Office Farm. But the sunshine seemed to have neither heat nor brightness, and the shade was cold through her paisley sleeves. When she turned off the public road and into the home woods, she wanted painfully to see and touch each of her children and draw them close, like a hen clucking her chicks under her wings.

It couldn't be, of course. They must not be raised in blinders. If they were to live in the world and be among its useful citizens, they should learn early their duties and responsibilities.

But not this young. *Please,* not this young.

Thirty-Six

O VER DINNER JENNIE told the family about the slave owner, and Pris and the boys were for leaving the table at once and hurrying up to the road in the hope of confronting him. Alick shook his head to their impassioned entreaties.

"I will not have you speaking with this man. You would be getting the worst of it, he would call you squeaking children and laugh in your faces, and you would not have saved the slave. But anything he has posted on our land you may rip down."

"Besides, he is likely halfway to Job's Harbor by now," Jennie said.

"And it's the grand reception the Winters will be giving him," Alick said. "He will be coming away considerably wiser for the experience."

"If it doesn't happen before that," said Jennie. "Suppose he should run into the Keelers? And I doubt the Jennisons would let him post anything on their land."

"Mr. Shaw wouldn't drive him off," Carolus said. "He's just the kind who'd like a whole crew of slaves so he could ride around on his big horse, cracking a whip over their bleeding backs."

William put down his spoon, and Bell Ann, who had been mystified until then, was horrified. "*Who* would be beat with a whip?"

"Mr. Shaw cannot be whipping slaves he is not owning," said Alick. "Eat your dinner, Bell Ann. Attend to yours, Carolus."

"But what if the slave ever turned up here, Father?" Sandy asked. "Looking for refuge? If slavery is legal, would you be bound to give him up?"

"In my mind slavery is a crime. Does that answer your question? But

I would not like a confrontation, knowing I could be arrested under the law, fined, perhaps imprisoned."

"Nobody would arrest *you*, Papa," Priscilla protested.

"And if they did, we would organize a raid on Tenby jail!" Sandy sounded as if he could hardly wait. "Everybody would go, most of Whittier and half of Maddox, and the General would ride up, but first he would send a messenger on a fast horse to the Governor."

"That's just the kind of thing Seven Frye would love to do!" Priscilla said. "Bolivar is *very* fast."

Alick acknowledged this statement with lifted eyebrow, and Pris flushed and returned nervously to her dinner.

"Or Robin," suggested Carolus. "*He* would be gone like Paul Revere."

"By Judicker, I was thinking of myself," Sandy said indignantly. "I'm thin and light enough, I could ride like the wind on a fast horse, if we had one."

"I'm lighter than you!" William cried. "I could go on Shonnie!"

Alick sat back, laughing. "Och, the hero I would be! Bonnie Prince Charlie would not be in it with me. I could be running for President after all that. I am almost sorry to disappoint you, but in my bones I know the missing man is a long way from here."

"And you must always trust your father's bones," said Jennie. "He's known them all his life, and I've known them for almost half of mine, and have always found them utterly dependable."

"What bones?" Bell Ann asked, bewildered, and was cross when everyone laughed.

The boys planned to go Indian-hunting in the afternoon. They had not searched for artifacts for all summer, and time was growing short. Where would they go? They knew they could not dig on other people's property without express permission, but what hadn't they yet explored on their own land? Sandy quickly took command. The last time when there was a tide low enough for clamming off the river end of Misery Wall, they had seen where rough water had tumbled away some rocks at the base, and fragments of clamshell showed in the hollows left. "Not many, but you don't know what is behind and beneath."

But first they went up to the road to see if the slave-owner had dared nail signs on their trees. "Something in my ears is moving in and out like bellows," said Jennie when they all went out at once. "The sudden silence."

"Och, but they are a passionate crew! I would not want them to be meeting him coming back. They would be forgetting their manners entirely."

"They would send him away deaf, at any rate," said Jennie. They were walking toward the Yard. The old apple tree was now wearing a thick crop of little green jade marbles. The morning breeze had dropped, and the river that had been a sash of crumpled peacock taffeta had become a widening band of robin's-egg blue satin. The apple tree's sprawling ancient limbs cast motionless shadows in precise silhouette. Across the pasture the animals stood or lay under the trees in pools of plum-colored shade; even Brisky was too somnolent to come whickering to the fence. Gulls rested motionless on the roofs at the Yard, and *Artemis* was becalmed above the barn.

It was the moment of warning that the southwest wind was about to rise, and the day would be pummeled into violent motion. "It is so beautiful," Jennie said. "I shall never get used to it. But then I think of the man Jerome, and something slams down between us and the beauty like a solid iron portcullis. As if we have no right to it. That abominable Fitzwater has dropped slavery into our lives like poison in our well."

Fitzwater had left a turbulent wake through the town. Some of the men coming back from dinner were loudly resentful. "By Judas, I'd like to serve a warrant on *him* for driving spikes into two of my best sugar maples!" one said. "That's mutilation, ain't it?"

"Yes," said Jennie with feeling. His fleshy face cracked into a complexity of seams.

"Met your young ones on the warpath."

"All they needed was war paint and tommyhawks," somebody else said. "Even that little one." They laughed and went on. By the rowans she met Harry, spoke to him, and for answer received neither the ambiguous syllable nor the finger touched to his hat brim. No wonder; the children and the dogs were coming down through the woods behind him.

They had divided into patrols to cover the road from the post office to the Keel land. No posters had been left up anywhere, not even at the Shaws'.

"We met Harry," Pris said, "and I asked him about it, but he stared at me as if I were a cannibal queen who'd just been wafted from the Sandwich Islands and dropped spang in front of him on the Whittier road. Isn't that a stupendous figure of speech?" she appealed to her mother. "I could start a novel with it, but not today. I am going to sew with Thankful."

Bell Ann decided to follow the boys Indian-hunting, because being with them could lead to inconceivable adventures. Priscilla's relief at losing her small shadow for the afternoon was transparent; there was too much to tell Thankful. Septimus had asked permission to call, and the request was more important than its denial. And there would be more, Jennie knew; Septimus' voice couldn't have been idle in that empty house even if his hands had behaved themselves. And if there *had* been a slight pressure of her fingers when he assisted her in and out of the gig, or the fingers had been carried to his lips, telling it to Thankful would be as delicious as the event itself.

When Jennie was alone she was too restless to settle down to finish the letter to Ianthe. Too many things had happened since it was interrupted yesterday. That transparent globe encasing the River Farm world in its own singular and intimate atmosphere had been knocked askew on its axis, just enough so that life here would never be the same again for any of them, even for Bell Ann in her vociferous innocence.

The wind off the water was now too boisterous for her to read in the orchard swing. As a salve to her conscience she should be useful, but darning would be carrying virtue too far. She compromised by beginning a pair of stockings for Bell Ann. She accomplished an inch of bright red wool ribbing before she wanted to hurl it across the room. She restrained herself, but she left it. Packing up a basket of molasses-raisin cookies and a jug of water, she went into the rough waggish humor of the wind.

In the hot lee of Misery Wall she examined the fragments of bone and ancient charcoal the boys showed her, and dutifully ran her thumb over the worked edges that had made thumbnail scrapers out of felsite chips. There were two broken points, and a modestly shining William held out his personal find: an almost perfect, pale gray, leaf-shaped knife. Sandy was notably generous about giving him credit; Carolus said William had a Gift, but thoughtfully refrained from patting his head.

Bell Ann had been playing in a tide pool among the ledges, sailing a fleet of large mussel shells loaded with periwinkles from one port to another. Jennie took off her shoes and stockings and slid her feet into the warm water, and Time's precipitate pace immediately stopped for her; this hour existed only in this place, and nothing else could have any relationship with it.

They all sat around the pool pleasurably wiggling their toes in it, eating their strupach and sharing with the dogs. They were on a little island of calm with the sound of water all about them; it broke against the prow of the Wall, and sent miniature combers splashing across the cove, translucent blue-green marbled with streaks of foam and crested with dancing light. Whenever one hit a rock it burst upward into plumes of diamonds.

"Miriam was here," Bell Ann said suddenly. "She came through the woods."

"It's too bad she didn't stay to have a strupach with us," Jennie said.

"She ran away from her chores," William volunteered. The twins went on steadily munching, gazing at the tumultuous cove as if mesmerized by the glitter. "She couldn't stay very long."

"She stayed long enough to tell *them* some ghost stories," Bell Ann said. "Maybe about those pirates that used to sail up the river and kill everybody."

"They never did *that*," said William. "Well, maybe one or two, but not *everybody*. They mostly just buried their treasure here and there, but nobody's ever found any of it."

"Well, it was ghost stories anyway," Bell Ann insisted, "because they told me I wouldn't like it, and to go back and sail my boats."

"Did they let you listen, William?" Jennie asked.

"Och, aye!" he said with a grin.

"And you'll have nightmares tonight!" Bell Ann said triumphantly. "They won't let you sleep at the fort anymore, you wait and see!"

William was not alarmed. He took another cookie.

"Look!" Sandy shouted, and pointed. Out on the river two ships ran before the wind, all sails set and bellying, vivid new ensigns flying. *Undine*, named for the water spirit, and *Venus*, for the foam-born goddess, the sister ships of the Dalrymple twins, were racing home.

The watchers by the wall were all drawn to their feet, even Bell Ann. Jennie winked away a blur in her vision, and she heard William's slow deep breath beside her.

"Lionel's a dite ahead," said Sandy. "Leander must be jumping on his hat, he's so furious."

"All he needs is a capful more wind," Carolus said. "*Venus* can do it."

"Then she'll have to get through the Narrows first, and wouldn't I love to see *that* duel! Gemini!" Sandy jabbed Carolus in the ribs. "Care to lay a wager?" Then he caught his mother's eyes and grinned. "Wouldn't be more than one of my chores against one of his."

"Done!" said Carolus. "You lug all the wash water next time, Alexander, because *Venus* will pass Hospital Point first."

"Oh, you'll be doing the lugging, Professor," Sandy retorted, "because *Undine* will do Captain Lionel and me proud."

William had not looked away from the ships as they flew onward. "They should both win," he said in a low voice, and Jennie knew he wanted victory not for the twin captains but for the twin ships; so superbly alive they were to him, he could not bear for one to lose.

"Well, it could be a dead heat," Carolus said, and Sandy graciously agreed that stranger things had happened.

Thirty-Seven

J ENNIE WONDERED AT supper time whether any of them had given another thought to the slave owner once he had disappeared. Certainly he was not mentioned. Pris came home with her hair done up; Thankful and Candace must have spent the entire afternoon with curling papers, brush and comb, and legions of hairpins. Her face was framed by quivering curls like little springs, and the rest of her hair was severely brushed upward, braided and twisted and wound with ribbons into a cylinder springing strangely from the crown of her head.

"Very interesting, dear," Jennie said. Alick nodded gravely, which could mean anything. William and Bell Ann were less than quietly astonished. Carolus was a little too polite, as if otherwise he would have fallen down laughing, and Sandy said she would have done just as well glueing on a patch of curly shavings and a dory plug. Priscilla's impassive disdain may have been due to the fact that it hurt to move her face.

Apparently Ianthe was not offended by the new coiffure, and the curls were tight enough not to be damaged when Pris leaned her forehead against the cow's side. She came back from milking like a princess turned dairymaid by a wicked stepmother but resolutely maintaining her aristocratic self-esteem. She ate her supper in an unnatural silence (on her part), as excruciatingly erect as if she were hanging by the beribboned cone.

She went to bed very early. When Jennie looked in on her later on, she lay in untroubled sleep with her hair loose and free.

"She must have taken it down the instant she could get away from us," Jennie told Alick. "And we needn't worry about seeing it on an empty stomach tomorrow morning, because she can't possibly do it all up by herself."

"That is a blessing." He went on reading, but she wondered how much he was taking in. The experiment with Pris's hair was a weathervane, whisking about in variable winds, and there would be more experiments. As a female, Jennie accepted the inexorability. It was for Alick that she felt a profound concern, knowing that in the depths below his common sense and his saving humor he was crying out for Time to stand still.

The nearest he had ever come to admitting it was when he had asked, "Are they only loaned to us?"

Gael that he was, seeming never to lack for words, he could hide himself behind them very well. Only Jennie knew that the young boy still existed, born to a widow and cheated of a father sent to die in America; a boy who was refused an education, who had known early that he was an embarrassment to the legitimate Linnmore heirs because his dead father had been the first-born son. When he left Linnmore, it was as a fugitive with no time to collect the few possessions that bound him to his dead; he had been wearing his bonnet, his plaid, and his dirk when Nigel died, so they had come with him; they now lay in a chest in the spare room. Once during the journey he said, "I have left no one behind me, only graves." Of Mata the garron, he had hardly spoken, and just once he had mentioned his grandfather Linnmore's Doune pistol, a shawl of his mother's weaving, and a pair of silver buckles from his father's shoes.

But with the years, and the children, Jennie had come to realize how much more there was. It had been not only his world, but his father's, so wound about and crisscrossed with the prints of Sandy Gilchrist's short existence that his son had walked every day of his life in his father's footsteps. He had seen, breathed, heard, and done all that his father had experienced before he became a soldier. If ghosts walked, young Sandy Gilchrist surely walked the moors and glens of Linnmore.

It was from this that Alick had gone away, to build with Jennie a world where no other Gilchrist had ever been, and never calling himself by that name. Watching Alick with his children, seeing how eagerly he had taken on the role of fatherhood, Jennie saw that he had become his own father, making up his losses to himself by giving his children everything he had ached for. But Time, at once best friend and enemy, would leave them in his arms for just so long, and then move them, one by one, away.

Earlier in the summer Pris had been invited to go home with the

Clements after the picnic and visit with them and the Mackenzies; she was slightly older than the oldest children in the two families, but she was comfortable with them all. At first she had talked about it so much that she incited the twins to irritation and envy. But it had been some time now since she had mentioned it, and the picnic was about to happen. Perhaps she felt too old for such simple pleasures now that she was a young woman sought after by an older man even if her parents didn't allow it. By Friday morning Jennie was tired of the suspense and went out to the barn to catch Pris when she was milking.

With her forehead against Ianthe's warm side, Pris sang softly to the rhythm of the milk squirting into the pail. It was a Gaelic milking croon Alick had taught her; his mother had used it. It praised the cow for her shining eyes and her velvety coat, her sweet breath and her loving heart, the goodness of her milk, and the richness of her cream. No knight in his castle, no chief in his great hall, had better. She was dearest of the dear, fairest of the fair.

The croon and the milking finished together. Pris set the pail to one side and kissed the complacent Ianthe between the horns. "I hope Bell Ann and Louisa are such a loving pair," she said. She watched fondly as Ianthe joined the others in the pasture. "She was the dearest little calf, like a fawn," she said. "It is hard to believe she was such a baby once."

"Spoken like a true parent," said Jennie. "Pris, if I am to be milking for a week, I want to be prepared for it. Do you or don't you intend to go back to Maddox after the picnic?"

Pris was honestly surprised. "I didn't think I *could* go."

"Why in the world would you think that?"

"Because you and Papa might be thinking I would manage to meet Seven there, somehow."

"I have never dreamed of such a thing, and I'm sure your father hasn't either."

"I didn't know," Pris mumbled. "Nothing like this has ever happened before. I did think of writing him," she confessed in a rush, "but how could I have mailed it? You can't do anything in a secret around here except in your own room."

"I agree," said Jennie wryly. "And, if you're a parent, your door must always be opened to a child. Wait until you reach *that* position in life."

Pris laughed uncertainly. "I don't think I'd have really done it anyway. I was so angry that day, I wished I could lie to you and deceive you. But all the time I knew I couldn't, and that made me angrier."

"I know exactly what you mean," said Jennie. "Very well, then, are you going?"

"Yes, and you and Papa needn't put me on my honor. I won't try to meet him, and if he comes seeking me, I'll tell him he must go away."

"He will be impressed by your integrity."

Priscilla's expression suggested this would be cold comfort. "You won't mention any of this to *them*, will you?" she asked. "Because you can trust me; no one needs to watch me."

"We wouldn't dream of mentioning it," Jennie said.

"Thank you, Mama," Pris said. "You are a very good friend." She was on her way to the spring house with the milk. Jennie, walking back to the house, was thinking of telling Alick about the conversation. Just as she reached him, Bounce shot out to bark at Harry Shaw. Alick, by the rowans, whistled the terrier back and told him to sit down and be quiet. Harry came on, limping with a rhythmic lurch to the right at every step. His hat brim was pulled down lower than usual, but not enough; as he passed them they saw his right cheek scraped and raw. He had quickly jammed his right hand into his pocket, but not before they saw it was red and puffy, and Jennie had the distinct impression of a blackening eye. He could not hide his swollen mouth.

"Good morning, Harry," Alick said. "What has happened to you?"

He didn't stop. "Riding Major last night," he said indistinctly. "He wouldn't have it. Threw me. *Vicious!*" he slung back at them and walked faster, making the lurch more pronounced.

"That hand looks ugly," Jennie said.

"I will have a closer look at it and send him home for fomentations if need be."

"His mother can't be very sympathetic, if he took the horse without her permission. He was likely vigorous with the whip, too."

"A wee whisper in here," he tapped his temple, "tells me it was not a resentful beast but a stramash somewhere last night in seas of rum."

The first loaves for the weekly baking had gone into the oven when the family sat down to breakfast, and now they were out, perfuming the house, and the second batch was baking. The boys were going a long way beyond Misery Wall this morning to get mussels for the picnic, and Bell Ann wanted to go, but it was too far for her. She disagreed loudly and stamped her foot at her mother. She was given a slap on her bottom and sent upstairs to reflect upon her naughtiness. Jennie prepared to boil a ham for the picnic.

Pris was chopping candied lemon and orange peel to go into a blueberry cake she had created, and as soon as Bell Ann had stamped her way upstairs and slammed her door, she said, "I am thinking of a novel. I have already started to write it, in my head."

"A romance?" Jennie asked lightly.

"Certainly *not!*" Then she guffawed in her old way. "Well, there will be lovers, but also a murder. It is my considered opinion that there is many a murderous maniac hiding behind a perfectly ordinary, even rather nice, face. My villain will not look a bit sinister, but rather like Mr. Lockhart, or even as gentle and pure-eyed as William. I'll use The Language of Flowers," she rambled on. "Someone can leave little warning nosegays around, you know the sort of thing. And somewhere there will have to be a mouldering mansion, either far back in the country or out on a cliff. We don't have a cliff around here, but I'll put one in, and there will be ghosts of drowned men lurking about."

"It sounds enthralling," Jennie said.

The dogs began to bark; it was Moses and Orono.

Priscilla came out too, and Bell Ann pleaded from her window. "Mama, I apologize for stamping my foot, and please may I come down and see Orono? Because what will he *think* if I don't bring him his piece?"

"All right, come down," Jennie called back. "We will talk later. There is cut-up turnip in the pantry."

"What happened to you, Moses?" Priscilla was asking. "Orono didn't kick you, did he?"

"Orono wouldn't ever kick me," said Moses, unsmiling. "Nor anybody, unless he was driven to it." He touched his bruised chin. His right hand, like Harry's, looked sore. "Took a tumble on the rocks last night."

"I was only teasing about Orono," Pris said winningly. "I know he is a perfect gentleman." Bell Ann arrived, out of breath and smiling confidently at everyone, kissed Orono and stood watching him eat his wedge of turnip. Pris and Jennie decided on a smoked salmon cured by Mr. George Gunn himself.

When Moses left, Bell Ann walked up to the road with him and Orono. Pris and Jennie sampled the salmon. "Delicious," said Pris. "Do you suppose Moses really fell on the rocks last night and battered his chin and his hand?"

"You didn't see Harry this morning. *He* claims Major threw him."

"That is *it!*" said Pris. "Harry has bothered Miriam again. He may have even turned brave on rum and gone down to the Keel. But I suppose we'll never know," she said regretfully.

Bell Ann came in, saying, "I don't know why I can't marry both David and Moses."

"Having two husbands at the same time is against the law," Pris told her.

"And so is stamping one's foot at one's mother or father," said Jennie. "We will have our little talk now, Bell Ann."

Thirty-Eight

T HE SATURDAY VISITORS had left their farms as soon as the morning chores and breakfasts were over, and when the wagons reached River Farm, and the horses put in the pasture, there was a second breakfast down in the orchard. In the exchange of general news, Harm Clements settled the twins' wager about *Venus* and *Undine*; he was superintendent of the Mackenzie shipyard and was thus at the waterfront all day. *Venus* had sailed into the Pool six minutes before her sister.

Carolus didn't openly exult, but his dancing eyes and the way he slapped his hand over his mouth as if to hide a grin were enough to turn Sandy's face to ruddy granite. He sat immobile with his back against a tree, pretending that he was not seething. Jennie wasn't sorry for him; he was too eager to inflict these wounds upon himself. Meeting Alick's eyes for an eloquent instant, she knew he was thinking that Sandy, like her, was a desperate optimist.

Harm went on telling how the twin captains came face to face on the wharf, glaring at one another like a man and his fetch trying to destroy each other with a look. Then they had passed without a word, a relief to some and a disappointment to others, because on occasion one captain had been known to accuse the other of deserving to be keel-hauled or worse, and then they would go at each other like two fighting cocks and have to be forcibly separated by their mates. Not too much blood was ever spilled, and that night they would be drinking toasts to each other at the usual family celebration.

The next news was about the slave-owner. He was supposed to have left Tenby by late yesterday afternoon, sailing up the Penobscot River to Castine on a fishing boat. No livery stable in either Maddox or Tenby would let a rig go that far with a stranger who was not a State-of-Mainer.

It was the sort of day which could have gone on forever, or at least for a few more hours, but the sun was an inexorable timekeeper, and there was livestock waiting at home. At the last moment, when the men were putting the horses between the shafts, the youngest Mackenzie girl and the Clements boy, who had been Bell Ann's henchmen all day, said she was coming home with them; she could visit with one family while Pris visited with the other. Bell Ann had Evelina Ermintrude all dressed and Bear in his best waistcoat by the time the parents were consulted. Lucy and Kate were agreeable, and Pris said she would be close enough if Bell Ann was homesick.

"I won't be homesick. I won't be homesick!" Bell Ann insisted at the top of her voice, and wrapped her arms around first one parent and then the other in fervent entreaty. Eddie Clements had invited Brisky home, too; he had no pony, and Brisky had been unusually gracious today until he'd had enough nursery duty. Luckily he had simply become uncatchable, instead of making his point by standing on someone's foot.

Finally the wagons drove out, escorted by the dogs like outriders, all the goodbyes and Bell Ann's last orders ringing out behind them.

"She will fall asleep halfway," said Sandy, "or else they will all be deaf. She is drunk with exultation."

"And I will *not* kiss High Cockalorum," said William. "Why, that old rooster'd peck your eye out fastern'n you could spit. *She* never kisses him!"

"Do you wish you were going with them?" Alick asked. William loved Harm's oxen.

"No, *ma'am!* I have more important things to do. Right now it's tending those birds!" He sped off like a young Mercury. "And no kisses!"

Jennie told the twins to stay away from the barn until she had milked Ianthe.

"Would you not like me to be milking Herself?" Alick asked, straight-faced.

"I know you have a touch to beguile any female," she told him, "but it is a disgrace for me to be intimidated by a spoiled cow. Either Ianthe and I accomplish a meeting of minds tonight, or tomorrow you may enchant her to your heart's content."

Ianthe by now was so anxious to be milked that she was not fractious. She seemed to take "Believe me if all these endearing young charms" as a personal tribute.

"Tomorrow morning I'll try 'There is a lady sweet and kind,'" Jennie told Alick. "Priscilla has given her a tremendous idea of herself."

For supper they finished the smoked salmon with tomatoes from Hector Mackenzie's experimental greenhouse, and Lucy's blackberry tarts.

The meal was no quieter than usual; the boys filled up the gaps as spilled water runs into every seam and crevice. At least William and Sandy did. Today Carolus's voice had cracked when he was shouting insults at the opposing team in a ball game, and he was afraid it would happen at the table, giving Sandy a chance to make him suffer for winning the wager. But the three boys went off to the fort like comrades-at-arms.

Watching them ramble down across the shadowy field and then disappear into the woods as if in the blink of a cosmic eye, Jennie said pensively, "I wonder if they are trying to raise the ghost of a pirate who will tell them where his gold is buried. Or the Norseman Carolus thinks built a hut where his bit of old stone corner is."

"They would be trying this with *William* present?" Alick asked skeptically.

"Perhaps he found out by accident what they're up to, and they have to take him along to keep him quiet. Well, if that's it, it will blow over as quickly as it did with us and the stone circle, once they're back to school and there's no more sleeping at the fort."

"Was your father knowing about this ghost-raising?"

"I'm sure, because he and his brothers must have gone through the same things at our age. How could we help it? A stone circle only a few miles across the moor from us, besides all the spells and charms and omens and warnings, and bred-in-the-bone superstitions around us as thick as the heather. Vincent Taggart would have been in sheer heaven; he could believe in ten different terrors a day."

"What ghosts were you raising?"

"We were rather afraid of ghosts then, because Mary Ann was, and we thought anything that could frighten Mary Ann ought to be left alone. But on the night of the spring solstice one year we made a visit to the Circle. We waited until dark, and Sophie was sound asleep. Mary Ann went to her own cottage, and Papa had friends in."

She was back there now, trembling with excitement and pride at being included in Ianthe's and Sylvia's schemes. "I know exactly how William must feel," she said, a little misty with nostalgia. "Alick, I couldn't number the proofs of the Circle's powers, the supernatural events sworn to on Bibles, and—," she laughed, "the babies conceived at the Stones. They weren't magnificent like Stonehenge, but rather squatty and dumpy, like a conclave of fat dwarfs, but oh, the *authority* of them!"

It was a night when a dry gale was blowing towers of black cloud across the sky, so that one instant it was very dark and in the next the crescent moon came sailing into sight, an arc of cold white radiance. Oh, stay with us, dear goddess, great Luna! she mutely prayed, eyes uplifted, stumbling and being yanked up by a sister on either hand. Strangely, it was as fearsome in the light as in the dark, except that when the light was blotted out one heard more in the wind.

"You know how it sounds, blowing across the moors," she said. Alick nodded, chin in his hand, watching her as he sometimes watched the children, with a sober mask over affectionate amusement. "We kept hearing cries in it, and thudding feet; the slopes were alive with what we could not see. Not sheep; there was still deep snow in the hollows, and they were safe in the folds for the lambing. We scampered on, clutching each other's hands, and then when we reached the Circle—what with the flying lights and shadows, and everything in motion, we thought the Stones were moving. The dwarfs were dancing!"

She put her hand to her chest, laughing and breathless. "I can still feel it there. I can *see* us now, tumbling away head over heels, dragging each other up, afraid to cry out."

"And afraid to look back," said Alick. "Am I not knowing what *that* is like?"

"We couldn't possibly have run the three miles home, but we felt as if we had, and we were in our beds before we could be missed. The dogs must have been under a spell, because they didn't give us away when we crawled in all scratched and panting. We slept in one bed that night, with the dogs on our feet."

"And did you never go back?"

"*Never!* Somehow we lost all interest. Now I think Papa knew more than we gave him credit for. If our three are up to anything, one good fright will end it."

"A stray goat from the Keel could be Blackbeard in the flesh," said Alick, "or Lucifer himself."

Alick had survived growing up next door to a Fairy Hill, above a loch named for either a phantom dog or wolf, and stabling a water horse; Satan-as-goat held the hill behind the mansion. As a grown man he had believed in the ghost of a murdered exciseman. Now, having put them all away, he was not disturbed by Jennie's imaginative suppositions; they were as reasonable as any, if there must be a reason to turn the new comradeship into a conspiracy.

Placidly he wound the clocks, his Saturday night ritual, while Jennie roamed through the house in her nightgown, brushing her hair. Bounce was called in; Darroch preferred to stay out, it was so warm. Without someone upstairs to sleep with, the cat hurried ahead of them into their room. They lay in the dark and talked about the day, what each other had missed; laughed or were thoughtful. Out in the kitchen, Bounce jumped down from the camp bed and came cautiously in to settle down under the bed with a faint scrape of toenails.

Garnet sang herself deeper into the atavistic jungle she roamed in her sleep. A jaw-straining yawn overtook Jennie, and then another. "Bell Ann must have been asleep for hours now," she said. "Well, it won't be like the last time she was away overnight." She thought she said it aloud, but afterward she wasn't sure. Alick didn't answer, and she was falling asleep too fast.

Her menses were on schedule when she arose on Sunday morning. Alick was already out in the kitchen building the fire while she washed and dressed. She had hated the messy process since the first shattering surprise of it; her sisters would have prepared her, but she had begun earlier than they expected. She had raged through their rooms shouting that she would not put up with it. When she was exhausted, and sipping chamomile tea between hiccups, they convinced her that she must, and would, put up with it. It was not the end of the world; look at *them*! They were right, but it changed from a horrible fate visited on an innocent child to a horrid nuisance that had to be planned *around*, not only with special laundry, but dates marked on the calendar. Up to now dates had meant holidays, birthdays, and other happy occasions; now they had a darker aspect. There were certain things you *must not do* on those days. Challenging fate, she washed her hair and went in wading and didn't die of it; she found out that her sisters had done the same.

But it was like being made guardian of the family monster, which you may not secretly destroy so you can get on with your life. In time it became more manageable, and she knew she was lucky to have such an uncomplicated and healthy set of organs. So had Pris, and she'd made sure that Pris hadn't been taken by surprise in the first place.

She went out to the kitchen and put on her boots and apron for the barn. "I am on time," she said to Alick.

"Are you disappointed?"

"I don't know. — No!"

He set the porridge pot over the flames for the water to boil, walked across to the windows, and stood looking out at the opalescent sky. She went to stand beside him.

"Are *you* disappointed? Because if you are—"

"We will begin again? Och, no! Not that I would never welcome the wee soul, but the five are giving us all the surprises we need, and they have only just begun." He held out his arms to her.

"When this week is over," she said into his shirt, "watch out for a wanton woman in your bed."

The way he laughed was something known only to the two of them.

The day was hot, and the heat and the heavy flow of her first day gave her reason enough to stay at home.

The boys were very late this morning, heavy-eyed, and moodily silent when Alick told them that if it happened again there'd be no more sleeping at the fort. Even William had lost his luster, but he did rouse up to say the mosquitoes had been something fierce, and two porcupines kept squealing at each other for half the night.

Jennie told them she was not going to church and gave them the choice. There was a faint brightening.

"God is too busy to care whether we're there or swimming in the river," Sandy said.

"If He isn't busy, He should be," said Carolus severely. "There are some very bad things going on in the world."

"Mr. Lockhart might be saying you should be faithful even when God is not looking," Alick suggested.

"Isn't He supposed to be all-seeing?" Carolus asked. "So He should know, and we are not being sneaks about it. Besides, what is one Sunday out of the year when the only other times we don't go is if we are sick or it's a blizzard?"

"I would tell Mr. Lockhart," Sandy said pompously, "that I could not respect a God who would be so petty."

"What do *you* think about God, William?" Jennie asked him. He had been listening with his head cocked like Bounce.

"Well, sometimes I think He is there, and other times I think He may be gone away, and that is when the bad things happen. Where was He when Jesus died? Papa would never let anyone hurt any of *us* like that," William went on. The twins looked at him as if one of the dogs or Garnet had suddenly begun to speak. "You can't really *love* God," William said, "because you can't see Him and He is too grand. You cannot even *like* Him. You wouldn't dare. But the Great Horse—," his face lit up, "*He* is different."

The twins burst out laughing, but William was not offended. "Aye, and a handsome, generous beast he is," Sandy said.

"You two," said Jennie to the twins. "Did Bell Ann tell you, or did you overhear her talking to herself?"

"She told William," said Carolus. He held up his right hand. "Mama and Papa, we swear we will never tell it anywhere else, and we would never laugh at her."

"I wouldn't," said William, "because how do we know he is not there?"

Thirty-Nine

B Y MONDAY MORNING, Ianthe and Jennie were a congenial pair; Jennie mined songs from her deepest memories and enjoyed every moment. Carolus had no chance to loll about watching while Sandy carried all the wash water; his father put him to work whitewashing the inside of the Necessary, where he whistled like a catbird trying to imitate six birds simultaneously. Singing was risky these days, but there was no risk of a whistle breaking.

William wiped dishes and helped to collect the laundry. When the twins finished their chores, they took axes and the crosscut saw and went into the eastern woods, where yesterday they had found a blowdown on the way to the trout pool. Shallow-rooted, a great spruce that looked as monumental as the Rock of Gibraltar could be freakishly felled by a stiff summer wind, and take others down with it. William looked longingly after them and the dogs, but when he had finished pegging clothes to the lines and spreading sheets and towels on the grass, he could go to see how the twins did.

They had a dinner of the trout the boys had caught yesterday, with spinach and boiled potatoes. In the afternoon the twins harnessed Perry to the wagon, took William and the list of the staples that were getting low, and drove to the Whittier store. It was cooler today, and they were always thoughtful about tying the horses in the shade; but if a horse showed an inclination to overtake everything else on the road, they were only too happy to oblige, which had led to some sessions with the grindstone. Perry was the least eager to race, and the sight of Alick at dinner testing the edge of the breadknife with his thumb was enough to

293

remind them not to urge the horse. They also left their money at home to avoid temptation.

Jennie, secure in the confidence that all her children were enjoying themselves somewhere else, sat down at the orchard table to write letters.

The boys brought home a flyer describing the recent arrival, by Whittier vessels, of American goods and foreign imports ranging from Italian and English silks to snaths and scythe stones. One could furnish a house either plainly or elegantly, supply tools for a carpenter or a farmer, provide everything for a trousseau, outfit a man for Sunday or work, replenish an apothecary's shelves or a tavern's cellar.

"The place was thronged with a great multitude," Carolus said poetically. "You could not have heard yourself think, Mama. And if they weren't talking about the goods, they were talking about Mr. Fitzwater. He is this week's sinner."

"*Ariel* looks handsomer than ever, now that she's been to sea," Sandy said. "I walked over to look at her. She'll be gone again in a week."

Taking your heart, my son, Jennie thought with loving pity. William, who had been stolidly munching his way through a hard heel of bread, said, "I wanted to speak to Captain Whittier, but there were too many people around."

The twins looked disconcerted, if not actually alarmed. It was so fugitive Jennie couldn't be sure of it, yet the impression remained with her, and William was confusedly reaching for the butter knife and dropping it on the floor, ducking down to get it.

"And did you *think*," Carolus said acidly to the back of his head, "that Captain Whittier would tolerate the impudence of a pipsqueak like you asking him if he brought a runaway slave home?"

"Even *we* would never dare." Sandy was so blatantly sanctimonious that Jennie felt like slapping him, and Carolus too. William sat back on his heels and looked up at them with his eyes full of tears.

"I wouldn't—I *wasn't*—," he protested.

"You *two!*" said Jennie crossly. "I don't know what to make of you! William didn't deserve that."

"I suppose not." Carolus gave her a sheepish grin and reached down a long arm to haul William to his feet. "I beg your pardon, young Wim."

"So do I, Old Go-to-loo'ard," said Sandy. William smiled with innocent relief. Almost in the next moment all three were gone, like birds. When she went out to collect and fold laundry, there was neither sound nor sight of them and the dogs. They would be back by chore time, and she would still be baffled by them.

Late on Wednesday, David came walking down the road with a pack on his back. The horses saw him first; Blanchard's sharp whinny set Brisky off, and the dogs picked it up, informing the boys, who were just returning from an afternoon on the river. They ran with the dogs to meet him at the pasture bars, where he and his horse were having a reunion somewhat hampered by Brisky's interference until Blanchard threatened to nip him.

The family was used to David's absence, but whenever he came home, it was to a joyful welcome. If he came listless and blank-eyed with the inevitable let-down of finishing a commission that had entirely absorbed him for weeks, the well began to fill again when the first Glenroy (human or beast) hailed him. When, at the worst, he wore the invisible armor of the loneliness that was peculiarly his own, the process of renewal might take longer, but it would happen.

Today he looked extremely happy—and not just to be home again, Jennie thought, when he took her in his arms and kissed her. The first time she had kissed him, seeing him as a desperately isolated child, he had been rigid and she thought she had offended or frightened him. But the infant Priscilla's unqualified adoration made the first breach; he had learned to take and to give affection. The David whom Jennie welcomed today in a noisy cluster of boys and animals was a handsomely confident man.

The boys were intrigued by his back-pack. He took out his pocket notebook and wrote, "Geraint brought it from England. Carries everything. Left my satchel with Robin and Pris at the wharf. Pris will bring it home."

They must have made up their differences, Jennie thought comfortably.

Supper had a party flavor, even without the girls. David had come from Boston on the Heriot ship *Alice Heriot*; they had seen her sailing upriver earlier. Geraint's leg was mending and he used a cane now. David brought Gwynneth's love, and gifts from himself: a new book by James Fenimore Cooper, *The Prairie*; for the boys, the back issues of a new magazine founded this spring in Boston, *The Youth's Companion*. He had subscribed to it for them. Bell Ann would have a new book of paper dolls, and there was a little marquetry keepsake box for Pris. The boys took the magazines and went into the winter kitchen and silence; Jennie would give them fifteen minutes before she mentioned dishes. The men sat back and lit their pipes.

The difference between David's return this time and all the others was as manifest as the fragrance of the night-scented stocks when the sun left them, or an aura around the moon presaging sure changes. If he had come to terms with his father's ghost, would it be like this? Alick must be noticing—he was as sensitive as a barometer—but he would not give her a glance across the table.

David had seen Tony; he had spent a morning sketching around the docks and had ended up at the office and warehouse of the Daughters Line. He and Tony had a meal together in a nearby tavern.

"I asked him why he hardly ever came home," he wrote. "He said that Maddox isn't changing fast enough." He looked quizzically at them as if they should understand what he did not. He had never known about Mairi Mackenzie, sixteen years old when Tony had been sixteen, Mairi the sweet singer with the long chestnut hair. They had been innocent and vulnerable, and she had been taken from him and given to a middle-aged man who needed a housekeeper, a nurse for his children, a woman in his bed. It was worse than if she had died, because then she would have stayed forever as Tony had known her. *She cannot fade, though thou hast not thy bliss, Forever wilt thou love, and she be fair.*

David's last news—and obviously saved for last—was that he would be painting a portrait at the Heriots'. "I can work for you until Monday," he wrote Alick.

"*Glé mhath!*" Alick slapped his hand on the table. "I have one man out with the summer complaint, and there'll be more out the next day."

"Is it Mr. and Mrs. Heriot you are painting, or all the family?" Jennie asked.

"None of them. A young girl, Mrs. Heriot's niece. She brought her back from Boston on the *Alice Heriot.*"

David was good with children. His father had painted exquisite miniatures of the General's children, immobilizing them by the forbidding power of his presence. But the eyes of David's subjects looked out forever at a face that first fascinated, and then charmed, because it told them so much without a spoken word.

Forty

O N SATURDAY AFTERNOON there was no wind for sailing, and the boys and David went swimming off Misery Wall. Alick spread his papers on the orchard table and worked on his ship. She was still a secret, kept from the children until Alick was about to set sail with Stephen for the down-east forest where, in one sense, the ship would actually begin. Jennie, between trips to the house to add water to the Saturday baked beans and tend the fire, read in the swing, with her workbasket on the opposite seat in case her conscience intruded too brazenly between her and her book. It had not by the time the boys' voices were heard in the woods. Alick rolled up his plans, and on cue Ianthe reminded the world that milking-time was imminent.

The beans were simmering and browning their way to delectable perfection. Jennie measured the dry ingredients for the johnnycake, then put on her boots and milking apron and went gratefully out into the cooling day. Alick was meditatively considering the crop of rowan berries. He was partial to a rowan-and-apple conserve, but the birds usually stole the berries as they reddened; rowans by the door were lucky for them as well as the house.

David and the boys were coming down from the wash house, towelling their wet heads. Darroch was rolling in the grass to finish drying his heavy coat. Bounce acted his name, jumping around Darroch like a clockwork dog. Suddenly he hurtled out into the road barking; simultaneously Brisky lifted his voice, and the General's small open carriage drove into view.

Robin was driving, and Bell Ann was between him and Priscilla. It was obvious that she was the only one enjoying herself.

William ran forward to take the horse's head when the carriage stopped. Priscilla had thrown off the robe and was half out already, caught and steadied by her father; Robin sat gazing stonily before him. His color was extremely high. Bell Ann stood up and cried, "*David!*" He lifted her out, and she wrapped her arms around his neck and said, "I love you, David." She kissed him loudly on each cheek. The twins went around to Robin's side, trying not to show an indecent curiosity, but he ignored them; his jaw was set so hard it looked painful, as if he were fighting a toothache.

Priscilla was so angry she was exalted by it. "Thank you, Robin, for a *most* enjoyable drive," she said with exquisite sarcasm. Robin's slowly indrawn breath paled his nostrils and lifted his chest; it was as eloquent as her irony. She turned her back on him with an insulting swing of shoulders, and Robin icily addressed the space between the horse's ears.

"It is a *tragedy* your *hero* was too busy to drive you home."

She spun around. "He *is* a hero!"

Bell Ann charged out past them with her dress full of apples for the animals. William grabbed one and fed it to Benjamin, the carriage horse.

"*Hero!*" Robin sneered theatrically. "To hear you go on, anyone would think he *swam* all the way to Castine and back with the bottle in his teeth." Alick and David were quietly removing the girls' belongings and David's bag from the carriage. Robin was so distraught he saw no one but Priscilla. Jennie was dismayed, and the twins and William were enthralled.

"He was there and back in twenty-four hours!" Priscilla said. "Who knows how many lives he saved?"

"Ye gods and little fishes, woman, the scare was pure hysteria! Let one idiot hear the word 'smallpox,' or think he hears it, and all the other idiots go up in smoke, screaming 'Plague'!"

"Thank you, Allan Robert Mackenzie, for calling me an idiot. I appreciate discovering my own identity." They were equally splendid in their passion.

"The crewman on the *Maid of Erin* died, did he not?" Pris sailed on. "And you seem to forget that the two passengers were already ashore and mixing with the populace."

"Father Boyd with the old scars of it on his face, so he could not be giving it? And the man with a medical certificate guaranteeing that he'd had it?" His eyes acknowledged her parents for the first time. "I saw the paper myself, and so did Guy, and the Deputy Collector of Customs."

"How do you know it wasn't forged?"

"Oh, leave off, Pris," he groaned. "You grow devilish tiresome! The fact is, Frye hogged all the attention, as usual. He was frittering around the wharf showing what a fine leg he has, in case an Irish heiress came off the ship and fell instantly in love with him. Well, none came, so he whipped off up the bay for vaccine to save a town that didn't know it needed to be saved."

"You're jealous because you didn't think of it!" she taunted him. "You were on the wharf too!"

"Working," he said, but she trampled that.

"*You* could have had the glory, *you'd* be the hero, *then* let us hear *you* call it nothing but the hysterics of idiots!"

"His horse was a hero," Robin said. "So were the men who sailed him across the bay from Belfast to Castine on a windy night, risking their lives—"

"And *his!*"

"Because he convinced them they would be saving a thousand souls from the Black Death."

"Oh, you—you—*pig-headed! Conceited!* You spoiled *whippersnapper!*"

Robin laughed savagely and leaned over the seat toward her. "And another thing: you were mighty happy I was on the wharf a little later, weren't you?"

Pris's head snapped back as if he had struck her across the face. With her hand to her mouth, she turned and ran into the house. Robin slumped in the seat with his chin on his cravat, gazing at the toes of his boots. The twins didn't move. William was frozen at the horse's head. David had disappeared during the duel.

Alick and Jennie, without a visible signal between them, came together at the side of the carriage. "Are you not wanting a cold drink, Robin?" Alick asked. "To cut the dust of the road in your throat?"

Robin's sideways look said it was not the dust that burned his throat. He pulled himself up and turned to face them. "I apologize for such a display of temper in your presence," he said formally.

"You may have had severe provocation," Alick said; he understood well the wounds of jealousy. "What is this about smallpox?"

Robin said, "You can let go, William. He is not going anywhere until I give the word. The *Maid of Erin* came in, carrying coal," he went on, tiredly. "She'd left off passengers at Portland, but two came here. Father Boyd to perform some baptisms and weddings in the county, and an Englishman, a *bona fide* traveler visiting His Majesty's late colonies. The ship was quarantined in the Pool when the Captain said he had a man down, but he doubted smallpox. And yes, the man has died and been buried in the town cemetery. He was Catholic, being Irish, and Father Boyd said prayers at the grave. But Dr. Waite says it was not smallpox, and he was aboard almost the instant the ship docked. He let the priest and the Englishman go ashore, and as far as I know nobody fled from town in panic. Fled for glory, though." He shrugged. "Well, Septimus brought vaccine back, and Dr. Waite has used it all on the non-vaccinated, so the heroic dash was good for something, I suppose."

"Why was Pris glad you were on the wharf later?" Sandy asked. Robin seemed not to hear. He took up the reins. Just as Benjamin began to turn, Bell Ann came pelting back from the barn, crying, "Robin! Robin!" He stopped the horse and looked down at her with world-weary kindness.

"Thank-you-for-my-ride," she chanted. "When is your birthday party? Because I can go this year!"

"There will be no birthday party, Bell Ann," he said austerely. "I am returning to college early to do some concentrated studying."

Her eyes filled with tears, but she gallantly stiffened her shaking mouth and ran into Jennie's arms. William bit down on his lower lip.

"Robin, if it's Pris's fault," Sandy said anxiously, "you shouldn't pay her any heed. *We* never do when she gets up on her high horse."

"It doesn't profit to make hasty decisions," Carolus said. "Always leave room to change your mind tomorrow." This patronizing advice was marred when his voice slipped off key, but Robin's lips never twitched.

"My decision is irrevocable. Good afternoon, all." He turned the horse's head and drove away.

"Good afternoon, all," said Carolus in a bass voice, and he and Sandy cracked into wild laughter, attacked each other, fell down, and began to wrestle. Bounce threw himself into the tangle, and William was overcome by giggles. Bell Ann lifted her wet face from Jennie's apron.

"He didn't really mean that, did he, Mama? It was just because of the fight."

"We'll find out sooner or later," Jennie said. Bell Ann took it for the magic of 'we'll see,' and ran to watch the scramble. Darroch circled it, making bass comments.

"*Well,*" Alick said to Jennie.

"The word of a thousand meanings," she said.

"Mind you, I understand how he feels about that young man."

"Oh, so do I. And I understand her, too. But I don't think it's time yet for Mama to bustle around her."

Pris came out dressed for milking, walked by them without speaking, and skirted the melee of dogs and children as if it weren't there.

The others were told before they went to their chores not to mention the affair.

"If we aren't supposed to say anything, why did they do it in front of us?" William asked with sincere curiosity.

"You may well ask that," said Carolus.

"I just did."

"They were swept away," said Jennie, "and *we* should have swept ourselves away at once and not listened."

"We were all too fascinated," said Carolus. "It was as good as a play."

"Go," said his father.

When the workers met at the supper table with clean hands and faces, and feet where necessary, Priscilla said with great poise, "Before we begin, let us put something out of the way. I didn't enjoy having an audience, but Robin didn't seem to mind in the least, and there were things that had to be said. So—," airily, "they were said. And they were all the truth."

"You mean what Robin said, too?" Sandy asked.

"Robin," she said, "is merely an impetuous young boy, not unlike yourself."

"Not unlike yourself," Carolus said in a baritone voice. The hilarity was kept down by the power of Alick's lifted eyebrow.

"He doesn't see the larger scene," Pris went grandly on. "In fact, Bobbety cannot see past the end of his nose. A good many people *were* anxious, because they had never been vaccinated, and so they were exceedingly happy that Seven did this great thing."

"But Robin was right," Sandy argued, "anyone could have done it; it's just chance that Seven was free. And he wasn't the only one mixed up in it."

"Oh, *really*!" said Pris. "I had hoped to say a few words of explanation and let that be the end of it. *Please!*"

"Yes, please," said Jennie. "That is a polite command, meaning *no more*."

"But she's costing us the party!" Sandy protested.

"And just when Bell Ann and I could go," said William.

"Enough," Alick said. He tempered it for the young ones. "He may be changing his mind yet."

"He will if Pris apologizes," said Carolus.

"*Never!*" said Priscilla.

"We hear, Mrs. Kemble," said Jennie. "Now give us the news. Surely something else must have happened besides the smallpox scare."

"I can tell you everything *I* did!" Bell Ann said. "Beginning last Saturday, I can remember every single, solitary thing."

"We have been fearing that," said Carolus.

"Darling," Jennie said, "we want to make it last. So tomorrow you may tell us about the first two days, and every day you will tell us about two more days, until you have told it all."

"Who will be assigned to listen?" Carolus asked.

"Oh, we'll share it out," said Jennie with a smile.

Sandy asked Pris why she'd been glad Robin was on the wharf that day.

"I don't know what you are talking about." Priscilla stared him down. Their father asked what was going on at the Clements and Mackenzie farms, and the conversation was steered away from Priscilla.

After supper Jennie and Priscilla left the boys with the dishes and Bell Ann in her room for a reunion with all her children. They walked down to the babies' graves. It was very quiet in the woods as the birds settled for the night.

Pris was preoccupied and sad. If she regretted the war with Robin, she should have known better than to provoke it. But she had done so, and now she had to dree her own weird, to quote Mr. Lockhart and Jennie's father. Jennie was casting about for the most tactful thing to say when Pris said unexpectedly, "Posy Pulsifer was at the wharf that day too. She'd delivered a batch of shirts to a North Carolina captain, and then she waited to watch the *Maid of Erin* come in. My, but Posy's handsome, in a gigantic way!" she said. "She wouldn't keep from staring at me. It made me feel peculiar, and the other girls noticed it."

"Strange," said Jennie, hoping that was profound enough to close the subject.

"Seven and I only said 'Good day' to each other on the wharf, Mama," she said. "We were perfectly proper. Harmony Clements is madly infatuated with Guy Rigby, and that was the reason we were there, so she could gaze on Guy, and Cath Mackenzie could adore Robin from afar. He thinks she's a mere infant. Little does he know how young *he* is. But both girls think Seven is the handsomest man in Maddox, and *they* didn't think he was hogging glory when he rode off on Bolivar. *They* thought he was superb."

"Well, even Robin admitted the vaccine has been useful," Jennie said diplomatically.

"What else could he do, if he is to be honest?"

"What happened later?" I didn't mean to ask that, Jennie thought. She was about to say, "You needn't answer," when Pris turned an agonized face to her and wailed, "Mama, how does something spread around that you thought—that you could *swear*—was absolutely private?"

Septimus and the empty house. "I don't know," said Jennie, "but I think the city is the only place where you can keep secrets. In the country they are blown about like dandelion fluff. What happened?"

"It is so nasty I can hardly speak of it. Nothing like this has ever happened to me before." She stared at the little gravestones, biting her lower lip. "Some boys from North Whittier were loitering around the wharf. Their names don't matter. We were ready to leave; we'd seen all there was to see, and Dr. Waite had come and gone. We had to walk by these boys, and I called them by name, all unsuspecting." She spoke in a rapid monotone. "Then they began saying things about the empty house that day. What were we doing there? they asked. And then they answered themselves." She swallowed and turned her head to look into her mother's eyes. "It made me sick to my stomach. I felt smeared with filth, dirtier than honest cow manure or rotten rockweed. Harmony is so peppery, and Cath wanted to talk back, but I pulled them along. We would have walked straight away but they moved around before us, smirking and jeering, but not too loud; there were men working on the wharf, and Robin and Guy were busy with the Irish captain. I kept praying nobody would hear what those wretches were saying about Seven and me."

It is past, Jennie thought. Too late for rage now. Be calm. "How did it end?" she asked.

"Robin!" Her short explosive laugh sounded more like a sob. "Can you believe it? He just happened to look around. . . . I don't believe he heard what they were saying, but he saw their faces and knew they were plaguing us. He and Guy came straight over. They sauced him, and he ordered them permanently off the wharf, and he said if he knew of them molesting us again he would have them arrested and warned out of Maddox, and their parents would be told why. Mama, he was just *splendid*."

"Not a young impetuous boy, in fact." Jennie couldn't resist that.

"No, not then," Pris agreed. "He rose to great heights at that moment. Of course I thanked him. I didn't mind accepting his offer to drive us home today. Naturally I didn't expect that the mere mention of Seven's good deed would provoke him into such a childish outburst."

"Oh Pris, Pris!" said Jennie. "Talk about a bull in a china shop! You admit he saved you from an ugly experience, and you were mighty glad of that. But when you know how sensitive he is about Septimus, why didn't your gratitude keep you from fighting it through?"

"Because he is so unfair! You heard him! He simply wouldn't admit the truth! Of course I know you and Papa are partial to Robin," she said sulkily. "So I can't expect—"

"Now *that* is unfair," said Jennie, "and you know it. We are partial to our children, and that is why we take such pains with them. Now just think back," she went on. "How would you have felt if Robin *heard* what those boys were saying? Would you expect him to believe it or ignore it?"

"He should not believe it," she said stiffly, staring straight ahead. "That is what I would expect of him."

"But if he *had* heard, and ignored it like a gentleman, would you have been grateful enough not to nag him about Septimus on the way home?"

"*Nag?*" Priscilla was incredulous.

"Yes, nag. He is young, as you say, Pris, and Septimus has the advantage of being an older man, independent, and extremely self-assured. Not only the girls think he's the handsomest man in Maddox— he thinks it too." She shook her head when Pris began to object. "A little vanity is not a sin, my poppet. We are all vain about something, you know that. We can all be humiliated too, even Septimus. There must be older men who can crack that enamel of self-confidence with a look, because they make him feel as callow as he makes Robin feel."

"Like Papa," Pris murmured. "And I've been doing it to Robin. I never thought. Oh, Mama, now I am mortified." She pressed her hands to red cheeks. "Every time I call him a child or a mere young boy, I am really wounding him when I only want to make him angry. I can *hear* myself! How could I have been so *awful*? I shan't blame him if he never speaks to me again."

"Coventry may start at home," Jennie said dryly. "Your brothers and sister think you've blown up the birthday party. You are hoist by your own petard."

"What can I do about that?" She showed some spirit. "Humble myself again? I did it once last week, when I had dinner at Strathbuie House. I pretended what happened at the time of *Macbeth* was all my fault, but now I would have to grovel, and I *won't*."

"A simple friendly note of apology, no groveling, should do it," said Jennie. "I don't think he'd want you to abase yourself. He wouldn't believe it, for one thing." Pris's mouth refused to turn up.

"If his parents and Frank can't persuade him to have the party, everyone will survive the disappointment," Jennie said.

"But I'll still be the malefactor, as if I didn't have enough burdening me down. First there was that nasty talk, and now *this*." She was trying not to cry. "How far will it go? Am I going to be shunned as a loose woman, a wanton? Now is your chance," she said sourly, "to say 'I told you so.' "

"I needn't. You've just had one of the more painful experiences in growing up. The gossip won't last long because there is always something new coming along."

"*I* can never forget it; and how did it ever start? I could swear there was no one in sight that day when we drove in."

"Someone could have been down at the creek and looked up at just the right instant to see. Well, I won't tell you to forget it, because you can't do that, and you shouldn't. Remember the lesson, my darling, but don't brood about it."

"If Seven hears about it, he will think I am worse than poison ivy," Pris said. "Perhaps he'd already heard it. On the wharf that day, he was courteous to us as a group, but I could have been just *anyone*! I hoped for a private glance, and I felt like a fool. I thought it was because of the way you and Papa dressed him down, but now I wonder."

"He knows about gossip, Pris. It shouldn't worry him if it doesn't afflict his career. Young men together don't discuss romance, at least not in a form you'd recognize. The real harm is done when they initiate the rumors and name names."

"Mama, you *can't* believe that Septimus—I know you hate him, but surely you can't think he'd do anything like that!"

Jennie put her arm around Pris's unyielding shoulders. "No, I don't believe it; he is much too intelligent. He values his position, and he will find a way to end the gossip if he hears it. And Pris, I don't hate him, but he made a reckless wager that day, and you are the loser. *That's* what I hate."

Pris suddenly sagged against her. "I don't care so much about the talk if it doesn't mean that he will stop caring about me," she said forlornly. "What does idle talk mean if you truly—" She shut it off, but the unspoken word rang like a carillon of bells. *Love.* Pris doubled over as if with cramp and hid her face in her hands.

Alick walked into the clearing, halted, then came forward lightly as the cat. "Robin?" his lips questioned.

"*Septimus,*" hers answered.

He made a gesture of resignation and sat down on Pris's other side and took her into his arms. She turned blindly to him and put her face against his shoulder. He spoke to her just above a whisper in the Gaelic that had always meant a safe cradling, from the moment when she was born into his hands.

Forty-One

S UNDAY BEGAN AS a classic weather-breeder. There was no dew on the grass, and water kept boiling away so that the porridge needed particular care. The air had an exhilarating property in which distant objects and sounds were seen and heard with the sparkle and ring of crystal.

Pris arose as clear-eyed as Bell Ann, singing out "Good morning!" on the way to the barn.

"So that tempest is over," Alick said cautiously, and Jennie knocked on wood. Last night they had left Pris alone, at her request, and she came home after she heard the boys pass by on the waterside track to the fort, and Bell Ann was safely asleep. Without speaking, Pris had kissed each parent goodnight and gone upstairs. This morning it was as if nothing had happened, but they were wary in their relief. Pris was an obedient and honorable girl, she would not defy them, but were tears to be part of daily life from now on?

Bell Ann came fairly dancing into the kitchen. "It is so good to be home, and I have *everything* to tell you!" She had brushed her hair and tied it back with a red ribbon. Her part wasn't straight and the bow was lopsided, but it was her own work. "Lillias Mackenzie parts her own hair, and Annie Clements makes her own *braids*. Where is that lazy William?" She pattered out.

"Will we have at least ten more years of peace with that one, do you think?" Alick asked.

"We can live only one hour at a time, and we have thousands of hours until then. Think of it, my darling. We are rich beyond the dreams of avarice!" She came up behind him where he was stirring the porridge and seized him around his lean middle, escaped before he could turn and seize her.

"Wait until tonight, woman," he threatened her.

The twins left first for church. David was saddling Blanchard while Alick and William were harnessing Diana, and Bell Ann begged to go with him on Brisky, but he convinced her that he was going too far for her and the pony; he had promised Blanchard a long session. Bell Ann knew a firm *no* when she met it.

"Oh, well!" she said carelessly. "I have too much else to do anyway."

David rode beside the chaise up the road and then turned the white horse left toward the Shaws', the Keel, and eventually Job's Harbor. He was bareheaded, the coarse coal-shiny hair falling across his forehead and around his ears. He was wearing a favorite old corduroy jacket with big pockets for sketching materials and food. His shirt was open at the throat, and a plaid handkerchief was knotted around his neck. Astride Blanchard he looked like a gypsy who had made an uncommonly good trade at a horse fair. Pris blew him a kiss. He returned it, laughed, and rode away.

"If I hadn't known David all my life, I would wonder so much about him," Pris said. "I wonder anyway. Because he is not talking all the time, like the rest of us, he seems to be full of secrets. Do you think he has ever been in love?"

"If he has, it's another of his secrets," said Jennie. Mrs. Shaw bowed as Major overtook them. "Good morning!" Jennie called after her. She doubted there would ever be more between her and the woman than a bow and a greeting, but her earliest opinion of Mrs. Shaw had been completely reversed.

"No, you don't, *mo chailin*," Pris told Diana. "Ladies do not race gentlemen, at least on Sundays. —What about now, Mama?" she asked slyly. "This portrait David is about to begin?"

"Mr. Heriot's young niece?"

"Oh, she is a niece, and young, but not a child!" Pris was in her glory, springing this on her mother. "She is nineteen, spoiled, and rich; she traveled with a maid, how do you like that? She is very pretty, I must admit, though it pains me. Like a porcelain figurine. Somewhere between here and Boston our David was lost. He is *hers*."

"How do you know all this?" Jennie asked.

"The maid told the Heriots' hired girl, who told Sibba and Eliza," she said smugly. "And they told *me*."

"Really, Priscilla," Jennie protested. "Tales at second-hand are bad enough, but at third-hand—!"

Pris was unabashed. "But listen, Mama, on the trip the maid was sick enough to heave up her rations for the past month—it wasn't that rough, but she's never been to sea before—and Jacinth, that's the girl's disgusting name, never paid her any heed once she'd set her cap for David. Mrs. Heriot looked after the poor woman."

"What makes you so sure she is Circe to David's Ulysses?"

"Mama, I saw them *arrive*."

"Did you spend every afternoon on the Maddox docks?"

Pris said huffily, "I went with Cath and Harmony because *they* wanted to, and that's when I saw the *Maid of Erin*. The other time was when I had dinner at Strathbuie House, and that is when I saw the *Alice Heriot* come in."

"Forgive me, dear," Jennie said. "Go on." They were passing the post office. The post office dog was in sole possession of the premises, taking the air on the mourner's bench.

"She came down the gangplank, all dainty in cornflower-blue, leaning on David's arm and smiling brave little smiles all around, gasping that she had been *ever* so frightened when they saw whales, but Mr. Evans had been such a strong arm and support." Pris panted and rapidly fluttered her lashes. "She kept looking up into his eyes and *palpitating*. It was enough to make me gag. It was even too much for Robin, who is not the most sensitive person in the world. He said he wanted to save David before he drowned in plain sight of all." Her theatrical groan made Diana's ears twitch. "It was probably too late even then. At his age it is likely to be fatal. Mama, she is a *flippetygibbet*!" Spoken with impressive despair, as: *She is a witch, a sorceress, a Harpy, Cybele, Medusa.*

"Perhaps all he sees in her is an exquisite subject."

"She commissioned the portrait herself, without waiting to consult her trustees in Massachusetts. But they will pay, the maid says. They always do, because otherwise she will have a tantrum. And *this* is the creature David is head over heels about! Don't you *care*? she asked accusingly.

"Yes, my darling, I care, but David is a grown man. When you children are grown long past turning the grindstone or being sent to your room to reflect, we shan't be able to do anything about you either; even when we're sure you are making the most ghastly mistakes. All your father and I can do is hope and pray."

"That the Great Horse will put his hoof down if you can't?" Priscilla grinned. "But Mama, if David is a Sleeping Beauty, he should at least be awakened by a true princess, not a flippetygibbet of a man-eater."

They were coming up to Three Corners, and Diana as always was exhilarated by the company of her kind and needed all Pris's attention. The usual cluster of youngsters was at Crit's Brook where it tumbled from the woods, but making no unseemly noise on the Sabbath. They'd done well to slide out from under parental eyes for these few minutes. The twins were separate with Miriam and Moses; they didn't seem to notice their mother and sister drive by. The gray-haired black man was walking slowly up the hill with three decorous young children. "Good day, Mr. Henderson," Pris said as they passed him, and he lifted his hat to her. "I met him when we went for the dory," she said to her mother. "He makes all the shoes and boots, and does the weddings and the funerals, too."

The sermon today was on slavery, and the minister was so impassioned that, if there had been the prospects of a war to end it, a good half of the male congregation would have enlisted before the next Sunday. All the hymns Mr. Lockhart and his wife had chosen dealt with Liberty, and the church members gave forth mightily.

Captain Blackburn and Carlotta had come together. The moment Jennie and Pris were out of church and alone for a moment, Pris was whispering, "They look so handsome together. It's *perfect*."

"Don't be marrying them off," Jennie cautioned her. "They are simply good friends."

"Oh, to be that free!" Pris said enviously. "I don't mean now, but when I am grown. Of course I would have to be a professional woman or a widow. Dr. Neville is both."

"I don't think she considers herself lucky for losing her husband."

"But now that it's happened, look how independent she is," Pris argued. "A widow can do almost anything, if she has the means."

Jennie drove home. The brook babbled along in solitude, and the peace of a hot Sabbath noon lay over Crit's Cove. All at once Priscilla said tensely, "Mama, Mr. Fitzwater is back. I didn't tell you earlier because I didn't want to spoil the day. But when Mr. Lockhart was preaching, I could swear he had met that man yesterday and wrote his sermon while he was still seething. I know how *I* felt."

"Where did you see him?" Jennie asked. There was a familiar sensation in her too vulnerable stomach.

"He was at the post office yesterday when we came home. We stopped for the mail in case the boys hadn't come for it. He was sitting on the mourners' bench, smoking a cigar. You could tell Mr. Phipps didn't like having him there, but he wasn't doing anything outside the law. I suppose you can't call nasty boasting illegal."

"What was he boasting about? His extensive lands and a manor house that would make Montpelier look like a squatter's cabin?"

"*Worse*. That he'd have Jerome before the week is out. Up in Castine someone swore to him the man must have left with *Ariel*. Old Cathcart said—," she twisted up one side of her mouth and clenched an imaginary pipe in toothless gums, " 'How do you know they warn't lying like Tophet, and your man was hid pretty close by? Them Castine men lie as easy as a cow—' Well, I won't say what the cow does. Mr. Phipps said, 'Ayuh, they're famous for it.' Then this loathsome slave owner said, 'You can't joke me, old men. I've had a sixth sense about this place for a mighty long time, and I'm not going home without my property secured in irons.' "

She described it as if she were watching it now. "Mr. Cathcart spat right at his feet and walked away. Mr. Phipps stood there just staring at him, and he laughed and sat back and stretched out his legs. 'I'm offering a hundred dollars now,' he said. Mr. Phipps said, 'The man who takes blood money will never live to spend it. Or it will bring him grief by the wagonload.' Fitzwater, wearing his nasty grin, said, 'You see I'm not posting anything. Enough talk around, and the bees will come to the honey.' Robin was red with rage by now, and not because of *me*."

"The man is a villain," Jennie agreed. "He leaves a poison track wherever he goes. Let's hope the boys don't hear of him, or we shall have Mr. Fitzwater served up for Sunday dinner, and I don't fancy that."

But the twins had heard of it before they reached home. Carolus was long-faced, Sandy was embattled.

"If he hangs about here long enough, he'll be riding out of town on a rail. Tarred and feathered first."

"And who will be officiating?" Alick asked.

"All of us, of course! We don't want his kind around here. He ought to be warned, and if he thinks it might happen, it would be a long time before he shows his face in town again."

"Enough of that," Alick said. "We won't be polluting the day with him. He is not to be mentioned during the meal, is that understood? You can be thinking instead what you will be doing with your free afternoon."

They immediately became silent, but with a good appetite.

Forty-Two

B Y SUNRISE ON Monday morning the eastern sky looked like a dirty fleece dyed an unpleasant shade of red. It was the forerunner of a vicious southeasterly gale, with hurricane winds and extreme high tides. All hands turned out to secure everything that could be blown or swept away, small boats were hauled ashore and made fast well above the reach of the tide, wheelbarrows put inside, with anything else that could be picked up or knocked about; vegetables and apples were gathered, the animals were back under cover by noon. At the Yard the men were busy all morning, preparing for the water to rise above the wharf and into the workplace. Alick closed down at noon to give the men time for their own preparations.

David had ridden early to Maddox to begin the portrait; he would find a bed in town for the night. Before dinner the boys went to the fort for their bedrolls, allowing the girls to accompany them. They were all so charged up with the energy generated by the coming storm that no one gave Fitzwater a thought. They were as joyfully wild as the cat, who raced about with her tail straight up and climbed one tree after another.

In the afternoon the family settled in to ride out the gale, as snug as raccoons in their winter den. At chore time the twins and Priscilla dodged out into the rain and wind, carrying lanterns because the barn would be so dark. The dogs went too, but Garnet curled herself tighter in her chair. Alick went with William, who was very pleased, and Bell Ann was kept in. She was dour about it, and her lower lip was expressive.

"Come and make scones," Jennie invited. "Put on your apron and wash your hands."

All five had picked blackberries on Sunday afternoon, and tonight

312

they had bowls of blackberries and cream with the warm scones. Afterward they sang until they were hoarse: songs learned from their parents, songs from school and from friends, songs that were simply *around*, like the air they breathed. The twins stayed up late to go down to the Yard with their father at the midnight tide. Jennie would have enjoyed it, but someone had to stay in the house with the lamps and candles, and the boys would be of more use to their father.

Everything was secure. There was barely a quiver through the new ship, and the boys took this as a good omen for her life at sea. They went to bed as happily as if Fitzwater didn't exist. But they would remember him tomorrow; there was no chance of *his* being swept off by a flood tide.

After the human life had quieted for the night, the house expressed its own life through its faint shudderings and creaks. "As long as she creaks, she holds," Alick quoted. There was reassurance in the working of the beams and timbers through the long sustained attacks of wind. Jennie had often been kept awake by storms while Alick slept, but had never been frightened by one, even as a child when the gales swept in from the North Sea. There had been a long time after April died when neither she nor Alick could sleep in a storm, only lie there listening and thinking of the small grave under the pounding rain or drifting snow. They would get up, make a hot drink, and read to one another; whether either one listened or not, the time would crawl past till they could sleep again, or it was daylight.

When the lulls were longer than the gusts, the storm was going away. Jennie fell asleep during one of the lulls. Her last conscious thought was of the man Jerome, as if it had been waiting all day to catch her when she was the most defenseless. He's been safe somewhere in this, she thought. Safe, dry, and a good distance from here.

In the morning the wind had shifted to the southwest, carrying the distant cannonade of the rote on open shores outside the river and across the peninsula. The sun rose through a silver haze. Gulls and crows flew down to inspect the leavings of the tide; ripped clusters of rowan berries lay blood-red on the ground. They'd be gone by night, eaten by birds between the comings and goings of people and animals. The water butts were brimming; an invitation to wash that Jennie declined, not aloud, and the children all took care not to mention it.

David came home early in the morning, to work on the blowdowns in the woods. He went down to the Yard with Alick to look around, and Pris walked part way with them, then she was off to stravaige on her own, wearing a pair of her father's old breeches, one of Carolus's belts to hold them up, and a shirt of Sandy's. The twins were eating more breakfast, because once they were in the woods with David there'd be no coming out until noon. It was William's and Bell Ann's turn to wash dishes, and they were trying to speed the twins.

"Other people have important things to do too, you know," Bell Ann admonished them. "I must see to my playhouse; it's probably a disgusting sight." She opened the door for Garnet and cried gladly, "Miriam is coming!" Miriam was indeed just coming from the woods. William and Bell Ann plunged happily into the drenched field to meet her.

Her dress was soaked halfway to her waist from wet bracken. She was limping, and one little toe was swollen and bleeding where she had struck something hard. She had been crying.

"Let me put something soothing on it," Jennie said, but Miriam shook her head.

"It doesn't signify," she said. "I'll get over *that*." Looking straight at the boys she said in a hard young voice, "He's taken. The sheriff and Fitzwater came for him this morning."

The twins' faces drained of blood and expression, and William's eyes and mouth went round as if he saw horror upon horror. Before his mother could reach him, he was running from the house, and she was after him. Carolus overtook her.

"Let him go, Mama." She could feel a shaking in him through the hand closed around her wrist. "We will know where to find him." He shepherded her back to the house. *He is no longer a child*, she thought through her distress. *It is not just a matter of outgrowing jackets.*

Sandy's teeth were clamped over his lower lip. Bell Ann had gotten into a rocker and pulled her knees up before her like a bulwark. Miriam was scrubbing hard with her fists at new wet streaks on her cheeks.

"So Jerome has been at the Keel," Jennie said. The twins appeared too stunned to respond to this.

"Ayuh," Miriam said hoarsely, "and they are taking him to Tenby Jail this minute. They came in a wagon for him. Pa tried to keep them out, and the sheriff was real polite, but he had a warrant. None of us would tell where Jerome was, no sir! We just stared at that Fitzwater, even the little ones, like a flock of dafties." She grinned, and then tears came into her eyes. "Wouldn't let on we ever *heard* of the man. They fetched Constable Jennison along, and he wasn't liking it one bit, and Mr. Swallow wasn't pleasured either, but we weren't blaming *them*. And then Jerome—" She snuffled and groped in her damp pocket for a handkerchief. "He walked out like a man. Nobody was going to drag *him*, and he told the sheriff he wouldn't be chained. 'I wasn't planning to,' Mr. Swallow said. 'We only chain murderers.' That *thing* went on raving fit to bust about having Pa in court, and Mr. Swallow told him none of that, he had his man, now they'd git. There was several spoke up and said he ain't riding alone, but Mr. Jennison said he'd come to no harm with him and the sheriff."

She blew her nose and rubbed it dry until it was red. "Mr. Henderson said calm as calm that *he* was going. And that *thing* looked him up and down like he was a tub of guts and gurry and says, 'And who might you belong to, boy?' Oh, we were some proud of Mr. Henderson then! 'I am Mr. Isaac Henderson,' he says, as if Fitzwater was the nearest thing to nothing that ever feet hung on and was called a man. 'I was born free, as the Apostle Paul said to the centurion.' And that shut old Sharkmouth up some fast and some tight."

Bell Ann left her chair and put her arms tightly around her mother. "Will they kill him?" she asked in a whisper. Jennie smoothed her hair, saying, "No, darling." The unity of Miriam and the boys was as dominant as another human presence in the room.

"Will they whip him with a big whip?" Bell Ann whispered.

"Mr. Jennison and Mr. Swallow would never do that," Jennie promised her.

"Jerome's decently dressed, and he's fleshed out some," Miriam said. "We took good care of him, but he's earned his way. He made us the handsomest table you ever saw, out of some oak boards Pa found floating once. And a real beautiful gate to the cemetery." She was ashy with fatigue.

"Would they be passing here about now?" Sandy headed for the door.

"Long gone," she said hopelessly. "They came early, before daybreak, so as to get him to Tenby Jail before there'd be many folks on the road. Besides, there's nothing you could do, except see a sight to make you sad for the rest of your days."

"Oh, *damn!*" Sandy cried in a choked voice. He drove his fist against the door. Bell Ann quivered under Jennie's hands, and she sat down and took the child onto her lap, cuddling her and rocking gently.

"Somebody told," Carolus was quiet about it. He didn't move his head, but his eyes shifted toward Sandy, and Sandy's eyes answered, confirming what their mother already knew.

"Pa had everybody up before him," said Miriam. "Just in case. But he's satisfied nobody there said anything, even the little ones and the foolish ones. They know better; it's the law of the Keel."

"*So.*" Carolus tented his fingers into a church roof and touched his mouth with the steepled tips. "Somebody was sneaking and prying around the Keel who had no business there."

"He *wanted* some business there," Sandy came away from the door looking sharpened and predatory. "But they marched him off with an honor guard, you could call it."

"I'd best be going," Miriam said. "I'm at Oakeses' today." This was something to be cheerful about, and she tried to be.

"Wait," Jennie said. "Would you take Bell Ann along to play with Sarie?"

"I'd be happy to, Mrs. Glenroy," said Miriam.

"Then wait a few minutes, and have something to eat."

She tipped Bell Ann from her lap. "Go up and change your shoes, and dress Evelina," she said. "And put on a fresh apron." Bell Ann was already halfway up the stairs, voiceless with her good luck. Jennie poured a cup of tea for Miriam and fixed a slice of bread and butter and jam, and the girl ate hungrily in spite of her distress.

William wouldn't have gone to his father, that was forbidden during work hours except in a family emergency. Besides, when William was grief-stricken he could not hide behind a stoic face, and there was no doubt now of his violent emotion.

As if Carolus could read her mind, he said curtly, "I'm off to find him. He's likely up in the haymow. He was always talking about how it must feel to be a slave. He was always hoping out loud Jerome would never be caught."

"Had nightmares about it," said Sandy, avoiding Jennie's eyes. "I'll look in the woods behind the Squaw Rock. You know that place he used to call a cave when he was little?" He and Carolus were in such a hurry they collided in the doorway.

Bell Ann came downstairs carrying Evelina Ermintrude; both wore their best aprons. Jennie put six of the morning's eggs in a basket with a jar of Hat Shenstone's blueberry honey and gave it to Miriam to carry.

"Don't tell Brisky," Bell Ann whispered when she kissed her mother goodbye. "If he doesn't see me go by, he won't know. I'll ride him when I come home."

"I won't tell," Jennie whispered back. Alone, she sank down at the table. "*Whoosh*" She blew the word out. "Now I know how a hot air balloon would feel if someone shot it!" Children did not keep you young; Alick was right about that.

Her three sons had not only known where the slave was, they had known *him*. Their deception was a reality upon which she and Alick must act. While ostensibly studying the stars and being kept awake by mosquitoes, porcupines, and curious raccoons, the boys had been going down to the Keel at night. No wonder they were late some mornings, heavy-lidded and heavy-footed.

They had been lying to their parents by omission, and they had broken a family rule by roving around at night without permission when they were supposed to be settled at the fort until morning; she felt as if a portion of weakened cliff had crumbled away from her feet. Children always had a secret life, but the twins were reaching the boundary beyond which the secrets were deeper and darker. This time they had involved William, and he was too young. She supposed she could never exhume the reason why William was even with them at the fort.

It was another landmark; the point at which you realize that from now on you would not always receive straight answers from your children.

David and the three boys arrived all together. William had hay on his clothes and kept scratching inside his shirt, but his head seemed to have been just dipped in a water butt to wash away dust and tears. The boys woodenly faced their mother, waiting. They are suffering for their deception, she thought; they have become acquainted with Jerome, and now they are paying a more awful price than we could exact. She longed to comfort them all in her arms, but there could be no comfort for what they knew.

"No matter how sad and angry you are," she said, "there is no excuse for being careless in the woods. David is in absolute command. William, for goodness' sake, take that shirt off and shake it outside." Oh, my Sweet William, she thought, when you were crying for your kite, you couldn't have dreamed of this.

William obeyed while Carolus and David collected axes and the crosscut saw from the shed, and Sandy filled a water jug.

They went down the road to the old apple tree at the turn and across the lower pasture toward the eastern woods; William was a small, forlorn, dark figure trudging behind.

Garnet came talking from somewhere and bunted Jennie's shins. When she was picked up, she braced a paw against Jennie's cheekbone, and the pads smelled of mossy damp earth.

"Your father will have some unhappy business this noon," Jennie said to her, "and your mother wishes he would come home this instant to hold hands with her."

Forty-Three

P RESENTLY SHE BREWED fresh coffee on the unlikely chance that Alick would receive her message by a hitherto dormant gift for mind-reading and break his rule about never leaving the Yard in business hours.

He didn't come, but Pris and the dogs did. Both dogs were muddy and odorous from splashing across the flats and rolling in kelp and rockweed. In breeches and shirt, with her hair tied tightly back from her face except for a lock that had gotten loose and flopped over her forehead, Pris looked like a long-legged boy. The resemblance to Nigel did not stab Jennie as it once did, but it was always there. Alick had known Nigel as child and youth, but he never mentioned the likeness; it was as if he were denying its existence.

"I had a glorious time all by myself," Pris said. "Why don't you run away? I'll guard the portcullis." She sat on the floor to take off her boots. "Whew! What a bouquet!" She tossed them outdoors and Bounce ran after them. "Don't you *dare* bring them back to me! —Where is Bell Ann?"

"Miriam stopped in on her way to the Oakes house, and I let Bell Ann go with her."

"She must have been in heaven." Pris went into the pantry, and called back with some displeasure, "Look at those dishes!"

"Have some coffee, and bring it here. I have something to tell you." This brought Pris out at once, but her happy expectancy was at once destroyed by the news.

"Whoever took the reward, I would like to drive that hundred dollars down his throat!"

"So would I," said Jennie. "So would the boys. They are devastated,

318

William especially. Pris, they have been going down to the Keel at night, so they know the man, which makes it worse. He is no longer a fact, he is a person with a face and a voice."

"Oh, *Mama*," Pris whispered. "What will happen to him now? Mr. Lockhart was exactly right Sunday! How can this country *allow* it? I could *cry*, but I would rather use *these*!" She lifted her fists.

"I don't know when I realized," Jennie said, "that half the people on this earth seem to exist to be plundered, enslaved, or slaughtered by the other half, and so it has ever been. On our way across the ocean your father read the Bible from 'In the Beginning' to 'The grace of our Lord Jesus Christ be with you all, Amen.' All through the Old Testament he was in a furor. '*Dia*, I could like to be confounding Dr. MacLeod with *this*. How would the wee MacArthur be explaining *that*? Murder and rape and the slaughter of infants! The pages run with blood! With Jehovah for a god, a man is not needing the Devil!'"

"Did he really say that?" A spark of amused admiration shot through the murk.

"Indeed he did." Jennie stood up. "Well, Pris, if you wash the dishes for the children, it will be another star in your crown, but clean yourself up first. Those breeches smell as rich as the dogs. Not that I don't like it, you understand. I adored it when I was young. But I know why Mary Ann used to drive us out of the kitchen sometimes."

"Someday I am going to visit Pippin Grange and walk on the shore of the North Sea." Pris took a jug of tepid rainwater upstairs. "I'll have one nice thing to remember from today," she called back. " 'The bliss of solitude,' your Mr. Wordsworth calls it."

Jennie guessed that the bliss was attributable to Septimus Frye's debonair doppelgänger, strolling with an exquisitely feminine Priscilla beside a summer-blue river; this Septimus knew all Keats and selected bits of Byron, and recited them beautifully to the ethereal girl in floating pastels, while a hoyden in shirt and breeches sloshed and skidded through wet kelp in a wind that ripped at her hair and burned her nose and cheeks.

Priscilla was setting the table for dinner and Jennie was slicing ham to fry when David came from the woods. He had left the boys digging in the crater made where a great old spruce had been uprooted. Sandy thought he'd found an Indian hand axe in it, and they had come to a layer of clamshells. That the boys could think of anything else but Jerome was encouraging.

When David took a towel and went to the washhouse to sluice away the morning dirt and sweat, Pris said, "I wonder how he got on with his painting yesterday. If he was able to think at all, with her working her wiles on him while he felt himself drowning in the dark pools of her eyes—they must be dark, Mama, her hair is black. Did I tell you? She looks French. They will be calling her *petite* instead of puny or mingy, which she is. A pindling bundle of sticks."

"Who are *they*?" Jennie asked.

"Oh, what passes for Society in Maddox," Pris said disdainfully. "They consider *me* a monstrosity, as tall as a mast pine, and—" It was lost when the dogs erupted in the dooryard and the silver jumped out of Pris's hands and crashed on the floor. She ran outside, whistling on two fingers, but the dogs were streaking down the road to join a bedlam of demonic howls and eldritch war cries. The three boys were leaping like pagans at war about the man who ran half-crouching through a fusillade of hard green apples.

William was a dancing imp from hell, shrieking with exultation when he knocked Harry's hat off and Darroch seized it. Bounce flew at Harry, but Pris caught the terrier with a lunge that threw her onto her knees. She knelt on the ground struggling to hold him, and calling to the boys to stop. Between their own delirious uproar and Darroch's bass like a great drum throbbing through a battle, they were beyond hearing.

The rampage had sprung up so quickly that for a moment Jennie was spellbound by what she was seeing and hearing. Harry came on at a shambling trot, trying to protect his head, and the boys followed, driving apples and insults at him. Jennie made a snatch at the nearest sleeve, but she was no more to Sandy than the wind blowing past him. She ran into the house for the bell and came out ringing it with all her might. Harry swerved by David and went on, audibly panting, his eyes wild. There was blood on one hand where Bounce must have nipped him, and a long tear in his breeches.

With the bell ringing as if by its own frenzy, with David confronting the boys, and Alick coming up behind them, there was no contest. Alick collared a twin with each hand and walked them rapidly toward the house. William kept Pris between him and his father. Bounce squirmed in her arms, crying his urgent desire to see Harry off the premises. Darroch was tearing up Harry's hat, an entertainment which gave the other men a reason to remain behind tactfully until Alick herded the twins inside. His grip was as hard as his face; Jennie saw the white knuckles.

She touched David's shoulder and pointed to her left hand, then at Bounce, then at Harry. David nodded, and went after him.

Alick released the twins inside the door. Carolus was pale, tightly composed, and very straight. Sandy was still radiating such passion that his father's anger could not reach him.

"We didn't throw stones," he said. "Only apples. He deserves stones."

Priscilla came in, with William on the far side of her. She was solemn, a little too much so. "Pris you might see if the potatoes and the greens are done," Jennie said.

"Yes, Mama."

The three boys ranged themselves in a line by the table, and Alick stood against the door.

"I am waiting," he said, ominously gentle.

No eyes refused to meet his, but no one spoke. In the next room Pris dropped a pot lid in her hurry to return. William was the farthest from his mother, his hands behind his back, his chin up; no tears. This was the same little boy who had stood blindfolded and giggling in a circle, rapturous at being included in a game. Now it was no game.

"*Dé tha seo?*" Alick asked softly. "What is this? Is it that my sons have gone mad, all three at once? When you speak the truth you are never whipped, even if it is a truth your mother and I are not liking to hear. Now, what is it? Has he insulted your sister, or kicked one of the dogs?" He examined each face, and waited.

"I will be hearing the truth," he said finally. "And we will stand like this here or out in the barn, if it takes until midnight."

"Have you heard about Jerome?" Jennie asked quietly.

Without looking away from the boys he said, "Yes, it was all over the Yard. But what has that to do with this disgraceful stramash?"

William couldn't contain himself. "Harry told where Jerome was!"

"And how did you know it was *Harry*? Were you hearing it with your own ears? Or does one of you have the Sight?"

Sandy was holding in, but only just. "It has to be Harry, Father," Carolus said. "He was making a nuisance of himself down at the Keel because of Miriam, and Moses drove him off. Do you remember the day he came to work all bruised up?"

"But there is more than one black man at the Keel," Alick said. "How would he know which one was the slave?"

"He must have heard someone call Jerome by name," Sandy said. "They don't know how long he was skulking around, watching and listening, before one of the dogs saw him," Sandy said. "There's a place on the hill above the settlement where you can watch Mr. George's house, and the comings and goings around the well and the shore. That's just the kind of filthy scurvy critter he is."

"But why Harry?" Alick insisted reasonably. "You are not knowing everyone who goes to the Keel, to hire a man or who ties up at the wharf; someone on the lobster smack, for instance."

"It has to be Harry," Sandy said doggedly.

William had hardly twitched a finger or shifted a foot through this, so there was no warning. "Jerome was *mine!*" he shouted. "*I* found him!" He backed off from the rest, doubling his fists at them. "*I* saved him! They *can't* take him away after all this time! He was *free!*"

He stumbled blind and wailing toward his father and pressed his face into Alick's chest. Alick held him with one hand, caressing his head with the other, while William wept into his shirt.

His despair had undone the others. Each twin was trying in his own way not to break down; Priscilla made a sound between a snort and a sob, and ran into the pantry. Jennie had a thickness and a prickling in her throat and nose. I am glad Bell Ann is not here, she thought.

Finally Alick took out his handkerchief, wiped William's face, and commanded him to blow his nose, keeping an arm around him. David came in soundlessly. No one looked toward him but Jennie, and he shook his head. He had not caught up with Harry.

"Which one of you will tell me?" Alick said to the twins.

They sat around the table while the boys told the story by turns. It had begun on the afternoon when Alick and Jennie drove to Job's Harbor to look at young Job Winter's boat. Pris was reading, Carolus was working on his herbarium, Sandy studying Bowditch, William was whittling masts for his model, and Bell Ann was playing with her dolls. Then Septimus rode in. They were glad to see him, it had been very jolly, but some time during the fun William disappeared. That was nothing new; he could have been bored and found his own company more interesting, especially if Bell Ann was too enamored of Septimus to go trailing after him.

The other boys themselves became bored with Seven and Pris quoting poetry at each other—no one added *and flirting*, for which Jennie blessed them—and decided to go sailing. But the dory was gone. They knew that William must have gone out alone to try to sail; every time they refused to take him he'd threatened furiously that he would teach himself. Trying not to panic, they took the skiff and rowed out to where they could look up and down the river, and then they saw the dory on the shore a good way upstream. So they turned that way.

The dory was made fast below a thick patch of woodlot south of Crit's Cove and the Foss land. It belonged to an elderly couple who were so devoted to their fine old pines and oaks they couldn't bear to have them turned into lumber; but with the family grown and gone, and rheumatism in the parents' bones, no one visited the magnificent creatures these days.

And here they found William, not alone; he sat cross-legged on the ground, watching a young black man eating bread and cheese from the Glenroy pantry. The man froze at sight of them, but William moved quickly in front of him. "What do *you* want?" he demanded.

They told him they wanted only to see that he was at home before their parents came back. "The man was so frightened the sweat was running off his face like rain," Carolus said. "Well, we'd been frightened not long before, thinking old Wim had managed to drown himself."

William had deliberately broken the rules about his being alone on the water, though he had been sensible enough not to try stepping the mast. He had taken food with him and rowed to the Cathcart woodlot because he had always wanted to prowl around it on his own and climb the particular pine the Cathcart boys once used for a look-out tower.

Halfway up the tree, he knew there was someone above him. He expected another boy, perhaps Rupert Foss, but it was not a boy's scuffed shoe that dangled before his eyes as he pulled himself up. He heard harsh breathing among the thick old branches overhead.

"Who are you?" he had asked tremulously. "I don't mean any harm. I will go away." He was shaking so hard he could barely hold on.

"Don't you go falling, now," a man answered. "I don't mean *you* any harm, li'l boy." His voice was kind, William thought, and foreign; he had never in his life heard a southern black speak. But when he saw the black face looking down at him through the pine needles, he understood all at once—afterward he didn't know *how* or *why*—and said the first thing that came to him.

"I have food."

He had the man's story and his name by the time the twins found them. Jerome had come north in *Ariel*; the captain hadn't known he was aboard, or pretended so, until the ship was well offshore and running into heavy weather, and there was no question of returning him. He had a strong stomach and good balance and made himself useful to earn his passage. At Parson's Cove they had brought him ashore after dark, and the captain took him out to a family farm well away from the main road, where he would be safe until he could be sent on to Canada. He built new cupboards for the woman of the house; he ate at the table with the family and was treated as a human being. He was happy until the day he heard hounds coursing far off in the woods. The family assured him that the dogs were trailing rabbits, that no one here hunted human beings with dogs, unless they were trying to find a lost child or a missing hunter. But he could not fight the terror in his very bones, and he had run away in the night.

On the last day aboard *Ariel*, someone had told him they were passing the Keel, and what sort of place it was. He knew that it was well to the south of Parson's Cove, and he thought that if he walked long enough on the river shore he would come to it. He had traveled at night, keeping far away from buildings and possible watchdogs, and spent his days dozing like a cat in the woods where there was no cutting going on, praying that no one would come upon him. But it had happened to him on his third day.

The twins put him into the dory and covered him with the sail, because there were other Sunday sailors on the river; they took the skiff in tow and rowed down to the Keel. The wind and tide were against them, but the dory had two sets of oars, and William took his turn.

"He pulled like a man," Sandy said. "You'd have been proud of him. But Judas, we were some skittish when we rowed past here, for fear you were home and would give us a hail. We *flew* by."

At the Keel they gave Mr. George a brief explanation. He drew Jerome aside and talked with him a few minutes, then a child was sent to fetch Mr. Henderson. "Jerome is very brave," William said. "Even when he was so afeard, he stood straight and looked Mr. George right in the eye, man to man."

"But you could tell how glad he was to see a black man," Carolus said. "They hugged each other." He thanked the boys and shook hands with them; when they left he was being taken away for a hot meal.

The three were now partners in a conspiracy, and William had begun it. It gained him privileges; he was permitted to go to the fort, and thence to the Keel. He was very proprietory about Jerome, and they humored him. But though he might have felt possessive about the man, the twins knew the meaning of responsibility; they solemnly explained to their parents that they couldn't simply drop off the man and never give him another thought.

So at night they had walked through the woods to the Keel to see him, coming back in the dark.

"What did Mr. George think of this?" Jennie asked. "You were told some time ago not to make nuisances of yourselves down there."

"Mr. George didn't know we were there, most times," Carolus said candidly. "We mostly talked to Jerome when he was making the gate for the cemetery. That's apart from the houses. There'd always be other boys and girls there too. Everybody likes Jerome. *Liked*," he added, swallowing, his eyes growing very bright.

One evening Miriam wanted to show them the handsome oak table Jerome was making, so they had gone home with her. They could hardly believe their luck when they came upon the fistfight in the field above the wharf. Harry and Moses were going at it hammer and tongs, but suddenly Mr. George had walked into the circle of watchers, breaking up the battle and ordering the spectators away.

"Mr. George looked *ten feet tall*," William said, "and Harry scuttled like an old crab running for his rock."

"Mr. George said, 'Moses, you see him off the premises,' " said Sandy. " 'But don't you lay a finger on him.' " He grinned at the memory, but it turned into a grimace. "They were both pretty well banged up."

The story was finished, and they were limp with reaction, dry-mouthed and hungry. They went for more water, trying not to clatter the dipper; no one even whispered. David let Bounce out and went behind him to pace the dooryard with his hands behind his back. Priscilla went to drain the vegetables. Alone, Alick and Jennie looked across the room at each other in tacit agreement that their children had left them once again without answers, but that answers must be found; or at least the right questions.

When the boys came back, Alick asked courteously, "And did it never occur to you to let one of the Whittiers know that the man was safe?"

He received three shocked stares. "You aren't supposed to tell anything like that," Carolus said, with a kindly tolerance for such surprising ignorance. "It is the Law of the Keel."

"But surely it's a different matter with Captain Whittier," Jennie said. "He must have felt responsible for Jerome."

They didn't even attempt an answer to this, but were not rude about it, merely patient.

"Captain Whittier will have to hear your part in this," Alick said. "That is one of the laws of *here*. Now to take up other matters. William, when you found the man you were disobeying me, and the rest of you have some guilt for that day." He looked across at Priscilla. "When you were left in command, where was everyone, even Bell Ann?" Pris went speedily back to the pantry where she began noisily taking down plates. "You lads deceived us about sleeping at the fort; you were out roving around at night instead. I hold Carolus and Sandy more responsible than William."

"He wanted to go!" Sandy sputtered. "He could hardly wait to go!"

"But you are older," Alick said implacably. Suddenly the winter went out of his eyes, it was as if a warm and relaxing wind followed on a blizzard. "There will be no grindstone," he said. "But there will be no more sleeping at the fort. And we will be having your most solemn promise that Harry Shaw will be invisible to you. If you meet him face to face, *he is not there*. Do you understand that?"

They did.

"No matter what you are feeling in your bones, he is innocent until proven guilty. Do you understand *that*?"

Someone sighed, but they all nodded.

"*Glé mhath*. Now, is it not dinner time, Jeannie? The hunger is at me like a ravening beast."

Forty-Four

T HE BOYS PAID close attention to their plates, but they were not very hungry, even for fried ham. They must have told David the story in the woods that morning. Jennie was not jealous because he knew it first; in him they had the nearly perfect older brother. But she thought that some unborn children were missing a nearly perfect father who, for whatever reasons, was the captive of an extremely imperfect father of his own.

Pris offered the boys freedom from the dishes, and they went back to the work with David, taking Perry to drag out logs. William rode the horse into the woods, and Jennie hoped he was enjoying it, just a bit.

"They needn't expect me to be this generous for long," Pris told Jennie. "I simply wanted to shoo those long faces out of the house. But I am very proud of them!" she said defiantly. "I think they did exactly right, and they do not deserve one *ounce* of punishment. They are suffering enough, and for a just cause."

"We are proud of them too, *mo nighean*," Alick said. He and Jennie went out, and she reached for his hand. They stopped in the dancing shadows of the rowan boughs; most of the berries that had strewn the ground in the morning had disappeared. He turned her toward him and gave her a little shake.

"Tell me the great joy is at you, Jeannie *mo chridh*, as it is at me. Who has three sons like ours? Beginning with William, they were never hesitating between right and wrong, and like men they kept their word." He gave her an exuberant kiss. "Och, I am sorry for their sorrow, the man is their friend. But I rejoice in them."

"And do you rejoice in *that* son?" She pointed at Darroch, sleeping in the road among bits of Harry's hat.

"*Ochone!*" said Alick. "The disgrace of it, and at his age, too. We are owing Harry a hat, such as it was. They can pay him from their pocket money."

"Pay an invisible man?"

"I will do it, and collect from them." Darroch awoke and rolled voluptuously on the ruins. "The *bodach* has never had a gift he liked better," said Alick.

The boys worked in the woods with David and Perry all afternoon. Pris went to the Bastos to plan Thankful's wedding dress. Thankful didn't want to be married yet, even if the parents were willing, and they were not. Courting was too much fun not to make the most of it, so the dress would be designed many times before she needed it.

Miriam brought Bell Ann back in late afternoon. Mrs. Oakes had been sympathetic about Jerome, and plenty of others were too, but what good was sympathy?

"Now they've got Jerome up there like a criminal," Miriam said bitterly. "It is awful at home, not just for him being took, but the disgrace. We never lost anyone like that before, the Law coming for them."

The boys were unnaturally quiet at supper time. They'd worked hard all afternoon, but tiredness didn't account for their willingness to let Bell Ann do all the talking, until she was told she had better turn her attention to her supper. No one took advantage of the vacuum, but no one seemed weighed down with sorrow, either.

The meal continued in silence until Alick laid his knife and fork across his plate and wiped his mouth. A signal that Jennie almost missed, and couldn't have described, passed among the boys.

"There is something we would like to discuss," Sandy said in his deepest voice. "William will introduce the subject because he introduced the subject in the first place, you might say." He gave William a gracious flourish of invitation. "Speak on, William."

"We want to buy Jerome and set him free." The words flashed up like sunstruck spray. Jennie looked past the bright faces at Alick. The flicker of his eyelids was the involuntary reflex to a blow aimed but just missing. O Lord! she thought. O Lord in deed and fact, why can't You be *Deus ex machina* this very instant? I would forgive You for everything else. I would build You an altar on the public road and light candles on it every day.

"We realize the price will be very high," Carolus said, "but if you will pay it, Father, we won't take any pocket money for as long as it takes, and work outside to help. I will give up college. I don't know what the going price for a slave is, but—"

"That's *indecent!*" Pris said. "The 'going price' for a human being!"

"We must be hardheaded," Carolus said loftily. "If we wish to free him, we must buy him first."

"Oh, well, you can have my savings," she said with a shrug.

"Mine too, said Bell Ann. David touched William's shoulder and nodded at him; William's response was speechless but brilliant.

It is a good thing that Reason prevails with me, Jennie thought, even if it occasionally totters on its throne. Otherwise I would be happy to mortgage everything we have rather than disappoint those faces.

"We are not rich." Alick spoke in the measured cadence which meant he was trying to find his words. "I am not in a position to make an offer for a valuable property, no matter how much I want to. The man could ask thousands of dollars, knowing that I could not be paying it, and his power and revenge would taste all the sweeter."

"But we can't just let him take Jerome away!" Sandy's voice shot up an octave, but no one smiled. Carolus was pleating his lower lip; William gazed at his father with dark, glistening, hoping eyes.

"Papa is right!" Pris said, "and I *hate* it!" She left the table and ran through the rooms to the stairs. Bell Ann slid off her chair and came to stand within Jennie's arm.

"Most of Whittier and Maddox would want to contribute, I am positive," Carolus argued. "They should have a chance to try. *We* should have the chance!"

"Who knows what Fitzwater will really do, until he's asked?" Sandy asked passionately. "He might have heavy debts and snatch at a good offer, never mind power and revenge. Money in the hand is aye the sweetest singer." he said sententiously, and Alick smiled.

"So you are composing your own axioms now. Give it to me in the Gaelic and I will be doubly impressed."

"But we need to do something right now, before the sea flattens out so they can sail," Sandy insisted. "Carolus and I can commence tonight, going from house to house. If we can ride, we will cover a good distance before it is black-dark." He stood up like a soldier. Alick closed his eyes and rubbed his forehead as if to erase a pain. "Sit down, Alasdair," he said. Sandy hesitated, then sank back into his seat, averting his face from the others.

Alick opened his eyes. "I was never intending to let Jerome go without a battle. If the decision is between obeying conscience and avoiding ridicule and humiliation, there should be no contest. Tomorrow I will be having a word with this one and that one, all of them respectable and some of them well-to-do. If I can form a delegation, and if we can do business—and I am warning you against great expectations—we will pay, and then everyone who wishes to will have a chance to repay us."

The great wave that had swept the boys through the afternoon had left them exhausted but not defeated. No one moved at first, until William jumped up and ran around the table. He hugged Alick from behind, nuzzling against the side of Alick's head, and kissed his cheek. "Thank you, Papa!"

Alick reach around and hauled a giggling boy into his lap. I suppose my Sweet William will lose that giggle when his voice changes, Jennie thought, and he will measure out his hugs. But isn't it wonderful to have them at all?

The boys carried wash water after supper. Bell Ann, having both parents to herself, made the most of it. They sat on her bed and listened interminably, it seemed, until she had almost put herself to sleep. She was tucked in, kissed, and left to tell Bounce the last part of it again in drugged fragments between yawns.

For the rest, Jennie organized a reading-aloud session to put their minds on something else besides what would happen tomorrow. Later when they were in bed, and she made the rounds, the boys were all still sure that by tomorrow night Jerome would be a free man; they would fall asleep believing it.

Pris was sitting up in bed brushing her hair by candlelight. Jennie shut the door behind her, and Pris said at once, "Do you think it will happen, Mama? I've been like the mouse in Hickory Dickory Dock, up and down all evening."

"Thank you for keeping quiet about it. They can create quite enough fervor without encouragement." She began unpinning her own hair. "I am trying not to think of *afterward*."

The brush moved slowly through the long fair hair. "What a day this has been. At least a hundred hours long." Her voice dragged like the brush, and her lids were heavy. "But whatever happens tomorrow, Mama, it will still be just the beginning. We can't ever ignore slavery now. If Jerome stays, the sight of him will always remind us of it, and if he goes, we will never forget him and how many more there are."

"Yes." Jennie kissed her forehead. "Good night, my love."

David had gone to bed, and Darroch was ready to come in; he smelled of the wind captured in his thick coat. "I can wish *you* sweet dreams," she told him. "Darling Darroch, we need someone like you, with no worries, no nightmares, and no hopes to be shattered." She gave him a piece of hard gingerbread and he held it politely in his mouth without chewing until she left him.

The bedroom was lighted by one candle on a chest of drawers. The flame fluttered in a draught as wind rattled at the windows and cried in the chimney. Alick sat on the side of the bed still dressed, leaning forward with his elbows on his knees, his head hanging as if he were asleep. Garnet undulated around his legs, arching her back to be grazed by his loosely-clasped hands. Impatient, she made a piercing demand.

"Is that all you are wanting of me, *mo coraid?*" he asked. "Well, it is easily granted." He scratched behind her ears and rubbed her back, and she fell over purring.

Jennie shut the door behind her, and Alick lifted his head. In the tremulous light the lines in his face were like seams in granite. She had for an instant the horrifying illusion that he had aged ten years in the last half hour. When she sat down beside him it went, but he looked as tired as she was.

"I would not mind all the effort," he said, "if I was not knowing he will only laugh at us. I should have given them no hope."

"But we teach them one must always try, even if—"

"They are children; they can afford to fail," he said. "We are their parents, and they think we can accomplish anything. When I was singing to them in the cradle, I never expected to be as helpless now as they were then."

Her arm felt heavy to lift, but she ran her hand back and forth across his shoulders and down his back as firmly as he had stroked the cat.

"When a parent fails," he went on, "it is a betrayal. I blamed my father for dying and leaving me, and cheating me of the glory of a soldier for a father. But I was old enough not to be blaming my mother for *her* death.

I knew who was responsible! Was not the minister saying at the grave, 'Our Lord God has seen fit to call her to Himself'? What did *He* want of her with all his multitudes? *I* was the lonely one!"

"Alick," she whispered. She laid her cheek against his shoulder. Scarlet wheels spun against her eyelids.

"We have raised them not to blame God," he said. "So they must be blaming someone, and this time their father, who could once do anything, will be the one. Priscilla and the twins may understand in time, but were you not seeing how William looked at me tonight? If only he had not come to hug me! I will feel that for the rest of my life."

"Do you really think that was the last hug?" She roused up. "I forbid you to talk like that! What they will remember about you is that you listened, and you stopped everything to try to help."

He looked sheepishly around at her. "Save me from the sins of self-pity and vanity. I blame it all on the weather. With the wind, and the heaviness in the air, you are climbing uphill all day."

When they were in bed, they lay for a time without speaking, listening to the wind. As long as it blew from that quarter, Fitzwater would be held in port, which would only draw out the misery.

Jennie didn't want to think of the slave in the jail, but it was inevitable. Sheriff Swallow would be kind, but it would be like the kindness granted a man the night before his hanging. How could she sleep knowing this?

"What are you thinking?" Alick asked her.

"Sometimes I think of Andrew and Elspeth Glenroy," she said, not wanting to mention Jerome. "I have so often imagined them coming ashore in Maddox. I wonder if she was ever brave enough to sail, and where they landed."

"Because you were kind to a woman in trouble," he kissed her hair and her temple and cheekbone, "we are here. And I would not be without you anywhere else, in heaven or on earth as a king among gems thick as the stars, and gold flowing like rivers. I would not choose immortality on Tir-nan-og without you." He kissed her throat. "And without those five upstairs. Now go to sleep, or we will be making it six upstairs."

Forty-Five

I N THE WINDY morning David wished Alick luck before he left for a day of work at the Heriots'; he had made it clear that he would contribute to the fund. Alick decided to take the boys with him to Maddox rather than keep them on edge with suspense all day. However the matter turned out—and he was no more hopeful than he had been the night before—they had owned a part in it ever since William climbed the watch-tower pine in the Cathcarts' woodlot and said bravely to the black face above him, "I have food."

For the boys, the deed was as good as done, and they would be present at the victory. William hoped they could go to Tenby and welcome Jerome when he left the jail; Alick was shaving in the pantry, and Jennie knew he was hearing all this with dismay.

"Don't be too sure of anything," she warned them. "You could be terribly disappointed."

"Don't worry, Mama," Carolus said merrily, "we have been knocking on wood like maniacs, and calling on all the gods we could think of."

"Can you hear how rough the sea is?" Sandy asked. "Do you hear the rote this morning? If it was meant for Fitzwater to be gone by now, they'd have been able to sail before this. We must have reached old Aeolus."

"Will someone be watching out for Mr. Eubanks, please?" Alick called out. The meeting moved out to the rowan trees, still talking.

"*Children*," Pris said, but with affection.

Thad Eubanks arrived, and Alick put him in charge for the day. He and the boys left in the wagon with Shonnie when the other workers were still coming in; Harry had not returned to work yesterday, and he didn't come this morning.

"They may be about to bring assault and battery charges," Jennie said. "I wouldn't put it past them. Oh well, we have enough witnesses to swear that the boys didn't try to break his bones with iron bars."

"Mr. Shaw might sue for damages to Harry's hat." Pris ruffled Darroch's head. "Och, it's the great hero you are, Darroch Mor."

"Well, girls, let us get to the washing," Jennie said. "Come weal, come woe, the work has to be done." The damp southwest wind blew strongly from the sea, but the misty sun was hot in the lee behind the house. It was good to be strenuously busy out of doors, and the atmosphere was cheerful until the work was almost done and there was time for reflection.

Pris said, "I am trying to be positive about something, but it seems to be all positively *bad*."

Then Bell Ann began to sing as she spread pillow slips on the ground, and Pris couldn't help laughing. "Do you *hear* that? It's one the boys sing when they're mucking out, about Miss Bailey, who hanged herself with her garters and haunted her seducer until he paid for a decent burial."

"Well, it's a jolly tune, and I'm sure she doesn't understand the words. Let's pretend we don't hear her."

They picnicked at noon out in the playhouse—Bell Ann's choice. In a circle of dolls they ate deviled eggs, a salad of beet and lettuce sprinkled with chives; buttered oatcakes and currant jam. Then they went to pick blackberries, accompanied by a choir of crickets invisible beneath a tapestry of Michaelmas daisies and black-eyed Susans, wine and scarlet wild rose leaves and hips.

"I wonder how David is getting along with What's-her-name?" Pris said. "I wonder how she can stand it, running on and on like a brook and knowing he doesn't hear a word of it? Of course, he'd be gazing at her all the time, and that must be satisfying. She can't know she is simply a composition to him. I *hope*! David is such an innocent."

"She may be a perfectly charming girl."

"*Charm*!" Priscilla spat it out. "We all know about *that*!"

"You think Septimus is charming."

"But that's different. Septimus *is* charming, but I'm sure *he* is sincere. He can't help being himself any more than Darroch can." The Newfoundland blinked amiably at her from the shade.

A butterfly would have been a better comparison, Jennie thought, but since the butterfly was frequenting other gardens these days, she could be tolerant. She had always cherished butterflies, even the plain little ones, and thought collectors were murderers. When Septimus was netted, it was doubtful that Priscilla would be the one to capture him; she was probably one of his memories by now. If he sold insurance to Ronald Heriot, he must have already met Jacinth, but Jennie did not mention this.

In late afternoon the wagon came home, and Alick's face was unreadable, which told everything. The boys were very quiet, even William was stiff with control. Alick told them curtly to go and change their clothes, he would attend to the horse. Pris kept Bell Ann occupied with picking flowers from the border for the table, while Jennie stayed with Alick as he unharnessed Shonnie, let him drink, put him into the pasture, and returned the harness to its proper place in the barn. "It was no surprise. I will be giving you the story when there's time. I am going to the Yard now."

"Aren't you famished for a cup of tea? Or a reviving dram?"

"My throat is a desert, but so is my soul at this point. Tomorrow's Tenby delegation may have better luck, at least *they* are hoping so." He nodded toward the house. "But it is not the hope they had this morning, soaring like an eagle till you cannot see him because your eyes are only human. It was a sad, grim drive home. I gave them turns with the driving, but it was not making the wagon any less a hearse."

She put her hands on his shoulders and kissed his cheek, and kept her arm in his as far as the rowans. Bell Ann ran out and took his hand and went on with him, confidently chattering.

"So it is finished," Priscilla said softly behind Jennie. "I knew from the first glimpse. I could have cried."

"Some Tenby people are trying tomorrow. Who knows? If he thinks both towns will pay—" She left it there, and Pris knew better than to pursue it.

The boys went straight to the shore to pitch storm rows of rockweed from the beach into a pile in the field for later use on the garden, and the girls changed into old dresses and went to join them. David rode in, knowing that the quest had failed; Ronald Heriot had been one of the delegation, he wrote, and had come home in a very bad temper.

Jennie erased the words and wrote, "I hate this. I want it to be over with, quickly. How does the portrait proceed?"

"Very well," he wrote. He did not quite smile, but there was the impression of a neutral gray sky infused suddenly with light and color. Nothing flamboyant for David, but it was there. She remembered the way he used to make his eyes meet hers as if it were an effort, but one he couldn't resist. And then a not-quite smile followed. "The *gille* is in love with you," Alick had teased her.

He is in love now, Jennie thought, but not with me, and I hope the girl is worth it.

"Will we see it when it is done?" she asked.

"I want you to see it," he wrote. "I have never done anything like it before." She knew he was speaking as an artist.

In their room that night, Alick talked, walking about the room while she lay in bed and watched him by candlelight.

They had stopped at Parson's Cove on the way to Maddox and talked with Captain Whittier on the wharf, where *Ariel* was being made ready for her next voyage. The boys told him how they had discovered Jerome and taken him to the Keel.

Sandy courageously took the initiative, considering that he wanted a berth on *Ariel* one day. "We were obeying the Law of the Keel, sir. That is why we didn't tell anyone."

"Sir, nobody made us swear to it," Carolus said, lest Mr. George be held responsible. "We just felt it was the right thing to do. But we understand now we should have told you."

"We'd have been glad to know he was safe under cover, but I know the Law of the Keel," Captain Whittier put his thumbs in his waistcoat pockets and spoke with nostalgia. "When I was a boy, scudding all around town in everybody's mess and nobody's watch, I'd have no more broken the Law of the Keel than I'd have sauced my father. I used to go codfishing with George Gunn. He had a pretty little wherry one of their—uh—citizens had built. Never laid eyes on the man, but he was an artist." Captain Whittier was gazing years astern. "George's father was Mr. George then. Beard down to here." He measured on his chest. "We thought Jehovah looked like him, not the other way around. I could always come back to the Keel if I kept my mouth shut. Of course I knew there were some strangers, but if I sighted one by chance, I never let on."

Then William piped up. "We are going to buy Jerome and make him free." Captain Whittier's reminiscent smile disappeared.

"Good luck to you," he said. "My brothers and I drove to Tenby as

tight as we could behind the Sheriff's wagon. We cornered Fitzwater at
the jail and asked his price. He blew smoke in my face and told me I had
better be thankful he wasn't taking me to court for kidnapping and grand
larceny. Said my brothers and I and every soul at the Keel were guilty of
abetting the commission of a crime, receiving stolen goods, and anything
else a shrewd Yankee lawyer could come up with. He understood there
were some in New England who were real geniuses if they were paid
enough money, that being all Northerners were interested in."

The Whittier men had walked out. "None of us has been fit to live
with ever since. I can hardly wait to get to sea again, and my brothers
threaten to sign on." He laughed, the way one laughs when something is
not funny but tragic. "If there's a fund raised, we will contribute, and
generously, no doubt of that. But don't say 'Whittier' to him."

The Whittiers' experience put the first frost on the boys, but it was
not a killing one. Fitzwater had a reason for hating Captain Whittier, but
it was unthinkable that he should not be impressed by the General, who
had been a friend of George Washington. They could not imagine that
he would not be awed into agreement.

In Maddox they had gone directly to find the General in the office at
his wharf; he was already thinking about the matter. He and Alick
composed a short note, inviting the recipient to join the Cause, in person
if possible. The General's handwriting was illegible, but his clerk Guy
Rigby and Alick each wrote a good clear hand, and made ten copies
between them. The General signed them all, and the younger boys were
sent to take the notes around town. Guy Rigby rode Young Joshua to
deliver the more distant ones, but first he was to leave a letter at the hotel
for Fitzwater, requesting an appointment at two in the afternoon.

By noon they were back with the answers. All but one were accep-
tances, and most of these promised to bring someone else along. One
man felt a delegation would be useless, but he would contribute if he was
wrong. Only one was a point-blank refusal.

"No wonder." The General had been contemptuous. "Can't quarrel
with his bread and butter. That's where his wife's money comes from, you
know. Building slavers, importing black cargo. Old Boston family, high-
principled Puritan crew, but they never let principles stand in the way of
profit. Slave-owning branch of 'em in Georgia."

"Who is this man?" asked Jennie.

"No one we have any dealings with," Alick said, "so don't concern yourself. Colin knows the truth through Lydia's Boston connections, but he never speaks of it for fear of visiting the sins of the fathers upon the children."

"Well, as long as it is no one we bow to, I am not curious," Jennie said. "Not very, anyway."

Alick and the boys had had dinner at Strathbuie House and the boys enjoyed the meal far more than their father did, guessing what lay ahead. They wanted to attend the meeting, but Alick said they had played their part; he gave them money to buy school supplies for themselves and the younger ones, and told them to be back at the mansion by three.

"The end is short and sweet." He filled a mug with water from the pitcher keeping cool on the western window sill. He stayed there close to the night, the wind pouring through the spruces and scenting the dusk with them, the crickets in the warm grass.

"He laughed at us, the slime," he said tightly. "He was most impartial with his insults, not even missing young Guy, who had pledged a month of his pay. The lad went white as clabber, then red, and his fists came up; Colin put a hand on his shoulder and kept him in place. We were all gentlemanly—no one was giving him any satisfaction—but he was raising the lust to kill in more than one breast."

He drank more water and came back to the bed.

"I will not be telling you all. The fact that he *exists*, and has been sitting up there drinking with the creatures who aye follow where the rum and the wine run free, making a mock of us all, with that poor devil lying in jail—just the *fact*, mind you, turns me into a murderer in thought if not in deed." He sat down heavily on the bed and began to take off his boots. "It must be the blood of my Highland ancestors crying out in me, my hands still itching for a claymore to split his skull and stop that laugh forever. But something did, for a breath or two. We were walking out, with him snickering behind us, when the Methodist minister turned, and said, 'May God have mercy on your soul.' Solemn and quiet, like the judge in the high court when he puts on the black cap. For a moment the man lost his wits and was glaring like a corpse before they close its eyes and bind up the fallen jaw. Then he let out a great jackass bray as if he was never hearing anything so funny in his life. There was not a one of us in that room who was not waiting for him to fall down dying of the joke."

He shook his head and sighed. "But it never happens when you are aching with the wish for it. *Dia,* it is always one you cannot spare who goes between two ticks of the clock."

She rose to her knees and began kneading the back of his neck and his shoulders. They were iron-hard at first, and she thought her hands would ache before the rigid muscles began to change under her strong fingers.

"You tried," she said. "Everyone has tried, beginning with William. 'Try never was beat,' they learned in the schoolyard, but this time Try *was* beat, and viciously. But Alick, *mo chridh,* you are not responsible, and they must know that."

He didn't answer in words, but leaned back against her, into her arms.

Forty-Six

I N THE NIGHT Aeolus changed his mind, and the wind swung to the northwest with a force that shook that end of the house like the concussion of an explosion. A cold gust blasted into the room and knocked the light china pitcher off the window sill; the crash brought Jennie upright out of sleep, crying, "What was that?"

"What is what?" Alick murmured, turned away from her, and sank again. She slid out of bed into a wintry gale that flattened her thin nightdress against her body and set her to shaking and her teeth to chattering. Stars like new-minted silver coinage filled the window panes, and by their light she pulled the rag mat from beside the bed to the window and laid it over the puddle. The curtains flapped insanely at her, and she felt absolutely naked to the wind. The china pitcher hadn't broken; she set it on the rug and closed the window. In the sudden lull she heard bare feet thudding overhead and the boys' windows being closed. She went through the parlor to the front hall and listened at the foot of the stairs. There were no voices; whoever had shut the windows was back in bed and probably halfway into sleep again, luckier than Jennie, who knew she was awake for the rest of the night, and resented it. She could just make out the face of the grandfather clock; it was only a little past two. Wouldn't it be nice if one could stop time by stopping the pendulum? Just this once to hold morning back?

She returned to her room, used the chamber pot, and bundled into bed again, pulling up the extra coverlet. She was glad the others could sleep, but there was nothing for her to do but think, and nothing to do about her thoughts except to endlessly circle them, as if all at once a change of view would reveal the great Answer.

This is when I could write in my journal if I still kept one, she thought. She had stopped keeping it the night when she could not force herself to write *April left us today*. Think of all the priceless things I have not set down, she thought. What a waste! But I could begin again; I could begin today, if I had a blank book to write in.

She took her stockings, slippers, and dressing gown out to the winter kitchen to put them on. Darroch's tail beat on the floor; when she lit a candle he regarded her with a benevolent interest that demanded nothing. She set the little kettle to boil, and brought the slate and chalk from the summer kitchen and settled herself at the table. Contemplating the blank slate, she thought, *tabula rasa*, perfect image of my mind at this instant.

The kettle began to boil, sounding like miniature bagpipes. She had just made the tea when the hall door latch clicked, and Alick came in, shutting doors noiselessly behind him. He was dressed and carrying his boots. "Are you ailing?" he asked anxiously.

"Not ailing, but I couldn't sleep. When the wind came around, it knocked the pitcher onto the floor and woke me."

"I'll be stepping outside first to smell the weather." Darroch went out with him. When they finally sat at the table, and he was cutting slices from a new loaf on the breadboard, he said with a smile, "Is this not reminding me of our first breakfast together? A rusty pannikin of water and a bit of dry bread you could crack your teeth on?"

"Don't forget the luxuries like that very salty ham, for as long as it lasted, and all the springs and streams to drink from afterward."

"And the hard cheese, so strong it could have walked along with us."

"But we were thankful to have it." She held up her cup, and he touched his to it in a salute. "To the memory of that brew you made from hawthorn and whortleberry leaves. It put the heart back into us. And the cormeille roots we ate, and the sorrel broth."

"The one blessed hare, and the trout."

"My mouth waters now," she said. "When we reached Fort William, Nancy's bread and butter, and proper tea with milk and sugar, tasted like Paradise, but nothing else in this world ever tasted like the food we ate as fugitives. And no one could understand it who had not also been a fugitive."

A black face among pine needles. "Jerome would know," she said, chastened. "How could I forget him? The seas will be flattening under this wind, and they will sail. Unless—do you think the Tenby delegation—"

He shook his head before she could finish. "No, and I am dreading the end of this day."

Jennie felt tired and cross, and even more tired for keeping it to herself when the children seemed to have multiplied to ten and filled the house. No one mentioned the Tenby delegation. The twins were thoughtful and animated by turns, as if they hoped for the best but were preparing themselves for the worst; hope seemed dominant. William was extremely perky, and Pris pulled a long face behind his back and shook her head, which Jennie pretended to ignore.

The boys went back to the shore to pitch the rockweed left from the storm, and Bell Ann went with them, always in hopes of discovering she knew not what in the tangle, but it was sure to be something to treasure. "A dead body," William suggested, "and you could plan the funeral." This unlikely prospect struck her as very funny. "And you can dig the grave!" she answered pertly.

"Goodness, I hope they don't really find anything," Pris said. "A dead gull would upset her and William terribly."

Jennie wrote to her younger sister Sophie, contentedly wandering the hills of home as she wrote. She had not once said to herself, *I will never see them again.* As long as she never said *never*, she could browse on memories as peacefully as a sheep on those slopes. There was a *never* for Linnmore, she had known it the day she left, but not for the fells and tarns of her childhood and Pippin Grange, within the reach of the wind off the North Sea.

After that she wrote a friendly letter to Robin at college, filling it with everything she could think of, like raisins in a pudding. "Would you like to add to this?" she called to Pris, who was cutting out a school dress for Bell Ann from an outgrown one of her own.

"No, thank you," Pris said distantly. "I hope you haven't mentioned me."

"I couldn't very well omit you from family news, but I haven't embarrassed you. Read it for yourself, and see."

"I will take your word for it. Don't send him my love, please."

"I would not dream of it," said Jennie. When the others came in, they had already washed the rockweed off their feet and legs, and they wanted a strupach. When they'd eaten it, sitting in a high-spirited row on the bench outside, she invited them to add to Robin's letter. The twins each wrote a few lines about their activities, William wrote candidly that he was sorry about the birthday party. "Dear Robin," Bell Ann wrote very slowly and clearly, "I love you. I am still your best friend." They also sent their love to their English cousins, in Sophie's letter.

"Now you may all take a walk to the post office and get these into the mail," Jennie said, "and you needn't hurry back if you see something fascinating."

For the four, the mood of the day would continue as airy and iridescent as a soap bubble dancing away on a breath of air; for Jennie and Alick, and Priscilla to a lesser degree, its fragile beauty was heartbreaking, because at any instant now its life would end.

David came home while they were at their evening chores and told Alick and Jennie that the Tenby attempt had failed. The wind was flattening the seas so fast that the General and Captain Bristow had no more excuses for holding *Lady Lydia* in port, and Fitzwater would be sailing with his prisoner at noon tomorrow.

"We'll wait until after supper to tell them," Jennie said at once. "Otherwise no one will want to eat." They were all thinking of William. It would not go deep for Bell Ann; something else would soon be occupying her mind. The twins would be angry for a long time, but it was not in their nature to brood. But William's tragedies endured; a dead bird or a drowned mouse could sadden him for days. He still sometimes cried out in his sleep for his kite. The death of a pet, or of someone he knew well, especially another child, could haunt his nights for weeks. His imagination was as much a torment as it could be a joy.

We cannot shed William's tears for him, Jennie thought, but I will be glad when tonight is over with. Then we must face the fact that Jerome is sailing back to captivity, and William will be suffering every mile of the voyage with him. And it won't end there.

They had a favorite supper, slices of cold oatmeal fried to golden-crusted splendor, eaten hot with either molasses or maple syrup, crisp pork scraps, and tart applesauce. When they were through eating, and the men sat back from the table and lit their pipes, Alick called William to him. "Are you too old for this?" he asked teasingly, slapping his thigh. William perched on his knee, and cocked his head whimsically at his father. "Och, the weight of you!" Alick pretended to wince. "And the long legs down to the floor. I will have to be finding another wee lad to fill my lap."

"I will be your wee lad, Papa," Bell Ann said jealously.

"But what would I do without my wee girl?" He drew her to him and kissed the top of her head. Still holding her, and keeping a restraining hand on William's knee, he said softly, "The Tenby folk were no luckier than the rest of us. Fitzwater will be leaving with Jerome tomorrow."

William twisted suddenly and put his arms tightly around Alick's neck and his face against his father's shoulder. Sandy abruptly went out, and Carolus followed him. Priscilla said sternly, "Come and help me, Bell Ann," and the child went to her like a sleepwalker, her dark gray eyes wide. David looked critically at his pipe, as if to avoid seeing the sheen in Alick's eyes as he smoothed and patted William's back, and murmured in the boy's ear. It would be in the language with no *yes* or *no* in it, but a treasury of tenderness.

When William straightened up, his eyes were dryer than his father's, but his round face seemed to have lengthened out; all at once he looked older than twelve. David was printing on the slate. He held it up before William, who slid off his father's knee and followed David to the back stairs.

When the door closed behind them, Alick read the slate aloud. "Come up and paint on your new kite," it invited.

"That may help as much as tears," Jennie said. "Well, at least they all know. Do we dare take a long breath? Or even two?"

"They are growing up," Alick said, "and I can fairly hear my gray hairs springing forth."

"Soon people will be calling you 'distinguished.' The best I can hope for is a 'respectable matron of mature years.' Well, rather that than 'ripe.' Decay is expected to swiftly follow ripeness."

Priscilla, clearing the table, said with something approaching awe, "I hope I will be able to cope as well with my family, when I have one."

"Coping, is it?" Alick was sardonic.

"Oh, my dear, we aren't coping," Jennie said. "We are simply trying to take everything as it comes without loosing our footing."

"You'll have been noticing," said Alick, "that we were needing David just then."

"But David is here because *you* were here for him, so it all comes back to you. Come along, Bell Ann." She steered the child into the pantry.

When the light had gone from David's skylight, he and William came downstairs. Jennie was pleased to see William yawning and seemingly at ease. While he was scrubbing off paint stains in the pantry, Pris asked him when they would see the kite, and he said carelessly, "Oh sometime when there's a good wind to fly him." He came out to his parents, drying his face, still without tears.

"May we go to see Jerome off tomorrow?"

Forty-Seven

D RESSING FOR TOWN on Saturday morning, Jennie said to Alick, "I feel as if I were going to a funeral. Only the black gloves and ribbons are missing. I keep harking back to the fateful Sunday. William has always been such a good little boy. Why did he choose that particular time to disobey?"

"Because he is twelve, and it is time for a wee rebellion now and then. But if you believe in Fate, it is Fate that blew him to the Cathcart shore. To his sorrow."

Crossing the bridge, they saw the Boston packet, *Lady Lydia*, at the wharf. She was elderly but staunch, and Captain Bristow was as wedded to her as to his wife. She was riding high on the tide, her ensign flying out straight in the northwest breeze. After the sea wind that had kept the kiln smoke blowing back over the town, the scene was as high-colored as if straight from a child's paint box. On Saturday the General's local enterprises were closed, but today his wharf was crowded beyond the men who had business there and the ever-present boys hoping to catch or cast off lines.

Corny wasn't in the Strathbuie stableyard. They put Perry in the paddock and walked down to the shore. Bell Ann was restrained between her parents; the others went in pairs, William and Carolus, Pris and Sandy.

A group of men and boys from the Keel stood out among the rest like rocks in a stream. Moses touched his hat somberly to Jennie and Alick. Most of the watchers on the wharf were serious and low-spoken; even the most light-minded would behave with decorum under the General's eyes

345

and on his wharf on such an occasion. Only the children were active,
darting among their elders like minnows, excited without knowing why.
Occasionally a noisy one was reined in and told to stand. David was
nowhere in sight.

The General stood by the gangplank with Captain Bristow, Guy
Rigby, and the first mate. Fitzwater waited apart in the shadow of the
bowsprit; his new friends evidently thought it was safer to drink with him
under cover than to be seen in public with him on the General's
premises. He wore a fixed half-smile, half-sneer, as if viewing rustic
yokels at a fair.

A line of boys were perched on the lime shed roof like gulls, and
suddenly one of them rose up and cried, "They're coming!"

The silence in which the wagon arrived remained unbroken except
for the heavy, hollow clop of hoofs on the planks and the rumble of
wheels. It was a stillness that made Fitzwater uncomfortable. He kept
wiping his face and his neck with a large handkerchief, though it was not
hot.

The sheriff and his deputy rode on the seat, the deputy driving; the
two black men sat on boxes in the wagon bed. Mr. Henderson was
familiar to Jennie from church. Jerome was a much younger man, bare-
headed, with broad shoulders, leaning forward over folded arms braced
on his knees. He was not manacled that Jennie could see. She had felt
earlier that they were dressing for a funeral; now the occasion seemed the
prelude to a public execution, and she wanted to run away. As if her hand
in Alick's arm communicated this, he patted it.

The crowd remained quiet, a child was shushed. Pris had taken Bell
Ann and gone to speak to someone, but now she came quickly back,
looking strained. "I do not want to see this," she said.

"You have to see him," Carolus told her sternly. "He is our friend."
Sandy's hands pressed down on William's shoulders hard enough to turn
his fingertips white. William was so still Jennie could hardly see him
breathe.

Fitzwater stepped out in front of the horse. "That's far enough," he
shouted. "Now hustle him aboard! None of your infernal flummadiddles!"
He went to the back and began to unhook the tailgate, but he was gently
moved aside by the deputy, who was bigger and broader. The sheriff
stepped down and strolled over to the General as if to pass the time of day.

"Now, Mr. Henderson," the deputy said, "you just hand over that box
you been roostin' on, and I'll put it down so you can step on it." He

steadied the elderly man and made encouraging noises until he saw him with both feet on the ground.

"Why isn't the prisoner manacled?" Fitzwater bawled, and there was a ripple of snickers. He swung around angrily but all faces stared solemnly back at him.

"He's still in my custody till he goes aboard," the sheriff said blandly. "He doesn't need irons."

Fitzwater reached into the wagon and grabbed Jerome by the arm. "Git out of there, you black bastard!"

The General's cane struck the side of the wagon, just short of Fitzwater's shoulder. "There is no need of rough handling or rough language, sir."

"There's a need to protect my property, *suh*!" He swung his head nervously from side to side. "I'm not deaf—I hear things! Rum talks, and it's been warning me."

"You sure that warn't the rum horrors talking, Mister?" The voice disappeared under a wave of laughter.

"Have no fear, sir," the General said contemptuously, "we are orderly here."

"*Orderly*, when one of your so-called *estimable* citizens steals a valuable property and a whole community conspires to hide it?"

"Around here most of us don't believe a man is property, like a horse," the General said. "I am shamed to admit that there are some who think if a man's black he's less than a man. But thank God there are few here. Very few." He aimed his cane at the ship. "Sheriff Swallow will see him aboard. There's been a place prepared for him, and you are not to use your irons on my vessel. Captain Bristow will see that the man is decently fed and exercised as far as Boston, and any abuse on your part will be dealt with as is the Captain's right."

"Don't worry! *I* don't aim to damage a prime property."

Suddenly William was gone from Sandy's hands in a headlong charge for the wagon. The twins caught him, and in the struggle he was all arms and legs and a butting head. "My goodness!" Pris whispered. "Sweet William!"

"Sir," said Carolus to the General in a proud, carrying voice, "we would like to speak to Jerome." Fitzwater swung a threatening arm at him. "Shoo! *Git*!"

"Let them," the General said. "They are not going to steal your *property* before your eyes." He nodded and the twins hoisted William into

the wagon and swarmed aboard behind him. They crouched around
Jerome, talking to him as if they had a year of words to crowd into five
minutes. The broad dark face turned to each speaker, and once—
unbelievably, in his situation—he smiled. Often he nodded and spoke.
He used his hands to illustrate something and they listened respectfully.

"How long is this damned gibble-gabble going to last?" Fitzwater
shouted at the sheriff. "Do you call the turns or does *he*?" He pointed at
the General, who was watching the scene in the wagon with a mellow
smile.

"My prisoner had himself lots of company while he was in my jail,"
the sheriff said imperturbably. "A few more won't hurt."

The twins finally shook hands with Jerome, and he looked long into
each face; then he leaned forward and took William's face in his big
hands, and spoke to him alone. When he ceased to speak, and straightened up, William gave him a hard, convulsive hug, then bolted from the
wagon in a wildly clumsy leap, staggering and almost falling before he
found his footing. Alick made a start as if to go to him, but stopped. His
and Jennie's enlaced fingers twisted and squeezed with a painful urgency.

"He is crying!" Pris said, crying herself.

"Stop that, Pris," Jennie commanded, pressing her shoulder. "We
cannot do that here."

The twins jumped down behind William and walked him away,
Sandy holding his elbow and Carolus's fingers hooked inside his collar.
William's face was contorted with a grief he didn't try to hide. They went
straight past their parents, who didn't attempt to stop them. Other
persons spoke quietly to them as they left the wharf, but they didn't
answer. They were like young soldiers surviving their first battle and
leaving dead comrades behind, trying desperately to be men enough not
to show what they had been through. My poor darlings, Jennie thought,
this is only the beginning for you.

"I will *not* watch him go on board," Pris said, and ran after them. Bell
Ann seized her parents' hands in a cramping grasp, trying to pull them
along. A ruddy young man leaving the wharf lifted his hat to Jennie and
shook hands with Alick. "This is a sorry day for Maddox," Ronald Heriot
said, "and your boys in particular, it seems."

"He is their friend," Alick said. "They would have given everything
to see him free."

"It is a sin and a crime, this business. — Am I invited to your October
launching, Glenroy?" The men talked, but Jennie heard nothing of it.

She was watching what her children could not bear to watch; Jerome jumping down from the wagon and walking toward the ship. He was a well-built man, wearing shirt and pantaloons surely of Keel homespun, and decent shoes. She remembered that Mr. Henderson was the Keel shoemaker. He walked beside Jerome now, his hat crumpled in his hands, but Jerome was as alone as Fitzwater as he walked toward his last captivity; no other person on the wharf had ever known or would ever experience what he knew so well. He walked as if he had always been free, with a high head and an easy stride. At the gangplank Fitzwater made as if to elbow Mr. Henderson aside, but Guy Rigby tripped over something invisible and fell against Fitzwater, while Mr. Henderson went up the gangplank with Jerome. Guy received a splatter of applause.

The two black men shook hands at the head of the gangplank. The older man came ashore wiping his eyes with a bandanna, and Jerome stood in impassive isolation, his head lifted toward the breeze as if he were filling his lungs with the wind of freedom that blew across the town to him; the same wind would presently fill the sails to take him away.

Fitzwater ran up the gangplank, and Jennie abruptly turned her back. Above the trees across the road the flag blew out straight against the sky, a steady rippling ran through its clear crimson, white, and blue. She remembered her first sight of the flag when the brig *Paul Revere* came up the river, she had not dreamed then that it would become her flag, and until now she had loved it beyond question. She wondered if Jerome was watching it, and if he accepted the truth that it was not *his* flag. Generations of slavery and a few abortive attempts to escape could eventually breed mute acquiescence, she supposed.

"Jennie?" Alick murmured.

"I don't want to see them cast off," she said.

"No more do I." He reached around for Bell Ann, who protested. "I want to see them raise the sails."

"Not this time, *mo graidh.*"

It was not a tone to argue with, but she compromised by walking importantly across the road ahead of them, and opening the gate onto the Strathbuie grounds. She was invited in by Ozzie the Newfoundland.

The boys sat on the top bar of the paddock gate like three crows. Bell Ann and Ozzie headed matter-of-factly for the kitchen, where Pris was with Eliza and Sibba and, possibly, macaroons and custard tarts.

Suddenly William's face flared scarlet. "If nobody watched the ship out of sight, Jerome will come back. I *know* it!" His passion defied reason; he forbade it even from his father, who did not attempt it.

"The General should clear everybody off the wharf! If they aren't too witless and gormless to go anyway. Don't they know they could *sink* that ship?"

Carolus retorted that the whole world, present company and their friends excepted, was witless and gormless. "We sail along like that stupid man in *Candide*, thinking that this is the best of all possible worlds. And then something happens, and we race about like Chicken Little, screaming that the sky is falling."

"And too few doing that," said Sandy cynically. "Otherwise, why hasn't slavery been stopped by now?"

Unable to provide any answers that wouldn't be platitudes, his parents were relieved when Corny came limping and puffing. "Gorry, warn't that an occasion? She's gone, pretty as a picture, all sails set, and Fitzwater with a face like a meat axe. Wouldn't I like to nudge him over the side, accidental-like, when nobody was around." He chuckled, then guiltily rubbed his hands over his face. "The General says will you folks wait up? He wants a blether, he calls it, and the Missis would be pleased to give you a cup of tea."

The boys decided to start for home on foot and let the wagon catch up with them. Priscilla thought of an errand on Main Street, which would save her from tea with Robin's mother. Jennie was in no mood for socializing, but one didn't walk away from old friends, and she would appreciate a cup of tea, they'd had only a light meal before they left home.

Bell Ann was blissful, she loved visiting Strathbuie House. She was invited to have tea in the kitchen; Eliza could be trusted to see that she ate bread and butter before the sweets, and not too many of those. The adults sat at the end of the drawing room that looked over the Pool and the river. *Lady Lydia* was out of sight now, and the hot strong tea was bracing, even without the rum the General offered around.

"Shocking, shocking," he growled. "I feel like fumigating the wharf after that one's been on it. I don't know how long the nation can carry on like this. Been a burning question ever since I can remember, but greed always wins out. Come into the library, Alick, before I forget myself and use bad language before the ladies. We'll have a smoke. I've been sent some of the sweetest leaf you'll ever taste."

Lydia reached for Jennie's cup and filled it. "You may as well sit back for another half-hour at least, Jennie, though I know you are dying to get back to your little Eden and take off your shoes and stays. Tell me, have you seen the girl that David Evans is painting? The money is tainted by slaving interests in the past, but of course that is not the girl's fault."

"I haven't seen her, but Pris says she is exquisite." At least that was *one* of Pris's words.

She *is* exquisite," said Lydia. "But there is either no brain behind those velvet eyes, or there is a frantically conniving, greedy little slut. The Heriots must be just waiting for her to put a foot wrong so they can ship her back. I tell you, Jennie, I am glad Robin returned early to college. I have no wish to see him seduced before he is nineteen."

"A *slut?*" said Jennie quizzically.

"That's a bit strong, I admit. But then I was always jealous of these born coquettes. They had the boys dazzled out of their wits while we big girls felt like elephants in ruffles."

"You didn't do too badly," Jennie said.

"Eventually. But it was a long journey. — Oh, who knows, Jacinth may be in reality a sweet child who would carry calves' foot jelly to old ladies and read them their favorite psalms, but she *appears* to be dedicated to standing Maddox young men on their heads so their brains will spill out through their ears. Not that most of them wouldn't think better with their feet," she added, "except perhaps Septimus Frye. He's the brightest of the galaxy."

"He may be collecting *her*," said Jennie.

"I hope David Evans is a man of sense, and sees her only as an attractive composition. She walks as if it is her duty to appear once a day before adoring subjects, always on a male arm. Most look blinded by glory, but with David you cannot tell."

Septimus, Jennie was thinking. It was no surprise. Off to fresh fields and pastures green; a girl who adored playing the *femme fatale* and had the opportunity. Pris would by now be safely relegated to his past. Now if only she did not encounter the afternoon promenade on Main Street, with Septimus as today's courtier.

Forty-Eight

P RISCILLA WAS WAITING for them out at the stables, feeding chunks of apple to the two old ponies. She had met Mrs. Heriot on Main Street and heard that David had refused to accompany Jacinth to the wharf, saying they couldn't spare the time from the portrait.

"At least he can stand up for himself in *some* things," Pris said with mournful satisfaction. "Of course it *could* mean that he didn't want to share her."

They did not catch up with the boys on the way home, but found them already there; the Keel wagon had given them a ride. Everything was very quiet, except for Bell Ann's description of each object she had seen in every room she had entered with Sibba on the first floor of Strathbuie House. But that soon went dry for lack of response from William, usually a loyal audience.

There were no baked beans tonight, but Moses Gunn had left a big handsome pollack in the springhouse. Stuffed and baked, with potatoes roasted in their jackets and a garden salad, it would be a banquet for anyone who had the appetite for it. They should all be hungry in spite of their emotions, though she had doubts about William. He had not spoken to anyone, as far as she knew. This worried at her while she prepared the fish for the oven. They had changed their clothes and were doing chores now, and Alick was down at the Yard to inspect in solitude the day's progress on the *Lincoln*; the work day had ended soon after they drove in. William might follow him as soon as his work was done. Yes, he surely would; she felt better.

Pris came with the milk buckets and cloths to wash, and Bell Ann was with her, grumbling.

"William is very sad, Bell Ann, can't you understand that?" Pris asked her. "He has lost his friend."

Bell Ann did not wish to be understanding, but sensed she would be in a minority and changed the subject. "Anyway, he went with Sandy down to the beach, and they wouldn't let me go too. What do you think of *that*, Mama?" she asked with artful pathos. "They let the dogs go, but not their little sister. Is that *fair?*"

"You may spend all tomorrow at the beach if you want," Jennie answered. "Now clean yourself up and help with the supper, like the good girl you are."

"I know he has lost his *friend*," Bell Ann said, "but he cannot be sad about it *forever*. That is *selfish*."

"*Tais-toi, mon enfant*," said Pris. "You and I will go gather things for the salad."

"And you can teach me French," Bell Ann said graciously.

Jennie was left alone except for Garnet, who was assiduously washing her face and ears after her supper of raw pollack.

This was one of the times when routine was a salvation of sorts. Of course it didn't keep one from thinking; it didn't stop the pictures from appearing in one's brain, each brilliant scene dissolving into the next. But to keep one's hand productively busy at the same time was a feat of concentration comparable with tightrope walking.

She made dressing for the salad, so much of this, so much of that, a cautious pinch of something else, and then a good whisking. She knew where the girls were. William and Sandy were together, that was good; Carolus was likely to be with them by now, and that was *very* good. The twins had been so protective of William at the wharf; it was a revelation in which she could not help rejoicing quietly.

Someone crossed the summer kitchen, and Sandy appeared in the pantry doorway and leaned against the jamb. His thin features looked even thinner, his eyes meeting hers were not dulled but distant, as if he were seeing oceans beyond her, and she was unsubstantial against them. Then all at once his gaze changed focus and took on the familiar pugnacious sparkle.

"Somebody ought to swear!" he said hotly. "Why is everyone so *gentlemanly?* I know some good words, but I can't use them where you and Father are, and Pris won't let us even shout ordinary around the cows."

"I know all about wanting to swear," Jennie said. "We had to go a long way from the house and shout our bad words into the wind. Usually by the time we came home we'd have walked off most of our bad tempers."

One day he'd suddenly ask her what used to make her angry enough to run away and swear. It was inevitable, but now wasn't the time.

"Anyway," he said rapidly, "I have made up my mind, and that helps some."

"Made up your mind to what?"

"When I'm of age, I'm going into the Revenue Service or the Navy, and work at putting an end to slave smuggling." The words snapped out. "It has been illegal since the Act of 1808, but it goes on and on, and the smugglers outnumber the enforcers. I knew all that from Captain Blackburn, and Mr. Lockhart is passionate about it. He calls it an outrage, brazen, *vicious*—he cannot think of words enough. But all I have been seeing is my own ship, my own glory. Now everything is different for me. We can't fight slavery on land, but we can fight it on the sea. Of course I still intend to be a captain, only she'll be a government ship. You just watch me."

"I'll always watch you, Sandy, and I'm watching you now with so much pride I can hardly stand it." For the first time this afternoon her hands felt unsteady. "Have you told your father?"

"No. William went down there, but I still had thinking to do. That old log in the mint ought to be preserved for posterity, there's been so much thinking done on it." He was the cocky fifteen-year-old Sandy again, but for a few minutes the man had been there. "I'll go and tell him now."

In a half hour they were all back with the dogs, except Carolus. Sandy was buoyant, and William composed. "I am going to help Sandy catch the slave smugglers," he told Jennie. "Then I will come back to shipbuilding. Papa understands."

"You can't go on a ship!" Bell Ann said jealously. "You are too young."

"I expect to grow up," William said. Bell Ann looked forlorn, and he added generously, "You will grow up too. You can't go to sea, but you can do other things."

"*What* things?" She gave him a withering glare. "This is not *fair*."

"Exactly what I say, love," Pris told her. "We should do something about that." Bell Ann was eagerly gratified. "Yes, let's."

Alick said across the room to Jennie, "I am thinking we will all sleep better tonight." Everything they didn't need to say was implicit in the statement.

"The fish is coming out of the oven," Jennie said. "Will someone ring the bell for Carolus?"

"He is in the house," Pris said. "I saw him from the garden. He came from the woods and went in the front door." She went to the hall and called, but there was no answer. "He must be asleep," she said, coming back. "We're all tired enough."

"I'll climb the rigging and scan the sea with my trusty telescope." Sandy ran up the stairs shouting, "Avast there, lads! All hands on deck!" There was a murmuring, then an explosive exchange of words, and Sandy came down again, by bannister to judge by his speed and the thump of his arrival. He ran out to them, crying, "Carolus is going to destroy his work! He's already begun!" He was white and aghast, and the others were shocked voiceless.

"*Stay here,*" Alick said to Sandy. He took the stairs three at a time, yet when he stood in the boys' doorway he might have just strolled across the hall from the attic. He waited until Jennie joined him. Then he knocked lightly on the open door, and they went in.

Carolus sat on the side of his bed, his dark head bent over the portfolio on his knees. He seemed to have frozen in the act of tearing out a page; it was half-crumpled in his hand. Alick sat down beside him, took the page and smoothed it out, and leisurely examined the detailed painting. Carolus did not lift his head or twitch a finger.

"What is this?"

"My business." Carolus hardly moved his lips.

"It is the business of all of us," his father said. "We know what is at you, my son, but you cannot be destroying the evil by destroying this." He touched the portfolio. "What could *you* have been doing against slavery? Your time will come."

"How can I fritter my life away with *plants*? What do they matter beside a man's freedom? When I read William Bartram's book, I wanted to visit the South. I *dreamed* it. I could *taste* it. I thought, I will go there when I am a man. Now I know what it is really like, I couldn't breathe in the presence of slavery! And now that I have met one man, it has all come down on me like a landslide, and I am as useless as a butterfly."

"Who has said that a butterfly is useless?" Alick asked softly. "Mr. Lockhart is not thinking that, and he is a minister of the gospel."

Carolus lifted his head and gave them a desolate look. "I cannot stop thinking of *him*. He was happy for a little while, and then—Oh, can't you see how *babyish* all this is?"

Jennie caught the book before it touched the floor. She sat down on the other side of him. "None of us can stop thinking of him. The memory of watching him go aboard the packet will always be with me."

"Then can't you see why I don't want to ever look at this stuff again?"

"Then give it to us to keep for you," Alick said. "I promise you, if you destroy this work, you will be destroying a whole summer of your life, and ours, because we have all been concerned in it one way or another. And you will be forever regretting that you punished yourself and us. Not to mention the minister, who has made you his colleague in this research. We will be taking the book into our keeping if we cannot trust you."

"Remember this, my love," Jennie said, "Jerome is a craftsman. What would he say to your demolishing your work?"

The braced shoulders under her arm rose and fell to an audible release of breath. "William told him about it. He bragged on all of us. You too, both of you. Jerome could remember his mother a little, but he was bought very young." There was an odd clicking and snuffling in his nose and throat. "A little boy, really."

"When this is finished," Jennie suggested, "you could dedicate it to Jerome, to mark the time—"

"When I ceased to be a child?" he asked cuttingly. He straightened his back. "Oh, I will go on botanizing; I can't much help loving it. But it will be a different world for me. All the time I will be wondering what I can do against slavery."

"When you are old enough to act, the way will come to you," Alick promised. "Now will you come down and eat supper? You will be needing your strength for the years ahead, and you won't want to be mucking out tomorrow morning on an empty stomach."

After William had gone to bed, she went up to him. He was lying on his back with his hands behind his head, gazing out at the twilight. He said gently, "Don't read to me tonight, Mama."

"Very well, dear." She set down the candle. "May I sit here, just the same?"

"Of course, Mama!" He gave her a beaming Sweet William smile. If he had reached the watershed between small-boyhood and the thorny fields that were neither hay nor grass, she would not be surprised; it was typical of William to be quiet about it. But she had a constriction in her chest and midriff. Changes were coming so thick and fast you had hardly time to recognize one before the next one was upon you.

William suddenly raised up on one elbow. "Where do you suppose he is now?" he asked.

"I wouldn't know, darling. Sandy should have an idea of the distance."

"If I wrote him a letter, where would I send it? He can read! Mr. Fitzwater's brother taught him. He was a good man, but he died. We could give it to one of the captains who stops in at Charleston."

"You've thought it all out, haven't you? It is a wonderful idea!" She couldn't imagine Fitzwater allowing Jerome to receive a letter, but William smiled with a sleepy peace. She kissed him, and was absurdly grateful for his arms around her neck.

It was no surprise the next morning when the older three came in to Sunday breakfast agreed that they were not going to church. "We have nothing to praise God for today," Carolus said. "It is *men* who do good or evil."

"I think God is the word for the good in us, and the Devil is for the evil in us," said Pris.

"I don't think I am evil," William said anxiously.

"When I say *us*, Sweet William, I mean all humankind."

"Go to church or not," Alick said. "God will not be caring whether you come or go. If we are to believe the Bible, He is not just there, He is everywhere. And if He is offended because you do not sit in a pew on Sunday mornings, why is He not offended by a man like Fitzwater?"

"The Great Horse will trample that man under his mighty hoofs!" Bell Ann cried. "Wait and see!"

"He had better not forget to trample Harry too," said William.

"A great many people must have prayed for Jerome to be free," Carolus said. "But it didn't work. I remember when we prayed to God to save April. We did it three times every day when we were staying at the Bastos'. We went out to the playhouse to do it."

"I know now I'd have prayed to Odin or Zeus," Pris said, "or to a rowan tree, if I'd thought it would work. And our chances would have been the same."

"The point is, God didn't save April," said Carolus, "any more than we saved Jerome."

"I told Mr. Street so," Sandy said. "He said God answered all prayers, and sometimes we didn't like the answers, but they are God's will. That made me angry with God."

"So we decided," Carolus said, "we were not going to pray to someone who says *no* all the time to the most important things, like saving little children. Of course, I am perfectly willing to thank Him every time He does a good deed, if He really does it by thinking about it, you know. But it's likely by accident, like *not* stepping on an ant just because you didn't happen to see it."

"I *never* step on ants," said Bell Ann, "because they have to take care of all those baby ants in eggs."

"Mr. Lockhart says that the universe is a miracle that continues to renew itself through all eternity," Pris said. "Do you think whoever created that can really bother Himself with millions of human ants?"

"Fair is fair." Carolus picked it up. "We don't blame Him for the terrible things like slavery. We know people do them. Because He gave us free will, He is not responsible for us in any way."

"I think today we should admire His works with a dinner under His blue sky," said Alick. "We should give Him all the credit due for a day like this, whether He intended it or not, before He drops winter upon us."

"*Clams!* While the tide is still down!" Sandy was out of his seat. "Who else is digging?"

Everyone was, especially the designated dishwashers. Jennie waved them out, and when they and the dogs were gone, she and Alick cleared the table.

"They were trying to raise God," she said. "Two five-year-olds and a seven-year-old. We sent them away from home to spare them, and all the time they were so desperately trying to save April . . . and then to lose her."

"But listen, *mo graidh*, what did they do then? The best thing! They repudiated Him. Now they respect, but they do not beg, expect, or blame."

She said, smiling, "You make them sound so wonderful!"

"They are! Because they are ours!" Then he knocked on wood with the knuckles of both forefingers. David, coming in just then, found them laughing.

At noon they went to Kilmeny's Cove for a picnic. It was on the far side of Misery Wall; ordinarily it caught the full sweep of the prevailing winds, so the family used the inner side of the Wall more. But with the wind still in the northwest, and held off by the height of forested land above, the lee was perfect. An erratic block left by the last glacier stood in the middle of the sand and pebble beach. Today Alick and Jennie occupied its shadow while the children played like porpoises in the cove, with Darroch in their midst trying to rescue someone. Bounce went out no further than his belly, ducking his head for anything that looked intriguing on the bottom. David sat on the rocks below the Wall, letting his clothes dry on him while he sketched.

Jennie saw and heard it all through a shimmer of remembrance. The cove was profoundly personal to her and Alick. In their first spring of owning River Farm, they had discovered the little cove on the far side of the Wall on a day of tumultuous winds. The cove lay in a space of sunshine at their feet, a sparkle of sapphire and aquamarine over a pale bottom of finely ground shell; it turned to dull silver and amethyst as the clouds moved over it. At the foot of the steep embankment of alder and bracken, the boulder stood alone like an altar to a primitive god, and all around it the beach looked hot and inviting after the chilly, windy, shade of the woods. Out where the lee ended there was a line between the cove's taffeta sheen and the river's wind-whipped dark blue and galloping crests.

"It belongs to a land where sin has never been," Alick said. They called it Kilmeny's Cove from then on.

Forty-Nine

M ONDAY MORNING MIRIAM was there early to start the washing. It was the first day of school, so the usual hail-fellow-well-met greetings were bypassed in the confusion. Bell Ann changed her dress and ribbons three times before Jennie stopped her. She bustled about putting things in her school bag and taking them out again until Pris made the hard and final decision for her. William was quite cheerful, as if the spell of Kilmeny Cove were still on him. Last night he had written several drafts of his letter to Jerome, and would write more before he was satisfied. He was taking his Baltimore clipper ship model to school, and Bell Ann's sample of work was the gingham apron she was wearing. They left early to visit and play in the schoolyard.

Miriam was quiet, and Jennie didn't mention Jerome, but Miriam brought up Harry when they were having the ritual coffee. "I didn't see that Harry coming to work this morning."

"He hasn't been here ever since the boys pelted him with green apples," Jennie answered. "Someone will be asking for his place if he doesn't intend to come back."

"I suppose he feels rich as a king, but he will suffer for it," Miriam said somberly. "One way or the other, he will suffer." A light had gone from her, but something else was in its place, not definable but evident.

She left at noon without stopping for dinner, to help with jam-making at a house up the road, and Jennie and Alick ate alone, always an enjoyable experience for being so rare. Alone together they were Alick and Jeannie, who could discuss almost anything without questions or

360

comments from around the table. The lack of a crowd would make any topic refreshing.

She told him about Miriam's prophesy about Harry. "Of course, being Garland Shaw's son must have already guaranteed trouble for him," she said, "and I was sorry for him until now. Do you think his father let him keep that money?"

"We don't know *if* he is the betrayer."

"There is too much evidence against him," she argued.

"They think that at the Yard, and they haven't been quiet about it. The *stramash* with the boys might be just the thing to give him a good excuse to leave. Well, I will be having an answer from his own mouth before the day is out. —And if I had another half-hour to spare now, I would be taking my wife to bed."

Taken by surprise, she burst out laughing, and jumped up, arousing the dogs. " 'Come with me and be my love, and we will all the pleasures prove!' " She held out her hand, and he took it and kissed it.

"It's so nice to be foolish without shocking our children," she said. "Farewell for now, young man. We shall meet in the gloaming."

Priscilla was home before anyone else, out of breath and luminous-eyed. The others liked to lallygag sociably on the way home; she had run alone almost all the way from the post office. Triumphant as Bounce, she laid Friday's *Tenby Journal* on the table before Jennie and pointed at a shout of capital letters and exclamation points: SHAME! SORROW! RIGHT-EOUS WRATH!

They headed a letter to the editor, set in large type and sharing pride of place with municipal crises, political debates, violence on the New Brunswick border, returning ships, a fire on the docks, and the death of a prominent citizen because of a runaway horse. The writer of the letter was, respectfully, Septimus Frye.

"Read it," Pris murmured reverently; then she read it aloud over Jennie's shoulder with appropriate emphasis.

" 'Dear Sir: On Thursday and Friday last, two delegations of local gentlemen, the Maddox contingent led by General Colin Mackenzie, and the Tenby group led by Mayor Sylvanus Macomber, waited upon Mr. Edward Fitzwater at the St. David Inn. The parties consisted of leading merchants, attorneys-at-law, shipbuilders and captains, educators, clergymen, public officials, and other citizens of great integrity. They made a most solemn and heartfelt request of Mr. Fitzwater; that they might purchase the man whom this writer, and I hope this newspaper, cannot in all decency and honor call by the opprobrious epithet of SLAVE.'

"*Opprobrious*," Pris breathed past Jennie's ear. "Imagine him knowing and using such a word! 'These gentlemen,' " she continued, " 'were contemptuously received by Mr. Fitzwater, who declared with a most vulgar sarcasm that he was honored by so much attention, that he missed certain faces whose owners were no doubt absent by reason of their guilty consciences; these were fortunate not to have been already arrested, as he had ample grounds for prosecuting them for abducting and sheltering the unfortunate man. Both the Maddox and Tenby committees bore his contumely—,' " Pris's pronunciation was wrong, " 'like the gentlemen they are.

" 'The man Jerome has been lodged in Tenby Jail, where Sheriff Swallow has made him as comfortable as possible, and local persons have brought him nourishing food. A free man of color has been allowed to stay with him to offer companionship and courage. It is understood that Senator Albion Hardy is attempting to have Mr. Fitzwater's claim set aside and the man declared free, but the time is woefully short and hope is faint. Fitzwater prepares to sail at noon tomorrow.

" 'America will never be the Land of the Free while the loathsome institution of Slavery is allowed to exist. As for the anonymous wretch who carries the slave-owner's blood money in his pocket, let him be warned that he will soon discover, like Lady Macbeth, that his hands are incarnadined forever by blood that will never wash off, and all the perfumes of Araby will not disguise the stench.'

"Isn't he magnificent?" said Pris. She repeated his name with the religious awe with which she used to read Mr. George Washington's signature on the General's framed letters from his friend. But Jennie had to admit it was a most stirring letter and deserved the attention shown it by the editors.

"Wait until Papa reads this!" Pris gloated. "He will see that Seven is not just a chuckle-headed coxcomb."

"We never accused him of being chuckle-headed," Jennie said. "He is an extremely bright young business man. But this is surprising, I agree. It shows deep conviction, it gives me a different perspective."

"Thank you, Mama. Now, may I write him a letter to tell him how impressed I—*we* are? I will bring it to you to read, of course."

"Of course," Jennie agreed. Pris ran upstairs, taking the slate and the newspaper, and Jennie found the mailbag dropped on the bench outside the door. A package from Ianthe was in it. It would include some small item for each of the family, but the package was addressed to Priscilla, and Jennie laid it aside. She sorted the rest, putting personal letters in the bedroom to read later with Alick.

Pris brought down her letter, written on the thick, rich initialed stationery her Aunt Sophie had sent her at Christmas. "It's too elegant for ordinary use," Pris said, "but this is far from ordinary. I don't know how many drafts I wrote on the slate; I wanted to be short but eloquent."

"You are both," Jennie told her. "It is gracious, not stilted, not effusive, but exactly right. I like this especially: 'Jerome touched our hearts in a way to make us remember him forever.' "

"I *was* going to use something from the Bible, or from Shakespeare, if I could think of it, but all at once that came to me." She took the letter and read it to herself, smiling with naïve pride. "And it's true too, isn't it? True to our own experience."

She left the letter in the parlor; after Alick read Septimus's letter in the newspaper after supper, she would bring hers out for him to approve.

"Papa cannot say I am too forward, can he? I was hardly personal at all. I said 'we' and 'us' throughout."

"I am sure he will give you high marks," Jennie said.

"Then do you have anything strenuous for me to do? I feel so *energetic!*" She spun around and strained fingertips toward the ceiling. "I could bound like a deer. I could leap into the air and take wing—"

"Do it outdoors, dear, and don't bound or fly so far as to not be back for supper."

Pris gave her a reckless hug, called to the dogs, and went out. Jennie saw her running down through the field; the monarch butterflies fluttered up from the goldenrod, with Bounce making useless leaps at them.

The twins came home in good spirits, passing the younger ones on the road. They agreed that Septimus's letter was a masterpiece of composition. "You'd never guess he could sound so educated," Carolus said. "Do you think he did it all himself?"

"Of course he did!" Pris was very flushed.

"But where was he Saturday afternoon?" Sandy asked innocently. "I didn't see him on the wharf, and he's not one to be shy."

"He was waiting, I am sure, for the last-minute message from the senator!"

When Alick came up for dinner, she didn't stand gazing at him as he read but made herself unnecessarily busy in the pantry. When he finally called to her, she went to his side, looking carefully blank. "Yes, Papa."

"A good letter." He tapped the newspaper. "The lad has a grand store of words at his command, and uses them well. It is surprising to find him such a thinker."

"Yes, isn't it?" She agreed diffidently. "And what do you think of *my* letter? I speak for all of us, of course."

"Och, yours is fine too. Post it, but don't be enclosing your miniature or a lock of your hair, or one of your gloves." They both laughed.

"That would give him a dreadful shock," Pris said. "He'd think I was proposing. He would be in a rare old pittapation, wouldn't he?" She kissed the top of Alick's head and took her letter upstairs. In the morning she would carry it to the post office, thickly sealed.

William came home eager to get to work on his letter at once so David could take it to Maddox in the morning, where all the captains were. Bell Ann came later, she had walked home with Lily Shaw. She was very set up with the triumphs of her day and determinedly silent about the defeats.

The pulse of the family was slowly correcting itself.

After supper Alick went to the Shaws' to talk with Harry. He took Bell Ann along; coming home from school she had promised Lily that she would somehow manage to see Lily's playhouse. They came back in a very short time, but Bell Ann was running ahead, talking about the playhouse before she could be understood. Clearly, she had seen it.

Pris, David, and the twins had gone walking on the shore toward the Bastos', Jennie and William and the dogs were outside the kitchen door in a warm twilight ticking with crickets. William lay on the grass near the bench, watching for the first stars. Alick sat down beside Jennie and lit his pipe.

It had been a very quiet walk to the Shaw house, which was veiled from the public by a grove of locusts and maples. The lane led between the cow and horse pastures; Major had trotted to the fence to take a closer look at Alick and Bell Ann. The shadows were long, the birds flew. Bell Ann held Alick's hand tightly when they entered the grove.

"I thought it was *enchanted*," she told her mother. When they emerged, there was the spotless house with no sign of its having a mistress, no climbing roses or one small flowerbed. Garland Shaw was waiting for them where the wheel tracks curved toward the barn. He must have seen them turning in off the road.

"The great yellow and white dog is standing behind him, growling," Alick said. "Why he didn't send the beast to drive us off, I couldn't fathom, unless even Shaw would not be letting the brute tear a man to pieces before the eyes of his wee girl. 'What do *you* want?' he growled like the dog. Och, the charm of the man! *Princely* is the word. Harry was standing in the barn doorway with a dung fork in his hand, looking deformed without his hat. Headless, you might say. I called to him, 'Harry, will you be coming back to work?' He consulted the toes of his boots for a bit of an eternity, and answered from far behind his teeth. If he hadn't shaken his head, I'd have made no sense of it. Even his father looked as if he was wishing to shake him hard until all his parts fell into place. It strikes me the man has bullied the lad since he took his first step.

" 'I reckon you have your answer, Glenroy,' Shaw said, and waited for me to go. But in those few minutes Bell Ann had disappeared. 'If you don't mind,' I said, 'I'll be waiting for my daughter.' Shaw went stumping off to the barn, and both men disappeared within it. But the dog remained. It stood on guard like a—"

"*Wolf!*" said Bell Ann, delighted.

"Listen to her! *She* wasn't the one to quell the beast by looking it in its yellow eyes. For all I knew the playhouse was far off in Fairyland, and there I stood alone. When I reached for my pipe its hackles rose even higher. It is not a wolf, but I am not sure it is a dog."

William, sitting Indian-fashion on the grass, was leaning tensely forward. "It may have been a dragon in disguise," Alick said, and William grinned. Bell Ann nodded proudly at him.

"I am not sure of that, either," Alick said seriously. "Mrs. Shaw would not be allowing it to blow out fire and soot up its surroundings, though it would be a handy way to be drying out wet kindling. Well, I whistled for my daughter, and it tipped its head—," he demonstrated, "and sat down for the concert, so I whistled up a bit of a jig and a reel, and he liked best 'The Devil's Dream,' which is better on a fiddle than a whistle, but your hero of a father carried on, and all the time the head was going this way, and that way—"

Bell Ann held back her giggles with fists against her mouth. William's upper lip was long and severe, as he tried not to give in.

"And me praying I wouldn't go dry," said Alick. "I think the beast would have eaten out of my hand, if it was not eating the hand first. Then out came the two little lassies like fairies, and at sight of them the great amadan fell over on its back and paddled its big feet in the air."

"And then what?" said William.

"Och, it jumped up and frisked around the children like a puppy, and never gave me a look. Man to man, William," he said, "it gives an excellent imitation of a dog."

"It *is* a dog, Papa!" Bell Ann squealed. "His name is Jacob!"

"But it would be good if he really was a dragon," said William. "That's the kind Mr. Shaw would have." He rolled over on the grass laughing as if he had been bottled up too long.

"One more thing," Alick said. "I gave Lily fifty cents for Harry's hat. She wrapped it in her handkerchief and put it in her pocket. A most courteous wee girl, if a trifle shy."

"I will pay you my third," said William between wheezes. "I make it sixteen and two-thirds cents, but I am not mean, Papa, I'll give you seventeen." He was off again.

"Lily's playhouse is beautiful," Bell Ann told Jennie. "It is a real little house, and she has a *whole* set of china dishes with flowers on them. She asked me to come and play, and I said I will, no matter what her papa says."

"What does her papa say?"

"He doesn't like Glenroys, but Lily says he doesn't like anybody, hardly. He is very cross with Harry now. Anyway, I *am* going. Some day," she added with a defiant thrust of her chin.

Fifty

B Y LATE TUESDAY afternoon the final copy of William's letter to Jerome lay on the kitchen table, well-sealed, and addressed only with the one name, Jerome; he could not bear to print *In care of Mr. Edward Fitzwater*. "I don't call it *care*, what *he* does!"

David would take it to Maddox in the morning, and Ronald Heriot would hand it to one of his captains who would be stopping at Charleston. Fitzwater lived in the city, and the captain was to find a way to put the letter in Jerome's hand; at least that was the promise to William. He had written about the ship his father was building, of school and what he liked and disliked about it, and his particular friends. He said that Harry Shaw didn't come to work any more because everyone hated him for what he did. He gave an earnestly detailed biography of every animal on the place.

"All my family sends you good wishes," he had written at the end. "I will write to you again. This is from your friend, Billy." Under that he printed his full name. "He always called me Billy," he explained to his parents.

The twins each added a few lines, more to please William than from any conviction that Jerome would actually receive the letter. The messenger would try to find him, no doubt of that, but if Fitzwater could win out on enemy territory, he would certainly be master on his own turf. But William was as satisfied as he could be. He still cried out in his sleep, "Run, Jerome!" Perhaps that would stop once his letter began its journey.

Jennie alone saw David come home near suppertime that Tuesday. The children were dispersed between barn and henyard, but she saw him from the pantry window, and was charmed by the mythic character of the scene: a man riding a white horse out of a dark wood. Usually he dismounted and unsaddled Blanchard by the drinking trough, but now he rode straight past the house toward the shore. She went to the door to watch; his action was so unusual that even the dogs were dumbstruck, gazing after him, then looking around at Jennie and tentatively wagging.

He met Alick and Thad Eubanks just beyond the old apple tree, and handed Alick a note. Alick read it and passed it over to Thad, and spoke to David with his hand on the horse's neck. She could read nothing at this distance on his upturned face, but no one was smiling. Thad was obviously reading the note twice, shaking his head as if in refusal to accept what his eyes saw. He pushed the note back at Alick, who read it again; then he turned and looked out at the river.

David came riding back without glancing toward the house, but she knew he had seen her. "My God, what has happened?" she exclaimed to the dogs, to prove that her throat hadn't been suddenly paralyzed. She walked to meet Alick, wanting to run. Thad touched his hat to her and went on; his face was hard. The muscles around Alick's mouth stood out pale and taut. He was rubbing his forehead hard as if in great pain from either inside or out.

"*Alick.*" It was all she could manage. Colin is dead, she thought. Or Lydia. Robin? Please, not Robin. Anna Kate, Hector—she ticked off the list. One of the children. Please not any of them. Then she heard herself saying, or rather croaking, "Is it *Stephen?*"

"How can I show this to them?" He put the note into her hand. David had written with a soft black drawing pencil on a leaf from a sketchbook.

"*Rights of Man*, just in, spoke *Lady Lydia* outside Boston harbor Monday morning. The man Jerome went overboard in heavy seas off Cape Ann Sunday morning. Took Fitzwater with him. They went down before a boat could be launched. Bodies not recovered."

"They must know," Alick was saying. "There is no sparing them this, but *Dia*—!"

"I saw *Rights of Man* sailing upriver this afternoon," Jennie said. "She passed *Lochinvar* and *Marmion* going out in company. It was a heroic sight, and to think she was carrying this news!"

"Jeannie, how will we tell them?" The tone was naked entreaty. "Tell *him?*" William had come out of the hen house with a basket of eggs and was crowing realistically at High Cockalorum.

His parents looked miserably at each other. But there was always a first thing to be done, if you could put your mind to it. Jennie groped and found it. "They should have their supper first," she said. It was what she always said. "We have put a good face on matters before; we can do it now."

"Jeannie, there is no way you can be optimistic about this," he said, "desperate or otherwise. How will you be able to swallow food?"

For a moment a salt and icy wave was flooding her eyes, her nostrils, her mouth, and she knew what Alick had experienced when he read not only of the deaths but the manner of them. Nausea raised its own waves. She took his hand for her good as well as his, and rubbed it hard between hers.

"There is always that most useful malady called Something-Going-About. We can be feeling the first queasiness, and they are always too involved with themselves to notice what we are doing."

She was right. No one seemed to notice that the adults, including David, lacked appetite for chicken fricassee.

William was the quietest, but it was the silence of satisfaction. He had accomplished his letter; it would be almost like talking with Jerome again, especially if Jerome answered it. He had written happily to a drowned man.

"When Septimus goes into politics," Carolus said, "maybe he will work for the vote for women. If they had it now, he would never have to make a speech. He could simply cavort around in his best suit, riding Bolivar, taking his hat off to every woman he met, and they would trample each other down to get to the ballot box."

"Listen to you!" Priscilla said. "Already so conceited, and so *young*! Raving on as if women needed men—or fifteen-year-old boys—to tell them how to *think*. Women would not declare war. I suppose that is stupid?"

"No," said Carolus, "and I don't mean *all* women. But most women. *Some* women," he hastily corrected himself. "Some men, too."

"He has to add that," said Sandy, "because he is afraid of what Pris will do to him when she catches him alone."

"What? What?" Bell Ann clamored. William giggled.

"Eye has not seen, and ear has not heard," Priscilla said sepulchrally, and then broke out with the laugh that always set everyone else off like a flaming stick thrown into shavings.

They couldn't keep the meal going forever, and there were lessons to do. The moment had come, and David saw it. He left his chair and went around to Bell Ann, touched her lightly on the top of her head. She twisted around to look up at him; their lines of communication were always clear. "Mama, Papa, may I be excused to take a walk with David?"

"Take your spencer, dear," Jennie said. For David she shaped the words *Bless you*, and received a moment's glance of commiseration. Bell Ann put on her knitted spencer and they went out with the dogs.

After all the laughing, the four older ones had suddenly gone as motionless and alert as foxes. In their growing up, each of them had been removed more than once from the scene by David when his or her presence was not desired. Now they wore identical *What have I done?* expressions.

"Nothing," she said aloud. "You are not guilty of anything that we know of." She tried to smile at that, but knew by their response that it was a failure.

Alick read the note to them. It was very short to carry such a message, and it was over in an instant. Pris's hand stopped halfway to tuck back a lock of hair, William was a boy of stone when Jennie touched him. Then Sandy snatched the note from the table and read it for himself. He crumpled it and threw it down, but Carolus reached for it and smoothed it out. Priscilla took it next, and laid it back beside her father's plate.

"Excuse me," she said almost inaudibly and went outdoors. Carolus followed her; Sandy made a kind of growl and left. William arose from his place, away from Jennie's touch, and said politely, "Excuse me, please."

"My little son, come to me," Alick said in the winning Gaelic, but it was no more to William than Jennie's arm had been. He walked to the front hall and went up the stairs.

Alick folded his arms on the table and slumped over them. "Whatever they need of us, we have failed them."

"What else could we do but tell them the truth? They made him their business, so there is no escape." Jennie took Sandy's place next to him and stroked the back of his neck.

"But I wish they need not be learning such brutal lessons so young, and yet too old to be rocked to sleep with promises that tomorrow will be better. William—" He could not speak for a moment. "To see him ravaged like that, it is tearing at my heart like an eagle with a rabbit."

"Hold me," she said. They leaned together into an embrace without words that lasted until Garnet came in the open door and wound round and round their legs.

"Come out of here," Alick said. "I've had enough of this room." They

went outdoors, the cat with them. The light powdered with gold everything left open to it, beyond and between the pure dark cobalt shadows.
Gulls coursed slowly, and high, seeming to vanish into the zenith as into
an azure mist and then reappearing as a flash of translucent wings. For a
few minutes it was so silent it was as if Jennie had lost her hearing. She
was actually relieved when the cat cried and reached up on her as far as
forepaws could go. Jennie picked her up, and the cat fitted her head
under her chin and delicately sniffed at the hollow of her throat.

Alick touched her cheek and then the cat's head with his forefinger.

"It would be too simple to cry," she said, "and make it just another of
those sentimental crises of family life. Besides, this is just too awful for
tears, not only what we suffer for the children, but all the circumstances
and the pictures that won't let you go. . . . Oh, we will weather this.
Think what we have weathered already."

"Now we will be weathering the death of their innocence," Alick
said. "If only William had not disobeyed and taken the dory out by
himself. But I have not the cruelty to tell him that he began it."

"Look and listen," she said. "Not a one of them is within sight or
sound. But we know where William is, and we can go to him, at least."

"The silence is eerie," he said. "It is as if they have all been blown
away from us to Kilmeny's Land. At this instant I am not even sure we
will find William upstairs."

" 'A land of love and a land of light,' " she said. "That is what we have
tried to create for us all here. Unfortunately the rain does fall, and the
wind often blows, and sin has been, and still is, around us. But the love
and the light—Alick, *mo chridh*, I think we do tolerably well at that."

He took her free hand and kissed it. "You are the one," he said. "You
gave it to me. They are not fairy children, they are ours, and they are not
to go to bed each keeping grief a secret. After Bell Ann is tucked away,
we are going to talk about Jerome."

"If they will do it."

"Why should they not? They are half-Gael after all, and I have not
seen any of them at a loss for words before, have you?"

"No," she admitted.

There was a sound behind them of bare feet in the summer kitchen,
and William came out. He kept his face averted and muttered something
about going to the Necessary. Alick stopped him with a hand on his
shoulder. "You are not to go anywhere else but there," he said to the
defenseless young face, "and then come back here at once."

"Yes, Papa," William mumbled. When Alick lifted his hand, he was gone like an arrow from a bow. Jennie put Garnet down and went in for the bell. "It is not exactly the harp of the sky," she said.

"We should have named the dory Kilmeny," he said. "Not just the cove."

"It's not too late to christen her."

"Och, she's been called 'the dory' all her life, she wouldn't know how to be answering to a proper name." He gave her a shadow of a smile as she began to ring the bell.

They straggled in from different directions. There were no obvious signs of tears except with William, but their faces were defensively locked and shuttered against intrusion; paradoxically it made them look younger than they were. Do they expect us to tell them to brace up and get on with living, Jennie wondered, when they are still staggering under the weight of all that happened because two innocent souls came face to face in a pine tree?

"After Bell Ann is in bed," Alick told them, "we are having a meeting about Jerome. You will have from now until then to think about what you will say, but your mother and I will expect something from each of you." He nodded at Priscilla. "You didn't know him, and neither did we, but we will say something."

"I will think about it now." She went to her room, and the boys went to theirs.

"I think Jerome's mind was made up when he boarded the ship," Jennie said. "I remember his face. I thought he was saying goodbye to freedom, but now I know it was something else."

"It is a pity," Alick said, "that Fitzwater cannot be remembering through Eternity the black hands that killed him."

They sat around the table in the light of the afterglow, which gave the scene the mellowed varnish of a painting: *The Glenroy Family*, by Reynolds or Raeburn or Copley. Bell Ann was missing, but the obligatory dogs were there. David was the watcher in the shadows, about whom imaginative viewers would wonder.

William sat out of reach of either parent, huddled and aloof. He would not speak first, and Jennie was afraid he would not speak at all; he had become untouchable in all ways.

"Alasdair, then." Alick sounded unshaken by William's refusal.

Sandy began gruffly, self-conscious at first. "Mr. Lockhart made me memorize bits of Shakespeare, and the one I keep thinking of, because it best fits Jerome, is 'His life was gentle, and the elements/ So mixed in him that Nature might stand up/ And say to all the world, this was a man!' " He waited; no one so much as moved a foot. "Jerome was a man," he went on, "and he was a proud man. He'd die rather than be dragged back, but he took the oppressor with him. He had the courage to go over the side, knowing he was going to drown too. I hope I can be as brave."

His voice had not cracked once.

"Carolus?" Alick said.

"I don't know if I can do as well as Sandy," he said. "But I am glad he took Fitzwater with him, and I hope old Fitz had time to know what was happening. Our lives will be different because we knew Jerome. The first plant I name will be for him, and that way his name will live forever, even if people don't know what they are saying. Thank you," he added with a very young uncertainty.

"You both spoke well," Alick said. "Priscilla?"

"I saw him just once, the last day," Pris said, quietly. "But I saw that he loved my brothers and they loved him, so he must have been worth it. I know he made you three into a band of brothers, and I didn't think that could ever happen. He made me proud of you, too. I wish he hadn't died. I wish we could have saved him—I'll always wish that." The dulling light was momentarily trapped and glistening in her eyes, then was gone as she looked down at her folded hands.

Jennie was next, not knowing what she would say, absurdly at a loss under the combined gaze of her children and husband. She took a long breath. "Someone called Death 'the last best friend.' Perhaps that was so for Jerome. But in the time that he was here, he found many friends, and you three boys and the Keelers must have been the best, before the last one." She wanted to stop there, but they seemed to be waiting. "I am supposed to be talking about Jerome, not you, but you are inseparable from him in my mind. I am in his debt for what he brought out in you, and taught your father and me about our children."

This time she knew it was enough.

"Parents are never wishing to see the children grow up," Alick said. "But there is nothing we can do, any more than I could stop a tree from growing without hewing it down. But now in a very short time you have taken a great leap forward, and it was nothing to do with your mother and me. Carolus says our lives will be different; he is right. Jerome showed you the face of slavery, and now it is no longer something other people, *grown* people, talk and write about. You cannot shut your eyes and ears and say it is not your concern. He has left you that legacy. You may not be wanting the burden of it, but its time will come, and Jerome will aye be in your minds and hearts."

A chair creaked, Bounce scratched.

"Now, William," Alick said very softly. "You began it. That is why we are sitting here like that. So you must be speaking now."

"I *am* going to speak," William answered with brave composure. "Jerome was my friend. He always called me li'l Billy, and he showed me how to do chip carving. He kept his promises. He told the truth. He said to me in the wagon, 'Don't you fret and worry, li'l Billy, I won't be beaten no more.' And he won't be." He folded his hands on the edge of the table, and became as he was before.

Jennie put her palms over her eyes and blinked rapidly in the dark. Pris was blowing her nose, the twins squirmed around in their seats, loud with their feet and clearing their throats. Alick was as motionless as the unhearing David. Gradually the atmosphere changed, it was as if the boys had come to a resting place at the peak of a heart-breaking climb, and were relieved, if not overjoyed, to have the journey behind them. Someone stifled a yawn, but no one seemed either able or willing to move.

William's letter to Jerome still leaned against the pitcher of fresh flowers in the middle of the table. Just as Jennie wished she had spirited it away, William's hand flashed out and took it, and he stood up.

"I'm going to send this," he said in a bright clear voice. He ran out, with Bounce dancing around him. The twins rose as one and followed, Darroch lumbered to his feet. Priscilla ran back in and took the flowers from the vase, and followed the twins. This time David went out with her. Alick and Jennie were left alone in a house echoing as if it had just been emptied by a supernatural cataclysm, and like survivors they reached for each other.

"Can't I go?" Bell Ann asked from the winter kitchen doorway. "I have my shoes on, and my wrapper."

"You should have been asleep an hour ago," Jennie said automatically.

"Well, I wasn't." She was not pert about it. "I have been sitting on the camp bed with Garnet."

"Pris," Alick called from the door. "Tell William to wait, we will all be there."

Bell Ann ran forward and took her parent's hands.

The tide was low in the cove. The dory lay on the shining wet flats that reflected the sky like water. William and the terrier had run through the shipyard out onto the long dock, and the twins had caught up with him. Pris and David were almost there. Darroch, hearing the others coming, waited courteously for Jennie and Alick. They walked beneath the loom of the new ship, Mr. Lincoln's figurehead gazed sleeplessly through the twilight.

The ship was impressive in her huge solitude; by day she was a helpless giant swarmed over by Lilliputians.

"What does a ship on the stocks think, when she is alone?" Pris had asked when she was ten.

"She dreams of being free," a small Sandy had answered.

The outgoing currents ran swiftly by the end of the wharf; little white crests came hurrying and rippling and splashing about the spilings. William stood at the edge, looking back past the others for his father and mother. The letter showed in his hand, held against his chest.

Priscilla distributed flowers among all the rest. Bell Ann did not object to the dripping stems, but asked mildly, "What are these for?"

"You'll see," said Pris. They clustered at the end of the wharf; William tossed the letter and it scaled like a large white leaf down into the moving water. Pris threw her flowers after it, and the others threw theirs; Alick secured Bell Ann by a handful of wrapper and nightgown, so she would not throw herself overboard in her fervor.

The letter was borne swiftly away among its escort of flowers; they watched it until the last little glimmer was sailing past the Whaleback, and then William turned and walked up the wharf alone. The twins tramped after him, heads down as if into a gale. Pris put her arm through David's, and they strolled behind the boys. With Bell Ann between them, Jennie could not reach for Alick's hand, but she thought with yearning of their bed and an end to this day.

William had stopped under the bowsprit and Mr. Lincoln's other-worldly gaze. He was a very small figure in contrast with the construction towering above him, and when Bell Ann pulled free of her parents and ran to him, she became a tiny thing in her fluttering wrapper, like a white moth. "William, I have something to tell you, and you better listen," she said. Her voice rose imperiously above the noisy pantings and snufflings as the dogs explored territory they did not often visit. Alick and Jennie stopped where they were, half-hidden.

"The Great Horse came straight down and took Jerome to heaven," Bell Ann said. "The men on the ship didn't see that happen, because the Great Horse is indibisible, unless he is coming to get *you*. *Then* you see him. Jerome is up in heaven *right now*." She pointed skyward past Mr. Lincoln and the bowsprit. "But Mr. Fitzwater is *not*. That is a true fact."

Would William now thrust her away as an infant speaking infantile nonsense? The watchers waited in suspense to see if he had grown too wise and too old in the last week; they prepared to receive a wounded Bell Ann.

"I hope the sea serpent *ate* him," William said. "There's one around Cape Ann, you know. They used to see him all the time there, or maybe it is a *her*. It was even in the papers. But now people are afraid someone will laugh at them if they say they saw it. *I* know it's still there, or its children, and I am *not the only one*," he said significantly. "And I hope it ate that man alive."

"He prob'ly did. I am as sure of that as I am of the Great Horse." She sounded serenely ageless. "William, can I take your hand?"

"I reckon so," said William.

Fifty-One

B Y THE TIME Priscilla had taken herself to bed, drooping and yawning, the others had long since fallen asleep like so many rocks dropping off a cliff. Jennie was now roused enough to set bread to rise for morning. No matter what her personal climate happened to be, a woman could make bread even if she could not order her universe. Alick took a turn with the kneading, and David made a pot of tea. When the big earthenware bowls were covered and set aside, and the room was full of provocative yeasty promise, they sat at the table and drank their tea in a customary silent communion. The three needed no pretense of conversation after all these years.

When Jennie and Alick went finally to their bed, she rolled into his arms, murmuring, "I'm so glad the Great Horse is indibisible. It's almost as useful as being invisible."

"And don't be slighting the Sea Serpent," Alick said. "A lovely pair they make. I would be praising them forever."

He roused everyone to eat an early breakfast by lamplight; reveille was sweetened by a meal of fried dough with syrup and bacon, instead of come-day go-day porridge. They did their chores afterward, and then had a good hour for the neglected school work. Alick heard William's spelling on the front stairs, Jennie drilled Bell Ann on number-facts in the parlor, and the twins did mathematics in the winter kitchen. Upstairs Pris memorized Greek nouns.

The change among the children was neither audible nor visible, but as subtly authentic as the first promise of still-distant rain after a long dry spell, or the exact moment when the tide turned. It was the anticipation of fresh life to be lived, beginning now, without forgetting what had led them up to the Now.

When they had left for school in a perfect September morning, and Alick had gone to work, Jennie baked bread, put together a vegetable soup to simmer all morning, and worked in the garden. When Alick came home at noon, he too was serenely preoccupied, which was usual for him when a ship was so close to launching. They didn't talk about what had happened, but about what they would be doing. The day had become hot, in September fashion, and after Jennie tidied the pantry she bathed and changed into a cool yellow Swiss muslin, and went out. Now there was no doubt that she was exquisitely alone except for the dogs, who were sleeping at the back of the house against the cool granite foundation, and Garnet was somewhere on her own. A long shrill squirrel-buzz of indignation suggested the woods behind the wash house.

She picked up a basket of bruised windfalls to take out to the pasture gate. After handing out apples, scratching foreheads, dodging the cows' enormous wet kisses, and ignoring Brisky's attempts to convince her he should be allowed out, she went to the shore. There was no breeze, and she walked under a blue and white ceiling gracefully patterned with delicate plumes and lacy tatters of cloud, which diffused the sun's fire to a white and shadowless light.

The tappings, climbings, poundings, and rhythmic thuds from the Yard, the ringing of hammers on iron, the echoing crash of dropped planks, scraps of voices and whistling, underlined the quiet. Gulls flew in and out of the gauzy clouds, and the osprey family exchanged signals as they surveyed the river and two brown-sailed fishing boats becalmed on ice-blue water.

Downstream a breeze was born, and strengthened as it traveled, and took on a cool edge, blowing a chill through Jennie's thin dress. The sky's filmy lace and plumes began to disintegrate. The water darkened from ice-blue to bluebird. Jennie sat on the log in the wild mint and watched the river come alive under a sea breeze. Any vessels that had been waiting outside could now sail upriver with the tide and the wind. Already a bowsprit was just appearing past Misery Wall, and then a flying jib, and the ship sailed entirely into view, like a tall white cumulus cloud in her new canvas. She was Stephen's vessel, *Bel Fiore*, dressed for a happy homecoming.

If the children had been there, they would have been running back and forth, shouting and waving. Jennie didn't move from her log. She sat there with her arms folded tightly across her chest. Her eyes kept misting. She had not been afraid when she and Alick crossed the ocean, but ever since their lives had become irretrievably involved with ships, she saw it as a miracle that such fragile beauty could ever survive and return home.

She waited on the log until a man in the crosstrees of the *Lincoln*'s mainmast let out an unearthly whoop. Satisfied that Alick knew Stephen was back, Jennie arose and went to the house.

Supper that night was the happiest meal they'd had for some time. "I don't know how the dear man was managing it," said Alick to Jennie under the exuberant din, "to have come home today, but there was a time when I'd have said the fairies had a hand in it."

"Heavens, I hope *not*," said Jennie. "Stephen would be having to pay for it sooner or later; you know how they are."

Though he was always Captain Stephen to the children, as a compromise between familiarity and formality, Stephen received the affection due the Favorite Uncle. Three genuine uncles in England and Switzerland were three birds in the bush; Captain Stephen was the one at hand. He had a batch of Wells nephews and nieces whom the Glenroys did not resent; they had their own unique relationship because Stephen had been their parents' dear friend before any of those nieces and nephews were born. Only Priscilla sensed the mystery of the past that bound them, the younger ones were satisfied that the bond existed.

Whenever he came home, they never expected to see him until he had been back for several days. When, the next afternoon, the dogs left Jennie in the orchard to run toward the house, she knew from their voices that it was no stranger, and she laid aside her book and stood up, half-curious, half-reluctant to lose sparse reading time. A black horse was tied under the rowan trees, and a tall man in blue was crossing the lawn, talking to his hospitable escort. It was Stephen, looking very fit, brown, and young, even with the new slight gray around his temples. When he saw Jennie, his smile broadened, and he held out both hands to take hers.

"If I had my druthers," she told him, "I'd be like Bell Ann and half-hug you to death. I am so *happy* to see you and not your fetch." She reached up and kissed his cheek. "Consider that a sisterly salute."

"A brotherly reply, then." He kissed her.

"You have an air of extraordinary success," Jennie said. "As if nothing went wrong anywhere at any time, the Fates have singularly blessed you, and you have come home a rich man."

He laughed. "I don't know how rich, but a happy man." He tightened his hold on her hands. *"Jennie,"* he said.

"Yes?"

He didn't answer, and she sensed that he was trying to choose and arrange his words before he spoke again.

"I am waiting, Stephen," she said with gentle amusement.

"Later," he said. "If I have an aura of health and wealth, yours is of eternal youth. You look younger than you did when I went away."

"La, sir, where did you learn such pretty ways? You have not been merely sailing and trading, you have been frequenting drawing rooms."

"I might surprise you. —Now I am going to the Yard, and if I can pry the Old Man loose, we will both be back." He cut off through the orchard to the road, the dogs going happily along.

She went up to the house. The black horse, Pedro, grazed under the rowans, while a pair of foolhardy pullets wandered around his feet. Stephen's hat was on the bench, and Garnet was examining it from crown to brim.

Jennie brought out a bottle of French claret and gave three wine glasses a final polish. She set them on the tray with the wine, then she went into the bedroom and looked at herself in the oval glass.

"Vanity, vanity. All is vanity, Eugenia," she said. "But when a woman is about to be forty she has a right to a few harmless frailties." She turned her head from side to side, satisfied that her chin and jaw and long throat appeared almost as young as Priscilla's. "You preen like Priscilla too, you besom," she said. "It's luck she's never caught you at it." She winked at herself, and did the polka with an invisible partner out to the kitchen.

The men came in about a half hour. Alick opened the wine and they drank a toast to Stephen's return. "Man, it's grand having you back," Alick said. "And none too soon, with the plans for you to approve, and to be going into the woods before winter."

Stephen laughed and shook his head. "But not the ship today, Alick. Today is singular for another reason. I have gifts for you all, but I have not unpacked them. I could not wait to show you this. And if you think I am blushing—," he was, incredibly, "I have a mighty powerful reason."

He took a flat velvet case from an inside pocket, slipped out a gold-framed miniature, and gave it to Jennie with a diffidence she had never seen in him before. A woman gazed up at her, neither beautiful or plain; a face with strong features, yet a feminine face, soberly meeting the eyes of strangers with a poise that verged on—no, not arrogance, that was a hateful word. *Hauteur?* That was worse.

"I wish I could have brought the original," Stephen said. She handed the miniature to Alick, exclaiming, "Oh, Alick, look at *this!*" Her gaiety sounded artificial in her own ears. She was upset about that, afraid the men had caught it, and angry with herself for her cold and shaky hands. What is *at* me? she thought in exasperation.

But Alick, studying the miniature, was maddeningly oblivious. "When will you be marrying her, or have you done so already?"

"It will be in the late spring," Stephen said. "In Maine. She wants apple blossoms and lilacs."

"Alick, how did you *guess?*" Again her voice clanged discordantly to her, but not to them.

"Och, the answer is not far to seek, when a bachelor is handing you the likeness of a striking woman and wishing he could have brought the original. *Beannachd leat, mo coraid!*" The men shook hands. "If you are finding half what Jennie and I have, you will be a fortunate man."

"Thank you, Alick," Stephen said. "Jennie?"

"Congratulations, Stephen." She put her hands on his shoulders and kissed his cheek. She was coldly unsurprised at the great difference between this and the kiss of welcome in the orchard; it was as if he had become another man. "Now tell us everything!" she commanded, and this time she could look into his face as the woman had looked into hers, keeping her secrets.

"Her name is Christina Cameron Maclean," he said. "I am trying to sound nonchalant about this, but I don't think I am succeeding." He couldn't stop smiling. "She is mistress of a large sugar plantation in Barbados."

"And will you live there?" She took the miniature from Alick and pretended to be eagerly examining it.

"Good Lord, no! I could never stomach it there for long. I am a State-of-Mainer, and Christina wants to live where there are four seasons. It is the call of her ancestral blood." He walked back and forth in the kitchen as if a lover's energy would not let him rest. "We will build in Maddox."

"And what about the great plantation, man?" Alick asked.

"She is turning Achnacarry over to her younger brother. He has been her superintendent for some time and he can hardly wait for her to go; he makes no bones about it." Primed by Alick's questions, he went on talking about the business, and Jennie was alone with Christina Cameron Maclean, who had dark chestnut ringlets clustered over her ears. Her splendid shoulders rose from a bodice of corded sea-green silk, and a green stone on a gold chain lay in the hollow of her strong throat. Her eyes were as uncompromisingly green as the stone and the silk. Greener than Lucy Clements' eyes, unless the artist had exaggerated. Neither staring nor about to smile, they regarded the viewer with the perfect, reposeful equanimity of a woman who knew her own worth. Jennie wondered if the miniature had been painted before or after Stephen had declared himself.

"*Jennie?*" he said. She looked up brightly at him. Alick was pouring some more wine. "Come, let us drink a toast to the bride," he said.

"To Christina," Stephen corrected him. "She wishes to be Christina to you both from the start."

"Christina is a good Highland name," Alick said. "So are Cameron and Maclean."

"She is both Highland and Lowland. The Elliots went out from the Borders in the 1600s and began one of the first sugar plantations there. Through marriage into another Border family, they became owners of one of the largest plantations on the island."

He sounded like his usual amiable and moderate self now, but for Jennie the change was indelible. She had often seen him with young women—he was never a hermit when he was ashore—but this was different. He was about to marry, and the Stephen she had known for nearly half her life would disappear except from memory.

"Her Lowland ancestors came as free men, gambling that they would survive the tropics and make fortunes," he said. "Some did not, but the Elliots succeeded. Christina's great-grandfather Cameron was the Highlander. *He* had no choice; he came to Barbados in chains, sold as a slave by the Crown." His voice was dry, which made the words burn all the more.

"After Culloden," Alick said. "Massacred on the field, or hanged, or sold into slavery."

"Yes. He was lucky to have survived to be sold. As happened in a great many of those cases, he was bought by another Scot who immediately struck off his chains and hired him as a free man. Young Cameron became indispensable, married one of the daughters, and to make a long story short, one day it all became Achnacarry, the Cameron holdings. The granddaughter, Christina, married the descendant of another Stuart supporter, but he died of yellow fever when he was still a young man. They had two daughters."

"I am sorry for that," Alick said. "Sorry for them both, for her to lose him, and for him to lose it all. But she survived for you, and I have great joy for you."

Stephen turned expectantly toward Jennie, who said, "Tell me about the girls. Will they be coming with you?"

"They are at school in Scotland. They will come in time, as soon as we are settled. They are about the ages of the twins and William."

"What will she do in the long months you are at sea?" she asked. "After her busy life in Barbados?"

"She swears that she will be with me, part of the time, at least."

"As if she is not already brave enough," Alick said. "Marrying a Yankee sea captain in the first place."

"A sugar plantation in Barbados," Jennie said, "sounds as exotic as the court of the Russian Czar."

"You will be having awkward questions from the children," Alick said. "Slavery is a raw wound with us at the minute."

"I heard about it at dinner at home last night," said Stephen. "But I can meet your children with a clear conscience. Our family has always done business with Achnacarry because the workers are free men, adequately housed and paid, and a man may rise on merit. There is also a school on the plantation. The Camerons and the Macleans have been abolitionists for generations. Neil Cameron and Duart Maclean never forgot that they came to Barbados in chains."

Alick said softly, *"Glé mhath, glé mhath!"*

"The children will likely exile their father and me if you aren't here for supper tonight," Jennie said. "And I'd like David to see the miniature."

"My dear Jennie, I cannot stay tonight. I came only to bring you my news, but if you ask me for tomorrow night, I will be here."

"Done. Do you still have a taste for mussels?" This was becoming easier, but she knew she was going to be very tired when it was over; she could hardly wait for Stephen to leave, and that made a catch in her throat.

"I will be getting back to the Yard," Alick said. They walked out to the rowans, where Pedro affectionately nosed Stephen as if to make sure of him after such a long separation.

"We will give Christina a Highland welcome," Alick said. "Rory will be composing a pipe tune just for her." He clasped Stephen by the arms. "*Dia*, Stephen, it is *grand* to have sight and sound of you! Be ready to make a long evening of it, we have a ship to build!"

Stephen watched him walk toward the Yard. "And there goes a good man." Without looking away from Alick he said, "Well, Jennie?"

"Well, Stephen?" The unsaid and unknown hovered between them like a feather held aloft on their breath.

"I think this conversation began some time ago, in the orchard," she said, trying to make light of it.

"But it is different now," he said seriously. "That was when I wanted to tell you about Christina. Now I want to ask you about her."

She felt a sort of fluttering, as if the unsaid and unknown had somehow gotten into her chest and had wings. "What in particular do you want to ask?" She sounded reasonable.

"You will be Christina's friend, will you not?"

"Was there any doubt of it?"

"Yes." It was a word of quiet regret, as if he were sad to be saying it, and to her of all people. "Jennie, my own people don't know about this. They know *of* her, of course, but not about her and *me*. I came here as soon as I could, to my dearest friends, as sure of them as I am of myself. I wanted them to rejoice with me because I am not going to be alone any more."

There was no taint of accusation or self-pity, but she was debasingly ashamed of herself.

"Oh, *Stephen*. How could you even have doubted me? *No*." She put her hands over her ears. "I don't want to hear that! It's not that I don't want to be Christina's friend. It's—" She wanted passionately to be honest. Another woman would have understood without the explanation, even if she could tumble out anything half sensible. But how far could she go, even with the best of men? Excluding Alick, of course. Alick understood without reservations, but they had been intimate friends before they became lovers, and they had been two halves of a whole since then.

"Try me, Jennie," Stephen said. "You were never good at dissembling."

"I was afraid I had lost my first American," she said. "I was thinking that after I have known you for eighteen years as one person, now I am going to know you as someone else. Spoken aloud, it sounds very foolish and selfish, and I could think of quite a few other shameful words if I put my mind to it."

"You believe that I cannot be both your friend and Christina's husband? Jennie, I am not a friend like that!"

"I know what you are, Stephen," she said penitently. "I don't know why there was even a second of doubt. You never doubted Alick and me. But Alick was perfect in his response, and I have been a disgrace. I'm burning alive with shame. Stephen, I am so happy for you, and if you love Christina we will love her too."

Stephen's reaction was so instant and complete that at once she felt that she was telling the truth; she would do anything for him.

Stephen was a forty-two year old romantic who wanted the whole world to be in love because he was. She had hurt him, and made the hurt well again; and if she couldn't love or even *like* the painted image when it became flesh-and-blood woman, she was honor-bound to keep an open mind and heart. At least she would have something in common with Christina, who might be at this very moment depressed by Stephen's euphoric expectations that she would adore his family and friends, when all *she* wanted to adore in this world was Stephen. Jennie felt a strong twinge of sympathy.

"We are going to ask the General to give her away," Stephen was saying. "She says she will be honored."

Fifty-Two

THE SHIP WAS to be called *Dolphin*, which meant no choice between wives or assorted daughters. Dolphins had been blithe companions and sometimes guides to ships at sea since the first deep-water vessels set out; for Stephen they were always a delight, always beautiful.

The plan was to sail up Penobscot Bay to Belfast the day after Election Day. Stephen had hired a broad-beamed schooner built in her owner's dooryard for the express purpose of carrying lumber, and she was called the *Wooden World*. At anchor she looked as ungainly among the swifter craft as a loon on land, but when the wind filled her big mainsail she was a different creature. She was not fast, but she was steady, and when she was so heavily loaded that the seas could wash over her decks, she still went through them with the smooth equanimity of a whale. The owner and his son were captain and crew.

The oak for *Dolphin*'s keel would come from a family woodlot in Maddox, where Stephen had already chosen the tree. The tough locust wood for the trunnels was also there. But the hardwood for the ship's timbers, the white pine for her masts and spars, and the well-nigh indestructible hackmatack to hold the skeleton together, would all come home by water.

While Stephen was collecting supplies to keep the woods camp going (hiring his own ship's cook to guarantee good feeding), Alick organized the woods crew. Once on the site, he and the master of the woods crew would select and mark what they wanted, according to the plans, and the crew would commence felling the trees; Alick would come home overland on the Belfast–Portland stage, which had a halt at the St. David Inn in Maddox.

Stephen intended to stay in the woods until the last load went out by hired ox team, and he would come home with the *Wooden World*. His position as a ship's captain meant nothing here, but he could man one end of a crosscut saw as well as anyone, even if he was not an artist with an axe, and he could shoot and fish for the pot. It was not in him to wait at home to see the makings of *Dolphin* unloaded on the Yard dock.

The Wells boys had spent some of their happiest hours in the woods above Belfast; their grandfather had acquired the acreage after the War for Independence, and many a Wells ship had once been part of it. Each boy had sworn that whenever he built his own ship most of her must come from this wilderness.

"Stephen is like a lad going on holiday," Alick told Jennie in bed. "He will be living his boyhood again, but this time the ship will be his own. And then there is the lady." He laughed. "*Dia*, the man is three ways in love at once. It would be consuming a lesser man entirely to have it all burst upon him at his age like the dawn of Creation."

The dispassionate, imperious face in the miniature floated in the dark behind Jennie's eyelids. "Wait until he encounters the hard fact of two captains in one household," she said. "I hope for his sake that she is so tired of managing the sugar plantation she will never look back with regret."

"In the midst of a Maine winter," Alick said.

"They will likely be sailing on blue tropical seas then. What would a captain's lady do to keep busy at home when she has been a woman of business? Never mind. Let us talk about *us*." She moved closer. "We have never been separated for a night, and I have been trying not to think of it, but there it is. It is going to seem forever. . . . And I know how you feel about being on the water."

"Och, she is like a duck, they tell me, and we will be sailing so close to land we can always be putting a foot out to stop her. I wish you could be going."

"So do I," she said wistfully, "it will be like sailing a foreign coast but knowing it is a part of home."

On Election Day the weather was mild, with no warning patches of mackerel sky, no menacing sundogs, no loom of the land in that certain light which meant an easterly. The twins arose with cogent reasons for going with their father, even missing Muster Day. Sandy would be able to practice with his sextant and compass aboard a seagoing vessel;

Carolus could add to his botanical knowledge in the woods. Captain Blackburn and Mr. Lockhart would agree they should not miss such an educational experience.

"You have been talking about Muster Day since the last one. Enjoy it." Alick said.

This ended the discussion, and William was seen by his mother to smile at his porridge.

Alick and David rode out early to vote. The Town House was on Parson's Cove; the land for the building and the Pound behind it had been given by the Whittier family when the community ceased to be South Maddox and became incorporated as the town of Whittier.

Any of Alick's men who were eligible to vote would do so before coming to work, but the Yard's operation was in full swing when Alick came home. He gave Jennie a bear hug the way the twins liked to do.

"All the while I am gone," he said, "I will be thinking about coming back to you."

"*Dolphin* is the lady to occupy your heart and soul for the next week, and I do not resent her. But once you board the stage in Belfast—"

"*Dia*, the horses will not travel fast enough for me."

"I beg your pardon," Priscilla said behind them, short of breath.

"Pris!" Jennie swung around in alarm. "Why aren't you in school? Are you feeling ill?" The girl looked pale.

"Ah!" said Alick pleasantly. "Here is the young woman who has gone into business for herself."

She looked from him to her mother and lifted her chin. Her voice trembled slightly. "I came home to talk to you both before Papa went down east. I didn't expect you to see it before I told you about it, Papa."

He was unsmiling now. "There it was, tucked in snugly between a notice of firewood to sell and an appeal for someone to clean privies. I had time to be reading the whole board because a clutch of voters had come from the Town House to discuss the ballot and try to remember what their wives had asked them to fetch home."

"I suppose I should have told you before today," Priscilla said, neither humble nor insolent. "But I was afraid to."

"Afraid of *what*?" Jennie asked. "What in the world is between you two?"

Alick gave Pris a little bow. "Explain to your mother, *mo graidh*." She reddened, and was annoyed by it.

"I gave Thankful a card to put up in the store for me." she said, so rapidly Jennie almost didn't understand. "I didn't realize it would be there so soon. It says I will do sewing to order. I realize I should have told you. *Asked* you." The words shot out in angry little bursts. "I shouldn't have done it at *all!*"

"Why on earth shouldn't you?" Jennie asked. "We'd like to have been consulted, but that does not mean we would have forbidden it."

"Most parents would." She was armored in pride like a porcupine in his quills.

"We are not most parents," Jennie said. "You do us an injustice if you can think that, after nearly eighteen years with us."

"I know that, Mama, but even *you* might jib at my putting my name up in public like that, and mentioning breeches, even if I did say they would be for little boys." She was impelled by their silence to go charging on. "I realize I have no rights until I come of age!"

"That is not true, *mo nighean*," Alick said.

"Legal rights, I mean." Her voice was thickening toward tears, and Jennie hated that.

"You cannot marry. You cannot be meeting young men without our permission," Alick said evenly. "You cannot leave home. But this—this we could have been discussing."

"I can tell you're displeased with me, Papa," she said stubbornly. "You think I have shamed you."

"Priscilla, why are you determined to make a battle out of this?" Jennie asked. "We are surprised, that is all." Surprised, and secretly overjoyed by this child of hers, though she maintained a judicious pose.

"I apologize for not telling you, I mean *asking* you first." The armor was down by now, the red rapidly fading toward mere pink. "But I was feeling desperate. Like a wild bird kept in a little cage and trying to beat its way through the wires. Well, not as terrible as that, but there is this longing to do *something*. I must take a step for myself, and I cannot endure to wait. Besides, I *hate* Greek grammar!"

"My darling, how could we have known that?" Jennie asked.

"With all the anxiety and distress about Jerome, I could hide behind it. So I did. But now with Papa going away, I thought about it all the way to school, and I wanted to tell you both *now*. So I came back. I just wish Papa hadn't seen my notice first."

"Well, Pris," Jennie said, "I would like to have heard about it from you first, but I can understand your reasons. Speaking for myself, I am proud of you. Of course, your father makes up his own mind." They both looked hopefully at a stoic Alick.

"I was not tearing the card off the board with a torrential spate of Gaelic imprecations," said Alick. "I may have created a small sensation by reading it so carefully and then walking away without turning white to the lips. Mr. John Wesley Whittier offered his congratulations on a spirited daughter with a good head on her shoulders. He sees great things for you, and I agreed."

"Oh, *Papa!*" She looked the way she did when she received her pony, "I shall insist on paying my board, and—"

"Not as long as you still do your share of the chores," Jennie said, "but if you are madly successful and have no time for milking, I will reconsider your offer. I suppose we can turn the little bedroom into a sewing room for you."

"I am going to work," Alick said. "You and your mother should sit down with a fresh pot of tea and discuss. Is that not what ladies do?"

Pris, looking after him, said, "I *adore* him. I hope there is another one like him for me, but how could there be? —I intend to keep my business after I am married, and Mama, I hope I can be like you with my children. You are always fair even when you must feel like shaking us."

"Tell me, Pris, what made you advertise breeches? You've never done them."

"Oh yes, I have. For Bear, many a wee pair." They both laughed. "Mama, anyone who can make a nice dress or a man's shirt can surely sew breeches for a little boy. They have to be stoutly stitched, that is all, and not look like the ones Mrs. Kilburn puts on her boys, as if she basted them together from old blankets."

Over the tea she said suddenly, "Of course, I may not acquire any customers. I have had to face that. But I would not know if I had not tried, would I? Thankful said quite a few women read it and no one clucked or pulled a face. Rates are favorable, it says, so that should help."

Jennie agreed, but they decided that it would be tempting Providence to rearrange the small bedroom before Pris received her first order. She would also have to explain to the Lockharts why she was leaving the classes; her parents would talk with them later.

Tuesday morning the *Wooden World* came slowly down the river under her great brown mainsail with the traditional hatful of wind, and tied up at the Yard wharf. It was early enough so the family could see Alick off before the children went to school; the dogs were shut up in the house. The twins had put aside their disappointment, with Muster Day only two days from now. They leaped back and forth between the wharf and the broad deck, anxious to help load, but no man allowed anyone else to handle his axes. *Bel Fiore*'s cook, a large rosy man who was a good advertisement for his talent, showed that he was no pampered genius; he alone carried the grindstone aboard.

William had charge of wheeling down the jugs of spring water, and Bell Ann sat on Alick's tarpaulin-wrapped bedroll so no twin could snatch it. Priscilla and Jennie had spent a very hot Monday afternoon roasting three chickens and baking a large molasses cake for the men to eat on the way.

There was a holiday atmosphere among the woods crew, except for two who morosely anticipated either being seasick in rough seas or becalmed on a glassy one on a day of hot sun. The skipper's son was helping to swing gear aboard as if it were sacks of feathers. Pris was watching, which may have helped; he was exhilarated enough to make Vincent Taggart even more foreboding than usual.

The skipper said they'd have a fair wind driving the old girl along once they were outside the river and heading to the east'ard. Vincent shook his head sorrowfully about that; Jennie wanted to ask him if he foresaw serpents or an undersea earthquake. Alick, conferring with Thad Eubanks about Yard business, seemed to have no misgivings, even for a man who once swore he was born to be drowned if he escaped the hangman. Stephen was as Alick described him, a lad going on a holiday. Apparently there was nothing he could think of this morning that would not make him smile.

He came across to where Jennie sat on a sawhorse. "I wish you were sailing with us," he said. "The bay on a day like this must be experienced to be believed. In all my going to sea I have never seen a fairer sight than our own islands, and then, far across the water and the crowds of sail, the blue Tenby Hills rolling along the sky. Penobscot Bay rivals Naples and Rio de Janiero, at least for me."

"I would love to be going today," Jennie said. "So would all my children. Only Muster Day can assuage their grief."

"When *Dolphin* is launched for her maiden voyage," he knocked on the sawhorse, "we shall all sail the entire Gulf of Maine."

Unless Christine has other ideas, Jennie thought, and was immediately ashamed of herself. "I will dream of it from now until then, Stephen," she said.

"*Dreams*," he said smiling. "Are they dangerous for a man of my age?"

"Not at any age, if you can transmute them into reality, which you seem to be doing with singular élan. The ship *and* the lady—or should I put her first?"

"Without the ship in the first place, there would be no lady. At least not one I could marry." He kissed her cheek, kissed both girls, shook hands with the boys and Thad, and went aboard.

Alick and Jennie had said their goodbyes before the children were up. They had never been parted for a night ever since they walked away from Linnmore. His leaving now was not frightening—the new ship was already an inextricable presence in their lives—but still there would be a persistent sense of incompleteness until he returned.

Now he gave her a discreet husbandly embrace and a wink. Bell Ann was predictably dramatic about the parting, but the boys were manly, even William. Priscilla gazed long at Alick and said devoutly, "Please be very cautious. We cannot do without you."

"Nor can I do without any one of you," he said. "So there will be no jumping horses if the fancy is suddenly seizing you, no going down the river to fish, *no* sailing the dory under any conditions." He included them all. "And when you are working on the woodpile, keep your attention on your work and don't be gaping around you like a plowboy in Fairyland."

"Papa, *you* watch out for the bears and the mooses!" Bell Ann cried.

"And the lynxes and the painters," William said severely. Alick smiled. "Och, we are even."

Fifty-Three

S LOWLY THE SCHOONER moved out into the stream, all creakings and
flappings until she found her invisible track; her sails tautened and
the ripple of her passage from bow wave to wake sang in the morning.

"Goodbye, Papa!" Bell Ann's voice flew above the others. "Don't go
near the side!"

"He will be careful," Jennie said. "Come away now." She took Bell
Ann's hand. The twins and Priscilla were already leaving, but William
stood alone at the end of the wharf gazing after the schooner as long as
it was safe to do so.

"Been pretty weather for so long," Vincent Taggart said, "they're in
for something by the time they sack all their gear into the woods.
Wouldn't be surprised if they make camp with the rain putting the fire
out and pouring down their necks. Maybe even early snow."

"You know what the Old Man tells you, Vinnie," Thad said. "Better
to be silent than to sing a bad song."

"But you cannot fight the signs," Vincent said stubbornly. "All that
laughing and foolishness—they'll be cussing before the day's out." He
tramped off the wharf in an irreverent group of fellow workers, and was
heard declaiming above their teasing. "That fat cook making a show of
himself, hefting the grindstone. He'll find out he ain't bound for no
garden party!"

Thad shook his head at Jennie. "Mistook his calling, that one. Ought
to hire himself out for funerals. He could dress all in black and walk
behind the coffin shaking his head and sighing like a gale of wind."

"I suppose we need someone like him to make the sun brighter and the sky more blue," Jennie said.

"Just so long as you don't let him get you all anxioused up, with your man gone."

"Vincent's been Job's Comforter for too long to fret us now," Jennie assured him. William trotted past them and joined the older three, who stood looking up at the *Lincoln's* figurehead.

"Poor man," said Pris. "He's already dreading a life on the ocean wave."

"No, he is gazing thoughtfully across the trackless wastes," said Carolus. "Seeking far horizons."

"Cathay," said Sandy. "The first landfall. They should have dressed him like a sailor; those go-to-meeting duds look mighty queer. It's a wonder they didn't put a hat on him, unless they didn't want to cover all that yellow hair."

"He has pretty blue eyes," Bell Ann said.

"If he wasn't elected Governor yesterday, I hope it won't ruin the fun when she's launched," Carolus said.

There was an inevitable anticlimax when they had all left for school. For Jennie, knowing that Alick was not at the Yard or in Maddox but away by sea, there was a fringe of loose ends fluttering in an erratic breeze. There was more than enough for a proper housewife to do; while she was trying languidly to decide between cleaning cupboards or going over the winter clothing, Priscilla came home, elated by the Lockharts' blessing. They would miss her, but they wished her well, and Mrs. Lockhart had even promised her some business. Mr. Lockhart hoped she would keep up her reading, and the parsonage library was always open to her. When he emigrated, he had brought his considerable collection of books with him.

She helped Jennie wash floors, talking all the while. The tinted drawings, lyrical descriptions of fabrics, and colors with exotic names in the fashion book Ianthe had sent her were at this point delectably fanciful fairy tales. Priscilla was a realist when she needed to be.

"Supposing I do have customers," she said. "It will not be for riding habits, or walking dresses, or morning frocks, or ball gowns. The fanciest work will be little girls' Sunday dresses and petticoats. Sometimes a wedding dress, but not a rich and elegant one."

"I don't imagine all those great dressmakers began at once with elegance," Jennie said. "You don't know what you will be doing someday. You may be living a life where you will dress like that yourself."

Pris hooted. "Mama, you are even more of a romantic than I am!"

"A romantic is not the worst thing to be, but I am not romanticizing now, merely pointing out that the byways of life are very strange indeed. The life that I expected to live one day is as opposite to this one as China is to Maine."

"But you crossed an ocean, and I shall never do that," Pris said wistfully.

"How can you be so sure? Let us finish these beds and think about dinner. It will be just you and I this noon, do you realize? Has it ever happened before? I don't think so."

"May we picnic?" Pris at once dropped years. "We should have roasted a chicken for *us*. They will be eating theirs soon aboard the *Wooden World*. It will be like a pleasure excursion, it's such a beautiful day. Let's go to the beach, I don't care if it is low tide."

The twins came home from school, bringing the mail, which they spread out on the kitchen table, looking for the current copy of *The Youth's Companion*. Sandy took it, and went upstairs to change into work clothes. Carolus tidily sorted the rest of the mail into proper categories. Jennie expected no letters, but there was always the chance of surprise. Priscilla said edgily, "Oh, Carolus, do stop being such a fussy old maid—"

She was too late. Carolus pounced just as she saw her letter, and snatched it out of reach, smiling like the fallen Son of the Morning. "O-ho! What have we *here*?" He held it to his nose. "French *eau de toilette*? I can't be sure." Priscilla made a futile lunge, then backed off with her hands thrust deep into her apron pockets; fists, her mother was sure. Even the rims of Pris's ears looked too hot to touch. "*Carolus*," Jennie said warningly.

"But Mama, I am entranced. An epistle inscribed in the finest cop-perplate to Miss Priscilla Glenroy, River Farm, South Whittier, the State of Maine. Why didn't he add 'Planet Earth, The Universe' while he was about it? Then—'Infinity!' "

"Give your sister her letter, Carolus," Jennie said.

He handed it to Priscilla with a deep bow. "Don't be selfish, sister mine," he entreated. "Please share it."

"Not even under the threat of death," she said glacially, and left the room.

"You'd better be getting to the woodpile," Jennie told him.

"But Mama, it's from Septimus Frye." Across the hall the parlor door shut with a finality just short of a slam. "Aren't you interested?" Carolus persisted.

"It is your sister's letter." Of course she was interested, uncomfortably so, but it was not the twins' business. Sandy came downstairs, cheerfully ignorant until Carolus told him. Priscilla was shut away for some time, obviously waiting until both boys were at work on the woodpile; they had a daily stint of at least an hour a day, sawing six-foot logs into stove lengths to be split by David and Alick.

They ate their after-school strupach and went out to the woodpile, and Priscilla returned, looking very composed. "Shall I make us some tea?" she asked. As if they'd had a sentinel posted, the twins came inside at once.

"Well, are we going to hear it or not?" Sandy asked her.

"Not," she said succinctly.

"In the absence of our father who art in Belfast, or should be by now," said Carolus, "it is our moral duty to protect our sister."

"Oh, twaddle," said Pris. "Someone fetch a fresh bucket of water."

"I fear she is lost," Sandy said. "And not to a gallant sea captain."

"Or a great scholar," Carolus continued. "But to a man who sells insurance. Great Zeus, how drab."

"Mama, am I obliged to hear all this?" Pris asked with melancholy grandeur.

"Pretend they are a pair of young roosters learning how to crow," Jennie suggested. There was an immediate outburst of cockcrows of such variety and virtuosity that even Pris couldn't help laughing. William came home amazed and delighted to a kitchen full of exuberant cockerels, and at once became one of them.

Bell Ann was not entertained. If she had anything to tell—and she always did—it would be saved until there was less competition. She kissed her mother and went upstairs to change from her school dress, then she took her slice of bread and apple butter outdoors, and a treat for Brisky. As the boys finally settled down to work, Priscilla went for a walk with her letter safe in her apron pocket. She allowed the dogs to go; they would ask no impertinent questions.

Jennie wondered if she would be invited to read the note. It was doubtless his formal thanks for Priscilla's commendation of his published letter. If his prose was a bit fulsome and he tossed in some poetry besides, no one had ever yet been carnally seduced by the written word. Jacinth was as rich a catch for a young man on the make as Frank Mackenzie, and she was beautiful, besides. Poor David, she thought, but canceled that. To pity David was to demean him. He had always regarded pity as a slight, to be ignored.

Bell Ann turned up for chores, but was unusually quiet about it, and had not much appetite at supper. Jennie contrived to touch her forehead by pushing the black hair back from it; the child was not feverish. Neither was she belligerent, but she was clinging, pushing into Jennie's lap before the meal was over, trying to curl herself up as she did when she was small. Jennie guessed that she was missing Alick too deeply to be able to say it without crying. Alick had never been away for a night in all the children's lives, but the older ones could freely discuss his absence, wishing they were with him deep in the alien forest; they hoped he would hear wolves howling.

"Fine music," old Mrs. Shenstone had told them. Her father had remembered wolves singing to the moon and how he, as a small boy, stayed out fearless and alone on frosty nights, listening, raising a howl of his own and being answered, and wishing the music would never stop. "He always had tears in his eyes when he remembered," she said. "Howling was friendly, you know. Wolves liked singing together."

When they asked her if it was true that she had raised the last wolf in these parts from an orphaned pup to a gray-muzzled elder who died in his sleep stretched out before her kitchen fire, she laughed.

"So some said, when they was wanting to make me out a witch. But they never came nigh to plague me when Remus was alive, and afterwards they thought he was still guarding the place." She wiped a tear away from her eye with a finger tip. "He was a lovely singer," she said.

Now at the table they talked wolves, panthers, lynx; creatures that had become legendary in this area, which had been densely settled for years. As they talked, David sketched the animals. William leaned on his shoulder as he did on Alick's, and collected all the drawings afterward to take to school the next day.

Jennie went upstairs with Bell Ann; a little babying was called for, and she read her to sleep with *Puss in Boots*, a favorite. When she went downstairs, David and Pris had gone for a walk in the sunset and the boys were studying.

"I *hate* problems," William whispered, hunched over his slate.

"Can't you hate them quietly?" Carolus asked.

Jennie took him into the summer kitchen. Having to read the

problems aloud to her brought his mind back from the woods, and he did the work, not rapidly—William was ever moderate—but correctly.

In the twilight Pris and David returned from their walk and set up a chess game. William wrote twenty-five sentences (most of them very short), using twenty-five new spelling words, and was done before his eight o'clock bedtime struck. He went out and was gone so long that Jennie followed him with the dogs.

"Find William," she said to them. Bounce, unbelievably a descendant of wolves, was not keen to go far from her and the lighted windows, but Darroch found William lying on his back in the road looking at the stars. She watched with him for a little while. The night was very still except for an owl far in the woods, and perfumed with September's distinctive essence, half summer and half an autumnal sweetness.

"I wonder if Papa is looking too," he whispered. "It's queer to think he can see the Dippers and Polaris and everything. There was a shooting star a little while ago. I hope he saw that. I've learned bushels about the stars this year, from Sandy. He must know them all," he said respectfully. "You would not believe all the constellations and the names. Mama, it is so *crowded* up there! And not just at night, but even when the sun is shining. I used to think they were sleeping all day and just came out at night."

"So did I."

Outside the door he said, "Goodnight, Mama. I will look at the stars until I fall asleep." He reached up to kiss her cheek.

"Good night, William. Sweet dreams," she answered as if this were a very ordinary occasion, and no sadder for her than it was for William.

The twins finished their work in time for a chapter of *The Pioneer* before nine, when they too went outdoors. They did not come back at once. Who could resist those stars? The boys were growing up fast; they needed to store hours like this one to take out and cherish when they no longer had the time to live them. She hoped that would never happen to her children, but it was like wishing they would always remain children.

They were still outside when she left Pris and David to finish their chess game and went to bed. "Give them fifteen minutes more," she said to Pris, "and then whistle." But they came in without being summoned. They stopped in her room on their way upstairs, smelling of soap and water, and giddy with the stars and tomfoolery.

"Pris and David are like an old married couple out there," Sandy said. "We think if they just settled for each other it would save them and the rest of us a great deal of trouble."

"What we receive for brothers-in-law is crucial," Carolus said. "David will be perfect for Pris because he is already part of the family."

"And he is twelve years older than she is, and *she* is too young to be thinking marriage and knows it, and you two are *far* too young to be so officious about your sister's business. Now that I think of it," Jennie continued pleasantly, "you will never be old enough to meddle in it, because it *is* her business, and your father's and mine until she is of age."

"Yes, Mama." They kissed her and left. In the candlelight they had looked as bright-eyed and innocently alert as Bounce. They had neither apologized nor capitulated while giving the impression of a graceful retreat until a more auspicious time. Priscilla was to pay for her autocratic ways in the past when she had been much taller than they.

Jennie lay back to read, and then Priscilla came and sat on the edge of the bed, brushing her hair. "David won, but just barely," she said. "I wonder if Jacinth knows chess, but then I don't suppose anyone who looks like that needs to know chess. I asked him when the portrait would be done and he said 'Soon.' No qualifications. Just 'Soon.' " She took the letter from her pocket and laid it on Jennie's open book.

It was an unexceptional but well-expressed message from an older young man to a sheltered young miss, written with perfect grammar and propriety. It thanked her for conveying her family's appreciation of his piece in the *Tenby Journal* and promised that Jerome's death need not be in vain.

"My future career will be dedicated to exorcising the evil of slavery forever. I thank you once more," he concluded, "and present my most respectful good wishes to Mr. and Mrs. Glenroy, your brothers who were so much involved with Jerome, and my particular compliments to Miss Bell Ann."

He was, faithfully, Septimus Frye, who then wrote a postscript signed by Seven F. "The red carnations in my mother's garden are so handsome this year. I enclose a bouquet in spirit, to perfume your day."

"Don't you think he sounds like a statesman already?" Pris demanded, snatching the letter back and reading it.

Well, all statesmen began as politicians as oaks grew from acorns, and one could credit the man with sincere and honorable motives, even if he knew very well that letters like the one in the *Journal* were enough to put a man before the voting public as a vigorous young warrior and reformer; a man worth watching from all sides. One thing was certain, he did not intend to lead a prosaic life.

"I shall save this to have when he is famous," Pris said. "Wait until Papa sees it! You know he has already begun to change his mind about Seven."

"Why won't you let the twins see it? I am curious," Jennie said. "After all, he speaks of them."

"Oh, Mama, you know how they are! They would pounce on the red carnations and shake the life out of them, like Darroch with Harry's hat. I'll find another way to convey his mention of them." She leaned forward to kiss Jennie on both cheeks. "I hope you sleep well, and Papa too." She grinned. "You should have smuggled his plaid into his bedding, then he'd be sure to sleep. I hope he doesn't wake up with Something sniffing at his hair that's about a hundred times bigger than Garnet!" Obviously she didn't believe in the Something. She ran up the steep stairs as Jennie used to run up the stone staircase at Tigh nam Fuaran.

Jennie blew out her candles and was immediately wide awake. It was not strange to be in bed alone, because sometimes she retired before Alick did. But as she lay there watching the stars over the black peaks of the western woods, and listening to the crickets and the little tickings and small creaks of the house, she was suddenly aware of what it must be like, that first night alone for a woman who knows her husband will never return to their bed.

For a woman who loved him, she qualified it; many a widow who stood long-faced in black at the grave must have smiled in the dark as she rolled to the middle of the bed and had all the covers to herself, luxuriously floating not only on feathers but freedom.

But for a couple who had grown as inseparable as two seeds in the core of an apple, to have the fruit brutally riven apart as by an axe—she felt as if the house itself had shuddered in an earthquake. She sat up breathing hard, clutching her knees. Nothing has happened, she thought, but you have *too much* imagination, Eugenia.

There was the quick pad of Garnet's feet on the floor, the tread of a very small tiger. She landed on the bed with a considerable impact and took her usual circuitous way across the coverlet as if creeping up on the Unknown. She touched Jennie's hand and then found her face with a cool nose and brush of whiskers. Vibrating to an as-yet soundless purr, she settled down by Alick's pillow. Jennie began to stroke her.

" 'Tiger, tiger, burning bright,' " she murmured. " 'In the forests of the night.' " The purr became audible. " 'What immortal hand or eye/ Could frame thy fearful symmetry?' "

Remembering the rest of Blake's poem put her to sleep.

Fifty-Four

S HE THOUGHT OF Alick before she was fully conscious, and when she woke up in a cool pewter-colored dawn, she didn't linger in bed. Washing her face, putting on her robe and slippers, she imagined the cold dew-dripping hush of the forest broken by the groaning, yawning, coughing, and snorting as the men crawled out of their blankets. Alick was always a quick and quiet riser; he would either be amused or depressed by the dawn chorus, depending on how well he had slept.

Garnet spoke without opening her eyes, and curled up like a woolly caterpillar. Out in the kitchen the dogs were gone, and someone had cleaned out the cold ashes and laid the new fire; Alick always did it at night, and last night she had forgotten. While she was lighting the kindling, David and the dogs came in, with wet feet and a scent of morning.

"You must be the good brownie of the house," she told David.

"But not good enough to attempt the porridge."

"A small thing." She set water to boil over the flames and went back to her room to dress. Upstairs Pris was rousing the others; Bell Ann sounded whiny. She didn't beg off chores and she was hungry at breakfast, but she was fractious.

With the sun burning away the damp and the mists, it looked like another fine day. "They must be already at work," William said. "I wonder if Papa made porridge for them."

"Not with *Bel Fiore*'s cook on deck and being paid for it," said Sandy.

This conversation took them through breakfast. Talking about her father cheered Bell Ann. Lily Shaw had a most disagreeable papa; Bell

Ann never needed to have *her* good fortune pointed out to her, but she was surprisingly sensitive about the other little girl's deprivation.

David rode away, the Yard men came, and the second day of Alick's absence was under way; one day nearer to his return. Jennie commenced staunchly on her list of tiresome tasks; the first was an hour of knitting on Bell Ann's new stockings. Pris had her work spread out on the table. Snipping the tiny stitches of a French seam sewn eighteen years ago by a London *modiste*, she said "Bell Ann had a bad dream last night and crept into bed with me. She was not very clear about the dream, but I think there was a goblin in it."

"She misses her father even in her sleep," said Jennie. "She will likely do better tonight. — I was thinking that you and I might saddle Diana and Shonnie and go riding one of these delicious mornings. Not tomorrow—I must bake or be like the Old Lady in the Shoe."

"And Thursday is Muster Day," said Pris. "We could go on Friday if the weather holds. But Mama, could we possibly drive to Maddox instead? Whittiers won't have what I need for the insertion and the panels. Much as I'd like to ride, once I have begun this it will be torture to be held up."

"If we waited until Saturday, the boys could try on their new boots."

"If that is what you would like," Pris said to her work. "I did think you and I might go alone."

"Darling, I would love to go alone with you, but the other children and the new boots are facts of life one cannot ignore."

"I know you can't cut yourself up in little pieces so we can each have one of you to ourselves, but don't you ever feel as if you *are* chopped up, and wish you could be the whole *you* again, all yours?"

Jennie laughed. "Sometimes, when I would like to do something on the spur of the moment and can't. But it is all part of the human condition. I wouldn't change my life for any other, and now I don't really feel like a whole person unless I know where you all are. Your father and I manage a little private time for ourselves, and it is enough."

"But sometimes not," Pris said shrewdly. "Did you say, 'We will marry to have six children' or 'We will marry to be always together'?"

"Children are the lovely dividends," Jennie said.

"Thank you, Mama. But parents *should* have a private life," she said didactically. "*Everyone* should have, unless they are too young and silly to be trusted." She went on meticulously clipping. If there was a message in her statement Jennie was not about to delve for it.

"Now that you are in business," she said, "I expect to pay you when you sew for any of the family."

"Charge my own mother?" Pris straightened up and stared at her. "I never would! It's enough for you to pay for the materials, but for the work—no." She shook her head vigorously. "Besides, it would look as if my family was keeping me afloat!"

"Then will you compromise? We could agree to consider each case on its own merits."

Pris relented with an abashed little grin. "I think we could do that."

It was mid-afternoon when Jennie finished her last chore on the day's list, tidying the drawers of the chest under the Simon Willard clock. She went out light-hearted with virtue and liberation into the hot and aromatic day.

Pris was putting away her sewing, and they would take cold lemonade and gingersnaps out to the orchard; the others would be home soon. Jennie went to the springhouse for fresh cold water, and she was still inside gazing at a pan covered with thick yellow cream and trying to decide on some elegant use for it besides butter when the dogs began to bark and Brisky raised his voice above theirs at the sound of hoofs. She went outside, smiling, sure it was Carlotta's Michael; he was thirsty, and knew where the drinking trough was.

Instead there were two men on horseback, Garland Shaw on his chestnut roan and Sheriff Swallow on a lively but gentlemanly gray. His rider was also gentlemanly, lifting his hat to Jennie, while Shaw slumped in the saddle. In the shadow of his hat brim his small, fine features looked swollen and blotched, and he was red-eyed and stuffy with a severe hay fever.

"Good afternoon, Mr. Swallow, Mr. Shaw," Jennie said cordially. She snapped her fingers at the dogs, who came back to her. "This is a pleasant surprise, but if you wish to speak to my husband—"

"We know he's gone, Mrs. Glenroy," the sheriff said, "and if I had my druthers I'd have hung back till he was home. But this won't wait. Do you suppose I could speak with your twins? In your presence, of course."

"You could, but they are at school," Jennie said. "They should be home soon."

"Why?" Pris had come out from the house. "Why?" she repeated, polite but insistent. "What do you need of them?"

"Now, miss," the sheriff said, "let us wait until they come, and we can sit down together and sort this out all right and proper."

She was not soothed by kindly adult tolerance. "Have they been witness to a crime? What sort of crime?"

"My boy was murdered last night," Shaw said hoarsely. "That's what our business is with your boys."

Priscilla jerked back as if struck by an immense fist. Jennie said, "Harry?"

"I only had but the one." Shaw spat the words at her.

The fact was so staggering that she remembered only vaguely, as of no consequence, his reference to the twins. "Mr. Shaw, I don't know what to say, I cannot believe it."

"I can," he said sardonically. "I've seen him cold and stiff in his blood, staring at the sky. Levi Winter's dog found him in the ditch early this morning." She knew then that his eyes were not fiery from hay fever, and she thought at once of Harry's mother.

"Mr. Shaw, I am sorry," she said, just managing not to stammer. "If there is anything at all we can do for you or Mrs. Shaw—"

"You already done too much, birthing them two whelps."

Priscilla's hand fumbled for hers and clamped on it hard enough to numb.

"Now, Garland," the sheriff said. "I am the investigating officer, and you have said enough for now. We will go inside, thank you, ma'am." They dismounted, and she saw Shaw's shaking hands as he tied his horse in the shade of the barn.

Jennie felt such a humming light-headedness that she wondered if she were about to have a stroke. All the while she was walking toward the house, and Pris was still crushing her hand. The garish sunshine of nightmare fell across the bare table, and the flowers in the center blazed in her vision with an unholy fire. She waved the men toward chairs. I feel shock and pity, she thought. What else could it be?

"Thank you, Mrs. Glenroy," the sheriff said, but Shaw would not sit down, or take off his hat, or stand still. Bounce watched him suspiciously. Jennie sat across the table from the sheriff, and Pris pulled a chair close to hers. Alick, Alick! She was calling deep inside. It was of no use even to recognize the cry, or she could lose herself when she needed every drop of self-possession; she knew already why Shaw and the sheriff were there, and it was as impossible to believe as Harry's death.

"Now, Mrs. Glenroy," the sheriff began softly, but Shaw was at her first. "It's no secret your boys spread it around that Harry took the reward for the nigger! That's a lie! He won the money in a lottery. He was always gambling. Drinking in the tavern over the creek, playing cards, wagering. He warn't brought up in those ways, and they killed him, but your boys was the instrument."

The sheriff said, "Hold your tongue, man. Mrs. Glenroy, there is no way to do this easy. Do you know where your twins were last night?"

"At home here, doing their lessons and then going to bed." Now that the battle was joined, she was infused with energy.

"Can you swear to them being in bed all night? No chance they got up while you were sleeping and went out?"

"No chance. I was not sleeping well, and there are stairs that creak."

"But they would know which ones, wouldn't they?"

Pris started to rise, Jennie drew her down again. "This will all be straightened out, Pris."

Pris said in a shaking voice, "But they are saying—"

"I am just asking questions."

"Ayuh," said Shaw with a skull's grin. "Why was my boy found with his pockets turned out and his coat stolen, to make it look like some tramp knifed him and robbed him?"

"Perhaps because it *was* some tramp," Pris retorted.

"To return to your question, Mr. Swallow," Jennie said, "when the boys go to bed, they stay there until morning. They are tired enough to sleep."

"Did they go out earlier in the evening, with your knowledge?" He would have seemed a very pleasant man under other circumstances; she remembered how he had been with Jerome.

"Yes, they went out for natural reasons before they retired." She kept her eyes on his broad, amiable face while her head kept wanting to turn and watch Shaw prowl. For all her sympathy, she felt him as a malignant entity waiting to do evil to her and hers.

"Can you say how long they were gone?" the sheriff was asking.

"Not exactly. Nine is their curfew on school nights. They read a little while when their lessons are done, then they go out for the usual reason. When they come in they wash their faces and clean their teeth and go upstairs. I went to bed while they were out, but my daughter and David Evans were playing chess." She put her hand on Pris's arm. "Do you know how long they were out, Pris?"

There was a convulsive little twitch in Pris's shoulder, but she made an effort to sound like a young lady with nothing to fear. "I do not know the exact time, sir, but I know it was not long enough for me to notice.

David and I were close to the end of our game when they went out, and they were back in time to see him win. They had been watching the stars."

"It was a fine night for stars," the sheriff said.

"Need their knives for studying the stars, do they?" Shaw asked. It was close to a snarl.

"They have only pen knives, Mr. Shaw." Jennie gave in to the shameful relief of hating a man whose son had just been murdered.

"There's other knives about a place. They could have a butcher knife stowed away. Mebbe two knives, and a change of clothes because of the blood."

"Enough, Garland," the sheriff said.

"This is ridiculous," Pris spoke with a hard young disdain. "They wore the self-same clothes they went out in, and I *know* by the way my brothers behaved that they had not just committed a murder."

"How was that?" the sheriff asked.

"They had been teasing me all day about a letter I received and wouldn't let them read. They began again when they came in. They were full of mischief." She turned to stare Shaw down. "They wouldn't. They *couldn't*."

"Thank you, missy," the sheriff said. "It seems your boys have a reputation for prowling at night, Mrs. Glenroy. Not sleeping at home."

"In the summer they camped at the fort, that's the ruin of the old Mannering place, and they went to the Keel at night to visit Jerome. We knew nothing of *that* until Jerome was taken; we hadn't know of their connection with him. Then they were forbidden to go back to the fort to sleep."

"That's what you *say*," said Shaw. "Do you stay awake all night so you can swear on the Bible that all your young ones are in bed? Or mebbe the Bible don't mean any more to the Glenroys than the truth."

"Garland, I'll have to ask you to leave," the sheriff said, "if you interrupt just once more."

"Mr. Swallow," Jennie said, "are you about to accuse the twins of causing Harry's death?"

"Not necessarily, Mrs. Glenroy. But do you deny there was bad blood and the boys had already attacked him?"

"With *green apples?*" she said incredulously, and succeeding in astonishing the sheriff, who looked to Shaw for confirmation.

"My boy left the Yard on account of it!" Shaw shouted. "He was afraid they'd ambush him next time and do real bodily harm. And they did."

"They did not!" Pris shouted back.

"He come home that time all beat up, and they'd set the dogs on him too." He gestured at the recumbent Darroch, who did not wake up.

"The *terrier* nipped at him when he ran, and tore his breeches, that is true," Jennie said. "My husband and David Evans had put an end to the green apple attack. Harry was in a fist fight at the Keel, earlier," she insisted. "The boys saw it happen, and we all saw the marks the next day."

"Mr. George Gunn admits that, Mrs. Glenroy," the sheriff said. "We went to the Keel this morning. He said some of the young ones objected to the deceased being there, and young Moses squared off with him before Mr. Gunn could put a stop to it."

"Could Mr. George Gunn vouch for all the Keelers last night?" she asked.

"Yes, he could," the sheriff answered. "It's well-known that nobody is allowed away from the Keel after sundown, just so none of them can be blamed for any deviltry."

"Well, then, my daughter and I and David Evans can vouch for the twins," she said, "and our word is as worthy of respect as Mr. Gunn's. They believed at the Keel that Harry took the reward, and we believed it, but so do a number of other people. Some questions should be asked in other places, Mr. Swallow."

"It warn't the nigger your brats was anxious about," said Shaw. "It was the hundred dollars. They took him down to the Keel to hide him until they calculated the price was up as far as it would go, and then they'd sell him."

Jennie knew a primitive passion to take him by the throat; he was so meager it should be quite easy to strangle him. I am right to hate this man, she thought. Pris was nearly choking from trying not to cry with rage at her helplessness. Shaw grinned, but the sheriff was not amused.

"Go outside, Garland," he said frigidly, "or I will personally escort you." He half rose, and Shaw went out, growling at the dogs to get out of his way. He left the door open and sat down on the bench, muttering and huffing.

Jennie snapped her fingers to call the dogs inside. "If I hear one scrap of your talk against my sons, Mr. Shaw, I shall bring an action for slander." She shut the door.

"Now, little girl," the sheriff said winningly to Pris, "try to compose yourself. The burden of proof rests with the law. Your brothers will not be unfairly treated."

"They already have been," she retorted, "by these suspicions!"

Jennie looked past the man's broad shoulder and through the window behind him. The twins were just emerging from the woods, swinging their book satchels. Carolus was looking up at the treetops and sky, following a gull's course as if the whole scene were entirely novel to him. Sandy charged on as if he could hardly wait either to eat, or to astonish his mother and sister with some dazzling navigational fact.

Pris saw and her wet eyes widened; the sheriff turned to look. For a moment the kitchen was very quiet, the dogs had not yet caught the message. The boys recognized Shaw's horse outside the barn, but not the sheriff's, and they stopped to pat both horses, and then loped toward the house, on the *qui vive* with curiosity.

"Do they look guilty to you, Mr. Swallow?" Jennie asked in a low voice. He did not answer her. The boys disappeared past the end of the house, and then Sandy called buoyantly, "Afternoon, Mr. Shaw." The dogs sprang up, and if Shaw answered, their noise drowned him out. As the boys came in, Carolus gave Shaw a quizzical backward glance. Sandy said with glad surprise, "Mr. Swallow!"

"Is that gray yours?" Carolus asked. "He is a real beauty, Mr. Swallow."

"Ain't they the clabber-faced innocents?" Shaw said behind them. "My God, beats all how some devils can look as holy as Jesus."

"You had better stay out, Garland," Swallow said. "Or better yet, leave. I'm not partial to arresting a man who's just been bereft, but I am about to, on the charge of impeding an officer of the law in the performance of his duties. Now you go home to your wife. The poor woman's been left all soul alone with the body of her son. You should be fetching some woman to her."

"*Harry?*" It was a husky whisper from one of the twins. "Is Harry *dead?*"

"You'll go as soft with them as a rotten pear," said Shaw.

The sheriff waited, expressionless. The twins looked bewilderedly from one man to another, unconscious of danger. For Jennie, it was like seeing them as small boys walking in ignorance within reach of a great rogue wave, too far for either her hands or her voice to reach them.

Shaw gave up, and turned away from the house as if he ached in every limb. With his departure a cold tranquility came over Jennie.

"Mr. Swallow would like to talk with you," she said to the twins.

"How did—how was—what *happened?*" Sandy got it out hoarsely, in fragments.

"He was stabbed, and that's what I want to discuss with you boys," the sheriff said. Pris quickly pressed her fist against her mouth. Carolus turned from her to the sheriff and then to his mother, a pucker deepening between his dark eyebrows.

"We have not seen any strangers," he said. "We almost never do on this road, except for peddlers."

"Sometimes we see tramps," Sandy offered, "but hardly ever." They thought that was all he had come to ask them; Shaw's slurs, if they'd heard them, were forgotten.

But when the sheriff made his purpose clear, in a very few minutes the twins were white-faced. Sandy had to swallow each time before answering, but always replied. Carolus visibly stiffened, he seemed to grow taller before his mother's eyes. He had to wet his lips when he spoke, but his answers were clipped, his *sirs* crisp. Pris remained motionless within the circle of Jennie's arm. I am Mama, Jennie thought; I have absolutely no right to disintegrate or to long helplessly for Alick. That won't bring him, and I will not allow any harm to our children.

"You boys were pretty well hawsed up about Harry Shaw claiming the reward for the slave, weren't you?" the sheriff asked.

"Yes, sir, we were," said Carolus. "We thought it was a terrible thing to do."

"And when you heard Jerome was dead, you thought Harry Shaw just the same as murdered him."

"Yes, sir," Sandy answered. "I am sorry for what happened to Harry. We didn't wish him dead, but we still think he did a dastardly deed."

"When you went out last night before you went to bed, where did you go?"

"We were in the barn a few minutes talking to the animals," Carolus said. "Then we went out and began looking at the stars. There's a big rock up by the springhouse, and we sat on that."

"And you didn't go out on the town road at all, and maybe meet Harry Shaw coming home? Not planning anything, but just happened to meet up with him? Or maybe," he sounded sympathetic, "you *were* hoping to meet him and just shake him up a bit, to scare him the way Jerome was scared? But things got a mite out of hand. Was it that way, lads?"

They could not speak as the implication struck home; someone actually believed them capable of murder. *Imagined* them doing it.

"And I suppose," Pris said sarcastically, "they just *happened* to have a carving knife hidden somewhere—none of *ours*—and took it along with them in case Harry would be walking home at just that moment. And then they came back into the house talking about the stars and teasing me, and not a spot of blood on them."

"Would you like to see my knife rack, Mr. Swallow?" Jennie asked. "None are missing."

Shaw crashed the door open, shouting, "A murderer can hide anything anywhere! Like what they took off my boy's body after they butchered him, and their bloody clothes! Likely had some clean rigs stowed away for the purpose, and where's *his* coat, eh?"

Sandy clung to the table as if he was about to faint, and the sheriff reached out a hand, but Pris was there first. Carolus looked absolutely blank. Shaw cackled, dreadfully, at Jennie.

"A murderer can hide anything. —We don't know why you and your man left the old country, do we?"

I would welcome a swoon, Jennie thought, but it would terrify the children even more.

The sheriff said angrily, "Garland Shaw, I am taking you into custody now." He went around the table, and Shaw sprang back with a lunatic agility.

"I'll clear out, but who's to keep you from letting this woman cozen you around her finger so you won't have this pair of scoundrels in the lock up by night?"

"I will see you to your horse, Garland," the sheriff said. "The matter of obstruction will be taken up later."

When he was out of sight the rest didn't move, but stood as if caught fast in a deadly bog. Jennie was about to pull free and reach the twins but he was back too soon.

"He's gone," he said. "Mrs. Glenroy, I have a warrant, but it would be more agreeable if you consented to a search of the boys' room, the barn, and the springhouse."

"Search the whole house!" Her voice flew with wildness, and she reined it back like a kite in a strong wind. How could it possibly be that someone knew about Nigel? How could her children be seen as murderers?

"Thank you," Mr. Swallow was saying. "If you'll come along with me, you might feel better about it."

Carolus dropped to his knees and put his arm around Darroch and his face in the dog's neck. Bounce would have gone on the search too, but Pris caught him up and thrust him into Sandy's arms; dazed, Sandy hugged the terrier to his chest and was ardently kissed about the ears.

Jennie led the way across the hall, but the sheriff demurred at searching her room; it would not be necessary, he said. "Folks like you and Mr. Glenroy, from all I've heard of you, would not connive at hiding evidence."

"Nor would we have murderous sons, Mr. Sparrow." She said it without malice; he was a decent man, uncomfortable about his duty, but he would do it nonetheless. He would respect their privacy as well as he could. She took him into the small bedroom, pulled out drawers and opened the chests, even the one where their Highland clothes were kept.

She lifted out Alick's plaid and held it while he knelt and carefully ran his hands through folded layers. She saw the blue and green plaid folded over Alick's shoulder as he walked before her on that hill where a May snowstorm had caught them, and she saw herself wrapped in it while she dried her clothes after the fall in the flooded corrie.

The sheriff arose stiffly from his knees. "Now the boys' room, please. Are you feeling faint, Mrs. Glenroy?"

"Never fear, I shan't swoon." She actually smiled at him as she started up the stairs.

He glanced in at the girls' rooms, but dismissed them. She took him into the attic; by luck it was hotter than usual, especially in areas where bloody clothes might be hidden. The kites rustled and whispered over their heads, disturbed on their roost. He was tactful enough not to mention their beauty, presumably because the twins might never be flying their kites again.

He didn't ask to see David's room, perhaps on the theory that David was as estimable as she and Alick were. In the boys' room he went tidily through each chest of drawers, looked under each bed and inspected by candlelight the long, deep closet under the eaves. Finally he said, "Thank you. I reckon we are done here."

Going downstairs behind him, looking at his broad shoulders and the thick waves of prematurely white hair, she had a flash of the old fantasy that she was dreaming, and would presently wake up into a reality from which she had been exiled for what seemed years but had been only minutes; she seemed to have known this man always, but not what he was doing here.

The sight of the three waiting at the foot of the stairs demolished fantasy or the hope of it. The sheriff cleared his throat. "Now, Mrs. Glenroy," he said with a forced heartiness, "there will be no more proceedings until your husband returns. I will leave the boys in your custody, but they must not step off the property at any time. Have I everybody's word on that?"

Jennie nodded. Carolus snapped, "Yes, *sir!*" Sandy said, "We have been waiting a year for Muster Day."

"You will have to miss it this year. Your word?"

"Yes, sir," Sandy said glumly.

"I shouldn't think their word would be much good to you," Pris said, "if you think they are thieves and murderers."

"Now, little girl, remember what I told you about the burden of proof."

"I do not believe that, Mr. Swallow," she said politely. "If they are supposed to be innocent until proven guilty, why should they be treated as guilty from the start, with no more proof of it than we can give of their innocence? Except that we *know* they are innocent, but you have the right to say something which you do not know at all."

"You are a good girl who loves her brothers," the sheriff said, "and you are an intelligent girl, too. Uncommonly so. Now, when your father comes back he will be seeing a lawyer, and then you will understand more about the workings of the law and its protection."

"Sir," said Carolus. "Isn't there anyone else but us?"

"Not yet," Swallow said honestly. "But I will be asking more questions." It was cold comfort and he knew it, but he would not lie.

"I will be looking around the outside premises," he said, picking up his hat. "Alone. Is any place locked up?"

"No," said Jennie. She walked to the door with him like a hostess and they saw some of the Yard men on their way home, hesitating uneasily near the rowan trees.

"Good day, Mrs. Glenroy," the sheriff said to her in a clear loud voice. "Thank you for your help."

"You are entirely welcome, Mr. Swallow," she answered in kind; she looked past him and smiled at the men.

"I am making enquiries in every house along the road," the sheriff said to the men, walking toward them. "You must know about Harry Shaw. You seen any strangers about?"

The young ones were all cock-a-hoop to assist; there had been a pack peddler on the road at noon, about to buy his dinner from Mrs. Phipps at the Post Office Farm.

"I will see him. What more do you boys know?"

Harry had been drinking rum and playing cards at a house in North Whittier last night. The narrator's brother had been there. When the game commenced to go against Harry, he left it. Ever since he came into money he had been afraid of losing it one way or another; he kept it with him all the time, and a sure way to plague him into a rage was to ask him how he'd gotten it. He'd taken to carrying his pistol. Last night he had left early, more worked up by the teasing and the losing at cards than he was by any fear of having his pockets picked on an empty road. But who in Whittier would do such a thing?

"That is just the question," the sheriff said gravely. "Do you know about what time he left the Nickerson house?"

"Early, my brother said. Hadn't much more than struck eight. They asked him if he was going courting now that he was rich. —You find his pistol?"

"Not yet. I didn't know he had one," the sheriff admitted. But the time was exactly right for the twins to meet Harry around nine, and of course the sheriff was thinking it. Now Jennie hated his courtesy, thinking he was ruthless behind the personable mask; now he would be looking for that pistol.

"Thank you, lads," he said. "Well, Mrs. Glenroy asked me to have a look around in case someone's hiding in one of the outbuildings." Pleasantly he refused their help, saying he would give a shout if he cornered the man; the dogs would be a help. He went toward the barn with his eager new friends, and the men touched their hats to Jennie and went on.

She returned to the kitchen and the frightened eyes, and saw the two five-year olds and the seven-year old who had prayed and prayed for April. She held out her arms, and they rushed to her and made a tight knot of four.

Fifty-Five

N OW," SHE SAID finally. "Loosen your grip, everyone, so I can speak. The truth for us all to remember is that *nothing* can happen to you, because you are innocent, and because I am your mother and I will not let anything happen to you. Nor will your father."

They stared at her in agonized concentration, as if her words were the antidote for a killing poison, and they drank every drop with a tremendous hope that it would work, terrified that it wouldn't.

"Once I promised your father a ship, when we wanted to leave Scotland, and I promised that she would not sink with us in mid-ocean, and I was right. Thank goodness William and Bell Ann are lallygagging on the way home, so they have missed all this."

Suddenly Sandy began to retch. Pris ran for a basin, Carolus jumped up to keep Sandy from toppling to the floor, and then held his head while he vomited into the basin until the spasms brought nothing. Jennie sponged his face with a cool wet cloth. He pushed his face against her breast, shaking.

"They could hang us," Carolus said distinctly, and she heard Alick's voice as he straightened up from Nigel's body, saying, *I am a hanged man.* They had argued then in the brilliant May sunshine, with the larks singing and the burn bubbling at their feet. She had sworn from there to Fort William that she would not let them hang him, and she had won; she had never admitted the possibility of losing. She took Carolus's shoulder in a punishing grip.

"It is not going to happen. Do not *even* think of it. Now, go and get the pail of water I left in the springhouse. Pris, we'll make that lemonade."

Sandy pushed away from her and went into the pantry. He blew his nose and washed his face. Pris joined him, saying, "Help me squeeze lemons."

For a few moments Jennie was alone, almost reeling, thinking, What must I do next? I must talk with *someone*, and all I want is Alick.

Pris's hand on her arm and her frightened "*Mama!*" brought her back.

"I am all right, Pris. Just frazzled, you might call it." Her smile was meant to assure, but it did not. Pris's throat was working as if she too might retch. She whispered, "They don't ha-ha-hang children, do they?"

"Not these two," Jennie said robustly.

The cold lemonade soothed their throats, and they calmed enough to eat a few gingersnaps, but not as if they were tasting them. They kept going back to the lemonade.

"Now we must think about the little ones," Jennie said. "We will have to behave as if nothing is wrong, and it is going to be very hard. David will help, and I hope I have sufficiently frightened Mr. Shaw into holding his tongue around town, so the children should hear no evil gossip in school." Until it becomes public news, she added to herself.

"What about Lily?" Pris asked. "She must know that someone killed Harry."

"We can only hope that Mrs. Shaw does not allow her husband to rave in the child's presence."

"There is that pack peddler!" Sandy said suddenly, but it was a straw that fragmented to dust at a breath, and they knew it. Why would he have still been in town, eating in the Phippses' kitchen, if he had killed and robbed Harry last night? But they were buoyed up by possibilities. If there was one stranger in town, there could be another, or more than one. By night it might be all over, if the sheriff and his deputies kept looking and asking.

"You can't tell who might have seen what," Sandy said. "Already there could be a new scent to track down. I'll wager—" He grinned at his mother. "I'm sure of it. We've been so frightened we can't see past our noses. We forget we are not the only people in Whittier."

"Except that, right now, we are the only *prisoners* in Whittier," said Carolus. "Under arrest even if we are not in jail. If we can't go to Muster Day, everyone will wonder why. William and Bell Ann will be like a hornets' nest with their questions."

Sandy's recovery had been brief. "And what will Mr. Lockhart and Captain Blackburn think on Friday morning?" He folded his arms on the table and put his head down on them with a groan.

"Couldn't we be quarantined at home for something serious?" Carolus asked. "Say we have been exposed to scarlet fever?"

"There is none in town," Pris said hopelessly.

"Well, we can be kept in for something mysterious that might turn out to be contagious. We will all stay home together tomorrow, and then there is only Friday for us all to miss school."

"Dr. Neville would have to impose the quarantine," Jennie said. "It would be asking her to lie."

"But she would do it for you, wouldn't she?" Pris begged. "Isn't she your friend? And *ours*?"

"I would never ask it of her," Jennie said, "and I don't believe she would do it, even if she wanted to."

By one of those bewildering little miracles which now seemed to have been going on for many hours instead of one, they recaptured confidence. How could such a disaster fall on *them*? The more they talked, the smaller their risk grew, until it became slight enough to blow away like a thistle gone to seed. Or almost that, but not for Jennie, and she doubted it was so for them behind their gallantry.

They now regarded Harry with a respect they had never given him in life. He had been killed within sight of home; selected for this awful honor, he had become a hero in reverse.

"Someone followed him home through the warm cricketty night," Pris said, using her own childish word. "Once he thought he heard footsteps like an echo of his, but when he stopped to listen, there was nothing there." As Pris softly spoke, the boys' breathing was shallow, their eyes and ears as sensitive as a butterfly's antennae; they were out there too in the forest-scented night. "Before Harry could turn up the lane to the farm, walking faster now because the air and the walk had cleared his head of the rum fumes, *It* struck."

Almost everyone knew about the money. There were many choices, and many hours of questions ahead, but Pris might be able to shorten them, the twins claimed. The way she described the murder, she might very well have the Sight. They urged her to meditate until she received a clear picture of the murderer. "You stare into space, making your mind empty," Carolus coaxed. "Or stare at some small bright object like a swinging locket. You mesmerize yourself."

"I don't know how *not* to think of something," Pris protested. "I was just imagining. Making it up out of my head."

"No, you were not," Sandy said. "You were *there*." Behind his intransigence there was a plea, and she heard it. She left the room; Jennie, seeing the tremble of her lower lip, walked with her to the hall. Pris gave her a despairing look, shook her head, and went upstairs.

The boys finished the lemonade and went out to work on the woodpile. They seemed so cheerful that Jennie wavered between dismay and relief; anything was better than the demoralizing fear that had struck them like a cholera epidemic, but when this new hope dissolved in their grasp, as it must, their fall would leave them lower than before.

She knew she had to rid herself of this paralysis, waiting for Alick like an animal frozen in fear. All their friends would be outraged, but could help only with that and sympathy. The General would be distraught because she had not gotten word to him at once, and so she must; she knew a little flare-up of hope like tiny flames from embers. He had powerful friends; there might be one among them whose influence, by whatever diverse channels, could reach the sheriff.

But she and Alick had never yet presumed on their friendship with the General, and she knew with a conviction that killed the little flames that she could not do it now without Alick's agreement. No, the man to see first was Young Mr. Dalrymple, who was their lawyer whenever they needed one, which was seldom. And now we bring him a murder; leave it to the Glenroys to be sensational, she thought with morbid humor.

She was peeling apples for a pie when Pris came downstairs, wan and grieved beyond tears. "I cannot concentrate, I cannot see or feel anything, or even guess! Mama, I don't have the Sight. I knew that, but they wouldn't believe it. I am betraying them."

"No, you are not!" Jennie said sharply.

"But what will I tell them?"

"I shall tell them. Go and put on your fishing dress." She went out to the woodpile and praised the work the twins had done. Their smiles were determined but chary; they had not completely deceived themselves.

"Pris cannot help, perhaps because she is trying too hard," she told them. "I'd like you three to take your rods and catch us a mess of trout for supper. You are not to badger her. Enjoy yourselves as much as you can, and remember what I promised you earlier."

She embraced each one. When they had gone, she no longer had to guard her face, and sagged, aching, into a rocker; she felt like a carpet that had been hung on a line and beaten with switches.

William and Bell Ann came home excited about Muster Day (and no school); Bell Ann seemed to have recovered from the first night of missing Alick. They changed their clothes and had their strupach, and were quite nice about giving each other a chance to relate the events of the school day. When Bell Ann went out to see Brisky, William confided that Lily hadn't been in school because Harry had died, but Bell Ann didn't know that. Rupert Foss knew *how* Harry died, but had not told anyone except his closest friends. Not even his younger brother and sister knew. He had been told by his father to keep his mouth shut, after Levi Winter stopped at the farm that morning early, and had a bowl of hot tea, and told about his dog finding Harry's body.

They had all seen the sheriff riding by the schoolhouse in the afternoon.

"Yes, he has been asking questions along the road," Jennie said. "He was here."

"I hope he comes again!" William said hungrily. Mr. Swallow had become a new hero of his ever since he had kept Fitzwater in place without lifting a finger; William was more impressed by the sheriff's having actually been in this house than by Harry's death, which seemed hardly real to him except in the incidental details.

"Do you think they told Lily that Harry was killed with a knife?" he asked thoughtfully.

It was all Jennie could do not to wince at the last word. "Probably they said he died of a sickness," she said.

"Well, he did," said William. "He caught it from taking blood money. Blood money begets blood. If you touch it, you will die."

"Just the same, it was very wrong to kill him," she warned. "And it is awful for his family."

William shrugged. He was too young yet for the perspective to imagine vividly a man lying dead in his blood, with open eyes that saw nothing and would never see again. He knew Jerome had disappeared beneath the waves; Harry was to blame, now Harry was dead. But *dead*, without the sight of it, was just a word; Harry would be no loss to him.

When Bell Ann came back, Jennie sent them to see how well the fishermen were doing. She had not yet been able to give in to tears, which might have been a release, and now she could not. She laid her head on her arms on the table, thinking, I must build a fire and make pastry, and scrub potatoes; but she could not move.

The door latch behind her clicked with the effect of a pistol shot. She sat up drunkenly and through blurred vision she saw David; she held her head as if it were literally whirling. He pulled a chair up to hers, took her hands in a large warm clasp, and studied her face as if he intended to paint it.

She told him everything, filling the slate again and again. With David she was not Mama, who had the solution for everything, but a woman in need of a friend. When she had finished, he took the slate and wrote, "I knew about Harry. It was all they could talk about at the store, but no mention of the twins. What can I do?"

She asked him to stay with the children tomorrow while she went to see Mr. Dalrymple; she would like him to be with her, but the children needed his presence more. He agreed, but reminded her that Mr. Dalrymple was a captain in the Maddox Militia and would not ordinarily be available on Muster Day, when each town had its own exercises.

"Another day cannot make things worse," she said. "Friday then, and after I have put matters in his hands, I will see the General. I would rather wait until Alick is home, but Colin will be very upset if he is not notified at once."

" 'Very upset,' " David wrote, "is an understatement." He offered to take William and Bell Ann to the muster at Parson's Cove and make a long day of it. He would likely see the minister there, and Captain Blackburn was a Militia officer. He would tell them the boys would not be at school on Friday; they were a bit off-color and their mother was keeping them quiet for a few days.

"Do you want Dr. Neville to come?" he wrote.

She thought for a moment how *good* it would be, the presence of another woman, one who would not go into spasms of horror or lamentation. Then she shook her head. "It would only burden her, because she couldn't help."

Supper was a triumph of great activity. The trout were all eaten, and the apple pie was one of Jennie's best. Why cannot I be such an artist when I am happy? she wondered.

William and Bell Ann talked incessantly about Muster Day. "Next year, Carolus and Sandy will be soldiers," William said. "Then, in two years, I will be one too."

"Why can't girls be soldiers?" Bell Ann asked, and was insulted when William laughed.

"I guess I will be a soldier if I want to." She gave him a petrifying stare.

"I wouldn't be surprised," Carolus said.

"If any girl could accomplish it, she would," Sandy agreed. "Likely get to be a colonel."

Bell Ann smirked at William, but he was not devastated. They wouldn't know until morning that they were going alone with David; Jennie had asked Pris if she would like to attend.

"My place is with you and the boys," she said.

"Thankful will be expecting you to admire Simmy with her."

"Not if I am taken with the same distemper the twins have. William can tell her about it. It *is* a distemper, Mama. It is worse, it is a fatal disease. If anything happens to the twins, I will want to die myself."

"We will all come through this, Pris," Jennie said as if her faith were fathoms deep, and no gale winds ever dipped below its surface.

The boys worked on their lessons; Bell Ann had a list of spelling words, but her good humor disappeared as bedtime approached. She was whining again, mopey, wanting to be held, and in tears at last. Rather than let her disturb Pris once she had fallen asleep after this dreadful day, Jennie put Bell Ann into her bed.

"You can have Papa's side," she said. "That will keep you from missing him so much."

"I do miss him," Bell Ann said pathetically. "But—" She stopped off the words by putting her thumb into her mouth, which she rarely did these days.

"But what, sweetheart?"

"I don't know what," Bell Ann said around her thumb. She lowered her eyelids as if dramatizing drowsiness.

Jennie read *The Sleeping Beauty,* and Bell Ann was asleep by the end of it, thumb still in her mouth. Under the circumstances Jennie decided not to combat that. Garnet lay under Bell Ann's free arm; she was as soothing as chamomile tea and a hot water bottle combined.

William went to bed, and the twins and Pris followed soon after; they were bone-tired. When they were all in bed she went up to kiss them, and no one mentioned the day or tomorrow. It was as if they were trying with all their might not to think, wanting only to disappear into sleep, be lost in it, undiscoverable, *safe.*

David was making tea when she came downstairs. He had a sketch pad beside his cup, and from time to time he added to what he had begun. Jennie sat in a rocker with her feet up, sipping tea, and looking vacantly into the shadows beyond the lamplight, trying to imagine Alick at this moment, the way William was always doing. But she could not place him in the far, foreign territory, and the worst of it was that she was too tired to go stumbling and groping through the dark to find him.

David turned a page, and the slight rustle aroused her. She took the slate and wrote, "David, I am so grateful for you. We all are."

"What do you think I feel for all of you?" he wrote back.

"We all exist *because* of you."

He had no answer for that. He worked a few minutes more on his sketch, then closed the pad and put it in his pocket. He went out with the dogs, taking the teapot along to turn the leaves out in the flower border. She remembered as if from the distant past that she had intended to set bread tonight, but dismissed the memory, and went upstairs to look at the children by candlelight; they were all sleeping heavily. William smiled as he slept, knowing he would wake up to a holiday. Sandy was in a defensive huddle, and Carolus slept straight and flat like the effigy of a knight on his tomb. Pris had wept a little in her privacy; the letter from Septimus lay on the coverlet, as if she had been reading it just before she blew out her candle, and had gone to sleep holding it. Perhaps she had taken some comfort from it and had floated off in a pretty fantasy like an Elizabethan love poem.

Downstairs, the dogs were back, and David had gone to his room, but he had washed the teapot and their cups and spoons.

She slept in snatches, broken by Bell Ann's erratic jumps, twistings, and mutterings, which drove Garnet to the foot. Finally Jennie got the plaid from the chest and spread it over the bed. Something of its influence must have reached Bell Ann in her tormented sleep, because she became quieter. Jennie, rested now by her naps, kept a fold of the plaid in her hand, imagining the scent of the Highlands was still captured in the wool. In the Highlands she had slept deeply under the plaid, and now she glided into sleep again, without dreams.

Bell Ann was a deep-breathing little bundle under the dark tartan when Jennie woke. She felt everything at once, before the sense of it took shape; Alick was gone, the twins were in peril. She ached from not having moved for hours, and was more tired than when she had gone to bed; she was unable to move and yet she must, though her legs might go out from under her.

They did not. Strength, if not vigor, was returning with each move she made. Morning fog lay against the windows, but there would be a red sun to burn off the mist from a diamonded landscape and a river changing from opal to aquamarine.

If there was anything to be thankful for, it was the weather; they could be outdoors today. But for how long would their kingdom be open to them? As she reached the kitchen she was attacked by such a paroxysm of chills that she could hardly move or see. A hot mug was pushed into her hands, and her fingers were fixed around it, and other hands securely covered hers.

"Good morning, David," she said through her chattering teeth. He led her to a rocker drawn up to the stove and lifted her feet onto the oven hearth. An injudicious swallow of tea burned all the way down and spread the fire through her chest, and while she gasped, the chills went. David made elaborate preparations for the porridge, and this worked as he intended; she laughed at him and took the caddy of dry meal away from him before he could turn the lot all at once into the boiling water.

Bell Ann slept on, and David went out to help William. The twins and Pris did their work without songs, whistlings, or badinage; they did not find it hard to be listless and lack appetite at breakfast.

"You three had better stay home today," Jennie said. "To be on the safe side in case you have caught something. That means I will stay with you."

"Oh, *drat!*" said Carolus, to add authenticity.

Priscilla said wearily, "I really don't care, the way I feel." Sandy did not reply. He went into the winter kitchen and lay on the camp bed with his hands behind his head, his eyes shut. David wrote on the slate and beckoned William to see.

" 'I will take you and Bell Ann,' " William read aloud. "*Truly?*" he asked David, who solemnly nodded.

"I am deeply sorry you cannot go," William said nicely to the others, and then in a small explosion of delight, "I'm glad *I'm* not catching anything!"

Jennie sent him to wake Bell Ann; he was to take her clean clothes to her and say, "Hurry, get washed and dressed, if you want to go to Muster Day." The surprise approach was to fend off a bad mood, and it did. There was only a short argument about her dress, which she lost; Muster Day was no occasion for the Paris frock. She complained that the dress would be too short before she could ever wear it out.

"It is made so it can be let down," Jennie said. "Your gingham is perfect. It is even patriotic: red, white, and blue. But you may wear your best bonnet."

"I am sorry you cannot go, Pris," Bell Ann said sweetly.

Jennie packed the largest dinner bucket with provender for a plain meal, plus bowls, forks, spoons, and mugs. There was always someone selling hot fish chowder or baked beans at the store on Muster Day, and switchel and lemonade out on the field.

Bell Ann was not to go wandering alone; she was to go across to the store and tell one of the Whittier ladies if she had to use the Necessary. "And do *not* put it off too long," Pris said, "because you know what could happen."

"I don't know what you are talking about," Bell Ann said pertly. "I never have accidents."

William was likely to vanish when they arrived, and not find the others until dinner time. Jennie told him to take charge of Bell Ann for a short time during the morning, and then again in the afternoon, to give David a chance to breathe.

"She cannot talk his ears off," William argued, "and he doesn't even have to hold her hand. She is his shadow; he could not lose her if he tried."

"He might wish to lose her now and then, William," Jennie said.

"To draw? But—"

Carolus pinched his ribs. "Wake up, Wim."

"Oh!" said William brightly. "Yes, Mama."

When they had driven away in the chaise behind Shonnie, Pris said, "Did you see the way she cocked a snoot at us? She thinks she is competing with me." Her smile was sad. "I remember when I had to accept David's not being mine alone; I thought I had awful troubles then. Do you suppose he gave up Muster Day in Maddox with Jacinth? My goodness, on whose arm will she go tippy-toeing along, flirting with the troops? At the dance tonight she must expect to be the belle of the ball, and the worst of it is that she *will* be." Then she clutched her mother's wrist under the rowan trees. "Mama, I am so *frightened!* Last night I was tired, and I was trusting in you and Papa, so I slept. But when I woke up, it was all there again, and it makes me want to vomit, or worse."

"Sweetheart." Jennie put her arms around her. "We must all hold together and get through these hours the best way we can. I am so thankful those two are gone for the day, and I am praying that they won't hear anything. But I don't intend for us to sit around this house staring at the furniture and each other. We had enough of that yesterday."

They were a sorry crew to take on a picnic, except for the dogs, who had enough zest for all. They walked a long way through the woods past the fort, to their boundary with the Keel. The adjoining section of Keel woodland was old-growth forest, a stand of white pine, used very sparingly; the Gunns had an almost mystic reverence for the grove, as if it harbored gods and a spirit lived in each of the most ancient trees.

"They always apologize to an old tree they are going to cut down," Carolus said, "and tell it what they need it for. Miriam says so, anyway."

"If nobody will believe us," Sandy said, "we will not let them hang us. We will run away to the Keel and hide there forever, unless we sail away on one of those ships that stop there and are never seen again."

"We will creep back at night like Indians," said Carolus, "and say goodbye to you and Papa. I hope we will sail to the Spice Islands or Far Cathay. The vegetation must be remarkable there."

"Let me know in time to supply you with clean smalls and a change of stockings," Jennie said. "Will you want towels?"

"How *can* you!" Pris cried, and the boys looked at their sister with embarrassment and even distaste, because she was not playing the game.

"Come and swim," Jennie invited. They had brought changes of clothing, and Jennie and Pris went in among the trees to change into the bathing dresses Pris had made. Down on the shore, the boys stripped to their drawers. There was no sandy little cove here, but shallow, pastel, finely pleated slopes of petrified lava slanting gently into water that today was as still as a garden pool. A rising breeze from the west drifted languidly through the tops of the old trees and skimmed down to the river a little distance out, brushing it with brief glittering kisses.

It was astonishing, the power of the water to buoy them up, not only in the physical sense, though that was a part of it. They were lifted and supported by the slightest, nearly effortless motions. A pressure of the toes on the pebbles that looked like gems through the sunstruck water, a gliding stroke of the arm, a wriggle of the fingers like small fish in an aquarium, and one was unable to keep from smiling, and then laughed and struck out to swim.

It was pure unthinking bliss with no *before* or *after*. Ospreys piped over the river and ships sailed it slowly in light airs. Time seemed to stand still as one had always prayed for it to do. Pris sat on a ledge submerged to her waist, supple in drenched blue linen, her yellow hair flat to her skull, and the long locks falling to her shoulders with the water running off in little streams.

"Mermaid ho!" Sandy shouted, dived, and seized a foot. She squawked like a startled gull, and he popped above the surface holding a long seaweed beard to his face, saying, "It is only Neptune, my dear!" Carolus swam under water in a contemplative way, as if studying the bottom. Darroch paddled from one to the other. Bounce rolled on old crab bodies on the shore.

It was a theory, Jennie's father had said, that when the earth was new they were all fish, and she used to wonder if Mr. Wordsworth was hinting at it when he wrote, 'O joy! that in our embers/ Is something that doth live,/ That nature yet remembers/ What was so fugitive.'"

The three came out of the water very hungry; with the elasticity of youth they were sure that when she handed everything all over to Mr. Dalrymple it would be finished. There were things about the law, Carolus lectured them over their food, of which they had never dreamed, and a few words from an astute lawyer would end this stupid misunderstanding. If there was any foot-dragging, the General would have the whole kit and caboodle up to Strathbuie House and give the affair its quietus. They imagined it in gloating detail, and Jennie had not the heart to remind them that, while the General would be a granite rampart of moral support, he could not, and would not if he could, manipulate the Law. This was not the old country, where the local aristocrats owned and controlled whole villages; where the squire, the laird, or the chief might easily hold the local law officers in his debt.

The boys' glib optimism infected Pris, and Jennie let it go on, thankful for the surcease. The twins pointed out the track to the Keel, visible almost to the settlement, and laughed about shepherding William home in the dark when he was half asleep and thought an owl was a ghost moaning. Some day, with permission from the Gunns, they would show Jennie and Pris the elegant gate Jerome had made for the cemetery. If they longed for their father, they hid it, but they hated going home; spirits descended as the sun westered. When they came within sight of the house, sunk in the cold blue shadow of the woods, they walked in a deadening fatigue with feet scuffing through the grass. The dogs had been trotting along at a steady pace, with no side excursions, but they suddenly sprang ahead; David was just driving up to the open barn doors.

Bell Ann saw them coming and stood up, calling, and was forcibly seated by William, but he could not stop her voice.

"There must be times when David doesn't mind being deaf," said Carolus. "But it will be a kindness to Shonnie to get her quickly away from the poor beastie." They dropped their gear outside the house and went across to the barn.

Pris hurried too. It was as if David's strong, male presence magnetized them in the absence of their father. Jennie herself was glad to see him; with David she need not be competent and courageous. The twins stayed with him, unharnessing Shonnie and putting the chaise in the barn. Pris went up to the washhouse to rinse away the salt water, and William and Bell Ann ran to their mother.

Bell Ann hadn't stopped talking since they'd driven in. She was gloriously sticky with molasses taffy, and she had eaten a ripe banana; the soldiers looked beautiful, and she had hardly not jumped when they shot their guns. Captain Blackburn was so handsome; kings must look like him. She almost didn't know Mr. Foss with his polished buttons and shiny boots. She could not wait for Carolus and Sandy to grow up and join the troops.

She stopped all at once to seize and hug Garnet as if she and the cat had been separated for months. William rolled his eyes at his mother. "She behaved very well," he said. "She fell asleep on the way home; that is what gives her all the git-up-and-go now." He signed comfortably. "I don't have to tell everything tonight, I reckon it will spin out into a week, and then I can do better. — Another horse tried to bite Shonnie, and Shonnie was furious. That was quite exciting," he said moderately. "I had a banana too, and we had clam pies, and David drew when I took charge of Bell Ann. There was a fist fight, two big boys from North Whittier, but the men stopped it." That had been a disappointment. "I told Thankful Pris and the twins were coming down with something. But none of 'em look very sick to *me*."

"It passed off," Jennie told him. "So to cheer ourselves up for missing Muster Day we went to the shore to swim and eat." He smelled of dust and heat and clean little-boy sweat. She wanted to squeeze him, but restrained herself. "It helped to make up for our disappointment," she said.

"I'm glad," he said generously. "We had races, but I didn't win any."

"Did that spoil your day for you?"

He smiled broadly and shook his head.

Fifty-Six

B ELL ANN FELL asleep all at once halfway through *Rapunzel*, and Jennie
arose from the bed and let down her own hair, which she had simply
tied out of the way after she rinsed it in rain water. She sat down before
her mirror to brush it. She had not looked closely at herself since
sometime on Tuesday, and she wished she were not looking now. She
hoped it was only the way the sunset light slanted across her face that
showed shadows where none had existed. Her eyes were dull in dusky
hollows, and deep parentheses bracketed her mouth. She leaned forward,
unbelieving; this could not be how she appeared to the children, it *had*
to be the light, which was not softly roseate but harshly red and filling the
room with cruel illusions.

She turned from the mirror and braided her hair swiftly, keeping her
eyes on Bell Ann's sleeping face. Alick now seemed so far from her it was
frightening, as if the longer she endured without him the farther he
would go, until he would simply dissolve out of sight.

She hurried out to the others. William was trying to review his work
for school tomorrow, and yawning until his eyes ran water constantly.
She sent him to bed. The other three, like her, were now showing the
strain. She lit the lamp early, and with a loosening of the tightness in her
chest and belly she saw that the smooth, healthy bloom seemed to return
to their faces. By lamplight she too lost the ugly lines and smudges.

"We are going to read," she said firmly. "Who will begin?"

When they had gone to bed, she went up to kiss them goodnight
again; whether they wanted it or not, she needed it. There were tears on
Sandy's face. She pretended not to notice, though she wanted to sit on

his bed and take him into her arms. Carolus was too casual, and Pris pretended to be absorbed in her reading.

Downstairs David had put the little teakettle to boil over the spirit lamp, and was slowly leafing through loose sketches in a portfolio.

"David, I'm sure Bell Ann and William consider you either their patron saint or a guardian angel," she wrote.

"A slightly worn one. But I would not have missed it. What about you?" He was appraising her face.

"We bumbled along. Going to the shore for the day was the best thing we could do. But we are up and down like those toy monkeys on a string."

"I sent a note to Dalrymple by Joel Whittier; he was going to the Maddox ball last night. I asked for an appointment, but you will be the one to see him. I shall stay here, as we agreed."

"I hate to keep you from your work." She gestured toward the portfolio. "Sketches of the Muster? May I see?"

He smiled and laid the folder open. That smile of David's! When the children were small, they would work to make it appear, and she was comforted by it now.

At first he showed her the quick and sometimes humorous drawings he had done that day. Beneath them the portfolio was filled with pencil, ink, and water color sketches of one girl. Jacinth, of course; sitting in a swing, thoughtfully leaning against a post, cutting flowers, smiling with the Heriot children around her, reading with grave attention at a garden table with her head on her hand.

David was not awkward as he spread the work out for Jennie to see. He was not blushing. He laid one large sheet aside, and wrote, "This is the most like the portrait. It is the one we chose."

Exquisite was the word others had used, even while disliking her, and it was the only word possible, if the watercolor likeness was true. A girl with a blue dress and dark curls crossing a green-and-gold-dappled lawn, smiling in gentle surprise and welcome. If this was how she regarded David while he worked, it was a wonder he'd been able to hold his brush at all, to trace the bare throat and the touching hollow that invited kisses, young breasts, and the long line of hip and thigh subtly suggested through layers of translucent muslin. White and deep pink flowers dripped from her hands.

"Oh, David," Jennie murmured, forgetting that he could not hear, but he must have felt a faint vibration of the air so close to him. He looked across at her with unwavering silvery-gray eyes.

"She is lovely," she said, carefully shaping the words. "Like the face that launched a thousand ships."

"I have wanted you to see this," he wrote. Your work, she thought, or the woman? Then she was afraid her lips might have moved with her thoughts, he watched her so closely. She reached for the slate and wrote, "I have heard how pretty she is, but I had no idea of her beauty."

"The oil is better than this." He tapped the paper. "*She* is." He was not diffident like a boy, he was not like Stephen making his confession. He was as unruffled as he had been when he was thirteen years old, and appeared at the door to live with them. He knew his own mind then, and he knew it now, as well as he knew that his work was much more than merely good. *Take me as I am; you will never do better.*

Why should Jacinth not take him as he was? He was gifted; he was both attractive and fastidious in his person, he had a natural unselfconscious dignity, a sense of humor, and he was well able to keep a wife, even one without money of her own. He was already well-known across the state for his walls and soon would be sought out for his portraits.

A strong-headed girl who had not known him all her life might have some difficulty adjusting to someone who had been his own man ever since he was William's age. He had become that when he watched his father drive away, and he had run after the wagon, trying to call "Da!" in his unused voice, and the man never looked back. On that day David ceased to be a child.

I hope she is worth it. She thought the hope was deeply buried, but his smiling mouth answered, "She is."

She went upstairs again to be sure no one was lying awake, but they were all sleeping, there was no pretence of it. *She* could not sleep. She sat by the open window in the dark, listening to the crickets. She tried to settle on David and Jacinth, but she could not. Finally she slipped into bed with a caution that made her ache.

The changes in Bell Ann's breathing as she went from dream to dream were disturbing, and her mother kept expecting the goblin to make his entrance; perhaps the past day's soldiers would hold him off. Bell Ann rolled over and burrowed against her; now Jennie was hot and prickling as if with a torturing heat rash. I will disintegrate at the first kind word from Young Mr. Dalrymple tomorrow, she thought, if I cannot have a few hours sleep. But she could not even weep to break the Iron Maiden clamp of nerves. The magic of Alick's plaid had been shattered.

Bell Ann flounced suddenly away from her, spoke in tongues, and her breathing became more regular. Jennie crept out of bed and walked around to cool herself. She felt her way upstairs in the not-quite-dark of a starry night, and listened, but they were all profoundly asleep. But then, none of them was sharing a bed with a twitching, muttering child who had driven even Garnet away.

The clock struck two. It was an hour for horrors to beget horrors that came in troops of demons, safe in the night, to inflict wounds of which she must not speak, not because she was brave, but because she was Mama.

The desperate optimist had died somewhere along the way, but a desperate coward remained, who wanted only to sleep. *Alms for oblivion.* She'd have given a fortune, if she had one, for just three hours of oblivion; a dreamless black absence from her brain. *Alms for oblivion.* Shakespeare. But what was the rest of it?

Trying to find it, picking over and shaking out rags of memory, she began imperceptibly to sink. Bell Ann slept quietly. The descent quickened; she knew it and would not move a finger or a toe as the words came to her: "Time hath, my lord, a wallet at his back wherein he puts alms for oblivion."

All at once she was waking up, surprised but not grateful that she had slept. The windows were only a bit lighter than they had been at two o'clock. It was raining too, with a light seductive patter that should have kept her sleeping for another hour at least. Bell Ann's fists and knees bored into her back, and she lay cramped and aching at the very edge of the bed. There would be no possibility of going back to sleep, even without the crowding; the day was already besieging her, and she was racing through everything to be done before she went to Maddox. She did not know yet how she could explain to Mr. Dalrymple. Perhaps she should write it all down. Yes. Get up now while it was quiet; write, correct, rewrite, go directly to the point—

She eased herself away from Bell Ann, a fraction at a time, holding her breath. Just as she began to swing her legs over the edge and lever herself up, Bell Ann clutched at her with a two-fisted grip on her nightdress, pulling her back with surprising power. Jennie slumped onto the bed and shut her eyes. I love this child, she thought, but why has she no mercy?

"Is he out there?" Bell Ann whispered, rising to her knees behind Jennie.

"Who?" Jennie asked. "Is it your bad dream again?"

"*Sh, sh!* He might hear you!" She crawled around into Jennie's lap, took her mother's head in steely small hands and whispered, "The man who is going to burn the house down."

Jennie's head snapped back. She said, "Burn the—" Bell Ann's hand clapped over her mouth. In the dim light and so close to Jennie's face her eyes looked huge and black. "Stop, stop!" she hissed.

"Darling," Jennie whispered. "There is no one outside. You have been dreaming!"

"No! I really saw him, and he told me he would, if I told you!" She held onto Jennie and tried to look out the west window. "He would come from there—he may be listening." Her straining whisper must have hurt her throat, because she put her hand up to it. "I was bad," she said, "and you didn't know it, and it just gets worse and worse." She twisted around again to look out the window.

"It's locked," Jennie lied, cradling her. "We will talk in low voices, but we needn't whisper. Now tell me what gets worse and worse. The bad dream?"

"No! It isn't a dream! I never lied to you before, but I didn't know how not to lie, because he said he would burn us all up in our house." She was shivering, and Jennie pulled the plaid around her. The child had to talk out her nightmare until it ceased to exist.

"But everyone knows I lied," Bell Ann insisted, "and that is why they act so strange, and you have those." She put out a forefinger and delicately touched the shadows under Jennie's eyes. "It's because I am so bad and disobedient, and it makes you sad." She began to cry, not loudly but with a sobbing that was almost unendurable for Jennie. She rocked her, murmuring, "There, there." So much for all their efforts to be natural for the little ones.

"Bell Ann," she said against the child's hair, "how can I be sad about what you did when I don't know what it was? If we seem strange to you, it is because we all have been worried about something else."

"Missing Papa?"

"That is part of it. Now tell me what you did that was so terrible."

Bell Ann's head came up from her breast and turned toward the paling window.

"There is no one there," said Jennie. "Believe me! Tell me what you have done."

"The day that Papa went, after school when everybody here was talking about something else, I ran away."

"Where? You could not have gone far."

Bell Ann raced headlong into her awful truth. "I walked home with Lily that day, and I told her I would come and play after I changed my dress. "I *promised* her, Mama, even though I knew you wouldn't let me go. But when everyone was busy, I made believe I was going to see Brisky, and then I just ran away."

"And did you see Lily?"

"No, because I didn't go to the house." She spoke slowly, as if she were watching herself walking alone on the road between bars of shadow and sun. "I got to their lane, and then I heard a baby crying. I really did, Mama!" She sat up on Jennie's lap, ablaze with conviction. "I looked everywhere, under the bushes, and even in the ditch, and then I stood still and shut my eyes, and listened the way Carolus told me to listen for a bird, and I heard it again, just a little cry, and it was across the road in *our* woods."

"Are you sure—?"

The hard little palm was pressed across Jennie's mouth again. "I *am* sure! I thought somebody left us a new baby, and I went looking for it, and I was thinking how surprised everybody would be when I brought it home, and what we would name it, and what Sarie Oakes would say."

It was either an extraordinary dream or, needing to confess her wrongdoing, she had concocted this adventure to romanticize the circumstances. But her fear of the firesetter was genuine; he must have existed in a separate nightmare.

"But I didn't find the baby," Bell Ann was saying, "because of the man. The Wizard." He had been elevated to a title, and she whispered it.

"Did he look like anyone we knew?" Mr. Shaw, perhaps; that would not be strange.

"No, *I* never saw him before." She was decisive. "He had a beard, but it wasn't nice and neat—it was all frowsy and tangled. He had a blue coat like a soldier's, but it was dirty, and some of the buttons were gone. And he had an old black hat with a partridge feather in it. It shaded his eyes."

"And where was he? Did he come along the road just then?"

"No." Bell Ann was unequivocal. "He was in our woods, not far from Gibraltar. Well, a little way inside, so you couldn't see him from the road. He was sitting under a tree, whittling. He had a knife like the one Moses cleans fish with. Oh, and it was the old grandfather pine we call 'the Y tree.' I almost forgot that." The elderly pine, deformed in youth, had divided into two trunks growing from one.

This dream was becoming a little too vivid for comfort. "He has a funny little short pipe," Bell Ann said, as if she were observing him now, and Jennie at once smelled strong coarse tobacco. "He had his legs stretched out and one crossed over the other, and there was a hole in the bottom of one boot," she continued. "He must be making believe he is a tramp, because people would be afraid of a Wizard. I am." She bunched herself up tightly in her mother's arms under the plaid.

"It is daylight now," Jennie said. "All the evil spells fade away in daylight." Not quite all, but Bell Ann did not have to learn that yet. "Did you speak to him?"

"He spoke to me. He said in a funny laughing kind of voice, 'What is a little lady like you doing here?' I said, 'These are my woods, and I am looking for the baby.' And he said, 'There is no baby, little miss,' grinning as if everything was comical, and I was the most comical of all." She was irate. "I hate it when grown-ups do that!"

"So do I," said Jennie. She was taut with suspense, and afraid of communicating it to the child, but Bell Ann was well away now, and nothing could stop her.

"I told him I heard the baby as plain as could be, and he said it was a catbird, he heard it himself. And then he said, 'Ladybug, ladybug, fly away home. Your house is on fire and your children will burn.' "

Sweat trickled down Jennie's back, her nightdress was clammy with it. "You say that yourself whenever you see a ladybug," she pointed out.

"It is different when I say it," Bell Ann said. "I love the ladybug, but I knew he did not even like me, and it frightened me, and I started to go, and then I heard the baby again. Mama, it was not a catbird."

Jennie, it was no dream, she thought.

"I said, 'There, do you hear it?' and he put down his knife, and he was not laughing any more." She pressed hard against Jennie as if to glue herself to her mother.

"He said, 'Go home as fast as you can, Ladybug. I am a Wizard, and if you tell anybody about me, I will know with my magic powers, and your house will burn down, with you and all your family in it.' " She drove her head painfully into Jennie's breast. "And now I have told." She was shaking. "And I know I heard a baby," she said in a muffled voice.

"Come," Jennie said. She helped Bell Ann into her wrapper and slippers, and put on her own. "I am bursting," Bell Ann confided, sitting on the chamber pot. "Don't leave me!"

"I shan't."

Out in the kitchen, in spite of the lazy greetings of the two dogs, who did not want to rouse up enough to go out, Bell Ann's fear returned. "Don't light a candle," she implored. "He might see us."

"Darling, do you think anyone could be outside and Darroch and Bounce not know it? See how sleepy they are."

"If he is a Wizard, he doesn't even have to be here to burn us in our beds."

"No one can do that, Bell Ann. He was trying to frighten you away, and he did." She urged her onto the camp bed and wrapped her in the plaid. "*There are no wizards*. I am your mother, and I *know*. And so does the Great Horse." She lit a candle, and set the kindling alight in the stove. The thin sticks were topped by a curly mass of bright shavings lovingly whittled by William. She replaced the covers and stood there, listening and waiting, not for the voice of the flames in the chimney, but for something that hovered just beyond the doors of conscious thought, something too vague, too tenuous for a word as strong as *hope*. But it was there, conjured up by William's curly shavings, now consumed in aromatic death.

Shavings.

On Tuesday afternoon, then, a stranger was loitering on Glenroy land, almost opposite the Shaws' lane. He had threatened a child with burning her house down if she told of him. What she believed was a baby's cry could have been made by a gull or a catbird, but the man was not imagined. He had been there late Tuesday afternoon, whittling with a knife considerably larger than a pen knife, and sometime during Tuesday night Harry was stabbed, and died. There should be shavings.

"I wish Papa would come home," Bell Ann murmured.

"I hope it isn't raining on their camp, don't you?" Jennie made her a mug of cambric tea. Bell Ann drank steadily, stopping only to yawn. Her eyes kept closing. Confession, Mama, and daylight had vanquished the Wizard for now, and it was a long time till tonight. Jennie took the mug before limp fingers could let go, Bell Ann curled herself up and went instantly to sleep.

Jennie drank tea and fed the fire. The clock struck five, but Bell Ann, safe in the oblivion that Jennie had craved, heard nothing from the world and surely met no wizards. Jennie returned to her room and dressed for going out into the rain. Then she went upstairs to wake the twins. When she crossed the threshold there was a whisper from Sandy's bed. "I'm awake. I thought you were a ghost."

"Take your clothes and dress downstairs," she whispered back.

He didn't ask why, he was already pushing back the covers. William, sleeping, lay on his side facing the window; the rain ticked away secretively on the roof close to his head. She woke Carolus by taking the hand that lay outside the quilt and gently squeezing it until he began to stir, sighing and scowling, and then his eyes flew open and stared as if he did not know her. She put her finger on her lips and shook her head at him. Sandy was already leaving the room.

"Are we running away?" Carolus murmured drunkenly.

"Not far. Come downstairs to dress."

The cat was on Pris's bed, and gave her a few courteous blinks and slept again. Pris awoke as she always did, clear-headed and poised for action, but this time with dread that nearly cut off her voice. "What has happened?"

"Bell Ann has been telling me her dreams," Jennie said. "It has not been all a dream. Dress for the wet."

In the winter kitchen, Bell Ann had turned to the wall, Bounce was against her back, and Darroch was a long black mound beside the camp bed. Jennie doubted that anything could wake the child until she was ready. She shut the door between the two rooms, and in the summer kitchen she gave the others mugs of hot milky tea, and bread and butter. They ate and drank like automatons while they listened to her, their eyes fixed on her in the candlelight as if they were powerless to shift their glances. Pris was alert, but the twins were too bemused by their sudden waking from exhausted sleep to quickly take in anything.

"There should be shavings somewhere near Gibraltar," Jennie said. "Under the Y tree." At the mention of the rock and the old tree, light began to seep back into dulled eyes. "Shavings should be proof that a stranger was recently about," Jennie continued. "In case Mr. Swallow is not inclined to take Bell Ann's word for it."

"He will never make her back down," Pris said with grim pride. "When Bell Ann knows she is right, she is constant as the Northern Star."

"Lucky for us she thought she heard a baby," Sandy said.

"When I think he could have harmed her, I am sick," Jennie admitted. "But he simply terrified her into rushing home. She insists it wasn't a bird."

"She still cries over the *Babes in the Woods*," Pris said, "and she was very jealous about the Oakes baby. She must have thought she was about to find a real Babe in the Woods, and save it." Her eyes glistened.

"Well, she may have saved her brothers' necks," Carolus said. He was brightening with every instant, like a sunrise, "Someone else may have seen that old army coat and the black hat and the beard, unless he traveled by night. Perhaps Mr. Swallow has heard of him already. That should help."

"What are we lallygagging for?" Sandy was already at the door.

"No, wait," said Jennie. "You boys cannot leave the property, so you must go by the upland pasture and the Blueberry Ground, and reach Gibraltar through the woods. Pris and I will come by the road and meet you there." She held an arm of each while she emphasized her instructions. "And remain well *inside* the woods, do not even come out to the ditch. If Mr. Shaw should be abroad this early, he would swear you'd been out in the road. Stay behind Gibraltar till we come." She made them wear their thick worsted jackets to keep them from becoming soaked through in the dripping woods. They protested, but obeyed. "And be *quiet,*" she said as they went out. "Be Indians."

"What if Bell Ann wakes up?" Pris asked. "Should I wake William to stay with her?"

"No, let him sleep. I doubt if she will wake soon; it is the first real rest she's had since Tuesday night. The dogs are with her, and David will be up soon. Did you ever know him to oversleep?" She sat down at the table and wrote on the slate, "David, Bell Ann may have the answer. She will tell you if she wakes up before we come back, the twins and Pris and I. William is still sleeping."

She propped the slate up against the sugar bowl so it would face him when he came downstairs. She and Pris put on their cloaks, and when they went out into the dark morning the rain was so light they scarcely felt it. The boys had already disappeared. No voices or hoofs were heard from the barn as they passed it, walking on the grass and not speaking. The air was soft and still, smelling of wet earth and leaves, and low tide in the river; a few birds whisked among the branches, dislodging small showers, but they were always quiet at the end of summer except for the wavery song-trials of young birds. Usually there were crows somewhere calling at any time of year, but not this morning, and the gulls would be feeding out on the flats.

The loudest sound in the world for Jennie was that of their steps on the road, and they were consciously walking as lightly as they could. Neither spoke, and they met no one; once something was startled in the bushes and fled away through deep wet bracken. They didn't see it, but they knew it was four-footed, not human.

Gibraltar was the children's name for an exposed rock formation raised like a pulpit above the road. River Farm's granite-based upland was covered with forest, berry patches and thickets, and summer pasture, crisscrossed with trails made by human and animal feet. It was all superb country for Indians, explorers, or Robin Hood, but Gibraltar was a phenomenal gift to a family of imaginative children.

It had been a besieged fortress of the Cathars; the heights from which the infamous Old Man of the Mountains sent his assassins to prey on pilgrims to Jerusalem; it had experienced English, Scottish, and American wars. It had been the prow of Magellan's ship, the *Golden Hind*, the *Mayflower*, a Roman trireme, an Indian war canoe, and the *Constitution*.

It became Gibraltar after Stephen had described that Rock to them and its history; the last siege and defense had been a year ago, fought by all the boys from up and down the road and a few determined girls. Spanish or English, the side didn't matter. It was a long, splendid, noisy affair, an appropriate farewell to childhood for many of the warriors.

Now there were not enough boys of the right age with the freedom to make up a fighting force or a good crew, but William sometimes went there alone or with Bell Ann, and they lay on it on their stomachs, hoping for someone to go by on whom they could spy like Indians.

This morning little streams trickled down its granite surface, and the young trees and ferns which had seeded themselves in the crevices drooped and dripped.

Fifty-Seven

ACROSS THE ROAD the Shaw stone wall emerged from the woods and traveled with them to the wide gate across the Shaw lane. The grove was a thick black blot in this lachrymose light, hiding the house where Harry lay in his coffin. There were no animals in sight; they were either inside or sheltering in the grove from the light rain. A family of crows arriving just then to shatter the stillness would have sounded like a chorus of angels, Jennie thought.

"I cannot believe it about Harry," Pris said unsteadily. "But I keep thinking how he must look, dead. *Killed.* How can they stand being in the same house with him? And Lily, that poor child!"

At this moment the twins appeared on Gibraltar's crest, waving and grinning like happy travelers, and then disappeared. Jennie had not seen such bright faces since the sheriff's visit. She and Pris stepped across the ditch at its narrowest. All around them they heard the soft drip of water as they walked in among the thick-trunked old spruces and white birches, whose fallen yellow leaves gave an illusion of scattered light. The boys met them behind Gibraltar with a sort of Indian war dance, chanting in hoarse, cracking whispers, "We found them, we found them!"

They dragged their mother and sister ruthlessly to the great Y-shaped pine. The broad, bright shavings shone up at them like the gold coins Jennie had once carried in a velvet bag around her neck.

Carolus put his palms devoutly together, and rolled his eyes upward. "Whatever led him to this tree, God bless it," he murmured. "And let us not forget our little sister, guided infallibly by the Great Horse."

The piece of pine from which the shavings had been whittled lay

438

nearby, the bare wood as bright as the shavings. The layer of old pine needles was scraped and kicked up, with distinct grooves where boot heels had rested when someone stretched out his legs.

"We have not touched a thing," Carolus whispered. "But see here." He sank to his heels, and pointed to a thread of blue worsted glued to the trunk by a drop of pitch.

"I am afraid to believe it," Sandy said shakily. "They could still say it was us."

"But not beyond the shadow of a reasonable doubt, I told him." Carolus was in no doubt at all. Suddenly he and Pris giggled like William and Bell Ann, then subdued themselves, not easily, when Jennie shook her head at them. "Keep your voices down. We don't want anyone else to know yet." Like Sandy, Jennie was half-afraid to believe.

"What do we do?" Sandy asked. "Mount guard over these while someone goes to Tenby for the sheriff? That would take hours."

"Why not the deputy sheriff for Whittier?" Carolus suggested. "That would mean just going to North Whittier, and then it would be up to Mr. Nason. If neither of us is allowed on the road—David?"

"Am I useless, and invisible as well?" Pris asked acidly. "You two could keep each other company here, and keep *quiet* if you can possibly manage it, and I will ride Diana to North Whittier. I would *love* to."

Carolus hushed her with a swift, almost threatening, gesture. He was listening for something through the delicate drip and rustle. Then they heard the small, fragile, debilitated sound that was not from a catbird ghosting through the underbrush, and not from a gull unseen in the gray sky above the forest roof. They listened for it to come again, though their hearts were beating almost too loudly, trying to sense where it originated in the darkness beyond them where the growth was more dense.

"Again, come again," Sandy whispered as if in pain, and they heard something again, very slight but enough to send them all into the depths, ducking under or crawling over fallen giants, sloshing into boggy moss and standing puddles, sprinkled lavishly whenever someone hit a low-hanging bough. The women's hems and shoulders were heavy with wet, the overheated boys shed their jackets and tied the sleeves around their middles. A red squirrel's alarmed passage overhead brought a fresh shower.

Finally Jennie stopped them. "We could go in circles forever in here," she said. "We need the dogs."

"*Please*," a light voice implored, almost too faint to be heard. It was as if a tree had spoken.

Sandy shot away like Bounce, and Carolus plunged after him. Jennie stopped to release Pris from a dead branch that had caught her hood like a goblin hand, and then all was suddenly quiet again, except for the drip and a small woodpecker's tapping. The twins had disappeared, but the branches were still shaking from the boys' rough passage. The women pushed through and found them standing by a tall moss-draped spruce whose lower boughs swept the ground. A thin, high, despairing voice came from beneath them.

"Theo, are you there? Are you back? Please, God—" Then another single little wail: Bell Ann's baby.

At once Jennie was on her knees. The boys held back the boughs, and she crawled inside the natural tent. The aromatic essence of the forest was displaced by the pungency of sickness, sweaty clothing, and involuntary uncleanliness; this was somewhat diluted by the healthy redolence of horse and barn coming from the heavy blanket in which the woman was wrapped into a long bundle. A cracked earthenware mug stood near her head, beside a hard heel of bread half covered with ants.

"*Theo?*" the bundle quavered.

"I am Jennie Glenroy." Jennie crawled closer, and a dim oval of a face turned toward her, with eyes like holes in a piece of sheeting, and the twisting dark shape of a mouth trying to speak. Her breath was sour and hot with fever.

"Don't try to talk," Jennie told her. Heaven knows what I am inhaling, she thought fatalistically; it was too late now. "We will take you out of this place to a dry bed and warm food. Where is the baby?" She felt gently along the edge of the horse blanket, and touched a tiny living face and felt the miniature breath on her fingers.

Her reaction was a violent compulsion to take the child at once, shelter it in her arms, *save it*—she sat back on her heels, willing herself into a reasonable frame of mind.

"Sandy and Carolus," she said evenly, "go home and fetch the litter from the Yard. No one will be there yet, so you needn't explain."

"Yes, Mama." The departure was a thudding, thrashing escape from something which appalled them more than the shavings had elated them. Pris parted the branches and knelt to look in.

"What shall I do, Mama?" she asked. "Shall I carry the baby home? I would be glad to."

"*No.*" The woman spoke quite strongly.

"Of course not," Jennie told her. "We will take you both when my sons come back with the litter. Pris, love, go after them. Begin heating a kettle of bath water and make up a bed in the little room. Oh, and ask David to go for Dr. Neville, and to stop at Mr. Nason's house."

"Will you be all right?" Pris asked. "What if *he* comes back?"

"Do you see him?" The woman tried to push herself up on one elbow. Jennie said, "No, but we will leave a note for him." She slid her arm beneath shoulders so skeleton-like under damp and odorous clothes that she was revolted, but she held the woman firmly and lowered her back to an improvised pillow of some rumpled coarsely woven stuff. "He will be glad for you and the baby. Go along, Pris." If he killed Harry, he will not be back, she wanted to tell her.

Her legs ached, and she sat on the ground and stretched them out. What am I taking into my house, among my children? she wondered with a sad resignation. But there was no choice, and she could keep the children away from the sickroom.

She could not tell whether the woman was unconscious now; she had to lean over to hear her breathing, and the baby had ceased its small noises. What if they were both dying while she sat here? She should be glad they had been found in time so they would not die alone. But if the baby died, Bell Ann would never forgive the Great Horse, and that must not be. She rejoiced at the swooping arrival of curious and sociable chickadees, but they did not stay long enough. The little woodpecker worked overhead, well out of sight. She had no watch, and time had been at a sodden standstill since Bell Ann's grip kept her from getting out of bed this morning.

The two wrapped in the blanket were still breathing, but only just, it seemed to her, and there was an odd catch in the woman's throat. The baby would simply sleep away in its mother's arm; Jennie sought the woman's free hand in the tumble of blanket, to hold it while she passed from a world that must have used her very cruelly.

She could hardly find a pulse in the bony wrist. Tightly holding the hand, she laid her head on her drawn-up knees and waited. The fact that the boys might now be cleared swam in and out of her consciousness like a fish glimmering among growing seaweeds.

When the boys came with the litter, Pris had given them a shawl for the baby; Jennie removed the child from the mother's hold with a skill learned from detaching toys from sleeping children. The ragged blanket around the baby must have been soaked in urine and dried unwashed more than once. The baby was naked beneath it except for a ragged scrap of shirt, and it was a boy. She wrapped him snugly in the dry shawl and left the old one where she dropped it. He was as light in her arms as a bundle of twigs gathered in an apron, but he moved his limbs slightly, she thought and hoped. She handed him out to Carolus so she could crawl out; then, taking him, she moved aside while the boys began chopping branches. They had brought their hatchets in their belts.

When they had cleared enough away to take the litter in, she beckoned them aside in case the woman might be aroused enough to hear. "She is very sick and not able to attend to herself," she said.

"We know," said Sandy wryly. "Even with the scent of the cut branches."

"Hold your breath when you lift her, and be thankful we found her, for your sake as well as hers."

"Yes, *ma'am.*"

The litter was a strip of sail canvas long and wide enough to transport a man, with varnished maple poles pushed through broad hems on either side, sewn by sailmakers. The boys laid it on the ground beside the woman, and with a skill Jennie had not expected, they quickly raised her, still wrapped in the horse blanket, and set her on the litter. Sandy lifted her bare head to put the improvised pillow beneath it, while Carolus fastened the buckles of the canvas straps attached to the poles.

"The mug too?" he asked his mother.

"I don't think so."

The sick woman's hair was a long, lank tangle, darkened to a dirty brown by grime and sweat; sunken eyes slept in hollows bruise-colored, as if each one had been struck by a fist. The fevered and emaciated flesh was merely a covering stretched over cheekbones and jaw that seemed sharp enough to break through the skin.

The boys looked quickly away from her and took their agreed positions, Sandy leading. They would change places several times on the way. Jennie went ahead with the baby.

"Walk carefully," she said, "and rest when you need to."

"We cannot get there too soon for me," Carolus said. "I am not very happy about the view from here. And I wish I had not seen *his* face. I've never seen—"

He hushed himself before Jennie could, and they went the rest of the way without speaking except for a few words when they changed places. She knew that he had been about to say that he had never seen a small baby who might be only a few breaths away from death.

The sky was lifting and lightening from low cloud to a white ceiling, which became translucent and began to take on an ethereal blue so subtle one doubted it at first. They heard High Cockalorum and his juniors bringing up the sun, and by the time Jennie and the boys emerged into the field behind the house, the high priest and his acolytes had succeeded and were now praising themselves. Long opalescent rollers of cloud drifted seaward across the river before a new northwest breeze.

Pris opened the door and the dogs burst out, wild with welcome and unbearable curiosity. Even Darroch was prancing like a pup. Jennie whistled them away from the boys and the litter and let them see the baby; they sniffed delicately at the small face, the fragile eyelids flickered and there were mouse-like stirrings inside the shawl. Bounce whined and trembled; Darroch was like a benevolent uncle who says, "A very nice baby indeed."

"Put the litter on the camp bed," Jennie called after the boys. Bell Ann and William came running from the hen yard.

"I knew there was a baby," Bell Ann shrieked. "Let me hold it, Mama!"

"Not yet," Jennie said. "You may have a little peek, but you cannot hold him until we know whether or not he is sick." Bell Ann gazed with rapture at the wizened, bluish little face. William said interestedly, "He looks like a tiny monkey."

"He does not!" Bell Ann protested. "He is *beautiful*. And I just the same as found him, a real Babe in the Woods." She ducked her head to kiss him, but Jennie swung him out of reach.

"Not yet. Have you finished your chores?" Bell Ann, balancing on tiptoes to keep watching the baby, didn't answer.

"No," said William.

"So they are all telling me from out there. Go back and finish, and then we will see about your breakfast."

"David cooked scrambled eggs for us and made toast on a fork," William said with reminiscent pleasure.

"Off you go, then."

"But what about the sick lady?" he asked. "Pris would not tell us anything, and David has gone away in a hurry."

"I will tell you everything you need to know," Jennie promised, "as soon as Dr. Neville has been to see the lady and this little boy."

"My little boy," Bell Ann crooned. "Wait till I tell Sarie! I can hardly wait to hold him. Can he sleep in my room, Mama?"

"He is very weak, Bell Ann. He will need special care." She saw in William a pity and sadness that changed his eyes for that moment from a child's to a man's. He took Bell Ann's hand and started to tug her away. "We will finish up and then get ready for school, Mama."

"You are not going to school," she told them. Bell Ann was instantly ignited with happiness, but William said flatly, "Why?"

"Bell Ann must have told you about the man she calls the Wizard."

"When we were eating breakfast." He had clearly been impressed by Bell Ann's escapade. "I don't believe in wizards," he said with a mildly patronizing kindness, "but he is a bad man. Do you think *he's* the one—"

Jennie smoothly interrupted. "We don't know anything, and we must not talk about him to anyone until Bell Ann tells Mr. Swallow about him."

"Could he come back?" Bell Ann moved close to Jennie, looking fearfully about her. William itched, literally, with uneasiness, vigorously scratching his bare calves.

"I doubt it," Jennie said. "But the sheriff has to know about him before you can tell anyone else about him, either of you. When it is over, you may talk until your tongues wear out."

The dogs ran to meet the first men coming in, a perfect audience, and Bell Ann all but giving off sparks. Jennie held her by the shoulder. "Do I have your promise? Yours too, William? Without all the oaths and other furbelows?"

"Yes, Mama," they said. Bell Ann wanted a last look at the baby. She was not discouraged, she was doting. "I will think up names for him," she called over her shoulder as William dragged her toward the henyard.

The boys were waiting for her in the kitchen doorway, in a respectful uneasiness as if they did not know what to do next. "When this is over," she said to them, "I shall hug you until you yelp for mercy. In the meanwhile, wash your hands and get yourselves some breakfast. Pris, you might as well fill up on eggs, too."

"Mama," Carolus said somberly, "do you know what is under her head? Harry's coat, and the knife slashes and blood are plain."

"*Good*," she said briskly. "Now you can smile again, and eat a good meal."

"How can we eat in the same house with them?" Pris whispered. "And what if we had not gone there, and no one heard the baby's last cry?" Now that it was over, she was white and trembling.

"Don't think what might have been, or what might be," Jennie said. "We four found them and brought them here, and we can always be glad of that." Her eyes embraced, if her arms did not. She went into the winter kitchen. The woman lifted heavy lids; it was almost an insuperable effort. "*Theo?*"

"Not yet, but here is your little boy." She laid him in the curve of his mother's arm. "What is his name?"

There was no answer. "Would you like some water?" Jennie asked.

"Yes, please."

Pris was there at once with a cup and a towel. Jennie laid the towel on her arm, and raised the woman's head from Harry's coat until she could sip. After a few swallows she opened her eyes wide and tried to look around the room, then back to Jennie's face. Her eyes, bloodshot and shiny, were blue. "Theo said he would take us to a nice place."

"Yes, and here you are. Soon you will be comfortable in bed."

"I am not very clean." Her voice kept sinking, but she was disturbed.

"We will bathe you," Jennie promised. You have saved my sons, she wished she could say.

"But you can't, you are a lady! Theo will do it. Where is he?" She was trying to raise her voice, but it exhausted her.

"He will come soon. Would you like milk to drink?" But she was asleep or unconscious in the next instant. If you cannot speak, Jennie thought, the coat can. But I want you to live, you *deserve* to live, and he does too; she touched the baby's cheek with a finger.

Pris would not eat with them, but stayed in the winter kitchen with the woman and child. William and Bell Ann were sent up to the road to watch for Dr. Neville. The boys were not euphoric yet; silently they ate their way through mounds of scrambled eggs, and Jennie took a small portion. When the baby suddenly cried, they all rose involuntarily, and Pris called out to them, "Don't come, anyone. I am here."

"I don't want you holding him, Pris," Jennie said.

"I shan't." It was quiet after that; the boys returned to their meal, and Jennie went on tiptoe into the other room.

Pris knelt by the camp bed, delicately squeezing drops of milk from a twist of clean linen handkerchief onto the baby's tongue. Slate-blue eyes large in the little monkey face were fixed on hers. She dipped the twist again into the cup on a stool beside her, and repeated the process, and the small petal of tongue came out again.

"That's my little hero," she whispered to him, while his mother lay like one already dead. But, with one grand affirming salute to life, her son managed to get a fist free.

Fifty-Eight

I N MID-MORNING Jennie, Carlotta, and Pris drank coffee in the summer kitchen, waiting for the sheriff. David had gone on to Maddox and would deliver explanations to Mr. Dalrymple. The twins had taken William and Bell Ann fishing to occupy them; if Bell Ann could not sit by the baby or go to school to dumbfound everyone (especially Sarie) with the true tale of the Wizard and the Babe in the Woods, she could see no sense in anything else. "She is as crawly as an ant hill," William said.

They were fishing from the dory at the mouth of the cove, within easy summoning distance when they were needed, and the water was as calm as a silk coverlet.

Wearing one of Bell Ann's baby nightgowns, and guarded by Darroch, the infant slept in the cradle the boys had brought down from the attic. His mother had been bathed by Carlotta, and she was so frail the two women easily carried her to the small room adjoining Jennie's.

"You may as well burn her clothes," Carlotta said. "They were not much to begin with, and they are beyond redemption now."

She was ill with either a childbed infection or something which had set in when she arose too soon after the birth and took to the road with her man. She was very anemic. She had been bleeding, not heavily but almost constantly, she told Carlotta when she roused somewhat during the examination, fortified by warm milk and brandy. She was not sure of much else except that they had been coming a long way from where the baby was born; she could not say when that had been. She thought they had been several days in the woods. Theo had brought her the horse blanket from somewhere. She had actually smiled about that.

"I knowed he must have just took it," she said with a ghost of pride.

"From a barn when no one was home. He warn't afeard of dogs. He learned how to charm the fiercest dogs when he lived with the gypsies once."

After that she was too tired to speak, except to ask for Theo; the baby now seemed to have no importance.

"Theo is rightly named," Carlotta said cynically. "He is God to her."

David had given her enough information so she came prepared; in her emergency chest she kept supplies of old sheeting and worn blankets, and she had stopped at Kilburns' for goat's milk, and borrowed a nursing bottle. She had brought a short gown for the mother, and they placed her on a pad of old blanket and sheeting because of the slight bleeding and her helpless incontinence.

"She is dying," Carlotta told Jennie. "Between the infection and the bleeding, she has nothing left but adoration for Theo. He brought her the coat for a pillow because her head hurt, and he had her brought to this place, she says, and he will be here soon to sit by her. She will die believing it. I suppose there are worse deaths."

"At least she will not have to see him hanged," Jennie said.

At first Carlotta knew only that a woman and child had been deserted in the woods by the man who had probably killed Harry Shaw and decamped with the money. When Jennie told her of the twins' involvement, she was staggered.

"Dear God in heaven, why did you not send for me?"

"Everyone has a call on you, and what could you have done?"

Pris had gone into the other kitchen, to sew by the cradle. "But to go through this hell alone," Carlotta said, "without your husband—"

"David was here, and we all supported one another. I hardly dared to think about Alick, and I am still so caught up in the whirlwind, I shan't drop to earth until the sheriff has been here and says the twins are clear." Her throat dried. "What if she cannot talk to him? What if she is gone before he comes?"

Carlotta put a hand on her arm. "Jennie, she is not going to die in the next few hours, perhaps not in the next few days. But even if she is too weak to talk, she has already talked to me about the coat, and there is Bell Ann's story."

"And there is Theo—somewhere! I could laugh except that I would sound like a maniac even to myself."

Thankful Basto tapped at the open door and came in, alarmed by the sight of Carlotta. "Is Pris really sick, or the boys? William said at Muster Day they were catching something." She was carrying a covered jug.

"No, dear, it's none of us," Jennie told her.

Thankful blew hard with relief. "Beef tea," she said, setting the jug down. "Mama sent it. It's good for everything that ails you. I almost said that ails man or beast." She giggled. "Lord! I am some *glad* nobody in *this* house has the high fantods."

Pris appeared in the doorway, smiling like Bell Ann at the thought of astonishing Sarie. "Come and see," she murmured like a sorceress, and suddenly there seemed to be a dovecote in the winter kitchen, with all the cooing and crooning.

"Not only Bell Ann is enamored," Jennie said. "Only Garnet is disenchanted. She has not been near, even from curiosity. . . . Tell me what his chances are, Carlotta."

"Well, he is severely undernourished," Carlotta said, "and undersized too. I judge him to be about six weeks old. His mother has no milk left, if she ever had much. A few more days, and—" She lifted her long hands, then dropped them in finality. "But you may have found him in time. His strength is astonishing, under the circumstances. Have you felt him grip your finger? I have." She looked down at her cup, and spoke with a new softness that was almost shyness. "Jennie, when his mother is gone, I shall take him. The Overseers of the Poor will be grateful, because then he will cost the town nothing." She looked up quickly. "You are very quiet. Had you decided—?"

"Only Bell Ann, and she is not the last word in this house, much as she would like to be. Carlotta, for the past two days I have been trying to hold fast from one hour to the next. I expected that at *this* hour, *this* morning, I would be trying to tell Young Mr. Dalrymple that my twins were suspected of murder. But of one thing I am absolutely certain; I am not expecting another child by any *means*."

Carlotta's smile was that of a woman in love. She went in to see her patient again and then stopped by the cradle where a girl knelt on either side. "Every time he fusses, give him a few swallows, Pris," she said. "You might alternate the milk with water. He needs all the moisture he can take." She was now the kind but always objective doctor, but Jennie knew better. Live, baby, she implored. Live for the mother who is going to raise you.

Carlotta would not be back tonight; she had calls to keep her busy from now until dark. She expected no severe changes, but would return in the morning. Jennie saw her off, and then she herself returned to the small bedroom.

The young woman must have once been what was termed "a nice-looking girl." Carlotta had washed her hair, and it had dried to a natural fluffy brown like soft feathers. Long lashes softened the blue shadows under her eyes. She had a short, well-shaped nose, but it was hard to guess at her swollen and fever-blistered mouth. Her sharp jaw and corded throat, and the scrawny hands lying relaxed on the coverlet, looked as pitifully aged as the long eyelashes looked childishly young.

"Mama." Pris was just audible from the doorway. "Mr. Sparrow is here."

This time she could fully appreciate the handsome bigness of the man and respond to his courtesies almost with confidence. The deputy sheriff was with him, a portly young man who was trying to keep an authoritative all-business expression in the presence of two attractive girls.

The sheriff had the note David had left for him with Deputy Nason. Jennie told him about Bell Ann's confession and how they had followed it up, finding the shavings, and then the woman and child. She took him in to see the baby; Darroch placed himself between the man and the cradle until she beckoned him away. The deputy remained to make conversation with the girls, plainly a pleasure he had not expected when he rode to Tenby with David's note.

Jennie led Mr. Swallow to the bedroom, and tried to awaken the sleeper, sensing that the name *Theo* would do it, but she jibbed at such a deception. "I can tell you what little she said to me, and Dr. Neville will be able to tell you what she told her. And then there is this."

She took the coat from off a chest and handed it to him. "It is Harry Shaw's coat," she said. "It was under her head, and I can assure you my sons did not put it there."

After he examined the coat inside and out, he sat down in the chair beside the bed. "Not that I am casting aspersions on you or the doctor, Mrs. Glenroy, but I would like to talk to her."

"*I* would like you to, also," she said. "God knows I wish she could tell you everything herself."

"You have made her very comfortable. Some folks would have thought twice." He leaned close to the sleeping face, and said just above a whisper, "Speak to me," and she was at once gladly awake.

"*Theo?*" Her hands began to twist around one another.

It was confirmation that they had not invented the man. "He is on his way," the sheriff said. He took one of the girl's restless hands and held it. "How long has he been gone, do you remember?"

"I can't tell the days," she said anxiously.

"No need to fret yourself, my dear." He patted her hand, immensely reassuring. "Did he give you something before he went away?"

She put her free hand up to her neck. "It hurts. . . . He brought me something." She frowned, sighed. "A coat," she said finally. "And then he went away to find this place for me. He had *money*," she said with naïve pride. "He can always find it."

The sheriff laid her hand down. "Go to sleep now, and he may be here when you wake up." Obediently she shut her eyes, smiling. He arose, his broad comely face austere.

"Seemed a sin to lie to her, but it is not likely she will ever know," he said out in the hall.

"He is everything to her. She has not even asked for the baby."

Jennie rang the bell to call in the fishermen, and the sheriff wrote in his notebook while he waited. When they came, Bell Ann was called in; the three boys cleaned fish by the water barrel, and Pris and Thankful joined them.

Bell Ann was happy to have a new and respectful audience, since the boys had severely discouraged her; for fear, Carolus said, that she would wear out the tale and begin to decorate it with literary details. Alone with her mother and Mr. Swallow, with Mr. Nason taking down her words, she sat in her father's chair, smelling rather fishy, her bare feet tucked up on a rung, and told her story. The sheriff's questioning was both tactful and skillful, but she did not waver in her description. She knew what she had seen, and when.

"And I *knew* there was a baby," she said. "He is our new baby now. Did you see him? William says he looks like a monkey, but *I* think he is lovely."

"Do you think his mother will give him to you?" Mr. Swallow asked.

"Oh, she can stay too. We have room." She slid out of the chair and tiptoed into the winter kitchen. Darroch stood up and looked into the cradle with her.

"I reckon I don't need to ask any more questions here," the sheriff said. "Thank you, Mrs. Glenroy." He went out, carrying Harry's coat. The twins, Pris, and Jennie walked with the men to the barn where the horses were tied. William was diverted by the chance to stay alone with Thankful, while Bell Ann sang to the sleeping baby.

"*Sir*," said Sandy, "are we in the clear or not?"

"On the face of it," the sheriff said dryly, "there's more than a reasonable doubt. The man was there on Tuesday night, according to your Bell Ann. The girl said he brought her the coat and said he had money, and then disappeared. Nason and I will ride along and look for those shavings. Old Y-shaped pine close to your high ledge ought to be easy to find, but I doubt we'll need that evidence."

"Where do you think he is now, sir?" Carolus asked.

He didn't answer, but went on stuffing Harry's coat into a saddlebag. Then he swung himself up into the saddle and sat looking down at them.

"He is on a table in the morgue at Tenby Infirmary," he said without inflection. "The man was found early this morning in a barrel in a lime shed on a Tenby dock. Blue coat, boot with a hole in it, curly beard, and all. They'd been careful to ram the black hat in with him. Partridge feather got broken. He was beaten to death."

The children were shocked, but what surprised Jennie most was her lack of surprise; as if it were all fated, it could not be otherwise.

"He could have been any tramp, from anywhere," Swallow went on. "I never expected to find the answers down here. He had signed onto a lime carrier to leave early this morning. He was drinking in a tavern last night with some of his new shipmates, and they left him there playing cards. We will find the men who did him in," he said with a chilling assurance. "Harry's pistol too, maybe."

"He didn't keep Harry's money long, did he?" Sandy said. "It's true that blood money begets blood." He was neither satisfied nor vindictive, but thoughtful.

"But the worst thing," Carolus said bleakly, "was leaving those two to die. That was as cold-blooded as lying in wait for Harry, and it was worse because they were helpless and innocent. I hope he had time to remember that before he was dead." Jennie laid her hand on his arm. It was shaking.

"Oh Lord!" Mr. Swallow said with very human dismay. "I hate having to face the Shaws with that coat. The only good thing about today is giving you the word." He spoke particularly to the twins. "You two have stood up to this like men."

"Except when no one was looking," Carolus said, causing a little wave of relieved laughter.

"Of course, your mother and sisters weren't exactly standing around wringing their hands."

"That, too, went on in decent privacy," said Jennie.

"Let me show you where the shavings are!" Sandy burst forth. "If I don't go for a run and use up the way I feel, I'll explode into bits too small even for kindling."

"Come along," the sheriff invited.

Fifty-Nine

F OR THE REST of the day after the twins came back, they alternated between pure exultation, which sent them out to make the woods echo with savage whoops, and a restraint that made them tiptoe and speak low in the house, from which a life was slowly departing. Harry's murder would probably remain far more personal to them than that of the unseen and unknown Theo, simply because he *had* been unseen and unknown, even though they had been suspected of his crime. The Wizard would fade in time for Bell Ann; for William, he existed only through her. For Pris, the baby might erase the gruesome image of the barrel in the lime shed. But Jennie, in spite of her relief and gratitude, and the emotional and physical demands of caring for the mother, knew that she could easily be as haunted by the sheriff's description as by Shaw's description of Harry's body. That these murders had occurred in such intimate contact with the Glenroy world, that this world could have been threatened, that it had swung perilously on its frail axis and shivered above the abyss, would have made her head spin if she had not so much else to do. Baking, washing, ironing—wasn't it all wonderful? She could hardly wait to start.

As his mother's time ran out, the baby was gaining his. Since they had brought him home this morning, he had already become perceptibly stronger in voice and movement. The boys admired his fists and the feet on the pipestem legs, saying he would be a big man, well able to take care of himself. When Jennie held him to her shoulder and patted his back to raise wind, and he produced a very small but emphatic belch, they applauded. They called him Hercules, which was grudgingly accepted by

Bell Ann. "For the time being," she warned them, "till I make up my mind."

They had a picnic sort of meal at noon; it was too hot to build a fire to cook their fish. Thankful returned early with a basketful of new bread and a pound of butter, and a message from her mother; when the time came, Mrs. Basto was to be sent for at once, at any hour of the day or night. This mystified the younger children; Jennie could see it in William's eyes. *What time? What for?* She forestalled spoken questions by sending them all to dig the rest of the potatoes. Bell Ann would rather hang around the cradle than pick up potatoes and put them in the basket, even with the promise of a swim afterward, but she was sent anyway. The older girls sat outdoors deciding the details of Thankful's wedding dress, with the cradle moved to the summer kitchen so they could hear the baby. Darroch left nursery duty to go with Bounce to the potato patch, where life could become riotous when the little pig potatoes began flying back and forth. The children would have to pick them all up afterward, except for those which the dogs had bitten.

Jennie heated beef tea on the spirit lamp and took some to the small bedroom. The long eyelashes were fluttering, and Jennie lifted the woman and held a teaspoon to her lips. She sighed and slipped back to sleep again without taking anything. "I must have a name for you," Jennie said softly. "What shall it be? Florinda? Charmain? Rosamund? Or Mary Ann, for someone I loved very much when I was young?" Without opening her eyes, the woman smiled. Now that she was safe, clean, and warm, and Theo was on his way to her, she was a girl again, she looked bathed in the elixir of youth, with trust and innocence restored to her, and even the hollows of her eyes and the shadows under them seemed the texture and color of violet petals.

Jennie sat in a rocker with her feet on Andrew Glenroy's chest, reading Washington Irving's *Tales of a Traveller*. She suspected that if she began to drift, the barrel and its passenger would be adrift with her, blue coat, black hat, partridge feather and all. The windows were open to one of those long, still afternoons peculiar to September, neither summer nor autumn but the intermission before the first swamp maple flamed out and the brackens turned tawny. Crickets were louder than birds, and the children's voices down in the field sounded as far away as the ships.

Jennie fell asleep as effortlessly as the day flowed toward sundown. The grandfather clock aroused her, striking three. She felt refreshed and actually hungry for the first time since Wednesday morning. Then she was dismayed to think the girl might have died while she slept; but she lived on, her breathing shallow but regular. Out in the kitchen, Pris had made a pot of tea, and Hercules was comfortably drugged by a recent ration of goat's milk. Down in the field, the potato harvesting had ended and been replaced by something like a demented combination of round-ers, cricket, and Rugby football, with the dogs racing in and out of the chaos and Bell Ann shouting as loud as anyone. From across the road, the horses, pony, and cows watched with that utterly entranced attention which made them such a satisfactory audience.

Jennie poured a cup of tea for herself, and she and the girls were sitting on the bench, Jennie with a new-minted appreciation of laughter as a gift given where it is deserved, when Miriam came around the corner of the house past the woodpile and the rainwater barrel. She answered their greetings gravely. Pris asked her to have a cup of tea and one of Mrs. Basto's raisin buns.

"No, thank you, a mug of cold water'll do me fine. I just had lemonade and apple cider cake at the Phippses. It was real arregorical. But I'm thirsty again."

"Help yourself," said Jennie. Miriam stopped short inside the door, staring at the cradle as if at a hallucination. She wet her lips. "'Tis true, then," she said huskily. Jennie arose and went in.

"What is true, Miriam?"

"Is there—was there—" She was overwhelmed as Jennie had never seen her before. "A woman *too*? In the woods? And it was *you* who found her?"

"Bell Ann heard the baby cry, the rest of us found him and his mother. Has the story traveled so fast since this morning?"

Miriam shook her head, her eyes still on the hooded cradle. "My Auntie Mab read it in her cards last night. And she only took them out because Pa was away fishing. He don't approve of the cards, so we wouldn't have known till we heard it somewhere else. But she saw a woman and a baby. And *death*." Death was a presence, a masked and hooded entity in some grotesque old masterpiece. He would carry a scythe, and a skull would grin behind the mask.

"Mrs. Glenroy," Miriam said reluctantly, "Could I see her? It's not prying. But I have an awful queer feeling about this." Her eyes beseeched.

The room was half-submerged in the aureate light coming in under the half-drawn shades, so that the girl lay in a gilded slumber on a bed that seemed to float above ankle-deep shadows. Miriam passed Jennie and took hold of the low rail at the foot.

"Why, *Saffy*!" she said in the clear voice of an amazed child, and the girl's eyes opened in the violet-blue hollows and gazed straight at her.

"Is that little Mim?" It was very dim, but distinct. With an effort that made Jennie hurt in sympathy, she lifted one hand and beckoned; then it fell back on the coverlet like a hand of marble.

At once Miriam was kneeling by the bed, holding the marble hand against her cheek. "Oh, Saffy," she said in a voice full of tears. "Where did you go? Why didn't you ever come back?"

Jennie went out and shut the door. In the sanctuary of her room she stood by the front windows without seeing down through the orchard trees to the diminishing riot in the potato garden. The truth, when she knew it, would have the everything-in-its-place inevitability of a Greek tragedy. Eight years ago, when Bell Ann was conceived in love, Harry Shaw raped the fifteen-year-old pauper who was the family slavey. Now she had come back, and she had brought Harry's death with her.

In a little while Miriam tapped at the door and came in. "She's sleeping," she said. "She drifted right away from me."

Jennie waved her to a chair and sat down on the bed. "Saffy," she said musingly. "*Sapphire*. Was she able to tell you much?"

Miriam sat straight with bare feet together and her hands folded.

"Mostly she wanted me to tell my folks she'd never sold herself on the streets. She couldn't find her kin in Boston, but Old Cap'n Alley left her with decent folks who had a bake shop near the harbor, and she worked there, and she met a good boy, a sailor, and they were pledged. He was lost overboard." One small sniffle. Jennie got up and gave her a handkerchief. "Then, after that, she stayed with the old folk until they died and a nephew took the shop and put her out. Theo," she frowned at the unfamiliar name, "he knew who she was, and he took care of her. She is waiting for him now. She says he is good, he brought her here to see Lily, but she thinks she got up too soon. And she hasn't seen Lily yet. . . . I had to put my ear right to her mouth. . . . Way he hurried her onto the road I wonder if he was in trouble?"

Jennie nodded. "It could be."

"She wanted to go to the Keel, but he wouldn't let her. I reckon he didn't want questions," Miriam said shrewdly. "I think he was in bad in Boston."

"So they slept in the woods, and she has not yet seen Lily, and Theo is dead."

"*No!*" Miriam cried out, then hastily muffled her mouth.

"They think he killed Harry for his money, and then *he* was killed over in Tenby for the same money. We found *her* in the woods this morning. She wouldn't tell us her name," Jennie said.

"She was always clear in her head about what she aimed to do, and no soul alive could make her change course. My folks tried." She sounded elderly and sad. "She's been gone so long, but she never forgot Lily. She wasn't Lily then, just her baby, no matter how she got it. Mrs. Glenroy, she's come a long way and it's about killed her. Couldn't—isn't there some way?" she pleaded. "Just one little sight of her? Lily needn't know who she is."

"Lily isn't allowed here, Miriam, and I don't know who could go to the Shaws now, and tell them Saffy's here. What good would it do?"

"I suppose you're right," Miriam said disconsolately. "You know, she worships that Theo, but she never mentioned the baby, even when I asked about him."

"It is probably because she is sick and confused, but he will go to a good home," Jennie said.

"With *you?*"

Jennie smiled at her eager response. "No, but you won't be disappointed when you find out."

Miriam lowered her head and gazed for some time at her feet. Then she sighed and stood up. "I will bring you back your handkerchief all washed, Mrs. Glenroy."

Thankful had gone, and Pris was alone with the baby; the others were all swimming. Miriam watched the baby eat and accepted an invitation to hold him. She had nothing to say, but looked a long time into his face. It occurred to Jennie that this nameless child was a half-brother to Lily Shaw, and if he lived, he would grow up in the same town, but neither Lily, nor he, nor the Shaws were ever likely to know.

When Miriam had gone, still refusing a raisin bun, Pris said with mild wonder, "Miriam cried for her, didn't she? I think I will likely cry later, but Mama, as long as she is living you believe that anything can happen."

"Dr. Neville gives no hope of that, I'm afraid."

"Then she will never have to know what happened to her Theo." She shuddered. "The way Mr. Swallow *described* it. . . . And by now Harry is buried. *Harry!* I don't believe it, any more than I could believe it about

Caroline." With a sad little smile she asked, "Do you think the Great Horse will come for Harry?"

"Mercy! Let us hope that Bell Ann does not begin to ponder *that* question out loud and at length."

"I believe this infant needs his napkin changed," Pris said. "You are a very leaky little boy," she told him. "As Thankful says, having more experience than me, it's all in one end and out the other." She carried him to the camp bed and laid him on a towel. Jennie did not offer help, but watched with amusement and some pride as Pris efficiently washed and powdered him and pinned him into one of Bell Ann's napkins. She had been too young to attend to any of her brothers, but just since this morning she had become uncringingly expert. But then, Pris did everything well.

She wrapped Hercules again and handed him to her mother, then picked up the pail of the latest napkins to take up to the wash house and put to soak in a tub. "Why don't you go and swim with the others before supper?" Jennie suggested. "I am sure you can trust me with him."

Pris grinned. "Thank you, I shall. I haven't changed my mind, you know. This experience hasn't convinced me I was born to be simply a mother and nothing else. You're not offended, are you?" She stopped in the doorway.

"No, because I never thought I was born to be simply a mother, either. I had my ideas too. I would have begun a school in the Highlands if America had not beckoned me so enticingly. But there is nothing simple about being a mother, whether you're a hen, a cat, or a woman."

"I only hope I manage so well," said Pris, "because I intend to have a family once I have my business established." She went out swinging the pail and whistling. Jennie told Hercules he was beautiful, yes he *was*, and he stared up at her with eyes the color of ripe blueberries.

When David came home, the children were doing their chores and the baby lay awake but quiet in the cradle. Jennie had new potatoes and carrots cooking and pork scraps frying in the big iron skillet where she would later fry the day's catch. The dogs had been fed, and Garnet, who had been skulking around the outer edge of things all day, came in for her supper, shunned the cradle, and hastened into Jennie's room.

David looked as if nothing unusual had transpired that day. His serenity meant he knew the boys had been cleared. He visited the cradle and gave Hercules his forefinger to grip; the two regarded each other long and soberly. When he straightened up, his lips said, "The mother?"

"She is still with us, but not for long. What about Mr. Dalrymple?"

He wrote the answer. "I told him what happened, so he would have the straight of it when the story came out. He sent you all his heartiest congratulations"

"Thank you again, David. I don't know what we would have done without you. And I mean that more every time I say it. How is the portrait coming?"

"Almost there." He gave her a faint smile and went upstairs.

She mixed up a skillet cake, half cake and half pudding, to cook on top of the stove and be eaten with heavy cream dusted with sugar and cinnamon. Supper was an unusually quiet meal. Everyone was tired enough to give all attention to the food and not waste energy in conversation. The dessert rated some muted applause, and William said pensively, "It is too bad the lady can't have some of it. And Hercules is too young to appreciate it." He did not object when Jennie ordered early bed. "Me too," Sandy said unintelligibly through a yawn. The only one to object was Bell Ann when she found out that Pris intended to sleep on the camp bed with the cradle beside her.

"It is not fair!" she wept. "I just the same as found him, and I cannot do *anything*!"

"You can hold him," Jennie said. "Come upstairs and get ready for bed, and then you can come down and sit in the rocker and hold him." Bell Ann was so tired she made heavy weather of it on the stairs, and in the end Jennie had to undress her. When her nightdress went over her head she fell sidewise, curled herself up and put her thumb in her mouth, and was asleep for the night.

William had followed them upstairs, and Jennie went in to speak to him. He sat crosslegged on his bed, holding one of his models in his hand and sighting along the bowsprit.

"Darling," Jennie said, "you had better wash those feet before you put them between the sheets."

"Oh, fiddle," he said amiably. "I should've hid them from you." He patted the bed and she sat down beside him. "That lady is going to die, isn't she?" he asked.

"All we know is what we see. Dr. Neville doesn't think she has any strength left. But she is in no pain, she just sleeps, and perhaps she has pleasant dreams."

"Bell Ann says Hercules is going to stay here if his father doesn't come back, because then he will be an orphan and we can be his family."

Was he apprehensive about this? She couldn't tell; he looked at her as he always did when he was worried, moved, or in awe. "Because," he went on, "she is just like me with Jerome, but she is littler, she cannot understand everything. If the baby dies, or if he goes to the Poor Farm, what will she do?"

"Dr. Neville thinks he may survive, and he will not go to the Poor Farm. There are people who would love to have him."

"Bell Ann would, and I reckon I wouldn't mind." Old moderate Sweet William. She gave him a companionable squeeze.

"Your father and I cannot be selfish. After all, we have five of you."

He bounced up onto his knees, laughing. "What will Papa say about all this?"

And *all this* is so much more than you know, Jennie thought. "Go downstairs and wash your feet, love," she said to him.

"I washed off the salt water after I swam," he protested, "and my feet were clean then."

"Ah, but where have they been since?"

Downstairs Pris had begun feeding the baby, with the dogs watching and David sketching the scene. The twins were washing and wiping dishes. They were bleary-eyed and sagging, endangering the crockery. "Go to bed," she ordered them. "I will finish up."

"You are a prince among women," Carolus told her.

"Indeed," said Sandy. A haphazard kiss landed on her cheekbone.

"But wash your feet first," she said, "if you can manage not to drown yourself in the rainwater barrel."

In a few minutes she heard William giggling out there, and she called, "No water fights! Everyone up to bed with clean feet in the next fifteen minutes!" It was pure bliss to be forbidding water fights and setting deadlines. She would sleep tonight; even sitting up with Saffy and waking up whenever the girl stirred, she would be able to fall asleep again. She looked forward to it without guilt. There was nothing she could do for Saffy except to make her feel cherished, to promise her Theo would come, and to hope that her heart would gently stop before she began to be afraid without him.

David went for a sunset walk with the dogs; Jennie finished the dishes and helped Pris to make up the camp bed. Pris went upstairs and came down in her nightgown and wrapper, "They are all sleeping so hard up there already, it's as if they've been put under a spell," she said. "And I am already sliding under it too."

They moved the cradle closer to the camp bed, and Jennie put a new candle in the holder on the table so it would burn all night. "I hope he won't wake you too often."

Pris stretched out under the covers and folded her hands behind her head. "Oh, this feels as lovely as a cloud should be." She looked half-lost in a lyric dream, like a maiden in one of the old Italian paintings, lacking only the little Cupids shooting arrows and dropping roses. "I will survive," she said languidly. "What about you?"

"I can survive anything, knowing the boys are safe. Good night, love." She kissed Pris and left her, carrying another new candle for Saffy's room, which now lay in a twilight rosily tinged by the afterglow over the black western woods. She set the candle on the nightstand beside the bed and moved a straight chair close to it. The supplies for tending Saffy were on a chest of drawers, and she put a washbowl on the chair and brought what else she needed to the bed. She changed the padding under Saffy, and washed her as gently as possible. The girl awoke enough to make her sleepy protest that Jennie was a lady and Theo would do it. She refused both milk and water.

Jennie put the candle across the room and set the basket of soiled clothes out in the hall. In her own room she undressed and bathed with slow motions, hoping there would not be any sudden calls on her; she was sure she couldn't quickly escape from this heavenly lassitude. Garnet was purring from the bed, and the sound turned Jennie's eyelids to lead weights. She went into the sickroom carrying a pillow and a knitted blanket and made herself comfortable in the rocking chair. Garnet followed her in, making a wide circle around the bed, and got up into her lap, warm and heavy.

"What a nice girl you are," Jennie murmured, and put her head back against the pillow and shut her eyes. Then she remembered Harry Shaw had been buried today. For the first time in the whole affair, she wept. Tears ran out the corner of her eyes, and her throat ached as if with the quinsy when she imagined Mrs. Shaw taking out and examining her memories of a baby she had borne, who fed at her breast, who had delighted her with his first smile, his first steps, his first words. It was hard to imagine that even Mr. Lockhart could give any solace to this monolith of a woman, but the service would have been well attended; the neighbors were kind. Jennie knew from Thankful that her parents had gone, even though they had been discouraged for years. All would show respect, bringing what flowers still bloomed in their dooryards. Certainly those persons whose family funerals Mrs. Shaw had attended should have reciprocated, Jennie thought with sad humor, wiping her eyes on a corner of the blanket.

What of Lily through all this? Had she been forced to see Harry in his coffin, her hand taken and made to touch his? Told to kiss him? Dressed according to barbaric custom in black? What dreams would be hers, and was she ever held like Bell Ann and rocked back to safety?

At least there was still a young life in the house for Harry's mother, an assurance unthreatened by the knowledge that Lily's mother had come back to see her child and now lay dying of it.

But what a savage truth to fling in Garland Shaw's face, what a revenge for his attack on the twins! My God, how I would love to tell him that! she thought, knowing she never would. Presumably he had not always despised his son, and to bury his only child should have scarred even him.

She slept deeply and woke up while the clock was striking ten, surprised not to be in her own bed. Candlelight shivered slightly on walls and ceiling; outside the crickets went on and on. She listened for Saffy's breathing, but Garnet had begun to purr as soon as she felt Jennie rouse, and drowned everything but the crickets. Jennie slid out from under the cat and the blanket, and the cool floor under her feet completed her waking.

Saffy was still breathing. The room was cooler, and Jennie put another light blanket over her. She went out in the hall and listened at the foot of the stairs; someone was lightly snoring, a peaceful, serene sound. In the winter kitchen Pris slept on the camp bed with her face turned toward the cradle and her hands under her cheek. Darroch lay on the other side of the cradle; he greeted Jennie with one beat of his tail, not lifting his head from his paws. Bounce was curled up behind Pris's legs, with his chin resting on her ankle. His eyes shone out at her through his forelock. "Stay," she whispered.

There were signs that Pris had been up and attended to the baby not long ago. He slept, dry and replete, as well as she did. Pris, you're a marvel, Jennie thought. Wait until I tell your father.

She went back to the rocking chair in Saffy's room. Garnet was stubbornly limp, and moving her from chair to lap was like trying to shift a large bag of sand with the contents constantly slipping from one end to the other. Then Jennie's pillow needed prodding to support her neck, but finally all was arranged and she could think of Alick without interruption.

He would never forgive himself for not knowing, for not sensing something, or for going at all, and he had enough scars already. I will mend you, *mo graidh, mo chridh*, she promised him, and the children will, and the ship waiting to be launched, and the ship waiting to be born.

The last words trailed off and sleep rose around her like a warm bath, and all the colors of the spectrum danced on her eyelashes in the instant before her eyes closed.

"*Theo!*" Saffy's voice was distant, and Jennie sat upright, staring toward the bed. In her lap Garnet was alert. The girl was panting, attempting to push herself up, whimpering, trying to speak and laugh at the same time. "*Theo,*" she repeated.

This is the end, Jennie thought, and a happy one; she sees him. Garnet jumped down and ran across the room, not in escape but with her tail straight up and in greeting, and a figure moved from the shadowed doorway into the candlelight.

"I knew you would come," Saffy said clearly. The man was *dead*; he had been *seen* dead, and Garnet was surely not welcoming a ghost.

It was to Alick's credit that he asked no questions, not even with his face. He reached out to Jennie and they embraced, but they didn't look at each other, only at Saffy, who had fallen back with tears running from her closed eyes.

"Go to her, Alick," Jennie whispered. "Be Theo. She has been waiting for him, and he is dead."

He sat down beside the bed and reached for Saffy's hand, but it eluded him and wavered to his face. "You shaved it off," she murmured. "That's good. I hated it."

He took the hand in both of his and held it to his lips; Jennie thought she had never loved him more.

"I thought you went away on a ship." It was barely audible.

"Och, I—," Alick stopped and made a palpable effort to speak without his accent, by not saying enough for her to realize he was a stranger, and keeping it to a near-whisper. "I would not leave you."

Her smile was beatific. "I know you would not." She rested while she collected more breath. "Will you bring her here?"

He looked at Jennie, who nodded. "Indeed I will," he answered.

"They call her Lily." The last word almost faded to nothing but he heard it, and he turned an astonished face toward Jennie. *Have I heard aright?*

"Yes," she said. "This is Saffy."

"A *Dhia!*" he whispered.

Saffy's fingers were trying to curl around his. She was gone far beyond words, but not beyond adoration. Her eyes brimmed with all she could not say, and then, easily and quickly, she died.

Alick felt for the pulse in her wrist, then in her throat. He rose and came to Jennie and they embraced again but didn't speak. Garnet polished their legs; her purr and the crickets outside made the only sounds.

Sixty

W E CANNOT LEAVE her like this," Jennie said at last. "Nora said to send for her at any hour of the day or night." They went out arm in arm, listening at the foot of the stairs, and then tiptoed across the winter kitchen, the cat hurrying ahead. The dogs rose and quietly followed them out into the summer kitchen. Alick shut the doors between and reached for Jennie again, and the dogs went into the transports earlier denied them.

"I will tell you everything," she said, "but she must not be left."

"I am feeling," he said, "as if I have strong drink taken. For the love of your husband, will you not be giving the man a wee strupach before he sets out to fetch the woman? I have walked from Maddox this night like a tinker with my bedroll on my back, a welcome change from pounding in the stage from Belfast, mind you. Then, with my throat dry as the road, I come into my house and find my daughter sleeping in the kitchen with her hand on the family cradle, where an irresponsible fairy has left her wean to be fostered on us, and I must quench the innocent beasts' natural joy at beholding their master, and follow to the next candle, where I am just in time to hold a strange lass's hand while she dies believing me to be her lover."

"That was an eloquent speech, even for a Gael," she told him. "Almost a poem, the Wanderer's Lament. If I can bear to let go of you, I will find you a meal and tell you all. I don't suppose another hour will make much difference to poor Saffy. Or I could wake the twins or David to go."

"No. Let them sleep. I want time for you and me, then I will be going for Nora."

She lighted a lamp and put the kettle on, and brought out cold food and the last wedge of the skillet cake, while he washed up at the sink. When he sat down across from her in his shirt sleeves, his skin glowing from the cold water, she said, "Do I look young enough to be your wife? I feel as if you're about David's age, and I could be mother to you both."

"You look tired to the bone," he said seriously, "but beautiful. You are worn out with sitting and nursing the girl. How came they here? Did our children find them on the road and bring them?" he asked wryly.

"In a manner of speaking," she said. She reached out to him. "Would you take my hand? It began so quietly, the day after you left, the day before Muster Day. But for Harry it began on the Tuesday night."

The news about Harry was jolt enough, but that his sons should be named was unbearable, even in retrospect. He walked back and forth, white about the mouth as if in pain and speaking in a torrent of Gaelic. "My children in such peril, and myself not here to drive it off. And the terror that was at my wife! I will never forgive myself!"

She stopped his pacing by holding him in one place. "Alick, you would have been proud of us. We did the best we could without you, *because* of you, because we knew how you would want us to be."

He gave her a savage smile. "And how was that? I would have been a madman. Shaw grieved or not—I'd not have had him in my house."

"The sheriff was a gentleman, and Garland quieted when I told him we would bring an action. It is over, Alick, and I don't want to remember those two days as long as I live," she said, "except for the great blinding revelation when Bell Ann confessed her naughtiness."

She coaxed him down again and told him the rest; the Wizard, the shavings, Bell Ann's perfect description, the coat, and Saffy's innocent contribution when the man was already dead.

"Only the Gunns and you and I know who she is," she said. "It'd be the last thing the Shaws need to know, or the town. Carlotta should be told the connection, but otherwise they are just anonymous wanderers."

"We will not begrudge her a corner here to lie in," he said. "And we can give her a name. We are good at that!"

He left with the lantern, and Jennie went to get dressed. Pris stirred when she passed, but neither she nor the baby woke. Jennie felt light-headed but capable, as if she could go on for hours now.

Alick was back with the Bastos in a little over a half hour; it was nearly midnight.

"I didn't want to send for Minnie Ledyard at such an hour," Nora said.

"I can lay out the poor girl alone. It's just the company of it, having someone else."

"I will help," Jennie said calmly. "If I could wash her while she was living, I can do it now. Tell me what you will need."

"I've brought most of it. I keep it ready," Nora said matter-of-factly. "You can supply the warm water."

When they returned to the men talking in the kitchen, Saffy lay in fresh sheets, bathed and brushed; she was wearing one of Jennie's best cambric nightgowns, with a lacy collar softening her gaunt throat and lace-edged cuffs around her emaciated wrists.

"It's not likely she ever had anything that nice in her life, poor lamb," Nora said. "Still, you can't tell what she might have come away from to follow the man. Could have folks crying their eyes out for her now, but they'll never know what happened to her, will they?"

She had a cup of fresh tea and one of her own raisin buns and butter. "I have my second wind now," she said comfortably. "I don't mind it a bit being midnight. Been too long since the old man and I went strolling under the stars." She gave Nick a mighty nudge in the ribs, and he grinned; Jennie saw them for a moment as they must have been when they were a courting couple.

"And *you* two," she said to the Glenroys, "don't you sit up with her. What does she care? You were with her when it was needful. I know sitting up with the dead's thought to be respectful, but it is what you do for the living that counts." Collecting herself, putting on her shawl, she said, "They'll likely put her in the graveyard over to the Poor Farm. That always seems a shame to me, and they've not even a name to scratch on a stone."

"We will be keeping her here, Nora," Alick said. "Tomorrow I will be building her coffin. I have some perfect boards at the Yard."

"The boys and I will be over after dinner to dig the grave, then," Nick said. "I reckon we can do that much."

Jennie and Alick and the dogs walked out with them in the cool starry night, as far as the Squaw Rock. They came back yawning and weaving, as if trying to hold each other up; they undressed in the dark and sagged into bed and into each other's arms. Jennie felt like one great pulse or hundreds of little ones; it was a mercy they all beat in time, she thought drunkenly, her head on Alick's shoulder, and he was holding her as if someone would try to forcibly take her from him.

She was very aware of the closed door between them and the small bedroom, of Saffy lying with folded hands in starlight while, unseen by her, the Big Dipper emptied itself outside the top sash of the north window.

Goodnight, Saffy, Jennie thought, but not goodbye. You will not be alone there, the babies will be with you.

Alick had left his bedroll in the summer kitchen, and as the house gradually came to life this token of his presence was discovered by one child after another. It was the first morning ever that at least one parent was not up before the children; Jennie and Alick lay listening to the traffic on the stairs, hushed for Saffy's sake, then the occasional yelp of joyful surprise when the bedroll was discovered. The muted din occasionally penetrated closed doors.

Jennie had never felt so much like lying in bed, except after childbirth or with a rare indisposition; it was as if she could lie there for hours in Alick's arm, heavy as a comb of honey, every cell filled with the sweetness of knowing they were safe and Alick was home.

But after innumerable cups of tea at midnight, the call of Nature was peremptory, and she had to get up. "Come back to bed," Alick invited. "They are famous without us out there."

"Pris will be wanting to milk, unless I am willing to do it, and I would rather tend the baby."

"Och, I was forgetting Himself."

Out in the kitchen David went on imperturbably building the fire when havoc broke loose at the sight of Alick. Dogs barked and bounded about; Bell Ann launched herself at him and fastened to him with arms and legs. He reached out for William and kissed them both, then releasing himself from Bell Ann's four-limbed grip, he took Pris in his arms. She said tearfully, "Oh, Papa!" Smiling, he held her off, then drew her to him and kissed her again. "I don't know why I want to cry when I am so happy," she said.

The twins stood back grinning, until he took one in each arm and held them to him, resting his cheek against one head and then the other, his eyes shut, keeping the boys there until he could speak. Then he sent them off with a slap on the rear.

"To your chores now, and I will be fixing breakfast for heroes."

"And it isn't even Sunday," William marveled.

"It is more than a Sunday, it is a new holiday your mother and I have just ordained." He touched William's head. "Go now." Bell Ann held back.

"But Papa, you haven't seen our baby yet!"

"I will be seeing the baby while you are looking after your friends out there."

When she had gone, he and David shook hands. "You were here when I could not be," he said. "I will never forget that, and I thank you."

"David went far beyond the call of duty," Jennie said. "He took William and Bell Ann to Muster Day, for *all* day."

"Och, a man of supernatural courage!" Alick said.

David asked about the timbering expedition. "We found what we needed for *Dolphin* in two days," Alick said. "Man, there is enough there for a fleet of ships! We may be building our own line one day." He was interrupted by a small fussing from the cradle. Jennie moved, but Alick was faster. "I must be looking at this heroic baby before Bell Ann casts me off." He scooped Hercules up in his wrappings, expertly cradling the head, murmuring to him. The baby stopped fussing. "Intelligent child; he understands the Gaelic," Alick said. Settling him comfortably on his arm, he began walking.

"Hercules looks much less like a baby monkey today," Jennie said, "and he has a bit of pink." She and David watched Alick walking back and forth, singing as he had sung to his own. "He is making a cattle thief out of that child," Jennie said to David. "Promising him a great future in looting the neighbors' pastures and poaching the Laird's salmon."

"And the baby is taking it all in," David said.

Alick finished verse and refrain, and looked at them with a smile. "He is trying to speak. He may be a genius, this fairy wean."

"Alick," Jennie said tentatively, "if Carlotta had not spoken for him—"

She didn't need to finish it. "Holding him is dangerous," Alick said. "The wee bottom in one hand and the wee head in the other, that is seduction, *mo ghaoil*. I was loving him at first sight—who would not? The little thing is so helpless. But she is the one who needs him. Think of all the wee bottoms and heads her hands have held, and none of them belonging to a child of hers." He tipped up his arm and met Hercules' kitten-stare. "She cannot quite be making a child of Michael now, can she, my bonny boy?"

Priscilla was the quiet one through breakfast, and she followed Jennie when her mother went to tidy her and Alick's room. Bell Ann was rocking the baby.

"She is gone, isn't she? I guessed, because you have not been near that room since you got up, and last night I dreamed that people kept going back and forth."

"That wasn't quite a dream. Mrs. Basto was here and we attended to her. She died a little after ten. Your father had just come home, and she thought he was Theo. He held her hands without the slightest idea what it was all about, and she died smiling."

Pris sniffled a little. "I am so glad for her, and I think Papa is the best man in the world."

"So do I," Jennie said. "We will put her with the babies and have a private service at the grave."

"Mr. Lockhart will know just the right words to say, and that will make us *really* cry." She blew her nose. "What about Hercules?"

"Are you going to weep bitterly at the thought of giving him up to someone else?"

"*No.*" Pris was emphatic. "Not as long as they treat him as their own child and not as a pauper boarded out by the town to someone who simply wants the money."

"I'm sure the selectmen would find a good home for him. But Dr. Neville wants him."

"That's all right, then," Pris said with satisfaction. "It is more than all right, it is perfect. Except for Bell Ann," she added wryly. "What with the baby and having Papa home, she is beside herself. It's like having a half-dozen Bell Anns. She will be howling her head off by suppertime."

"I am afraid of that," Jennie admitted.

It was Saturday, and no men would be coming to work; presently Alick would go down to the Yard and begin to build the coffin. Jennie gathered the children together and told them about the death.

The twins took it with a sober lack of surprise. William was more acquainted with death than he had been six months ago; he had know Caroline, Jerome, and Harry, and for a day and a night life in his home had revolved around a dying person as it revolved, so happily, around his father now. But whatever he was thinking, he was not telling it.

Bell Ann had the most to say. Sitting on her father's lap, she said confidently, "The Great Horse will come for the lady. But where will she be planted like a flower to wait for him?"

"Where the babies are," Jennie said.

"They aren't there," Bell Ann corrected her. "Only their stones." Jennie agreed. She waited now for questions about the living baby, but Bell Ann didn't ask, and she was reluctant to open the subject. Jennie, you've aged this week and you have become a coward in your old age, she told herself.

Bell Ann was fascinated by the idea of 'the lady' lying there in the small bedroom. She slid off Alick's knee and whispered in William's ear. He pulled his head away and rubbed his ear, and said crossly, "I *know* it!"

"But you don't know *everything*. You don't know what she is doing in there."

"She isn't doing anything. She can't. She is just lying there like somebody asleep."

"Because her soul has fled," said Carolus seriously, and this swept away the dam for them all. What was a soul, where was it kept, where did it go? Bell Ann denied the whole idea. The lady would wake up when the Great Horse came for her and ride laughing to Heaven, and that was *that*. She drank her milk like a man who has won his argument in the tavern and tosses down his ale with a flourish.

"Would you like to see her?" Alick asked suddenly.

"Yes," Bell Ann answered at once, "because I never did." William nodded, keeping his eyes on Alick's face. "*I've* seen her," Sandy said curtly.

"She doesn't look the same now," Jennie told him. "I think you twins should both see, so you remember her differently."

"We will be doing it now," Alick said, arising.

"Wait," said Pris. She went out to the flower borders. The twins gazed after her as if they would like to follow and keep on going. Bell Ann drew her upper lip down long and made a face at William, who turned stiffly away. Pris brought in a little nosegay of stocks, white alyssum, and Sweet William. She walked ahead of the others. Bell Ann took her parent's hands, William kept close to Alick's free arm. The twins followed, looking unnaturally gawky and uncomfortable. The dogs, intrigued by this strange conduct, were told to stay behind.

When Alick opened the door, Jennie felt a sickish qualm in case there had been some dramatic change in the night, but in the morning shade, clear as springwater, Saffy looked the same. In the lace-and-ribbon-trimmed nightgown she lay between the lavender-scented sheets as if waiting for her bridegroom.

Bell Ann whispered loudly, "Mama, she has your best nightgown on!"

"I thought it would be nice for her to wear."

"For when the Great Horse comes," Bell Ann agreed.

Pris went forward and put her flowers in the curving hollow between shoulder and throat, then stepped quickly back as if Saffy's lids might begin to open.

"She is pretty," William said in a low voice.

"And *young*." Carolus sounded amazed. "I can hardly believe it, the way she looked when we brought her home."

"She still looks just about starved to death." Sandy's voice was jerky and loud. "And I guess she was." He left the room and Carolus was close behind him.

William seemed unable to move or stop staring at Saffy. Alick took him lightly by the nape. "Come along," he said, in Gaelic, and William came along. The dogs began barking outside, and William sprang free from his trance. Bell Ann pulled loose and ran after him. Pris was more decorous, but just as greedy for a distraction. They heard Bell Ann's gleeful shout, "There's Moses!"

A wagon and horse awaited outside the rowan trees; the wagon, even its wheels, looked to have been scrubbed clean with stiff brushes. The chestnut and white horse was as massive as the shire horses Jennie had once known, with great hoofs and hairy fetlocks and a huge head, which the boys patted and stroked respectfully wherever they could reach. His harness was glossy and unpatched, the metal parts polished to a fiery brightness. The boys called him by his name, Kenneth, and he accepted their adulation with a massive grace.

Moses and another boy jumped down from the wagon bed. Mr. George Gunn himself was the driver. When he saw Jennie and Alick he stepped down and came toward them under the rowan branches, taking off his hat. He was a big, swarthy man with heavy features and black eyes; his thick black hair and beard were neatly trimmed, and what showed of his shirt was brilliantly white; so were the boys' shirts. They, like the horse, were dressed for an occasion.

"Good morning, Gunn," Alick said, going to meet him.

"Good morning to you, Glenroy." Spoken in a deep, courteous rumble by one laird to another. "Good morning to you, Mrs. Glenroy, and Miss Priscilla. We have come for her."

Nothing else was needed; the two Keel boys were already unloading the coffin from among sheaves of fresh bracken, Michaelmas daisies, and branches of scarlet maple leaves.

"Show them the way," Alick said to the twins.

"How did you know?" Jennie asked George Gunn.

"We knew she'd go with the tide last night; that is what takes them."

"We would have been keeping her here, you know," Alick said. He gestured toward the woods. "With our family."

"You are good people, but she came to us once, and that makes her one of ours. I began the box when my girl came home yesterday and told us. I knew I was saving those boards, didn't know what for. They came from the handsomest old grands'r of a pine you ever saw, and I don't begrudge her them." He addressed Jennie directly. "My wife lined it real soft with some stuff we salvaged from a wreck off the Goslings years ago, in case you worry about her being comfortable. There's a pillow and a coverlet, too."

"Thank you, Mr. Gunn." She felt almost as tongue-tied as Bell Ann, who had been flattened by Moses' dignified demeanor.

"Maybe you could help me shift her, Glenroy," George Gunn said. "It's not proper for the lads to do."

When they had gone in, Jennie sank gladly onto the bench. Priscilla sat beside her, and Bell Ann hitched herself onto her mother's lap. William went down to the garden to pull a carrot for Kenneth.

"It is so sad," Pris said, "but it is beautiful too. I only wish she could know. What good does beauty do you when you are dead? It is not for you; it pleases the living."

"It shows that she was a person meant to have love and respect," said Jennie. "She is not tossed away like a nothing."

"She will have love and respect," Bell Ann said, "when the Great Horse comes for her. He is much larger than Kenneth," she said complacently. "And more beautiful too."

"Bell Ann, you make everything so simple," Pris said. "But who is she, Mama? *They* know."

"She lived at the Keel once," Jennie said. "Miriam recognized her. They will protect her name now as they did then."

"Here they come," Pris said. The twins, pale and stern, were helping to carry the coffin. David, Alick, and George Gunn came out last. The chest of polished pine was replaced in the wagon, and the ferns and boughs laid over it. The men shook hands, and Jennie and Pris were formally taken leave of. George Gunn mounted to the wagon seat, the boys beside him. Taking up the reins, he did not at once signal the horse.

"If you're ever of a mind to," he said, "come and see where we have put her to rest, behind Jerome's gate."

It seemed for a while that morning that their lives had been knocked so far out of joint that nothing would ever really be simple again. Each was disoriented in a different way. Jennie and Alick began briskly to shake the family into some sort of order. Bell Ann and William were sent with a note to the Bastos explaining that the men needn't come. The twins saddled Shonnie and Perry, who needed the exercise as much as the boys needed the change, and rode to tell Carlotta what had happened and deliver a note from Alick to Mr. Ledyard, the town clerk, stating that an unknown young woman had died in his home at approximately half past ten last night; for the cause of death, Dr. Neville was the person to see.

Pris walked to the post office to collect the mail, which no one had remembered since Tuesday.

"This morning we were all going to Maddox to do some shopping and for the boys to try on their new boots," Jennie told Alick.

"We should have put them all in the wagon and told them to make a day of it," he said. "Then you and I could be barricading ourselves in the house and have our way with each other."

"And what about the fairy wean in the cradle? Do you remember how they *always* woke up when—"

"Och, the spoilsport you are." He pulled her onto his lap.

"I would love to continue this indefinitely," said Jennie, "but they all have a habit of hunger at regular intervals, and Nora brought us two chickens last night."

The twins carried back word from Carlotta that she would be there in the late afternoon to take the baby home; Bell Ann was out riding Brisky, and the boys were instructed to keep their news to themselves. After dinner, which Pris called a Feast of Thanksgiving, Alick and Jennie took Bell Ann for a walk. The tide was up, the air was warm, and the fields and alders twinkled with chickadees and goldfinches. They walked along the ledges and bits of pebbly or sandy beach upriver from the Yard. There was enough breeze to fill sails and toss sparkles across the blue river, and cause a pleasant splashing around the rocks. At the edge of the woods, yellow birch leaves drifted like snowflakes toward earth and water. The autumnal voices of nuthatches sounded from deeper among the forest trees.

Bell Ann chattered, sang, whistled, and sometimes walked silently in an almost visible aura of joy. She stopped on the shore wherever she could collect enough flat pebbles to play Ducks and Drakes. She had never been able to skip her stone more than once; this afternoon, while she stared in disbelief, her pebble made three skips, and then she repeated the feat.

"Wait till I tell William!" she gloated. "Before he knows it, I will be winning all the time!"

This moment of triumph seemed a good omen. There was even a handy shelf of rock where Jennie and Alick sat while she practiced. When her aim grew wild, Alick invited her to sit down and rest her arm for a time.

"When you go back to it, you may be doing even better than before," Jennie said. "And while you are waiting, you and Papa and I can have a talk."

Sitting between them, wiggling her bare, wet feet in the warm sand, her hands on her knees, she said agreeably, "What about?"

"About Dr. Neville, first," said Jennie. "You know she is all alone, she has nobody."

"She has Polly, and Michael."

"Yes, but they are not family," Jennie said.

"Michael is," Bell Ann insisted. "Brisky and Diana and Shonnie and Perry and Ianthe and Louisa are in our family, aren't they? And Hettie and High Cockalorum and—"

"We know all their names, my own," Alick said. "But we are talking about human family. She has no wee girl or boy of her own, because her husband died before he could be their father."

Bell Ann nodded, but she was poised for sudden moves. *We* could always tell when Papa was leading up to something, Jennie thought.

"Young Hercules has no mother or father," Alick said.

"He has us!" she cried. "He has *me*! I just the same as found him, the way William found Jerome! William couldn't *keep* Jerome, because of that man. But nobody can take Hercules away from us, because he has nobody but us." Gaelic blandishments meant nothing now. "You said— you *promised*!" she raged at her mother.

"Darling, I did not ever say we would keep him, and I was wrong to let you think it. We cannot be selfish. We have been given so much to be thankful for, *we* must give, do you understand? We all have each other, but Dr. Neville has no child, and the baby has no mother, so they belong together."

"I hate you, I hate you! I hate *her*!" Bell Ann tore away from them and went storming over the rocks in the first full-blown temper tantrum they had seen for some time, and no room handy in which to put her. "I hate you, I hate you, I hate *her*!" she went on shouting. Branches, stones, driftwood, anything she could lay hands on, were hurled into the water and anything too light to fly was kicked and trampled when it fell to earth.

The first time it had happened, Alick's dismay was painful to see. "I am sure you never had a temper tantrum yourself," Jennie had told him, "so you cannot understand. You think your baby is either a changeling or she has turned into a little monster. Well, she simply has to roar out her rage, but we needn't listen. She cannot learn too young that this may be understandable behavior, but it is not acceptable."

A few sessions of howling herself out in isolation had done away with tantrums, so Alick was not quite so dismayed now, but he was shaken. Bell Ann was throwing handfuls of sand, having used up everything else, and chanting hatred between sobs.

"I should have prepared her," Jennie said ruefully, "but my mind has not exactly been rapier-sharp this past week."

"*Dia*, what you were going through without me!"

"If you reproach yourself for not being here, I shall walk away from you, though not so noisily as our daughter. I am glad we're far away from the neighbors. — It has gone on just about long enough." She looked at her watch. "In sixty seconds it will be either a handful of cold river dashed into her face, or a spank where it will bring the blood down from the brain."

As if a secret warning system functioned deep in Bell Ann's head, she quieted suddenly and sat down where she was, hugging her knees and staring at a sailing wherry on the river as if trying to turn it to stone and sink it.

"We are going back now, love," Jennie called to her.

Bell Ann sighed noisily with an exaggerated lift and corresponding droop of her shoulders. "I s'pose you would not leave me here alone," she said scornfully.

"You suppose exactly right, *mo nighean*," Alick said.

"I will be so glad when I am not treated like a baby anymore." She refused to take their hands.

When they reached the house, she went grimly up to her room, ignoring the cradle on the way. The boys and David were elsewhere, and Pris was sewing. The tantrum wasn't mentioned, but in a little while Jennie went upstairs and found Bell Ann sleeping with Bear in her arms and a hand stretched out to Evelina Ermintrude, who had been dressed in her best outfit.

It was late afternoon when Captain Blackburn and Carlotta drove in. The dogs woke Bell Ann, and she came downstairs to the pleasant hubbub of which the baby was the heart. She shook her head when Alick beckoned to her, and pretended not to hear Jennie's summons, but stood far off from everyone, her hands behind her. "Good afternoon, Miss Bell Ann!" Captain Blackburn saluted her.

"Afternoon," she said dourly.

"Come and help me dress him, Bell Ann," Pris invited; Carlotta was tactfully standing back. She looked especially handsome and young, and very happy. Bell Ann ignored both her and Pris.

"How long will this last?" Sandy asked his mother behind his hand. "Until he's a grown man?"

"I pity us all," said Carolus. Jennie shook her head at them.

Carlotta said suddenly, "Bell Ann, might you and I talk by ourselves for a few minutes?"

"I s'pose," said Bell Ann stolidly, knowing she must be polite even if no one deserved it.

"The parlor," Jennie said to Carlotta. Bell Ann walked stiffly, clumping her feet, and Jennie shut doors behind them. Alick and the captain were talking ships, William sat on the camp bed watching Pris dress Hercules, and the twins were listening to the men.

"I shall miss him," Pris said to her mother as they maneuvered a dress over his head, "but it will be nice to be back in my own room again, and wake up thinking about my business."

"Hercules Neville," said William to the baby. "That's who you are."

"Somehow I don't think it will be Hercules," Jennie said. The door into the hall opened, and a self-conscious silence struck the room as Bell Ann walked confidently into it, her face long and serious, but not with grief or rage. Carlotta came behind her, also serious. Bell Ann looked up at her as if exchanging a secret message, and Carlotta nodded.

"His name is Simon Roy Neville," Bell Ann informed them. "For his grandpapa and his papa. That is to say," she explained condescendingly to the attentive faces, "they *would* have been if they had not got sick and died. So it is all right to say they *are*."

She looked at Carlotta and received another nod; conspiracy was thick around them. "And I am his aunt," she announced. "As soon as he can talk he will call me Aunt Bell Ann. Nobody else will be his aunt," she warned her sister and mother. "Not his real aunt, with a s'tifficut to hang on my wall, with all pretty writing, *and* a gold seal on it."

"A *what?*" asked William.

"A certificate," said Carolus. "Don't you understand English? Hurrah for Aunt Bell Ann!" he shouted, and the rest took it up, everybody clapping hands, and the boys adding a few soaring whistles to the loud acclamation. Bell Ann went pale, and then red; all at once overcome, she rushed at her father.

Sixty-One

O CTOBER WAS ALWAYS a bittersweet month for Jennie and Alick. A beautiful month enhanced the poignancy of April's loss, because it had happened in a beautiful month too. But a stormy month was worse, with the house a prison. It had been a long time since the old scars had severely pained them when the leaves began to turn, but Jennie was always glad to have her birthday behind her, even though in itself it could be a happy time, especially for the children. This year the twins and Pris had given her a heart-shaped locket engraved with all their names; April was in her proper place between William and Bell Ann. William had made her a little hinged mahogany box, decorated with the chip carving he had learned from Jerome. Bell Ann gave her a picture she had embroidered at school, a bouquet of daisies, buttercups, and red clover, in a blue mug, attended by a blue butterfly. It had been smuggled home in the dinner bucket in a grimy condition. Pris had washed and pressed the work, and Alick had framed it.

His gift was a finely woven lidded sweetgrass basket, wound around and around with string and fastened with multiple knots. He handed her his penknife, and sat back to smoke his pipe and impassively observe. The children were nearly hysterical with suspense and laughter before she made the cut which demolished the whole lunatic network.

The basket was so light it felt empty. It was not. It held an elegantly executed pen and ink drawing of a piano with candles at either end of the keyboard, and Jennie was playing it. Alick hadn't told any of the children what his gift would be, but Pris and the twins had guessed it at once.

William was mystified when his mother so extravagantly hugged and kissed his father.

"It is very nice, but why did you fasten it up like that when it doesn't even have a frame?"

"We don't need a *picture* of a piano," Bell Ann said. "We should have a real one."

"And we will have," Alick said, "when Tony escorts it from Boston when he comes home for Christmas."

"My whole life is changed!" Bell Ann cried. "I am an aunt, and now we will have a piano! I hope you can play tunes on it, Mama."

"Just you wait!" Alick told her.

David's package was a thick folder of music, ranging from works of great composers to music for dancing and the songs of the day. "Tony chose it all. I wanted you to have it now so you can be practicing your fingering." With characteristic unselfconsciousness he made it clear that, if he could not hear, he could watch her as she played. She began that night to practice at private moments on the invisible keyboard of her piano.

The day before the scheduled launching of the *Enoch Lincoln*, Jennie drove Diana to Maddox through a countryside bewitched with autumn. There had been a few light, glittering frosts which led to warm days and southerly winds; the first killing frost had yet to arrive, and no one was expecting a change in the weather until this phase of the moon ended, even Vincent Taggart.

The Governor, a modest man, wanted no formalities beyond the launching ceremony, but he would happily shake hands with all the men who had built the ship, their families, and other guests of the builders, providing they didn't number in the hundreds. Mr. Babb was supplying the wine, and the honors would be done by the captain's fiancée. The ship would then sail directly to Portland carrying the Babb and Lincoln parties. With nothing for Jennie to do now, she was driving to Maddox.

She drove with a sense of freedom edged with the consciousness of virtue. The week's work was done, the traditional shortbread was baked, and she had a genuine errand in town, so she was not being frivolous. The twins needed some new books, the bookseller in Maddox had ordered them, they had arrived, and Jennie was to collect them. She was also looking forward with happy greed to his stock of new novels. The other errand, which David could have very well done, was to tell the General that he was welcome to bring his present guests to the launching, he needn't have asked. He was forever bringing someone home from his trips to Boston, and New York, being intensely proud of what Maddox and Whittier had become.

Pris had a customer, her first; a woman had broken her wrist and couldn't complete her children's winter clothing. She was new in town and had no friends or relatives to call on. She saw Pris's card in the store, and Pris was riding Shonnie there this morning to take measurements and bring home the work.

The momentum of daily living and the pervasive excitement about the imminent launching had been such in the last month that the Shaw affair had been left far astern, though none of them was forgetting it, or ever would. They still half-expected to see Harry slouching by the house, and at times the dogs roused up noisily for no visible reason. Jennie had given in to the naggings of conscience and compassion and had written a note to Mrs. Shaw, expecting and receiving no answer. She still drove behind Major, but not to funerals, it was said. Lily wore black-and-white checks, and black ribbons on her hair. Bell Ann reported that Lily could not stop staring at her red ribbons, and one morning Bell Ann had offered an exchange for the day. It became a custom; on the way home from school each day they changed back, and Bell Ann's new skill as a maker of bows was still deceiving Mrs. Shaw.

Turning the small bedroom into a sewing room for Pris could not exorcise Saffy, but she was a touching little spirit. Simon Roy Neville, now Carlotta's legal son, was in full pink bloom. He smiled, he talked engagingly to his toes, and his brown hair had become ringlets as silky as the best embroidery floss. When he firmly conveyed Bell Ann's finger to his mouth and chewed on it, she was beyond words; she liked to think hers was the only finger so honored. After a fervor of bib-making (one for every day of the week) she was learning to knit stockings for him.

Passing the Goward pastures, Jennie saw Bethiah and her father carrying full buckets across a field to empty into a watering trough. Bethiah was too old for elementary school now, and her life at fourteen was spent between house and barn chores, and once a week a long day of church-going in Maddox. The family had become so puritanical that Muster Day had been forbidden to the children, and a rare visit to the store or the post office was all Bethiah could anticipate. Jennie could not imagine the sullen child becoming a docile drudge; secretly she must be counting off the months until she could run away.

Good luck, Bethiah, Jennie thought. I am sure you never meant
Caroline to die, and you are repenting it with every breath.

David would be working outdoors today, in this exquisite autumn
light. He had been painting Ronald Heriot for several weeks, and Heriot
wanted his yard behind him in the portrait; he would appear as he was,
a shipbuilder and proud of it. When David had finished Jacinth's portrait, he had wanted the Glenroys to go at once to Maddox to see it, but
Jacinth begged to put it off until Mrs. Heriot held her planned reception
to exhibit her husband's portrait. It would be so *nice*, Jacinth said.

"What she means," Pris said cynically, "is that she wants no more to
do with David's family than she can help, so we cannot come separately,
for then she might have to hold conversation with us."

After painting all morning, David rode with Jacinth in the fine
afternoons, or drove her in the livery stable's new light and stylish chaise,
which the irreverent called the Courting Carriage. He was leasing it by
the week, and Blanchard grazed in the Heriot paddock while David and
Jacinth ranged for miles behind a fast-trotting Morgan.

He must have been beautifully free of jealousy; he surely knew that
Jacinth was not sitting at home at night with her watercolors or her
workbasket in a town where she could go to almost everything, and with
a different escort each time: concerts, lectures, the Dancing Club series,
always with supper afterward.

Septimus was undoubtedly one of her partners. At the top of the hill
where Jennie had met him that day and he quoted Shakespeare at her,
she half-expected to meet him again, like a ghost always encountered at
the same spot. Such a storm in a teacup there'd been over him, and then
the message about a red carnation in that letter: "Alas for my poor love."
He must have given the *Language of Flowers* to half a dozen young girls
and had written them the same words. He was a talented young per-
former if he could keep his balance between Jacinth, who was pretty and
rich, and Frank, who was the General's daughter and one of the heirs to
the Daughters Line.

"You staying long enough for me to put her in the paddock?" Corny
asked Jennie at Strathbuie House.

"I think so, Corny," she said, "the day is mine, and I intend to browse
my way along Main Street like Columbine. Do you remember her?"

"When there is nobody left who remembers that cow," he said, "it'll
be a mighty different world. Why, if we was to come back into it, we
wouldn't know ourselves or where we was."

"Well, on a day like this, the far future is the least of our worries," Jennie said.

"Ain't it a pretty one," he agreed, giving her a hand down. "Makes you forget winter's on the road." Ozzie advanced in stately welcome and paced beside her to the house. The oval garden was entrancing in color and perfume even this late in the year. She stayed there for a few minutes, watching the birds drink and bathe. The surrounding trees turned it into a secret garden; at one time it could be seen from some upper windows of the mansion, but not now through the bronze, coppery, and green foliage.

As usual in mild weather, the back door into the house stood open, and the kitchen voices were heard along the stone-floored passage. Eliza's baking scented the air with a different perfume from that of the garden.

Ozzie led the way like a genial butler, and she received a greeting like Corny's. (Lydia Mackenzie had long since given up trying to mold her help into a servant class.)

"What are you baking?" she asked. "It smells heavenly."

"Corn gems," Eliza said. "There'll be some going up with her coffee. My second batch this morning. The General may be watching his figure, but not at breakfast. He and them two went through a dozen with grape jelly. I guess they don't serve anything like that in those castles. I hear tell the kitchen's so far from the dining rooms, food must always be cold when they get it."

"Do his guests live in a castle?" Jennie asked. Sibba's thin young face was quite transfigured.

"Oh yes! I never waited on anyone who lived in a castle before!"

"The Markweeze de LaFayette was here before her time," Eliza explained kindly. "Mine too, if I was to be honest. But land of love, Sibba, there's been folks here who live in houses just as grand as castles, and likely a lot more comfortable. Only in America we don't call them castles, and we don't have earls."

Sibba's attitude was subdued, but not her eyes, which gave Jennie a sparkling sideways look. "Anyway, they are so *pleasant* from what I thought dukes and earls would be. You'd never think that young boy is a *lord*."

"Ayuh, Sibba's real taken with 'em," Eliza said dryly. She added another flowered cup and saucer to Lydia's tray. "You'll be going up, won't you, Mrs. Glenroy?"

"The missus is up and bathed," Sibba said. "She is doing her hair."

Jennie went into the passage and out to the main hall. It was illuminated from the skylight two floors above, indirectly from open doors on both sides; and sunlight reflected off white woodwork, mirrors, and the polished parquet. Sibba had come behind her. Her small, narrow face intent, she pattered into the library.

"Are you finished with your coffee, sir?"

"Yes," a man answered, "and very fine coffee too. Strathbuie House brews the finest coffee I have had in America, from South Carolina to Nova Scotia."

If Sibba answered, Jennie didn't know. A long, narrow blade had pierced her head from one temple to the other; she *saw* it, ripping through the veil of years, and the shreds of time falling away in smoking wisps.

She hung dizzily to the newel post, shouting inside her brain, No, no, *no*! It cannot be! It is impossible. It is an accident! —You are not insane, you are only haunted. You cannot run because you are having a waking nightmare.

Whatever else Sibba had said, he was answering. "Thank you, my dear. Strathbuie House is your home, I understand."

"Until I am grown and married, sir." Oh, Sibba was responding, it was in her voice. Jennie saw Morag and Aili responding, and everyone else of those days. It could not *be*, but it was enough of a coincidence to make one feel knives in the head, and why could she not move?

"And will you set your cap for one of the General's captains?" How young he sounded.

"I liked a boy once who would likely be a captain one day if he had not of been lost at sea."

"My poor lass," the man said. "But you are still almost a child. All is not lost. I have had a terrible loss in my life, but here I am, and none the worse." He laughed. The familiarity of that sound was another blade, but Jennie still denied its existence on one level while recognizing it on another. "So take heart, wee Sibba. — I have finished my letters. I shall find the General now." A chair creaked, and Jennie heard steps. She was free, she picked up her skirts and ran up the stairs. At the top she turned right into a corridor, and then she could run no more. She leaned against the wall, trying not to sag to the floor.

Either her heartbeat or the silence from below was like surf in her ears, and then through it the question, with neither humor nor kindliness: "Who was that who just ran up the stairs?"

So he had seen her. She strained to hear, trying not to pant.

"Mrs. Glenroy!" Sibba said ardently. "She is a good woman. Her husband built the ship they are launching tomorrow."

"Thank you. Run along, dear," he said absently. Jennie's pulse had quieted. She even heard the rustle of Sibba's dress and apron as she left the hall, and the loud authoritative voice of the tall clock, but she heard no footsteps crossing the parquet to the front door. She had run up the stairs at Tigh nam Fuaran more times than she had walked them. Was that recollection holding him immobile? She flattened herself against the door of a linen closet, feeling behind her for the latch; one step on the stairs and she would disappear and wait in the lavender-scented dark as long as she needed to. It took all her concentration to keep from shaking, and to combat what was more treacherous, the desire to *see*.

Sibba would be coming up next with Lydia's tray, and she could not sit down and drink coffee and pretend to gossip. Downstairs there were slow steps across the parquet to the front door, a reflective pause there, and then the door opened and closed again.

She moved to the turn and listened. When she was sure he had not closed the front door in a ruse and was still waiting inside, she sprang across the open gallery to the back stairs. It was like the dream of a headlong plunge toward an abyss, and she had no wish to sprain an ankle and be as captive as a criminal taken to the hangman. She groped for her handkerchief and held it to her lips as she reached the open door at the foot.

Two astonished faces turned toward her. She said apologetically, "I've been taken with chills and I refuse to pepper you all with a Glenroy cold. Will you tell the General and Mrs. Mackenzie that we will be expecting them and their guests at the launching?" She was actually saying it, and they were looking interestedly at her, not incredulously. "I am sure Mrs. Mackenzie will be happy that I've gone, under the circumstances. Goodbye, everyone."

"Take care," Eliza said after her. "Brew yourself a good pot of mullein tea!"

"I will!" She could hardly keep from running down the passage to the open back door with Ozzie barking behind her. Outside she *did* run toward the walled garden, and across it like the wicked who flee when no man pursueth. Past the far gate, she walked as fast as she could, breathing through a seared windpipe, and with a stitch coming in her side.

Of course Diana was at the far end of the paddock, running with Young Joshua, and Corny was not in sight. Her dry mouth kept her from gathering up enough saliva to wet her lips and whistle. The brick house shone rosily through the trees, birds sang, the horses played in the sun.

The scene so innocent in itself had become garish with nightmare, the way the Fairy Hill by the Pict's House had been changed on that day by Nigel's death. His *death?*

Corny called to her from a window upstairs in the carriage house. "I wasn't looking for you this soon, Mrs. Glenroy."

"I began to have chills. I think I had better go home."

He disappeared, and she heard him whistling from the window at the other end and saw the horses turn their heads. By the time he was downstairs and outside, Diana was one of several at the gate. He rewarded them all with sugar lumps, then took Diana out, talking to her all the while he was harnessing her to the chaise. He seemed maddeningly slow and clumsy, though she knew he was not. But supposing Nigel had changed his mind about going to the wharves and was even now strolling toward the stables? She shut her eyes and at once was so dizzy she thought she was actually falling, and opened them again quickly.

"There you are, old girl," Corny said to Diana. "Mrs. Glenroy, are you safe to drive?"

"Oh, yes!" She even smiled. "Besides, Diana does not need a navigator."

She took his hand and stepped onto the mounting block and then into her place, with Corny huffing solicitously behind her in a pungent effluvium of strong tobacco, horse, and hay. Once settled with the reins in her hands, she felt stronger; in a minute she would be safe out in the lane. But in that minute a bare-headed boy in green riding clothes, his shirt open at the throat, rode in on Robin's horse Sinbad. Diana was enchanted. For Jennie it was chaos again as the boy pulled up, his hand lifted toward an absent hat. Smiling and mannerly, he waited for her to speak.

"Good morning," she said, and it must have sounded sane because his smile widened and he answered in a light, young voice, Nigel's accent just tinged with the Highlands. "Good morning, ma'am!"

His thick hair was brown, sun-bleached at the temples, and his innocently friendly eyes were greenish, but just the way he sat the horse, the length of thigh, the carriage of the long head, the cleft chin, and most of all the smile—they were all Nigel's. Except for the coloring, this was Nigel at fifteen or so. *And* Priscilla.

Yet the image of Nigel's death had been pressed into her brain long ago, like a seal into hot wax.

The scene had not been eternal after all, she was driving out, and behind her Corny was asking, "How did he suit ye, young one?"

"I wish I had him at home!" Voice preparing to break, like the twins'. "He's keen as mustard! I've never ridden a more knowing horse."

"He's Robin's horse," Corny said. "He knows what a boy wants."

She slapped the reins lightly on Diana's back and drove out into the lane. Diana resisted being turned up Ship Street instead of down. It was not the way home. But *down* was the way to the General's wharf, the store, and the shipyard, and it was the way Nigel had gone.

The struggle of wills took all of Jennie's attention. They went up to the flagpole and around it into the west-bound traffic of Main Street. She drove the short distance to Quarry Lane, which ran downhill to the bridge; once Diana saw that, she gave up gracefully, no doubt convinced that she had won the argument.

Going up the hill on the opposite bank, Jennie fought a compulsion to stop and look back at the Mackenzie dock, to see if Nigel stood out for her even at this distance. But of course he would not. Maddox had its share of tall men. What difference if he had turned florid and corpulent or stayed handsomely lean? Lot's wife's curiosity had been fatal. All that Jennie really needed now was to have Alick within touching distance.

She was soaking with perspiration inside her clothes, her hair was damp. She threw off the light lap robe, and as soon as the houses thinned she took off her bonnet. She took in nothing on the ride home, though she realized sometimes that someone had spoken to her and she must have answered, but she couldn't have told the names. It was a surprise to suddenly find herself driving through the woods and out into sunlit open space, with the river at the foot of the field, the ship's masts showing above the Yard, and the dogs running to meet her. It was like waking from one of those dislocating dreams, still under its spell, and then slowly realizing it had been just a dream. How could he be here, when they had left him dead?

Pris came behind the dogs, and she told herself there was absolutely no resemblance between her daughter and the strange boy.

"You are home early," Pris said.

Slipping so easily into the mother's role, Jennie felt like laughing aloud with relief.

"When I stopped at the General's, I had a feeling I might be taking cold, so I didn't go to the bookstore, I came home. David can fetch the books home tomorrow."

"How are you now?" Pris gave her a hand down.

"I think it has gone. Perhaps it was my imagination, because I didn't want to be away from home on a day like this."

"It *is* perfect, isn't it? For me, anyway, now that I am gainfully employed. Oh, Mama, sometimes I can hardly believe it! Breeches, flannel shirts, a schooldress for the little girl, and a Sunday dress as well. That will be like dessert." They unhitched a fidgety Diana and let her have a drink. The bell at the Yard signaled the noon hour.

"I am so sorry to burst in upon your quiet meal with your father," Jennie said.

"Oh, fiddlesticks," said Pris. "It will be all the nicer, just the three of us without children."

The scent of haddock chowder heating made Jennie's stomach roil. "I must change out of this dress at once," she said. "I have been far too warm. Undo me, please."

When she shut her bedroom door behind her she felt like a fox who has escaped the hounds, bedraggled, panting, gone to earth at last, to lie there until strength returned. Something—the Great Horse?—saved him from knowing what his bloody end would be when they had found and stopped his earth while he was out of it. She and her sisters had always fiercely identified themselves with the fox. But at this moment she *knew* as she had never known before.

She stripped off everything, and stood on a towel and sponged herself with cool water from her forehead and nape down to her heels, letting the air dry her. Alick would soon be walking up to the house; in the next few minutes she must collect herself enough to sit through a meal and act as if she were not terrified. She began to collect clean underclothing, leaving off stays so she could breathe easier. When the door opened and Alick came in, she was not yet ready to face him. Helplessly she closed her eyes and shook her head. His hands clasped her around the waist.

"What is at you?" he asked in the Gaelic, and she could not answer. He held her harder, almost shaking her. "Tell me!"

She opened her eyes and looked into his face. His fear of the unknown was deepening the lines in his thin cheeks, paling his mouth. She thought almost dreamily, We will never grow old together. Then his fingers dug brutally into her ribs, and she said with a gasp, "*Nigel*."

His eyes went wide and he asked her, still in Gaelic, what she was meaning. She put her hands on his shoulders, wet her lips, and said, "He is at Strathbuie House. He and his son are the guests Colin wishes to bring to the launching."

He watched her as if she were raving. "Were you seeing his face? Did you meet him?"

"No, but I heard his voice."

His hands loosened slightly, and so did his face. "You were hearing a voice that reminded you of his."

"That is what I have been telling myself, but Alick—listen!" Now her fingers were digging. "I was going up the stairs to Lydia's room, and I heard him talking to Sibba in the library. Alick, it was like a knife pinning me to the spot. Then I knew he was coming out, and I ran up the stairs." Her voice became hoarse, and he poured water into a mug and gave it to her. "He saw me from the back, and he asked Sibba who had just run up the stairs. She said it was Mrs. Glenroy, whose husband built the ship about to be launched. She went to the kitchen, but he stood at the foot for a time, and then he went out. I ran down the back stairs. Alick, I knew my mind was not tricking me when I met the boy at the stables. He is about the age of the twins, Not blond, like Nigel, but Alick, I *saw* Nigel in him! Just the way he sat the horse, and held his head, and Alick, I saw not only Nigel but Pris."

"Then I did not kill him," he said dazedly.

Seeing him take the blow in his turn brought back strength to her. "We cannot meet him," she said. "It is that simple. Is there any way we can postpone the launching? Remember, Colin said they have passage home on the *Frances Mackenzie* next week."

"Listen to me," he said. "We will eat with Priscilla now, and be such actors as Shakespeare would have honored, and afterward we will talk."

They embraced and kissed with all the fire of a long deferred first embrace, or a last one.

The chowder was easy to eat after all, and Priscilla was so euphoric that she needed only a smiling comment or an occasional question to keep her going. It was not often that any one child had sole possession of the parents, and the experience was always heady, unless it was disciplinary. Afterward she washed the dishes; when Jennie and Alick went out she was singing "Greensleeves."

There was a scalding irony in the fact that she and her father, in total ignorance of each other's existence, were some few miles apart.

Alick went down to the Yard to put Thad in charge, and Jennie walked through the field to the babies' graves, telling the dogs to stay with Pris. Garnet followed quietly. When she was safe inside the woods, Jennie expected her tormented stomach to eject her dinner, but it didn't;

a small enough victory when the war was about to be lost. She knelt by the graves and made herself uselessly busy so she would not be staring glassily into space like Evelina Ermintrude when Alick came. Garnet lay on April's grave, and when Alick walked into the clearing the cat playfully rolled onto her back and kneaded the air with her forepaws. He dropped to his heels and scratched her belly.

"We cannot be putting off the launching," he said.

"But you are well-known for being meticulous," Jennie protested. "Supposing there is some little thing wrong you have just discovered, to put it off for a week or so."

"*Dia*, when Babb was here a week ago, we were only waiting for the proper tide! We would have to be inventing a serious error and turn all the men into liars for the occasion, even supposing we could notify Babb in time and he could apologize to the Governor. The tide won't be this perfect again until into November."

"Then must we simply wait until *he* comes riding in and alights from Colin's barouche and sets eyes upon us?"

He reached out to her across the small graves. "Let us be standing up while we still can," he said. "My legs are breaking."

They walked to the stone wall and she sat within the circle of his arm. It was growing darker as cloud cover slowly edged over the sun, and it was sharply cooler. Alick rested his chin on her head and said thoughtfully, "It smells of rain."

"What if, after this morning, he already senses something?" she asked. "If they refer to us as Alick and Jeannie, those names are common enough for Scots, but Lydia has always called me Jennie, and if she should add that I was born in the north of England—! Alick, I am like a person who is lost in the snow and is ready to lie down and go to sleep and die in it, because I don't know in which direction to move." Why did he remain so quiet? His heart was not even hurrying. "Can we be arrested? You for attempted murder, and he could add seduction, as he threatened to do. I am surely an adulteress in the eyes of the law, and all the children but Pris are illegitimate."

It was odd how coolly she could lay it all out like that; it was as if she had gone so far beyond the first impact that now she was numb.

"We are American citizens," Alick said. "Our government would not surrender us to a foreigner who has no proof of his accusations."

"But if they are made *at all*, they could damage us. You know these things kill like an infection in the blood or poison in a well. Think of all the children, not just Priscilla!" She sat up and twisted to face him. "Could he legally claim Pris?"

"Again, *mo chridh*, how can he prove it? Yes, she looks like him but that does not prove she is his flesh and blood."

"Then what if he bargains with us? He will not disturb our life here with scandalous accusations if we give him his daughter." The numbness was giving way to returning agony. "Oh, I know all these things cannot be proved beyond the shadow of a doubt, but the filth is left forever. A month ago," she exclaimed, "I thought nothing as bad as the murder could happen to us again! And all the while he was on his way to us. God must be paying us back, saying, 'You see, I was here all the time, and I know what you did.' Our children will hate us as David hates his father."

She began to laugh, knowing that hysteria would have her in a moment. Alick seized her by the upper arms and shook her.

"Jeannie, Jeannie, be quiet now!" he commanded her. "Breathe as deeply as you can, but slowly. If you could endure hell without me, surely you can be struggling out of it *with* me." She obeyed him, but in a way it would be a relief to give in to the even temporary mania.

"Now listen to me," he said. "They will never hate us, because I am not Evans, and you are not a poor mad wraith of a woman. We will tell them the truth, and they will believe it. Nothing else in the world matters to them but you and me."

She laid her face against his chest where she could hear the steady beat of his heart through the linen. "I know why Bell Ann loves that," she said. "So if we can be brave enough, we will prevail."

"That is about the size of it. There is a proverb in the Gaelic, I am sure, but I cannot remember it." He turned her face up to his, and she put her arms around his neck. "So now we wait, and pray to the Great Horse to make us valiant, if he cannot send us a miracle."

"You understand," he said somberly, "I am glad I am not a murderer. My hand must have been shaking so, I couldn't find a pulse. But when we were running away because I thought I had killed my cousin, I wanted no miracles. I knew what I could do, until we reached Fort William, and then the terror was at me, but I still wished for no miracles." He smiled then, and bent his face to hers again. "But there was one, anyway. *You.* And now that I know I am no murderer, I am praying Fate for a miracle to strike him down before he can ever set eyes on us."

"It would certainly be easier for us than valor," she said.

Sixty-Two

BETWEEN THE SEASONAL storms and the chilly fog mulls of autumn, summer had given them a long succession of encores. By supper time, this day, seen in retrospect, had been the almost unbearably perfect bow. The raw, rain-scented evening was the first chord of the overture to an eternal winter, and Nigel was the malignant spirit responsible. That he was ignorant of his influence made no difference; the day that he came on stage, summer fled, blowing kisses and scattering dead flowers. The ship would be launched under lowering, perhaps wet, skies; for the first time the sun would not shine on a Glenroy vessel when she took to the water.

The presence of Nigel would be a far more terrible catastrophe than rain, but Jennie could not help connecting the two in her mind. He had once been sunshine in her life and then, overnight, disaster.

Reading was no narcotic for her that evening, nor was chess for Alick, judging by the ease with which David kept winning. "My heart is not here," Alick said. "It is with the ship. What is she thinking alone down there in the dark, waiting?"

"Probably she can hardly wait to sail out into the world," Pris said. "Like me. Papa, you are always a fidget the night before a launching." She gave him an indulgent look. "How will you be able to endure it when your own ship is ready?"

"He will likely sleep aboard to keep her company," Jennie said. "What I am thinking about tonight is the weather. We may be launching in a cold rain. I hope the Governor is not frail; he looks it in his likenesses."

It was a logical pair of reasons for their absentmindedness, unless David suspected something. One could never tell about David. She sometimes credited him with mystic powers, as if his silence were a self-imposed element in which he heard not only the music of the spheres but the thoughts which ordinary persons did not even know they were thinking. It was certain that he noted a good deal more than the rest of them. Tonight he may have caught little looks and touches meant to be secret, but which told him something was wrong.

At bedtime she put extra blankets on all the children's beds. She had promised Alick she would keep from thinking about what might or might not happen tomorrow, or at least to try, but that was hard when she stood by Pris's bed, and the candlestick shook slightly in her hand. Just so she had looked on Nigel sleeping. It would be a blessing, she thought cynically, if he *had* gotten florid and corpulent, it might obliterate the Sun God forever.

Downstairs again, without conscious planning she went to Andrew Glenroy's chest to take out the plaid. She knelt there for a few minutes, holding Alick's bonnet, remembering the day he had put it away forever, and how she had missed it. His dirk was wrapped in Kirsty Dallas's small tartan guilechan. In another life, she had once seen him hold it to a man's throat.

She felt utterly weary and resigned, except—and this brought her up as if she'd stumbled into a nest of thistles—where Priscilla was concerned.

When Alick came in she was in bed. He raised his eyebrows at sight of the plaid. "Your old charm against evil."

"But I don't believe it is going to work," she said. "Alick, no matter what you say, I cannot imagine meeting him, looking into his eyes, shaking hands with him. I cannot imagine being a courteous stranger with Nigel Gilchrist. I should have to have such control over my mind, and my body too, that I would be a witless automaton."

He undressed quickly and blew out the candle, and got into bed and took her into his arms. "Go on," he said.

"Alick, I understand that you are glad you didn't kill him, and *you* must understand that I loved him! I adored him from the first glimpse. I'd never had such feelings in my life, and I didn't know what was happening to me. It was as if I would die if I couldn't have him. Part of the awful tearing grief I felt later was because I loved him, and he was killing that before my eyes."

"Yes," Alick said. He obligingly tightened his arms.

"Years later, when I thought of him dead, he was pitiful, less of a villain than a dangerously wrong-headed boy. But he is alive, and hale, and well-to-do. He has probably gone on compounding his crimes against the folk of the glens and the moors. They all must be scattered to the four winds by now."

"It is not likely that he has seen the light on the road to Damascus," Alick agreed.

"Alick, with all that was between us, how can we look each other in the face and pretend we are strangers? How can *you* and he?"

"We will be doing what is necessary." The soft-spoken finality always signaled to the children that the argument was over. "You will be perfect tomorrow. So will I. So will he."

"If you and I could hold hands all the while, I might do well, but how would that look to the Governor and all the Babbs? Mr. Glenroy's wife fastened to him like a cluster of burrs on a dog's ear?"

"Och, what a bonny picture you are making of yourself! *Sleep.*"

But the argument continued in her head. He will know Pris is his, by the date of her birth, because of course they have talked about her, and us, all innocently enthusiastic. Nigel will be as passionate to claim her as we are not to allow it. He *will* demand, he *will* bargain, he *will* threaten.

"You are as stiff as a bundle of pokers," he said.

She was ashamed to tell him she was still on the roundabout. But salvation came out of nowhere, a floating fragment from the last little pool of peace yesterday, when she still believed the servants were discussing strangers. Later in her panic she had forgotten it, and even now she didn't recognize its significance.

"Sibba and Eliza were utterly charmed, they ran on about how nice these folks were, they never knew them dukes and earls could be so common, and the boy was a good young one, you'd never think he was a *lord.*"

The effect was dynamic. Alick sprang up in bed. "And you were not *connecting* what they said?"

"To what? After I heard Nigel's voice, I was completely shocked, I knew nothing else except that he was alive, and *here.*"

"I know, I know, *mo chridh.*" He took her in his arms again. "But Nigel the Earl of Kilcorrie! *Dia*, my wits are all adrift!" He began to laugh. "How did he do it? Was he making away with everyone between him and the title after the bodach died? I wonder if Archie succeeded after all and had a little while at it, at least. The castle would be suiting Christabel fine, though I doubt it would be snug as winter at Linnmore. It is that old, they were always keeping the cold and the wind out with great tapestries, and were frostbitten ten feet away from the hearth. I wonder how Archie's Countess of Kilcorrie was enjoying the chilblains that came with the title."

She was offended by his humor. "But it can make no difference to our situation! Nigel is Nigel, even if by some coincidence he should become heir to the British crown! I am still his wife, and we are both supposed to be dead to one another."

He hugged her the way the twins did when they were in the highest spirits. "Amadan that I am, my brain has been away with the fairies, not to be remembering what happens when a man touches pitch, never mind his rank. It entraps him. Och, we are doubly safe from the Earl of Kilcorrie! If he raises a cry against *us*, he besmirches and perhaps loses his wife, his countess who is not really his countess. *You* are, *mo ghaoil*. I kiss your hand." He did so, merrily.

"But it is no joke. He could be quite safe, I might be no threat because over there I may be legally dead. But here, in our village, the scandal could ruin us."

"But to go by the size of the boy, he was not waiting too long to discover whether or not you were legally dead. A fact he would not be wanting known at home. Once he knows you exist, he will never be knowing a moment's peace for fear of the pitch reaching the castle, Edinburgh, the church, the House of Lords, and bastardizing young Lord Gilchrist before the world. If he has more of a family, there is a flock of wee Honorables to consider." He cuddled her as if she were Bell Ann. "Och, *mo chridh*, whatever he could do to us is nothing to what he would do to his own. He might adore Priscilla on sight, knowing she is his, but he cannot be claiming her. The price would be the sacrifice of the rest of them, his wife, the children, their good marriages, all their prospects."

"It is going to be even harder than I feared," Jennie said. "My head wants to reel like the drunken tailor in the pipe tune."

"I am swearing to you, he will be helping to make it easier for us for his own salvation. He will be hoping and praying all the time that we will never send that one fatal word to someone in Scotland."

She said with a flash of savagery that startled her, "That will pay him out for standing there with his watch in his hand while the thatch burned. God knows whatever became of them and all the others who must have been dispossessed ever since. I could ruin him for that!" She subsided against him. "I am so tired. Do you think we will sleep?"

"Yes," he said. But she could not.

"How long do you suppose he lay there that day? If Parlan had taken the horses back, did he wake up alone and make his way home, or did they come for him with a litter expecting to find a corpse?"

Alick didn't answer, and she knew he was asleep. She could not help smiling in the dark. For him it was solved, and she had prattled him to sleep with her supposings and wonderings. But she was so conscious of Nigel he might have been under the same roof. Her entire body knew of him. She lay there listening to the rising wind in the chimney and feeling an insidious chill which was not in herself, even though it seemed to be. After all the optimism with which the launching had been anticipated, the weather was entirely appropriate. "Give not a windy night a rainy morrow, to linger out a purpos'd overthrow," Shakespeare had written, and he knew whereof he wrote.

How could life possibly remain unchanged by the knowledge that Nigel lived, even if they met and parted without a word or glance of recognition? Yes, they were glad he was not dead, but they had built a world around that supposed death as an oyster built a pearl. Now the wonderings were coming thick and fast, and she had no business letting them in.

When Alick woke her, she didn't realize she had actually fallen asleep; then she was half-sick with remembering, and angry because he had waked her. She turned away from him and put her arm over her eyes.

"The Great Horse has sent us a miracle," he said. He went to the front window and opened the curtains. "Come and see."

She stared blurrily at the gray panes. "*Rain*," she said crossly. "A soaking northeaster. I knew it would happen, and so did you."

"Look again." He bundled her into her robe and walked her to the window.

It was not raining out. It was snowing, and hard, on a northeasterly gale that swept the snow across the fields like billows of smoke, and shrieked around the house, and wailed and whistled through cracks they had believed to be well caulked. The sudden extreme cold made it a blizzard rather than simply an October snowfall.

"There is no way we will launch in this," Alick said. "Only a fool would do it, and the Babbs are not that. I am hoping there are none among my shipwrights who think they should be fighting their way here this morning. It will not be giving up by noon and leaving us a fair afternoon."

"A one-day reprieve," she said. "It would represent everything to a man condemned to hang; he would be thinking that in the next twenty-four hours anything could happen—until they took him to the scaffold the next morning."

Then she was immediately ashamed; in the gray light he too looked gray, as if she, not the storm, had suddenly brought winter to him. "I apologize!" she said. "My darling, I am wearing you out with my vapors, and I promise you that all this day, and tonight too, I shall not mention you-know-whom." She kissed him with loud smackings, the way Bell Ann liked to do, and finally he smiled.

"The fire is dancing a jig out there," he said. "Come and dress before it."

With the house full of children staying home from school, David not going to Maddox, and Alick there because nothing was going on at the Yard except for the storm whistling about the waiting ship and the snow blowing across her decks, there was neither time nor privacy for vapors.

The children were keyed up by the unexpected; divided between wanting the snow to last for sledding, snowmen, snowfort, and snowball fights, and wishing for it to go away quickly so the Governor could come and the ship could be launched. Bundling up at chore time to dive headfirst into the storm was an adventure that Bell Ann bravely shared. They'd groan enough about it in mid-winter, but the novelty of it in mid-October swept them on, because of course the weather would clear and go back to being October again.

When the family were pleasantly occupied with their varied interests, Jennie took a mid-morning nap curled up around Garnet for a hot-water bottle, and woke feeling stronger and more confident; the power would come from somewhere to buoy her up to the occasion, and the day in between was looking more and more like the miracle Alick called it.

The evening was spent as all their stormy evenings were, with games, singing and reading aloud. Jennie was tired when she went to bed, but not sickly so; she had an ethereal sensation of detachment from the world outside her house. For one thing, nothing was certain about tomorrow. The storm could keep up, or, if it cleared, the temperature could stay down and keep the roads iced and dangerous. The launching could put both ship and workmen in peril.

She woke in the night to a stillness so sudden and profound it was like the aftermath of a great explosion. She decided sensibly that the clocks had just finished striking and the wind had nearly died out. She got up and went across the cold floor to the front windows and looked out on a landscape in which the snow gave off its own light, like phosphorescence, and cold diamonds of stars were appearing among funereal plumes of cloud. The river lay black between the white fields, and the woods were the impenetrable and haunted black forests of legend. Even the orchard trees partook of the mystery, and the sprawling old apple tree at the turn was really the sacred tree of an earlier race and still possessed its powers.

Though she was shivering after the warmth of feather bed, quilts, and Alick, she was fascinated by the scene; she could hardly imagine it gaudy with color and alive with movement even down to the myriad little lives in the grass. This was a perfect vision of the eternal winter. This is how it would be, she thought, if the sun burned out.

Suddenly, into this composition of blacks and whites, the lights of a ship came slowly past the eastern woods, her dimly illuminated sails glimmering like great wings. The storm was going away, and a ship had left Maddox on the tide. She would be well on her way when daylight came, and twelve hours from now, unless there was dangerous icing, the ship *Enoch Lincoln* would be launched, and it would be over, come weal or woe.

Would another day of delay make things better or worse? When the boys were in trouble, she had needed Alick; he was here now, what more did she need? As cautious with this as with a tooth which had finally ceased to ache, if one could only keep one's tongue from it, she returned to bed.

Sixty-Three

WITH THE FIRST direct rays of the rising sun driven at the house in spears of light and warmth, the snow on the roof began to melt and run down the spouts into the barrels; the snow on windowsills shrank and dripped away. Snow thudded off the eaves and loaded branches, and the woods sent up wraiths of steam that vanished in a sky of new and milky blue. Shrubs and grasses appeared spikily through handfuls of trembling diamonds, and soon yesterday's paths showed wet and bare.

Indian Summer, or St. Martin's Summer as Jennie had known it at home, had arrived. The launching would take place. It was scheduled with the tide, at approximately two o'clock. School was dismissed at noon so the children could see the Governor, and they began arriving shortly after noon, all except Lily, and were expansively taken in tow by William and Bell Ann. Some had been at earlier launchings because fathers or brothers worked at the Yard, and these were looking forward as much to punch and cakes and the bagpipes as to seeing the Governor.

Bell Ann at last could wear the Paris frock of embroidered rose-pink muslin. The precious ruffled pantalets must have made her legs feel cluttered and impeded, but for the moment she felt ravishing. William placidly wore his Sunday suit as a matter of course.

Lucy and Harm Clements and the Hector Mackenzies came early. Jennie felt unable to hold a sane conversation with old friends, though Alick seemed to have no difficulty. She told them she was behind in her preparations and Pris and the twins were helping. They would visit after the launching; another example of her desperate optimism, since she didn't know what her condition would be then.

She mixed gallons of punch and claret lemonade in the sail loft, which had been tidied up for an informal reception. Pris and the twins brought down trays of glasses and mugs. The boys were also in their Sunday suits to meet the Governor, with the understanding they could change as soon as the ship had sailed. Jennie wore her green and gold cambric; she would feel more comfortable in it because of its pleasant associations. She would put on her bonnet when propriety demanded it. Pris had taken a pale yellow dress from the trousseau, and, using the original skirt as a slip, had given it a new full one of Roman-striped cotton gathered into a wide girdle at the waist; she wore a short sleeveless jacket of the same vivid goods, leaving the yellow sleeves and round collar free. It was different, and dashing, and Jennie was proud of her; at the same time she was afraid for her, no matter what Alick promised, and she was fearful of showing it whenever she met Pris's eyes.

Outside, workmen and their families strolled around the Yard doing homage to the ship and their work on her. Decorated with bunting, she was a passive queen awaiting either sacrifice or coronation. Rory was walking up and down the wharf warming his pipes, and inevitably the children were drawn to him. The nearest neighbors came on foot; young Job Winter rode in and was at once made welcome by Alick, and then, after he paid his respects to Jennie and met Pris with a sunburst smile of unabashed pleasure, he was adopted by the twins, who took him to visit the ship.

A number of Whittiers arrived in chaises and traps. Carlotta and Captain Blackburn came into the sail loft to speak to Jennie. "Where is Simon Roy?" Bell Ann cried. "He is going to miss his first launching!"

"And his first cold, I hope," Carlotta said. "With all the barking I hear lately, and all at different pitches, we could easily get up a Seals' Chorus."

Jennie was surprised at how easily she laughed, shook hands, asked for elderly parents, ailing spouses, and news of seafarers. At any moment now the General would arrive, and perhaps the Governor's party at the same time, and then—she sailed over what lay between—in less than an hour it would be all over. By not imagining The Between, she fancied that she could keep herself in this heady state for as long as possible.

The dogs had been shut up in the house, so there was no warning before Bell Ann came pounding into the sail loft, Sarie trailing her, shouting, "Mama, the General is here!" She felt as if she were turning to stone on the spot. Why hadn't Alick come for her? Now she had to walk out there all alone. What was he *thinking* of? She took Bell Ann's hand, keeping her from rushing out again, and took Sarie by the other, and walked up to where the dark green barouche was just stopping under the trees, the horses facing her. Alick was standing at one side. She forced her face into the dignified, but not haughty, smile which she had practiced before her mirror. It felt like a grimace, but she knew it was not.

Priscilla came behind her, and whispered an exclamation of either surprise or annoyance, which was explained by the sight of Robin on the box handling the reins. "Robin's back! Robin's back!" Bell Ann sang out and pulled away from her, seized Sarie and dragged her toward the barouche. William, of course, was already between the heads of the two horses, and Sandy and Carolus were coming up the bank from the Yard, assuring Job Winter it was time he met the General. Brisky was saluting the horses at the top of his lungs.

Jennie was aware that others were gathering around, either boldly or shyly, but they were presences in a dream, only sensed, never distinct. Pris caught up with her, and Robin solemnly lifted his hat to them both. Still in a dream she felt Pris's arm drop away from hers, and she walked toward Alick. Septimus Frye's new trap was close behind the barouche, Bolivar already hitched to the rail, and Septimus was standing by Alick like a friend of the family. He was a fashion plate in fawn, with skin-tight trousers and a sapphire silk cravat.

Alick held out his hand to her, and she put hers into it and turned to face the barouche.

Lydia's favorite capuchin color was kept from clashing with someone's flame silk pelisse and bonnet by Mrs. Heriot's nun-like dark blue marocain between them. The dark-eyed girl wearing flame could only be Jacinth. The General and Ronald Heriot sat opposite the three. "Jeannie!" the General called to her. "Every time I see you, you have molted a few more years. Life with this hard-bitten Highlander must agree with you."

"One of Colin's more gallant speeches," Lydia said. "But he is right, dear Jennie." Mrs. Heriot smiled and bowed to Jennie. She was a very pretty, fair woman of Dutch ancestry; Ronald Heriot had found her in New York. He stepped down and took off his hat to Jennie and Pris, and turned to offer his hand to the ladies. Robin alighted unsmiling and assisted Jacinth.

Priscilla pretended to see Septimus for the first time, and said in a rather high, vivacious voice, "How nice to see you again, Mr. Frye!"

"How nice to see you, Miss Glenroy." And then they both laughed. Robin glanced gravely at them across the barouche and went to take the horses from William. David materialized—one moment he was not there, and then he was—and Jacinth gave him a smile that said the thought of him alone had sustained her all the way from Maddox. Her arm slipped through his, and they walked away as if no one else existed. Robin looked quizzically after them and then grinned at Jennie.

"But where are your guests, man?" asked Alick, offering the General a shoulder to steady his descent.

"Oh, they've gone," the General said, puffing. He braced with his cane against the jolt of the step to earth. "Matter of fact, they left at midnight on the *Adina Leslie*. She was bound for South Carolina with a stop at Boston, and once he heard that, he was all of a fever to go. *There!*" He was down. "Where's Lincoln? Wouldn't do for him to be late and we miss the tide again. — No, this storm yesterday brought out the nerves in Kilcorrie. Hated to miss the launching, and the boy was wild to see it, but his father thought if winter set in this early in these parts, he'd feel safer waiting in Boston to sail for home. Been gone from his family and business too long, he said." He kissed Jennie's cheek and, grunting, bent to kiss Bell Ann. "Capital feller, I'd like to keep him for a month. Great company talking, wizard at billiards, and he thought this bit of the States was the finest kind."

"I saw him." Jennie heard herself saying and then explained, as if the earth were not still rocking under her feet. "I was awake a bit after midnight, and I saw *Adina Leslie*'s lights on the river. They had to be— She was like a graceful phantom gliding along."

"Robin, this is my friend Sarie Oakes," Bell Ann was saying. "Robin goes to college," she told Sarie. "He is very intelligent."

"Thank you," Robin said. "Will you young ladies do me the honor of escorting me to where I may have a good view of the launching?" He took a hand of each and walked toward the Yard.

Pris and Septimus stood at Bolivar's head murmuring and laughing secretively around his nose, which made his ears twitch. Jennie suspected that Alick's ears were also twitching while he was apparently listening to Ronald Heriot, but if he felt as she did at this moment, Septimus was a very minute mote in his eye, hardly painful at all.

She and Lydia looked from their children to each other and communicated rueful amusement, as if to say, What can one do?

"What a perfect day for a launching!" Mrs. Heriot exclaimed. "And she looks to be a most handsome vessel."

"They are here!" Simmy Mayfield shouted between his hands from up by the house.

It was over, most of it recorded by David with Jacinth leaning worshipfully on his shoulder.

The Governor had captivated everyone with his unpretentious charm; Captain Babb's fiancée, though a bit flustered with nerves, had broken the bottle of wine on the first attempt. The eyes of the figurehead watching her had put her off a bit, she said afterward, much more so than those of the flesh-and-blood Enoch Lincoln. Rory piped the ship down the ways with his new tune, "Hail to the Governor"; Captain Babb's crew (brought with him) raised the sails, and now the two Lincolns were on their way to Portland with a strong fair wind and full sunshine, and somewhere there was built within the ship a bit of rowan wood.

The last of the watchers, whistlers, and wavers on the wharf saw off the Governor, he was waving his hat back at them; a slight, youthful, fair-haired figure among the solid, smiling Babbs, under the snapping and booming spread of her canvas. One of the crew was originally from Maddox, and he was taking the ship downriver; her captain was standing so close to the wheel that someone remarked that his hands must have been itching something fierce to take a holt, the way his intended was hanging to his arm for dear life.

Jennie, Lucy, and Anna Kate stood amid the rest with linked arms, smiling mistily; Jennie for reasons that had nothing to do with this fair ship, but with the ghost she had seen at midnight taking away forever the image of Nigel dead in the heather and leaving behind the memory of a voice and a smiling boy. Goodbye, Nigel, she thought. Cherish that bonny boy of yours! Pris's brother, but here ignorance is surely bliss.

The ship was about to pass Misery Wall, and they began to straggle off the wharf, to be startled by a loud blast from the pipes, and Alick standing on a barrel in their way. True to form, he had left his coat somewhere. William, being a host, was no acolyte and coat-bearer this time, and the silk tartan waistcoat was gorgeous in the sun.

"Everyone to the sail loft!" he shouted. "Give them a good blow, Rory. Lead them in!"

Rory struck up a march, and Alick jumped down. He fought his way through a surprised and expectant school of persons following the piper as herring followed the torches until he found Jennie, and swept her away from the others. "I beg your pardon, ladies," he said to Lucy and Anna Kate, "but I need my wife. Och, and you too, Anna Kate. No offense to you, Lucy, *mo graidh*." He kissed her cheek and hurried the other two women away with him.

"A *dance?*" Jennie said in his ear.

"Have I not been wanting one?"

"What are you smiling about, Anna Kate?" Jennie asked her.

"Och, who would not be smiling at the thought of a dance?"

When they were all inside, he stepped up on a bench and clapped his hands for attention. "Now, ladies and gentlemen, big and small, I have been promising my wife and myself a dance for so long the bitter shame is at me. So this is our dance, and my wife and I will be opening it with our children and our Highland friends, and the young man the Glenroys could not do without."

They were quietly gathering without being summoned. When he jumped down Jennie pinched his arm. "How long have you planned this?"

"Since *before*," he said. "But we would be dancing, no matter what."

He led Jennie onto the floor. David followed with Pris, then William and a suddenly self-conscious Bell Ann. The twins faced Hector's and Anna Kate's daughters, whose parents came next, then Rory's son and daughter, Mr. Lockhart and Rory's nimble wife made the eighth couple.

Facing each other, they were poised and ready for the warning from the pipes; gulls could be clearly heard outside, and Brisky's voice. Then Rory's fingers danced on the chanter into "The Wind that Shakes the Barley," and the dancers swung into the swirling intricacies of a Highland reel. The adults moved with grace and skill and the children turned into demon dancers, but never putting a foot wrong. The whoops rang like war cries. The audience was stamping and clapping out the time, and even the Methodists were seen to be joining in. The General was pounding his cane on the floor.

When the reel was over, the dancers went amid applause to the water pails and punchbowls, wiping their faces, congratulating each other and themselves, laughing, winded.

"You two were wonderful," Jennie told William and Bell Ann. "You kept up like real little Highlanders."

"And I'm not even hardly out of puff," Bell Ann bragged.

Carlotta and Captain Blackburn came to make reluctant farewells. "I would love to stay, but I have patients," Carlotta said. "It's been far too long since I have danced, and I am sure Nicholas was as famous in the ballroom as at sea, though I don't know how either of us would do in a Highland reel. Certainly not like you two."

"It is a form of divine madness," Jennie said, "and Alick was born with it."

Alick smiled. "Far from divine to some minds," he said. "More to the other extreme. But man, it was fine, was it not? The little ones skipping like bewitched lambs, and the minister too!"

"Man, I was a dancer before I was a minister!" said Lockhart.

As Carlotta left, David brought Jacinth to them. "I am Jacinth Heriot," she introduced herself, holding out her hand to each with a charming little bob like a genuflection, as if she were meeting royalty. "What a wonderful *wild* dance!" she said. "I declare, I saw a *far different* David from the man I thought I knew. Unplumbed depths!" She rolled her eyes at him with a shiver of lashes, and said with a fetching earnestness, "How I have *longed* to *meet* his family! He has written *volumes* about you all!"

With her lively eyes a shining deep brown, and a beautiful mouth, she was as exquisite as her likeness, and if she was neither subtle nor especially intelligent, she was probably as enchanting to watch as a pretty kitten, with the advantages and dangers of being a nubile woman.

"It is so nice to meet you at last, Miss Heriot," Jennie said, including David in her smile. He looked quite as usual, but then, he was David. "Still, we feel we already know you."

Jacinth looked gratified. "I am sure you *do*. No one is ever able to keep me a secret, not even David. Now he is going to show me your lovely grounds."

"Grounds, is it?" said Alick. "Och aye, you could call it that." David took her away toward the open double doors at the far end. "She was not intending to waste time on the *cailleach* and the *bodach*," he commented.

"What would she have left to *say*? Perhaps it is enough for David to look at her. She *is* lovely."

"Everyone is lovely to me today. Shall we be having a polka?" He went to speak to the North Whittier family who would provide the rest of the music. She wondered if Septimus was included in that *everyone*. He and Pris had disappeared, but Robin was apparently indifferent, joking with a group of young men around the claret lemonade.

The musicians were a father-and-son pair of fiddlers, another son

played the flute; and a dogged, stocky daughter of fourteen or so commanded silence with a warlike roll of the drums. Her father announced
a polka, and Vincent Taggart, first man on the floor with his wife, said
loudly, "I'm some glad *I'm* not a Methodist!"

A contradance was to follow the polka. Jennie elected to sit it out
with Lydia, and Alick joined the General and Ronald Heriot. In the brief
intermission for tuning fiddles, catching breaths, wetting throats, and
choosing partners, Lydia began talking about her recent guests. For
Jennie she might have been speaking about just anyone; it was as if after
all these years Nigel had become a stranger at last.

He was a handsome man, Lydia said, blue-eyed and fair; he was
charming and humorous, but he had once suffered greatly. "It was very
tragic," Lydia said. "His first wife went out riding one day, and her horse
came home, but she did not. They searched the hills for days, but they
found only her hat."

"How terrible for him," Jennie said, willing her lips not to curve at the
memory of that hat. Septimus had come in alone and was having a drink
of punch; Pris must have captured Bell Ann and taken her home to
change her dress before she damaged it. David had returned and delivered Jacinth to Mrs. Heriot, who sat just beyond Lydia, and had brought
them cups of claret lemonade. He looked extremely distinguished today,
and now extremely happy since he had been out in "the grounds" with
her, presumably in some secluded spot.

"Months later that year," Lydia was saying, "one of the servants was
visiting in another town and recognized a riding habit among the old
clothes for sale in the market. The woman said her children had found
the clothes in a remote glen, so they think she was kidnapped and
murdered by one of the bands of whisky smugglers roaming the hills."
Nigel had won her; there was a genuine tremor in her voice when she
said, "He was hardly more than a boy, and he nearly went mad with
grief."

"Isn't it wonderful that he was able to remake his life!" Jennie said.

The drum summoned the dancers to take their places for Hull's
Victory. David arose from his chair beside Jacinth, and she handed her
cup to Mrs. Heriot and also stood up, smoothing down her flame-colored
silk, adjusting a black curl. She was looking toward the dance floor, her
lips parted with a childlike expectancy. David crooked his arm for her to
take; her smile blossomed, and she put her hand not on David's blue
sleeve, but in the hand of Septimus, who had crossed the floor so swiftly

that he appeared before her like a figure of magic. Neither he nor Jacinth gave David even a casual glance, though she must have brushed against him as she passed.

David looked after them as if he could not believe it had happened, that he had somehow mistaken what he saw. Then the music began, and there was no mistake; out there on the floor Jacinth was radiantly tapping her foot as if she could hardly wait to fling herself into the dance with Septimus. Slow color seeped onto David's high cheekbones; Jennie's own face was burning. She could not go to him any more than she could stride onto the floor and take the girl's wrist and twist it until she yelped with pain. David walked toward the open double doors at the end and went out.

"I have never," Lydia said, distinctly through the music, "seen a more indecent display of dimples than what these two have just given us. I beg your pardon, Gretel," she said, "but the girl is a hussy, and Septimus Frye is a brazen little jackanapes."

"No apology is needed." Mrs. Heriot's amiable simplicity was missing. "I have had just about enough of that young lady. She has simply been leading David Evans on because she feeds on being admired, and besides, what would she do with her afternoons!" Her round blue eyes did not flash or snap, but they were exasperated beyond question. "The sooner I pack the minx off to Boston, the happier I will be. I should apologize to you, Mrs. Glenroy."

"Not at all," said Jennie. "David is a grown man. He makes his own choices and must abide by the consequences. But I cannot help feeling for him. If Pris were here she'd have not let him escape, she'd have forced him out there to dance, and hope she could trip Jacinth up."

"That is just what she needs. No one has ever done it."

"Where is Pris?" Lydia asked. "Robin had hopes, I know, but he'd die rather than admit it. He's on the floor with some buxom lass, having a good time if it kills him."

"She should not have gone off like that," Jennie said, rising. "Her father will be wanting a dance with her." The curious thing was that Nigel did not now come into mind when she said *father*, when the association had tormented her for all these recent hours. "I will fetch her."

She found her shawl and unobtrusively left by a side door. The twins were in the complicated dance, and Alick was talking with some men across the room.

The mid-afternoon was still warm in the sun, but already the shadows of the western wood were spreading down through the field, swallowing the house in a cold blueness. Bell Ann and a clutch of little girls were running around in the leafless orchard, Bell Ann no longer in embroidered pink muslin. William and friends were in the pasture, taking turns riding Brisky bareback and rewarding him with apples. He was so pleased at being one of the crew that he trotted like a champion, no kicks, no nips, no obdurate halts to throw a rider over his head. His elders watched aloofly. Jennie called to William from among the visiting horses. "Have you seen Pris?"

"No, Mama!" he answered. One of the boys spoke to him, and he called back, "Rupe saw her going over the whaleback a while ago."

"Thank you, Rupe!"

Pris sat crosslegged on the beach below the whaleback. She was hidden from the road by a barrier of wild rose bushes turned dark red, thick with orange hips. In her Roman stripes she looked like a forlorn gypsy maiden in a romantic painting, except for the fair head. Her shadow stretched down to the water, into the white ruching of foam that edged the wavelets. She must have heard Jennie's step in the coarse sand behind her, but she didn't turn her head.

"What is wrong?" Jennie asked. "You are missed at the dance. Your father arranged it for all of us, you know, so you are as much a hostess as I am."

"I cannot help that." Pris's voice was congested with crying. Jennie went down on her knees beside her, and turned Pris's face toward her.

"*Don't!*" Pris wrenched her head free. When she was about to wipe her face on her sleeve, Jennie gave her a handkerchief.

"Usually I am the person without one," she said.

"I cannot seem to stop this." Pris blew her nose. "Oh, Mama, I have been such a *fool!* Please don't hate me for it, I hate myself enough for the whole world!"

"Why?" Jennie sounded calmer than she felt.

"Because when I wrote him that letter you read first—remember?" She stopped and blew her nose again. "Well, I put a spray of forget-me-nots in it!" she wailed. "I did! I had no shame! I could cover myself with sackcloth and ashes!"

"As long as you don't threaten us with joining a convent," Jennie said. "I remember his letter of thanks, and the red carnation. I looked it up: 'Alas for my poor heart.' And you thought he meant it for you alone."

Pris nodded abjectly. "But that's not the worst. I wrote *more* letters to him and smuggled them to the post office, and sometimes Thankful mailed them." She was not merely pink, she was a deep hot scarlet from her throat to her scalp. "I *know* you and Papa will never forgive me that."

"Go on with the story." Jennie sifted through the sand for yellow periwinkles.

"I told him I didn't expect answers, because it could make trouble here, but we would meet at the launching. Oh, Mama, how I babbled on! I enclosed poetry, I talked about love songs and romantic novels. I made a perfect idiot of myself, all the time thinking of those imaginary red carnations." She searched for a dry corner of the handkerchief.

"So, today—," Jennie prompted her.

"We had the polka together, and then we came out to be free of the children, and I could hardly wait—I'd been dreaming of it all this time." She turned to Jennie in anguish. "And all he wanted to say—he didn't even take me into his arms and say he was sorry to have to tell me—he just *said* it! I am too young to interest him, I must grow up *much* more, and by that time he will be interested in someone else, so I had better put him out of my mind forever. And *then*—," her lower lip trembled, "and then he went back to the dance. On *our* property!" she said in outrage. "He is prancing around in *our* sail loft. He should at least have had the decency to leave at once!" She stood up. "I am going up to the house and stay out of sight. I can go around by the woods, and no one will notice me."

Jennie arose and held her back. "You may go home and wash your face with cold water, but then I want you back at the dance. Your father will be missing you soon."

"But Mama! Face *him*?" She looked ready to cry again.

"Why should he drive you away? Where is your pride, my girl? Besides, think of David. Jacinth has chosen in public between him and Septimus, and very cruelly. David was good enough when they were alone, but she would not dance with him, not when she could choose Rodger Dodger of the Dimples."

Pris giggled, though there was a choke in it. "I *hate* her for doing that to him! Where is he? I must find him."

"No, he is better alone," Jennie said. "Wherever he is."

"But what will he *do*? He was so completely hers; this could kill him."

"Not David. He will finish Mr. Heriot's portrait, but he will be iron as far as Jacinth is concerned. He will not only not hear her, he will not even see her."

"Do you think she expects her portrait was done for love?"

"David is no fool. She will receive her bill."

"Now I can hardly wait to go back in there." She rinsed the handkerchief in cold salt water and washed her face with it. "How do I look?"

"Better. You can always call it sunburn."

Pris spread the handkerchief on a log to dry. "Thank you for coming to find me. I was furious at first, but then I was glad. Now I am going to accidentally step on Jacinth's feet. Mine are so nice and *big*," she said smugly. "I can really hurt."

As they came around the barrier of wild roses, Septimus and Bolivar were just going up the road at a sporting gait, and Jacinth sat beside Septimus. The boys yelled and waved at them, but they didn't look back.

"Are they eloping?" Pris exclaimed.

"Who knows?" Jennie said. "Perhaps they are going on a long ride to be alone. She will have to be engaged after this, or the Heriots will ship her out so fast her head will spin off her neck."

"I would love to see that! But now I've lost a chance to stamp on her feet."

They laughed. "I will just tell you one thing more I would like you to do." Jennie stopped her at the foot of the steps. "Hull's Victory" was rollicking to a breathless conclusion and a rush to the cold drinks.

"Anything, Mama," Pris said fervently. "Anything for my best friend."

"Well, your best friend would like you to walk up to another friend and ask him if he is too proper to dance with a lady bold enough to ask him that question."

"*Robin?*" She made a face.

"It won't commit you. But you have been friends all your lives. Why not carry on?"

Sixty-Four

T HE CHILDREN doing the chores, and Jennie and Alick were sitting on
the bench in the chill of the sunset; the wind had dropped, the air
was cool enough for Jennie's shawl and Alick's coat. It felt pure and
gentle against the skin, scented with the stocks and an invigorating spice
of woodsmoke from the supper fire. There would likely be frost tonight.
Winter was coming, but not quite yet, and not an eternal one.

Voices of birds and children from the henyard, the whistling (two
different tunes) of the twins as they cleaned up the road where the horses
had been, sudden bursts of barking from Bounce when he was overcome
with excitement while he and Darroch were tracing the foreign scents of
the day—all sounds carried through the quiet with the penetrating
quality of bells. Pris was milking; she would be singing to Ianthe, her
forehead against the cow's warm flank, the two of them joined in a
communion of spirits. David had ridden away on Blanchard before the
dance was over, but he left no note, so he would be back later, even if it
was midnight.

Jennie and Alick had not spoken for some time, their hands just
touching. Not a finger, not a toe wished to move. Garnet endeavored to
work her head under Alick's other hand.

"Can you not be leaving the man of the house in peace?" he asked her,
but he gave in and she laid her chin on his thigh.

Jennie asked out of nowhere. "What is his business? Colin mentioned
a business."

"Och, he has built a distillery in the castle grounds! The Crown has
been issuing licenses, and whisky will now become a gentleman's drink,

509

though I am thinking there is still plenty of the other sort made in secret places to put a few shillings in the poor man's pocket." He chuckled. "He calls it 'Dew of Kilcorrie.' Is that not poetic?"

"A peer in trade," said Jennie. "A new breed. I suppose his title will help sell it. Doubtless he is decked out in full Highland dress on every possible occasion, as if he were a true Highlander and not a traitor."

"And with his own piper," Alick said.

"I wonder if he married Miss Lamont of Rowanlea."

"If he did, she brought him a nice dowry in money and land both. More room for sheep, more grouse moor and deer forest and salmon loch to lease to rich Sassenachs." He said it without expression; the passion ran too deep for the fuss and froth of words. The Clearances were still going on.

She told him the story he had given Lydia Mackenzie about her disappearance. "If he felt in his heart that I was dead, after someone recognized my riding habit at Fort Augustus—that is where Kirsty would have taken it—why did he not notify my family?" She answered herself, "Because he was afraid I might still be alive? No matter how or in what terrible circumstances? At Linnmore I would have been a difficulty to them all, so it was good riddance to bad rubbish," she said, not with hostility.

If that was the way it had happened, what did it matter now? She had known what he was before she ran away that day. "By the time my trunks reached Sylvia, with no message—and they had taken their own good time about it—Sylvia already had my letter from Fort William. I have never stopped blessing Nancy MacNichol."

"My Highland pride is offended because he left me out of the story," said Alick, "but I understand. A missing wife alone, perhaps murdered, is easier to talk about than a wife missing with another man."

He leaned back against the wall, his hands folded behind his head, and stretched out his legs. Across the river, the afterglow fired windows and gave the spruces a patina of bronze.

"You wondered what he looked like now," he said. "Well, I would like *him* to be seeing what the embarrassing trouble-maker of Linnmore has become."

"He knows, I am sure. Colin is so proud of you he must have talked and talked—and how Nigel must have been hating it behind the charm!"

"*Hearing* is not *seeing*—the children, the Yard, my men, a bonny ship, and myself the builder; and myself the laird of this place, and you the begetter of it all, not just the mistress. But it is perfect as it came about. We partook of the same miracle. As long as he never catches a blink of us, he knows nothing, and neither do we."

Voices: Pris, Bell Ann, and William were talking outside the barn. "You need not worry about the politician again," Jennie said. "He and Jacinth simply danced away from Hull's Victory, out the door, over the hills and far away, like the song, perhaps to visit another empty house. He had better be prepared to marry her, or lose her. Mrs. Heriot was livid, and Mr. Heriot looked fit to hurl thunderbolts.

" 'The minx,' Mrs. Heriot called her. Septimus had just come in from telling Pris she was too young for him. Honorable up to a point, I will give him that, but he left her crying and went in to claim Jacinth from under David's nose, and to *dance!* That was the crowning outrage."

"Pris danced with Robin and young Job Winter, and more, and she was not seeming so sad."

"Pride, Alick. She took it like a soldier, finally. We should be proud of her; she deserves it."

"I am always proud of her, *mo chridh*. Proud of all of them." The twins were coming up the road with the dogs; there was a meeting when everyone talked at once. "At the moment, not a care," Alick said. "Their worst stramash would be music to me, as long as they are safe."

"I have been thinking, Alick," Jennie said tentatively, "that some day when Pris is older, do you think we might send her to Ianthe? To be placed as an apprentice and learn fine dressmaking?"

"How many minutes, hours, days, weeks, months from now?" he teased her. "*Dia*, I know she is too bright and too ambitious to be caged. But let us not be talking of it tonight."

"Not for a long time." She kissed his cheek. "I had better be attending to our supper. Speaking of poetry, isn't that the pure essence of it?"

"Tonight will be that," he said.